More praise for *The Wonder Worker*

"Enthralling . . . For fans of Howatch's earlier novels about the Church of England, this is familiar and juicy territory. . . . In those novels, Howatch captivated readers with beautifully told struggles between earthly and spiritual forces. She does it again in *The Wonder Worker.*"

—*The Cleveland Plain Dealer*

"[A] compelling story . . . After seventeen novels, including the acclaimed series about the Church of England, Howatch continues to write impressive fiction imbued with moral questions. . . . Howatch engrosses the reader in this splendidly wrought, provocative novel of spiritual ideas."

—*Publishers Weekly* (starred review)

"A look at the ways and means of healing, both spiritual and physical . . . A good cup of hot tea and reading *The Wonder Worker* is a sure cure for a dreary winter."

—*Florida Times Union*

"This book is so well written that readers will race through it."

—*Library Journal*

Also by Susan Howatch

Absolute Truths

Mystical Paths

Scandalous Risks

Ultimate Prizes

Glamorous Powers

Glittering Images

The Wheel of Fortune

Sins of the Fathers

The Rich Are Different

Cashelmara

Penmarric

The Devil on Lammas Night

April's Grave

The Shrouded Walls

Call in the Night

The Waiting Sands

The Dark Shore

The Wonder Worker

The Wonder Worker

A NOVEL BY

Susan Howatch

FAWCETT COLUMBINE
The Ballantine Publishing Group
New York

A Fawcett Columbine Book
Published by The Ballantine Publishing Group

 Published in the United States by Ballantine Books, a division of Random House, Inc., New York, and distributed in Canada by Random House of Canada Limited, Toronto.

Originally published in Great Britain as *A Question of Integrity* by Little, Brown, London.

Grateful acknowledgment is made to the following for permission to reprint previously published material:
HarperCollins Publishers Ltd.: Excerpts from *A Question of Healing* by Gareth Tuckwell and David Flagg. Reprinted by permission of HarperCollins Publishers Ltd., London.
Music Sales Corporation: Excerpt from "We'll Meet Again" by Ross Parker and Hughie Charles, copyright 1939 (renewed) by Irwin Dash Music Co., Ltd. All rights for the Western Hemisphere controlled by Music Sales Corporation (ASCAP). International copyright secured. All rights reserved. Reprinted by permission of Music Sales Corporation.

http://www.randomhouse.com/BB/

Library of Congress Catalog Card Number: 98-96533

ISBN: 0-449-00150-4

This edition published by arrangement with Alfred A. Knopf, Inc.

Cover design by Ruth Ross
Cover illustration by Honi Werner

Manufactured in the United States of America

First Ballantine Books Edition: November 1998

10 9 8 7 6 5

Contents

Part One

ALICE

The Romantic Dream

Life is a pilgrimage. It is a pilgrimage to health. It is also a pilgrimage of health. We have it on our journey, always partially, always imperfectly, always with an admixture of that illness which is its opposite or the mark of its imperfections.

CHRISTOPHER HAMEL COOKE

"Health and Illness, Pastoral Aspects,"

an entry in *A Dictionary of Pastoral Care*

1

We all have our favourite addictions to which we turn when we are under stress. For you it is food, while for others it can range from chemical substances to spending money or constant contact with others in order to avoid alone-ness.

GARETH TUCKWELL AND DAVID FLAGG
A Question of Healing

I

I can remember exactly when the miracles began. It was when I first met Nicholas Darrow and fell in love with him. Can I write that and avoid sounding like a romantic schoolgirl? No, so I must start again. I'm not a schoolgirl and being romantic is pointless. What had romance ever done for me, I often asked myself, and the answer was always the same: zilch.

So let me reject any statement which reeks of romance and write instead: I can remember exactly when my life began to change out of all recognition. It was when I first saw Nicholas Darrow and glimpsed a life-style I had never encountered before.

That's better. That's more truthful, and truth matters. I suppose in the end it's all a question of integrity.

The meeting with Nicholas was quite unplanned. No doubt religious people would speak of divine providence, but I wasn't religious—not after slogging my guts out to look after Aunt. What had God ever done for me, I might have asked myself, and the answer would always have been the same: zilch.

It was the March of 1988. I was trying to get a permanent job because I needed extra money to pay for more nursing, but I'd messed around with temporary work for so many months that all the shine had been stripped from my *curriculum vitae*, and when I explained about Aunt I could see my would-be employers thinking: family problems, unreliable, forget her. However, if Aunt was to stay out of the geriatric ward she had to be cared for by a rota of nurses from a private agency, and I had to earn the largest possible salary to—no, not to make ends meet; that was impossible, since the nursing care was so expensive, but at least I could postpone the evil day when Aunt's savings finally ran out and I had no choice but to consign her to one of the National Health dumping-grounds.

On that particular morning in March I had unsuccessfully tried to flim-flam my way through an interview with a personnel officer who had behaved like a sadist. Trudging away from the hideous office block which housed her, I felt in a mood to jump off Tower Bridge.

I was in the City, that square mile of London's financial district which always seems a world away from what I call Tourist London: the grand West End streets crammed with monuments of our Imperial past, and the grand department stores crammed with frenzied shoppers. On London Wall, that wide, bleak highway just south of the Barbican, I paused to work out which was my nearest tube station but by that time I was so overpowered by the desire to binge on a high-calorie lunch (mushroom quiche, chocolate-chip cookies, rum raisin ice cream) that I was incapable of coherent thought. To make matters worse the heavens then opened, the rain bucketed down and I realised I'd left my umbrella in the office of the sadist. In disgust I looked around for shelter, but there were no shops to be seen, only office blocks, and no buses, only taxis which I couldn't afford. I hurried towards the nearest side-street but when I turned the corner I found no sandwich-bar where I might have sheltered but only older, grimier office buildings. The street was narrow and soon became cobbled. I started to slither in the vile high heels I'd worn for the interview, and the next moment I wrenched my ankle. It was then, as I leaned against the nearest wall to take the weight off my throbbing foot, that I glanced further down the street and saw the church.

It was washed, shining, serene, an oasis in the midst of a desert. Automatically I limped on over the cobbles towards it.

I knew I had never seen the building before but I guessed it was one of the City's many Wren churches. As I drew nearer, the roar of the traffic on London Wall receded. I heard the birds singing in the churchyard and saw the daffodils blooming among the ancient graves.

Suddenly I forgot the misery of the morning. I forgot the sadistic personnel officer, and I forgot my dread that all the well-paid boardroom cooking jobs in the City would nowadays be awarded to girls called Caroline or Sophie who looked like the Princess of Wales, possessed Porsche-driving merchant-banker boyfriends and lived in the fabled streets around golden Sloane Square. I even ceased to be aware of the slapping, slashing rain. I was remembering the day long ago when Aunt had taken me on a tour of some of the City churches. They had strange names such as St. Andrew-by-the-Wardrobe, St. Botolph Aldgate and St. Lawrence Jewry—and this church, I had just discovered, was called St. Benet's-by-the-Wall; I glimpsed the name as I stumbled past the painted board outside. On reaching the outer door, which stood open, I plunged into the shelter of the porch. The relief of escaping from the downpour was considerable. Breathing hard I smoothed my wet hair, gave my spectacles a quick polish and prepared to take refuge in what I assumed would be a quiet, deserted interior.

I heaved open the inner door and stopped dead. The church was packed. I gazed open-mouthed, jaw sagging. What was all this? What could possibly be going on? I'd thought nothing happened in the City churches any more. I'd thought they were mere clerical museums maintained for their architectural interest. During all the times I'd done temporary work in the City I'd never realised the churches were still active . . . But of course my work as a cook meant that I was never around in the lunch-hour to witness such a phenomenon.

This particular church was obviously very active indeed. The whole building seemed to be pulsating. Automatically I stood on tiptoe to try to glimpse what was going on, but I was too short to see past the forest of suits. Surely men didn't go to church any more? Maybe the building had been hired for some sort of yuppie rally . . . I pictured an American guru holding forth on the wonders of capitalism before hosting a buffet lunch in the crypt. (Californian wine, barbecued nibbles, chicken-with-everything, coleslaw in tubs.)

I had just realised I'd forgotten I was hungry when more people came in behind me and I was propelled towards a dark, pretty woman of about forty who was wearing a badge inscribed: ST. BENET'S: FRANCIE. I muttered an apology as I bumped into her, but she merely whispered with a smile: "Welcome!", a reaction which astonished me so much that I found I had the courage to ask what was going on.

She said: "It's our Friday healing service. It's just started. Stick close and I'll get you behind the wheelchairs so that you can see."

I had no interest in watching a church service of any kind, least of all something so peculiar as a healing service, but since she was being friendly I didn't like to be impolite. I followed her as she eased her way through the throng to the side of the church, and when I stood at last behind one of the wheelchairs I took care to whisper my thanks, but she was already on her way to attend to the other late arrivals. Turning back towards the altar I began to absorb the sight which met my eyes.

The interior of the church was so unlike the usual Wren design in which the stalls face each other across a wide central aisle that I was sure the space had recently been rearranged. The wide central aisle now dissected a semi-circle of chairs, set in curving rows and catering for a much larger congregation than Wren would have envisaged. The distant altar looked as if it might date from a previous century, but both pulpit and lectern were modern, carved in the same pale wood as the chairs. The windows were clear; I supposed that the Blitz had blown out the old stained glass. The walls were a creamy white, non-clinical, almost luminous, and the panelling which rose some twelve feet from the floor was sumptuously dark in contrast. All the brass memorial tablets gleamed. Despite the greyness of the day there was an overwhelming impression of light, and despite the presence of so many people there remained also an overwhelming impression of space. With extreme reluctance I had to admit to myself that I was intrigued.

Beyond the lectern and seated facing the congregation were two clergymen, one silver-haired, one red-headed, but my glance travelled over them without stopping because I had finally become aware that someone was saying, in a pleasant, casual voice devoid of histrionics, exactly what that utterly silent, utterly fascinated audience wanted to hear.

I looked into the pulpit and saw Nicholas Darrow.

II

Anyone who thinks I'm now about to describe some rip-roaring 1980s version of testosterone on two legs is going to be disappointed. But on the other hand, anyone who thinks the clergymen of the Church of England are all wet wimps in frocks is now going to be very surprised indeed. I myself was amazed. I had no time for clergymen (what had the clergy ever done for me? Zilch!) and had long since decided they were all damp-palmed hypocrites, so I was hardly expecting the pulpit to house an ecclesiastical version of a film star, but nonetheless the moment I saw Nicholas Darrow I felt my stomach churn in a way which reminded me of everything I'd always wanted but never come within a million miles of having.

As he stood in the pulpit it was hard to judge his height, but he was certainly no dwarf. The cut of his cassock was hidden by a surplice so it was also hard to judge his build, but I sensed he was well proportioned, slim without being slender. I was too far away to see the age-lines on his face, but I guessed him to be somewhere in his forties; he had an air of confidence, an aura of natural authority which people usually only acquire in mid-life. His unremarkable brown hair was short, straight and neat. His pale eyes I assumed were either blue or green. His skin was stretched tautly over his prominent cheekbones and the tough line of his jaw. There was no way he could have been described as classically handsome—and yet no way he could have been written off as unattractive. As he continued to talk with such low-key, easy grace, I found I was particularly noticing his elegant hands as they rested lightly on the curving edge of the carved wood.

There was a crucifix on the wall behind him and he was talking about Jesus Christ—well, he would, wouldn't he?—but I couldn't focus on what he was saying because I didn't really want to hear it. I had no time for all that Bible rubbish, couldn't understand it, didn't need it. What I needed was money, loads of it, enough to pay for masses of nurses for Aunt and masses of sessions at a health-farm for me (or could one lose four stone instantly by just having liposuction at an upmarket clinic?), and once I was slim I'd want a stunning house in Chelsea with a beautiful kitchen and a lavish bedroom with yards of wardrobes which contained oodles of designer outfits in size ten—well, twelve, one had to be realistic—and I'd want a gorgeous Mercedes in the garage and a handsome husband who loved me and four stunning children—not necessarily in that order, of course—and oh yes, an elegant cat, very furry, who would travel with us in a custom-made basket from our home in Chelsea to our country house in Gloucestershire which, inevitably, would be just a stone's throw from the rural retreats of the Royals . . .

I had just realised with self-loathing that I was knee-deep in the most pathetic romantic dream, quite unsuitable for any woman of thirty-two who had no choice but to be a hard-bitten realist, when the sermon—homily—chat—whatever it was—ended and I became aware that Francie, the welcomer, was once more by my side. I whispered to her: "Who was that clergyman?" and she whispered back with pride: "That's our Rector, Nicholas Darrow."

As Darrow left the pulpit one of the other clergymen, not the young redhead but the silver-haired veteran, limped to the lectern and began to read, but I mentally disconnected myself again. I was thinking how beautifully the Rector moved, as beautifully as the actors I had seen on the West End stage in the old days when I was a schoolgirl and Aunt had taken me to see a couple of the Shakespeare plays. But perhaps that wasn't a flattering comparison. No respectable clergyman would relish being compared with an actor, but nevertheless . . . I was still meditating on Nicholas Darrow's mesmerising stagecraft when the reading ended and Francie murmured: "Do you want to go up?"

"I beg your pardon?"

"Do you want to receive the laying-on of hands?"

"Whose hands? You mean . . . are you saying he touches people?"

"All three priests do. It's all right, it's absolutely above board, there's a long Christian tradition of—"

"No thanks," I said. "I'm not sick. I'm fine."

To my relief she made no attempt to argue but instead gave me her warm smile and turned her attention to the occupants of the wheelchairs nearby. I was still savouring my relief when someone muttered: "Excuse me," and I found myself being propelled sideways as people edged past me. Having wound up wedged against the wall I found myself next to a notice-board covered with requests for prayer. "Please pray for Dad who has cancer . . ." "Please pray for Jim who has AIDS . . ." "Please pray for Sharon, last seen two months ago . . ." "Please pray for the family of Jill who died last week . . ."

A voice in my head suddenly said: "Please pray for Aunt who's dying by inches," but I blotted out the sentence in shame. I didn't believe in prayer (what had prayer ever done for me? Zilch!) and I hated all that sort of thing and I particularly hated what was now going on in this church—I didn't know why I hated it so violently but I did hate it, I hated everyone and everything—in fact such was my uncovered rage, the rage I always repressed so efficiently that I had hardly been aware of it, that I wanted to grab a machine-gun and mow down everyone in sight—except that attractive man, of course—but no, why should I spare him? I hated all attractive men;

in fact at that moment I felt I hated all men, attractive or otherwise, because none of them had ever displayed the remotest interest in me. So why shouldn't I want to mow them all down? And after I'd done the mowing I'd shoot myself too because life was so vile, so awful, so hellish, and even when Aunt died I'd still have no hope of happiness because there'd be no money and no one would want to employ me and—

Somebody asked me if I was all right.

"Absolutely fine," I said. "No problems whatsoever."

The organ began to play quietly, and through my tears I saw for the first time how diverse the congregation was. In addition to the men in city suits there were young mothers with children, wrinkled old ladies, smart girls from the offices, women in fashionable clothes from some expensive patch of the West End. I also noted several camera-toting tourists, far off the beaten track, and even a yuppie with a bottle of champagne tucked under his arm as if he, like me, had been diverted on the way to lunch. The majority of these people remained onlookers, some obviously admiring, some more reticent, but all unable to tear themselves away as the minority made their way slowly up towards the altar. The woman in the second wheelchair was a stroke-victim like Aunt, and one side of her face was paralysed. I watched her with a growing incredulity. What did she think was going to happen? Did she imagine she was going to jump out of her chair and walk? I felt outraged. I also decided that this was the most embarrassing scene I had ever witnessed and that I wanted above all to leave.

Yet I stayed. I found I had to go on watching Nicholas Darrow, so calm, so grave, so dignified as he went about his mysterious work. He was placing his slim, long-fingered hands on the heads of those who knelt at the altar-rail, his face tense with concentration, his whole body exuding an integrity which I instantly recognised and which somehow, by some mysterious force, pinned me in position. I could always have walked out on a charlatan. But I couldn't turn my back with contempt on someone honest.

My eyes filled with tears again and this time I started to weep. Immediately I was horrified by my lack of self-control. What would Aunt have said in the days when she could still speak? She had taught me that to show emotion in public was disgraceful.

The image of Aunt suddenly filled my mind. What had Aunt ever done for me, a stranger might have asked, and the one answer I could never have given was: "Zilch." Aunt had taken me in and brought me up—my great-aunt she was, the aunt of my foul mother who hadn't wanted me—God, what a disaster my early life had been, but Aunt had intervened, spinster Aunt, once a hatchet-faced teacher in a grammar school, no one special, just another bossy old bag who could be both beastly and boring, but this particular bossy old bag had been there when she was needed and now *I* had to be there for her, just as she'd been there for me. Well, that was only fair, wasn't it? I owed it to her. It was a matter of principle. I mean, one has to have one's principles, doesn't one, and even though I wasn't bright enough to make a success of my education and even though I was so plug-ugly that I had to have baths in the dark (how I *hated* all that flab) and even though I was such a failure as a woman, unable to get married or even to lose my virginity—*even though* all these ghastly facts were true, I wasn't entirely a write-off because I was trying, trying, trying to ensure she died with dignity in her own home. Yet I was beginning to hate her for taking so long to die. I knew I was. But that was because I was so done in through lack of sleep. Or was it? Maybe I was just afraid that in the end the money would run out and she'd wind up on the geriatric ward and then all my slogging would have been for nothing. Oh God, what a mess my life was, but there was no point in saying "oh God" like that as if calling on him would change matters. The situation could only change for the worse, and what had God ever done for me anyway? *Zilch.*

I told myself I had to leave before I started to scream in despair, but before I could move a muscle I saw Nicholas Darrow touch the grey, bowed head of the stroke-victim in her wheelchair. The voice in my head instantly cried: "Oh, let her get up and walk!" But of course she didn't and of course I'd been crazy to imagine such a thing was possible. The poor woman was quite unchanged—or so I thought, but when the wheelchair was steered back down the aisle I saw she was very, very far from being unchanged. Her dark eyes were luminous with joy and her lopsided ugly old face was radiant. With her twisted mouth she had managed to smile.

I thought: bloody hell! And the next moment tears were not merely flowing but flooding down my cheeks. Then suddenly Francie was at my side again, the unknown friend providing comfort in an alien landscape, and I felt a bunch of Kleenex tissues being stuffed into my shaking hand.

At that point I lost track of the service for a while; all I could do was reduce the tissues to a soggy wodge and say silently to myself over and over again in despair: oh, shit! Francie asked if I wanted to sit down and I shook my head, but I knew this wasn't the wisest response. The world had become chaotic, devastating. I felt as if something had split the outer shell of my mind and revealed unspeakable horrors lurking in the primitive darkness below.

At last I realised the service was ending. A hymn was being sung. That reminded me of my schooldays when we had sung hymns at morning assembly, and that memory in turn reminded me again of Aunt, spending her money without complaint to send me to a little private school in Kensington.

The hymn finished. Wiping away my last tear I heard the silver-haired clergyman announce that counselling was available to anyone who wanted it; those in need could approach either the "priests" (how Aunt would have hated the use of that Romish word!) or the "Befrienders," who wore St. Benet's badges and would refer each person to the right qualified helper. At once I glanced around for Francie but she was busy with someone else. What a relief! By that time I wanted only to slip away and lose myself in the City's lunch-time crowds.

The silver-haired clergyman stopped speaking. Nicholas Darrow pronounced a blessing. The organ began to play again, and the next moment I realised that the clergy were processing down the central aisle to the back of the church in order to mingle with the departing congregation. I shrank back against the wall. Of course I had no intention of speaking to him; my pride absolutely forbade me to make such a pathetic exhibition of myself, and besides, I could never have drummed up enough courage. (Supposing he were to look at me and flinch with revulsion?) But at least I could stay in the background and watch.

The music from the organ was being drowned by the rising tide of conversation, and by this time Nicholas Darrow had halted by the door which led into the porch. Effortlessly he shook hands, effortlessly he smiled, effortlessly he found the right words for everyone. "Drink a toast to St. Benet's when you uncork that bottle!" I heard him say amused to the yuppie clutching the champagne, and then a second later he was talking to a young mother about the problems of her council estate in Tower Hamlets.

At that point I found myself wishing I did have the nerve to talk to him, but what was there to say? I could hardly declare: "I don't believe in religion or churchgoing or any of that sort of thing, but I believe in *you*—I believe you've got something so special that when you touch the severely disabled they become inwardly transformed—I believe what I've just seen with my own eyes, and that's why I want you to visit my home. It's because I know you could transform my aunt." If I said all that I'd just sound nuts and Nicholas Darrow would be put in an awkward position as he figured out how to get rid of me, so I had to behave properly and sensibly, just as I always did in the world which existed beyond the walls of this church, and behaving properly and sensibly meant keeping my mouth shut, going home and pretending for ever afterwards that nothing out of the ordinary had taken place.

Yet that other world, the world where I always behaved properly and sensibly and never made an exhibition of myself by crying in public, now seemed as far away as the other side of the moon, and the next moment I realised I was no longer shrinking back against the wall. I was moving towards Nicholas Darrow. I still didn't see how I could bring myself to speak to him but that no longer mattered because I was sure now that if only I could touch him, no matter how briefly, I could magically siphon off some of his extraordinary power and pass it on to Aunt.

What a fantasy! Yet at that moment it seemed a brilliant idea, quite the most inspired plan it was possible to imagine. Nearer and nearer I crept, inch by inch, and all the time I was edging my way stealthily through the crowd I was drumming up courage by saying to myself: he'll never know.

When I finally reached him he was shaking hands with a gushing middle-aged woman. I could see her face shining with adoration, but the next moment she was hidden from me because I had moved directly behind him. I was very, very close now, so close that I could even see the faint hint of silver in the brown hair at the nape of his neck. The moment had come. I drew a deep breath. Then I raised my hand and laid my index finger gently, for a split second, between his shoulder-blades.

All hell broke loose.

As soon as he was touched he flinched as convulsively as if I'd knifed him, and spun round before I could recoil.

"Who was that?" he demanded in a voice which silenced the crowd. "Who touched me?" And as we at last came face to face I saw that his light eyes were neither blue nor green but a brilliant shade of grey.

III

"*It was you,* wasn't it?"

"I'm sorry, I'm sorry, I'm sorry—"

"It's all right."

"I'll go away—I won't come back—I'll never do it again, I promise—" I was gabbling in the manner of one of those respectable middle-aged women who are caught shoplifting. My face felt as if it were in flames. I tried to edge backwards but everyone in the crowd seemed to have been transformed into pillars and I found myself hemmed in. Tears streamed down my face again and although I scrabbled at once to annihilate them I felt horribly humiliated. What was happening to me? I couldn't begin to work it out. All I knew was that I must be conjuring up an image of a drowned porpoise, and as soon as this revolting thought crossed my mind my humiliation became unbearable.

"I hate myself," I sobbed. "I hate myself, I hate myself—"

He interrupted me. Reaching out he clasped my forearms with his long, strong fingers and said firmly: "It's going to be all right. Believe me. It's going to be all right."

Both my arms began to tingle.

I fainted.

IV

When I regained consciousness a woman was stooping over me, a youngish woman, bottle-blonde, square-faced, kind-eyed. "It's okay," she said as my eyes focused on her. "I'm a doctor. You just passed out for a moment."

I said distinctly: "How bloody awful," and blotted out the world by closing my eyes again.

I heard her say to someone nearby: "Stacy's taking his time getting that glass of water—anyone would think I'd told him to dig a well . . . Ah, here's Nick again. Nick, she's all right but don't let her dash off—she ought to sit quietly for a few minutes."

"Right." His fingers gently enfolded my hand and at once I opened my eyes.

He was kneeling by my side, his face inches from mine. "You need some strong tea," he said in such a practical voice that I felt a return to normality was not only possible but imminent. "Do you think you're well enough yet to sit up?"

The young red-headed clergyman had finally arrived with the glass of water. Levering myself into a sitting position I took a sip. The church had emptied, I noticed, but although I was relieved to be spared a large audience I was still speechless with embarrassment.

Nicholas Darrow said casually, without any hint of condescension or annoyance: "What's your name?"

"Alice," I said, "as in Wonderland." If running away is impossible, one can always withdraw behind a mask of facetiousness.

He smiled. Daring at last to look at him I saw the lines creasing the corners of his eyes. I also noticed he had very even teeth, unstained by nicotine. "I'm afraid I can't offer you Wonderland," he said amused. "I'm no wonder worker peddling magic. But I can provide you with an easy-chair in my office while you drink that tea I prescribed. Do you think you can now trust yourself to stand?"

Ignoring the outstretched hands of the doctor and the redhead, I scrambled to my feet and followed him.

V

Nicholas led me through the vestry and down the stairs into an area which had once formed the crypt of the church. To my astonishment I found myself in a large, brightly lit room which might have been the reception area of a doctor's office. The decoration was in soft, muted colours, very restful, and each item of the teak furniture seemed perfectly designed for the space allotted to it.

Bewildered I said: "What's all this?"

"The St. Benet's Healing Centre. I specialise in the traditional Christian ministry of healing, and that means I work hand in hand with orthodox medicine. Val, the doctor who looked after you just now, has a branch of her National Health practice here, and we have our own psychologist too."

As he spoke I was absorbing more details. I realised we had entered the Centre through a route reserved for the staff and that the glass swing doors, now facing me, formed the official entrance; they opened on to a flight of steps which led up into the churchyard. An assortment of plants made me aware that the reception area was not without natural light. The windows, set high up in the walls, were at ground level. Various signs directed visitors to a number of destinations, but apart from the intriguing arrow marked MUSIC THERAPY, these signs failed to register in my brain. I was too busy noticing the comfortable chairs, the table with the magazines and the grey-haired receptionist sipping coffee behind her desk.

"This is Pauline," said Nicholas to me. "Friday lunch-time's quiet for her as everyone's at the healing service and I have no fixed appointments directly afterwards. I like to leave time to see people who come to the service and stay on." And having put me at ease by implying I wasn't wrecking his busy schedule, he asked the receptionist to make us some tea.

On the other side of the area was a door marked CONSULTING ROOM ONE, and when I followed him inside I found myself in more austere surroundings. Waist-high bookshelves stretched along one wall. A desk and swivel-chair were placed beneath the high window. A small round table flanked by two easy-chairs stood in one corner, and two matching chairs were parked in front of the desk.

"Have a seat," said Nicholas, closing the door.

"Where do you want me to sit?"

"Where you'll feel most comfortable."

I chose one of the chairs parked by the desk.

"And where would you like me to sit?" he asked, surprising me.

"Oh, behind the desk," I said at once. "In the swivel-chair." I had already worked out that once we were seated the desk would hide the lower part of my body.

As we settled ourselves I noticed that above the bookshelves was a portrait in oils of a striking blonde with dark blue eyes and a beautiful mouth, delicately painted but suggesting strong emotions effortlessly concealed.

"What an interesting picture!" I said, having stared at it for so long that some comment seemed to be required. Of course I'd instantly guessed who she was.

"My wife says a photograph would have represented her more faithfully," he said, "but I myself think the artist's captured the essence of her personality." As an afterthought he added: "Sometimes the essence of a personality is hard to perceive. In fact sometimes it's heavily masked by the physical appearance."

Below the level of the desk my left hand tried to push in the roll of fat which bulged over my intestines and I found myself picturing how I must have looked to him when I was unconscious. So appalled was I by this thought that I didn't hear his next sentence and had to ask him to repeat it.

"I was asking why you touched me just now in the church."

I made the obvious reply. "How did you know I had?"

He smiled, but although he averted his eyes I didn't think he was embarrassed. I sensed he was merely concentrating on the task of explaining his eerie awareness in the most prosaic language available. All he said in the end was: "I felt the power go out of me."

The words had an oddly familiar ring, as if I had heard them long ago in a different context, but I refused to be diverted by an uncertain memory. Intrigued I said: "What power?"

"The healing power. It doesn't originate with me—I'm just the equivalent of a channel, although the word 'channel' gives too passive an impression. Perhaps it would be more accurate to say that all human beings have a certain healing energy which can be jacked up by the main source of the power."

"But what's the main source?"

"God."

"Oh."

We fell silent. I can see now that he had wanted me to reveal my position on religion and my lack of comment was as eloquent as a five-minute speech.

"Christians like me are different from magicians," he said tranquilly at last. "Magicians like to believe they're the masters of the healing powers—they like to believe that they can bend nature to their will."

"And you?"

"Oh, we've no room here for ego-trips and personality cults. Our call's to serve, not to dictate and control."

I said "Oh" again but this time I sounded more respectful. He was talking about integrity. That was something I could understand, and even though the religious view was alien to me I could share his belief that pride and arrogance were destructive while a clear-eyed modesty kept one honest.

"I'm saying all this," Nicholas was adding, "because newcomers to St. Benet's are often overwhelmed by the healing service, even though we try to keep it low-key and unsensational, and often they feel there's some sort of magic going on. But there isn't. It's just that healing can trigger unfamiliar emotional responses, particularly when past wounds are exposed."

"You mean—"

"I'm saying that although it must have been both embarrassing and unpleasant to faint in public, there's no need to reproach yourself for what happened. If anyone was to blame it was me."

"*You?*"

"But of course! I was the one who hit the roof and made you the focus of everyone's attention! No wonder you were so shocked you passed out!"

"Yes, but . . . I'm sorry, I still don't quite understand what happened. Why did you react like that?"

"I was exhausted. The healing service always depletes me, rubs me raw so that my awareness is magnified. I think what happened when you touched me was that I knew you were in desperate need yet I felt I had no strength left to help you—and that in turn triggered a panic reaction."

I said stupefied: "But how could you possibly have known I was in desperate need?"

"By using my common sense. If your need had been less desperate you'd have collared me and demanded a private audience. As it was, you were so overwhelmed by this problem of yours—whatever it is—that you were beyond words altogether."

I said slowly: "I hadn't realised I was so desperate."

"That suggests you've been living with the problem for so long that you've grown to think of it as a normal part of life. Are you going to tell me now what the problem actually is? After making such a hash of our introduction I feel the least I can do to make amends is to listen if you want to talk!"

I was still trying to find the words to thank him when the receptionist arrived with my medicine, the strong tea.

VI

"*Put* a spoonful of sugar in it," said Nicholas when we were alone again. "It'll accelerate your recovery."

I would have helped myself to two spoonfuls but I didn't want to appear greedy. Restricting myself to one I said with care: "I don't want to bother you when you're exhausted."

"I'm better now. The adrenaline's flowing again."

"But even so, I should probably just go on bearing the burden by myself—"

"That's for you to choose, of course, but don't forget that this is a place where people can set down their burdens and get some rest."

Again my memory was jogged. "You're paraphrasing some quotation or other," I said. "I must have heard it at school long ago. I went to this small private school in Kensington and I hated it but I had to pretend I liked it because Aunt was making a financial sacrifice to send me there. I had this aunt," I said rapidly, "this great-aunt who brought me up. She taught history at a GPDST school south of the river, but I couldn't pass the exam to go there, I wasn't clever enough. That was such a disappointment to her but she refused to let me go to the local comprehensive. She didn't like comprehensive schools. In fact there were a lot of things she didn't like—foreigners, the Labour Party, Roman Catholics, the tabloid press, bad manners, pierced ears, long hair on men, bell-bottom trousers, *Coronation Street*, Concorde, policemen with beards, litter, hamburgers and cruelty to animals. She was a real old battle-axe. She didn't go to church. She said the Church of England was okay for the rites of passage because that was Tradition, but otherwise churchgoing was a waste of time—England was her religion really, I suppose, and she didn't have room for another. She didn't believe in God. But she believed in a Christian education because—" I stopped, diverted. "Wait a minute," I said finally identifying the memory which had been niggling me. "That's the New Testament you keep paraphrasing."

"It's an occupational reflex. Why did your aunt believe in a Christian education?"

"She said it was part of England's culture and that those who ignored it would end up culturally illiterate. She believed in morality too and said free love was designed by men to do women out of their rights. She never minced her words. In fact she was beastly to me sometimes, but I know that was all my fault for being such a disappointment to her. I wasn't the sort of child she could be interested in; I wasn't clever or pretty. 'You're devoid of charm!' she said once when I was depressed. I felt so awful letting her down after she'd done so much for me. She sent me to one of the best cookery schools to get my Cordon Bleu—she always tried to get the best for me, I suppose she thought it was her moral duty because I can't think why else she would have bothered. She talked a lot about moral duty—and about integrity. That's why she hated watching the politicians who were slimy on TV. 'They've got no integrity!' she'd say. 'They wouldn't recognise the word even if it was displayed in lights at Piccadilly

Circus!' Well, she stuck by her moral duty to me, I'll say that for her. She was a bloody-minded old bag, but she was all-of-a-piece and she practised what she preached."

Nicholas merely said: "When did she die?"

"A month ago after the last stroke—except that she hasn't physically died because her heart's still beating. She's still alive," I said in despair, and pressed my clenched fists against my eyes to smother the tears.

VII

I told him about the succession of strokes which had slowly destroyed her health. I told him of my struggles with the Social Services to get some measure of nursing help during the day so that I could continue to work part-time to pay the bills. I told him how Aunt's capital, always a modest sum, was now dwindling fast, especially since I had been obliged to give up my permanent job to look after her.

"And then after the last stroke," I said, "I found myself in an impossible situation. I couldn't cope with the additional nursing which was required—she now has to be turned every two hours—and I found I was getting so tired as the result of lack of sleep that I didn't have the strength for my temporary work. So I'm having to hire night-nurses but they're so expensive that I've got to go back to work full-time—and that means I have to get nurses during the day as well to supplement the care provided by the Social Services, and I doubt if I can earn enough money to pay for all this—in fact I know I can't, it's a losing battle, it's a nightmare with no end in sight, but I can't abandon her, I just can't—I've got to stand by her just as she always stood by me—"

"Of course you've considered the option of hospital and free care under the National Health."

"That was never an option. She had a horror of the geriatric wards. One of her friends died there, and I promised long ago after the first stroke—"

"I understand. What do the doctors say?"

"Nothing much nowadays. They probably think I'm nuts even to try to keep her at home."

"So it's a double-headed problem, isn't it? How do we enable your aunt to live her remaining days in her own home, and at the same time how do we ease this enormous burden on you?"

"Exactly." I felt so relieved not only by his acceptance of my stubborn, possibly stupid refusal to break my word that I was able to say: "You're not going to advise me to dump her?"

"I don't think such advice would be helpful."

"Because of the moral issue involved in breaking a promise?"

"That sounds as if morality has nothing to do with common-sense decisions about how to survive the consequences of one's actions! The truth is that after your aunt's dead, you'll have to live with the memory of how you handled her last days and you won't want that memory to include a crucifying guilt which will blight your future."

"So what you're saying is—"

"I'd rather meet you where you are, not where other people think you ought to be, and that involves respecting a decision which is still valid for you. In the end only the carer can know when there's no strength left to cope and when no avenue of help remains unexplored . . . What exactly is the medical prognosis?"

"Zilch—but I accept that and I'm not seeking a miracle cure. All I want is for her to go back to where she was before she had the last stroke. Then I could cope on my own again with just the help from the Social Services."

Nicholas said evenly: "I'm afraid the likelihood is that no physical improvement is possible and I'd be seriously misleading you if I gave you cause to think otherwise. However, here at St. Benet's we always make a distinction between a cure and a healing. Even if no cure is possible a healing can still take place."

"I don't understand."

"A cure is the disabled person who gets up from his bed and walks. A healing is that same disabled person coming to terms with his lack of mobility, transcending his anger and grief and becoming an inspiration to all those who visit him."

"Well, Aunt's quite beyond any of that."

"The healing can take many forms . . . Would you like me to call on her and perform the laying-on of hands? If she's strongly anti-Catholic I think I'd abstain in this case from administering unction, but the laying-on of hands is non-denominational and isn't even confined to Christian healers."

I was so overcome with gratitude that I could hardly find the words to thank him, but the next moment an unpleasant thought occurred to me. "Will her non-belief in God block the healing?"

"Not necessarily."

"But if she's basically hostile—"

He smiled and said: "Obviously I'd prefer a non-hostile patient, but the hostility may be a surface emotion of no particular importance and beneath it the built-in human desire to be well may be burning with an additional intensity . . . Can your aunt speak at all now?"

"No."

"How much does she still understand?"

"The doctors say she understands nothing."

"And what do you say?"

With difficulty I answered: "I think sometimes she comes back. I think sometimes she's still there."

We sat in silence for a moment. At last I whispered, still hardly daring to believe he was willing to help: "When will you come to see her?" And straight away he replied:

"Tonight. What's your address?"

VIII

Five hours later I was sitting in Aunt's bedroom and waiting for Nicholas to arrive. I had cancelled the night-nurse. I didn't want her flapping around and getting in the way.

Aunt and I lived in a little cottage in Dean Danvers Street, a stone's throw from Westminster Abbey and the Houses of Parliament. She didn't own the cottage; she had acquired it by securing a tenancy at a rock-bottom rent during the war, and now she was a "sitting tenant," still paying a pittance but safe from any attempt the landlords might make to evict her. For a time I'd hoped I could inherit the tenancy under one of the Rent Acts, but her solicitor had told me there were legal difficulties which made this hope an impossible dream.

The cottage stood amidst the little network of Georgian streets by Smith Square. It was a pleasant area but unfashionable. Not far away the yuppies were driving property prices sky-high in Pimlico and the mega-rich were busy refurbishing Belgravia, but Westminster, still mainly a mass of council flats, hostels for derelicts and pieds-à-terre for MPs, was hardly the place for anyone keen to display wealth and status.

Big Ben was striking as I sat on the edge of the chair by Aunt's bed. Often inaudible in the house during the day when the traffic was at its heaviest, the clock seemed surprisingly loud at night. Sometimes, in those dark hours before the dawn, I even fancied I could hear that gigantic mechanism ticking.

"There's a clergyman coming to see you," I said to Aunt, "but don't worry, he's not wet or stupid. I met him today by chance."

I paused but Aunt's gaze remained fixed on the ceiling, her blue eyes vacant. She had once been tall and robust but now she was thin and wizened, her hands like claws, her skin barely concealing her skull.

"This man has a Guild church in the City," I said, waving in front of her the pamphlet Nicholas had given me before I had left his office. "Remember the Guild churches and their special ministries which were started up after the war? They're closed on weekends but open during the week to serve the workers in the City." I pointed to the picture on the front of the pamphlet. "The church is called St. Benet's-by-the-Wall—it was built by Wren, damaged in the Blitz and completely rearranged inside just a few years ago when the crypt was converted into something called a Healing Centre. It stands in Egg Street just south of the Barbican."

No response. Nothing. I was just wondering idly if I'd get a reaction by shouting that I wanted to leap into bed with Nicholas and make love to him from dusk till dawn, when the doorbell rang and at once my heart thudded in a way which recalled Big Ben booming the hour. Adjusting my tent-dress I checked my make-up in the mirror and hurried downstairs to the hall.

He was not alone. Immediately I felt a pang of disappointment, but a second later I was despising myself for my stupidity. Had I really hoped for a cosy chat over Aunt's almost-corpse? How pathetic! Pulling myself together I did my best to smile in welcome as I registered the fact that the woman with him was the bottle-blonde who had attended me when I'd fainted.

"I should have warned you that we always work in pairs when we're paying calls," said Nicholas after the preliminary greetings had been exchanged, "and in this case, as your aunt's so ill, it seemed wise to bring a doctor with me."

"Val Fredericks," said the blonde briskly to me, and gave my hand a quick clasp before stepping past him into the hall. "I'm Nicholas's partner under the Acorn Trust."

"What's that?"

"Just an organisation which encourages priests and doctors to work together," said Nicholas, following her across the threshold and closing the door behind him, "but never mind that for the moment. Now, before we start I'd like to clarify a few details with you and Val would like to look at the patient. It is all right if she sits with your aunt while we talk?"

"I won't examine her," said the blonde quickly. "That would be trespassing on ground already covered by your aunt's doctors, but it would be helpful if I could observe her for a couple of minutes."

Having no objection I showed Nicholas into the sitting-room and took Val upstairs. To Aunt I said: "This is Dr. Fredericks. She's a colleague of that clergyman I told you about." And when Aunt remained corpse-like I said defiantly to the stranger beside me: "I always introduce her to visitors."

"Of course," said Val, as if it were perfectly normal to assume that someone in Aunt's state would care about the social niceties, and sat down in the chair by the bedside.

I returned downstairs.

That afternoon I had spent over an hour cleaning the sitting-room and I was glad to see my efforts showed despite the dark, faded wallpaper and the threadbare carpet. Most of Aunt's good pieces of furniture had been sold by this time, but I had managed to keep her three favourites—the grandfather clock, the desk and the bookcase—and these were now highly polished, glowing in the soft light from the lamps. On my way home from the City I'd bought some daffodils at the market on Strutton Ground and these were now arranged in Aunt's best Waterford crystal vase. Flowers always made such a difference to a shabby room, and Nicholas was noticing them; he was touching the petals briefly and the daffodils seemed to strain towards him as if he were exuding an invisible light. On the table by the vase was Aunt's cherished photograph of her golden cat, now deceased. I watched as Nicholas's fingers wandered from the flowers to the frame. "Handsome!" was his comment as he replaced the photograph on the table.

"That's Orlando on his twelfth birthday. He actually lived to be eighteen, but then he got kidney trouble and—but you don't want to hear all that. Sorry. Do sit down."

He smiled reassuringly, settled himself in the larger of the two armchairs which flanked the fireplace and pulled a notebook from his pocket. "Our conversation earlier was helpful," he said, "but there are more things I need to know. For a start, what's your aunt's name?"

"Beatrice Harrison."

"And how old is she?"

"Eighty-two."

"Did she ever marry?"

"No, she was too plain. She said a plain streak ran through the family and plain women never married."

Nicholas raised an eyebrow. "Never?"

"Well, she didn't. And I haven't. So she thought no plain woman did."

"That reminds me of the famous argument about dogs and cats: 'My dog has four legs. Your cat has four legs. Therefore my dog is a cat.' "

"I don't quite see—"

"It's using logic to prove an absurdity. But tell me more about this family of yours. Are your parents dead?"

"My father might be. He dropped out and went to Canada over thirty years ago and I've heard nothing from him since. My mother dropped out of my life too but she's alive and well and living in Manchester with her second husband."

"You see her sometimes?"

"Oh God, no! But I've got her address and I'll let her know when Aunt dies . . . Which reminds me, what have all these questions to do with Aunt and her illness?"

"Background information gives me a clearer picture of what to pray for. Is your aunt's doctor also your doctor?"

"Yes."

"Do you like her?"

"Him. Not particularly. Well, to be truthful, I never go near him if I can help it."

"That doesn't sound satisfactory. What's his problem?"

"Well, it's my problem, not his. Whenever I show up at his surgery he just goes on and on about the dangers of being overweight, and by the time I get home I'm so upset I have to binge to calm myself down."

"If he doesn't realise how much he's upsetting you I'd say the problem was very far from being yours alone."

"You mean—"

"I'm often asked to help people who express distress through their use of food or some other substance, and I can tell you that adopting an authoritarian stance and giving lectures is usually a complete waste of time. But let's get back to your aunt. Have you told her about me?"

"Yes, but there was no reaction. Mr. Darrow"—I drew a deep

breath—"if all goes well, what do you think might happen? I mean, what are the possibilities?"

"Well, there's always a chance she'll astound us by sitting up in bed and announcing that she's cured—I've seen some extraordinary things happen during my ministry—but as I implied earlier, although a cure's possible I don't think it's likely. What I always hope for, when I'm treating terminal patients, is that there'll be a chance to clear up the unfinished business which is oppressing not only the dying but those closest to them. If your aunt can no longer speak that makes my task more difficult, but sometimes important messages can be conveyed without using words at all."

"I'm just so terrified you'll get no reaction."

"If that happens I'd propose trying again next week. From what you say I think there's still a chance I can make contact."

"But I could be wrong in thinking she's still there sometimes—"

"You could be, yes, but I'm going to assume you're right. I'm also going to assume she can hear, since hearing is often the last sense to go, and finally I'm going to assume that she's *compos mentis* whenever she slips back into consciousness."

I said in despair, "That's a lot of assuming."

"But it's by no means an impossible scenario. Think of a pianist locked up in a room with a vandalised grand piano. He can clearly remember how to play the 'Moonlight Sonata' but the right noises are no longer available."

"But if the piano's beyond repair—"

"There could be one or two notes which still ring true. But the pianist has to be encouraged to search for them."

"And how do we do that?"

"Leave that to me. All you've got to do is to provide support. Don't worry if you can't believe in something code-named God. If you feel you can't in honesty pray, try instead to summon up the love you feel for your aunt and wrap it around her as if it were a very expensive coat and she were suffering from hypothermia."

"Okay, but—"

"If your aunt's surrounded by love then God will be present—no, never mind if you can't share that belief! The important thing is that you should believe that *I* believe it, and back me every inch of the way. So long as you're a positive presence there'll be no danger of things going wrong."

"How could things go wrong?"

"There's always a dark side to every situation. I believe you love your aunt, but I can see your relationship with her has its unhappy aspects. If that unhappiness is allowed to surface, the love will be obscured and the channel of healing will get clogged up by the wrong emotions."

"But you're the channel, not me!"

"No, this is a joint venture. Remember what I said earlier about the built-in human desire to be well? That desire seems to exist on the level of consciousness where all human beings connect, and we'll be operating at that level when we try to help your aunt. It's the level at which we're all potentially healers, all capable of bringing our special energy to the healing process and linking up—if only the channel can be kept clear—with the overall energy of our Creator."

"But you're the professional healer and I could only be just an ignorant amateur!"

"In a worldly sense, yes, but we're both human beings so the access to God is the same—and since we're equal before God it's pointless to quibble about status. The big challenge is not to become what the world describes as a professional but to harness one's energy properly and keep the channel unclogged."

"And are there techniques for doing that?"

"All healers, religious and secular, have their techniques. My technique is to try to follow the example of Jesus Christ, the greatest healer who ever lived. I'll always fall short, of course, but if I stopped trying I'd be done for."

"Why?"

"Ah well . . . I suppose it's all really a question of integrity."

Such was the strength of his personality that I suddenly felt I was capable of believing anything he believed in—God, Christ, the Holy Spirit—the whole Trinitarian caboosh. And despite his warnings not to expect a miracle-cure I was now convinced he could solve my problems merely by tapping Aunt with his index finger.

It embarrasses me now to think how naive I was.

What happened was far more extraordinary than that.

IX

"*Aunt,* this is Mr. Nicholas Darrow," I said too loudly when I returned to her bedside. "I told you about him earlier. He's the clergyman from St. Benet's-by-the-Wall."

Nicholas took Aunt's claw and held it as he murmured the conventional words of introduction. Then he sat down on the chair which Val had vacated and motioned me to take the chair on the other side of Aunt's inert body. Val herself had withdrawn to stand at the foot of the bed.

Without any trace of tension Nicholas said clearly to Aunt: "Alice talked to me today. I daresay she'd never normally discuss her worries with a clergyman"—with relief I noticed the omission of the Romish "priest," a word guaranteed to grate on Aunt's nerves, especially when used by a clergyman of the Church of England—"but her circumstances now aren't normal, are they, and she's so anxious to do her best for you."

He paused but there was no response.

"I'm familiar with illness," resumed Nicholas unperturbed. "That's because I work in the ministry of healing—I work with doctors, and my ministry's approved both by the Church and by the British Medical Association. So you can be sure Alice hasn't made a fool of herself and hired some shady wonder worker who has no genuine credentials. And you can be sure too that she's talked to me not because she wanted to gossip and not because she wanted to complain about the tough hand you've both been dealt, but because she was seeking help for someone who's special to her."

He paused again. Still no response.

"As Alice talked," said Nicholas undeterred, "I had several thoughts. The first was: what a wonderful thing you did, taking on Alice like that! But it must have been hard for you, a single woman no longer young, to cope with bringing up a child in addition to holding down a demanding job. My second thought was that you must have experienced considerable stress from time to time—you must have encountered numerous problems which hadn't come your way before, and you had to solve them without anyone to help you. My third thought was how heroic you were to try to keep all your anxieties from Alice—but Alice sensed them, didn't she, and thought you were disappointed in her. Well, maybe you were from time to time. Children don't exist merely to provide their parents or guardians with an unbroken flow of satisfaction. But wasn't the main problem the fact that you feared you might make a hash of this enormous task you'd undertaken? Weren't you afraid above all of falling short of those very high standards of yours? It occurs to me that far from being disappointed in Alice you were terrified that Alice would wind up being disappointed in you. Perhaps you were even afraid sometimes of breaking down and having to put Alice into care."

He paused a third time but there was no reaction from Aunt. She merely lay motionless, her gaze fixed on the ceiling.

But *my* face, I knew, was by this time expressing the deepest possible emotion. I was aware of my lips parting in amazement as my breathing became more rapid. The implications of Nicholas's monologue swirled through my mind, and I turned my head to stare at him.

He ignored me. "That's why I want to tell you what a success you've made of bringing Alice up," he said to Aunt. "Alice thinks that in your eyes she's riddled with faults, but she's got it wrong, hasn't she? You don't care about any run-of-the-mill shortcomings because all you've wanted is for Alice to be a woman of integrity, just as you are. Well, you've got what you wanted and now Alice has the guts to stand by you just as you always stood by her. She loves you and she wants justice for you—which is why I'm here tonight. Pain and suffering have ruled this house long enough, and now it's time for them to be challenged."

He stopped. There was no movement from the bed but I wasn't expecting that now. I was sitting bolt upright on the edge of the chair with my fists clenched.

Nicholas was saying: "I'm going to ask God for help but I won't be talking to the fake-God so many people still believe in, the one who's just a brutal tyrant enjoying an early retirement in the sky. I'll be talking to the working God, the one who's still creating the world and in consequence suffering alongside us, the one who never wills pain but slaves always to redeem it. And while I talk to him, please think of Alice, loving you enough to long for justice, and picture what you'd say to her if you could speak."

He leant forward. He'd been holding Aunt's hand throughout this monologue, but now he used both his hands to encircle hers before saying: "I'm going to recite three short prayers. Then we'll be silent for a while as we think our own thoughts and wish our own wishes. When I end that silence we'll all hold hands and I'll pray directly for help."

He started out on the first prayer, but my thoughts were now so chaotic that I was unable to concentrate. All I could do was wipe the mist from my glasses, but the moment they were replaced I was distracted again because I could now see his face with such clarity. I even noticed the way his cheekbones caught the light as he drew closer to Aunt, trapped as she was in the damaged body which had become so frail.

It was as the second prayer began that I remembered his request for support, and at once guilt needled me because I knew I should have remembered sooner. In an effort to make amends I cried out in my head: "Come on, Nicholas, *come on!*" for all the world as if he were battling some formidable opponent on the Centre Court at Wimbledon and I was bawling encouragement between the rallies, but when he stopped the spoken prayers to allow the silence to begin, the image of Wimbledon faded and all I could think of was Aunt, rescuing me long ago and making so many sacrifices to see that justice was done. Then I found myself shouting silently to the God Nicholas believed in: "Help her, help her—please, please, please—" and as the words rang out in my mind I knew how much I really did love her, silly, opinionated old bag, and how much I longed to prove to her that I was worth all the trouble she'd taken to bring me up. So I added to Nicholas's God: "Make it all come right!"—and at that precise moment my chaotic thoughts were swept aside as Nicholas finally rose to his feet.

He kept Aunt's claw in his right hand and held out his left to Val. She in turn reached out to me and I took Aunt's other claw to complete the circle.

When all our hands were clasped Nicholas said clearly, without fuss or melodrama: "In the name of Jesus Christ . . ." But my concentration broke again before he finished the sentence. I was looking at Aunt and the words GET WELL were ringing in my mind, but Aunt was corpse-like still, no change there, and in a wave of despair I looked away from her towards Nicholas. Instantly the despair was wiped out. I knew why. It was because I loved him, and the love was stronger than any of the negative feelings which were trying to penetrate our circle. I found myself saying to him soundlessly over and over again: "I believe in you, I support you, I love you," and as I directed this tidal wave of truth towards him he made one of his fluent, graceful movements, unclasping his hands and pressing them down on Aunt's head.

For several seconds he was motionless, his eyes closed, his whole body seeming to vibrate with concentration, but at last he withdrew his hands, crossed himself and said a final prayer. "May the grace of Our Lord Jesus Christ and the love of God and . . ." I lost track again.

I was trying to dredge up the courage to face the sight of Aunt, immobile and unchanged despite all our efforts.

". . . Amen," concluded Nicholas.

I managed to look at her. Nothing had happened. The entire exercise had been a complete waste of time, and now I felt not only deeply embarrassed but unspeakably angry. Releasing the claw I thought: how insane to beg God for justice! Everyone knew there was no real justice in this world, everyone. Life was always so vilely unfair.

"Alice."

I jumped. Confused by my rage I thought at first that Val was addressing me, but I couldn't think why she should be whispering.

I turned to her but she was silent. In fact she wasn't even looking at me. She was staring open-mouthed down the bed at Aunt, and a second later, as the shock hit me like a bullet between the eyes, I suddenly realised what was going on.

2

> You need help and support as you resolve to journey *with* your pain rather than to anaesthetise it at regular intervals . . . Key relationships are crucial.
>
> GARETH TUCKWELL AND DAVID FLAGG
> *A Question of Healing*

I

Nicholas was at my side in a flash. "She's blind," he said. "Take her hand again."

I collapsed to my knees by the bed, grabbed Aunt's claw and leant over her so that my face was inches from hers. "I'm here," I said. "I'm here—"

She whispered my name again but could say nothing else.

"Stay where you are," said Nicholas to me. Reaching forward he stroked Aunt's lank, sparse hair gently with his fingers. "Take your time," he said to her. "Alice is listening. She won't go away."

Aunt's face finally changed.

The gaze was no longer vacant. Her eyes were anxious. The muscles on one side of her mouth were twitching. Her shallow breathing became rapid in her agitation.

Before I could stop myself I was gabbling: "I'm sorry for all the times I let you down by not being clever or pretty, I'm sorry I wasn't what you wanted, I'm sorry you had to put up with me all those years, but I'm trying so hard to keep you out of hospital, I'm trying so hard to keep my promise—" I broke off, unable to continue, but Aunt was paying no attention. Her entire will was focused on the task of speaking, and the moment I fell silent she whispered for the third time: "Alice." I saw the veins stand out on her forehead as she made this enormous effort to communicate. Then as Nicholas laid a finger delicately against the twitching muscle at the corner of her mouth she uttered two words in succession. They were: "*Dear* Alice."

Everything changed. Past, present, future—all were tossed in the melting-pot, and when they emerged again the past had been rewritten, the present was transformed and the future was redesigned.

"This is what you wanted, wasn't it, Miss Harrison?" said Nicholas to her. "You wanted so much to talk to Alice one more time."

Aunt's claw tightened around my hand. I thought at first it was an involuntary spasm but it wasn't. The spasm didn't subside. She was using all her strength to hold my hand and utter another word.

Frantically I said to Nicholas: "I didn't hear that. What did she say?"

" 'Forgive.' "

"You're saying you forgive me?" I said to Aunt. "You forgive me for not being the sort of child you wanted?"

Aunt became more agitated. Her breathing was shallower, and one side of her face was now contorted.

"I think, Alice," said Nicholas at last, "that it's you who's being asked to do the forgiving."

"Oh my God . . ." I tore off my glasses with a sob and chucked them down on the bed. "Why, you silly old woman, what's there to forgive? You took me in and looked after me and—" I broke off as I realised Aunt was trying to interrupt. Again she said: "Forgive," and this time I recognised the word straight away.

At last I saw what was required. Clutching her hand tightly I said in my firmest voice: "Of course I forgive you. I forgive you because I love you. It's all right. Everything's all right, and you don't have to worry any more."

At once the strength flooded through her. She whispered clearly, so clearly that misunderstanding was impossible: "Best of girls. Such a blessing. How lucky I was."

Then as the power of speech was abruptly withdrawn, I sensed her slip away, at peace at last, into the uncharted sea which separated her from death.

11

Val had moved to feel Aunt's pulse. Wiping my eyes again I said dully: "Is she dead?"

"No." She laid Aunt's hand carefully back on the sheet. "The pulse is rapid but that's to be expected after all the exertion. There probably won't be any serious change for a while, but her own doctor should take a look at her." Unexpectedly she put her arms around me, and in the second before I started crying again I saw Nicholas slump down exhausted on the nearest chair.

Drawing away from Val I stumbled to the bathroom where I found my make-up was a mess, ravaged beyond repair. I washed it off and to my surprise found that my hand was steady. A great calmness had descended on me. Aloud I said to Aunt: "Bon voyage," and in my mind's eye I saw that dark sea stretching to the bright light beyond the rim of the horizon. In the near-death experiences I had read about in the papers, there was always a bright light at the end of the darkness. Aunt had said that was a hallucination caused by lack of oxygen to the brain, but it had long since occurred to me how odd it was that so many people should have such similar hallucinations. I'd thought hallucinations were as diverse as dreams.

When I returned to Aunt's bedroom I said: "I'll be okay now. I'll sit with her till it's over."

Val said: "It may still take some time. If you want me to call a nurse—"

"I'd rather wait alone."

"But you'll phone her doctor? I really think—" She broke off as Nicholas put a hand on her arm.

"Alice is all right," he said. "Alice can now make the decisions which have to be made."

My voice said: "Alice is healed." I passed the back of my hand over my hot forehead and marvelled that I hadn't understood before. "I was the patient, wasn't I?" I said. "You always knew there'd be nothing much you could do for Aunt, but you realised there was a lot you could do for me."

Nicholas merely said: "Healing's an ongoing process. We all need healing all the time, but each healing makes us fitter for the journey." He stroked Aunt's hair for the last time and said goodbye to her. Then, clumsy with weariness, he staggered downstairs to the hall.

III

Val said gently: "I know he didn't cure your aunt but he did help her. Now she can let go and die in peace."

"I'm sorry, I didn't mean to imply there was no healing there too. Of course it was a miracle that she managed to speak—"

"Oh, that wasn't a miracle. It was an unusual thing to happen and makes me wonder if the loss of speech was due more to the shock of the last stroke than to brain damage, but I've seen other patients speak in unlikely circumstances if the motivation is strong. No, the real miracle—and Nick hates that word!—was that you and she were able to complete the unfinished business."

"Val!" shouted Nicholas from the hall.

"I must go." She pressed her card into my hand. "Call me if you change your mind about the nurse—or if you simply want to talk."

I thanked her and led the way downstairs. I couldn't find the words to thank Nicholas but I clasped his hand tightly in gratitude.

All he said was: "We'll talk later," and within seconds he was gone.

IV

I sat by Aunt's bed as the night ebbed and Big Ben marked the quarter-hours. I was still thinking of Nicholas. Apart from Aunt, who in the beginning at least had only cared for me out of a sense of duty, he was the only person who had ever acted as if I had some value as a human being. I thought of the vast numbers of people he must know, the numerous claims on his time, his busy life in the heart of London. Yet he hadn't hesitated to set aside part of his evening to help someone who constantly found herself written off as a fat nonentity.

That reminded me of how badly I did at interviews and that in turn made me peer fearfully into the future. I was going to lose my home and there would be hardly any money left to inherit. I'd have to get a live-in job—probably in some institution so desperate for help that they would even employ a fat nonentity who hadn't had a full-time job for a while. However, I knew I'd be fortunate to have free accommodation, no matter how dreary the circumstances, so I said to Aunt: "I'll manage. I'll be all right."

Aunt's breathing changed before dawn. I almost called the doctor but I thought he might be angry, summoned from his bed when there was nothing he could do, so I never picked up the phone. Instead I held Aunt's hand. I wasn't frightened. Death was coming as a friend. He was wanted, welcomed. Aunt was ready now.

The breathing became much stranger, so I knew the end was near. That type of breathing had some special name; I'd read about it somewhere, probably in the medical column of a magazine or newspaper. Aunt had always taken *The Times*, but newspapers nowadays were so expensive that I had decided even the *Daily Mail* was an extravagance I couldn't afford.

Death came—and to my surprise Aunt looked different afterwards. She had been corpse-like for so long that I'd assumed no further change in her appearance would be possible, but although I still felt her presence in the room I saw the body had been abandoned. That was now just an arrangement of matter which had somehow lost its familiarity.

There were no tears—and no sleep either; I didn't feel tired any more. I felt as if I were on some drug-induced high, very peculiar it was, but wasn't morphine produced naturally in the brain in certain circumstances? I thought I had seen that too reported in some medical column. I liked medical matters. If I hadn't been so stupid I would have wanted to become a doctor—like Val, working alongside Nicholas at St. Benet's-by-the-Wall.

At eight I phoned Aunt's doctor, and while I waited for him to arrive I called Val to tell her what had happened. She was very kind. After she had said all that needed to be said she added: "Nick's always out of town on weekends, but I'll phone his colleague, Father Lewis Hall, and I'm sure he'll want to get in touch with you."

I'd forgotten it was Saturday and that the Guild churches of the City would be closed for the weekend. I wondered where Nicholas went. I pictured him in a beautiful country house with his elegant wife. What would he do with himself on weekends? Work in the garden? Play cricket on some village green? Read novels? Take the children on outings? (Of course there would be children.) I found I couldn't imagine him having anything so ordinary as a family life. And there was no point in day-dreaming about him anyway. I started to think of Aunt again.

Going to her desk I removed the will, which I had found after the first stroke, and broke the seal of the envelope. I knew she would have left everything to me, but I wanted to find out if she had left instructions for her funeral. She had. That militant non-believer who despised clergymen had written in a note attached to the legal document: "I hereby give instructions that my body is to be cremated after a *short* service conducted according to the rites of the Church of England. Every English person, regardless of religious belief, should observe the tribal custom of being buried by the English church. This is what being a member of Our Great Island Race is all about. (Churchill understood this perfectly.) NOTE: The readings must be taken *only* from St. John's Gospel, a work of extraordinary literary merit, and there is to be *no singing.* (Without a first-class choir singing is pointless.) Under no circumstances whatsoever should that ghastly but popular passage from the writings of Canon Henry Scott Holland be read, and under no circumstances whatsoever must anyone give some nauseating speech about how wonderful I was. The clergyman must refer to me throughout as Miss Harrison, not as Beatrice or—God forbid—Bea."

That seemed clear enough, but I wondered what the clergyman at the crematorium would think.

The doorbell rang to herald the arrival of Aunt's doctor.

V

At eleven o'clock that morning, after the undertakers had removed Aunt's body and just as I was beginning to realise how much there was to do after someone died, the doorbell rang again and this time I found Nicholas's colleague on the doorstep. He was the silver-haired clergyman who had read the lesson at the healing service, and at the time I had assumed he was just another decorous elderly gentleman in a clerical collar, but as soon as I saw him at close quarters I realised I'd been mistaken.

For a start, his silver hair was shaggy and allowed to taper into furry sideburns which gave him a rakish look. He also had yellow teeth (he reeked of nicotine) and sinister black eyes which conjured up images of gangsters. In a heroic effort to neutralise this villainous appearance he had encased himself in an exquisitely cut clerical suit, but this only made him look like an actor who had been hopelessly miscast.

"Miss Fletcher?" he said briskly. "I'm Lewis Hall, and I assist Nicholas Darrow at St. Benet's. Is this a bad moment to call? If it is, just say so and I'll disappear—and don't worry about giving me offence because I assure you I shan't take it."

I found this straight talk very refreshing. The detestable doctor had been unctuous to hide his relief that Aunt could now be struck off his list of patients.

"Thank you, Mr. Hall," I said. "Do please come in." As I showed him into the living-room I noticed again that he had a pronounced limp. Accepting my offer of tea, he bared his yellow teeth in a benign smile when I mentioned the word "cake."

"I'm always very partial to elevenses," he said.

I had made a large banana cake the previous day and although most of it had now gone there was still enough left for two generous slices. Mr. Hall took one bite of his slice and demanded: "Is this from Harrods?"

"No, I made it. I'm a cook. It's what I do for a living."

"I trust you have a top job at Buckingham Palace."

As I smiled, grateful for his kindness, I suddenly realised that he too was treating me as if I were a real person instead of a fat freak. I began to feel less shy.

"But I must stop drooling over the cake," he was saying briskly, "and start talking about you. First, let me offer you my sympathy. Even a long-awaited death can be extremely distressing when it finally comes. Second, let me offer you some assistance in dealing with all the things that have to be done. I understand there's no family available."

"Well, that's most kind of you, but—"

"At St. Benet's we have a team of people we call Befrienders—their main task is to listen to people in trouble, but occasionally it's appropriate for them to take a more active role, particularly when someone's bereaved and on her own. You talked to Francie, I believe, at the church yesterday?"

I said startled: "How did you know?"

"It's in Nicholas's case-notes—when you fainted she told him she'd spoken to you earlier. Now, we've often asked Francie to lend a helping hand in this sort of situation. You'd still be in control—she'll do as much or as little as you want—and if she gets on your nerves you can tell her to get lost. But she could be useful."

I found the proposal tempting. I remembered how willingly Francie had accepted my refusal to go up to the altar-rail for the laying-on of hands, how efficiently she had supplied me with Kleenex tissues, how tactfully she had avoided making a fuss.

"There are also spiritual matters as well as practical matters to be considered," resumed Mr. Hall purposefully after pausing to sink his teeth again into the cake. "Do you need a priest to conduct the funeral?"

"Clergyman," I said automatically. "Aunt wasn't a Catholic."

He at once apologised, explaining that although he was from the Anglo-Catholic wing of the Church of England he respected the fact that the Church was a broad umbrella, sheltering Catholics and Protestants alike. "And was your aunt a churchgoer?" he enquired between swigs of tea.

"No," I said, but I was so reassured by his willingness to tolerate Protestants that I decided to show him Aunt's funeral instructions. He laughed at the reference to Scott Holland. "What a character your aunt must have been!" he commented amused, and I found myself beginning to talk to him of the past. In the end I even mentioned my awful mother up in Manchester and my vanished father who if he was still alive was probably being equally awful somewhere in Canada, and all the time Mr. Hall listened and nodded and watched me with those sinister black eyes which were now so bright with kindness, but at last it occurred to me that I must be taking up more time than he had allotted to the call, and I brought this rambling monologue to a swift conclusion.

". . . and so there it is," I said vaguely, not sure what "it" was, but the next moment I was remembering that I still hadn't answered his question about whether I needed someone to conduct the funeral. "Don't worry about the service," I said hastily. "The crematorium people will have a rota of clergymen, won't they, and I'll just take whoever's on duty that day."

Mr. Hall, who was busy building a pyramid with the crumbs left over from his banana cake, said casually: "Nicholas would conduct the funeral for you."

I was astounded but somehow managed to say colourlessly: "I wouldn't dream of troubling him further when he's already done so much."

Mr. Hall's hand halted above his pyramid of crumbs, and as he looked at me sharply I sensed my response had intrigued him so much that he was making a rapid reassessment of my character. It occurred to me then that most women would have given a very different response when offered further pastoral attention from Nicholas Darrow.

"How very considerate of you," said Mr. Hall pleasantly at last, "but there's still no need to fall back on a clergyman from the crematorium rota. I'd be more than willing to take the service if you wish." And when I hesitated, fearful of being a bore yet tempted to accept his offer, he added kindly: "Think it over and let me know—and think over too what I said about Francie." Then he asked me if I wanted him to say a prayer before he left.

"No thanks," I said at once, but this flat refusal struck me as horribly rude, particularly when he had been so nice to me. "I'm very glad you called," I added in a rush. "Please don't think I'm not grateful."

He smiled, not in the least put out by my rejection of the prayer, and taking a card from his wallet he wrote on the back: MRS. FRANCINE PARKER (FRANCIE). A series of numerals followed as he added her telephone number.

"I'm glad to have met you, Miss Fletcher," he said, placing the card on the tray beside the teapot, "and do please give me a call either at the Healing Centre or at the Rectory if you need further help of any kind."

I thanked him, led him to the front door and watched as he limped down the street to the parking meter at the far end. His car was a dusty red Volkswagen Golf, workmanlike and respectable, but he drove it like a Porsche. I heard the engine roar and the tires squeal as he surged off around the corner into Smith Square.

A very peculiar clergyman.

Drifting back into the kitchen I mechanically began to make another banana cake.

VI

Apparently my healing, such as it was, had left my compulsion to eat untouched. But what had I expected? A craving for a liquid diet of a thousand calories a day? I might fantasise about losing four stone and winding up with the ideal husband, but at heart I knew this was just a romantic dream which hadn't a hope of coming true. I did feel a little better about myself now I knew Aunt had genuinely cared for me, but how could I ever feel more than a little better when I was still repulsively fat and likely to remain so? Stress always drove me to binge, and although I no longer had to cope with Aunt I still had to endure the strain of making a new life for myself.

I knew I needed the help Mr. Hall had suggested, but still I hesitated to phone Francie. I had taken a perverse pride for so long in struggling on alone; the struggle had given me a flicker of self-esteem, and besides, I had a horror of being a burden or a bore and putting myself in danger of further humiliating brush-offs. When I was much younger I had hoped to make friends but there seemed to be no place in the world of the thin for someone like me, and in the end I'd retreated into isolation. Loneliness was painful but at least it was silent, devoid of snide laughter and barbed comments. I was used to loneliness now. I thought of it as a chosen solitude and was only occasionally aware of being unhappy.

But this was a time when I regretted not having a friend. Picking up Mr. Hall's card I stared at Francie's number and told myself she wouldn't want to hear from a fat nonentity, particularly a fat nonentity with all sorts of tiresome problems, but then I remembered again her behaviour in the church. Like Nicholas and Mr. Hall, she had treated me with respect, just as if I was a normal person, and at that point it occurred to me that if Mr. Hall had recommended her she was most unlikely to refuse my request for help.

I finally succeeded in pulling myself together. I told myself that if I didn't grab this life-line I might turn into one of those embarrassing neurotics who staged suicide attempts in order to win a little care and attention. Pathetic! Whatever happened I had to keep sane, and keeping sane involved taking sensible action instead of cowering mindlessly in a corner.

I picked up the receiver and dialled the number.

VII

"*Oh good!*" exclaimed Francie warmly after I'd revealed my identity. "I was hoping you'd phone—I spoke to Lewis Hall this morning and he said he was going to see you."

I did stammer something about not wanting to interrupt her weekend, but she swept that remark aside, said she was sorry about my bereavement, she was sure I wouldn't have called unless I was feeling utterly ghastly, and would I like her to come over straight away? She always loved rising to the occasion, especially in an emergency, and no, it was no trouble at all, her children were away at boarding school, her husband was away on business in Tokyo and all she was doing was ironing a table-cloth. Where did I live? Dean Danvers Street off Smith Square? Super! She'd be with me in half an hour.

Exhausted after being befriended in this masterful manner yet more than relieved that someone would now help me reduce the chaos to order, I began to lunch on rum raisin ice cream, but I was no more than halfway through the tub when the phone rang.

The caller was Nicholas Darrow.

VIII

"*I've* just spoken to Val," he said as I remained speechless with surprise. "She told me the news. Was it easy at the end?"

I groped for the right words. It helped that the question was so direct. Years of living with Aunt had equipped me to withstand straight talking but to wilt in the face of diplomacy. Finally I managed to say: "Yes, suddenly her breathing changed, then stopped. There was no pain."

"Good. And how are you?"

"Bloody awful," I said, discovering in horror that I was unable to switch from being direct to being convoluted in the name of self-effacing good manners. "But that's okay, I'll be better soon, Francie's coming."

"Francie's very warm-hearted and extremely efficient, but be sure to let her know when you've had enough and need to be alone. Do you want me to conduct the funeral service?"

I did try to pretend to him that any old clergyman would do, but the words which came out were: "Yes, but I don't want to be a nuisance and take you away from your real work."

"Funerals *are* part of my real work and asking me to conduct one doesn't convert you into a nuisance. We'll discuss the details on Monday when I'm back in town—and meanwhile if you still feel hellish, even after seeing Francie, do please phone my colleague Lewis Hall. He likes getting calls on weekends when the City's deserted and the Healing Centre's closed."

After I had thanked him for this reassurance he said he was very sorry I was going through this difficult time, bereavement was a great ordeal, he'd keep praying for me.

Then he rang off.

Returning in a daze to the kitchen I slumped down again at the table and blotted out all my humiliating romantic dreams by finishing off the rum raisin ice cream.

I X

Francie was magnificent. She made an appointment with the undertakers to discuss the funeral details, she rang the doctor to find out where the death certificate had to be registered (he'd told me but I hadn't taken a word in), she made a list of the people who had to be informed (the solicitors, the landlords, the bank and various departments of the government's bureaucracy) and she drafted a most impressive notice for the "Deaths" column of *The Times.* She even offered to call my mother, but I thought that was unnecessary; my mother and I never communicated by phone. I did manage to write her a three-line note, but this so exhausted me that Francie said she would leave me to rest, a move which I thought displayed perfect behaviour for a Befriender.

She returned on Sunday with some flowers from her garden in Islington and offered to take me to her local church, but when I declined she didn't argue; she merely asked me to have lunch with her instead. I said no, sorry, I was too tired, and she didn't argue with that response either. Instead after promising to be with me when the funeral director called, she again excelled herself by leaving me alone.

The funeral director was seen as planned on Monday morning and in the evening Francie returned to the cottage, this time accompanied by Nicholas, in order to review the arrangements. Nicholas talked about the service and Francie talked about the catering. Afterwards I was so exhausted that I barely had the strength to binge. I was also starting to worry about the expenses I was incurring, but I decided to postpone all thought of my dire financial situation until after the funeral.

Some of Aunt's friends were still alive and no doubt there were numerous former pupils who remembered her, but during the long illness when she could no longer write, many had ceased to keep in touch. No more than thirty people turned up at the crematorium and less than twenty came back to the cottage, where I had spent many therapeutic hours preparing an elaborate buffet. I had been uncertain what to do about drink. Francie had said I shouldn't feel obliged to serve alcohol, but providing only tea or coffee seemed an inadequate way to revive people after the grisliness of the crematorium, and in the end I had splurged at the supermarket on some white *vin de pays.* The thought of lapping up the surplus after the guests had gone had cheered me considerably. The only reason, I was sure, why I never normally drank to excess was because I could never normally afford to do so.

To my relief my mother had decided not to attend the funeral but had spoilt this wise decision by sending the most vulgar wreath adorned with a revolting message. ("Dearest Aunt Bea—In undying gratitude for all your great kindness to Darling Alice—all my love, the memory of your goodness will never fade from my memory . . ." And so on and so on. It really is disgusting what sentimental depths people will plumb when driven by a guilty conscience.)

I myself had ordered a small bunch of cut flowers, since I knew Aunt would have disapproved of any tasteless floral extravagance, and on the ribbon encircling the stems I pinned a card inscribed: "In memory of a woman of integrity. A." I felt no need to drivel on about love and gratitude. Aunt had hated people stating the obvious. Aunt had hated so many things, funny old bag, but she would have liked the quiet, brief, dignified little service which marked her death. In the end the Church of England didn't let her down in delivering her precise version of the great British tribal rite which she valued so highly.

Nicholas read some sentences from St. John's Gospel at the start of the service, and later he read a longer excerpt. He had picked the excerpt himself and I had approved the passage without bothering to read it because I'd felt sure he would make the right choice. That was why, when I was finally listening to him reading the passage, I received such a jolt. " 'Let not your hearts be troubled,' " he urged, " '*neither let them be afraid*,' " and as those words rang out in the chapel I saw he was looking straight at me with his clear light eyes. Then I found I wasn't afraid, even though I had no job and no money and would soon have no home; I wasn't afraid of the future because Nicholas was there in my present, and as soon as I realised this I thought longingly: if only he could be in my future too! But that was just another of my futile romantic dreams, I knew it was, just as I knew I was only toying with such a fantasy because Nicholas was looking so attractive, so compelling, and I hardly knew how to bear the fact that soon I would see him no more.

He worked hard that day. He not only gave me a lift in his car to and from the crematorium but he also paused at the cottage afterwards to mingle with the mourners. On the outward journey we said almost nothing, but to my surprise I found the silence comfortable and I suffered no nervous urge to break it. On the way back I did speak, chattering inconsequentially as I savoured my relief that the ordeal was over, but finally I screwed up the nerve to stem my verbal diarrhoea by asking: "Is there really a life after death?"

"All my experience suggests the alternative is too implausible."

"But if Aunt's now ashes, how can one talk of a resurrection of the body?"

" 'Body' in that context is probably a code-word for the whole person. When we say 'anybody' or 'everybody' or 'somebody' we're not just talking about flesh and blood—we're referring to the complex pattern of information which the medium of flesh and blood expresses."

I struggled to wrap my mind around this. "So you're saying that flesh and blood are more or less irrelevant?"

"No, not irrelevant. Our bodies have a big impact on our development as people—they contribute to the pattern of information, and in fact we wouldn't be people without them. But once we're no longer confined by time and space the flesh and blood become superfluous and the pattern can be downloaded elsewhere . . . Do you know anything about computers?"

"No."

"Okay, forget that, think of Michelangelo instead. In the Sistine Chapel he expressed a vision by creating, through the medium of paint, patterns of colour. The paint is of vital importance but in the end it's the pattern that matters and the pattern which can be reproduced in another medium such as a book or a film."

I tried to work out how Aunt would have replied. She had always held that life after death was nonsense. "I've heard it said," I ventured cautiously, "that religion only came into being because people were so afraid of dying that they needed an excuse to believe life would go on afterwards."

"Oh, that myth's been disproved by modern scholarship! It turns out that religion was around for a long time before the concept of life after death evolved."

I was so surprised that I exclaimed: "Thank goodness Aunt never knew that—she hated having to revise her opinions!"

"But as a woman of integrity wasn't she interested in truth?"

"Yes, but she didn't think truth had anything to do with religion."

"We all have our religions," said Nicholas. "We all have our ways of grappling with reality in order to make sense of our world. And didn't you tell me that your Aunt's religion was England—or rather, nineteenth-century English patriotism?"

I laughed before protesting: "But England's real! You can touch it and measure it! Aunt didn't believe in anything which couldn't be touched and measured and verified scientifically."

"And is patriotism something which can be weighed and measured and verified scientifically? And justice? And all those other qualities your aunt believed in so passionately?"

I couldn't begin to imagine how Aunt would have replied to this, so I just said feebly: "But science is important!"

"It's very important indeed. But it's not the only window on reality."

I suddenly realised he was parking, switching off the engine, and with a shock I saw we were back in Dean Danvers Street. Nicholas paused. He had turned to look at me. His right hand, still resting on the steering wheel, was perfectly still, the long fingers relaxed. His left hand was lying carelessly on his left thigh as he faced me, and the left thigh itself, shrouded with black cloth, was set at an angle which brought his knee within inches of mine. When I could no longer meet his eyes I stared down instead at the gap which separated us and knew it symbolised a gulf which could never be bridged no matter how kind to me he chose to be.

Casually he said: "Come and see me at St. Benet's some time if you want me to help you find a more sympathetic doctor. I was disturbed to hear of your non-relationship with your GP."

"Well, I don't really need a doctor," I said at once. "There's nothing wrong with me that a diet won't cure."

"Okay, forget the doctor. But come and talk about food. Maybe you don't need to diet at all."

I was astounded. "How can you possibly say that?"

"Because you may only need to change your life-style." He paused before adding: "Think it over. I'd like to help if I can."

"But I couldn't afford—"

"There's no charge. We're funded by a charitable foundation and private gifts."

For one long moment the romantic dream consumed me and I dreamed of a future which guaranteed me regular visits to St. Benet's. But then I remembered the unbridgeable gulf and knew I could go no further. I had to fight against being lured on by well-meaning kindness into a world where he would always be unattainable. Better to be thankful for these few precious moments and then go on my way alone. I didn't want to wind up as a pathetic groupie, hanging around St. Benet's and becoming a nuisance, and I didn't want to end up in a doctor-patient relationship with him either. I felt too strongly; I knew I could care too much. Either I met him as an equal in his own world or I didn't meet him at all—and since the very notion of meeting him as an equal there was ridiculous I knew I had to wipe it from my mind straight away.

"It's very kind of you to want to go on helping me," I said politely, "and I'm very grateful, but I must stand on my own two feet now." And in an attempt to divert us both from such a difficult subject I added lightly: "Does everyone at St. Benet's behave as if even the most insignificant person has value?"

"I should hope so," said Nicholas dryly, withdrawing his hand from the wheel and opening the door. "We're supposed to be following a man who believed everyone was special, even those on the margins of society who feel themselves despised and ignored." And scrambling out of the car he began to feed coins into the meter.

Tears filled my eyes. I didn't know why but I at once hated myself for not controlling my emotions properly. Aunt would have been appalled. Furtively using my cuff as a handkerchief I heaved my bulk from the passenger seat, grabbed my keys from my bag and somehow managed to open the front door.

X

Well, I got over that bout of stupidity, of course I did, there was so much to do, food to take out of the fridge, wine to uncork, people to talk to—I didn't have time to give way to turgid emotions, did I, I had to keep up appearances, behave as Aunt would have wished, see that everything was done properly. Anyway, I was brought down to earth soon enough when I opened the first bottle of the wine and found it tasted like paint-stripper. That was a bad start. I noticed that Nicholas only had one sip from his glass and only two of the hors d'oeuvres which I had so enjoyed preparing. When he refused a third I was stupid enough to ask: "Is something wrong with them?" although I knew there wasn't because the other guests were tucking in happily enough and I myself had already put away at least six. In reply he said: "I'm afraid I never eat and drink much when I'm on duty in a clerical suit," which I thought was a clever excuse, putting the blame on clerical etiquette, but I was still oppressed by a sense of failure.

He left half an hour later, but he didn't leave me without a memento of St. Benet's; when I went out into the hall to see him off he surprised me by producing from his raincoat pocket an advance copy of the church's monthly magazine. "Hot from the presses!" he said with a smile. "I brought it because there's an ad in the back which might interest you. Someone's looking for a cook." And before I could comment he had wished me good luck and was gone.

It was as if he knew that the quickest goodbye would be the easiest for me to bear.

XI

By two o'clock everyone had departed and I was left in the kitchen with the last plate of hors d'oeuvres and several bottles of the paint-stripper. I did have another go at drinking the stuff—getting drunk to blot out the pain of parting from Nicholas seemed to make excellent sense—but the taste was so revolting that I abandoned this project and finished off the food instead. When I finally paused to read the St. Benet's magazine I found I had a craving for something sweet after all the savouries but I was clean out of rum raisin ice cream. Opening a packet of golden syrup biscuits instead, I began to thumb my way through the magazine to the advertisements at the back.

"Painter/Decorator, experienced, good refs . . . ," "Carpenter, no job too small . . ." Where did all these small-time tradesmen come from in the opulent square mile of the City? I supposed they lived in Tower Hamlets, the deprived borough to the east—or perhaps in Islington, the socially mixed borough to the north . . . My glance travelled on down the column. "CAT LOST, Clerkenwell Green area, favourite haunt St. James's churchyard . . ." I sighed, both for the lost cat and for beautiful Orlando, now deceased. "ACCOMMODATION WANTED . . ." I skipped this section and zeroed in on "SITUATIONS VACANT," but the first advertisement hardly seemed suitable. "Lady, semi-disabled, requires Christian woman to live in, light cooking, other help kept . . ." I was sure I didn't qualify as a Christian, and "light cooking" would hardly test my Cordon Bleu skills, but what was this next one? "Cook wanted, live in, non-smoker, SW1 area, must be able to cook delicious low-calorie dishes in addition to sophisticated cuisine for dinner-parties, references essential, salary to be negotiated, those without a Cordon Bleu need not apply . . ."

I was so intrigued that I forgot the biscuits and polished my glasses to make sure I'd read the ad correctly. I myself lived in SW1, the eastern end which, apart from the little Georgian enclave around Smith Square, was hardly considered a choice area of the City of Westminster. But beyond the council estates of Page Street and the charity housing around Perkin's Rents, beyond the market on Strutton Ground and the church at Rochester Row, lay Pimlico, where the yuppies now exercised their Porsches, and north of Pimlico lay the cream-and-white magnificence of Belgravia, the classiest part of SW1. A person who could afford to keep a live-in cook—not a cook-housekeeper but a cook—and imperiously demand a Cordon Bleu qualification (which meant the salary would be more than peanuts) wouldn't be living in Perkin's Rents and doing her shopping on Strutton Ground. Nor would she be renovating some tired terrace house in the Pimlico Grid and making shopping trips to Sainsbury's, Nine Elms. She'd be living in Belgravia, possibly in one of the Eatons—Eaton Place, Eaton Terrace, maybe even Eaton Square—and doing her shopping in Harrods Food Hall.

I decided I could take to life in Belgravia very happily, but did I have any hope at all of nailing such a glittering prize? Normally I would never have considered applying for anything so upmarket. Rich, beautiful people, I had always told myself, would never want to employ someone who couldn't mirror their glamour. However . . . I paused to examine my pre-conceived ideas. Someone who advertised in a church magazine wasn't going to be a run-of-the-mill rich bitch, and someone who advertised in the St. Benet's magazine was possibly not going to be a bitch at all. Perhaps she too believed everyone had value, and besides . . . would Nicholas have mentioned the job to me if he'd felt I had no chance of getting it?

A second later it dawned on me that he'd wanted me to apply—which in turn meant he'd seen no reason why I shouldn't be successful. Perhaps he'd even seen me as ideally suited to work for this person—but no, I was getting carried away by my dream of living within a stone's throw of Harrods' Food Hall and I had to return to earth at once.

By this time I was in such a state of nervous excitement that I had to have yet another golden syrup biscuit. Almost immediately I paid the price for all my bingeing that day, and as soon as I'd finished vomiting I crawled upstairs, flopped on my bed and passed out in utter exhaustion.

XII

When I awoke an hour later I knew I had to call the advertiser immediately before I started bingeing again out of sheer fright. Marching downstairs I grabbed the magazine, reached for the telephone and started dialling.

The woman answered on the first ring. I pictured her reclining on a couch in a sumptuous drawing-room while sipping tea—Lapsang Souchong, perhaps—from a Crown Derby cup. Beyond the tall Georgian windows the trees of Eaton Square would be swaying in an exquisitely delicate breeze.

"Hullo?" It was certainly an aristocratic voice, soprano and self-confident, and the manner proved to be aristocratic too, pleasant but steely, making me wonder if her charm was only skin-deep. A polite conversation ensued, effortlessly shaped by this formidable female. It was hard to guess how old she was. She could have been in her thirties but the effortless way in which she directed the interrogation made me suspect she was considerably older.

"What's your connection with St. Benet's?" she demanded sharply after asking the essential questions about my qualifications.

"The Rector conducted my aunt's funeral today."

Of course she didn't offer her condolences. What was Aunt to her? She didn't know me, and the idea that she might make an effort to observe the conventions of middle-class politeness obviously never entered her head. Instead she exclaimed with pleasure: "Ah, so you know Nick!" and for the first time I heard the genuine warmth in her voice.

Briskly she said: "Very well, this is the situation: I have a house in Eaton Terrace—the Eaton Square end—and there's a tiny flat in the basement for a live-in employee, just a bedroom, sitting-room, bathroom and kitchen. I have the most wonderful cleaner, a treasure who comes in almost every day, so apart from the cooking you wouldn't have to do anything except clean up after yourself in the kitchen—oh, and keep the basement flat spick-and-span, of course. I like to entertain a lot but otherwise there's only me to cater for—I'm a widow and my children are grown up. I go away now and then, and while I'm away I'd expect you to act as a caretaker—which is why I advertised in Nick's magazine; I've got to get the sort of person who's absolutely honest, even when she's unsupervised, and I decided my best course was to trawl a Christian community and ask the priest's opinion of whoever turned up in the net . . . Nick didn't mention you, by the way, when I placed the advertisement last week."

"I've only just met him."

"Never mind, he'll have summed you up accurately, he's psychic. Where was I? Oh yes, the caretaking. There's a burglar alarm—and I've also got a dog, but Mortimer goes everywhere with me so he won't be around to guard you while you're on your own. Are you likely to panic if you're alone in the house at night?"

"Not in the least."

"Good. Now, I'll pay the going rate and give the usual amount of holiday, but we can talk about that later if I decide you're suitable. When can you come to see me?"

"Well—"

"Shall we say noon tomorrow? I have a committee meeting in the morning, but I'll be home by eleven-thirty."

"Noon—yes—thank you—"

She gave me the number of the house. "Bring your references," she added, "and your Cordon Bleu certificate. I always believe in checking details—you mustn't think I intend to rely *entirely* on Nick's psychic powers. Now, is that all quite clear?"

"Yes, thank you, Mrs.—" I paused, waiting for the final piece of information.

"Lady Cynthia Aysgarth," came the crisp reply. "That's A-Y-S-G-A-R-T-H, like the place in Yorkshire. Thank you, Miss Fletcher." And she hung up, leaving me still scribbling that unfamiliar northern name.

XIII

I sat on the sofa, my brain automatically printing out the class-system data which had been accumulating there ever since the day over thirty-two years ago when I had drawn my first breath of English air. Lady Cynthia Aysgarth wouldn't have mentioned her Christian name in those particular circumstances unless it formed part of her title. She hadn't declared herself to be merely "Lady Aysgarth," so that meant she wasn't a life peeress or the wife of a baron, baronet or knight. "Lady Cynthia Aysgarth," requiring to be addressed as "Lady Cynthia," would be the daughter of an earl or a marquess—or possibly even the daughter of a duke. I had never met such a creature before in my life, but now was hardly the time to feel squeamish about the upper classes.

The following morning I reviewed my references. The personnel officer at my last permanent job testified generously to my competence as a cook, the temporary agency which had given me work vouched for my reliability as an employee, and Aunt's elderly solicitor proclaimed that as a human being I was sober, clean, courteous and with no criminal record. So far so good. But the main problem still had to be tackled: my appearance.

At six o'clock that morning I had washed my hair and trimmed all the split ends. I now spent half an hour applying make-up before wedging myself into my best outfit: the navy jacket and skirt with the navy-and-white polka-dot blouse, the navy shoes and the navy gloves. (Aunt had been very keen on gloves.) After contemplating myself in the full-length mirror I decided I looked drab but not actually repulsive. At least no one could doubt my respectability.

I was now well on my way to the next miracle. Leaving the cottage at last, I took the number eleven bus past Victoria station and began to walk west from Buckingham Palace Road towards the glistening mansions of Belgravia.

3

> Incidentally, compulsive eating is not simply greed, although you may continually berate yourself for your greed. A compulsive eater may well, for example, exercise an iron control in other areas of life and be very disciplined over things that cause other people problems, like the use of time and money.
>
> GARETH TUCKWELL AND DAVID FLAGG
> *A Question of Healing*

I

Lady Cynthia was a streamlined fifty-something with a large amount of layered, tinted, streaked, curled and cosseted brownish-gold hair, a creamy, velvety skin and cat-like green eyes set wide apart over high cheekbones. Her eyelashes, heavily dosed with mascara, were so long that I even wondered if they were false, but I thought she was probably old enough and classy enough to think false eyelashes vulgar. Her sculpted jawline hinted at a first-class face-lift, but maybe face-lifts too would be considered vulgar and the jawline was achieved solely by dieting. I guessed that in her prime she had been highly favoured by society photographers and hotly pursued by hordes of eligible young men.

She wore an exquisitely tailored dress, pale mustard in colour, and no jewellery apart from a rock or two on her fingers. Her manner was business-like but not snooty; indeed it became increasingly pleasant. Far from putting her off, my appearance seemed to reassure her. Fat girls didn't have menfriends who would cause trouble, and if they spoke passably and dressed sensibly, the odds were they would also know how to behave.

Lady Cynthia was delighted that I should live so near Smith Square, such an attractive little corner of London, and did I know some very dear friends of hers in Lord North Street called . . . But to the surprise of neither of us I didn't know her friends, and honesty compelled me to explain that Aunt had only been the tenant of her cottage.

"But what a heavenly place to be a tenant!" said Lady Cynthia kindly, unaware that Aunt had picked up the tenancy dirt cheap during the war when the Smith Square church was a bombed ruin and no one wanted to live in such a blitzed little patch of Westminster.

After displaying her kindness—which I appreciated—Lady Cynthia got down to business. My references were inspected. I was cross-examined with efficiency. The salary was disclosed (a bit mean but I had to remember the free flat) and the bureaucratic details skimmed in a survey which included vague remarks about national insurance contributions, tart comments on the hellish jungle of employment legislation and rapturous praise of her "divine" accountant who always told her exactly what to do whenever she jousted with the Inland Revenue. She then said I could use her car to do the shopping, and did I have a licence? I did, but I felt I had to add that Aunt's car had been sold some years ago and I hadn't driven since.

"So you'll be a bit rusty," said Lady Cynthia, apparently unruffled by this confession. "Never mind, I sold the Bentley after my husband died, so if you were to have a prang it wouldn't matter too much. Nowadays I drive a dear little thing called a Polo and it's so much easier than the Bentley to park." That concluded our conversation about driving, but I sensed Lady Cynthia had noted my honesty and savoured it. I also sensed that by this time she had decided to hire me.

I was taken to inspect the kitchen, which was oldish but not past its sell-by date. To my relief there was no Aga; one never knows where one may stumble across these cherished hulks, but personally I prefer an electric oven with a gas hob, both of which were on offer in Lady Cynthia's kitchen. Agas always remind me of Old English sheepdogs: warm, large and lovable but something I can happily live without.

I was then shown the basement flat which Lady Cynthia had described as "tiny," but I saw at once it was palatial to anyone threatened with the world of bedsits. Never mind that the front room was dark, sunk well below the level of the pavement. Never mind that the back room was gloomy, sunk well below the level of the garden. Never mind that the kitchen smelt musty and the bathroom smelt damp. After the previous cook's recent death from old age, the rooms had been freshly painted and there was no sign of mouse-droppings. The furnishings were sparse but that meant there would be room for Aunt's antiques. The flat also appeared to be devoid of central heating, but I noticed a couple of plug-in, oil-filled radiators, and anyway I was used to wearing several sweaters in winter in order to economise on heating bills.

"I have a rule forbidding calor gas stoves and paraffin appliances," said Lady Cynthia firmly. "The fire risk is too great. There's an immersion heater for the water, and there's a telephone which you may wish to have connected, but if you decide to do without please remember that my telephone is never to be used without my permission. Other rules include no parties, no more than three guests at a time and all visitors must use the basement entrance . . . Now the moment's finally arrived! It's time for you to meet Mortimer."

I suddenly realised my entire future was to be settled by Lady Cynthia's dog. Would he or would he not approve of me? As she went upstairs to retrieve him from her bedroom I could only hope feverishly that he was in a benign mood.

I was eventually presented with an animal which looked like a beribboned rat. "Isn't he adorable?" demanded Lady Cynthia, cradling him in her arms and gazing at him with a doting expression.

"Gosh!" I said, quite unable to dredge up a single lie which could pass for a compliment, and added idiotically: "He's very small."

"I hate big messy dogs," confided Lady Cynthia, apparently interpreting my "gosh" as an exclamation of rapture. "In fact I hate messiness of any kind." And as she continued to gaze adoringly at Mortimer, I finally saw her not as an aristocrat nor even as a beautiful, confident woman but as someone vulnerable, someone who chose to pour out her love on an easily managed little dog because big, unmanageable humans had in the past proved too hurtful with their muddled, messy demands which had led to muddled, messy relationships. For the first time it occurred to me to wonder how she had become involved with St. Benet's, and I wondered too when she and Nicholas had first met.

"Well, I'll check your references, of course," Lady Cynthia was saying, "but if I find they're satisfactory, I shall wish to offer you the job. I hope you feel the position would suit you."

It was hard not to shriek: "YES!" and punch the air in triumph, but I managed to say in my most repressed middle-class voice: "Yes, indeed. Thank you, Lady Cynthia."

"How soon can you start? Oh, wait a minute, you're clearing up after a funeral, aren't you, how beastly—of course you'll need at least another two weeks to get everything straight. Supposing you move in on the thirty-first and start work on April the first?"

"Yes, I'm sure I could manage that," I said without having the least idea whether I could or not.

"Splendid! What a huge load off my mind—I must phone Nick straight away to tell him the good news! I've already been in touch with him, of course," she added, opening the front door to show me out. "I would have cancelled the interview if his opinion had been unfavourable, but he assured me straight away that you were a woman of integrity."

My heart gave the impression of disconnecting itself, turning a complete somersault and plugging itself back into position all within the space of three seconds. I had a hard time finding the words to say goodbye, but seconds later I was surging along the pavement of Eaton Terrace with the job nailed, an income guaranteed and a home assured. Within the space of twenty-four hours my life had yet again been transformed.

I decided I was becoming thoroughly addicted to miracles.

I I

The next day Francie reappeared on my doorstep. Much to her surprise I had firmly rejected her offer to attend the funeral (of course she never realised how much I had longed for a little time alone with Nicholas) but now here she was again, apparently still delighted to see me, and with her this time was the young red-headed clergyman who had taken so long to fetch me the glass of water when I had fainted at the healing service. He was introduced to me as Nicholas's curate, the Reverend Eustace McGovern. "But nobody's called Eustace nowadays," he said, "so I'm known as Stacy." He talked like the characters in *Bread* so I knew he was from Liverpool, but he told me his parents had come from Dublin and I always felt Stacy was more Irish than English. He was very nearly beautiful, but true masculine beauty is rare and Stacy missed the mark because his pale skin was splattered with freckles; I decided straight away he wasn't sexy. He was so tall that he seemed to overflow the armchair I had offered him, and his limbs were so long that he knocked over the coffee-table when he impulsively stretched his legs.

"Really, Stacy!" scolded Francie, who treated him just as a nanny would treat a wayward child.

Francie was dressed in a tawny tweed suit. Her dark hair, disarranged by the March gale blowing outside, was still trying to wave in the right directions, but as I left the room to make coffee I saw her whip a mirror from her handbag to make the necessary repairs. If Francie hadn't been so kind I would have felt intimidated because she was so attractive. However, I knew now she was older than she looked. When discussing cookery during one of our meetings she had disclosed she had attended a finishing school in the late fifties, a fact which I calculated made her about forty-five.

By this time I had also heard more about her work as a Befriender, one of the team of volunteers trained in listening skills and assigned to meet those who turned up at St. Benet's for help. If more than a listening ear was required the Befriender would classify the problem and refer the caller to either Nicholas or Lewis Hall—or Val the doctor—or Robin the psychotherapist—or Daisy the social worker who liaised with the local authorities. Francie had started by working three mornings a week but now worked full-time.

"Francie's our Befriender-in-Chief," said Stacy that morning after Francie had explained how thrilled she'd been that I'd landed such a "super" job and how she'd felt she simply had to call in person to congratulate me. "She'd befriend the Devil himself if you gave her a chance."

"Stacy, what a thing to say!" Francie was genuinely shocked. "If Lewis were here he'd hit the roof!"

Stacy blushed and apologised but I could see he had no idea why Francie was making such a fuss. Francie, being very English, had taken his words literally, but Stacy, being very Irish, hadn't meant to be literal at all.

"How *is* Mr. Hall?" I said quickly, trying to divert her.

"My dear, a martyr to his arthritis, he's getting less and less mobile. I can't understand why he doesn't have that hip replaced."

"Maybe he wants to be in one piece for the Resurrection," said

Stacy, this time giving me a wink to signal that he wasn't serious, but Francie just exclaimed: "Stacy, *honestly!*" and looked scandalised again. That was when I realised that although Francie had many virtues, her sense of humour wasn't as well developed as it might have been.

"Stacy's substituting for Lewis this morning," she explained to me after she'd recovered from this latest clerical clanger. "In fact he's substituting for Nick too. You're representing the clergy of St. Benet's here this morning, aren't you, Stacy?" she added unnecessarily in a meaningful voice designed to remind him of his professional duty.

"Yep," said Stacy, guzzling one of my chocolate-chip cookies. "Wow, these are great, Alice!"

"Have another!" I said delighted, passing him the plate. "I made them myself."

"Brill!" He started guzzling again.

I wondered how old he was. Twenty-five? He seemed more like a teenager. "I miss my mother's cooking!" he was saying with a sigh.

I asked him if he had any siblings.

"Three beautiful sisters," said Stacy at once, pleased to be asked. "They're all older than me. Siobhan and Sinead have been married for some time but Aisling only got married the other day and I still can't believe she's gone, I'm going to miss her so much—"

"Where's she gone to?"

"Oh, just down the road from our Mam, but it's never the same after they get married and I've been feeling really down about it—"

"Stacy," said Francie repressively, "Alice has her own sadness to deal with. She doesn't need yours as well."

"But I was going to take her mind off the funeral by showing her my best picture of Aisling in her wedding dress!"

"Nevertheless I'm sure Nick would say—"

"Talking of Nicholas," I said in another heroic attempt to divert her, "I've been so absorbed in my troubles that I've never once asked you how you met him. When did you first go to St. Benet's?"

"Oh, I knew Nick long before he came to London to work!" said Francie, rising at once to the bait. "I was at finishing school with his wife Rosalind. She and Nick married in 1968."

"Oh, I see . . . And had they known each other long before they got married?" I asked this question not merely to satisfy my rampant curiosity but to divert her yet again from Stacy, now pigging out on a third cookie.

"Ages and ages! They were childhood sweethearts, so it was all madly romantic when they finally walked down the aisle."

"They've got two sons, both named after saints," said Stacy, having finished his munching and crunching, "and they live in a beautiful home in Surrey, a converted farmhouse it is, full of oak beams and antiques, and there's a garden which looks as if it was designed by angels and made in heaven. Mrs. Darrow's a very lovely lady and could make a flower grow just by blowing a kiss at it."

"You wouldn't think it from that description," said Francie acidly, "but Rosalind's actually a very successful businesswoman. She built up a floral consultancy specialising in weddings, and before the business was taken over recently she was managing a chain of florists in Guildford, Kingston and Epsom . . . But Alice dear, we didn't come here to chatter about other people—we want to hear about *you!* Do give us a blow-by-blow account of the interview with Lady Cynthia!"

I embarked on a brief summary. Fortunately Francie was so enthralled that she never noticed Stacy eyeing the last cookie as if he couldn't bear to see it looking so lonely on its plate.

"Does Lady Cynthia come often to St. Benet's?" I asked as soon as my summary was completed, and when Francie glanced away to reach for her coffee-cup I gave Stacy a quick nod. The cookie instantly vanished.

"Now and then she visits the Healing Centre," said Francie carefully, "but of course all that's confidential."

"Ah."

"Incidentally, Lady Cynthia's another person who's known Nick for ages—he got to know her husband's family back in the early sixties. Norman Aysgarth was a doctor of law who lectured at King's College London, but his father and Nick's father were both priests in the same diocese." Having replaced her cup in its saucer she rose to her feet. "Well, we mustn't outstay our welcome! Stacy, isn't there something you'd like to say to Alice before we leave?"

"You bet!" said Stacy. "Thanks for those biscuits, Alice—they were great!"

"I'll give you some to take home," I said pleased, and leaving Francie, lips pursed, in the sitting-room I led him to the kitchen.

"She's hinting that I should offer to say a prayer," said Stacy in a stage-whisper as I opened the biscuit tin. "Would you like that, Alice? I'll keep it short and sweet, I promise, but it'll get God nicely on the line if you want to have a chat with him later."

I was so disarmed by this vision of a sociable deity waiting hopefully in heaven with a receiver in his hand that I said at once: "Okay—pray away!"

For the first time Stacy became very sober and well behaved. He crossed himself, clasped his hands, bent his head, closed his eyes and said with unimpeachable sincerity: "Almighty Father, look after Alice in her bereavement, and by the power of your Holy Spirit enable us, your servants at St. Benet's, to look after her too. In the name of Jesus Christ Our Lord, Amen."

I allowed a respectful pause to develop before I said politely: "Thanks. Very nice," and dropped the remaining cookies into a plastic bag.

"Stacy!" called Francie from the hall.

"Come back to St. Benet's soon," said Stacy encouragingly to me, "and I'll show you the photos of my sister Aisling's wedding—and I'll make you coffee to go with them." He didn't wait for a reply but dashed away, tipping a picture askew as his shoulder brushed the wall, and bounded out of the front door into the street.

Francie said apologetically: "He hasn't been at St. Benet's long. I'm afraid he's a bit raw."

"I thought he was sweet," I said truthfully.

"Dear Alice!" said Francie, sighing in apparently genuine admiration. "Always so *nice!*" She gave me a quick hug before adding: "But I can't possibly go without offering you further help—you're going to have an enormous amount to do, clearing the house and moving to Eaton Terrace. Shall I come back tomorrow? I may not be able to escape from the Centre during the day but all my evenings are still free because Harry's had to go on from Tokyo to Singapore."

I'd already begun to wonder how I was ever going to be ready to begin life in Eaton Terrace by the end of the month.

"Thanks, Francie," I said, deciding I couldn't afford to be too proud to accept further help. "That's very good of you."

III

How I would have managed without Francie in the days that followed, I have no idea. Even though I didn't have to organise the sale of the house, the bric-a-brac had to be sorted out, the junk in the loft had to be carted away and the surplus furniture had to be shed. In the end Francie took time off from the Healing Centre to help me deal with removal companies, second-hand furniture dealers and house clearance firms, and when I did finally move into the basement flat at Eaton Terrace it was she who tipped the removal men, bought flowers to bring a blaze of colour to the dark little sitting-room and on impulse took me out to supper at a bistro in Chelsea. By that time I liked her so much that I felt sad to think our paths would never cross again.

"Of course we'll meet soon at St. Benet's!" she declared when we said goodbye, but I was now more convinced than ever that I had to sever the connection with Nicholas. Whenever Francie had gossiped cosily about "Nick and Ros," she had unwittingly underlined how stupid it would have been for me to involve myself further with him.

"I suppose we're all a bit in love with Nick," she had confided at one point. "He's so magnetic, isn't he? Such *charisma*, as everyone used to say back in the sixties! But he has a very quiet private life. Monday, Tuesday, Wednesday, Thursday and Friday he slaves away at St. Benet's and never socialises. Then late on Friday night he scoots down to Surrey to spend the weekend with Ros—he always goes, nothing's ever allowed to stop him, and it's obvious that by the end of the week he simply can't wait to see her again . . ."

After this conversation I spent some time feeling jealous of Rosalind the Wonder Woman, who was clearly one of those fabled creatures who "have it all"—stunning husband, stunning home, stunning career and (inevitably) stunning children—but so thankful was I to be neither homeless nor unemployed that it soon seemed ridiculous to envy her just because she had sensibly made the most of her good fortune in a world I could never enter. She'd been lucky in that world of hers, but now I'd been lucky in mine. I made up my mind to forget her—and that, of course, meant forgetting Nicholas as well. At least Francie's information had spared me the torment of wondering when Lady Cynthia would invite him to dinner. Unavailable during the week he would be out of town every weekend.

With a faultless display of common sense I resolved to devote myself single-mindedly to my amazing job in Belgravia.

IV

At first I was so overwhelmed, adjusting to my new life, that I could do little in the evenings after stacking the dishwasher except eat rum raisin ice cream and gawp with glazed eyes at the television screen. (Lady Cynthia had included a video with the TV—a most generous bonus.) However, eventually I became relaxed enough to draw up a very beautiful diet-sheet, the low-calorie meals all highlighted in serene pastel colours. This artistic masterpiece I fixed to the door of the refrigerator in my flat and afterwards I felt very hopeful and positive.

Meanwhile I had adjusted to the Polo, found the supermarket in the King's Road, mastered the kitchen appliances and tamed the monster Mortimer, whose special dogfood was delivered weekly from Harrods. Sad-eyed, shrill-voiced and tyrannical, he soon realised Lady Cynthia got cross whenever he confused me with his Harrods rations, so after our initial unpleasant encounters he kept his teeth to himself. Lady Cynthia supervised his meals, thank God. All I had to do was keep his food-plate clean and see that his bowl of water was topped up. A week after my arrival I catered for my first dinner-party (pear and Stilton soup, red mullet and red pepper tart, *crème brûlée aux kiwis*) and the eleven guests ate everything in a gratifying display of greed. The next day I overheard her saying to someone on the phone: "I've found this marvellous cook, but you'll never guess how I got hold of her! Through Nick Darrow's church magazine! Trust Nick to turn up a miracle when required . . ."

By this time I was burning to know why Lady Cynthia visited the Healing Centre "now and then," as Francie had put it, and I hoped I might eventually be enlightened by Lady Cynthia's "treasure," Mrs. Simcock, who came to the house four times a week to clean, wash and iron; she also supervised the window-cleaner during his visits, provided cups of tea for the man whom the gardening firm sent to tidy the back garden and walked Mortimer around Eaton Square every day before she went home.

Mrs. Simcock was sinewy, sharp-eyed, snobbish and devoted to Lady Cynthia, Mrs. Thatcher and the Queen. She would arrive at the house in Eaton Terrace in a designer coat (cast off by Lady Cynthia), very high-heeled shoes, and spectacles with diamanté trim, but she always worked in a track-suit and trainers; only the diamanté spectacles were worn throughout. Having decided that I wasn't snooty, Mrs. Simcock was becoming increasingly confidential over elevenses.

I learnt that Lady Cynthia's husband had died five years ago ("Drink," said Mrs. Simcock with relish) and that her elder son, Billy, lived in an institution as he was severely autistic. ("Barmy," said Mrs. Simcock with the unthinking cruelty of someone who has never experienced mental illness and never expects to.) I also learnt that the younger son, Richard, who worked for an oil company in Aberdeen, had recently married a Scottish girl. ("Not good enough for him," said Mrs. Simcock aggrieved. "She's got an accent and the best people up there don't have accents. Look at the Queen Mum.") I did suggest that Lady Cynthia was probably not expecting her son to marry a Bowes-Lyon, but Mrs. Simcock just retorted: "And why not, I'd like to know? She's good enough for anyone!" And that was when I discovered that Lady Cynthia was indeed the daughter of a duke, not the offspring of a mere marquess or earl. But her big mistake, I was gloomily informed, was that she had married beneath her as the result of a grand passion when she was too young to know better.

"Not only was he just the second son of a clergyman," said Mrs. Simcock with utter contempt, "but his grandfather was a draper—and from *Yorkshire!*" (I wasn't sure why Yorkshire made matters so infinitely worse, but assumed it was because Mrs. Simcock, a true southerner, hated anything north of Watford Gap.)

Still yearning to uncover Lady Cynthia's connection with St. Benet's I said purposefully: "I suppose Lady Cynthia became interested in the Church when she married into a clerical family."

"Oh no, dear, her husband was an atheist and all he wanted to do was kick the Church in the teeth. A real mess he was—nice-looking but a mess. When he was alive they lived in Flood Street—that was after the Duke died and Lady Cynthia inherited her share of the loot. Before that she and Dr. Aysgarth lived down the Fulham Road somewhere—I didn't know her in those days, but I worked for her in Flood Street. Then after Dr. Aysgarth kicked the bucket she moved here."

"But how did Lady Cynthia get interested in the Church?" I persisted, not in the least interested in all these classy locations and desperate to get my investigation back on course.

"Well, I expect she started believing in God, dear, some people do. Strange, isn't it, I've never been able to see it myself—although mark you, if I had an alcoholic atheist for a husband I'd be right there hammering on the door of the nearest church and screaming for admittance just to spite him. But of course Lady Cynthia's never spiteful, just saintly. My God, when I think what she had to put up with from that man—and she was so loyal, always standing by him—"

"I suppose being religious gave her the strength to cope."

"Daughters of dukes don't need religion for that, dear. Strength's inborn. But I'll say this for the Church: at least it gave her a holiday from that man every Sunday! She used to go to St. Luke's Chelsea when she lived at Flood Street, but now she goes to St. Peter's Eaton Square and if you ask me they're bloody lucky to have her."

In triumph I saw my chance. "What about that church in the City—St. Benet's?"

"Oh, that one! Yes, that's run by an old friend of hers, I know him, he came to Flood Street regularly while Dr. Aysgarth's liver was packing up for the last time. Name of Darrow. Peculiar," said Mrs. Simcock thoughtfully, "but nice-natured. Nowadays he helps her with Mr. Billy the Barmy—once a year she takes Mr. Billy to some sort of special healing service at St. Benet's. Of course it never cures him but it makes *her* feel better. Funny thing, religion . . ."

I pondered on this information but felt it could only be a partial explanation of the St. Benet's connection. Francie had certainly given me the impression that Lady Cynthia appeared there more than once a year.

I don't know whether Mrs. Simcock's stories about the tragedies in Lady Cynthia's life triggered the explosion of upsetting thoughts which, I can now see, had been gathering in my unconscious mind since Aunt's death, but on the day after my first dinner-party I sank fathoms deep into depression and started weeping in the lavatory, sobbing in the supermarket and generally giving way to the kind of emotional behaviour which Aunt had always loathed. In a paroxysm of grief I tore up my diet-sheet and made myself a Black Forest gateau, but that lapse just made me more depressed than ever, and the next morning, when I came within an inch of pranging the Polo, I realised it was time to start facing up to the cold hard facts of life. Supposing I lost my job, my home and all my new security? I had to treat the situation as an emergency and get help straight away.

With great reluctance, unwilling to re-establish the connection but seeing no easy alternative, I phoned the Healing Centre and asked to speak to Francie Parker.

V

"*Don't worry,*" she said. "It's very normal to get a reaction at this stage. Come over here as soon as you can and I'll be waiting with the coffee."

Shuddering with relief I headed for the tube station at Sloane Square.

As soon as I reached the reception area of the Healing Centre Francie led me into a very small, very private room and plied me with coffee while I destroyed numerous Kleenexes and reflected dimly, as I made fruitless attempts to check my tears, how much I hated myself for such a humiliating loss of control.

". . . and I even tore up my diet-sheet!" I bawled, finally sinking into bathos. "It was so beautiful—I'd worked it all out, right down to the last calorie—I've been reading all these marvellous low-cal cookbooks because Lady Cynthia likes to weight-watch when she's not entertaining—and now everything's ruined because all my will-power's gone and the only thing I can do is eat Black Forest gateau and rum raisin ice cream—"

"Hey, this sounds really upsetting." Francie, to her eternal credit, remained dead serious, demonstrating that there were times when a stunted sense of humour could even be described as an asset. "I'm so sorry, Alice."

I shed some more tears while Francie heroically maintained her sympathy, but having vented the worst of my misery I was at last able to pull myself together. "Okay," I said. "I feel better after letting all that out. I'll be all right now. Thanks for listening."

"Hang on," said Francie quickly as I hauled myself to my feet. "Now that you're here, why don't you have a quick word with Nick?"

"Oh no," I said at once. "No, I wouldn't dream of bothering him."

"But it's his job to bother when people are in situations as tough as yours, Alice! He wouldn't grudge you the time no matter how busy he was. Let me just see if—"

"No, absolutely not!" I grabbed a handful of tissues for the journey home.

"Okay," said Francie hastily, startled by my fierceness, "but won't you at least keep in touch to let me know how you're getting on?"

"Yes, of course. Thanks again, you've been wonderful," I said, anxious to show her she wasn't unappreciated, "but now I must go. There's shopping to do—things to cook—and anyway I mustn't take up any more of your time."

Hurrying out of the little interview room I blundered down the corridor to the reception area—and there, helping himself to coffee from the machine, was Nicholas Darrow.

VI

"*Oh,* there you are!" he said nonchalantly. "I was hoping you'd turn up. Do you have a moment to tell me how you're getting on with Mortimer?"

Well, I could hardly have said no, could I? It would have been so rude, and besides . . . all my will-power had evaporated. It was like opening the door of the freezer and seeing the tub of rum raisin ice cream; I knew that just a couple of spoonfuls were guaranteed to make me feel so much better.

Naturally there was no disguising my emotional state. I could picture my bloodshot eyes and blotched face, and it occurred to me, as I nodded my head to accept his invitation, that even a dead cod on a fishmonger's slab would have looked more appealing.

Seconds later I was again sinking down in the chair which allowed his desk to hide half my body from him, and he was closing the door of his consulting-room.

"I had a reaction this morning from all the stress," I said, feeling driven to explain my cod-like appearance, "but Francie's been great. I'm fine now."

He never queried this statement. He merely said: "I'm glad you felt you could turn to her for help. How's the job?"

"Brilliant! I cooked dinner for twelve last night. It was great fun."

"Is Mortimer still getting his food from Harrods?"

"They deliver every week."

"If I were you, I'd slip him a supermarket dog-biscuit every now and then. Give the poor chap a break."

I smiled, and when I finally dared to look at him I saw he was smiling too. He was wearing a very clean blue shirt, perfectly ironed—one of those modern clerical shirts where the collar is just a token strip of white plastic, barely visible—and he was also, I noticed with astonishment, wearing jeans. On all our previous meetings he had been so conventionally dressed that I had automatically classified him as a mainstream clergyman despite his unusual ministry, but now it occurred to me that he might be just as off-beat as Lewis Hall—not exactly a rebel and certainly not a rogue, but someone who was highly original, perhaps even a touch eccentric. But on the other hand, what did I know about clergymen? Perhaps nowadays hordes of them wore jeans whenever they weren't conducting services. I could well imagine Aunt declaring that the Church of England was going to the dogs by tolerating such informality, and tears filled my eyes again as I remembered her.

I took off my glasses and began to polish them. "I keep thinking of Aunt," I said to Nicholas, now visible only as a blur, "but they're good thoughts. It was so wonderful at the end. Thanks to you." Putting the glasses on the desk I groped in my bag for a tissue. "I'm glad she was able to die in peace at last. I'm glad I'm relieved of the awful worry and strain of those last months. But I miss her. And I miss my nice little home in Dean Danvers Street and the market at Strutton Ground and Big Ben chiming the hours and Orlando's grave in the garden—"

"Ah yes, the handsome cat."

"He had such a beautiful grave . . . I planted a rose-bush . . ." The tissue was soggy now. As I clenched my fists I pictured it being condensed to pulp in my palm. "But I mustn't be sentimental," I said. "Aunt despised sentimentality. And I don't want to be ungrateful when I've got so much to be thankful for—Lady Cynthia, a new home, a good job—oh, I do know, believe me, just how lucky I am! Aunt hated people who couldn't count their blessings."

"I feel I know exactly what your aunt thought about all kinds of things," said Nicholas wryly, "but what do you yourself think, Alice? Now that you're free to take charge of your life, what territories are you going to explore and what shape will your journey take?"

"I can't explore anything until I've lost weight. But that's okay, I'll do that once I'm settled, I don't need any help on that one, I'm fine."

He nodded but said nothing and for a moment we were silent. I was surprised by how comforting the silence was. It was as if my mind was being stroked—but that reminded me of all the times I had stroked Orlando's golden fur and I had no desire to start crying again. Chucking the sodden tissue in the wastepaper basket I rammed my glasses back on my nose. "I must go now," I said, "but it was very nice of you to see me. Thanks."

"Would you consider visiting St. Benet's regularly for a while? It might be useful to have a weekly slot when you could update me on your new journey as it unfolds."

"That's very kind of you," I said, "but no."

"I hope you're not refusing because you feel you'd be a nuisance, taking up my time."

"It's more complicated than that." I hesitated, aware that I was now skating on thin ice. Finally I said: "I don't want to get involved with the people here. I don't want to get involved with anyone anywhere while I'm so fat because being fat means one's always in an unequal position and no real relationship's possible. Take Francie, for instance. She's been wonderfully kind to me, but despite the fact that she's always behaved exactly as a Christian should I know that deep down she thinks I'm just a sad case, someone to be pitied rather than liked. When I'm thin, of course, everything will be quite different and I'll be able to meet Francie on equal terms, but right now . . . well, never mind, forget all that, it doesn't matter."

"I think it matters very much," he said. "I think *you* matter, Alice. I'd be undervaluing you as a person if I tried to override a decision you're fully entitled to take, but remember—the door's always open if you want to return."

That was the moment when I nearly lost control altogether and told him that if I returned I'd never rest until I could see him every day from Monday to Friday (although I did realise I'd have to cede him to Rosalind at weekends). A horrific monologue zipped through my mind. "Of course I know you'll never love me, but that's all right because I don't expect love, I'm not worthy of such a thing, the people I hope will love me always go away—which means it's less painful not to get involved—but even so I *would* like to keep seeing you, I would, because you're the first man who's ever treated me as a real person and I'm just so grateful—and yes, okay, I'll admit it, I do love you, but it's not a pathetic infatuation, I love you because I sense that at some deep level we connect, it's as if the bedrock of our personalities is made of the same stuff, it's as if—" I broke off this unspoken torrent of romantic nonsense when I suddenly realised Nicholas was speaking again.

"Let me just add," he said, not looking at me as he rose to his feet, "that I do understand what you're implying. You feel, don't you, in some way difficult to put into words, that the kind of relationship I'm now offering wouldn't make you feel at ease, and that therefore, if you came here as a client, the relationship would always contain an element that didn't ring true. If you do feel that, then you're right to refuse to see me in future. It's all to do with honesty, isn't it?"

We stood facing each other. His grey eyes were almost blue, reflecting the colour of his shirt. I looked away.

"There'd be no equal ground," I heard my voice say. "Here I'm so vulnerable and you're so powerful. There'd be illusions . . . difficulties . . . I couldn't cope."

"Fair enough. I accept that. But I'm sorry."

I was too emotionally pulverised to reply. Escaping from his office at top speed I left the Healing Centre and fled back to my collection of ice-cream tubs in Belgravia.

VII

Ten lunch-parties, three cocktail-parties and five dinner-parties later in the height of summer, when the English strawberries were glowing in the Food Hall at Harrods, the flowers were blooming in the lush gardens of Eaton Square and the Wimbledon tennis was fizzing (at intervals—the weather was dreadful) on television, Lady Cynthia summoned me to the private den she called her boudoir to discuss her future plans for hospitality.

By this time I was familiar with the pattern of Lady Cynthia's life. She certainly kept herself busy; no one could have accused her of being one of the idle rich. She took an active part in the affairs of her local church. She was involved with more than one charity concerned with mental health. She sat on committees, organised fund-raising events and cultivated a network of people who were in a position to help her with her good causes. This meant her entertaining was primarily inspired not by a self-centred need to stave off boredom but by a desire to be of use to others less fortunate than herself. I admired this very much, especially as I now felt sure she must often be lonely. She spoke little of her relations except for her younger son, hundreds of miles away in Scotland, and although she had many friends there was no person who visited the house more frequently than anyone else; my assumption that a rich, still beautiful woman would have at least one doting admirer had proved to be quite mistaken.

"Distrusts men, she does," said Mrs. Simcock darkly. "And after having an alcoholic for a husband, who can blame her?"

However during that summer, shortly before the Wimbledon tennis began to dominate the television, Lady Cynthia had attracted the attention of a VIP while attending a reception at the American Embassy, and when I arrived in her boudoir that morning with my notebook I found her in unusually buoyant spirits.

"I want to invite some people to a Sunday lunch," she announced as I sat down. "A traditional Sunday lunch, the kind of lunch which will make an American go home to Boston and swear that English food, properly cooked, is divine."

"Roast beef," I said automatically. "Yorkshire pudding. Roast potatoes—" My mouth was already watering. I decided I had cooked too many French dishes lately and was keen for a respite. "Horseradish sauce, gravy, three kinds of mustard—"

"Exactly!"

"Peas, creamed carrots, greens—and new potatoes to contrast with the roast potatoes—"

"Perfect!"

I sighed at the thought of what fun I was going to have. "Anything to start, Lady Cynthia, or do you want to plunge straight into the roast?"

"Let me see. No soup, certainly. Perhaps something cool and light—"

"Asparagus with hollandaise sauce? Dressed Cornish crab? Smoked eel terrine?"

Lady Cynthia dithered. "Asparagus would be heavenly, but since we're having so many vegetables with the main course . . . Dressed crab would be heavenly too, but everyone serves dressed crab nowadays so perhaps we should try to be more original . . . Did you say smoked *eel?*"

"*British* eel! It's delicious. You serve it with finely diced green capsicums—or blanched button mushrooms—or I could make a salad with—"

"Salad," said Lady Cynthia, fastening on the word with relief. "Americans love salads."

"Fine. And the pudding? Apple crumble, treacle tart—"

"I don't think we want anything hot. And strawberries at this time of year are such a cliché—"

"Syllabub, gooseberry fool, junket, summer pudding—"

"Summer pudding! Yes—with a choice of custard or cream!" Lady Cynthia, who was so careful with her calories, was certainly succumbing to the urge to splurge. I wondered if this was all part of her new buoyant mood.

"The lunch will be for six," she was saying with animation. "Five guests and me. The chief guest will be the American whom I want to convert to the glories of English cooking, and his name is Walter P. Woodbridge the Third. (You write 'third' as the Roman numeral three on the place-card.) He flew to Europe with President Reagan earlier this month and stayed on in England after the President had briefed Mrs. Thatcher about the Moscow summit. He's now checking up on NATO or something terribly vital, but it's all secret so I don't ask questions."

"How interesting, but I've just had an awful thought: might he be on a diet? Americans so often are."

"Walter doesn't need to diet," said Lady Cynthia happily. "He's very slim and fit." That was when I knew she was tempted to fall in love but trying to keep a cool head. I myself might have described Nicholas in exactly that tone of voice to a sympathetic third party.

I had a stimulating time planning the details of this feast, but on the Friday which preceded it the details changed when Lady Cynthia arrived back from the Wimbledon championships in a state of agitation. Rain had suspended play again and she hadn't waited for the Becker-Lendl semi-final. As soon as she arrived home she hurried to join me in the kitchen where I was preparing her low-cal dinner (stuffed peppers, green salad, stewed apple with no sugar added).

"I've done something I know I'm going to regret," she confessed, sinking down into the nearest chair, Mortimer clasped to her bosom for comfort. "In fact I regret it already. We're going to have an extra guest on Sunday."

"Fine, no problem—"

"It's the biggest problem imaginable—really, I can't think how I could have been so stupid! There I was, sipping champagne with Walter in one of those rather frightful hospitality tents, when someone shrieked behind me: 'Cynthia darling!' and to my horror I found it was someone whom I've been trying to avoid because, to be absolutely frank, she's become a bit much. We used to belong to the same set in the sixties and she was a great friend of my husband's eldest brother, but she made a disastrous marriage and went to seed and—well anyway, when I'd recovered from the shock of seeing her I said: 'Darling, *what* a surprise!' and in fact it *was* surprising because she was almost presentable, only the tiniest bit tight, and when she said how splendidly original it was of Richard to have married a Scot I actually felt quite warm towards her because such a lot of people were stuffy about the wedding and made snide remarks about kilts. So on an impulse I said: 'Darling, do drop in for a drink sometime!' and she said: 'Lovely—when?' which really put me on the spot, but I thought she might be all right if she had to eat at the same time as she was drinking, so I invited her to lunch on Sunday. However, when she cried: 'Whooppee!' and drank a glass of champagne straight off, my heart sank to my boots. The other guests will think I've taken leave of my senses."

"They know her?"

"All too well—with the exception of Walter, of course, who met her today for the first time. God, what *am* I going to do? Walter says don't worry, he'll take care of her, but he has no idea of the size of the problem. If she goes over the top she might well try to tear his clothes off."

"Gosh!" Up till now I had only experienced dramas of this kind on television.

"I think my only hope," said Lady Cynthia, too worried to be aware of my vicarious thrill, "is to invite yet another guest, someone who'll be able to whisk her away if she soars beyond the pale . . . Nick Darrow would be ideal, but he's never in town on weekends."

Immediately, as if to distract myself from all thought of Nicholas, I suggested: "What about Mr. Hall?"

"Lewis—of course!" Lady Cynthia was so struck by this idea that she almost dropped Mortimer. But then she hesitated. "He may not want to come," she said uncertainly at last. "We don't usually socialise, but perhaps in this case he'd make an exception to our rule." And seeing my baffled expression she added in an abrupt voice: "I have a special relationship with Lewis and go to St. Benet's every month to talk to him. He's my spiritual director."

I didn't like to say: "What's that?" so instead I murmured encouragingly: "I'm sure he'd want to come to your rescue." As I spoke I was realising I had finally uncovered Lady Cynthia's principal connection with the Healing Centre.

"Well, he certainly knows all about trying to cope with a society woman who drinks too much," said Lady Cynthia dryly. "He was married to one."

"I didn't realise he was a widower."

"He's not. He's divorced. But that was all a long time ago and he's never remarried. The great thing about Lewis," said Lady Cynthia, relaxing at last as she warmed to her subject, "is that he's thoroughly sophisticated so no decadent behaviour would surprise him, and he's thoroughly *au fait* with this woman's social background so he won't be inhibited about muzzling her if she becomes impossible. His father was at Eton with my father," she added casually, as if producing the trump card which proved Lewis could be trusted to triumph over anyone remotely louche, "and his mother's family owned that wonderful house in Sussex called Hampton Darcy which now belongs to the National Trust." And having delivered this little snippet from Debrett she dismissed me in order to make the crucial phone call. It was only later that I had the opportunity to ask: "Lady Cynthia, what's the name of this tricky old acquaintance of yours?"

"Venetia Hoffenberg. And may I just say, my dear, that I consider the word 'tricky' to be a masterpiece of English understatement."

I thought: this is going to be a real fun-lunch.

It never occurred to me that the inevitable drama would pave the way for the third miracle.

4

> We suggest you do not just focus on the issue of food intake. Rather, try to unravel the difficulties and deprivations that have led to compulsive eating . . . Are you using food to suppress uncomfortable feelings? Are you, literally, stuffing them down? . . . Or is food a way of filling up the emptiness within you?
>
> GARETH TUCKWELL AND DAVID FLAGG
> *A Question of Healing*

I

I went to Harrods for the beef and eel, Marks and Spencer for the vegetables and fruit and Sainsbury's for the more mundane ingredients. This tour exercised the Polo and gave me some interesting experiences in parking.

Back at Eaton Terrace I planned the approaching meal as if I were a general plotting a military campaign. The golden rule of English cooking is: never overcook the vegetables. But this is a hard rule to keep when several vegetables are on the menu, and on Sunday morning I was so absorbed in the challenges the lunch presented that I almost forgot to set my video to record the men's final from Wimbledon. (I had a mild crush on Edberg.) However, as things turned out I needn't have bothered. The weather was so foul that the entire match was postponed, but in the kitchen I was certainly grateful for the cool temperature. By the time I'd finished nursing each item to the pinnacle of eatability I still looked as if I'd been roasting in the oven alongside the beef, but at least the sweat wasn't actually sizzling on my forehead.

Since I'd set out the smoked eel terrine with the sweet red capsicum salad while everyone was drinking champagne in the drawing-room, I didn't get the chance to inspect the guests until Lady Cynthia buzzed me to remove the plates some time later. Mr. Walter P. Woodbridge III, I discovered, was tall and handsome with melancholy brown eyes which reminded me of Mortimer. Unlike Mortimer he had iron-grey hair, beautifully cut, and the usual American teeth, flawless and well flossed. When he smiled at me and said a courteous "thank you" as I presented him with the first platter of vegetables, I even decided he was good enough for Lady Cynthia—good enough, at least, to be her escort. Naturally I didn't want him to marry her and leave me homeless, but as Lady Cynthia was so cautious about men I decided my future was probably secure.

One of the other male guests had been elected to carve the roast beef, as Lady Cynthia had been nervous of entrusting this supremely British task to Walter P.W.III. Mr. Robert Welbeck, an old friend of hers, was the son of a knight, not a baronet, a misfortune which meant he had no title. (Lady Cynthia was always keen to tell me these details to ensure I got the place-cards right at the first attempt.) The untitled Mr. Welbeck was bald and portly, probably in his fifties. Despite the fact that he was a churchwarden of St. Mary's Mayfair and, presumably, a Christian, he didn't treat me as if I had any value whatsoever, and neither did his wife, a pencil-thin teetotaller who refused the potatoes. (I hate people who are strong-minded enough to do this.)

The next two guests I assessed were Lord Todd-Marshall (Conservative life-peer, no inheritable title, born middle-class, profession "something in the City," hobby sitting on quangos) and Lady Todd-Marshall (title acquired by marriage, also born middle-class, unpaid profession magistrate, hobby organising everything in sight). Lady T-M was better behaved than Mrs. Welbeck and gave a little grunt of acknowledgement when she had finished helping herself to all the vegetables including both varieties of potato. I decided she and her husband were standard Tory Party fodder, Lord T-M bulky in grey, Lady T-M stout in navy-blue, neither of them about to win a prize for unconventional behaviour.

Having passed judgement on the Todd-Marshalls I turned my critical gaze on the last two guests: Lewis Hall (no title but born upper-class, marital status divorced, profession clergyman, hobby directing spirits—or whatever it was he did with Lady Cynthia once a month) and the Shady Lady (born the daughter of a baron, title The Honourable, marital status widow, profession unprintable, hobby creating havoc).

Lewis was austerely and traditionally dressed in one of his tailor-made clerical suits, but still created the impression of a demagogue who preached hellfire and damnation in the pulpit and flirted with both behind the scenes. By now I was sure that this impression was deeply misleading, but I remained intrigued by his indestructible air of raciness. Of course he behaved beautifully. When our glances met he exclaimed: "Hullo, Alice! What a magnificent banquet you've prepared for us!" and he smiled, treating me as a real person instead of a robotic slave, before I moved on towards the Shady Lady.

The Honourable Mrs. Venetia Hoffenberg was tall, with fantastic hair, dyed jet-black and arranged to soar skywards into a knobbly hump which was nailed eccentrically into position by a couple of diamond hatpins. She had green eyes, false eyelashes, scarlet lips and a husky voice made huskier by a smoker's cough. She looked as if she could seduce six men before breakfast and still be capable of downing a bottle of champagne with a seventh. Appearing to be wearing pyjamas, she was also flaunting enough gold bangles to win instant admittance to Fort Knox.

"Oh God, what's all this rubbish?" she demanded disdainfully as I offered her my magnificent platter of vegetables. "Take it away and get me a drink! Which claret are you serving with this hunk of dead cow, Cynthia darling?"

"St. Estèphe, darling. The 'eighty-five."

"Damn it, I never drink claret less than ten years old—I'd rather have bloody Beaujolais!"

"Are you sure?" said Lewis, suddenly turning to her with his most charming smile. "Personally I can never resist a St. Estèphe of any age, although I admit I do have a soft spot for some of those sixties vintages. Have you tried the 'sixty-three lately?"

"Don't talk to me of 'sixty-three!" cried Mrs. Hoffenberg dramatically. "That was the most ghastly year of my life when I was crucified by a bloody heartbreaker and wound up married to a bloody clergyman!" She looked him up and down as if assessing his capacity to be bloody. "You married?"

"Yes and no," said Lewis cunningly, intriguing her so much that she allowed him to reminisce about how he had met his ex-wife in an air-raid shelter during the war.

Having finished serving the vegetables I began to circulate with the horseradish sauce while Walter P.W.III, appointed by Lady Cynthia to take charge of the wine, belatedly began to pour out the claret. I deduced he had been thinking so hard of Lady Cynthia that he had quite overlooked the decanters until Mrs. Hoffenberg's demand for a drink had jogged his memory.

In the kitchen once more I covered the remaining vegetables with foil, returned them to the oven to keep warm and ate a cheese sandwich to stave off the hunger pangs. In no time at all—or so it seemed—the buzzer sounded again. Abandoning the extra slab of cheese I'd just carved for myself, I sped back with the vegetables and found to my delight that the men were all having second helpings of roast beef.

"I haven't had such a magnificent Sunday lunch," Lewis was declaring, "since I took my grandson to the Dorchester to celebrate his twelfth birthday."

"The Dorchester? Oh, I can't be bothered with any hotel nowadays except Claridge's," said Mrs. Hoffenberg, whose voice had become gravelly. She was smoking between courses like an American—although the one American present was doing no such thing. She also appeared to have purloined one of the claret decanters for her own personal use. It was standing an inch from her glass and she'd put one of her gold bangles around its neck. I was reminded of an explorer claiming land by planting a flag.

"I felt my grandson should see the Dorchester as part of his education," Lewis was saying amazingly, "although I have to admit I'm never averse to a little escapade at Claridge's."

"Hell, darling, neither am I!" said Mrs. Hoffenberg, suddenly deciding to behave like Mae West in one of her celebrated roles. "Why don't we have an escapade there together sometime? You may be well over sixty but I bet you're not way over the hill!"

The other guests, who had been listening with expressions of polite disapproval, now stiffened in open-mouthed horror, like a gaggle of goldfish spotting a cat closing in on their fragile glass bowl. Lady Cynthia's face was a lovely shade of pink; I had never seen anyone look so stunning while being devastated by embarrassment, and I was aware of her Walter shooting her a burning glance, the sort of glance a gentleman of the old school gives to his beloved when he yearns to protect her from something which might sully her purity. I was offering the vegetable dish to Mr. Welbeck but he was oblivious of it. The sight of a Shady Lady vamping a clergyman was just too good to be missed—appalling behaviour, of course, and quite beyond the pale, but nonetheless utterly riveting. Out of the corner of my eye I saw his wife shift in her chair, and when he jumped violently a moment later I realised she'd managed to kick him. Hastily he began to scrabble for a potato.

"If you're generous enough to pay me that sort of compliment, I'm sure you'll be generous enough to share your claret with me!" said Lewis resourcefully, and removing the bangle he placed the decanter out of her reach on the other side of his plate.

"Spoilsport!" snapped Mrs. Hoffenberg. "Cynthia darling, wheel on another vat of St. Estèphe!"

"There's none left, darling. Alice, could you fetch some more Malvern water, please?"

Somehow I tore myself away, shot to the kitchen, grabbed two bottles of Malvern (one sparkling, one still) and streaked back to the dining-room just in time to hear Mrs. Hoffenberg announce: ". . . and the trouble with clergymen is that they're hung up on God and this makes them impotent."

"Really?" said Lewis, quite unabashed and assuming an innocent expression. "And have you done a survey to confirm that most worrying thesis?"

By this time Mrs. Welbeck was scarlet, Lady Todd-Marshall was purple and all the men except Lewis were holding their breath as tenaciously as if they were battling with hiccups.

"I don't need to do a survey, darling—I just *know,*" said Mrs. Hoffenberg dogmatically. "I was married to a clergyman and—did I ever tell you that I was married to a clergyman?"

"Several times, yes."

"Well, let me tell you, sweetie, that it wasn't just his wrists that were limp . . . Hey, pass that decanter back—I can't think why you had to go and swipe it like that!"

"I'm so sorry, how thoughtless of me," said Lewis at once, and poured the remaining claret into his glass before handing her back the empty decanter.

"Why, you absolute swine, you've nicked the lot!"

"Dear me, so I have! Well, I did tell you I could never resist a St. Estèphe—"

"Pig!"

"Venetia," said Lady Cynthia, "do shut up—there'll be port later with the cheese, I promise . . . Alice, you can take the beef out now."

I forced my feet to remove me to the kitchen.

When I returned, summoned by the buzzer to clear the plates after the men had finished their second helpings, Mrs. Hoffenberg was sulking in silence and the conversation had turned to Mrs. Thatcher's recent prophecy that there would be a golden age stretching far into the 1990s; Mr. Welbeck was saying what a wonderful thing it was that now even the middle-classes had the chance to become members of Lloyd's and live in affluence ever after, although Lady Todd-Marshall retorted that it was no use wallowing in affluence if everyone died of AIDS or got murdered by psychopaths, and what about that pregnant woman who got murdered on the motorway. But the men weren't interested in pregnant women getting murdered on motorways, and after murmuring soothingly how keen the government was on law and order they began to drool again over Mrs. Thatcher and her special relationship with Walter P.W.III's friend Ronnie.

In disappointment I retired to the kitchen and loaded a tray with the summer pudding, the cream and the cold custard. The Stilton was already on the dining-room sideboard, the pong kept in check by a covered dish.

When Mrs. Hoffenberg saw the summer pudding she said in disgust: "Oh God, it's all puddings today, isn't it—first Yorkshire and now this! Well, I'm going to give the food a miss from now on—where's the bloody port?"

"Venetia," said Lady Cynthia, furious by this time, "you're not exactly a credit to whoever taught you manners in the nursery, are you?"

"I'm not a credit to bloody anyone. Well, if you're not going to produce the port for another ten minutes, I'll have a brandy to keep me going—and make it a double!"

"The port's on the sideboard. Help yourself. And I hope you'll now stop talking about drink," said Lady Cynthia in a trembling voice. I knew instinctively that all her most painful memories of her alcoholic husband were being awakened, and I was sure Lewis knew that too for at once he leaned forward and said: "Cynthia, will you please excuse me if I too skip the pudding?" Then without waiting for a reply he added to Mrs. Hoffenberg: "The rain seems to have stopped. Let's take our glasses of port and inspect the garden."

"At last!" shouted Mrs. Hoffenberg. "A clergyman with initiative! A clergyman with pizzazz! A clergyman with—"

"Quite so," said Lewis before she could complete a word which apparently began with a "b." "Be sure you make a note of me in that survey of yours." Limping to the sideboard he poured a dash of port into a glass and tried to hand it to her but she waved it away. "I'm having a minimum of eight ounces," she declared. "It's the least I deserve after that rotten claret and ghastly meal." And pouring the contents of her water-glass into the flower arrangement, she grabbed the port decanter and filled the tumbler to the brim.

"Disgusting!" muttered Mrs. Welbeck, the teetotaller.

I whispered to my employer, who had faltered in dishing out the summer pudding: "Shall I do that for you?" but Lady Cynthia managed to say: "No, that's all right, Alice. Take around the custard and cream."

The French windows which led onto the balcony opened and closed as Lewis and Mrs. Hoffenberg withdrew, passing out of sight as they descended the flight of steps to the patio. A deathly silence began as everyone waited for me to finish my task and vanish, but as soon as I left the room temptation overwhelmed me; recklessly I pressed my ear to the panels of the closed door, but there was no difficulty hearing the explosion of outrage which followed.

Mrs. Hoffenberg was described by Mr. Welbeck as having "hit a new low" by exhibiting such "rock-bottom behaviour." Mrs. Welbeck said it was always far more repulsive to see a woman drunk than a man drunk. (Why? She never deigned to explain.) Lady Todd-Marshall suggested darkly that Mrs. Hoffenberg was ripe to appear before the bench on a charge of being drunk and disorderly. Lord Todd-Marshall made the middle-class remark that Mrs. Hoffenberg's performance constituted the sort of behaviour which drove people to talk about the "decadent aristocracy"—although of course, he added hastily as he remembered his hostess, he well knew that the majority of the aristocracy led thoroughly decent lives. Everyone, in other words, rushed to judgement. It was left to Lady Cynthia, the person most wronged by Mrs. Hoffenberg's old-soak act, to set her anger aside and say: "It's all very sad. She's obviously terribly unhappy. It's easy to criticise her, isn't it, but so hard to offer constructive help." I admired Lady Cynthia very much when she said that, and I was sure Nicholas would have admired her too.

I slunk away and started preparing the coffee.

Lady Cynthia hurried into the kitchen just as I was putting the demi-tasses on the tray. "Alice," she said without any preliminary chit-chat, "Lewis is going to take Venetia home now, but he wants a woman to go with him in case Venetia . . . well, in case she needs help there which it wouldn't be appropriate for a priest to provide. Would you—could you—"

"Yes, of course," I said. "The coffee's almost ready. Shall I—"

"Don't worry, I'll see to it. Thank you so much, my dear—oh, and don't take to heart anything beastly which Venetia said about that wonderful meal. Everyone else agreed it was a tour de force."

Nice, kind, thoughtful, generous Lady Cynthia. I hoped more fiercely than ever that Walter P.W.III would somehow restrain himself from sweeping her off to America. Removing my apron I grabbed a piece of roast beef to sustain me and hurried downstairs to fetch a cardigan.

By the time I returned to the hall the front door was open, Lewis's red Volkswagen was outside in the street with the engine running and Lewis himself was busy stuffing Mrs. Hoffenberg into the front seat while Lady Cynthia hovered anxiously nearby. Turning to me she said in a low voice: "This is so good of you, Alice," but in fact, as I well knew, it wasn't good of me at all; I was motivated not by virtue but by an enthralled desire to witness Life with a capital L. Walled off by my weight, isolated by feelings of inferiority and entombed for years with a maiden aunt, I'd become all too accustomed to life passing me by. Yet here I now was, about to chaperone a clergyman, tend a decadent aristocrat and roar around London in a foreign car to the accompaniment of squealing wheels. I was having a hard time concealing my ecstasy.

After I had wedged myself into the back seat we set off.

Mrs. Hoffenberg, astonishingly, was still conscious but by this time very woozy, and as we drove up Eaton Terrace she began to sing snatches of a countryish sort of song which I didn't recognise. Snatches of the lyric floated towards me along with a pronounced aroma of port. Her voice, raspy and torchy, reminded me of the nightclubs glimpsed in television dramas, low dives which the police inevitably raided for drugs.

The song seemed to be about the pain caused to the singer by a heartbreaker, a dream-maker, a lover who kept playing with fire. However the singer had now found someone else who would take the heartbreaker's place—fill the empty space—with the result that the singer's heart wouldn't be broken any more.

I was just wondering if she intended to sing this little number over and over again for the remainder of the journey when she suddenly abandoned the lyric and said with surprising clarity to Lewis: "That's an early Elvis song. Do you like Elvis?"

"I'm too old."

"Oh, don't be so stuffy! I bet *you* were a heartbreaker when you were young!"

"Any self-centred fool can break hearts. Nowadays I get my kicks out of mending them."

"Honestly? You mend hearts?"

"Mend hearts, refurbish souls, heal wounds old and new—"

"In that case, tell me this: do you think the best way to cure a broken heart is by 'filling the empty space,' as the song puts it, and having it off with someone new?"

"That's like giving a drink to someone with a hang-over. It may alleviate the pain for a while but it doesn't fix the problem which drove you to drink in the first place."

"Damn it, I'm not talking about bloody drink, I'm talking about bloody sex! Do you screw around?"

"No, I don't believe in exploiting people. I follow an alternative life-style."

"But darling, I yearn to be exploited by you! Send the slave back to Cynthia's in a taxi and swap to my life-style for the rest of the afternoon!"

"You'd be extremely disappointed. My arthritic hip's playing me up today."

"Oh, for God's sake! Why don't you get a new one?"

"No time. I'm too busy mending hearts broken by your kind of life-style."

"Very slick!" said Mrs. Hoffenberg crossly, but added with grudging admiration: "You're pretty damned weird but I like you anyway." And closing her eyes abruptly she began to snore.

"Are you all right, Alice?" said Lewis at last.

I assured him I was.

"We're nearly there."

Situated in a quiet Chelsea backwater the house was strikingly pretty, its front walls swathed in ivy, the flowerbeds beneath the windows ablaze with scarlet roses, but inside the place was a mess. Beyond the chaotic living-room, strewn with sections of the Sunday papers, the kitchen was littered with unwashed glasses, and flies were fastened to plates of unfinished food.

"Bloody hell!" muttered Mrs. Hoffenberg, who had woken up sufficiently to be steered into the house. Collapsing onto the sofa she stared around aggrieved. "What a tip! Never mind, the maid comes tomorrow and meanwhile I'll blot out the whole scene with a swig of VC. Get it for me, would you?" she added imperiously to me. "There's a bottle in the fridge."

"What's VC?" demanded Lewis.

"Veuve Clicquot, you idiot! What else?"

"Alice, would you please get Mrs. Hoffenberg a glass of water?"

"I don't want fucking water! I want—"

"Forget it. I'm not prepared to stand by and see you abuse yourself any further. I draw the line."

"Why, you miserable, mean, beastly, brutish old bastard—"

"Right. That's me. You've finally got my measure. Now lay off the booze, lie down on that sofa and pass out."

"But I might choke on my own vomit—I might wind up a corpse!"

"I'll make sure you're wedged in a safe position. Alice"—he stopped me at the door before I could fetch the glass of water—"come here for a moment, please, and stand beside me. Now Venetia, look hard at Alice. You're going to remember her. You're going to remember that she was here and you're going to remember that you and I didn't drink champagne—or do anything else. And last but not least you're going to remember my alternative life-style, you're going to remember I work at St. Benet's with Nicholas Darrow, you're going to remember that I'll always be willing to help you there if ever you decide to get your heart fixed."

But Mrs. Hoffenberg was no longer listening. She was sliding from the sofa to the floor, and a second later she was lying unconscious amidst the mess and the filth and the trash.

II

"*Go upstairs,* Alice," said Lewis abruptly, "find her bedroom and bring down the pillows and the duvet—or if there's no duvet bring at least two blankets. I'm sorry, I'd do it myself but my hip's so bad now I doubt if I could get up the stairs."

I did as I was told while he cleared the sofa of junk. Eventually we hauled the body up from the floor, dumped it on the cushions and swaddled it with the duvet. The pillows we used to wedge her in a non-lethal position. I was just adding the final touch by removing her shoes and tucking her feet out of sight again when Lewis said: "Let's take an extra five minutes to make this place less sordid. If I woke with a hang-over and saw such chaos I'd immediately want to hit the bottle again."

Our labours moved into a new phase. I loaded the dishwasher, threw out all the left-over food and wiped the kitchen counters. Lewis stacked the newspapers into a pile, emptied the overflowing ashtrays and found a Hoover which I used to remove the debris from the carpet. He also found two empty bottles of VC, one lying on the floor in a corner and the other standing forgotten on the window-sill.

As I switched off the Hoover I saw he was taking a closer look at the body. "Alice, what are these diamond hatpins doing in her hair? Is this a wig which she's skewered into position?"

"Wigs are never grey at the roots."

"True. Well, the hatpins are decorative but they could also be dangerous if they work loose. Can you take them out?"

I detached them gently but the mound of hair at once collapsed, resembling a birds' nest which had been vandalised. At Lewis's suggestion I then brought the water which he had asked me to fetch earlier, and he slipped one of his cards beneath the glass as I set it on the coffee-table. The inscription was still plainly legible. "The Reverend Lewis Hall, The Healing Centre, St. Benet's-by-the-Wall, Egg Street, London EC2 . . ." I stared, remembering how he had left his card with me at my home in Dean Danvers Street, and suddenly I had an impression of a pattern, an enigmatic, repeating signal from a source which was somehow both close at hand yet far away.

I looked up to find Lewis watching me with his sharp, shrewd black eyes. "You did well," he said. "I can see now you're efficient as well as sensible. You don't panic, you're too intelligent to ask unnecessary questions—and on top of all that, you cook like a dream! I shan't forget your help today, Alice. Thank you."

I felt so overwhelmed by this praise that I was hardly able to thank him in return. Slowly it was dawning on me that I might not be doomed to watch life always from the sidelines. Gradually I was beginning to grasp that although mainstream society might write me off as negligible, there might be another world where I could belong.

I said shyly to Lewis: "I liked it when you talked of an alternative life-style."

"Did you? I thought afterwards it sounded as if I were advocating a counter-culture, and that wasn't what I meant at all."

"What's the difference?"

"A counter-culture splits off from the mainstream culture and rejects it; it forms its own private little world. But the whole point of an alternative life-style is that it exists at the heart of mainstream society and intermingles with it." As he spoke he was looking down at the body on the sofa, but although his eyes were grave there was no contempt in them.

Suddenly I heard myself say: "Why does she drink so much when she must know, deep down, that getting drunk won't solve anything?"

"She's probably despaired of solutions. The despair's eaten away at her and created an empty space which in turn sets up a pain so excruciating that she feels she can only drink to blot it out."

"But I thought it was the heartbreaker who created the empty space!"

"No doubt he had a malign effect, but I'd guess her problem goes deeper than that. After all, other people have their hearts broken and don't wind up as alienated as this."

"Alienated from what?"

"From reality. Venetia's alienated from her true self and the life she was designed to lead. She's alienated from the very ground of her being." He turned away abruptly, adding over his shoulder as he limped towards the door: "I'll take you home."

Some time later in the car I said: "Maybe she'll come to St. Benet's."

"She might. But I doubt it."

"You think she'll feel too embarrassed by what happened today?"

"I suspect she'll repress all the embarrassment which someone like you would experience. She's far more likely to be angry with me for turning down her proposition."

"But you're a clergyman!"

"You may have noticed her opinion of clergymen wasn't too high."

"But even so . . . Clergymen don't usually accept propositions from shady ladies, do they?"

"Certainly not! But as the *News of the World* so loves to point out to its readers, there's always the chance of a rotten apple cropping up in even the best barrel of Coxes." He was changing gears as he spoke, and when the car slowed down I realised we were in Eaton Terrace.

"I'll come in and report to Cynthia," said Lewis, switching off the engine. "Thank you again for your help, Alice." And when he patted my forearm lightly in approval I found myself no longer thinking of Mrs. Hoffenberg, who must have had such a rich, privileged childhood, but of the father I couldn't remember and all the love I'd never known.

At once I felt the need to eat, but now that need made me shudder. I could only picture Mrs. Hoffenberg demanding the champagne, and in a moment of horror I knew why she both fascinated and appalled me so much. It was because when I looked at her I saw my own "empty space" reflected, my own despair which had resulted in alienation; it was because when I looked at her I saw the unloved, elderly wreck I could become. Automatically I struggled to count my blessings, just as Aunt had always insisted that I should, but it seemed to me at that moment that the only blessings worth counting were the ones I didn't have. I opened my mouth to blurt out to Lewis: "The ground of our being's love, isn't it?" but before I could speak I realised he was in such pain that he was unable to get out of the car. Hurrying around to the driver's door I tried to help him but within seconds he had decided to abandon his plan to report to Lady Cynthia.

"I must get home," he said. "Tell Cynthia I'll phone her."

"But are you okay to drive?"

"Let's hope so," he said dryly, and set off, still grey with pain, in the direction of the Pimlico Road.

I went indoors. All the guests had gone except for Walter P. Woodbridge III who was consoling Lady Cynthia for her ruined lunch-party. As I walked into the drawing-room to deliver Lewis's message, I found the two of them in the middle of a very smoochy snog.

Back in the kitchen I tried to put all the left-over food away without touching any of it, but my will-power failed. I finished the roast beef and summer pudding and knew myself to be no better than the drunk snoring in that disgusting house in Chelsea. I thought in misery: I *want* to get thin. I *want* to eat less. But what I want to do I don't do, and what I don't want to do I do.

Self-hatred overwhelmed me. I wept as I threw up later in the lavatory, but I knew that before the end of the day I would have started on the rum raisin ice cream.

If anyone had said to me at that moment that the darkest hour is always just before the dawn I would have wanted to commit murder, but the third miracle—my third great miracle of 1988—was soon to alter my life beyond recognition.

III

The first thing that happened in the run-up to the miracle was that Mr. Woodbridge's iron-willed pursuit of Lady Cynthia accelerated. There's no doubt that once these Americans get going on a mission there's no stopping them and in no time they're all over everywhere in their pale suits and deep suntans. Down in my dark little basement I polished Aunt's favourite pieces of furniture, watered my platoon of pot-plants which were guaranteed to thrive in twilight, and dusted the silver-framed photograph of golden Orlando as I wondered how soon my life at Eaton Terrace would end. I tried to be philosophical by telling myself I had always known the job was too good to last, but the truth was I had expected it to last some years and I was now bitterly disappointed.

I knew Lady Cynthia would always deal fairly with me and I never quite lost the belief, planted by Nicholas at Aunt's funeral, that I should go on in hope and not be afraid, but nevertheless it was a strain not knowing when the axe would finally fall. At first I had hoped that Lady Cynthia might merely have an affair, but I suppose I knew from the start that her religious principles ensured she never would unless marriage was certain. This meant, as I struggled to foresee the future, that the crucial question became: were they or weren't they? Mrs. Simcock, diamanté spectacles flashing, whispered to me over elevenses that Lady Cynthia had had enough tragedies in her life without taking on a foreigner who might prove to be impotent, and the sooner he was tried out in bed the better. Mrs. Simcock liked Mr. Woodbridge but could never quite forgive him for not being born and bred in England south of Watford Gap.

While I waited in mounting suspense I had to keep eating to calm me down. I often did think of seeking help at St. Benet's—not from Nicholas, who still had to be avoided at all costs, but from Lewis, who had looked at Mrs. Hoffenberg with such compassion after she'd passed out. However, I always told myself I was only eating so much because I was anxious about the future and that I'd get better by myself once I was more settled.

Francie phoned every two weeks, which was kind of her, but I always evaded her suggestions that we should meet; I had put on weight again and I was too afraid she would notice. Lady Cynthia never noticed because she was so bound up with Mr. Woodbridge, and

Mrs. Simcock never noticed because she was too busy watching out for the first signs of an affair, but I noticed because my best tent-dress became tight under the armpits and ceased to hang properly.

The blow finally fell in August. Summoned by Lady Cynthia to her boudoir I was told that she had agreed to marry Mr. Woodbridge. Since neither of them wanted a long engagement or a big wedding they were tying the knot in mid-September, when Mr. Woodbridge's assignment in London had finished, and sailing to America on the *QEII.*

Lady Cynthia was looking very beautiful and very happy and I couldn't grudge her such good fortune, but I was devastated by the news of this breakneck rush to the altar. I had hoped for a leisurely engagement followed by a wedding in the spring.

"Of course lots of people will mutter: 'Marry in haste, repent at leisure,' " she was saying buoyantly, "but I've waited years to meet the right man and now I've found him I'm not going to waste time because, who knows, life's always uncertain and there may not be much time left."

"That sounds very sensible to me, Lady Cynthia."

"Dear Alice, what a blessing you've been since you came here! Which reminds me, I must stop talking about myself and start talking about you. Now, my dear, this is the position: naturally I shall give you the very best references and naturally I shall tell all my friends what a success you've been—in fact I won't rest until I know you've found a job that's good enough for you! And your next flat, I'm sure, will be a lot nicer than that horrid little den downstairs which you've tolerated so nobly."

I was willing myself not to cry. If Lady Cynthia had kicked me out into the street I would have been dry-eyed, but her generosity, her kindness and her affectionate smile all combined to decimate my self-control so that I could hardly utter the required words of thanks.

She chatted on, saying that she planned to retain a base in London but had decided, for security reasons, to buy a flat and dispose of the house. Of course she would be coming back regularly to England to see Billy—she'd decided not to move him to an institution in America because he was so settled where he was—and of course she would be coming back to see Richard, who wouldn't be in Scotland for ever and might well wind up in London—or even in New York . . . The world was so small nowadays, wasn't it, and travel so easy; indeed the only difficulty lay in the fact that Mortimer would be unable to accompany her on her trips to England because of the quarantine laws.

"Mortimer will miss his food from Harrods," I said.

Lady Cynthia replied blithely that Mortimer would adjust.

Poor little Mortimer! Downstairs in my flat that evening I heaved a sigh for both of us, forced as we were to accept this radical change in our comfortable circumstances, but before I could become maudlin the third miracle moved a step closer.

The telephone rang.

IV

By that time I was on my own in the house, as Lady Cynthia was dining out with her fiancé. I was eating butter pecan ice cream (I'd run out of rum raisin) and watching *Brookside* on television.

"Hullo?" I said, turning down the volume. I assumed the caller was Francie since no one else ever phoned me. I knew now that having my own phone had been a ridiculous extravagance, but in the beginning I'd believed that I would soon be thin and luxuriating in a social life. "Is that you, Francie?"

"Not this time."

I dropped the tub of ice cream.

"It's Nicholas Darrow, Alice—is this a good time to call?"

"Just a moment." I picked up the tub. I set it down on the table. I switched off the television. And I took three deep breaths. Then I picked up the receiver and said: "Sorry about that. Yes, it's fine."

"Good, because there's something important that I want to discuss. Cynthia's told Lewis you'll soon be in the market for another job, and I was wondering—of course I'm sure you're thinking in terms of another job in Belgravia, but I was just wondering—would you be interested in working among people who pursue a rather different life-style?"

I heard the signal again, the repeating pattern I'd glimpsed when seeing Lewis's card, but this time the signal was no tentative tap but a blast on a trumpet. In my mind's eye the pattern emerged as a many-stranded rope, supple and powerful, and the next moment I felt as if the rope were encircling me like an expertly thrown lasso. The shock was profound. I couldn't speak. I could only submit as I was reeled in, inch by inch, from the sidelines to the centre, from a stunted existence to life in abundance—and suddenly I could imagine that life all around me, real life, the life I'd always wanted, and I knew that eventually it would fill the empty space which tormented me and end the degrading hunger I found so insatiable.

"I'd like you to consider joining our team as the Rectory's cook-housekeeper," Nicholas was saying. "And I assure you I see us as meeting on equal ground . . ."

V

There was more but I barely took it in. When I finally replaced the receiver all I could think was: it's the biggest miracle yet.

It never occurred to me that the proposal could be the logical outcome of a certain combination of circumstances. Later Nicholas did explain why I seemed to be the best person for the job and I did see that the miracle was a mere natural development which might even have been described as predictable, but at the time I was overwhelmed with wonder. I told myself I was going to be one of a family at last. Lewis would be my substitute father, Stacy would be my substitute brother, and Nicholas . . . Well, all that mattered was that Nicholas wasn't going to be in any sense my doctor and I wasn't going to be in any sense his pathetic patient, masochistically confessing my revolting habits. I was going to be one of a team, valued and respected as I did the work I loved. I was going to belong.

The tub of butter pecan ice cream was still sitting on the table, but at that point I got up and threw the tub in the trash.

The gesture gave me such a feeling of empowerment that I became euphoric. Romantic thoughts began to cascade through my mind, but I told myself severely that the last thing I was ever going to do was behave like some idiot who couldn't control her emotions. No one would ever know how much I loved Nicholas. For his sake I'd make sure there was no mess, and anyway I wasn't greedy. I knew he could never love me, so I wasn't going to crucify myself longing for a future which could never happen. All I wanted was the chance to work on his team and be treated as a real person. I didn't deserve more than that. After all, who was I? Just a fat lump who cooked. And as I'd been luckier than any fat lump had a right to be, I certainly wasn't going to wreck this miraculous chance of happiness by behaving like a lovelorn birdbrain.

I suddenly felt quite sure—in fact there was no doubt in my mind whatsoever—that once I started living at the Rectory I would be cured of all past pain, saved from all my present anxieties and set free to live happily ever after in a blissfully untroubled future.

I thought I was being so realistic but of course it's obvious to me now, as I look back, that I was still wallowing in the most dangerous of romantic dreams.

Part Two

LEWIS

The Unvarnished Truth

The counsellor has the temporal welfare of his client as his first consideration. He seeks to enable the client to return to his environment and then to live with a sufficient degree of usefulness and contentment. The Christian counsellor has that end in view too; but he asks a more ultimate question. To what purpose is this temporal welfare? Is not this life a journey? How can a man be fit if he does not know what he is fit for? . . . A man who has no sense of his ultimate purpose and destiny is not, in a Christian sense, well at all.

CHRISTOPHER HAMEL COOKE

Healing Is for God

Monday, 15th August, 1988: Cynthia's gone off her rocker. Love's finally unhinged her. Amazing! Sometimes I think the nineteenth century legal classification of women with lunatics really is justifiable, but nowadays, when everyone, even Mrs. Thatcher, is jumping on the ordination-of-women bandwagon, and the nutty clerics at the nutty Lambeth Conference have even been waffling about women bishops (whatever next, I ask myself!) it's not the done thing to make any remark even in jest which knocks any segment of the human race except white Anglo-Saxon males. I don't like this—and not just because I'm a white Anglo-Saxon male. I don't like it because what it's actually doing is taking a swipe at truth and introducing censorship under the guise of being nice to the downtrodden. Thank God that at least in this journal I can say what I damn well like so long as it's spoken in the quest for TRUTH with a capital T.

Anyway, where was I? Oh yes, Cynthia. She comes to see me today for an extra session and tells me she's definitely going to marry the Yank. Well, that's no surprise; I could see it coming a mile off, and I think this time marriage is right for her. There'll still be problems: guilt over Billy, yearning for Richard and so on, but I think that with the Yank's help she'll be able to cope, merging her old life with the fresh start she needs and deserves. So far so good. But then she goes clean off her rocker and tells me she's going to give her house to us. My jaw sags. The house is one of the few freehold houses in Eaton Terrace and it has to be worth at least half a million at today's inflated prices.

Heaving my jaw back into place I manage to say to her: "Are you really sure you want to burn this particular boat? Money's so useful when one starts a new life." But that cuts no ice. It turns out the Yank has a cool sixty million dollars and he's going to settle several million on her as a wedding present. Why should she need the proceeds of the sale of a chic little hovel in Belgravia? I tell her she should take more time to think over this magnificently generous decision, but she says she's got no doubts because she's sure it's God's will.

It always makes me very nervous when people talk like that. Reminds me of the patients at Barwick, the ones with all manner of inflated delusions. What a long time ago it seems since I was at Barwick! But working as a chaplain in a big mental hospital certainly teaches one a thing or two about unstable behaviour.

"A call from God? Tell me about it," I say, fearing the worst, but to my relief her response is at least rooted in reality. Apparently she remembered me telling her—at that lunch-party in early July when Venetia went on the rampage—that life at the Rectory was chaotic because we never had time to cook decent meals, pick up cassocks from the cleaner's, buy food and so on. She also remembered me saying we longed for a cook-housekeeper but couldn't afford one. "My gift will set you free to devote yourselves to the Healing Centre without any petty distractions!" she says shining-eyed. Bless her, she's so happy. And bless her, she's right. It would. But should she be making such an offer when she's in love and not responsible for her actions? We don't want the Yank turning up on our doorstep with a six-shooter in his hand and accusing us of conning a vulnerable woman out of a fortune . . .

COMMENT: Let's face it: the above entry shows me at what Val would call my sexist worst. On the excuse that I'm crusading for truth I've implied all women are as good as lunatics and made insulting remarks about the Lambeth Conference bishops into the bargain. I've also been vaguely anti-American, writing about that courteous and civilised citizen of the United States as if he's a gangster. So what's going on?

Obviously I'm ruffled about something. But what?

Okay, let's try and figure this out. Whenever I get a bout of being anti-women it's a sign that a little crack has appeared on the smooth surface of my (nowadays) successful celibate life. So what's caused this current crack and how long has it been going on? The strange thing is that although it's only today that I've become sufficiently aware of it to record the malaise here in my journal, I've got a feeling it's been around for at least a couple of weeks. Maybe longer. But I've been repressing it.

Nasty. All the worst things get repressed. Damn it, what can be going on? Do I deep down want to seduce Cynthia and kill Woodbridge? No. Cynthia's not my type, not bitchy enough. Well, not bitchy at all. But she is, after all, looking ravishing at the moment, and she is, after all, female . . . Ye gods, I'm right, this is a sex problem, ****** hell! (Mustn't compound the problem by sinking into blasphemy, even though nearly everyone's forgotten nowadays that "bloody" means "by Our Lady"—but I remember, so . . . Stop, I'm rambling—which is possibly a sign of premature senility—but on second thoughts the senility wouldn't be premature. *Hell!* I hate old age. Incidentally, should I revise my current practice and classify "hell" as a blasphemy? No. Not in 1988. I shall go on allowing myself to write "hell" here when under stress.)

Now, where have I got to? I've worked out that I have a sex problem of some description, which is bad news as, for starters, my spiritual director's no good on sex questions. Maybe I should sack him. Maybe I should book myself into the London Clinic and order a castration. Maybe I should simply drop dead. But I'm never going to remarry, never, never, never. I've always said I'd never remarry while Diana's still alive—and what a great excuse that's given me to avoid a new commitment, but I really do believe, as an Anglo-Catholic, that a divorced priest shouldn't remarry.

Or do I?

Oh, hell, hell, hell, hell, *hell* . . .

Tuesday, 16th August, 1988: Cynthia phoned to say she'd told Woodbridge about her call to give us the house. He replied that she was the most wonderful woman in the world and she could give all Belgravia to the Healing Centre as far as he was concerned—he'd love her whatever she did. So he's off his rocker too. *Folie à deux.* Amazing.

Cynthia gives me permission to tell Nicholas, and Nicholas, of course, thinks I'm the one who's off his rocker while Cynthia and Woodbridge are sanity personified. "What's the problem?" he says. "We need a cook-housekeeper. Cynthia knows we need a cook-housekeeper. She wants to give us some money so that we can get a cook-housekeeper. It all seems very straightforward to me, so why the gloom?"

It's strange how Nicholas, who's a clever, able and extremely gifted man in some ways, can sometimes be as blind as a bat and as dumb as a donkey. "Wake up!" I snap. "I've been that woman's spiritual director for three years and you've been her friend for far longer. If things don't work out for her in future she could turn around, accuse us of undue influence and say we've swindled her out of half a million pounds!"

Nicholas just scoffs: "Don't be so ridiculous! If you weren't so hung up on women you'd never imagine that Cynthia would do such a thing!"—at which point I tramp out, banging the door. Ten minutes later I trudge back to say sorry. "That's okay," says Nicholas, barely looking up from the letter he's writing. "I suppose your hip's bad again today."

"Sod the hip!" I yell, and tramp out again. This time he follows me. We sit in my room. I again apologise. He says: "What's really bugging you here?" And I answer: "Don't know. Mystery."

We sit in silence for a moment. Eventually he asks: "It's not Cynthia, is it?" and we discuss this possibility, but he winds up agreeing with me that I'm not scratchy because I'm subconsciously jealous of Woodbridge. "You'd never have made a success of counselling her," says Nicholas, "unless you'd faced up to any questionable feelings right at the outset." That's true. I still feel that because of my hang-ups I'm not the best priest to counsel women, but sometimes people are put across one's path and it turns out that one can, after all, be of use. I could always empathise with Cynthia strongly because she had an alcoholic spouse, and the empathy enabled me to give her the help she needed.

Once Nicholas concedes that I've no desire to bed Cynthia and kill her fiancé he says: "Of course I realise we have to be on our guard when rich women give us money, but I honestly don't think we're running a risk in accepting this particular donation."

I say: "All right, maybe the worldly risk is zero, but there's still the spiritual risk. We've got to be sure that this gift is acceptable in the eyes of God and compatible with Cynthia's spiritual journey."

Nicholas says: "Sure. Uh-huh. We must pray about that." Nicholas sounds much too glib sometimes. I know he's already made up his mind that the gift is God's will and should be accepted PDQ.

Well, maybe he's right. But what I want to know is: if my relationship with Cynthia is everything it should be (and it is), why should (a) her marriage and (b) her donation be stirring up the mud at the bottom of my unconscious mind and making me write about a crack appearing in my (nowadays) successful celibate life?

COMMENT: The simplest explanation, which is apparent in the above entry, is that Cynthia and Woodbridge are triggering memories of my sex-life with Diana. But then how do I explain my hunch that this new outbreak of anti-women fever seems to have been contracted well before Cynthia announced her engagement? The engagement may well have brought the malaise to consciousness by making me think about sex, but I'd bet heavy money the malaise didn't originate there.

Another explanation: could this be the veiled expression of a psychic twinge, an ESP-type feeling that danger's lurking ahead? (I might be projecting the unknown danger onto women by demonising them.) No, the only thing twingeing is my damn hip, and anyway in the ministry of healing, danger's always lurking ahead, that's normal. One false step and then the Devil whooshes everything down the drain in double-quick time—and that's exactly why one has to know oneself through and through and why one has to keep facing the unvarnished truth in order to understand what's going on; the more you know, the less likely you are to make a mistake and get whooshed.

I still enjoy the danger of this ministry, of course, still thrive on it. I'll never forget how I nearly died of boredom when I was married and working in an ordinary parish . . . Hell, there I go again, thinking about Diana, thinking about marriage, thinking about sex! How ironic it is now to reflect that when I was young I believed a man past sixty would have no interest in copulation whatsoever . . .

Wednesday, 17th August, 1988: Nicholas says after the morning mass as we return to the Rectory: "I've had a brilliant idea." This could be true, so I look interested. Nicholas does indeed have some brilliant ideas—alongside all the ideas that are as nutty as a fruitcake. It's always my job to help him discern which is which.

He says brightly: "I spoke to Cynthia last night. She said she was going public with the news of her engagement today, starting with Alice and the cleaner, and as soon as she mentioned Alice I saw a really spectacular opportunity for us. I've thought about it again this morning and I've prayed about it, and I'm now one hundred per cent convinced—"

He wants to hire Alice Fletcher as the cook-housekeeper. It's one of his nutty-as-a-fruitcake ideas. Any female employed in this capacity has to be not merely an old crone but also a dyed-in-the-wool lesbian.

I say calmly, reasonably, soothingly: "No, Nicholas. Not Alice. No."

"But after Cynthia's lunch-party you came back raving about Alice's cooking!" He's honestly baffled by my reaction. I'm getting worried about these moments when Nicholas is blind as a bat (with arrogance, in the mistaken belief there's no situation he can't handle) and dumb as a donkey (with the brains-on-ice complacency which results from overconfidence). Is it my imagination or are these moments increasing?

"Nicholas!" I bark. "Wake up! That girl's heterosexual, a virgin and all set to become infatuated with you—if indeed she isn't infatuated with you already! You can't possibly share a house with her!"

Nicholas halts at the foot of the steps leading up to the Rectory's front door and looks at me as if I ought to return to Barwick—as a patient. "Your trouble," he says, "is that where women are concerned you can't tell a diamond from cut-glass! This is Alice we're talking about—*Alice!* Isn't it patently obvious by now that she's quite different from all the groupies we have to deal with?"

"I'm fully prepared to admit she's a nice, well-behaved child with a talent for cooking, but—"

"She's thirty-two!"

"All right, she's not a child, she's a woman, but how mature is she? Isn't she in fact exactly the kind of emotionally needy girl, starved of affection and in consequence living on romantic dreams, who would fall in the biggest possible way for a charismatic, cassock-clad—"

"Look, forget all that for a moment and just try to look beyond your preconceived notions to the unusual pattern she's woven during the last few months. Alice has been put across our path. She keeps recurring in our lives, even though she's always been most reluctant to ask for help, and our meetings with her have established that (a) she's a woman of the greatest integrity, (b) she's sensible and level-headed in a crisis and (c) she's a first-class cook. Adding all these facts together, isn't it obvious that she's (a) the ideal woman to have a live-in job at the Rectory, (b) the only woman we know whom we'd trust to have a live-in job at the Rectory, and therefore (c) the perfect candidate for the position of cook-housekeeper?"

"Could you kindly stop a-ing and b-ing and c-ing me and get a move on into the house? I want my breakfast before I faint from lack of nourishment!"

"But seriously, Lewis—"

"You're deliberately foisting this nutty idea on me when I'm too peckish to think clearly!"

"—seriously, I'm sure this is right—and I'm not just thinking of ourselves now; I'm thinking of Alice. She's got enormous potential but her development's been stunted by the rejecting parents, the aunt who couldn't handle emotion and the weight problem which has made her socially isolated. What Alice needs now in order to realise her potential is a place in a community where she can feel valued and respected. Then she'd soon make progress, build a fulfilling new life for herself, conquer her eating disorder—"

"I'm all for Alice doing those things," I say, hauling myself up the six steps to the front door and wishing human beings had evolved with rubber hips impervious to arthritis, "but I don't think she should do them while living under your roof at the Rectory."

But Nicholas is as unstoppable as a tank. He gets this way occasionally when he kids himself his psychic gifts have served up some kind of special knowledge amounting to divine revelation. Although I taught him long ago to be humble when trying to discern God's will he's still capable of going over the top into sham-guru-land if he falls in love with a peculiarly dubious idea. That's yet another reason why I'm so valuable to him. I don't merely tell him when the ideas are unworkable; I also take him down a peg or two when he gets inflated. My function is always to present the unvarnished truth. But I'm having a hard time scraping off the varnish this morning.

"I know I'm right!" he says grandly. "You're being sex-obsessed as usual!" And sweeping past me into the house he surges towards the kitchen without a backwards glance.

I reach the top step, puff a bit to get a grip on the pain and then limp along after him to resume the battle.

When I reach the kitchen I find that Stacy, who's hurried on ahead of us to cook the breakfast, is making a diabolical mess scrambling eggs and frying bacon. Smoke's rising from the toaster and the coffee percolator's behaving as if it wants to lay an egg. If ever three men needed an efficient housekeeper, it's us.

"If you could forget about sex for a moment," says Nicholas, going on the offensive again as he switches off the toaster, cuffs the percolator and takes control of the eggs and bacon, "you'd see straight away that Alice is ideal."

I reply in my clearest voice: "It's no good. Within twenty-four hours she'd be worshipping you as a hero."

" 'No man's a hero to his valet!' " quotes Nicholas amused, and he even has the nerve to add: "I can think of no better way to prevent Alice hero-worshipping me than to invite her to live at the Rectory and see just how ordinary I really am."

"You? Ordinary?" remarks Stacy, pausing in his efforts to dig charred cinders from the toaster. "Don't make me laugh! But what's all this about Alice coming to live here? Sounds like a brilliant idea—she makes the best chocolate-chip cookies in the world!"

Hopeless.

I'm so cross by this time that I pile my plate high, grab a mug of coffee and march off to eat in my room. Sitting under the crucifix I gloomily picture the Devil, coasting around, sensing the possibility of an interesting *divertissement* and moving in for a closer look . . .

COMMENT: I overreacted. Certainly I deserved Nicholas's affectionate reproof: "You silly, cantankerous old bugger!" when he came to make peace ten minutes later, but although I do give up and consent to his scheme to employ Alice, I still feel I'm right about the danger she represents. (Or am I? Is it possible that in my own way I'm being just as arrogant as Nicholas? Worse still, could I be projecting my arrogance onto Nicholas because I can't bear to acknowledge it in myself? Triple-hell!)

But no, once I calm down and start thinking rationally I still believe, in all honesty, that employing Alice is a risk which shouldn't be taken. Can I perhaps rely on Rosalind to side with me and tell Nicholas that a heterosexual virgin isn't the best type of housekeeper to choose for a man who regularly induces pie-eyed adoration in vulnerable females? No. All Rosalind's going to care about is that Alice, who's at least three stone overweight and in consequence looks like the back end of a bus, is going to be of no sexual interest to Nicholas whatsoever. Or at least I assume that's the only angle which would interest Rosalind, but who knows what goes on in that particular lady's head? I hate that sort of bland blonde who behaves all the time as if she's auditioning for the role of ice-queen at the panto. It wouldn't surprise me if beneath all that permafrost she—

No, stop right there. I'm at it again, being anti-women and thinking of sex. What *is* going on in the cesspit of my unconscious mind? Well, I certainly don't want to go to bed with Rosalind.

It's time to thrash out this problem with my spiritual director.

Friday, 19th August, 1988: I'm going to have to sack my spiritual director. Simon's very good on prayer and he certainly helped me through that dry spell last autumn; he likes all the devotional classics I like; he understands how hard I work to master my hang-ups and he's even tolerant when I get turgid and ramble on about Great-Uncle Cuthbert. But he's no good on sex. Damn it, he thinks I subconsciously want to go to bed with *Alice* and that this is why I'm lathering myself into such a sweat about employing her! I say coolly (can't afford to be furious or he'll think he's hit the mark): "Thanks, but middle-class virgins have never been up my street." He then sinks to levels of unprecedented idiocy by commenting: "Maybe they should have been."

Hopeless! I want to hit him. Great-Uncle Cuthbert probably would have done—he always liked biffing people, but of course he lived in a more robust age when biffed people didn't automatically scream: "Sadist!" and run to the nearest social worker. What would Great-Uncle Cuthbert have thought of this latest spiritual direction fiasco of mine? In a way it's all his fault; I'm forever sacking spiritual directors because they never understand me as well as he did. Funny, cantankerous old bastard! I wonder what *he* really thought about sex beneath all his standard preaching on the subject . . .

Damn it, there I go, harping on sex again! Why can't I get my act together?

Having slouched home in deep gloom I confide in Nicholas. He give me one of those limpid, thoughtful looks of his and says: "Maybe the time's finally come when you should consider seeing a woman spiritual director."

I shout: "I'm not talking about my sex-life to any damned woman!" but as soon as the words are out of my mouth I know I'm up to my neck in hang-ups and I'm so furious that I bawl out: "Fucking hell!" and bucket back to my room at top speed. Disgusting! What *am* I going to do with myself? I'm in despair.

Nicholas arrives. He puts his arm around me for a second, then sits down at my side and waits. This is where Nicholas is so gifted. He can communicate an immense amount just by being there—concern, support, empathy, fellowship, fraternal solidarity—everything. I'm so lucky to have Nicholas in my life. I don't care any more about not having a son. I probably wouldn't have got on with a son anyway, and he couldn't possibly have done more for me than Nicholas has.

Nicholas stands by me when I'm in a mess, looks after me when I'm lost, forgives me whenever I've been thoroughly stupid. I'm luckier than any grumpy old codger has a right to be.

"It's my hip," I say at last. "It's bad today."

He doesn't tell me to get it replaced. He just nods and waits.

"Okay," I say, "it's not my hip. I'm still very bothered by my new outbreak of anti-women fever, particularly as I can't identify the incident that triggered it. It definitely wasn't Cynthia's engagement, and no matter what Simon may think, it's got nothing to do with Alice either—although I do admit I'm still worried about importing her to the Rectory—"

"Okay, stop right there and let's just take another look at this particular anxiety of yours. If Simon's facile psychological explanation is wrong, what exactly is it about Alice that makes you so anxious?"

Encouraged by this critical comment on Simon's diagnosis I say at once: "I'm sure she'll quickly become much too bound up with you—and then all the pent-up emotion emanating from her will swirl around on the psychic level and infect the atmosphere. Alice is a splendid young woman, just as admirable as you say she is, but if her feelings for you aren't dead neutral the Devil could use her as a Trojan horse to slither into St. Benet's and destroy your ministry."

"That's true." Nicholas is keen to signal that he's taking my objection very seriously now. He doesn't bat an eyelid at my old-fashioned religious language which I always feel expresses reality so much more effectively than that namby-pamby, mealy-mouthed psycho-babble which is so popular with liberal churchmen nowadays. He pauses for a moment to let me absorb how seriously he's behaving. Then he says very reasonably: "But do you think I hadn't thought of that? Look, if I find she can't handle the situation I'll ease her into another job—for her own good as well as ours. And we'll know soon enough if things don't work out."

I start to feel better. In fact I feel so much better that I'm even able to say: "But if Alice has nothing to do with my latest outbreak of anti-women fever, what is it that's triggered the relapse?"

"Did Simon voice any other theories?"

"No, he's hopeless about sex, clueless, pathetic—no use at all."

"But presumably you've talked to him about sex before."

"Yes, but during the two years he's been my spiritual director I've been on an even keel so I've never had to put him to the test."

"In that case, are you sure you're right that he's inadequate? It seems odd that an experienced spiritual director should be useless in such a very vital area—okay, I know he's eighty and a bachelor, but—"

"Believe me, Nicholas—"

"—he's useless. Right. I get the message." Nicholas ponders on this. I sense he wants to take a risk and try to help me unravel myself an inch or two, but he's on tricky ground because we both know we're too close to counsel each other; Nicholas is well aware that he mustn't usurp the role played by my spiritual director, but he's still very tempted now to try a filial—or rather, fraternal—probe into my soul. Nicholas always thinks of me as a brother, not as a father. I like that. It keeps me in my place and checks any urge I may have to behave like a sentimental old man who's never fathered a son. Great-Uncle Cuthbert got sentimental about me in the end, and it didn't do. All those lectures about how I should follow in his footsteps and be a monk! No wonder I rushed out and married the first girl I groped in an air-raid shelter.

"Maybe we ought to approach this mystery from a completely different angle," says Nicholas cautiously at last. "When were you last conscious of saying to yourself: 'I refuse to get my hip replaced'?"

"You're off your rocker!" I snarl. But I know he's not. Feebly I bluster: "I'm not talking about my damned hip!"

"Okay. But has Simon ever asked you about it?"

"What's there to ask?" I say, trying to calm down and present a nonchalant response. "The hip's a nuisance, but I'm not having it replaced. Hospitals are where you pick up an infection and come out in a box."

"You don't really believe that, do you?"

"Oh, sod off!" I say—very ungratefully, but I'm rattled. This is because my reason for keeping the hip is so pathetic for a Christian priest, so devoid of trust in God, that I'm thoroughly ashamed of it. "It's no one's business but mine!"

"Okay," says Nicholas equably again, "but I don't like to see you in pain and I don't like to see you being distracted from your work by a curable medical condition, and I've got a hunch—"

"I bet. You're a great one for hunches, some of them nutty as a fruitcake—"

"—and some of them spot on target! Can't you even bring yourself to tell me when you last said to yourself: 'I refuse to replace my hip'?"

"I've no memory of saying that to myself recently."

"Not even five—or six—weeks ago?"

I stare at him. He gazes back blandly, disclosing nothing.

"Well, maybe I said it to myself after Cynthia's lunch-party," I say crossly, "but so what? That doesn't connect up with my malaise. We've already established I don't want to bed Cynthia."

"I must be on the wrong track then, mustn't I?" says Nicholas vaguely, and leaving me feeling more baffled than ever he slips out of my room into the hall.

COMMENT: Nicholas certainly gave my soul a tweak there. I know very well that I have a religious duty to be as fit as I can in order to serve God to the best of my ability; I know very well that I should have that blank-blank hip replaced. Great-Uncle Cuthbert couldn't have *his* arthritic hip replaced, poor old bugger, but I'm not living at his end of the twentieth century and I don't have to be saddled with this problem. Nor do I have to be saddled with the reputation for cantankerousness which I've acquired as the pain has worsened. In fact if I had the hip replaced I might even become saintly, radiating sweetness and light! What an unnerving thought—but not half so unnerving as imagining what I might get up to if I were fully mobile, unfettered by pain and bounding around like a man ten years my junior.

The unvarnished truth, which I've never been able to commit to paper until this moment, is that I'm using my current physical disability as a chastity belt. Instead of lining myself up with God, as a priest should, to the point where I can rely on his grace to keep me in order, happy and productive, I'm hiding behind my arthritis in a blue funk—as Nicholas has obviously realised. And do I seriously think that a successful celibate life has anything to do with repressing my problems in this way and winding up physically disabled, mentally ill-at-ease and spiritually up the creek? No. The successful celibate life isn't about repression but about sublimation, which is a different kettle of fish altogether. Repression means refusing to think of sex, locking up one's sex-drive and always feeling exhausted—not to mention neurotic—because it takes such an enormous amount of mental energy to convince yourself nobody has any genitals. Sublimation means facing up to sex, standing eyeball to eyeball with one's sex-drive and, by the grace of God, figuring out how to expend all that energy creatively and productively in some way outside the bedroom.

I know all this, but as I wrestle with the unvarnished truth here it helps to set down the basics in black and white. Let me add, to cheer myself up, that in the past I've had many successful years as a celibate, lined up fruitfully with God and enabled to accomplish effectively the work I was called to do. I certainly didn't feel tormented by sex then—or even needled by it. I was pro-sex, benign but not tempted. Yet now I see so clearly that this ideal equilibrium has ebbed away and my sublimation is teetering into repression. Correction: has already teetered. Once the relationship with God drifts off course—once the integration of the personality is lost—then sex becomes a threat and women become the enemy.

All very unedifying. To be fair to Simon, I must state that he *has* tried to get me to talk about the hip and my unacceptable reason for keeping it. But I just shut him up. Why can't I ever find a spiritual director who'll wipe the floor with me as Great-Uncle Cuthbert did? Because nowadays spiritual directors aren't supposed to wipe floors with anyone is the answer, but what about a monster like me who goes on being monstrous until someone has the balls to use him as a floor-cloth?

At least Nicholas has just had the balls to give me a metaphorical cuff. Quite right too! I needed a smart biff to make me face up to what's wrong, but even though I've now confronted the fact that my celibate life is not merely ruffled but pathetically inadequate, I still have no idea what triggered this bout of anti-women fever.

Monday, 22nd August, 1988: A bombshell's exploded, rocking me to the foundations. I get a phone call from the police to ask if I'm the husband of Mrs. Diana Hall. I say ex-husband, but they don't care about the "ex." It turns out that Diana's had a heart attack in the street (outside Harrods—typical) and has been rushed to hospital. My name and number were in the front of her diary in the space allocated to information about the next-of-kin requiring notification in the event of an accident.

How sad that she had no close friends left who could tolerate her and no relations anxious to give her the time of day. How sad that there was no one else to name in that diary but me, the husband she despised and couldn't wait to be rid of. Of course she could have put down Rachel's name, but apparently she did have the decency to spare her only child from being rung up by the police if something went wrong. Or did she? It's hard to imagine Diana being that unselfish, especially as she and Rachel haven't got on for years.

On second thoughts I can see it's far more likely that Diana named me because she knew that as a priest I'd always pick up the pieces—and because she fancied giving me the hell of a shock, the silly bitch. No, no, I mustn't say that, mustn't write it! Poor Diana. How far I contributed to her rotten, wasted life I don't like to think. When someone goes down the drain, those closest to them should always take a good hard look at the past to identify their part in the fiasco. Few people do, of course. Too painful. But everyone should try.

I arrive at the hospital and find she's dead. So I don't get the chance to say "Sorry" for the final time. Just as well. She'd only have spat in my face. Funny how I always took it for granted she'd die of cirrhosis, and yet here she is, pegging out after a heart attack.

I try to say a prayer as I stand by the bed, but nothing happens. Suppose I'm in shock. All I can think of is that amazing kiss in the air-raid shelter and then making love to her later after the all-clear on the kitchen floor of her parents' empty house in Upper Grosvenor Street. Those wild, woolly days of the war . . . That was after Great-Uncle Cuthbert's death in 1940, of course, and before I became a priest. When I think what I used to get up to before I became ordained . . .

Easier to think of that than to think of my marriage. How Diana hated me becoming a priest! How she hated the psychic dimension to my personality too, never understanding how becoming a priest enabled me to harness this dangerous gift at last by using it to serve God by serving others. She never even understood what Christianity was all about. All my fault, I know that now. I completely failed to communicate to her the life-saving, life-enhancing nature of my spiritual beliefs. She just wanted me to go on being the raffish young soldier she'd met in the air-raid shelter. She couldn't grasp that if I'd gone on being raffish my self-destructive tendencies and that potentially lethal psychic gift would have done for me in no time. Great-Uncle Cuthbert was around to save me when I was fifteen but he wasn't around to save me later, when the war was over. God did that by calling me to the priesthood and giving me a framework and purpose which allowed me not just to survive but to flourish.

Yet I could never talk properly about this great miracle to Diana. I could never talk properly to her about anything. I failed her as a husband and I failed her as a priest. I should never have married her.

After a while she bored me in bed anyway. A disaster. Whenever I remember the humiliating failures of my marriage I want to bang my head against the wall in despair.

Well, I get out of the hospital, drag myself home (hip giving me hell) and try to find Nicholas, but he's away on business, I'd forgotten, and he won't be back till tomorrow evening. Some bishop wants him to sort out a problem that the local diocesan exorcist has failed to solve. We seem to be getting a lot of these special requests at the moment to eradicate unsavoury phenomena. Nicholas is a consultant to several dioceses now and says the paranormal's currently a growth area.

No one's at the Rectory. It's six o'clock, too late to go back to work. I'm just about to mix myself the stiffest of whiskies when Stacy clatters into the kitchen with the Communion wine salesman and announces that they're going to have a cup of tea. I growl: "Not today," and the salesman beats a hasty retreat. Stacy demands annoyed: "What's your problem now, for goodness' sake?" and I want to biff him. Insolent young puppy! (I'm very worried about Stacy but I'm not putting my reasons down on paper at the moment.) I say: "My wife's died." He's shocked, stammers apologies. He's a good boy really, but I don't think he's right for the ministry of healing and I'm even beginning to wonder if he should have been ordained. "Get me a whisky," I order, "and make it a double." He does, very efficiently. Maybe he should have been a barman.

After two double-whiskies I grit my teeth, go to my room and phone Rachel, far away in the north. She picks up the receiver. I break the news. I'm a priest, I'm trained to do this sort of thing, I work in the ministry of healing—I should be able to do this difficult but not unusual task standing on my head with my eyes shut. So what happens? I make a complete and utter balls-up. Rachel breaks down. Sobs ensue followed by wails of guilt-induced grief about Darling Mummy (whom she's shunned for some time) and what a tragedy it all was and how everything was my fault.

I long for another double-whisky and wait for her to hang up but she doesn't. Instead my son-in-law intervenes in his usual masterful way by grabbing the phone and saying: "Thank you, Lewis, for exercising your usual talent for upsetting my wife," and the receiver is slammed down before I can reply.

Five minutes later when I'm on my next double-whisky he calls back. He's a very able priest, he's a very successful suffragan bishop and now and then he even manages to be a good Christian. "I apologize for being too abrupt earlier," he says glibly. He's always very smooth. Silver-tongued Charley. Very gifted. "I was worried by Rachel's distress. That's certainly sad news about Diana—it must have been a shock for you, and I'm sorry. Is there anything I can do?"

Just stay away, Charley. Just resist that perpetual temptation to play Mr. Bossy-Boots. Just muzzle the urge to muscle in on this particular scene.

Aloud I say: "Look after Rachel."

"Naturally." He's at once ice-cool. I know he blames me for all Rachel's problems. "That's my job." Then my worst fears are realised as he switches on the pastoral power again and radiates Evangelical efficiency. "Okay, leave everything to me—I'll rejig my schedule and drive south tomorrow to organise the funeral. I'm sure you need to rest your hip."

Bastard! Usurping my role, treating me as if I were defrocked, incompetent riff-raff, harping on my hip and implying I'm over the hill . . . I'd like to slug him on the jaw.

I'm so upset that I hang up on him and try to phone Nicholas, but the Bishop's wife says she has no idea where he is.

I sit in my room, write my journal and get silently, steadily drunk.

COMMENT: Disgraceful! Quite apart from the fact that no priest should drink himself silly, I was actually conforming to Charley's opinion of me as a useless clerical has-been—and that makes me all the more furious about my abysmal lack of self-discipline.

Almighty God, please forgive me for all my terrible shortcomings as a husband and father and all the past pain I've caused my wife and daughter. Forgive me for not being more grateful that Rachel should have such a loyal and devoted husband. Forgive me for getting drunk and being such a stupid old fool. Please grant me the grace to do better in future. I ask all these things in the name of Your Son, Jesus Christ Our Lord, Amen.

Tuesday, 23rd August, 1988: I dream of Churchill making the V-sign. Then I dream I'm drawing a big V—for Victory, I suppose—in the sand on a deserted beach. Odd. I presume that Diana's death has triggered memories of our war-time romance. I wake up feeling like the inside of a tramp's boot. Triple-hell.

I get Stacy to celebrate the eight o'clock mass. He does it in the manner of Laurence Olivier playing Shakespearean drama—an attractive performance but frequently over the top. I know I should have a quiet word with him afterwards but I don't trust myself to do it properly.

During the morning I see a few of my people but I'm not much good. It's a relief when I arrive in church for the lunch-time Eucharist—although my relief ebbs when some drunk turns up and bawls out a pervert's blasphemy involving the Blessed Virgin Mary. Two of the Befrienders close in and steer him down to the crypt for soup and sandwiches. When I see him afterwards I find out that he's fallen through the welfare net which our government, worshipping the principle of "every man for himself and the Devil take the hindermost," has been busy destroying. I pass him on to Daisy and leave her ringing the Social Services to see what can be done.

At this point Francie asks to see me. We retire to my consulting room; she weeps; her husband's beaten her up again. He never beats her where it shows, of course. It takes a middle-class thug to beat his wife with cunning. I don't think there's any future for her in that marriage, but it's for her to say that, not me. All I can do is listen with sympathy and keep the Kleenex tissues flowing.

I get back to the Rectory at five-thirty and when I walk into the kitchen I find Nicholas. Thank God! He's stuffing some shirts into the washing machine and looking abstracted so I don't launch straight away into a recital of my troubles. I merely enquire after the paranormal problem which turned out to be just routine stuff in a council house. Then he asks what's been happening at the Healing Centre but although I give him a quick résumé I realise he's not listening. This isn't particularly surprising; one often feels like a zombie after an exorcism.

To wake him up I tell him Venetia Hoffenberg has phoned twice, and I pretend I've no idea who she is. "Now why should the name Venetia remind me of the 1960s?" I enquire with mock innocence to remind him of his pre-ordination days when he messed around with her fast set, but just as his concentration snaps back into focus the phone rings.

It's Venetia herself, and this time she finally gets the man she wants. As Nicholas takes the call I mix myself a drink and remember the scene a few weeks ago at Cynthia's when she got drunk, propositioned me and was rebuffed. Meanwhile Nicholas is saying: "He's not my curate. He's my colleague at the Healing Centre." Venetia knows that perfectly well, of course. She just wants to act as if I'm a nonentity so that she can wipe me more easily from her mind.

I'm still recalling my memories of that first Sunday in July when Nicholas at last replaces the receiver and I see to my astonishment that he's very excited indeed. "That's the only woman I've ever met," he's saying dizzily, "who can recognise a quotation from Wittgenstein!"

I think: so who needs a woman like that? But I suppress this sexist question, the latest manifestation of my anti-women fever, and manage to mutter some polite response before asking what's going on.

It turns out that by an amazing coincidence Nicholas bumped into Venetia yesterday when he headed for the local cathedral to recharge his spiritual batteries, and not only did she go to Evensong with him but she also promised to visit the Healing Centre.

This is certainly good news and may well indicate that Venetia is willing to seek help, but on the other hand she may have been motivated by no more than a chummy impulse so there's no guarantee she'll follow through on the promise. Not for the first time I reflect what an unusual relationship Venetia and Nicholas have. There's an affinity between them which isn't fundamentally sexual, although as with all friendships between a heterosexual male and a heterosexual female, the sexual dimension exists, sometimes harmlessly, sometimes not harmlessly at all. I'm prepared to believe Nicholas is correct when he says he's been put into her life to be her spiritual friend, praying for her regularly, but I'm not prepared to believe this relationship is without its worldly dangers. After all, that woman is worldly danger personified. She could seduce anyone from a millionaire to a milkman in between swigs of Veuve Clicquot.

"I'm going to save her!" Nicholas is saying, still addled with excitement. "It's been twenty-five years now since that man in her past wrecked her, but now it's all going to come right!"

He's in such ecstasy that I know it's time to take him down a peg or two. "You're not going to save her, Nicholas," I say sharply. "If anyone saves her, it'll be God and you'll just be his helper—although in fact I doubt very much if it's possible for you to work directly on this case. If she agrees to counselling, wouldn't you have to admit you know her too well to achieve the appropriate level of detachment?"

"Oh yes, yes, yes—" He's impatient. He knows it all. He's within an inch of going over the top and swanning around like a wonder worker. "Obviously I can't counsel her," he says airily, "but I can supervise her case, encourage her, see her regularly as a friend—"

"Just keep praying for her, Nicholas. That's all God's ever required you to do for Venetia. Leave the treatment, supervision and encouragement to others."

He sighs, knowing I'm right. The wonder worker vanishes and I'm facing a balanced priest again.

"Personally," I say, finally unable to resist letting my prejudice show, "I can't help thinking that the less personal contact you have with that woman the better."

I've blown it. Too bad; I was doing so well. Why on earth couldn't I have kept my mouth shut?

"Oh, sod off!" exclaims Nicholas exasperated. "Why do you always behave as if all women are out to seduce me?"

"Because they usually are."

"But you know perfectly well I've no desire whatsoever to go to bed with Venetia! You know perfectly well she's just an old friend, six years my senior, whose path only occasionally crosses with mine! Lewis, I know you have a certain problem at the moment, but can't you honestly see there's no need here to talk as if Venetia's a wicked temptress who can destroy a man's will-power just by the flick of her false eyelashes?"

Bingo.

Dear God!

The unvarnished truth finally dawns.

COMMENT: God must be thinking I'm as blind as a bat and as dumb as a donkey. And to think I even dreamed of V-signs last night! Of course the V wasn't for Victory! It was for Venetia.

Repression, repression, repression—how I've repressed the memory of those amusing, stimulating, erotic, deliciously dangerous interludes with Venetia at Cynthia's lunch! It's true I behaved impeccably throughout and made sure I had Alice to chaperone me when I took Venetia home, but underneath all that faultless behaviour . . .

No wonder Nicholas was asking me: "When were you last conscious of saying to yourself: 'I refuse to get my hip replaced'?" My hip was giving me hell that day but I distinctly remember telling myself I was never going to do away with it. I may have chosen to believe at the time that this was because I couldn't face a sojourn in hospital, but the rock-bottom truth was that I couldn't face life without my arthritic chastity belt; I knew, on an unconscious (semi-conscious?) level that I'd met a woman I fancied and was tempted.

But why exactly was I tempted? Logically Venetia should have left me cold. She's the same class as my wife, she's wasted her life just as my wife did, and she's a drunk, just as my wife was. Ah yes, but that's the point, isn't it? I failed to save Diana; I had a share in her ruin, and the guilt's haunted me ever since. But Venetia seems to be offering me the chance to assuage the guilt, redeem the tragedy, put right, in another place and in another time, all that went wrong with my marriage.

What a dangerous illusion to be harbouring! Now just you face up to the facts, Lewis Hall. Your attraction to upper-class women is always disastrous. That's because fundamentally they remind you of your mother—the bitch!—and after the first sexual ecstasy has evaporated, that reminder takes over and kills any desire (a) because the desire now feels incestuous and (b) because you couldn't stand your mother anyway. So you're then led down the thorny psychological path of splitting off the sexual relationship and dumping it on someone else, preferably the nearest working-class woman (so unlike your mother) available. Result? You wind up in unintegrated chaos with a split-level life and a failed relationship which produces nothing but suffering to yourself and to others.

No wonder I felt called to celibacy once my marriage had ended! After my career as a walking sexual disaster the only way I could live with the memory of all the shame and mess was to channel the sexual energy into a constructive cause and dump the destructive lifestyle. And that decision worked for me—or at least it did once I'd pulled myself together after the divorce, resigned from that dead-awful parish and taken that absorbing chaplaincy in the mental hospital, the job that led me into the ministry of healing. All right, so my life wasn't all purity after that; I wasn't a saint, and God knows I did get into a terrible mess in 1983 when I was kicked out of my diocese and wound up dead drunk on Nicholas's doorstep, but I picked myself up again, didn't I (by the grace of God), and I clawed my way back onto an even keel (by the grace of God) and I've been more or less *all right ever since* (by the grace of God)—until today when I realise that thanks to Venetia I'm in danger of going off my rocker again; I'm flirting with the insane delusion that now I'm a staid old priest working at St. Benet's instead of a raffish young soldier on leave during the Blitz, I can finally sustain a relationship with a woman of my own class without creating an emotional wasteland.

Talk about wishful thinking! Pathetic. The truth is that with my hang-ups I'm not fit for any woman, and although I always try to live in the hope that one day I'll be healed, I know damned well I'm not healed yet, not by a long chalk.

Merciful God, Almighty Father, what a mess I am, but thank you for giving me the strength to face the truth about myself, no matter how shaming and painful that is, so that having recognised my faults I may struggle afresh to overcome them and live a life more acceptable in your sight. And give me the grace, please, to be a good priest, mindful always of your will and wanting only to serve you as well as I possibly can. I ask this in the name of Your Son Jesus Christ. And in the name of the Blessed Virgin Mary, I beg you to help me make a new effort to forgive my mother for abandoning me all those years ago—help me, please, to treat every woman I now meet with respect in the knowledge that all men and women are of equal value in your sight. Amen.

Wednesday, 24th August, 1988: I feel better. Of course there's no question of me having any kind of relationship with Venetia, that cleverer, wittier, more eccentric, more arresting and infinitely more fascinating version of my wife. Besides, I don't want another alcoholic wife any more than she wants another clerical husband—although not even my worst enemy could describe me as "limp" (her word) in any vital department—and unlike Diana Venetia may well have the guts to make a go of Alcoholics Anonymous. So bearing those vital facts in mind, perhaps . . .

No. I'm lapsing into fantasy. Forget her.

I'm diverted from all this turgid introspection by the arrival of my son-in-law, swirling south from his diocese and sweeping all before him—undertakers, solicitors, Diana's neighbours, even the staff at the Healing Centre who happen to be in the reception area when he sails in, flashing his purple stock and his trendy made-in-the-Third-World pectoral cross. I feel like bashing him over the head with my crucifix. Fortunately Nicholas is there. Nicholas was so good to me as soon as I told him about Diana. He quite understands how I feel; he accepts my assertion that she was still my wife in God's sight even though in the eyes of the secular world we were divorced, and he never queries my statement that I'm the one who should have the responsibility of organising the funeral. But Nicholas also understands how Charley feels. Nicholas tells me Charley doesn't realise how connected I always felt with Diana; Nicholas says Charley honestly believes he's doing me a favour by muscling in on my territory. After all, my hip does slow me down. And Rachel is, as usual, on the verge of another breakdown. Charley's muscling in because he wants to be kind to a semi-disabled old man and because he wants to protect his wife from additional stress.

In the end I just say to Nicholas: "Okay, tell him to get on with it. I won't make a scene. He's not the only one who wants to protect Rachel."

I have to record that later Charley was very kind to me. He *is* without doubt a good man. The only trouble is I just can't stand him. I'd rather have an old-fashioned Evangelical, steeped in Protestant piety, than this subtle, silver-tongued power-broker with his mix-'n'-match selection of theological wares which range from biblical scholarship through trendy liturgy to questionable charismatic histrionics. I hate it when the Church tries to be fashionable in order to kow-tow to secular society. I even heard Charley ask Nicholas if we were planning to employ a woman deacon as the curate once Stacy moves on! And he knows I disapprove *utterly* of women deacons. Ordaining women as deacons is the thin end of the wedge which the feminists have now used (courtesy of the recent abysmal session of General Synod) to ensure that legislation to permit priestesses will be debated in a few years' time. Meanwhile the newspapers are constantly yammering about "women priests" whenever they're not bleating about acid-house parties, AIDS, child abuse, that filthy film *The Last Temptation of Christ* and all the other revolting aspects of our increasingly decadent society.

The Church's decadence in particular fills me with deep gloom. Imagine a mass taken by a priestess! Disgusting! The men in the congregation would be able to think of nothing but sex.

If the Church of England goes off its collective rocker and approves the legislation to permit the ordination of women to the priesthood, I'll bloody well go over to Rome!

COMMENT: That disgraceful use of the word "bloody" shows how disturbed I am, and as for the last two paragraphs of the above entry, they appear to have been written by some nutter who's behaving like a character in a Freudian case-book. But then a great many ordinary, sane, intelligent people, male *and female*, are talking like that nowadays whenever the subject of women's ordination comes up for discussion, and we can't all be nutters. The truth is that I genuinely believe women priests are incompatible with our great tradition. (Or am I just latching on to this convenient belief to satisfy my hang-ups? That's a very nasty thought, but no, it's so nasty that it can't possibly be true. I'm a traditional Anglo-Catholic and I'm perfectly entitled to believe, for the purest possible theological reasons, that women should not be admitted to the priesthood.)

All right, calm down, lower the blood pressure. I'm just very upset about Diana at the moment, that's all, and this is making me a trifle astringent in my comments about the opposite sex. Well . . . vitriolic, actually. Must call a spade a spade. *Vitriolic.* Very nasty. Wholly unchristian. In short, disgusting. Dear God, what a mess I am whenever I'm suffering from anti-women fever . . .

But at least being anti-women ensures that I don't start mooning over Venetia.

Monday, 5th September, 1988: The torn-out pages between this entry and the entry above have now been burnt. I decided to destroy my lengthy ruminations on the funeral. Looking at them today I felt that not only had I never read such maudlin, self-centred, self-indulgent twaddle in all my life, but that such revolting ramblings had no place in any journal kept as a spiritual discipline. Great-Uncle Cuthbert would have puked.

All that needs to be said about the funeral was that it was hell. Afterwards Nicholas allowed me to get drunk. I suppose he thought it would be therapeutic—as if I could exhaust the urge to blot out the pain in one fell swoop—but in fact I got drunk every night for a week. I sacked my spiritual director (but later reinstated him). I was unable to work. Nicholas sat up with me every night and listened as I reviewed the painful past and wound up rambling on and on and on, just as I always do when I'm very disturbed, about Great-Uncle Cuthbert—how he'd saved me, how I'd let him down by not becoming a monk, how disappointed he would have been with me if he'd lived, how guilty I felt for not fulfilling his high hopes, how haunted I felt whenever I fell short of his high standards, how I wished he'd come back and straighten me out, how I'd loved him, how I'd hated him, how I'd feared him, how I'd admired him . . . And so on and so on and so on.

Dreadful. Nicholas was a saint to stand it.

Refusing to abandon me at the weekend he took me home with him to Butterfold where I spent much time sitting in the garden, reading my favourite spiritual classics and trying not to get on Rosalind's nerves. As it was during the school holidays, his boys were there. The elder one's very boring, a hearty extrovert; the younger one's rather different but apes the older one so that they seem more alike than they really are. Nicholas tries hard with them but there's no real communication going on. Never mind, I'm sure the boys appreciate the fact that he tries.

Not for the first time I wonder how I would have got on with my own father if he had survived my infancy instead of pegging out with pneumonia after soaking himself on a grouse-moor. How would I have communicated with a soldier addicted to field-sports? What does one say to a simple soul who considers his mission in life is to kill things? When I was growing up I used to mind being fatherless, but now I can see I was spared endless discomfort. And besides . . . I got the paternal attention I needed in the end, didn't I? But I mustn't start drivelling on again about Great-Uncle Cuthbert.

Finally—today, Monday, the fifth of September—I get back to work. Almost the first person I see is Venetia. She's in the reception area waiting to talk to Nicholas. The Medusa locks are floating around her shoulders in a most unsuitable style for a middle-aged woman, but does she care? No. She's made up to the hilt and wearing a sky-blue T-shirt inscribed with the message MAKE MY DAY—THE NIGHTS ARE TAKEN CARE OF, a message obviously designed for some moronic teenage tart trying to be cute, but does she give a damn whether the message demeans her or not? No. She's also wearing navy-blue trousers, wholly inappropriate for a woman of fifty-plus with large hips, but does this unwise flouting of sartorial convention inhibit her in any way? No. Her green eyes look at me as if I'm some form of very low life which has just crawled out from under a stone, and we're all set, obviously, for a show-stopping reunion.

"Hi," she says in her gruffest voice, looking at some spot beyond my right shoulder.

"Good morning," I growl, and disappear at top speed into consulting room two.

I spend five minutes taking deep breaths and thinking what a stupid old man I am, but finally I stop feeling aroused and get down to work. I listen, I counsel, I pray, I perform the laying-on of hands, and to my surprise everything goes well. I was worried in case I was still too damaged to be an effective channel for the Holy Spirit, but of course God's no stranger to damaged mankind; he's constantly working in us and through us to achieve his purposes, yet it's still amazing what can be achieved, even by a battered old wreck like me, in the name of Jesus Christ, our mentor, the finest healer of all time.

In fact the older I get the more clearly I see that Christ must come first, first and first again with all those who practise his ministry of healing. It's not just that he reveals God's presence in a suffering world which cries out for redemption. It's because by following his example we kill the self-centred emotions such as pride and arrogance which can pervert the healing process, and by struggling always for humility—not the fake-humility made famous by Uriah Heep but the genuine humility which consists of facing the unvarnished truth and owning it—we remain honest, useful healers instead of dangerous, razzle-dazzle wonder workers consumed with the lust for power and self-aggrandisement.

My sessions end at eleven. I'm very tired but my mood is good and when I potter over to the church for the next segment of my day it doesn't take me long to revive. Unfortunately the drunk's back again at the lunch-time Eucharist, and Stacy, who's the celebrant, gets put off and becomes more like Laurence Olivier playing Henry V than ever. Nicholas, I note with relief, has a quiet word with him afterwards. I must tell Nicholas how worried I am about Stacy, but after the Eucharist I let my chance slip by because I'm too keen to find out what happened when he saw Venetia.

"Everything went well," says Nicholas pleased. "By the time we parted she was willing to agree that the Healing Centre was user-friendly and down-to-earth, not some airy-fairy outpost of the nutty fringe."

"So she's coming back?"

"She's agreed to have a trial session with Robin."

"Well done!" I say heartily, keen to give praise where praise is due, and I should end the conversation there but I don't. I find I just can't leave the subject alone. "Don't you think she'll need more," I hear myself say, "than Robin's brand of person-centred therapy?"

"Maybe, but I think regular doses of empathy for, say, three months would be more palatable to her at this stage than a dive into psychoanalysis. We want to ease her in gently, not frighten her off."

We discuss this further. I concede that person-centred therapy is an immensely useful counselling process, but I still feel Venetia's problems are so deep-seated that she needs a therapy which centres more on peering into the unconscious mind to detect the damage caused by the past. However, Nicholas disagrees and I have to remind myself he's more likely than I am to be right; he knows Venetia better than I do.

"The past has certainly damaged her," he says, "but in ways that are so obvious that I don't think any great peering into the unconscious is necessary. As I see it, the prime task is to restore her self-esteem because only then will she have the courage to believe she can triumph over the past disasters. Of course I could be wrong, but let's see what Robin has to say."

I'm so addled by the thought of Venetia that I'm stupid enough to ask: "Did my name come up at all?"

"No," says Nicholas, giving me one of his limpid looks. "Should it have done?"

Damn! He's realised I've put two and two together where Venetia's concerned and want to pant in some addled fashion over the result. It was bad enough him guessing long before I did that the trigger for my unbalanced behaviour was Cynthia's lunch-party, and that neither Cynthia nor Mrs. Robert Welbeck nor Lady Todd-Marshall was the woman who did the triggering. Should I now discuss the matter frankly with him?

No, I can't. I haven't got my act together yet. I'll just play it cool for a while . . .

COMMENT: A cowardly conclusion. The truth is that I'm so aghast at this lunatic lurch of mine towards sexual idiocy that I don't want to talk about it. That's pride; I hate to admit I could be quite such a fool. The subject must certainly be discussed with my spiritual director when I make my confession, but I'm under no obligation to discuss it with Nicholas and Nicholas has had to put up with enough rubbish from me recently. The least I can do is spare him any further senile babblings.

I just wish I had a spiritual director who knew something about sex. This is the sort of problem that exposes all Simon's weaknesses and makes him seem like a virgin of twelve. He's bound to say I should review my call to celibacy, but that would be a complete waste of time since I'm still totally unfit for marriage.

Or am I?

Dear God, supposing . . . No, no, no, no, *no.* I'm not getting married again. It would be a disaster.

But isn't it rather a coincidence that this eccentric and fascinating woman has glided into my life at almost the exact moment that I became a widower, free to remarry? Yes. It's a coincidence. And like most coincidences it means absolutely nothing. *Nothing.*

Hell, I wish I could drill it into my head that I'm sixty-seven and far too old for all this sort of thing . . .

Tuesday, 6th September, 1988: I receive a welcome diversion from my chaotic thoughts about chastity, celibacy and downright sexual lunacy.

Alice Fletcher, nice child, good girl, comes to the St. Benet's Rectory at 6:00 p.m. on the dot to be inspected by Rosalind, a terrifying ordeal if ever there was one, and Alice is quite right to be as nervous as she looks. She's wearing a kind of black tent which hides all the rolls of surplus flesh but makes her look enormous.

In contrast Rosalind is trim in peacock-blue, shoulders of her jacket thickly padded, skirt at knee-length, white blouse flounced over supremely elegant bosom. The blonde hair is a shade blonder than it used to be and is cut in layers which could only have been achieved at enormous expense. Not for the first time I think that those ice-blue eyes of hers could bore a hole through a wooden plank. In short she looks like a business tycoon—which she is, in her very correct, very mannered, very English-rose way. Before she came out on the right side of that take-over bid she was running a flower-business, and you can be sure all the little petals did exactly what they were told. Rosalind is one of the success stories of the 1980s, along with the estate agents and the interior decorators; she votes for Mrs. Thatcher and welfare cuts and that vaguely fascist concept which is pronounced "lawnorder." How Nicholas stands being married to someone like that I'll never know.

I don't see Alice received by Rosalind upstairs in the Rector's flat, but the child returns to the ground floor so white around the gills that Nicholas and I both rush to offer her a glass of sherry. She can hardly speak but manages to accept. Meanwhile Rosalind shows no sign of emerging from the flat so Nicholas takes over the rest of the interview. (This visit of Alice's to see her future home and formally accept the job—of course the acceptance is a foregone conclusion—was originally set to take place a fortnight ago, but was delayed because of Diana's death, my resulting incapacity and the fact that Nicholas had his hands full.)

Sherry in hand he takes the child off to show her the basement hell-hole which will be the housekeeper's flat. I don't go because my hip's blank-blank awful and I know I couldn't cope with the stairs. I'm sitting at the table, however, when Nicholas displays our antiquated kitchen. Alice, excellent manners well to the fore, tries hard not to look appalled.

Of course she's in love with Nicholas. Has to be. If she wasn't so mesmerised by him she'd turn the job down on the spot and rush back to Belgravia where one of Cynthia's chums could offer her a flat massaged by an interior decorator and a kitchen resembling the interior of a space-ship.

However, since Nicholas is clearly the most important person in her life at the moment she says: "It's all great—what an exciting challenge!" and behaves as if she's in Wonderland.

After she leaves, all my doubts about the wisdom of employing her resurface and I have to struggle hard to keep my mouth shut. To help win this struggle I switch from sherry to whisky.

While I'm swilling away morosely Rosalind comes tip-tapping downstairs from the Rector's flat to pronounce her verdict. Adjusting a blonde curl with an exquisitely manicured fingernail she says in her high, measured, English-bitch voice: "How terrible it must be to be quite so unattractive! If I looked like that I'd shoot myself."

I immediately decide that employing Alice is the most brilliant idea Nicholas has ever had and that I'm going to cure Alice of her eating disorder even if it's the last thing I ever do.

Nicholas says vaguely: "Darling, not all women can look as attractive as you."

"Oh, for God's sake!" exclaims Rosalind. "Nicky, you're always making excuses for these lame ducks you collect! One wonders sometimes who on earth you're going to make excuses for next." She somehow manages to avoid looking at me, but of course I know I'm lame duck number one. "All right, if the girl can cook decently I'm sure she's worth hiring, but you'll have to find another cleaner. Mrs. Mudd would destroy someone like that in five minutes flat. Get something ethnic and very meek from Tower Hamlets—or would you like me to do it for you?"

"Well, if you can spare the time—"

"Well, as I've got time on my hands at the moment and time is something you so seldom have—" But she's killing the barbed remark with a smile and he's smiling too, moving in for a kiss.

"Thanks, darling," he says gratefully before they lock themselves into a clinch.

I pour some more whisky down my throat to settle my heaving stomach and beat a hasty retreat to my bed-sitting-room.

COMMENT: No matter how successful I become in eliminating my unacceptable feelings about women, I know I shall always dislike Rosalind. As a priest I must still pray for her . . . but not just yet. I'd rather pray for Alice Fletcher.

Poor little Alice! I know she's very large but I think of her as little because I'm sure that on the psychic level, as opposed to the physical level, she's a small girl longing to grow up, marry a nice, normal husband and have at least three nice, normal children.

And why shouldn't she long for such nice, normal things, I'd like to know? I'm sick of these damned feminists with their padded shoulders and their obsession with careers . . .

Watch it. Remember that God's creation is amazingly diverse and that every strand of it is cherished. Christianity—real Christianity, not the fake stuff which so often passes for Christianity these days—isn't about preserving walls to keep out people you don't like. It's about bashing the walls down to welcome all people in.

Alice can sense that. She knows she won't feel excluded here, even if she chooses not to go to church. Obviously she thinks she's going to live in Wonderland among Miracle Workers, but she'll get over that. I just hope the inevitable disillusionment won't be too painful . . .

Friday, 9th September, 1988: Venetia returns to the Healing Centre and this time meets Robin to hear about Carl Rogers and his famous Person-Centred Therapy. I keep well out of the way.

Val and I have another tiff about homosexuals. "It's disgusting to call homosexuality an affliction!" she blazes.

"Whether the statement is disgusting or not is immaterial," I retort. "Is it true? That's the question."

"You're worse than the Pope!" she screeches and storms out of the room.

I feel most stimulated by this bold comparison. I hold no brief whatsoever for the Papacy (which is why it would be damn difficult for me to go over to Rome if the Church of England finally goes off its rocker and permits priestesses) but I admire the way John Paul II sticks to his traditionalist guns amidst the rising tide of secular fundamentalism (which is every bit as dangerous as religious fundamentalism). Imagine Val abusing me just because I want to pursue the truth! She's behaving like one of those secular trendies who believe everything's true—you just trot into the philosophical supermarket and select whatever "truths" you fancy. The vastness of human arrogance takes my breath away sometimes—and to wrestle with the truth you have to be humble. Anyway, what's Val, who's an active Christian, doing toting around this rubbishy relativism? Stupid, emotional, overwrought woman . . .

But at least she's diverted me from all thought of Venetia.

COMMENT: I must apologise to Val and explain that when I said homosexuality was an affliction I didn't mean it was something like leprosy or syphilis. I meant it was more like dyslexia or tennis elbow—nothing noxious but just a condition which means certain rewarding experiences have to be ruled out. After all, marriage and parenthood do represent rewarding dimensions of being human. Not to be able to experience them must be—no, all right, perhaps "affliction" *is* the wrong word. Perhaps "deprivation" would convey the truth better—or would that needle Val to new heights of wrath? I'm sure she'd never concede she was in any way deprived. People embrace relativism when the truth is too tough and painful for them to face, I see that clearly now. So the answer is not to bang away to them about truth but to try to meet them where they are, and—

Dear God, how difficult it all is! But please grant this irascible old servant of yours tolerance, patience, insight and wisdom when dealing with homosexuals.

And don't let me get in a heterosexual mess with Venetia the moment I start gasping for light relief after these turgid conversations with Val. Amen.

Friday, 16th September, 1988: It's Venetia Day. She comes to the Centre for her first real session (as opposed to last week's trial session) with Robin.

By a most carefully engineered manoeuvre I'm lurking by the coffee machine in the reception area when she emerges from consulting room three. I offer her a cup of coffee. She says sourly that this is "sweet" of me but she has to rush off to lunch at Claridge's.

So much for that. Serves me right. I don't know what I thought I was doing anyway, lurking around like a raincoated flasher on the prowl.

I go back to the Rectory for lunch and find Stacy chasing a mouse around the kitchen with a frying-pan. Bad news. The mouse escapes but Stacy breaks the frying-pan. More bad news. He then says can I persuade Nicholas to take him along on the next exorcism. I say: "You're not ready yet, Stacy," and he starts to whine why not. Impudent young whippersnapper! I growl: "Take it up with Nicholas," and retreat to my bedsit with a cheese sandwich and a bottle of Perrier water.

Rosalind may think her husband's soft on lame ducks, but Nicholas is very tough indeed when it comes to questions of spiritual fitness. He won't let Stacy participate in an exorcism unless he has much more evidence that Stacy's taking his daily spiritual exercises seriously. But Stacy's not interested in the essential groundwork. He just wants to be out and about playing Laurence Olivier at the altar, "relating" to people at the Centre and jousting glitzily with the Devil every now and then, but he's got to be made to understand that without the underpinning of a devout life he'll merely become—at best—yet another ineffectual "carer" in a cassock or—at worst—a wonder worker, boosting his ego by playing God.

I feel more convinced than ever that Stacy's going to be one of our failures, and I don't think Nicholas has taken the right line at all on the clouded subject of Stacy's sexual orientation.

COMMENT: I should worry about my own sex-life instead of worrying about Stacy's. After much prayer and endless cogitation (utterly unhelped, of course, by my spiritual director's alarmed whinnyings) I still feel I'm called to celibacy. I really can't go marrying again at my age. Rachel would be horrified. Charley would think it indecent. The grandchildren would be embarrassed.

The Venetia fixation is just a piece of senile soppiness.

I shall now forget her.

Friday, 23rd September, 1988: As soon as I open my eyes I think: Venetia Day. But that fact is now of no interest to me whatsoever.

However, by chance—and I really do mean *by chance*—I emerge from helping Megan with the music therapy session and I'm just heading for the coffee machine when Venetia staggers out of Robin's room and exclaims: "Thank God—coffee! Have you got a needle so that I can inject it straight into the vein?" And it turns out she's had an exhausting fifty minutes. I give her some coffee but before I can invite her into my own room she says: "Thanks," and zips off, complete with steaming Styrofoam cup, and I'm left feeling like an untipped waiter.

Nevertheless it seems that at last the awkward hostility has faded away and we've established some sort of *entente cordiale*. Naturally the relationship won't develop further, but I'm glad I'm no longer treated as a form of low-life normally resident under a stone.

Focusing with determination on other matters I manage to talk to Nicholas about Stacy, but Nicholas refuses to share my pessimism.

"Obviously Stacy needs to do more work in a number of areas," he says, "but I still think he's got great potential. He's warm-hearted, good-natured, capable of empathising with clients and caring conscientiously for them—"

"You're describing a potentially gifted social worker," I say acidly, "but social workers aren't priests. If he can't or won't do the basic spadework to ensure his spiritual health, how's he going to survive in the ministry of healing?"

"But he's making progress! Now that he's sorted out his sexuality—"

"*Sorted out?*"

"Okay, you think he's gay and won't admit it. If that were true I'd agree he had a problem, but—"

"But he *is* gay and he *has* admitted it!"

"You're being far too influenced by that one homosexual relationship. I agree that created great confusion for him, but the seduction of a teenager by an older man doesn't necessarily mean the boy won't grow up heterosexual, and since Stacy assures me he hasn't the slightest desire to be gay—"

"He seems to be very unsuccessful at finding a steady girlfriend."

"All that proves is that like a lot of immature men he's shy with girls. Is there the remotest hint that he likes to hang around with gays?"

"Well, since you ask, I didn't like the way the Communion wine salesman was eyeing him the other day."

"That's the salesman's problem but it needn't be Stacy's. Was there any sign that Stacy wasn't just being his normal warm-hearted self?"

"No. All right, you've proved I'm being a sex-obsessed old fool! Let's forget it."

"No, no, we won't do that," says Nicholas at once, anxious to show me that he's still capable of keeping his mind prised open an inch on this particular subject. "Obviously we must continue to monitor the situation in case you're right, Stacy's deluding himself and I'm up the creek. But I don't feel I have sufficient grounds to reopen the subject with him at the present time."

This sounds reasonable enough, but the trouble is I suspect this show of reasonableness is just that: a show. There's no way that Nicholas, in his heart of hearts, feels he's up the creek on this one. He's going through the motions of being open-minded, but his mind's wedged shut while he surfs along blithely on the big wave called ARROGANCE.

I'll have to return to the fray later and make sure I bring him down a peg or two, but in the meantime it seems there's nothing I can do about Stacy except learn to live with my anxiety.

COMMENT: It would certainly be convenient if Stacy were a heterosexual. It would mean we could all sidestep an area which is notoriously strewn with problems. But if he is indeed a homosexual, this wouldn't be a disaster. I've lost count over the years of the number of excellent homosexual priests I've met, particularly in the London diocese, but if Stacy's gay he *must* develop a strong spiritual framework which will sustain him throughout all the inevitable difficulties, or else he'll wind up a disaster for the Church.

To be fair, this dictum also applies to heterosexuals. I of all people should bear in mind that a poorly integrated heterosexuality can also cause havoc for the Church. But even Val wouldn't deny that society makes life more difficult for gays, and that's why they need all the spiritual sustenance they can get.

The truth—the truth which lies beyond all this business of sexual orientation—is that Stacy's got to grow up before he can be an effective priest. Whether he's gay or straight isn't the primary problem at the moment; the problem is his chronic immaturity. He's got to find out who he is and accept himself, warts and all, or how is he going to be of use to those who come to him for pastoral care? A healer must achieve a high degree of integration and self-knowledge before trying to work among divided, damaged souls; if he doesn't, he'll unwittingly project all the unassimilated aspects of his personality onto those vulnerable people with disastrous results.

I must pray hard that Stacy be led into the truth, no matter how difficult that truth may be to accept, and be given the grace, to face it, own it and integrate it into his personality; I must pray that somehow Nicholas and I can help him reach this long-delayed but absolutely essential maturity, and go on to serve God as well as he possibly can . . .

Saturday, 24th September, 1988: Cynthia gets married, quietly but smartly, at St. Peter's Eaton Square. What a refreshing change it is to attend the wedding of a middle-aged couple where neither party is divorced! (Woodbridge's wife died at around the same time as Cynthia's husband.) Afterwards there's a reception at Venetia's favourite haunt, Claridge's, but although there's a multitude of silver buckets oozing ice and Veuve Clicquot, Venetia's not there. She hasn't been invited. Fortunately. She's just joined AA and the last thing she needs to see is a phalanx of champagne bottles.

Little Alice is now on the brink of arriving in Wonderland. Because of the extraordinary state of the property market the sale of the house in Eaton Terrace was agreed with lightning speed and a most inflated price achieved. Alice is moving out on Monday, and Cynthia, generous to the last, is paying for the removal of Alice's worldly goods to the hell-hole at the Rectory. Nicholas tells me the word "hell-hole" is a misnomer now that the flat's been repainted, recarpeted, replumbed, rewired and de-moused. I'd like to see this miraculous transformation, but I still can't face those steep stairs.

I've really got to face up to having my hip done soon . . . when I've found a spiritual director who can discuss sex adequately and thus help me solve my current problem . . . and of course all that may take some time . . .

COMMENT: Great-Uncle Cuthbert would have been livid if he'd read that last sentence; he'd have known straight away that I was prevaricating. All right, all right, it's time to face the unvarnished truth again! The truth is I don't want a new spiritual director. Apart from the subject of sex, Simon's good. He's not perfect, but he's good.

But is he good enough? No. Not if he's useless about sex.

I can almost hear Great-Uncle Cuthbert snarling what Nicholas is probably thinking: "If you lack confidence in Simon, you'll wind up believing you know better than he does—which means you'll get an inflated opinion of your strengths and severe amnesia on the subject of your weaknesses and the entire relationship will soon be worse than useless. Sack him."

Yes, Simon will have to go, no question about it.

I must have a blitz on finding a new spiritual director.

The only trouble is I'm very busy at the moment and there are so many distractions . . .

Monday, 26th September, 1988: Little Alice arrives, wide-eyed, almost speechless with nerves, but professes herself thrilled with the reformed hell-hole. Alice has nice eyes, I notice for the first time, dark and velvety like the eyes of a golden retriever. I notice because she takes off her glasses for a polish, either because they've misted up as the result of her emotion or because she just can't believe the squalor of the old-fashioned kitchen, looking at its worst after Stacy finally broke the percolator and coffee went all over the wall.

Nicholas tops off his welcome by confessing that although the pest control van has recently called with satisfactory results, a new generation of our little furry friends (as St. Francis would no doubt have called them) will inevitably make future assaults on the Rectory. This is an ongoing struggle for supremacy we're engaged in here, not just a bunch of humans playing pat-a-cake with the occasional stray rodent.

Nicholas is just turning away after telling her which exterminators we use when Alice enquires shyly: "Isn't there a cat?"

Nicholas stops. Slowly he revolves, pivoting on the balls of his feet. Then he looks at Alice as he's never quite looked at her before and says flatly: "Rosalind doesn't like cats." He begins to turn away again but before he can complete the pivoting Alice exclaims, trying so hard to be helpful: "Oh, but I'd see that it never went into your flat and I'd keep it out of sight whenever Mrs. Darrow came to visit—and cats are so good at solving mice problems!"

Nicholas swivels back to face her. The balls of his feet are getting plenty of wear and tear today as he tries unsuccessfully to tear himself away from this conversation. The next moment he's saying respectfully: "Of course you're remembering Orlando."

A memory drifts into my mind of a very young Rachel reading a large, illustrated story-book. "Named after the famous marmalade cat, I presume," I say, deciding to flaunt my skimpy knowledge of children's literature.

"He was more a gold cat than a marmalade cat," says Alice, "but he was very beautiful and very bad news for mice. I just loved Orlando."

Nicholas sighs, and I know he's thinking of all the cats he loved before Rosalind decided animals were a bore, leaving hairs all over furniture and planting colonies of fleas on fitted carpets. "We always had tabby-cats," he says nostalgically, "when I was growing up."

"How lovely!" exclaims Alice enrapt. "Several at once or one at a time?"

"One at a time."

The two cat-lovers smile, united by their common passion. Then Nicholas announces with the air of someone making an executive decision: "We'll have a cat. You must come with me to help choose it." And with that knock-out exit line he departs for his study.

As little Alice nearly faints at the thought of cat-shopping with Nicholas, I wonder if this is really the most sensible of decisions.

COMMENT: Worry about your own sex-life, Lewis Hall, and leave other people to worry about theirs. Or, in less emotive language: trust Nicholas to manage Alice's hero-worship as skilfully as he manages everyone else's.

But "everyone else" doesn't live at the Rectory.

Oh, pull yourself together, you stupid old fool, and stop seeing women as nothing but trouble . . .

Tuesday, 27th September, 1988: I've just had the best breakfast in years, cooked by our new in-house serf, Alice. Even Nicholas, who's not interested in food, ate twice as much as usual. Stacy kept saying: "I can't believe I'm eating all this." For a blissful half hour the sin of gluttony reigned supreme at the Rectory, and the Devil did a tap-dance in our stomachs.

We're giving Alice a week to settle in before we implement Nicholas's new and excellent plan to hold a communal breakfast for the Healing Centre's leading personnel after the eight o'clock mass, but she's off to a flying start on day one. Nice, good, clever child. If only she didn't have a crush on Nicholas! But she conceals it beautifully, and no one except a dirty old psychic like me would ever know.

Rosalind turns up to interview hopeful cleaners; she's already dispatched Mrs. Mudd, who will no doubt find some other all-male household to terrorise. Rosalind is togged out in chic earth-brown, shoulders very boxy, and looks as if she's just about to join a shooting party with a Kalashnikov.

In that blissful Rosalind-free zone, the Healing Centre, I'm collared by Francie who tells me her husband's beaten her up again and that this time she's decided to leave him. I've heard that one before. It's difficult to appear credulous when one knows that if the pattern runs true to form she'll soon change her mind and resolve to stay with the villain. However, to my relief Francie isn't seeking my opinion of the situation; she just wants to open her heart to me when she's so upset. Fair enough. I'm a priest. I can take a heart being opened. But someone really should try to lead Francie out of this sado-masochistic relationship which is causing her so much pain.

I must talk to Nicholas about her again. Luckily I don't have to worry about the confidentiality rules here because she confides in both of us and makes sure we each know the other is *au fait* with the latest news. This is unusual. It's not unusual for members of staff to have problems, but they tend to share them either with Nicholas or with me and not with both of us. On the other hand, no one has a problem as serious as Francie's, so maybe she feels she needs both of us to provide sufficient spiritual support.

Thinking of women needing spiritual support reminds me of Venetia, whom I may just possibly glimpse flitting through the Healing Centre in less than seventy-two hours' time—although of course if I do see her it'll be the purest of coincidences.

COMMENT: Stop drooling over the thought of Venetia at the Healing Centre, you old fool, and just pray for her recovery.

(Dear God, help me to be a *priest* here, not a sex-obsessed pensioner! Amen.)

Friday, 30th September, 1988: Venetia Day.

Venetia turns up in a black trouser-suit, complete with waistcoat, and looks like a 1980s version of Vita Sackville-West. Maybe she's a lesbian. A lot of promiscuous women are. All that nymphomania is their way of kicking men in the teeth.

By the impurest of coincidences I'm just in the reception area telling Bernard that as office manager he should do something about the copier, which is chewing up paper again, when Venetia surfaces from consulting room three. She's been crying and she's trying to put on an enormous pair of wraparound dark glasses. Behind her Robin's hovering and fluttering, sending out caring signals but managing to look like a strung-out stick-insect. I make a short sharp gesture which implies: "I'll cope. Scram," and he vanishes. Robin's always empathy personified. No wonder he's stick-thin. Nothing like constant deep empathy for burning up the calories.

Meanwhile Bernard's declaring stuffily that we can't get a new copier because after the recent postal strike the new facsimile machine has to have priority; he refers to it as a "fax," which, with his northern vowels, sounds as if he's reading straight from *Lady Chatterley's Lover.* Abandoning him and his technological pidgin-English, I march over to the dark glasses and say without preamble: "Coffee?"

"Yep." She's not mincing her words either.

"Go and sit in consulting room two."

She does. Fortunately I've got no more appointments that morning as I'm supposed to be on duty at the church prior to the lunch-time Eucharist. Grabbing two mugs of coffee I prepare to apply first aid.

Venetia's slumped in the chair by my desk. Sitting down opposite her I hand over one of the Centre's regulation boxes of Kleenex and during the next five minutes I wait in silence as she soaks up the tissues one by one. At last she drags on the wraparounds again and says drearily: "Okay, I'll go now."

"Feel like a drink?"

She perks up. "Lead me to it!"

"All right, I'll take you to the Savoy for a pussyfoot."

"A *pussyfoot?*" she echoes appalled in the manner of Lady Bracknell.

"Don't let the lack of alcohol put you off. I'm a great one for pussyfoots whenever my liver needs resting."

We stare at each other while she decides whether or not to spit with contempt. But in the end there's no spitting. Instead she laughs, and at once I laugh too.

Before I leave I get Nicholas on the intercom and excuse myself from the lunch-time healing service. I also add that I hope he doesn't have to cope with our roving blasphemer who wants to bugger the Blessed Virgin Mary. The blasphemer was back yesterday, turned out of his mental hospital. Mrs. Thatcher's closed it down. Typical.

Feeling about thirty-nine years old I grab a taxi and sweep Venetia off to our nearest grand hotel. I even forget the pain in my blank-blank hip which once again has been giving me hell . . .

COMMENT: Of course I took her out entirely for therapeutic reasons. I thought it vital that someone should intervene at that point to stop her bingeing on alcohol. I knew how important it was to introduce her to the pussyfoot, so useful to those on the wagon. I felt strongly that she needed a nice little visit to the Savoy as a reward for enduring that difficult but no doubt very worthwhile therapy session. In short my invitation was a gesture made only with her welfare in mind and I had no ulterior motive whatsoever.

Hell, what balls I write in this journal sometimes!

But I really mustn't start thinking about balls . . .

Saturday, 1st October, 1988: I receive a note which reads: "Dear Lewis, Thanks. But you remind me of someone I've spent half my life trying to forget. He was wonderful too. Goodbye. VENETIA."

Triple-hell! Quadruple-hell! Multiple-multiple-hell!

I'm so cantankerous that Stacy tries to hide when he sees me coming, and Nicholas asks if I've thought of changing my pain-killers.

Bugger everyone! Bugger everything!

I'm *furious.*

COMMENT: Well, what did you think was going to happen, you addled idiot? A whirlwind romance? Talk about losing touch with reality! Pathetic!

This woman's trying to get her life in order. She doesn't want some old crock doddering along and screwing it all up.

LEAVE HER ALONE.

Monday, 3rd October, 1988: Another note arrives from Venetia. It reads: "Dear Lewis, Sorry. I overreacted. You're really nothing like him at all, I can see that now. Perhaps we might pussyfoot again sometime. Have you been to Claridge's lately? V."

I feel like opening a bottle of champagne but it's only seven o'clock and I've got a full morning ahead. I want to leap up on the kitchen table, beat my chest and roar like a lion, but damn it, I'm sixty-seven years old and I was barely able to hobble just now from my bedsit to the front door to pick up the post.

That blank-blank hip . . .

Suddenly I go berserk. I erupt into the study, where Nicholas is doing his spiritual exercises, and give him such a fright that the Bible flies clean out of his hands. Then I thump my fist on the nearby table and shout at the top of my voice: "SOD THE FUCKING HIP! I'M REPLACING IT!"

Nicholas's jaw drops but he's already realising that this wild behaviour is therapeutic, and a second later he's giving me an encouraging smile. After all, I've kept a stiff upper lip about that damned hip for far too long, and the restraint's only increased the stress.

"Congratulations, Lewis!" he exclaims. "An excellent decision!" And the die is cast.

A new life awaits me!

In ecstasy I dream of rejuvenation.

COMMENT: On reflection this was very far from being an edifying scene. Reasons:

(1) I'm behaving exactly like an unstable adolescent over Venetia and setting myself up for all manner of possible humiliations.

(2) Indulging in lurid Tarzan-like fantasies (vault onto table-top, beat chest, etc.) is hardly appropriate mental activity for an elderly priest. I'd have done better to visualise the dialogue with my spiritual director which must now ensue as I face up to the impending loss of my arthritic chastity belt. Am I or am I not supposed to remain a celibate? It's no good sinking into some grisly infatuation with yet another neurotic female drunk if I can only serve God properly by remaining single. I should remember that the entire acting-out of what was originally a mere suppressed carnal reflex could well indicate that I've been destabilised by Diana's death and in consequence behaving like a lunatic. I should also remember that nothing's changed but my marital status, and even though I'm now a widower I'm still the same man who likes to flirt with aristocratic sirens but go to bed with rough trade. How can I even think of remarriage when I know very well I've never managed to overcome this hang-up? Of course Venetia, in a peculiar way, combines the two types: she's an aristocratic siren *and* uninhibited rough trade. So maybe . . . No. Stop. I'm fantasising. Forget that.

What am I supposed to be writing? Oh yes, the reasons why the above scene was unedifying. (1) I'm behaving like a testosterone-crazed adolescent, (2) my fantasies were spectacularly unhelpful in solving the celibacy question, (3)—

(3) I should have thought more coolly before committing myself to do away with my chastity belt.

And (4) even though I usually manage to avoid blasphemy I must make more effort to avoid obscenity. "Sod the fucking hip" was hardly the best of sentences for a priest to utter, even though I was relieving an intolerable tension and even though only Nicholas was present. Language matters. Filthy language reflects a polluted consciousness, and how can God communicate with us if the channel of communication is clogged up with the psychic equivalent of mud? I must talk to Nicholas about this—I think he also has been rather too free-and-easy with the four-letter words lately, but we must now tighten up our spiritual discipline in order to keep fit. It's no good mindlessly reflecting one of the more yobbish aspects of contemporary culture; that's not what priests are for, and anyway, who needs more yobs? Human beings are at their most useful when they're trying to be civilised, not when they're rollicking around with their brains on ice.

What a splendid conclusion to reach! But there's just one point that still worries me: will the mere avoidance of the word "fuck" stop me thinking all the wrong thoughts about Venetia?

Tuesday, 4th October, 1988: After much thought I decide that I can't continue to pussyfoot with Venetia. But then seconds after reaching this supremely sensible decision I see that I have an absolute moral duty to continue because if I don't she'll feel rejected—and this would be most undesirable while she's in such a fragile emotional state. So I phone her and fix a date when we can go pussyfooting at Claridge's.

Not until afterwards does it occur to me that I could now be breaching professional ethics. Should I socialise with someone who's currently a client at the Centre? Even though I'm not conducting the counselling sessions I could still, as a member of the team, be considered involved in Venetia's treatment.

I'm so troubled by this thought that I do what I should have done earlier and confide fully in Nicholas, but to my relief he takes a relaxed view and says he would have intervened after the interlude at the Savoy if he'd felt the pussyfooting represented a threat to Venetia's welfare. "Robin and I both think you could play a useful part in helping her fight the drink problem," he says. "If you can prove to her that she can sit in a bar with a man and enjoy a non-alcoholic drink, that would be important."

But there could be two schools of thought on that one; I can imagine some members of Alcoholics Anonymous, for instance, saying that she shouldn't be in a bar at all until she's got a better grip on the addiction. However, if Nicholas and Robin are going to sanction the pussyfooting . . . I decide to keep quiet about the hypothetical objections of certain hypothetical members of AA.

"The one thing you mustn't do under any circumstances," says Nicholas, suddenly flinty-eyed, "is—"

"I know, I know—"

"In fact if you have any doubt at all about your ability to keep the physical side under control, you'd better opt out now before the friendship goes any further. I could explain the opt-out to her in such a way that she doesn't feel rejected."

"No need."

Nicholas allows a pause to develop before asking in his most colourless voice: "Have you done anything further about finding a new spiritual director?"

"Well, I've been very busy just lately, and—"

"I wish you'd go and see my nun."

Nicholas switched to this nun for spiritual direction when his male spiritual director died and left Nicholas a letter recommending her. Nicholas admires this woman enormously. She's a Roman Catholic, but that doesn't matter since nowadays we're all so ecumenical. She's been married in some dim and distant past. She's probably an exceedingly good, wise, spiritual old lady. But . . .

"No, I've got to have a male director," I say, but making a big effort I add: "That's not because of any defect in your nun. It's because of the defect in me."

"A woman might succeed in healing you even though all the men have failed."

I find I can only say: "No. Great-Uncle Cuthbert wouldn't have approved."

"Then get a male director you can respect," says Nicholas, very flinty-eyed again, "and get one fast. If you wreck Venetia now, at this most crucial stage of her life, just because you can't get your act together on the celibacy question—"

I assure him I'd rather be castrated than wreck Venetia, and five minutes later I feverishly start phoning my friends for information about any new star who's appeared in the spiritual direction firmament.

Two other London priests recommend this nun. Amazing! If I didn't know that Great-Uncle Cuthbert would never have trusted me to be honest with a female director, I'd think that God was trying to tell me something . . .

COMMENT: I'm still shilly-shallying around like an arch-ditherer over this spiritual direction business, and I *must* come to a decision. Here are the indisputable facts:

(1) I have to get a new hip in order to be fit enough to serve God to the best of my ability.

(2) With the new hip I could get into a sex-mess unless I sort myself out PDQ.

(3) If I don't sort myself out PDQ I might wreck Venetia.

(4) In order to discover if I have any viable future with Venetia I've got to discern what God requires of me at this stage of my life and what kind of life I'm supposed to lead to meet those requirements.

(5) In order to arrive at the correct answers to these crucial questions I need help.

(6) In order to get the kind of help I need so that I can (a) line myself up properly with God through prayer and (b) work out what has to be done, I must find an experienced spiritual director who knows which end is up when it comes to sex, and

(7) I must find this paragon *without delay*.

So far, so good. Now, let me think . . .

Maybe the words "without delay" are the crucial ones and that's why I automatically underlined them. The truth is, though, that unless one's exceptionally lucky, finding a new spiritual director—the right new spiritual director—always takes time, and if time is something I just don't have . . .

No, I'll have to stay with Simon for the time being. Better the spiritual director I know than the spiritual director I don't know, and I mustn't rush into a new association here just for the sake of speed. That could prove disastrous, far more disastrous than sticking with Simon until the right person turns up.

I hereby vow to keep conscientiously looking for the streetwise, sexwise spiritual genius who'll rescue me whenever I'm tempted to reach into my personality and push the button marked SELF-DESTRUCT.

Ought I, perhaps, to take a look at Nicholas's nun?

No, waste of time, she'd never cope with me.

Dear God, please transform Simon into a streetwise, sexwise spiritual genius! Amen.

Wednesday, 5th October, 1988: I demand an emergency appointment with Simon and get it, but when the time comes I feel lukewarm and want to cancel. Only the memory of Nicholas being flinty-eyed deters me.

So off I go, but it's a wasted journey. Simon just waves his middle-class fixation at me again and spouts drivel. Why does Simon, who had a perfectly respectable upbringing in a forty-room mansion in Northumberland, idealise the middle-classes like this? I'm beginning to think his idea of heaven must be Surbiton.

He says it does sound as if I might just possibly be having a call to marry again, but perhaps the call is not to marry Venetia, so like Diana, but to marry someone quite different, a nice middle-class girl, for instance, who would like nothing better than to cook and sew and keep house and who would look after me beautifully in my old age.

The trouble is that Simon, having been a monk for fifty years, has no idea whatsoever what the modern middle-class girl is like. She either has a career, drinks scotch and brutalises every man in the boardroom, or else she's dumped the children on the au pair and taken to fornicating with the house-husband next door.

I escape, feeling depressed, and head for Claridge's to pussyfoot with Venetia.

All goes well—what a relief! Maybe I'm putting too much faith in spiritual directors and not enough faith in my own intense desire to do nothing which would blight Venetia's chance of escaping from a living death into Life with a capital L. We don't sit too close together. I behave impeccably and she makes no passes. In short, we talk and laugh and enjoy ourselves in a boringly normal fashion, but the meeting works and before we part we arrange a date to go pussyfooting at the Connaught.

COMMENT: I'm extremely pleased and feel I'm in control of the situation—which probably means I'm not in control of it at all. "Let he who thinketh he standeth, take heed lest he fall . . ."

I'd better confide in Nicholas.

I can't be too careful here.

Thursday, 6th October, 1988: I swear to Nicholas I've been transformed into a knight in shining armour and Venetia's safe. He's impressed by my sincerity but not entirely convinced I'm incapable of making a balls-up at a later date. I at once declare that I'm now going to find a new spiritual director as soon as I possibly can.

Nicholas just says very politely: "I'm glad that's now top of your agenda."

To divert Nicholas from my humiliating flounderings over the spiritual direction question—not to mention my questionable flounderings over Venetia—I raise the subject of that other troubled woman, Francie Parker, who's still busy floundering with a sadistic husband, but Nicholas finds her situation as baffling as I do. She won't go to the police. She won't go to a lawyer. She won't go to a women's refuge or seek support from a women's group. She does periodically leave her husband, but she only goes to her mother in Kent and she's always back home within forty-eight hours.

"Do you think there's a risk," I say worried, "that this upsetting private life may affect her work as a Befriender?"

We mull over this possibility, but come to the conclusion that listening devotedly to other people's problems probably provides Francie with the perfect escape from dwelling on her own.

"She keeps saying her work's a life-line," Nicholas reminds me, "and there's no evidence of incompetence—on the contrary, everyone says how wonderful she is. In fact only this morning Alice said to me how nice it was to see Francie regularly again . . ."

We agree, not for the first time, that we can't force Francie to seek help and that all we can do at present is listen if she wants to talk. But I can't help feeling this isn't a very satisfactory solution.

After this conversation with Nicholas I leave the Centre and go upstairs into the church to do the ecclesiastical chores: I change the altar-cloth, tidy the prayer notice-board, put out a new supply of information booklets about our work at St. Benet's. I'm still pottering in this fashion when Francie herself slips in to pray. I loiter, pretending to be deeply engaged in checking the supply of Communion wafers, and eventually she approaches me. She says she's been giving thanks to God because her husband's sworn to reform.

I think: Almighty God, please show me what I can do to help this woman.

But I already know I mustn't collude with this new fantasy.

"Francie my dear," I say gently, very gently, so gently that I sound like a cuddly old priest in one of those ultra-sentimental Hollywood films long ago instead of a grumpy old codger battling through 1988 with an uncertain sex-life, "I seem to remember your husband's sworn to reform before."

"But this time he really means it!"

She *can't* believe that! Or can she?

"Well, if he breaks his word this time," I say, "you should consider taking a completely different approach to the problem."

She says she will but I can see she now thinks she's going to live happily ever after.

Of course it's notorious that abused women do get so mesmerised by the abuse that they become incapable of reacting rationally to their torment, but even so I find I'm still inclined to boggle.

Cautiously I enquire: "Have you told Nicholas this?"

"Not yet. But of course I will. Nick's so sympathetic," sighs Francie, momentarily letting her guard slip. "So understanding."

But there's nothing new there. Francie's just one of several women at the Healing Centre who think Nicholas is the cat's whiskers. This pardonable degree of admiration—mild hero-worship—vague crush—whatever one wants to call it—is quite harmless, merely part of the normal fall-out from a charismatic ministry, and Nicholas knows all about how to deal with these commonplace psychological projections; he's very skilled. Probably Francie's idealising him more than usual at the moment because her husband's so unsatisfactory, but she's basically a sensible woman and there's no danger of her going over the edge. I'm sure of this because I feel that if the danger existed she'd be confiding her problems only to Nicholas and leaving me well alone.

I light a candle for her before moving on to prepare for the lunch-time Eucharist.

COMMENT: I was lighting a candle for Francie but thinking of Venetia. That's spiritually sloppy. I must improve my concentration.

But how splendid it is to think that there's only five days to go before the next pussyfooting session . . .

Tuesday, 11th October, 1988: I meet Venetia at the Connaught and we pussyfoot together in a very amusing fashion. I'm delighted to hear that she's increased her sessions with Robin to two a week because she finds them so profitable. I'm also delighted to be able to record that I behaved IMPECCABLY.

The only difficult moment comes when I ask after her daughter, now twenty-two, who's working in Germany. Venetia sees little of Vanessa. The child was mostly brought up by Venetia's favourite sister who likes children. Venetia says this was for the best as she herself "couldn't cope." She's probably right, as it's no fun for a child to have an alcoholic mother, but guilt is engraved in every line of her face and I see this failure has exacerbated her self-hatred and her rock-bottom self-esteem.

However, this brief discussion of Vanessa takes up less than a minute of the conversation, and soon afterwards we're laughing again as if it had been instantly forgotten; Venetia's suggesting we should pussyfoot again next week and I'm agreeing, adding what fun it is to check up on all these grand hotels. Then she asks idly: "Are you rich?"—which is the sort of stimulating, no-nonsense question that a nice middle-class girl would never dare to ask, and I answer: "No, my cash-flow problem's so severe that I've had to sell the second Bentley and cut back on the weekly order of caviar from Fortnum's." The rich are always moaning about their cash-flow problems.

This amuses her but she refuses to be diverted. "As a follower of Jesus Christ," she says, "why don't you set up a charitable trust and give your money away?"

I explain that I have no intention of making a gaggle of lawyers and accountants rich by setting up a charitable foundation, but that if she's interested I'll give her a list of the charities I support. When she says: "Sorry," and looks ashamed I say at once: "No need to apologise—your query was justified. Wealth gives rise to all sorts of spiritual questions which need to be asked and answered."

But she only says: "I should have realised you'd be generous. After all, look at the way you're spending money now on a raddled old has-been like me!"

I hear the pathetic craving for reassurance, the longing that someone, somewhere, might believe she wasn't entirely disgusting.

"Where's the raddled old has-been?" I demand truculently. "I see only a courageous wannabe!"

She tells me that if I can see that I can see anything, but I've struck the spark of hope. Her beautiful green eyes become misty. The cigarette trembles between her fingers. "You're rather a dear old pet!" she whispers emotionally.

This is too much. It's bad enough having to act the Cuddly Old Priest for Francie, but to be diagnosed as a Dear Old Pet by Venetia is more than my aged flesh and blood can stand. "I'm not a dear old pet at all," I rasp in my best cantankerous voice. "I'm mean, stroppy and exhausting to know. Ask Nicholas or Stacy."

She rasps back: "Good, that makes two of us! Now we can stop pretending we're so adorable!"

We gurgle and giggle as we puff away at our filthy cigarettes, and I'm sure we both feel that life's suddenly very worth living indeed. Sailing home later in a taxi I remember an old Vera Lynn hit. " 'We'll meet again—don't know where, don't know when,' " I warble as if I were dead drunk instead of stone-cold sober, but in fact I do know exactly where and when. And I can hardly wait to go pussy-footing next week at the Dorchester.

At home I find Rosalind's staying the night; she's come up to town to meet a friend for lunch and see how the new cleaner's getting on. The new cleaner is very shy and industrious and answers to the name of Shirin, but her English is uncertain. I won't let her in my bedsit, not because I want to be anti-women, racist or xenophobic, but because I like my privacy and I'd rather hoover the carpet and wipe off the dust myself. I do this without fail every six months.

I want to tell Nicholas that I've behaved IMPECCABLY with Venetia, and as my hip's not so bad tonight I clamber up the stairs to his flat. He and Rosalind, sitting hand in hand on the sofa like a couple of teenagers from the chaste 1950s, are watching a rerun of *Fawlty Towers* on television.

Seeing that I've been driven to climb the stairs Nicholas jumps up at once, thinking something's wrong, so I hasten to reassure him. "I'm fine," I say, "and so's Venetia."

"Venetia Hoffenberg?" says Rosalind, making what I believe is known as a "moue" of distaste. "God, what on earth are you doing with that old wreck?"

As I bend my whole will towards keeping my mouth shut, Nicholas says mildly: "Darling, is that quite fair? You haven't seen Venetia for a while. She's changed."

"What a relief for her family! They've all assumed she'd wind up like her sister Arabella—a hopeless drug addict attended by a ghastly old gigolo."

"Well, tonight Venetia was just a scintillating nicotine addict attended by a ghastly old priest," I snap, unable to keep my mouth shut any longer, but Nicholas intervenes with formidable smoothness; Nicholas says with that limpid, casual air he's perfected over the years:

"I'm glad all went well. That's just the news I wanted to hear," and I calm down again straight away.

My hip's not so good now. Dragging myself downstairs I find Alice guarding the oven which is keeping my dinner hot.

"You don't have to wait up whenever I'm late home," I say, deciding that as she's been at the Rectory for over two weeks she'll be settled enough to survive a peremptory remark or two. "I can take the dinner out of the oven myself."

"I thought you might like a nice cup of tea if you were tired."

I'm so exhausted by the struggle not to behave like a Rottweiler with Rosalind that I'm not as grateful for this middle-class solicitude as I should be. "Forget the tea!" I bark, Rottweiler streak well to the fore. "Bring me the whisky bottle!" And I show her how to make a whisky-and-soda exactly as I like it.

"Would you like a glass of wine with your meal?" asks Alice, a little shattered by my bared teeth but speaking up bravely, and I discover with relief that she knows all about wine as the result of that superior cookery course she took. Moreover she reveals she only offered me tea because she thought that was the correct behaviour when dealing with clergymen at unusual hours.

What am I doing being canine and peremptory (i.e. rude) with this exemplary cook-housekeeper? Clearing my throat I ask her in my most mellifluous voice if she would be so very kind, please, as to bring me one of the half-bottles of St. Julien which I keep in a crate in the hall cupboard. Not only does she bring me this treat instantly; she uncorks it, decants it and fills my claret glass to exactly the right level.

Nice, well-informed, splendidly accomplished young woman! We're lucky to have her.

As I tuck into the most excellent meal I wonder if "Nicky" has told Rosalind yet about the proposed cat.

COMMENT: I must pray for Alice, doing so well in her new job.

I must pray for Venetia, struggling so hard to begin a new life.

I must pray for Francie, flailing around in that dead-awful marriage.

I must pray for dead-awful Rosalind.

I must pray for dead-awful me. Dear God, please help me conquer my Rottweiler streak. Amen.

Monday, 17th October, 1988: I read with horror that some American female "priests" (mustn't use the word "priestesses," Nicholas says; that insults them by conjuring up images of paganism) have broken the law and conducted a Eucharist in an Anglican church. And I'm still reeling from last week's news that the Shroud of Turin was a fake! Whatever next, I wonder, although in fact the Turin business doesn't matter much in some ways; they could never have proved the shroud was Christ's even if they'd succeeded in showing it was made in the first century. Far more depressing than the news about the Shroud was Mrs. Thatcher's assertion at the Conservative Party Conference last Friday that she was "too young" to retire. They're saying she'll go on for ever now—or at least all the way through the nineties to the Millennium. How are we going to cope with the continuing sacrifice of the weakest members of our society on the altar of that obscene god, THE MARKET?

I spend the day sunk in gloom but perk up when I pussyfoot at the Dorchester with Venetia. Needless to say I behave IMPECCABLY, and in the taxi home afterwards I sing "Lili Marlene." Funny how those old war-time songs live on in the memory.

On my arrival home I find Alice is waiting in the kitchen to introduce me to a small striped object which mews: the new kitten. Trust Nicholas to get his own way and grab a tabby. It's to be called James because Alice believes simple, unpretentious names make life easier for the owners. (Apparently polysyllabic "Orlando" proved tiresome when summoning the animal for meals.) At least Alice got her way about the name. Nicholas would have called it Walsingham or Canterbury or something stupid. His earlier cats were all called after a town steeped in ecclesiastical connections.

"Very nice," I say, stroking the kitten with my forefinger. "Is he house-trained?"

"Almost."

"Obviously a very superior animal."

Alice mixes me a perfect whisky-and-soda. She produces a portion of shepherd's pie which I can only describe as celestial. She pours me a glass of claret. I feel cosseted, pampered and in consequence extremely benign.

Maybe God's converted me from a Rottweiler into one of those smiling golden Labradors.

COMMENT: I don't think I'd better see the hand of God in a shepherd's pie which called me to gluttony. My powers of discernment are obviously up the creek. When am I going to find a new spiritual director?

Thursday, 20th October, 1988: I take time off to call on a couple of spiritual directors, but they're no good; they'd never survive me. Then I call on my orthopaedic man in Harley Street. He says he'll book me into one of those very expensive private hospitals. All right, I know I shouldn't be taking the private-medicine route, but I'm a paid-up member of BUPA and I'm too old for the alternative. No doubt Our Lord Jesus Christ would disapprove of this spoilt-rich behaviour, but he never had to face an operation on the National Health—and surely Our Lord would have had compassion for an old man who's scared stiff of pegging out on the operating table before he's had the chance to pursue his impeccable pussyfooting to an entirely respectable conclusion? When I'm asked about a date for the operation I say firmly: "As soon as possible," but my heart sinks when the fourth of November is suggested. I didn't think it would be that soon.

I've been so bound up lately with spiritual directors, Venetia and the hip that I've neglected Stacy, but at home that evening my anxiety about him is renewed when he says to Nicholas: "By the way, is it okay if I ask Alice out? I think she'd be a very acceptable girlfriend for a priest."

I don't like the way he puts this. It's as if he's a casting director selecting an actress for an important role in a film. It's also very often the case that men uncertain of their sexuality try their luck with a plain woman whom they calculate won't either let them down or behave in any way which is remotely threatening.

Nicholas says kindly but firmly: "No, I'm afraid that won't do, Stacy. I'm sorry, but if you date Alice and things don't work out that could lead to a difficult atmosphere here. It's very important, you see, when several unrelated people are living under one roof, that certain distances are preserved and certain boundaries never breached. One person with emotional problems can be a loose cannon, wrecking the equilibrium of the community."

This puts the well-known problem in unobjectionable—i.e. namby-pamby—modern language but I'd still prefer to say: "It's the Devil getting in and causing havoc." Doesn't that vivid metaphor convey more of the potential danger and destruction than the aseptic language Nicholas has chosen to use?

As I silently ask myself this question Nicholas is mentioning to Stacy the names of two young women who help part-time at the church, and Stacy's obviously grateful for the tip.

"I regard this as incontrovertible proof," pronounces Nicholas after Stacy's clattered away upstairs to the curate's flat, "that he's genuinely keen to find a steady girlfriend."

I just grunt, but when Nicholas starts spouting some fashionable modern guff about sexuality being a complex spectrum, I find I have to interrupt. "My dear Nicholas," I say testily, "the only reason why Stacy's playing the heterosexual card is because he's so keen to please you."

But Nicholas refuses to accept this. "That can't be right," he says obstinately. "He knows I'd affirm him even if he was primarily homosexual in orientation—he knows I'd never want him to forfeit his integrity by denying any part of his true self."

"Not so easy to expose the true self sometimes, though, is it? Not if you're a homosexual and certainly not if you're a homosexual priest. Easier to play the straight card and opt for the double-life."

"But Stacy's not doing that! He's a man with a homosexual past who's now realised the truth lies in claiming his heterosexuality!"

"Stacy's a mess. And talking of messes . . ." I raise the subject of Francie.

Mulling over our recent conversations with her, we discover they're identical. Again, confidentiality isn't an issue because Francie's given us carte blanche to discuss her case with each other, but this time I suddenly hear myself say: "There's something about this business with Francie that doesn't add up."

Nicholas is riveted. He knows a psychic twinge when he hears one, although we both know enough about psychic twinges to be very wary of them. I can see him thinking: he could be off his rocker. But he could be right.

"Go on with that," he commands, sitting bolt upright on his chair.

"Well, for a start, just why is she confiding in both of us? I'd say that was atypical. Surely in most cases the abused woman is at first very reluctant to speak of the abuse at all and then inclined to confide only in one person—who's usually female?"

"Generalisations can be misleading. Surely the point here is that

Francie's worked alongside us both for years and trusts us completely? In these particular circumstances—"

"But there's something else." By this time my elderly brain's clanking away like a steam engine as I try to correlate my psychic twinge with my rational thought processes. "Her story never develops, does it? It arrived fully-fledged and now it just goes on and on in the same groove."

"That could merely be because abusive relationships do tend to go round and round in the same circle."

"Yes, but—"

"What seems odd to me," says Nicholas unexpectedly, "is that having brought herself to confide in us—having taken the major step towards getting help—she consistently refuses all our helpful suggestions. I really did think that the idea of a women's group—"

But by this time I'm barely listening. My brain's now banging along at maximum speed. "We never see the violence, do we?" I interrupt. "She always claims that Harry, being a crafty middle-class thug, only hits her where it doesn't show. But supposing—"

"Supposing she's disturbed, much more disturbed than we've ever realised, and this report of the violent husband is a fiction designed to win our attention?"

We stare at each other. This is a deeply unpleasant theory. Quite apart from the fact that we're both fond of Francie, who's a good woman in her own way, she's our senior Befriender, someone who's done sterling work for us during the past four years. It's an important job, dealing all the time with troubled people. If she's now seriously troubled herself, she's going to be disabled and that would be bad news for the Healing Centre.

I say sardonically, trying to ease the tension with a touch of black humour: "Do I hear the Devil knocking at the door?" but the moment the words are out of my mouth I feel that joking about the Devil is hardly the best of ideas in such circumstances.

Meanwhile Nicholas is saying stupefied: "I just can't believe Francie would go clean over the top."

"I concede there's no concrete proof, but all we've got to do is wait a little longer. Fantasists always trip up in the end."

"Yes, but . . ." Nicholas is still grappling with his disbelief. "What's her motive?" he demands at last. "She could have our full attention at any time without resorting to fantasy!"

"Well, obviously she's after a different kind of attention and equally obviously it must be you she's gunning for. Up till this moment I've always thought that if her hero-worship was out of control she'd be confiding in you alone, but now I see she's much cleverer than I'd anticipated and she's using me as a smokescreen."

"Wait a minute!" says Nicholas sharply. "Are you sure you're not demonising her, projecting onto Francie doubts and suspicions which in fact belong elsewhere?"

"Certainly not!"

"Well, that's what it's beginning to sound like to me, although I promise you I'll keep an open mind. Incidentally, talking of your problems with women, have you found a new spiritual director yet?"

I have to admit I haven't.

Nicholas sighs, wishing I'd get my act together.

The conversation closes.

COMMENT: It occurs to me that we could have quite a demonic brew simmering at St. Benet's. If Francie's off her rocker and Stacy's going at ninety miles an hour down the wrong sexual street, there could be two separate disasters capable of engulfing us in scandal. Or am I just being a trifle unhinged now that the hip replacement's finally on the agenda and I'm having nightmares about the surgeon's saw?

I've sworn Nicholas, Alice and Stacy to secrecy about the operation. I don't want loads of visitors when I'm in hospital; I want no witnesses to the fact that after the carve-up I'm sure to feel a mess and look like a nonagenarian. Ah, vanity, vanity . . .

I shall miss Alice's cooking while I'm away. Her Lancashire hotpot tonight was a masterpiece, and I shall pray that some nice young man asks her out very soon. Should I try to find out why she doesn't go to church with us during the week? No. Most people don't go to church during the week and she's perfectly entitled to abstain. Should I try to find out why she doesn't go to church on Sundays? No. Maybe she's too shy to come to the eight o'clock mass I hold for a few members of the prayer-group on Sunday morning when the church is officially closed, and if I draw attention to her absence she'll feel shyer than ever. Anyway, how do I know what she gets up to on Sundays during those times when she's not at the Rectory? She might trundle off to St. Paul's Cathedral where she'd feel anonymous and comfortable. No, I must abstain from cross-questioning her and leave her to emerge from her great-aunt's brainwashing in whatever way suits her best.

Nicholas has explained to me that Alice was very much influenced by this great-aunt, a pig-headed old girl who thought churchgoing was rubbish but would have fought to the death to preserve the hatch-match-and-dispatch routines of the Church as Great British Tribal Rites. "Folk religion," as it's been called, may be absurdly quaint, but one mustn't underestimate its ability to bring Christianity into the hearts of ordinary people. Alice has a Christian background. One day she may care to explore it further. Whether she does or not is up to God, working either through us or in spite of us, and I must leave the matter in his hands. Besides, the best evangelism is a Christian life well lived, not a tactless nagging or unimaginative ranting at every unbeliever in sight.

Thinking of Alice reminds me that I forgot to check the refrigerator before I retired to my room tonight. I've discovered that her weakness is rum raisin ice cream, a most delicious luxury which she has to keep in the main kitchen because the refrigerator in the hell-hole's kitchenette is too small to accommodate anything in the freezer compartment except ice-cubes. By checking the freezer compartment of the main kitchen's refrigerator I can see how much bingeing she does. There was a lot going on at first, but the consumption's declined. Only six tubs a week now. Neither Nicholas nor I ever make any comment, and Alice never asks us for any help in fighting this dis-ease which must give her so much grief and discomfort, but of course we pray for her. I light a candle too after every healing service, and one day, I firmly believe, she's going to start to get thin . . .

Monday, 24th October, 1988: Venetia and I pussyfoot at the Berkeley. Haven't been there before, although of course I knew the old Berkeley. I remember a very steamy frolic there during the war.

Venetia talks about this man in her past, the man who messed her up to such a degree that she ricocheted into marriage with the wrong husband. What a mixed-up, pie-eyed, self-centred bastard this heart-breaker of hers must have been! But was he actually any more mixed-up, pie-eyed and self-centred than I was when I messed up Diana? Maybe not, but he was sixty-one years old and married *and* a priest, just as her husband was, and he should have known better.

Dear God, how easy that last sentence was to write! Yet who knows what I may be tempted to get up to when I'm sixty-seven, single and sporting a new hip?

My behaviour with Venetia is IMPECCABLE but I take a taxi home in dead silence.

Alice serves up toad-in-the-hole followed by jam roly-poly. I can't describe the sheer sensual thrill of eating such perfectly cooked English classics. I'm having a hard time trying to suppress all thought of the coming butchery but Alice's food calms me down.

James the kitten is now fully house-trained. Nicholas is supervising his education in the art of being a perfectly behaved cat. I might have known Nicholas would never be able to stay away from that animal. I ask him if he's told Rosalind yet that there's a cat on the premises, but he says vaguely that he hasn't told her because he didn't think she'd be interested.

Coward.

COMMENT: *I'm* the coward, secretly quivering about this blank-blank operation! And to think I won all those medals in the war! I *must* pull myself together—and I *must* stop worrying that I'll become a sex-maniac as soon as my hip's replaced.

Why haven't I succeeded in finding another spiritual director? Am I setting my sights much too high? Or is my desire for a new spiritual director in fact much too low?

I wish Great-Uncle Cuthbert were here to shake me till my teeth rattled . . .

Friday, 28th October, 1988: I've decided to stop looking for a new spiritual director until after my operation. This is because I'm in such a state now about the carve-up that all I want to do is savour what could be the last few days of my life.

I start the savouring by pussyfooting with Venetia at one of those new places, a Canadian high-rise called The Inn on the Park. Very stylish in that modern, transatlantic way which always looks so peculiar in England. The pussyfoots are what the Americans call "jumbo." Venetia and I agree they're magnificent.

I somehow still manage to behave IMPECCABLY.

COMMENT: If only I could stop the recurring nightmare that my surgeon will accidentally castrate me on the operating table . . . Am I sure it's sheer fear alone which is causing these fiendish sleep-patterns?

Maybe I'm just eating too much at dinner. Tonight Alice served roast chicken with all the trimmings followed by rhubarb crumble, and I stuffed myself disgustingly. To cap it all I find I now have a craving for rum raisin ice cream . . .

Thank God I'm seeing Venetia one more time before the fatal day. Meanwhile I only hope I don't die of overeating before I can even reach the hospital.

Wednesday, 2nd November, 1988: Venetia and I pussyfoot at the Hilton in Park Lane. Marvellous views of London. I finally get around to telling her I'm dropping out of circulation for a while.

"Where are you going?" she asks.

I say: "It's a sort of retreat. I'll tell you about it later." (Dear God, let there be a "later.")

I'm not sure what shape I'll be in when I escape from hospital. The specialist is encouraging, but he obviously doesn't like to commit himself to unbridled optimism in case I take one step with the new hip and drop dead with shock. He does mutter something about crutches, but I ignore this because I'm still well under seventy and I'm sure crutches must be for the real oldies, the pushing-eighty set, who haven't kept themselves fit by leading busy working lives and who have all kinds of things wrong with them in addition to arthritis. After all, there's nothing wrong with me except for my hip, and once it's replaced I'm determined to be gliding around like a lounge-lizard before I leave the hospital.

My surgeon also says I should have a "nice little holiday by the sea" in order to convalesce properly, but that's the last thing I need; I'd die of boredom. I want my dirty old bedsit and my services at St. Benet's and Alice's cooking. Who needs to sit around staring at the sea? Only old crocks who never dream of pussyfooting.

As all these thoughts shoot through my head, Venetia's saying something about what fun to go on retreat, will I be asked to beat myself with twigs, if so could she come as a beater, please, and does all this have anything to do with Jesuits.

"No Jesuits, no twigs," I say with a sigh, and think: just a saw and a Harley Street surgeon.

Venetia sighs too and says she'll be ripe for a retreat herself once she finishes this course of therapy, but I know her sessions are going well. She's beginning to toy with the idea of further education. She turned down the chance of a university education when she was young, and she's always regretted it. Of course she couldn't attempt a degree now, she says, but perhaps she could still do something positive with her brain instead of pickling it in alcohol . . . or did I think she'd left it too late?

I say firmly: "It's never too late," and promise that I'll find out details for her of London University's extra-mural courses.

I behave IMPECCABLY.

Unfortunately once I'm back home I go to pieces again. I eat two helpings of liver and bacon and two helpings of cherry tart with custard and I'm still hungry. All nerves, all an illusion, but the hunger seems gnawingly real, and when Alice offers me some rum raisin ice cream I can hardly restrain myself from eating the whole tub. The prospect of this operation is without doubt bringing out my entire neurotic side . . .

COMMENT: Disgusting!

I feel totally humiliated by my extreme pusillanimity and abject lack of self-control.

Thursday, 3rd November, 1988: My departure for hospital is imminent; I have to check in today for the assault tomorrow. I'm playing the final chorus from Bach's *St. Matthew Passion*—good music to die to—and wondering if I'll ever hear it again. In this life, I mean. And it's this life I'm interested in at the moment, thanks to Venetia.

How wonderful it will be when I'm slinking around like a fifty-year-old instead of hobbling along like an old codger with one foot in the grave!

COMMENT: The above entry is nothing but self-centred twaddle. Why aren't I praying for my surgeon and his saw? But I suppose that would be self-centred too, since I'm so anxious for the saw not to slip.

Dear God, as I go to meet my fate, whatever that is, please enable me to behave serenely, with dignity, and kill any impulse I may have to disintegrate into a gibbering food-fixated wreck. Amen.

Oh shit, why did I ever make the insane decision to submit to this blank-blank-awful medical nightmare . . .

Sunday, 6th November, 1988: I SURVIVED! My eyes opened on a day I'd convinced myself I would never live to see (yesterday) and I duly breathed a gargantuan sigh of relief. Couldn't do much more than that, though. Drugged to the eyeballs. But today I'm less doped up and more *compos mentis* so I'm having a little scribble. (Was it Hensley Henson who said that writing a journal was as addictive as drink?)

I'm very sore but the relief from the arthritic pain is absolutely unbelievable. Three cheers for my surgeon the healer! No, make that six. (The extra three are for my genitals, still intact.) By this time I'm so euphoric, relishing my survival, that I behave beautifully, so beautifully that everyone thinks I'm a Cuddly Old Priest. However, they soon find out what a mistake they've made. Within hours I'm getting crusty again, fed up with bedpans and all that rubbish, and demanding fresh pyjamas, new pillows, better food and drinkable wine. Nicholas walks in just as I'm bawling: "I hate hospitals!" and behaving very badly.

He says: "You silly, cantankerous old bugger!" and gives me a hug.

Yesterday, when I was glassy-eyed and dozy, he delivered flowers from himself, Alice and Stacy. Now he brings me Penguin's brand new reissue of Josephine Tey's *The Daughter of Time*—very appropriate, since the hero conducts his investigations from a hospital bed—and Iris Murdoch's *The Book and the Brotherhood*, which has also just appeared in paperback. The Tey novel I read when it was first published, but that was many years ago and I shall take pleasure in rereading it; Nicholas knows too that in these circumstances it's less stressful to read something familiar than something new. The Murdoch novel I shall no doubt enjoy—but later when I'm feeling less like a battlefield.

In addition to the books, he's also brought three get-well cards. Stacy's is rude, showing a bedridden old man ogling a nurse. Typical. Alice's is feline, showing a cat pawing a placard inscribed GET WELL SOON. Also typical. But Nicholas, original as ever, has chosen a postcard of his favourite Kandinsky painting and written on the back: "Aren't you glad to be living in the 1980s? With a new hip you're indisputably one up on Great-Uncle Cuthbert!"—a message which makes me smile.

In fact I feel so emotional as I paw over all these offerings that I can't talk much, but Nicholas understands and makes the silence peaceful.

I wonder what sort of card Venetia would have sent if she knew where I was and what had happened to me . . .

COMMENT: I hate the disruption of my religious routine as much as an athlete would hate the interruption of his training, but I try to maintain my equilibrium by regularly giving thanks to God for all the marvels of modern medicine. Nicholas brought the Blessed Sacrament with him, as arranged. He'll bring it every day until I come home. I didn't want to rely on some unknown chaplain. How lucky I am to have Nicholas to look after me, how lucky I am to have so much more than so many people, THANKS BE TO GOD, AMEN.

Saturday, 12th November, 1988: Little Alice visits me. I'm staggered. I banned Stacy, as I knew he'd crash around breaking everything and my nerves couldn't have stood it, but it never occurred to me to ban Alice. I never dreamed she'd want to see me.

"You're a very kind, thoughtful young woman," I say, unable to decide whether or not I'm glad to see her. I was so keen that no one except the hospital staff and Nicholas should see me when I was looking like a beaten-up old tramp.

Alice blushes, delighted to be praised, and produces a little tub of rum raisin ice cream from an insulated bag. Shyly she says: "I thought you might like a spoonful or two."

I immediately decide I'm very pleased indeed to see her, and several dollops of ice cream disappear down my throat in double-quick time.

As I guzzle this treat she says with care: "I'm cleaning your room. Nicholas thought it would be a good opportunity, but don't worry, I'm not letting Shirin in and I promise I'm not snooping." She pauses before adding serenely: "I do understand that you wanted to guard your privacy, but everything really was rather dirty, you know."

That's the moment when I realise Alice is finally at ease in her new job. She has sufficient confidence to imply in the nicest possible way: you filthy old man, your nicotine-stained, overcrowded, chaotic bachelor's bedsit offended against all the known laws of hygiene and was the most revolting health hazard I've encountered in my entire career as a cook.

At once I say: "Thank you, Alice. It's very good of you to take the trouble. I don't deserve such kindness."

"Why on earth not?" demands Alice, so relieved that I've taken the news of the invasion well that the last trace of her shyness disappears, but before I can attempt a reply she's extracting from her handbag an envelope of photographs and asking: "Would you like to see the latest pictures of James?"

The kitten is looking most attractive—and so is Nicholas, who's holding him. Nicholas is in all the snapshots.

"Isn't he lovely!" sighs Alice, and of course she means the cat.

Or does she?

I suddenly realise I'm starting to worry about sex again.

I must be on the mend.

COMMENT: I hope Nicholas isn't developing a blind spot about Alice. He can't afford to relax his vigilance, and I don't think he was monitoring the relationship closely enough when he decided to acquire that cat. Nicholas is dopey about cats and he can't afford any dopiness where Alice is concerned.

Is it my imagination or is Alice thinner? I notice she didn't bother to have any rum raisin ice cream.

Monday, 14th November, 1988: The soreness has eased and the freedom from arthritic pain still seems miraculous, but the bad news is that my specialist's muttered prophecy has come true, I'm obliged to use crutches whenever I leave my bed, and despite all my determination to believe otherwise I know I shall be unable to chuck them aside the moment I go home; so for a while I'll be sidling along like a drunken crab. To make matters worse—and this is why I won't be thrown out of here just yet—the physiotherapist has explained to me that I have to relearn my walking; because I didn't take action on the hip earlier I learned to walk in the wrong way and this is now handicapping my recovery. Triple-hell! How can I present myself to Venetia when I'm in such a patently decayed condition?

I'm so upset that I have a row with one of the junior doctors when he says shouldn't I be showing more Christian patience. Impudent young whippersnapper! I bare my teeth and growl. He flees.

Nicholas arrives. Trying to divert myself from my furious disappointment I badger him to tell me all the news, even the worst items, and eventually he abandons his high-minded decision not to bother me with our current cliff-hanger at St. Benet's. It turns out that Francie left her husband (again) but returned (again) after the usual forty-eight hours with her mother; the husband's promised (again) to reform and Francie refuses (again) to get any kind of help.

"So what else is new?" I say dryly to Nicholas, but apparently the answer isn't quite: "Nothing." Nicholas has suggested to Francie that she might like to talk to our tame psychiatrist up in Hampstead to try to examine the "destructive dynamic" in the marriage, but this very reasonable proposal has also been rejected by Francie, and Nicholas is now more willing to believe she could be fantasising. Our psychiatrist—a friendly, sympathetic female—has helped us before with battered women, and Nicholas feels that if Francie's problem really is a violent husband she would by this time welcome the chance of first-class medical help from someone who specialises in the field of abusive relationships.

"On the other hand," I comment cautiously, "maybe she feels that to see a psychiatrist is to admit she's nuts."

"She surely wouldn't be that naive, not after working for years at St. Benet's! Besides, I was careful to take the line that it was primarily Harry who needed the psychiatric help; I suggested Francie's interview with Jane would be more of a conference than a consultation as they worked out how to deal with him."

"So what did Francie say when she finally turned you down?"

"The usual. Harry would reform. No outside help was necessary. Her love would see them through."

"If Harry's the sadist she says he is, that's a grand illusion. If he's not the sadist she says he is, that's just the fantasy continuing. Either way she's up the creek."

There's a pause while we meditate gloomily on this verdict. Then Nicholas says: "I wonder if the reality's quite as clear-cut as that."

"What do you mean?"

"Well, Francie could be telling the truth when she says Harry's a sadist, but she could be lying about the nature of the abuse."

I stare at him. "You mean the abuse may not be half as bad as she says?"

"No, I mean it could be much worse than she says. Maybe she's so traumatised that she can neither put into words what's going on nor make any attempt to do more than let us know she's in trouble. That would at least explain why she's turned down the therapist, the self-help groups and the psychiatrist; she'd feel she was way beyond being able to articulate the problem to strangers."

I'm interested but sceptical. "What sort of problem do you have in mind?"

"A sexual deviation by the husband."

We mull this over and I find that running through a choice list of sexual deviations certainly takes my mind off my post-operative difficulty. I even begin to feel in the mood which that Victorian, Great-Uncle Cuthbert, would have described as "bobbish."

"So what's the next step?" I demand.

"I think all we can do at the moment is keep the lines of communication open, so I've asked Francie to come to see me twice a week for a ten-minute update on the situation."

"That means she's got your special attention!" I exclaimed. "You mark my words, Nicholas, those little ten-minute chats will soon expand into fifty-minute sessions!"

"I think she'll trip up and be forced to come clean long before that happens—if she's a fraud. And if she's not a fraud, then she deserves some special attention."

"But you're taking a big risk, Nicholas! If she *is* seriously disturbed and unacceptably fixated on you—"

"The truth is I still find it hard to believe that Francie's suddenly gone over the top."

"It's not sudden! These tales of wife-beating have been going on for some time! And besides, don't forget that even the most stable people can go off their rockers if a chemical imbalance develops in their brains!"

"That's true, but I see no sign of psychosis here. The most likely explanation is that she's suffering from an abuse which she's working herself up to articulate to me."

"I disagree. If Francie was being subjected regularly to some disgusting perversion, I think she'd have broken down by now or at the very least shown some sign of stress in her work, but she's still functioning normally, isn't she? Nobody at the Centre except us has the remotest idea she's in trouble, and in my opinion—"

Seeing I'm getting overheated Nicholas diverts me with what appears to be good news about our other major problem. "Talking of people functioning normally," he says, making a skilful interruption, "that reminds me: I almost forgot to tell you about Stacy. He took out Tara Hopkirk at the weekend. They went to a film at the Barbican and had a very successful evening."

Tara Hopkirk is one of the church cleaners. She lives in the Isle of

Dogs, always dresses in sweatshirts and outsize jeans, comes to the lunch-time Eucharist once a week and looks like the back end of a bus. In other words she's a downmarket, churchgoing version of Alice.

"Not much class there," I observe.

"So what? Stacy's hardly blue-blooded, is he, and Tara's a splendid girl, very good-hearted!"

I can imagine Tara feeling delighted by this surprising initiative from the curate, but what's Stacy feeling? I decide it would be wiser not to venture a comment.

Sensing my scepticism Nicholas switches subjects again and this time he talks about the latest case-conference on Venetia. Apparently he wants to pussyfoot with her in my absence, just to check that she's on an even keel without her regular fix of Lewis Hall. This first bout of therapy is set to end in mid-December, although she'll almost certainly need to continue the therapy after she and Robin assess her progress at Christmas. If she then feels she needs to explore the past in detail she can elect to try psychoanalysis, but that's a possibility which can be discussed later. In the meantime she's attending AA meetings and keeping off the booze. So far so good.

I give him permission to pussyfoot but tell him he's got to overcome his aversion to grand hotels in order to pussyfoot with style. Nicholas sighs. However, he's very fond of Venetia and he's passionately committed to her rehabilitation. He'll grit his teeth and face Claridge's for her sake.

"I was hoping to impress Venetia by walking like a much younger man when I next see her," I say, unable to resist confiding my disappointment to him. "But as it turns out I'll be looking older than ever and hobbling along on crutches. What am I going to say to her when she asks for an explanation?"

"There's no need to give any explanation at all. Just be enigmatic and elliptical."

"What on earth do you mean?"

"Say: 'I hope that one day I'll be able to tell you the whole story, but meanwhile—alas!—my lips are sealed.' "

"I like the 'alas'! But supposing she just laughs and accuses me of talking codswallop?"

"She won't. She'll be fascinated but tactful. After all, she likes you, doesn't she?"

"Yes, but—"

"Then she won't force you to talk about a subject which you've clearly labelled *verboten.*"

I feel more cheerful.

He gives me the Blessed Sacrament and we pray together. Then he performs the laying-on of hands, and afterwards I feel not just more cheerful but wonderfully better, full of hope, relaxed and at peace. The nurse comes in later, looking as if she wishes she were wearing a bullet-proof vest, but all she finds is this cuddly old priest sporting a soppy, beatific expression. "Well, whatever happened to *you?*" she asks astonished, and I explain that I've received healing from a great priest, devout, humble and well integrated—and in consequence capable of being wholly at one with the power of the Holy Spirit.

How magnificently far removed my Nicholas is from being a power-mad, self-centred wonder worker on an ego-trip!

I feel so proud of him.

COMMENT: I mustn't get so sentimental about Nicholas. I must stop writing "my" Nicholas, like a doting father mooning over his idolised son. Sentimental old men are embarrassing, and I don't want the one successful relationship in my life to get bogged down in gooeyness. Sentimentality always distorts the truth. I must never forget that Nicholas has his faults and his weaknesses, and that my job as his brother-in-Christ is not to view him through the rose-tinted spectacles of a sentimental affection but to see him through the clear lense of a genuine love. Only then can I be of *real* service, helping him if he stumbles, steering him back on course if he strays.

Almighty God, please keep Nicholas safe while I'm not at home to look after him. In the name of Christ, Amen.

Wednesday, 16th November, 1988: I'm to be allowed to go home tomorrow, but unfortunately I'm not through with hospitals as I have to have regular physiotherapy. But the physiotherapist seems confident that in three months' time few people will guess I've had hip trouble.

Good news.

Meanwhile my surgeon is most displeased to hear that I'm not going off for a little holiday by the sea. With asperity he declares that I mustn't rush back to work; I must walk a certain amount each day but avoid violent exercise of any kind; there must be no late nights, no driving cars and please could I seriously consider giving up smoking.

I'm so cross I want to shock him rigid by asking how soon I'll be able to have sex, but ragging a stuffed-shirt layman by implying I can't wait to commit fornication is hardly justifiable behaviour for a priest.

Keeping my mouth clamped shut I start to dream of pussyfooting . . .

COMMENT: Is my impatience with the surgeon and my longing to go home a mere normal desire to return to much-loved surroundings, or is there a psychic twinge involved? I keep praying for Nicholas as if I'm worried about his safety. So, to pose the question more bluntly: am I just being a stupid old man, playing the neurotic father with a man who's perfectly capable of looking after himself, or am I latching on to a hidden threat which has somehow taken root in the world of the unseen and is stealthily expanding to dangerous dimensions? It's hard to pinpoint this threat. All I know is that the Devil must be hating Nicholas's success as a Christian healer. What I might very well be sensing is that cloven hoof twitching as it revs up for the big kick.

Sometimes only metaphorical language can convey truth.

I felt the kick of that cloven hoof back in 1983 when my previous ministry was destroyed. What would I have done if Nicholas hadn't taken me in and rehabilitated me? I don't like to think. God acted through Nicholas, of course, redeeming the mess, renewing me, breathing fresh life into my shattered career. But I'll never forget the kick of that cloven hoof when I was self-satisfied, overconfident and doing so well that I no longer bothered to battle with my pride. I turned into a wonder worker, that was the truth of it. Even the best healers are subject to corruption, and perhaps the most successful are particularly likely to be booted down the drain into the sewer. Success breeds pride; pride distorts one's vision of reality; a distorted vision means you never see the kick coming from the cloven hoof . . . And then the next moment you're in the filth and smashed to pieces.

I see so clearly now that the wonder worker is the shadow side of the Christian healer. The wonder worker's there all the time, deep in the psyche, but so long as he's confronted and owned he can be subjugated. Once he's neglected or ignored he'll get restless and slide stealthily out of control. The healer's got to be very fit spiritually to see off that particular challenge, but see it off he must. It's a matter of life and death.

Watch out, Nicholas, *watch out!* You were the ideal healer whenever you visited me in hospital, but back at St. Benet's you're self-satisfied about Stacy's phony date with Tara and you're overconfident in your conviction that Francie's not deranged. If you're not careful, that arrogance of yours will blind you to reality, particularly if I'm not there to hold the unvarnished truth constantly before your eyes, and then one day . . .

One day all hell will break loose.

Almighty God, please help me get fit as soon as possible so that I can be of maximum use to Nicholas in fending off any kicks from the cloven hoof. Amen.

Thursday, 17th November, 1988: I leave hospital. All the nurses drool over me. I try to apologise for the episodes of truly appalling behaviour but the girls say they're always so glad to meet a patient with a fighting spirit. I seem to have established a reputation as a "character." Extraordinary.

I arrive home. To mark the occasion Alice is dressed in her best tent, now too big for her, and the kitten has a bow around its neck. My bedsit is so clean I can hardly bear to light a cigarette in it. I potter around, puffing away at my nicotine fix, and touch all my favourite items—the crucifix, the icons, my best books, my picture of Rachel and the grandchildren.

Alice has baked a magnificent cake which has WELCOME HOME written on the top in royal blue icing. I sit in the kitchen, drink Madeira, eat cake and feel very happy. Eventually I go to my room and phone Rachel. "Oh, and I've had my hip done," I say casually at the end of the conversation. "I'm okay now."

Rachel hits the roof. Why didn't I tell her I was having it done? Supposing I'd died—think what a shock it would have been for her since she hadn't even known I was in hospital! How could I have been so selfish? And how had I dared deprive her of the chance to send cards—flowers—presents—what on earth could the nurses have thought of her neglect?

"They didn't think anything," I say. "I never told them I had a daughter."

Rachel takes violent offence, bursts into tears and hangs up.

As usual Nicholas straightens us out. He rings her back and explains that I was trying to spare her anxiety.

I'm put on the line. Rachel sobs that she's sorry, she didn't mean to be beastly to me, she was just in shock, but now she's recovered she'll send cards, flowers, chocolates, champagne—

"Very nice," I say. "Thanks. Vintage Moët would do," and we finally manage to part on an affectionate note.

After this I feel in urgent need of a light-hearted interlude, so I phone Venetia.

"How was your retreat?" she enquires.

"Successful. How were your pussyfoots with Nicholas?"

"My dear, he tried to drink Coca-Cola but I wouldn't let him. It was sheer inverted snobbery—he wanted to cock a snook at Claridge's!"

"Disgusting! I've missed our pussyfoots. Can we meet?"

"Name the day."

"Tomorrow? At the Connaught?"

"No," she says, and for the first time she hesitates. "Not the Connaught. Somewhere larger and noisier where no one will pay attention to what we're saying."

I deduce she wants to talk about her therapy. "We could go back to the Hilton."

"Fine. Tomorrow at six-thirty?"

Almost delirious at the thought of pussyfooting I return to the kitchen and find Alice making soup for lunch. "If you're looking for Nicholas," she says, "he's gone over to the church."

I glance at my watch and discover with surprise that the time's much later than I thought. The lunch-time Eucharist will be beginning in ten minutes.

I'm anxious to attend, but for a moment I'm diverted because I've suddenly realised how odd it is that Alice never abbreviates Nicholas's name. Why has this habit never seemed odd to me before? Because it's not odd, is the answer; it's unusual but not odd. So why does it seem odd to me now? Because my psychic antennae are vibrating away, picking up any hint that Nicholas could be in danger and converting any unusual feature of the familiar landscape into a potentially sinister threat.

Apart from me—and apart from Rosalind, who clings to the "Nicky" he was called in kindergarten—everyone calls him Nick. I was the only one left who called him Nicholas, just as his father did, but I'm the only one no longer. Alice has annexed all three syllables so that she stands out from the crowd of Nick-people. Alice has taken a stand which makes her special.

The kitten's up to his old game of chewing my shoelaces. Stooping to pick him up I say casually, very casually, so casually that no one would ever suspect my nerves are jangling: "Alice, why do you never call Nicholas Nick?"

She pauses in the act of stirring the soup and gives this question serious consideration. "Nick Darrow's the star of the Healing Centre," she says at last, "but Nicholas Darrow is his whole self, not just the Nick-part but the other parts of his personality as well. There's the part he shares with Rosalind, for instance, and there's the part we see here when he's off-duty. And finally there's that very mysterious hidden part which is invisible, the part which enables him to understand people so well. It's a sort of *dimension*," she explains, not sure she's found the right word but confident she's describing something real. "I'm sure I'm not imagining it."

I stare at her. She reddens and starts stirring again. "Sorry," she mutters. "I'm sounding weird."

"Not to me. You're being most perspicacious," I say, keeping my voice casual, but I'm stunned. Little Alice, who can so easily be written off by people like Rosalind as a dull lump, has just displayed intelligence and intuition on the grand scale; she's described not merely the self which belongs to Nicholas but the psychic strand of that self, the gift which Nicholas never discusses except with me and his spiritual director.

I'd bet heavy money that no one at the Healing Centre knows about this hidden strand of Nicholas's personality. People know he's charismatic (in the technical sense), but the charisms of healing or preaching or teaching—or any of the other gifts listed by St. Paul—can be displayed by psychic and non-psychic alike, and outwardly Nicholas gives no hint of his psychic powers. They're private, dedicated to God, never to be flaunted or exploited for personal gain. It's only the wonder workers who use such powers for their own aggrandisement.

It's a long time now since Nicholas played the wonder worker. It's a long time since he used psychic parlour-tricks to boost his ego, a long time since he told fortunes by stroking the palms of pretty women, a long time since he pretended to relay messages from the dead by reading the minds of the living. He's offered his psychic gifts to God in humility, and as a result they're nowadays so seamlessly incorporated in his ministry that they've become a hidden asset instead of an ego-distorting handicap. Yet Alice has recognised the extrasensory perception which makes him exceptionally intuitive when dealing with clients and exceptionally adroit when dealing with paranormal phenomena. She's recognised it even though this extremely discreet and disciplined use of psychic power is beyond the recognition of most people. It takes a psychic to know a psychic like Nicholas—and little Alice, I now see to my profound astonishment, knows the Nicholas all the non-psychics never meet.

But wait a minute, maybe there's a simpler explanation. Maybe Cynthia said something to Alice about the psychic gifts. Both Cynthia and Venetia knew Nicholas way back in the Swinging Sixties before his ordination when he was playing the juvenile wonder worker and getting up to all manner of mischief.

But no, that explanation doesn't quite pan out. Cynthia might possibly have mentioned to Alice that Nicholas was a psychic, but she could never have described the psychic dimension of Nicholas's personality as Alice has just done. In Cynthia's eyes Nicholas was just someone who used to perform psychic parlour-tricks but who now wouldn't be seen dead with a crystal ball. She had no grasp of the fact that the gift was still used but in a completely different way.

I say idly as I stroke the kitten and pretend the conversation's about something normal: "It sounds as if you're a sensitive, Alice."

"A what?"

"A psychic."

"Oh no!" she says horrified. "I don't believe in that kind of thing at all. Aunt always said it was rubbish."

That great-aunt of hers was without doubt a pig-headed old trout. (What a curious piscine vision that phrase conjures up! But I'm too annoyed to amend the metaphor.) Austerely I say: "Well-developed psychic ability is a gift, like a talent for music, and like a talent for music it doesn't automatically make you a better person than those people who don't have the gift. That's because spiritual gifts and psychic gifts aren't the same thing, although since both deal with the unseen they can overlap."

"But surely scientists don't admit—"

"A true scientist should keep an open mind and examine the evidence—as scientists in America and Russia are doing right now in order to find out more about what they call 'psi.' Both countries have been spending fortunes on research in the hope that 'psi' can be used in espionage."

Alice is round-eyed with surprise but still valiantly sceptical. "Do you really believe that?"

"I believe they've been spending fortunes and doing research on the assumption that 'psi' exists. Those are matters of fact. What I don't believe is that they'll ever be able to harness the 'psi'-factor for espionage. 'Psi' isn't suited to such a concrete activity—it couldn't possibly be reliable enough because even the best psychics have blind spots and make errors."

"I don't believe in any of it," persists Alice stoutly, as loyal to Great-Aunt Beatrice as I am to Great-Uncle Cuthbert—ye gods, what power these eccentric old monsters acquire when they rescue abandoned children! I perfectly understand why Alice feels compelled to adopt a blind faith in disbelief, but I understand too that Alice, whether she likes it or not, has a psychic gift that she's repressed. However, with the great-aunt out of the way, it at last has the chance to open up—and to put her right on Nicholas's wave-length. She and Nicholas are two of a kind, I see that now.

I'm horrified.

COMMENT: Thank God Alice is a plain girl with no sex-appeal. But wait a minute. If she's got psychic potential has she also got physical potential? Let me try to see her in a way that censors out the fat.

That means I have to reverse my usual order of priorities. Instead of noting (a) bosom, (b) legs, (c) bottom and (d) face, I've got to start with the face and ignore the rest. An intriguing challenge! But let's have a go.

Alice has dark hair, which shines nicely when it's washed, and she's got those velvety-brown doggish eyes which could be more flatteringly described as doe-like. She has white, even teeth—she's a non-smoker, of course—and a wide, appealing smile. She's got an extremely well-endowed bosom, and—no, hold the censored portrait right there. What do I see? I see a potential version of the type of woman Nicholas misbehaved with in his disturbed preordination days. When I first met Nicholas in 1968 and helped him sort himself out he told me exactly what his preferred type of woman was. "I like steamy brunettes," he said. Then he went and married a blonde who wouldn't remind him of the girls with whom he'd sown his wild oats. Big mistake. I never wanted him to marry that woman. And now he's been married for twenty years and he's at that dangerous age, the mid-forties, and . . .

Do I hear the Devil knocking at the door?

Triple-hell! Alice will have to go. The situation's too dangerous. I know it's too dangerous, but how will I ever convince Nicholas? He'll think I'm just a nutty old coot, paranoid about women. Damn it, he's already accused me of demonising Francie!

I mustn't rush this. I've got to take my time and tread very carefully.

Dear little Alice, what a shame. I'm really very fond of her . . .

Friday, 18th November, 1988: I was going to write PUSSYFOOTING WITH VENETIA at the top of this entry and underline it in red ink to mark my joie de vivre. I was looking forward so much to doing that. I was looking forward to doing so many things, few of them realistic. Well, we all have our dreams that can never come true.

I don't want to record what happened but I know I've got to try. I always regard writing this journal as a form of therapy. There's a healing dimension to it. Or there can be, if one's not feeling too beaten up to be healed. So . . .

I meet Venetia at the Hilton, as arranged. She looks very smart in magenta, hips curving, legs flashing, Medusa locks spun around her head in rakish, snakish coils. Diamonds everywhere as usual. Eyelids sagging with false eyelashes. In other words she's looking exactly what she is: a true British eccentric.

I lurch in bumpily on my crutches and probably look like a centenarian escaping from an old people's home. I'm also in some degree of pain—not arthritic pain, thank God, but the pain of using muscles which have become unfamiliar and a hip which doesn't yet seem to belong to me. I don't mind the pain but I do mind the lurching. I mind it very much.

"My God!" exclaims Venetia appalled. "Was the retreat rather more than you bargained for?"

"I suppose it was. I kept wishing you were there with twigs."

She laughs before demanding: "What happened?"

"I hope that one day I can tell you the whole story, but meanwhile—alas!—my lips are sealed."

"How very inconvenient when you've come here to drink! Should I arrange for the pussyfoot to be administered intravenously?"

"I'll unseal a crack for the straw."

She laughs again and I order the pussyfoots, but I'm enormously relieved she asks no further questions. I know now I'll never tell her about the hospital. Why bore her with geriatric tales of hip replacement? It would only underline the fact that I'm sixteen years her senior and vilely, terminally old.

After a while she says: "You seem rather *piano*. Are you sure you're okay?"

I say: "Absolutely! Ignore outward appearances," and chatter brightly for a while about nothing.

However, soon another pause develops and I suddenly realise I'm not the only one having trouble relaxing this evening; she's uneasy too. "What's up?" I say, dreading some tale of an alcoholic binge, but that's not the problem at all. In fact there's no problem. She's just uneasy because she can't quite work out how to tell me how magnificently her rehabilitation's coming along; it's coming along so magnificently that already she's beginning to see a constructive, interesting future for herself. She tells me that once her first tranche of therapy comes to an end she wants to leave London and all her alcoholic friends and begin a new life elsewhere—on her own.

"I want to spend time in Cambridge," she says, not looking at me as she fidgets with the ashtray. "I want to try and get that degree I passed up when I was young. It all began when you said: 'It's never too late.' That was when I saw I shouldn't settle for less than what I really wanted, and when I discussed the idea with Robin he told me about the Lucy Cavendish College which is specifically for women older than the normal undergraduate. So I wrote off and got all the information and . . ."

She's going to read theology. She has to take an entrance exam, but she's had an interview with the principal and she thinks she has a good chance of making the grade. She was interested in theology long ago, but after that rogue cleric of a heartbreaker wrecked her she shied away in revulsion from anything to do with religion. Now it's time to make good that damage, time to get in touch with what really interests her, time to grapple with reality instead of running away from it.

I can see that it's probably not a coincidence that some of the more influential people in her life—the heartbreaker, the husband, Nicholas and now even me—have all been priests. The likelihood is that we symbolise an intellectual "attrait" of hers which she's repressed. She's still not religious, she says, but that doesn't matter because a lot of non-religious people study theology nowadays; it's such a magnificently rational intellectual discipline and far more in touch with the basic issues of existence than modern philosophy. She'd be unable to start the degree until next autumn, but she'll need the extra time to complete sorting herself out—oh, and she might do a course in New Testament Greek while she waits. That would give her a head-start, and since she's so old she wants all the head-starts she can get. She's going up to Cambridge tomorrow to take a look at some flats which are for rent. Of course it'll be hard to leave London, but . . . well, she's discussed the plan with Nick as well as with Robin, and she's sure now she has to seek fresh woods and pastures new.

"Or do you think the idea's crazy?" she says, suddenly losing her nerve. "Do you think I'm bound to fail?"

Venetia's whole future's at stake and I mustn't wreck it by creating some self-centred scene. As I pray for the grace to behave as I should, I know that when people genuinely love others, they don't cling; they don't try to imprison them for their own use or batten on them to serve their own needs. They open the palms of their hands and they step back. They set those they love free to do what they're called to do and be what they're required to be.

I say: "Bound to fail? You? Nonsense! You'll be enjoying yourself so much that you won't even remember what the word 'failure' means!"

"You really think I can do it?"

"I don't just think," I say. "I *know.*" I speak with absolute confidence and wind up sounding indestructibly positive. "What a long way you've travelled since we met last July, Venetia!" I exclaim. "I'm very proud of you, and of course I wish you every happiness in your new life."

But as I speak I'm aware of a terrible pain beginning. It's an old pain resurrected; it's chillingly familiar. It's the pain I felt when my mother said there was no place for me in Paris where she'd fled with her new lover. But I mustn't think of that now. I mustn't vent on Venetia all the rage which at my worst moments I still feel towards my mother, but how do I find the strength to control all my chaotic, unhealed emotions which are trying to muscle in on the scene and wreck it?

"There's something I want to say." She's whispering and I can barely hear her. There are tears in her eyes. "I want you to know"—she stumbles but recovers—"I want you to know that I can never thank you enough for what you've done. You've redeemed what *he* did. You've played it as he should have played it all those years ago. There's been no abuse this time, no exploitation, no *folie à deux*—and as a result you've given back what he took away: my self-respect, my hope for the future, my belief that life has value and meaning . . . Oh yes, Robin was wonderful, of course, and Nick too, but in the end it was *you* who finally rewrote the past and enabled me to believe in a future where everything was made new."

I forget my mother. I find I have the strength to say: "I'm glad I could help. I'm glad I was put across your path." Then I start to get into difficulties. I try to say: "I've so enjoyed our pussyfoots," but I have to grope instead for a cigarette.

"I'm sorry," she says very rapidly, very unsteadily. "Forgive me—I'm sorry—"

But I'm all right. When the crunch comes, I'm all right. I keep thinking of that shining future and how very, very much I want her to have it. "There's nothing to forgive," I say, "and no need to apologise." By this time I've found a cigarette but although I'm ferreting in my pockets for my lighter I can't find it. That's hardly surprising. It's lying on the table, and Venetia spots it before I do.

"Here—" She grabs the lighter. The flame flares.

"Feminist!" I growl. "Lighting other people's cigarettes is a man's job!"

The touch of humour helps. Laughing shakily she says have I ever thought of being exhibited in a museum as a relic. I try to laugh too and suddenly we're just a couple of friends chatting over our pussyfoots as if nothing's happened. But that's an illusion. Everything's happened, and soon it's time to part.

"I'll see you home," I say, stubbing out my cigarette, but she answers: "No, not this time. This is where I have to go on alone."

I don't hesitate. I stand up and offer her my hand. I'm a very small but very vital cog in the healing process which is now blinding my eyes and deafening my ears as it sweeps Venetia away from me, and it's very important that I don't break down.

"So long," my voice says, sounding almost debonair. "I wish you luck—all the luck in the world—and if you chicken out now and stay in London I swear I'll come after you with twigs and beat you all the way to Cambridge!"

She smiles but the tears are streaming down her face.

Then she turns and stumbles away.

****

(The asterisks represent the fact that I had to take a breather at that point. Couldn't give my pen the necessary steady push. But I'm better now.)

Well, back at the Hilton I down a double-brandy and stagger out, remembering my dream of gliding around like a lounge-lizard. How pathetic that dream seems to me now.

I collapse into a taxi. When I struggle out, the driver asks if I'm all right. I must look like death. I certainly feel ripe for a coffin. I go straight to my room and lock the door. Eventually Alice taps on the panels and asks if I want my dinner. I say: "No thanks!" and sound cheerful so that she won't worry about me. It's Friday night and Nicholas has already left for Surrey.

As I start on the whisky I remember Venetia mentioning that she'd discussed her plans with my colleagues. So Nicholas would have known what was in store for me, but she must have told him in confidence; otherwise he would have warned me in advance.

I'm sure he's thinking of me and praying for me now, but I don't want his thoughts and his prayers. I want him to be with me in person. I'm a smashed-up, carved-up old wreck and he's the only one who can help me. I want my Nicholas.

Five seconds later the phone rings. It's Nicholas. "Sorry," he says. "I wanted to wait at the Rectory till you got back, but Rosalind had invited some people to dinner and in the end I had to leave."

"That's okay."

"As soon as they've gone I'll come back and collect you. You can spend the weekend at Butterfold."

"No need for that."

"Well, I'll come back to the Rectory anyway and keep you company."

"No. You need your weekend's rest. I'll be all right."

There's a pause before Nicholas orders: "Buzz Stacy on the intercom and get him on the line. I want to ask him to drive you down here."

"No, Nicholas. Rosalind wouldn't like it. And anyway it's better for me to be alone at the moment." I know this last statement's untrue, but I've got to stop him wrecking his weekend and making Rosalind fed up.

Replacing the receiver before he can argue further, I lie down on my bed to give myself a break from the crutches, but after a while I realise that all I want to do is make for the nearest working-class pub and . . . But I'm too much of an old crock to make the trip worthwhile. Or am I? Not necessarily. A lot of tarts prefer old crocks. Gives them a break from all the plunging puppies. So . . .

A long time passes while I wrestle with temptations best not described. A very long time. Maybe even as long as an hour and a half. But finally I quit the wrestling match. Easing myself off my bed, I shed my clerical suit and stock, place my pectoral cross on the bedside table, heave my way to the wardrobe and take a look inside. Five minutes later I'm wearing my old corduroys, a sweater and an anorak. God knows what I look like; I take care not to glance in the glass, but I feel like a gambler who's lost all his money and is about to hit rock-bottom. Having checked my wallet for cash, I adjust my crutches, unlock the door of the bedsit and step into the hall to listen.

The silence hurts my ears. Looking at my watch I wonder how easily I'll be able to get a taxi. Can't phone for one. Don't want to call attention to the fact that I'm beginning my journey from a rectory. But I can get as far as London Wall and I'm bound to find a taxi there in the end. The only trouble is I don't feel like walking even up the street to London Wall. I'm tired and sore, but the emotional pain's so great that I can't stand it, can't live with it, can't rest till I've blotted it out—and got my revenge on my mother—by proving I can survive being dumped—and that means I can't just get drunk to kill the pain, I've got to—

I think about what I feel driven to do but because I'm so dislocated I feel no disgust. I'm totally out of alignment with God, totally disconnected. My whole psyche's screaming in agony. I feel as if at any moment I'm going to disintegrate—split into a million pieces—

I reach out to open the front door, but my hand never touches the latch because a sound outside makes me stop dead. Someone's inserting his key in the lock. Someone's coming to my rescue in the nick of time. Someone's pushing the door wide open and pausing on the threshold to survey the wreckage.

I'm face to face with Nicholas.

****

(Another breather required. Don't know when I've last found a journal entry so hard to write. But I can go on now.)

Nicholas steps into the hall.

We say nothing.

He takes his key from the lock, shuts the front door, sheds his coat. I turn back to the bedsit. Once I'm there I take off my anorak and hang it up in the wardrobe. I remove my sweater, which I put away neatly in a drawer, and I remove my corduroys which I replace in the wardrobe alongside the anorak. Then I put on my clerical suit again and my black stock. I replace my pectoral cross, and finally I haul my way to the kitchen where I sit down slowly and painfully at the table. By this time Nicholas has made some tea and mixed me a darkish whisky. Closing the kitchen door he sits down at my side and we drink. During all this time not a single word has been exchanged between us.

At last I say: "Rosalind won't like this."

"Oh, she'll understand."

This could be the overoptimistic view of the overconfident husband, but I don't argue with him. I'm just so glad to be rescued. Between sips of whisky I say: "It was all right. I let Venetia go and wished her well. I did what was required of me."

"It was a very great victory over adversity."

"Yes, she thoroughly deserves her new life and the last thing I want to do is stand in her way."

"I wasn't referring to Venetia."

The silence begins again. I drain my glass and reach for the bottle but he doesn't stop me. He just tops up the next dose of whisky with water.

Unsteadily I say: "No need to treat me as a hero. I just did what had to be done."

"That's what all the best heroes say."

"But just now I was all set to fall flat on my face in the mud!"

"I wonder. I think you'd have turned back long before you reached the pub."

"How can you be so sure?"

"After behaving like a hero you'd have found you had no valid reason to abuse yourself by taking a roll in the mud."

"Behaving like a hero doesn't alter the fact that I'm bloody useless at relationships! God, no wonder all the women I meet want to dump me in the end—I can't even get it right with my own daughter! I'll never get it right with any woman, I can see that now—I've ruined every chance I've ever had with the result that I'm currently washed up with nothing left to hope for—which of course is the fate I deserve because I'm worthless, useless, I let down every single person I care about—"

"You've never let *me* down," says Nicholas.

I scrub my eyes with my fists like an infant and bawl: "Shut up!" but he doesn't.

He says Venetia doesn't think I'm worthless or useless. She phoned him when she arrived home from the Hilton. She thinks I'm the best priest in London, in the Church of England and in the entire Anglican Communion. Venetia doesn't feel let down at all.

"Nevertheless she's still dumped me exactly as my mother did—"

"Exactly? Come now, Lewis, be honest! What's the unvarnished truth here?"

Then the fog clears from my mind and I can see that the past and present are quite dissimilar. My mother was on her way into the dark, to an existence which resulted in an early death. Venetia's on her way into the light, to live the life she's been designed to lead. "But the pain of loss still feels the same," I say dimly to Nicholas.

"What loss? Venetia has to travel on alone for a while, but Cambridge isn't the other side of the moon—it's less than seventy miles from London. And Venetia never said goodbye, did she? She told me she blew the ending by dissolving into tears, but if she'd stayed calm perhaps she'd have said not *adieu* but *au revoir.*"

I think about that. "She'll marry some academic," I say at last, "and even if she doesn't it'll be too late for me when she finally graduates from Cambridge. I'll be seventy and past it."

"Surely not! Think how boring that would be for your spiritual director!"

I try to smile but it's too difficult. However, I feel better. That's because I can hope a bit. I can believe Venetia might after all want to pussyfoot again with me one day. I can see clearly now that she didn't dump me. She parted, with great reluctance, from a man whom she said had rewritten her past and transformed her future.

I say uncertainly: "Maybe I'm not such a failure after all."

"You can be certain that in this case you were a very great success. Think of Venetia, setting out at last on a rewarding life—what was that famous sentence of Churchill's you used to like so much? Something about coming back from hell—"

" 'We came back after the long months from the jaws of death, out of the mouth of hell, while all the world wondered—' "

"That's it. And that was where Venetia was coming from. From the jaws of death, out of the mouth of hell—"

"I liked Churchill," I said. "He never used namby-pamby language." I thought again of Venetia having the chance for a worthwhile life at last after eking out a maimed existence for so many years, and suddenly I was exclaiming: "Why aren't I on my knees thanking God for all this instead of whining away like a child who's been deprived of a bar of chocolate?"

"Because when you were young you were deprived of very much more than a bar of chocolate."

I mutter a very rude word and guzzle some scotch before saying firmly: "I was better off without my mother. I was a bloody fool to mind being dumped."

"No, you weren't, Lewis. You were a vulnerable adolescent, not a bloody fool, and vulnerable adolescents are allowed to mind when their mothers walk out. It's acceptable."

"Not to Great-Uncle Cuthbert."

Nicholas says nothing. He says nothing so loudly that my ears tingle and I forget the scotch. It's time once more to burnish the golden memory of my saviour.

"Great-Uncle Cuthbert was right!" I declare. "My mother was a disaster, no use to me at all, I was well rid of her!"

Nicholas utters two syllables. They are: "Uh-huh." Meanwhile his face is so inscrutable that I want to biff it, and this mindless spasm of violence makes me uneasy. What's going on? Why is Nicholas behaving as if he's counselling someone who's seriously disturbed? Nicholas always plays along with me over Great-Uncle Cuthbert, always. We've got this routine. Whenever I drivel on about the old man, Nicholas nods and smiles and offers harmless little comments and eventually I feel better and shut up. But now for some reason Nicholas isn't playing that particular game any more; Nicholas is changing the routine.

I feel threatened. "Hold it!" I bark. "What are you up to? What are you thinking?"

"I'm not sure you really want to know."

"Oh yes, I do! I want the unvarnished truth—lay it on the line!"

"Well, when you talk about Great-Uncle Cuthbert, I sometimes wonder what it is you're really trying to say. It's as if you're revving yourself up to deliver a very unvarnished truth indeed but in the end your nerve fails and the delivery never happens."

"You're off your rocker," I say automatically and decide this judgement concludes the conversation. I don't want to think of the painful past any more. I want to keep my eyes fixed on the future, the future with a possible pussyfoot in it.

"Okay, I'm off my rocker," Nicholas is saying, "but there's still something I'd like to ask."

"About what?" I say dozily, mind on the imaginary pussyfoot.

"About Father Cuthbert Darcy, religious genius, Victorian eccentric, dictator, hero, monster, Abbot-General of the Fordite monks from 1908 until 1940. Did he, as a good Christian, tell you to forgive your mother?"

"Of course. He was faultlessly Christian throughout. He never put a foot wrong."

"So here we have an example of Great-Uncle Cuthbert as hero and religious genius, not as Victorian eccentric and monster."

I feel restless again, edgy, and all I want to do is sit quietly and dream of pussyfoots. Irritably I snap: "He did tell me, I assure you, to forgive my mother. It wasn't his fault if my attempts to forgive her never had any psychological reality."

"Whose fault was it, then?"

"Well, mine, obviously."

"You were a boy of fifteen. He was a tough, sophisticated despot in his seventies—"

"He was an extremely wise and holy man!"

"But he had the advantage over you, didn't he? You hardly met on equal ground and he was a formidable personality. I don't think he can be entirely blameless here."

"Well, he was. He was perfect. He saved me."

"I'm more than willing to concede that he gave you stability and affection and a sense of purpose, and that all those things were crucial in helping you to survive that adolescence. But what bothers me is this business of forgiveness. How far would you say he himself forgave your mother?"

"What do you mean?"

"Well, her scandalous life must have been an embarrassment to him—she must have made him very angry. And then he was put to a lot of trouble and expense, wasn't he, when he was obliged to make you a ward of court. That must have made him angry too. So—"

"He always said it wasn't for us to judge her."

"Then how did he explain the need for forgiveness to you? That would have involved making a judgement that there was something to forgive."

"Great-Uncle Cuthbert never explained," I say grandly. "He just told me what I had to do to survive. He said: 'You've got to let her go by forgiving her because if you can't let go you'll make yourself mentally and spiritually ill. It's all very simple,' he said. 'You must face the unvarnished truth and accept it in order to overcome this damage and be healed. Always pursue the unvarnished truth,' said

Great-Uncle Cuthbert, 'because that's the truth that comes from God. We sinners always try to varnish it to suit our own purposes, but we must never flinch from trying to strip off the varnish at every opportunity and see the truth as it really is.' " I stop and look at Nicholas expectantly. "Perfect, wasn't he?" I say proudly. "Faultless. He could be a tricky old bastard at times, I'm not denying that, but fundamentally he was a great man."

"Okay, I'll go along with that. But what was his version, Lewis, of the unvarnished truth about your mother?"

"It wasn't a version. It *was* the unvarnished truth. He said: 'Your mother's a slut and a disgrace and you're well rid of her. She's forfeited all her rights over you by her disgusting behaviour, but I'm here to look after you and so long as you do as I say you'll be safe and everything will be put right.' And I did do as he said. And everything was indeed put right. Well, most of it. Almost everything."

Nicholas embarks on another deafening silence. At last I manage to say: "All right, so he passed judgement on her. But it was the correct judgement, wasn't it? She *was* a slut and she *was* a disgrace and her behaviour *was* disgusting, and when she slunk back from Paris at last with VD and cirrhosis and wanted to see me again before she died, she *wasn't* entitled to see me again and she *had* forfeited her rights. And that was the unvarnished truth."

"Looks pretty varnished from where I'm standing."

"You're up the creek! You're off your—"

"Sure. Look, Lewis. For twenty years I've listened to you struggling to crack the varnish which covers this particular truth, but you've never succeeded in cracking it because you've never had the right tool to help you. But now, thanks to Venetia, the sledgehammer's finally materialised. Shall I put it in your hand or shall I lock it up in a cupboard out of harm's way?"

"You're totally—utterly—"

"Okay, I'll lock it up."

"No, wait a minute, wait, wait, wait—"

He waits. I think rapidly, chaotically, breathing hard. First I think: I just want to dream of pussyfooting. Then I think: you blank-blank coward. And finally I think: I've lost everything—what more do I have to lose?

So I say: "Pass me the sledgehammer."

Nicholas says neutrally, without hurrying: "Venetia has a daughter. She abandoned that child because she had so many problems that she couldn't cope with motherhood. Because of those problems she drank, she drugged, she slept around, she wasted herself. Now, supposing that abandoned child came to you and said: 'How should I feel towards my mother?' And supposing she said: 'Should I forgive her?' "

There are no words. I can't reply. I can hardly breathe.

"Think of Cynthia's catastrophic lunch-party," says Nicholas. "Didn't you tell me that Venetia was called a slut and a disgrace? On a surface level, the level where the varnish lies, that judgement was true. But below the varnish, deep down on the level which matters most, the judgement was radically false. Venetia's a far finer person than that, as we both know."

My eyes are blind. My voice is being smothered by something which feels like a concrete block sitting on my vocal cords, but I can still whisper. I say: "No one at that lunch-party understood the pain Venetia was in, how much she hated herself, how completely her self-esteem had been destroyed. If Vanessa Hoffenberg ever came to see me"—my voice is coming back—"if that girl ever came to see me, I'd say: 'Your mother was greatly wronged in the past. Don't stop loving her, don't turn your back—*forgive,'* I'd say, 'FORGIVE—no one's asking you to forget all the sins and omissions, but forgive and break the cycle of pain, tell her she's forgiven.' I couldn't tell my mother that," I say so indistinctly that my words are barely audible. "I wasn't allowed to tell her, I didn't dare tell her because I was afraid Father Darcy would be angry and I depended on him for everything. I was afraid in case he washed his hands of me and the court put me in an orphanage."

"He despised her, didn't he?"

"Yes."

"Demonised her, even."

"Yes."

"Didn't forgive her, did he?"

"No."

"Wasn't very Christian, was it?"

"No."

"So we see him here not in his role of heroic religious genius but in his role of eccentric Victorian monster. And as an eccentric Victorian monster, he didn't always get it right, did he?"

"No. But I have to believe he did," I say, fighting my way through a fog of emotion, "because otherwise it gets too difficult. I have to believe he got this right . . . although I suppose I've always known . . .

unconsciously . . . that he didn't get this quite so right as he ought to have done—"

"Stop there," says Nicholas, but I've already run out of words. I've cracked the layer of varnish from end to end but the underlying truth is still too terrible to face. I have to cover it up now, I realise, veil it in small talk, turn my attention elsewhere.

"Did you notice?" I say. "I called him Father Darcy, just as I always had to in the old days. Why did I ever start referring to him in our conversations as Great-Uncle Cuthbert?"

"Perhaps you wanted to domesticate him, make his memory easier to handle. He was such a tough customer, wasn't he, Lewis?"

I agree he was but insist gloomily that I loved him anyway. "Hit me over the head with the whisky bottle," I beg, "and shut me up! I don't want to talk of him any more."

Nicholas pours me another whisky.

Then after I've knocked it back he steers me to my room and puts me to bed.

COMMENT: I have to believe Great-Uncle Cuthbert was always right, because if I believe he got it wrong about my mother I'll feel so guilty I'll want to cut my throat. All those times she wrote and begged to see me again! All those times I proudly tore up her letters in front of Great-Uncle Cuthbert in order to impress him! All those times I . . . No, it doesn't bear thinking about, no wonder I repressed the whole putrid mess.

And I still want to repress it. I'm too battered at the moment to face something so profoundly upsetting. I just want to fall back into the comforting, familiar pattern of hating my mother and revering Great-Uncle Cuthbert. That way security lies. I shall feel safe, as safe as I felt long ago when I realised this mind-set would guarantee me a roof over my head.

I liked my little room in the guest-wing of the monastery. I liked flinging up the window in summer and smelling the new-mown grass of the lawns and hearing the far-off, non-stop drone of the traffic circling Marble Arch. I liked helping in the garden and learning carpentry in the workshop and being taken for a daily walk by one of the monks in Hyde Park, as if I were a dog requiring regular exercise. I didn't like the food and I didn't like the services in the chapel and I didn't like playing chess with Great-Uncle Cuthbert, but it wasn't a bad life. Most of the monks were kind. Funny to think of them all now . . . Ambrose the doctor . . . Francis the Prior . . . Yes, Francis was fun. I always thought he secretly fancied my mother, who stormed the house a couple of times to try and see me . . . though of course she never did. Great-Uncle Cuthbert forbade it, and I went along with his decision . . .

No, I can't face all that now.

But I'll have to face it eventually, won't I? Must face the unvarnished truth.

But not now.

Later.

Saturday, 19th November, 1988: I wake very early and write up my journal for yesterday. I've obviously experienced some sort of earthquake on the psychological level but I still don't feel I can deal with it and I'm determined to make no more demands on Nicholas. He's done enough. Do I need a therapist to help me process the information the earthquake has thrown up? Maybe. But first of all I've got to see my spiritual director and make my confession without delay. I shudder to think how close I came last night to going off the rails.

At seven I buzz Stacy and ask him to take the eight o'clock Saturday mass for the handful who turn up from the prayer-group; Nicholas has already left again to resume his weekend in Surrey. By nine I'm back once more in my old home, the headquarters of the Fordite monks, and making my confession. Simon's amazingly good. In fact he's so good that I even feel tempted to talk a little about the earthquake, and to my stupefaction he's most adroit, not making stupid comments and not egging me on when I run out of steam. It occurs to me that he has a head-start over any therapist I might consult because he knew Great-Uncle Cuthbert and can picture my peculiar adolescence all too clearly. In fact he can dimly remember me as I was then. Simon is years older than I am but he entered the Order in 1938 when I was seventeen and still quartered in the monks' guest-wing.

I leave feeling that I want to talk to him in depth about the earthquake. What an unexpected surprise! Maybe I'll never want to sack him again . . .

COMMENT: I'm going to survive.

Better still, if all goes well, I shall emerge from this upheaval with a new attitude to women. Or will I? It depends. It depends how far I can face up to the unvarnished truth and master it. It depends on whether I can achieve a genuine forgiveness of my mother. It depends on whether I can forgive Great-Uncle Cuthbert for brainwashing me and manipulating me and—

No. Can't think of that. Not now. Later.

Maybe I'll be healed but not cured. In other words, maybe I'll never now achieve a satisfactory intimate relationship with a woman but that won't matter because I'll be at peace as a celibate and benign towards women in general. No more sexist remarks. No more seeing women as evil temptresses. No more saying "priestesses" when I should be saying "women priests" . . .

Dear God, I hope the Synod doesn't approve the legislation for the ordination of women!

Well, it seems I certainly haven't experienced a miraculous cure, manifested in a conversion to the feminist cause. In fact I don't think I've experienced anything much yet except an enormous amount of pain and confusion, but buried in the midst of all that darkness is the spark of hope. "I'm going to survive," I wrote at the top of this section, and by the grace of God I shall.

Looking back on yesterday evening I see so clearly now how dependent Nicholas and I are on each other as we work together at St. Benet's. We're like two tightrope walkers on the high wire. Nicholas saves me when I lose my balance, and when he's tempted to play the Wonder Worker I'm there to rein him in. Yes, we've been very successful in outwitting the Devil's attempts to destroy us but there's no cause for complacency. Our old enemy's bound to try again to shake the high wire, and perhaps next time, having failed last night in his attempt to drag me down into the mud, he'll make Nicholas his prime target.

Well, that kind of language is all very old-fashioned and anthropomorphic, but I like to visualise evil in the form of a homicidal old bastard who's off his rocker, and I'm sure I'm right to be nervous about the future. My psyche keeps bleeping like an Early Warning System which is picking up news of an approaching nuclear attack. I suppose I could just be overwrought as the result of the earthquake, but I could also be unusually receptive, my psyche rubbed raw by stress.

How I wish Nicholas was back at the Rectory! I feel uneasy when he's too far away for me to keep an eye on him.

Sunday, 20th November, 1988: I celebrate Sunday mass. The crutches are a blank-blank nuisance, but I'm all right once I'm planted at the altar. All the prayer-group are there and the atmosphere's excellent. They don't mind me flailing around like some sort of mutant octopus. I suppose my specialist would say I should be resting, but so what? Celebrating mass makes me feel good. Getting back into my religious routine makes me feel even better. I know how to heal myself, thanks very much! I'll be throwing those crutches away in no time now.

To maintain my upbeat mood I get myself to St. Mary's Bourne Street for the morning Eucharist, and later on I turn up at All Saints Margaret Street for Solemn Evensong and Benediction. I know I ought to call it a day after this, particularly since the new hip's now acting stroppily, but I can't resist topping off this orgy of Anglo-Catholicism by dropping in at St. Edward's House for Compline. After all these services and taxi-journeys I feel physically feeble but mentally strong, very centred. If only I didn't get so tired! But I shouldn't find the tiredness surprising. This is the time when I'm supposed to be enduring an idle convalescence by the sea.

I'm sustained during my peregrinations—in icy, even snowy weather, I might add—by the magnificent lunch Alice cooks. She's supposed to be off-duty on weekends, but she cooks anyway on Sundays because she enjoys it. Stacy and I certainly enjoy the results.

In my bathroom that night I sing a Vera Lynn song. Then I fall asleep as soon as my head touches the pillow.

COMMENT: My psyche's quietened down as the result of the megadose of prayer and worship. Of course I was being neurotic earlier when I thought I could sense the Devil plotting to close in on Nicholas.

I look forward to a boring and unremarkable week in which nothing abnormal whatsoever occurs.

Monday, 21st November, 1988: I've just reread that idiotic last sentence. Short of saying to the Devil: "Do come in—so nice to see you!" and flinging open the front door of the Rectory with a smile, I can hardly have issued him with a more tempting invitation to unleash a volley of vicious kicks with his cloven hoof.

Switching to the language of psychology I can summarise the crisis less emotively by writing: There's a whole range of disordered emotions swirling at present around those most intimately connected with St. Benet's; I've been aware of these disordered emotions for some time, since I'm experienced enough to spot the symptoms, and the threats to our ministry became obvious today when various incidents occurred involving individuals who are either dysfunctional or alienated or neurotic—or possibly all three.

In other words, to call a spade a spade, the Devil made a multipronged attack and caused havoc.

The day begins well. I wake early, pray and meditate on a passage from the writings of Father Andrew, but as I dress (hip still feeling very much a foreign body) I remember an abnormality: although it's Monday morning Nicholas is still absent. Instead of returning to the City late last night he's stayed on in Surrey because this morning he has to drive down to the south coast. In Chichester there's to be a discreet gathering of those in the Church who exercise the ministry of deliverance, and Nicholas is not only reading a paper at the conference but conducting a seminar. Afterwards he plans to stay the night down there with friends before driving back to London early on Tuesday morning. He's spoken to me on the phone three times a day since our Friday evening session, but he'll be too busy to phone today. Never mind. I'm better now. I've recovered my equilibrium.

On the way home from the eight o'clock mass Stacy tells me he's going out with Tara again tonight, and he's so bouncy that I begin to wonder if I'm completely wrong about his sexual problems. Well, it wouldn't be the first time that Nicholas has been right and I've been up the creek. I decide to waste no more time worrying about Stacy at present.

So far so good. No kicks yet from the cloven hoof.

The morning passes uneventfully, and so does the lunch-time Eucharist. Another average day, I think as I heave myself home for lunch. Nothing to get excited about.

At the Rectory Alice serves a mushroom quiche, a big salad, plenty of cheese and warm brown bread. I see now I overreacted about Alice when I realised she had a psychic gift. I don't seriously believe, do I, that Nicholas would ever fall for her? He'd have to be completely destabilised for such a thing to happen, and I can't think of anything which would send Nicholas clean off his rocker. Any priest, of course, can suffer a breakdown if he gets the spiritual balance of his life wrong, but I'd kidnap Nicholas and see he got the best help long before his wobble on the high wire became fatal.

After lunch I take my usual short snooze in the bedsit before returning to the Healing Centre for a conference with Stacy; I'm currently training him in the delicate art of making pastoral visits to a mental hospital. Regularly we go to see our clients who have needed to be hospitalised, but because of my operation I've been unable to pay visits for a while and I need to find out how Stacy's been getting on.

He seems to have been avoiding a pastoral disaster but his notes are scruffy and inadequate. I drill into him how important it is to keep proper records but I'm careful to be encouraging as well and anyway he's too bouncy to be downcast. "Enjoy your evening with Tara!" I call after him as he bounds out of my consulting room, and he turns to give me a radiant smile. That Tara must be really turning him on. I'm astonished.

"And what are you doing tonight, you old villain?" he asks me so fondly that I don't even think of growling: "Insolent young puppy!" I say I'm going to the West End to buy a tape of Vera Lynn songs and then I'm going to be very "Establishment" and treat myself to a dinner at the Athenaeum.

"Who's Vera Lynn?" says Stacy, teasing me, and skips off with a laugh when he sees the expression on my face.

Yet again, so far so good.

I spend the rest of the afternoon chairing a finance committee meeting. Nicholas said I wasn't to do this, as I'm supposed to be convalescing, but anything as dull as a finance committee meeting is bound to be restful. Bernard, as office manager, makes a long speech about the new facsimile machine while I mentally switch off and pray for Venetia. I hate technology.

Back in my consulting room at five o'clock I'm just sorting through the pile of rubbish on my desk when I uncover a flyer for a special lecture tonight at Sion College. Some monk's talking about Benedictine spirituality in the modern world, and I particularly want to hear him because I've read several of his books; the special lecture is to celebrate the fact that he's just published another. Am I too tired to go? Certainly not! (I refuse to let this new hip get the better of me.) Leaving the Centre I hurtle down to the Embankment in a taxi and arrive at my destination ten minutes before the lecture's due to begin.

I'd forgotten the staircase that has to be climbed. Triple-hell! I scrabble away, trying to work out how to combine the crutches with the handrail, and various kind, well-meaning people offer to help but I brush them aside. There's nothing wrong with my arms and nothing wrong with the handrail. I can haul myself up, and if the hip doesn't like it, that's too bad.

Huffing and puffing I finally reach the top of the stairs, adjust my crutches and move forward into the beautiful library where all the Sion College lectures take place. A fair number of people are already assembled: clergy, theology undergraduates from King's and an assortment of the retired ranging from elderly gentlemen in shabby raincoats to little old ladies with hats like tea-cosies. They're all gossiping away in the semi-circle of seats. Moving forward into the room I spot a knot of militant homosexual clergy heaving ahead of me and automatically I veer away towards the front row. Then I stop dead. I've briefly registered the presence of a familiar thatch of red hair. Taking another look at these homosexuals, at least two of whom, so I've heard, spend their Saturday nights haunting gay bars and worse, I spy in their midst none other than the curate of St. Benet's-by-the-Wall, the Reverend Eustace McGovern. Moreover he's bursting with vitality and obviously having the whale of a time. No sign, of course, of Miss Tara Hopkirk from the Isle of Dogs.

He sees me a second after I see him and his face turns as red as his hair.

Altering direction I edge up the half-empty row in front of him and stop opposite his chair. "Good evening, Stacy," I say, and allow my glance to flick sardonically over his companions.

"Oh hi!" he says, trying to be casual but now crimson with embarrassment. "I thought you were going to the Athenaeum!"

"I changed my mind. I see you did too."

Stacy hangs his head and looks the picture of guilt. I feel humiliated for him.

Meanwhile the militants, all of whom are London-based and known to me, have realised exactly what's going on and are trying to work out how to protect their new chum. One of them makes the wrong move and drawls: "Lewis my love, I can't tell you how intimidating you look! Are you psyching yourself up to wallop us with those crutches?" But the ringleader of the bunch, a man I detest, shuts him up by saying crisply: "John, do you really have to play Dame Edna this evening?" and to me he adds in the friendliest of voices: "How are you, Lewis? I was sorry to hear you'd been in hospital."

"That's past history now," I say, "and I'm recovering fast."

To my surprise he asks a couple of other friendly questions, just the kind of questions a good priest should ask, and in the end he says with perfect sincerity: "It's good to see you again—won't you sit with us?" That's when I realise I've been outmanoeuvred. If I refuse, I'll look the most unchristian of swines.

"Move over, Dame Edna," he says to the silly one next to him, "and give up your seat to Father Lewis."

Meanwhile a couple of heterosexual priests have spotted my plight and are trying to rescue me. "Lewis!" calls one, and: "Over here!" calls the other, patting the seat next to him, but I suddenly see the funny side of the situation. "No thanks!" I call back. "I'm making a pastoral call on the gay community!"

All the queers cheer. Dame Edna vacates his seat, lifts away the chair in front of me and enables me to step forward into the right row. The very charming, very able ringleader—of course it's Gilbert Tucker—laughs as I plonk myself down next to him, and when he offers me his right hand I find myself trying to recall why I've always disliked this delightful priest so much—but the moment we shake hands I remember. Oh yes! He turns a blind eye to gay priests who kick chastity in the teeth, and says Jesus would understand and approve of their conduct. Wonderful! These priests have an unintegrated sex-life in which their sexual energy's not channelled into their work but split off from it into episodes quite contrary to their calling, yet Tucker has the nerve to claim his support for these creatures is backed by the most integrated human being of all time. Our Lord would certainly have been compassionate in considering such conduct. But *approving?* As the tennis star Mr. McEnroe would snarl: "You *can't* be serious!"

I spend the lecture seething that such behaviour should be tolerated in the London diocese, and I wonder what the great homosexual priests of the nineteenth century, all of whom rated chastity and obedience so highly, would have thought of such a debasement of their Christian standards.

When the lecture finishes, Stacy says a rapid goodbye to the gay set and mutters that he'll come home with me. In the taxi he starts to stammer something but I growl: "Later!" and shut him up. On our arrival home Alice, having been instructed earlier that neither Stacy nor I would require dinner, emerges from the hell-hole to offer us a meal, but I shoo her back to her television.

"We'll talk in Nicholas's study," I say abruptly to Stacy, and he creeps along behind me like a puppy that's already been whipped.

Dumping myself in the swivel-chair at Nicholas's desk I watch as Stacy crumples into the chair nearby. He's now looking so miserable that I know this would be quite the wrong moment to take a tough line, so I say in my kindest voice: "My dear Stacy, this isn't first-century Rome. You're not about to be thrown to the lions. I assure you you're going to survive this conversation."

But my dry humour, which is supposed to lighten the atmosphere, has the reverse effect and the boy bursts into tears.

I'm most surprised. After all, I hardly caught him *in flagrante* with another man. Obviously the scene at Sion College embarrassed him, but it had its funny side and I behaved sportingly enough. So, I ask myself, what's now triggering this melodramatic reaction? Can it really be just because he has no alternative but to admit the sexual preferences which were on open display tonight? Surely not! Nicholas has made it clear to him that facing up to one's true nature represents an important step on the road to maturity—and to being a good priest. So why are the taps now being turned on?

Quickly I say: "Stacy, whatever your problems, Nicholas and I will stand by you. There's no need to behave as if you're about to get the sack."

But obviously he has trouble believing this because the taps remain turned on. I spend a long moment trying to work out how they can be turned off, but in the end I just hand him the box of Kleenex nearby and say calmly but firmly: "Okay, what appears to be your primary problem here?" It seems plain that my first task is to encourage him to talk.

Slivers of information begin to dribble out of him. He confesses he said he was going out with Tara in order to convince me he was just like any other bloke—and he's tried so hard to get interested in girls, he really has. But no matter how much he likes them he doesn't feel comfortable when they're keen to "snog." (Revolting word.) He wonders if that makes him gay, but he doesn't want to snog men either. The gay activists say cheerfully that if he doesn't want to snog girls he must be gay but he shouldn't worry about snogging anything at the moment, since his prime task is to relax and grow comfortable with his true sexual orientation. But Stacy's not happy with this advice. He says that if he's gay it would "kill" his mother and "destroy" his three sisters, all of whom have no idea he was seduced in his teens by a much older man, and anyway he knows that what he really wants has nothing to do with gays at all. He wants to be a Nick-clone, married with two children and living happily ever after. That's what his mother wants. That's what his sisters want. And that's what he wants because his family means more to him than anything else in the world. He does so miss Siobhan—sob—and Sinead—sob, sob—and most of all his darling Aisling—sob, sob, sob, sob, sob—

Of course he's queer as a coot (imagine behaving like a stuffed dummy when a girl's keen for a kiss!) but I have to tread with great care here because the boy's so pathetically immature. It's time to play the cuddly old priest again. "I'm most extremely sorry to see you so unhappy, Stacy," I say gently, "and I can see now that this is a situation which has been putting you under a lot of stress. I assume you've discussed this problem in depth with your spiritual director?"

"Oh no!" he says surprised. "It didn't seem to have anything to do with prayer."

There's so much wrong with this statement that I'm struck dumb, but by a heroic effort I get my tongue in working order again after ten seconds. Meanwhile I note that Stacy's dangerously unintegrated, having split off his spiritual life from his carnal problems, and that his spiritual director (chosen with enormous care by Nicholas and me) has been unbelievably incompetent. In fact the man's got to be suffering from Alzheimer's. I can think of no other explanation that's plausible.

I manage to say levelly to Stacy: "Well, never mind your spiritual director for the moment. Perhaps the best way forward might be for you to see a therapist who has no connection with St. Benet's and who could talk all this through with you in neutral surroundings."

"Oh, I couldn't do that! I wouldn't want Nick to know I'm not on top of this problem! He thinks I've got it all sorted!"

"Then Nicholas must be disillusioned. Otherwise there'll be more incidents like the one tonight and you'll make no progress at all."

"I know you're a queer-basher, I know what you must be thinking, but just because I wound up sitting with the gays tonight doesn't mean—" He dissolves into sobs again.

"Look, Stacy," I say, still speaking kindly but aware of my patience fraying at the seams, "brace up, there's a good chap, and let's just clear up two fundamental misunderstandings. First of all the real error you made tonight was *not* that you wound up sitting with the gays. Amazing though this may seem to you in your distraught state, that's not a sin. The real error was that you lied to me about Tara and compromised your integrity. In a small community like this we can't afford to lie to one another and lead double-lives, because the essential falseness of such behaviour always winds up polluting the atmosphere and undermining trust. Do you understand that?"

He nods, snorting into a fresh Kleenex. He's nearly exhausted the tissues in the box by this time.

"Your lie this evening stemmed directly from the problems you're having about your sexual identity," I pursue, ploughing on doggedly, "and this is why it's urgent that you have help in finding a solution. It's also vital that you keep nothing back from Nicholas, who as your Rector is responsible for your welfare. Now, the second fundamental misunderstanding"—I pause to come up for air—"which is minor in comparison with the first but which needs to be corrected in the interests of truth, is that I'm not a queer-basher. I object to no human being on account of his or her taste in snogging. What I object to are the lies, the self-deception and the double-life which all arise from a poorly integrated sexuality. Do you understand what I'm saying?"

He nods again drearily and snorts into the last Kleenex.

I grab another deep breath and slog on. "Nobody's perfect," I say. "We all have our flaws, but our job is to recognise them, face up to them and take the appropriate action so that they can be transformed into creative, not destructive, forces within our personalities. Take me, for example. I've got a very flawed sexuality. I made a complete balls-up of my marriage and I've never been able to sustain a successful relationship with a woman. That's my infirmity, my handicap, my cross—call it what you like—and in a sense this puts me in the same league as the homosexuals, but I absolutely believe that the answer to a poorly integrated sexuality is *not* to lead a double-life and *not* to bob around low bars in order to pick up rough trade. During the course of my life I've proved that I'm at my most integrated—and happiest—when I'm celibate. Of course celibacy can be tough and I'm not pretending I've always lived up to the ideal, but by sublimating—not repressing but *sublimating*—my sex-drive I've managed to live a full, rewarding life in which I've been of service to others. And on the occasions when I did fall by the wayside, I've *never* deluded myself by saying my lapses were right, I've *never* demanded special consideration because of my handicap, and I've *never* been stupid enough to whine: 'Oh, Jesus would approve of my occasional nights on the tiles because that's the way I've been designed by God!' God didn't design me to be damaged. I got this way in the school of hard knocks and now I've got to work hard cooperating with God to redeem the mess . . . Are you listening?"

He nods but he's not. He's weeping silently again and there are no more tissues left in the box.

"What I'm trying to say," I resume, searching without success for a handkerchief, "is that there's no flaw or handicap so grisly that it can't be redeemed and translated into a positive force for the good. But first of all we have to acknowledge our flaws—we have to 'name the demons,' as the old-fashioned religious language puts it, so that they can be brought under control. That's why I'm suggesting you seek help from a therapist who specialises in your type of problem. You need to 'name the demons' so that you can conquer them and become a mature, well-integrated priest."

Stacy whispers pathetically: "I don't want a therapist. I don't have demons. I just don't want to snog with anyone at present, that's all. I'm sorry I got mixed up with the gays tonight, but I promise I won't go near them again."

Dear God, he's understood nothing! "Stacy—"

"All I want," says Stacy desperately, "is to go on living here with Nick and slogging my guts out to be the kind of priest he wants. Nick's the most wonderful guy in the world, and if I let him down and have to leave St. Benet's my life wouldn't be worth living, but I'm not going to let him down. I'm going to keep taking out Tara and eventually I'll snog her and then everything will be okay."

Once again my tongue ceases to function.

I'm appalled.

****

(Had to put the asterisks in—no words seemed adequate to describe the quality of the hiatus which then took place in the conversation.)

Ye gods and little fishes! The boy's in love with Nicholas—and this is no harmless hero-worship; this is homoerotic lunacy which will obstruct Stacy's journey to homosexual maturity and eventually bog Nicholas down with a pastoral problem the size of an elephant. Moreover—and this is the real killer-threat to St. Benet's—Stacy shows no desire to face up to his problems and no ability even to understand why he should do so. We just can't afford this sort of immature, unaware, unperceptive person on the team at the Healing Centre. In our kind of ministry we need to rely one hundred per cent on our colleagues, and how could one ever have sufficient confidence in a priest who's incapable of spiritual growth and psychologically as dumb as an ox?

We took Stacy on in the belief that he had potential, that he would develop and improve. But we were deluding ourselves. The boy's a disaster. If he stays there'll inevitably be a pastoral mess of the worst kind: either he'll make a catastrophic balls-up in treating a client or he'll get engaged to please Nicholas and then go cottaging in secret when the strain of a live-a-lie life becomes too much for him.

I foresee screaming headlines in the *News of the World*, the Archdeacon descending on us like the wrath of God and the Archbishop phoning the Bishop of London to ask just what on earth is going on in his charismatic backyard. The reputation of the Healing Centre would be tainted. Nicholas's ministry could well be washed up, closed down, wiped out . . .

Game, set and match to the Devil.

Still reeling from this kick from the cloven hoof I regain control of my tongue but find I can only say feebly to Stacy: "Look, I don't think we can profitably continue this conversation tonight. Let's wait till Nicholas gets back before we explore the situation further."

I'm in such a pole-axed state that I forget Stacy's longing to keep Nicholas in ignorance, and the result's a disaster.

"You can't tell Nick!" yelps Stacy in panic. "You've got to treat every word of this conversation as confidential!"

Triple-hell! Now I'm really stymied! But as a priest there's only one response I can give, so I give it. "All right, Stacy," I say. "I'll keep my mouth shut, but I can't stress too strongly that you should tell Nicholas everything before he receives feedback from other people and puts two and two together. How do you think you're going to keep the incident at Sion College quiet? Not only is he in close touch with Tucker about our AIDS programme, but he sees several of the other priests regularly at the local clergy meetings."

But Stacy just says desperately: "I'll talk my way out of that," and dissolving into sobs again he bolts at last from the room.

* * * * * * * * * * * * * * * *

(I'm getting fond of using asterisks to denote a horrifying hiatus.)

Well, I try to calm down but it's hard. My thoughts are scurrying all over the place. Surely Stacy doesn't imagine he can stay at the Rectory for ever? It's his second curacy and he's due to be here three years. Then he'll move on, just as a curate always should. But could he perhaps be seeing himself moving on not to a parish or a hospital chaplaincy but to a salaried job at the Healing Centre? We'd like to take on another priest some day, particularly now I'm getting older, and Nicholas has probably said as much to Stacy—who's now dreaming of a permanent niche for himself at St. Benet's. Yes, I'm sure that's it. Stacy must know his work leaves a lot to be desired, but obviously he's sidestepped that knowledge by kidding himself all will be well so long as he tries to be a Nick-clone. Dear God, what a mess . . .

If the situation wasn't so dangerous it would be tragic, of course—tragic and pathetic. Poor little Stacy. But what on earth am I going to do?

Unfortunately I must leave that question dangling as I have no idea how to answer it, and anyway it's time to describe the second kick from the cloven hoof.

Well, after Stacy's bolted sobbing upstairs to the curate's flat, I beetle to the kitchen, invade the refrigerator and eat three slices of mushroom quiche left over from lunch, a lettuce leaf, a small pot of coleslaw and a large bowl of rum raisin ice cream. I wash all this down with a double-whisky, generously diluted with repeated dashes of sodawater, and afterwards I feel more human. Back in the bedsit I soothe my nerves further by listening to Bach, and I'm just thinking that the possibility of sleep might not, after all, be remote, when I hear the doorbell ring.

I glance at my watch. Half-past ten. Too late for a social call, but certainly not too late for a desperate soul, drunk, drugged, suicidal, homicidal or just plain homeless who fancies some Christian attention. I struggle into the hall. Can I manage for a few seconds without my crutches? Of course—if I'm more or less stationary. Setting them aside I grab the rounders bat which we keep by the front door and prepare for action. I'm hardly an illustration of the command "Love Thy Neighbour" at this moment, but there's nothing particularly Christian about being foolhardy and although the City's crime rate is low there's always the chance of a priest-hating psychopath turning up. With my hand on the latch I peep through the spy-hole.

Bad news.

My visitor's Francie Parker and she's clearly off her rocker.

****

Francie hasn't been at St. Benet's today. She had to go down to Kent to take her mother to hospital for an X-ray. Perhaps the strain of her absence from St. Benet's has unhinged her—but maybe she would have become unhinged today anyway, whether or not she'd received her regular weekday fix of Nicholas Darrow.

I know straight away she's unhinged because her appearance is disordered. Francie's an attractive woman and she normally dresses well, but at this moment her hair's wild, she looks as if she's wearing a nightdress under her open coat and I'll bet her feet are clad only in slippers. I realise that either she wants to create the impression that she's dashed straight out of the house after an outstandingly brutal assault, or else she's so far over the edge that she has no idea she's wearing the wrong clothes. But whatever's going on she's in crisis. Discarding the rounders bat I warily open the door.

"Oh Lewis—"

Now that we're face to face it seems very clear to me that she's not a terrified, beaten-up victim reeling to the Rectory for help. She's rosy-cheeked, bright-eyed and mainlining on adrenaline—high as a kite no doubt, but I'd stake my reputation it's not violence she's high on. I'd also stake my reputation that I was right in my suspicions of Francie, Nicholas was wrong, and now we're up to our dog-collars in a grade-A clerical nightmare.

"Francie!" I exclaim, unable to decide what my opening sentence should be but knowing that these two syllables will buy me a little time to make up my mind. I clasp my small pectoral cross and pray for inspiration. None comes.

"Can I come in?"

"Of course—why not?" I say agreeably, waving her across the threshold. This may seem the height of recklessness, but I'm trying to be pragmatic; slamming the door in Francie's face will hardly solve the problem. What I've got to do is to defuse her by diagnosing what's going on and getting her to a doctor. After all, the likelihood is that I'm in no danger myself; it's Nicholas she's gunning for, not me.

But while I'm reaching this sensible conclusion I'm intensely aware that Francie might be operating at a level which defies sensible conclusions. I am, after all, a former exorcist, and even though I retired from the ministry of deliverance after getting booted out of my last diocese I'm not suffering from amnesia on this particular subject. The fact is I could be in as much danger as Nicholas would be if he were now here at the Rectory; if the Devil's annexed Francie's personality, then all manner of atrocities could happen.

But having acknowledged this most dramatic of possibilities, I decide it's unlikely that Francie is, in the classical sense, possessed. I see none of the famous symptoms, and Francie's certainly not vomiting all over me, wetting herself or going into a tail-spin at the sight of the cross on my chest. Much more probable is the theory that the Devil could be infiltrating the Rectory by riding on a mental disorder which was already present in her, and that means I've got to focus on the mental disorder, not the Devil, in order to figure out exactly how to handle this situation.

At that point I switch modes of thought. I don't stop thinking in the old-fashioned religious metaphors—that mental process is still continuing on one level of my mind and I keep a tight grip on my cross—but on another level I start thinking in the language of psychology. What sort of mental illness is Francie experiencing here? Is this just a neurotic acting-out or is it a psychotic episode? Is she a hysteric? Is this some sort of dissociated fugue? Or is she just pie-eyed while under the influence of a romantic love which has veered towards grand opera rather than soap opera? We all know how nutty people can be when they're in love but we don't normally judge them clinically insane and lock them up in a mental hospital until they feel better.

"Let's go to the kitchen," I say pleasantly to Francie after this lightning review of diagnoses ranging from the melodramatic to the banal. "It's warmer in there."

"Thanks!" Francie's genuinely appreciative, perfectly friendly. "Oh Lewis, I'm so sorry to call so late—what on earth can you be thinking!"

I try a touch of reality to see how she reacts. "I'm thinking you must be very cold in your nightgown and slippers."

"I was so terrified that I didn't even stop to dress!"

So she's still pushing the fantasy. But is she a hysteric who's hypnotised herself into genuinely believing that what she says is true, or is she well aware that she's lying in order to further a carefully constructed plan? I've no idea, but at least she's not hearing voices which command her to kill every priest in sight; I'm tempted to discard the possibility that this is a psychotic episode. I'm also tempted to discard the possibility that she's a hysteric. Francie's never shown signs of having a hysteric personality—although I need to remember that a traumatic incident can induce uncharacteristic reactions even in people not normally vulnerable to dissociative states.

"I'll make you some tea," I say, playing for time again as we enter the kitchen.

"Lovely—but Lewis, aren't you supposed to be convalescing? On second thoughts I mustn't keep you up when you're probably longing to rest! I'll just go straight upstairs to Nick's flat."

"I'm afraid you'll find it empty," I say blandly. "If you'd been at the Centre today you'd have heard that he's away on business."

This information really puts a spanner in the works. Glancing back over my shoulder as I fill the kettle I see the fury flash in her eyes before she regains her self-control and at that point I strongly suspect she knows exactly what she's doing. But on the other hand, as I have to remind myself, she'd still be cross about Nicholas's absence even if she'd hypnotised herself into a state which had little connection with reality.

"Nick's not here?" she demands incredulously, hardly able to comprehend such misfortune.

"Unfortunately not, but never mind, Francie, I'm more than willing to help you! As soon as we've had tea I'll call the police."

"*Police?*" This isn't in the script at all. In a flash she sees she has to forget her plan to bed Nicholas tonight and concentrate on preserving the fantasy of the sadistic husband.

"The man must be taken to court and charged with assault!" I say firmly. "He's obviously so dangerous that no other option is possible!"

"But Lewis, you don't understand . . ." Her bosom heaves. She starts to weep. It's Kleenex time again at the Rectory.

I decide to take a risk and initiate another infusion of reality. "My dear," I say in my dryest voice as I produce the Kleenex, "I'm afraid you must take it as settled that I understand all too well."

She flinches, staring at me not merely with anger but with a new rush of incredulity. Is this—*can* this be dear, sweet, kind, lovable Lewis, cuddly old priest, who never fails to be benign towards bouncy, flouncy Francie, the Befriender who's always so charming and chic? That pushover Dr. Jekyll, she realises with horror, has suddenly transformed himself into a most formidable Mr. Hyde, and her brilliant scheme for seducing Nicholas is now in very serious danger indeed.

"Sit down," I order, waving a crutch at the kitchen table, "and let's both observe a minute's silence. I need to make the tea and you need to reconsider your position."

Silence falls, broken only by the sound of Francie's tasteful sobs. I suspect she has no pressing inclination to cry; she's too furious. But she feels she has to go through the motions in order to conjure up the image of a deeply wronged heroine.

Meanwhile I'm reminding myself that I have to be very, very careful. I'm so keen to defuse Francie that I could wind up making a bad mess. What I want, of course, is for her to volunteer a confession and agree to accept medical help. What I don't want is for her to retreat into some new dream-world where medical help has to be resisted at all costs—or where she hears a voice telling her that arch-villain Lewis Hall must be killed in order to protect and preserve Her Great Love. Dismantling fantasies can be the psychological equivalent of dealing with dynamite. I can almost hear the screams of a dozen psychiatrists begging me to go no further.

"Now, Francie," I say at last when the tea is made and we're sitting facing each other at the kitchen table, "you mustn't think I'm not willing to listen. Tell me, please, every detail of this latest brutal assault which, as usual, has left no visible marks. You have my full attention."

But she's cleverer than I'd anticipated. She's prepared some evidence, and as it's evidence designed to be shown to Nicholas, it's deposited in a most strategic location. Jumping to her feet she sheds her coat, tears down the straps of her nightdress and displays her breasts.

Very nice. I'm exceedingly partial to breasts. These are a trifle scratched, but there's nothing there I couldn't overlook if I had other purposes in mind.

"Where are all the bruises?" I demand. "Where are the welts and cuts? All I see is possible evidence that when your husband last made love to you he clawed instead of stroked! That certainly proves he needs to upgrade his sexual technique but it doesn't prove he's a wife-beater!"

She's so furious now that she can hardly speak but she manages to hiss: "You swine! Of course everyone knows you're a repressed homosexual who's revolted by women!"

"Oh yes?" I say vaguely. "Who's 'everyone'?" As I speak I'm moving to the corner of the room and activating the intercom. "Alice," I say a moment later before Francie can dream up a reply, "come to the kitchen at once, please. Francie's here, she's very upset and I'm sure she'd like another woman to be present."

"No!" screams Francie, but the order's been given. Panic-stricken she wrenches back the straps of her nightdress and drags on her coat. Her hands are shaking with rage and also, I sense, with shock. We could be approaching the moment when she's too rattled to do anything except come clean.

I decide it's time to soft-pedal. "Sorry, Francie," I say regretfully, reviving Dr. Jekyll. "Believe me, I have every sympathy for you in your distress, but if I'm to help you survive this very genuine ordeal, we've got to agree on what the ordeal actually is." I metaphorically lob her a rope which she can use to haul herself to safety—if she doesn't decide to use it to hang herself. "Is the damage internal?" I say earnestly. "Is the damage in fact not non-existent but so appalling that you can't bring yourself to describe it?"

She decides to hang herself. That's sad. I was so hoping she'd reject this counter-fantasy and retreat into the truth. "Yes," she says, remembering to sob again. "Yes, that's it. The damage is all inside."

Do I snap the trap shut or not? I could say that in that case we should summon Val at once to gather the medical evidence for the police, but that proposal might well send Francie over the edge. Maybe I should back off and try to bring the confession to birth in some other way.

I'm still reviewing my options when Alice walks in, charmingly rotund in a cherry-red dressing-gown. This is obviously my evening for being stimulated by women in various stages of undress, but I regret to say that by this time I'm too exhausted to appreciate such unexpected treats. Revving up some energy from somewhere I smile at Alice and say: "How good of you to come so promptly, but I suspect we may not need you here after all. Do we need Alice, Francie?"

Francie shakes her head. She can't look at Alice, and this is probably because Alice represents normality, the world of sanity which will somehow have to be re-entered when this gala performance comes to an end. I'm now quite certain that although Francie's seriously nuts about Nicholas, so nuts that she requires treatment, she knows she's fantasising about the wife-beating, just as she knows she can't murder nasty old priests who are sceptical about her "ripping yarns." Flipping back into the religious mode of thought I confirm to myself: no possession; exorcism unnecessary; the laying-on of hands, prayer and community support required during and after the appropriate medical treatment.

And the Devil? He'll back off once she enters the healing process because he's not fundamentally interested in her at all. His interest is in the ministry of St. Benet's, and he'll look around for another Trojan horse to ride.

"Thank you, Alice," I say to my witness. "I'm sorry to have disturbed you."

Alice, velvety eyes wide with bemusement and fascination, withdraws with reluctance.

"All right, Francie," I say, instantly becoming much cuddlier. "I know I've been behaving like a brute, but that's only because I'm so anxious to help you and I can't help you unless I know what the truth is here. Now, let me take your last allegation absolutely seriously in order to prove to you that I'm one hundred per cent committed to your welfare. Should we send for Val so that you can have an internal examination? You may well be severely damaged, and I'd be failing in my duty as a priest if I didn't pull out all the stops to get you to a doctor."

I think I've done it. I think I've cracked it. Francie knows she can't see a doctor, but she doesn't blame me for urging this course of action, because (she thinks) I'm acting not out of scepticism but out of full-blooded Christian concern. The moment's come when she has to abandon the fantasy of the internal injuries, but that's a viable course of action now because I'm not going to be an unsympathetic brute, crowing over her humiliation, but a cuddly old priest panting to be pastoral—and isn't there something immensely comforting about the thought that despite all the horrors of the present scene I'm still rooting for her so hard that I'm oozing empathy from every pore?

"Oh, Lewis!" Francie whispers, teetering on the brink of unburdening herself, and as we sink down into our chairs again, she covers her face with her hands. Then she says in a muffled voice: "Give me a moment, would you? I've got to work something out."

This sounds promising. I wait in dead silence and will her to confess.

Finally she says, letting her hands fall but not looking at me: "I don't want Val."

"Okay."

"There's no internal damage."

"Okay."

"Harry *is* a monster, but . . ." She hesitates, needing reassurance.

"We'll treat this room as the confessional, Francie. I'll hold anything you say to me in confidence."

Tears well up in her eyes again. Reaching for the box of Kleenex I prepare to feed the tissues to her one by one.

"I've thought of divorce, of course," says Francie, dabbing her eyes genteelly, like a suburban housewife mourning the breakdown of a cherished vacuum cleaner. "But I've got no money and I know that

Harry, being a lawyer, would manipulate everything so that I only got a pittance. And he'd try and grab the children too, I know he would—I might well end up with nothing. So I've got to forget about a divorce. It's not on."

The odd thing is that I feel there's something phoney about this speech even though I can see every sentence is probably true. However, sometimes when people are under great emotional strain they do sound phoney. I decide my best course is to press on.

"But how are you going to stand being married?" I say in my most concerned voice as I ease another tissue from the box.

"I can stand it so long as I have my work at St. Benet's," says Francie. There's a pause before she finally adds: "And Nick."

"Uh-huh . . . Can you go on with that a bit?"

She does go on with it. In fact the dam breaks and everything streams out. She's madly, passionately, desperately in love with Nick, but she's kept it to herself because she knows that if anyone at the Centre realises she's in the grip of a grand passion instead of the usual harmless hero-worship, she'll be rated unstable and sacked, and she couldn't live without seeing Nick five days a week, especially as she's been having such wonderful chats with him about Harry's sadism.

I don't ask about the sadism. We've reached the stage where it's tacitly understood that the sadism is a fiction. Besides, I'm keen to sharpen the focus on Nicholas.

"But since you love him so much," I murmur, "I'm sure you must want more than mere chats. In the circumstances that would be only natural."

She nods, relieved that I'm being so sympathetic and non-judgemental. "But what you've got to understand," she says earnestly, "is that I can never marry Nick, even when he's free."

"*When* he's free?"

"Oh, I'm sure he'll divorce Rosalind soon! He'll want to clear the decks to prove his love to me!"

"Ah."

"But of course even if he's single we can never marry."

"No? But surely—"

"Oh, you mustn't think I'm so blinded by love that I've lost touch with reality, Lewis! Of course I'd risk divorcing Harry, despite all the difficulties, if the man I loved was available for marriage, but Nick'll never be available for me, will he? He could never marry a divorced woman. Not in his present situation. Not as Rector of St. Benet's."

"Hm."

"He could survive a divorce from Rosalind, of course. Nowadays that wouldn't affect his ministry at all—well, hardly at all, provided it was a friendly divorce with no scandal. But the problem for the divorced priest comes when he wants to remarry. He might get away with marrying a virgin—or a very devout, very presentable widow. But a divorcée . . . No, that would be impossible. It would offend a lot of people here—the trustees wouldn't like it—the Bishop would object . . . No, no, no, such a disaster must never be allowed to happen! Believe me, Lewis, I wouldn't do *anything* which would harm Nick's wonderful career here!"

"That's extremely noble and self-sacrificing of you, Francie. So how do you deal with this difficult problem of being deeply in love with Nicholas yet unable to marry him?"

"I'm willing to be his mistress. I came here tonight because I thought it was time I made that clear. Of course I know that's technically immoral, as we're both married to other people, but a great love transcends everything, doesn't it, because God is love and I'm sure he'd understand and forgive us."

With an enormous effort I ignore this dotty updating of the Ten Commandments and say with a patience which borders on the superhuman: "But Francie, wouldn't this too have an adverse effect on Nicholas's ministry?"

"Absolutely not!" she insists with shining eyes. "You see, *no one would ever know!*" She's mad as a hatter. She has no conception of the spiritual health and spiritual fitness needed to underpin Nicholas's ministry, no conception of how a double-life would destroy his integrity and finish him. She thinks the only problem is the danger of being found out. "I'm willing to be endlessly discreet for his sake!" she announces. "His welfare would always come first and I know I could make him happier than he's ever been in his life . . ." She waffles on in this vein for a while and ends in serving up some profoundly questionable ideas about the Darrows' marriage.

"Rosalind doesn't understand him—he couldn't possibly be happy with her—I'm sure she's hopeless in bed, whereas I—"

"Quite so."

"Of course we'd only have the occasional night together, but just the occasional night would be such heaven! Nick's so wonderful, so sensitive, so intelligent, so attractive, so—"

"Absolutely."

"And what's so miraculous is that my feelings are reciprocated! When I think of all the looks he's given me—and the special smiles—and the remarks which are capable of more than one meaning—"

I know straight away that this is a fantasy I should make no attempt to unravel. This one's for the professionals because it's the genuine article: the product of a sick mind, a lie which Francie genuinely believes to be true. The fantasy of the sadistic husband, in contrast, was a carefully constructed lie concocted for a specific purpose, and Francie knew all the time that the story was false.

The memory of this lie diverts me for a moment, but I want to haul her back anyway from the realms of fantasy so I interrupt her romantic drivel by asking: "Francie, can we just backtrack for a second? I quite understand now why you talked to Nicholas about Harry's sadism, but why did you involve me as well? What was the point of confiding in us both?"

She stares. This is certainly a question she hadn't expected and I see at once that she's not sure how to reply. Finally she says in an offhand way: "It seemed right somehow. Nick might have wanted to discuss the case without being hampered by the confidentiality rules. Well, as I was saying—"

Odd. I'm not sure what to make of this. I feel I've missed a trick somewhere, but I can't imagine what the trick is.

Meanwhile Francie's still raving about Nicholas. I wait till she pauses for breath and then say: "Francie my dear, there's no doubt in my mind that you're in a very tight corner, but don't worry because I'll stand by you and give you all the help I possibly can. What I suggest now is that we resume this very important conversation tomorrow when we're both fresh—and maybe Robin should sit in on the session. I feel I need assistance here in order to give you the very best advice."

"Oh, but I don't want Robin to know! I don't want anyone but you to know! I owe it to Nick to preserve the maximum discretion!"

"Of course. But Francie, how are you going to manage your work in these circumstances? I really feel you need some input from Robin as you try to deal with all this—"

"No, no—I can handle everything! My love's transforming me, you see, allowing me to work better than ever—it's a gift from God, and God will guide me through the future!"

"But my dear, gifts from God seldom come packaged with user-friendly instructions, and he'll almost certainly be calling other people to guide you—"

"Exactly! He'll call Nick, and Nick will give me all the advice I can ever need! So there's no point in bothering Robin, is there?"

I'm getting nowhere and I've *got* to get this woman into therapy, if not into hospital. I'm most reluctant to give the fantasy a shove, but perhaps if I'm ultra-careful I can risk a small prod.

"Francie," I say, "I fully accept how strongly you feel about Nicholas, but I really do think I'd be negligent if I didn't mention a couple of facts for you to consider. The first fact is that it's very hard for an outsider to work out what exactly goes on in any marriage. The second fact is that the Darrows' marriage has lasted twenty years, and this length of time is almost certainly not without significance. Are you sure you understand the role Rosalind plays in Nicholas's life? I'm not at all sure I do."

Naturally she doesn't want to hear any of this. She tries to block off the implications of my speech by crying passionately: "I love him, I love him, I love him!" but I've put a little smudge on the glorious Technicolor landscape of her grand passion, and with any luck she'll soon become depressed. People can never conceive of the need to seek help when they're in a state of euphoria, but give them a touch of depression and they're more inclined to beat a path to the doctor's door.

"I can see your feelings for him are very strong, Francie," I say truthfully, knowing I have to lay on the sympathy with a shovel now to calm her down, "and that's why we should continue this discussion tomorrow—just you and I—when we're both fresh. Then we can do the subject justice. Now before you go, let's pause to pray that this very challenging situation will be resolved in a way pleasing to God—who cares, of course, for the welfare of both you and Nicholas."

She raises no objection and somehow I manage to rearrange these words into a pattern which is both a genuine plea to God for help and also a soothing reassurance to Francie. I'm very tired now and all my ambivalence towards this sick woman, who's revelling in her destructive fantasy, is relentlessly sapping my energy, but Francie finds the prayer meaningful and snuffles with emotion. Grabbing a handful of Kleenex for the journey home she whispers: "I'm sorry I said such awful things to you earlier."

"You were very upset, I realised that."

"Of course I know you're not really a homosexual."

She sounds very sure. Maybe I looked a little more greedily at those breasts than I should have done. In haste I say courteously: "Let me escort you to the front door."

In the hall I ask her where her husband is, and when she says drearily: "Hong Kong," I receive a glimpse into the heart of her sickness. The world's so small nowadays. Successful men go jetting all over the place, and usually not with their neglected wives who wind up craving all the love and attention which no longer come their way.

Poor Francie.

But dear God, what a kick from the cloven hoof . . .

****

Well, it's still the evening of Monday, the twenty-first of November, and the third and final kick, the one that's aimed to knock St. Benet's clean off its foundations, is still to come. But when Francie leaves, I don't know that. As soon as the tail-lights of her car have disappeared down Egg Street, I heave myself back to the bedsit, slump down fully dressed on my bed and pass out with exhaustion.

Before I lose consciousness I send an arrow-prayer to God thanking him for enabling me to help Francie with a fair degree of success. I've cracked the lie without driving her over the edge; I've softened her up for therapy; I've kept the lines of communication open, and I've ensured our parting was friendly. With any luck, I tell myself, I'll have her in Robin's consulting room by the end of the week and eventually Robin will serve her up to one of our tame psychiatrists—and then we'll give her sick-leave and I'll make plenty of pastoral visits—and when she's better she'll see the need for marriage guidance counselling—and she'll no longer be a threat to Nicholas—and everyone will live happily ever after . . .

I'm almost unconscious by the time I complete this rambling sentence, but I still have time to think: thank God Nicholas is so strong, so stable and so well integrated that no woman on earth could knock him off his rocker.

The next moment I'm asleep.

I'm awakened abruptly less than twenty minutes later by the slam of the front door. I open my eyes—and shut them again almost at once because I've left the light on and the brightness hurts. But my ears are active. I hear running footsteps. I hear Nicholas shouting: "Lewis!" and by the time the door of the bedsit bangs open I'm sitting bolt upright on the edge of the bed with my heart pounding like a piston.

Nicholas's pallor has a greyish tinge. His eyes are slate-coloured with some violent emotion. He's trying to speak but he can't get his words out.

It's catastrophe-time at St. Benet's. Grabbing my crutches I try to haul myself to my feet but I'm too stiff, too disabled, and all I can do is sit down again. "What is it?" I'm demanding rapidly, fighting back the panic. "Nicholas, for the love of God, tell me what's happened!"

In a shaking voice he says: "Rosalind's left me," and as I stare at him in stupefaction he sinks shattered onto the nearest chair.

Part Three
ROSALIND
The Nightmare Scenario

The healing of relationships with other people is not merely a pastoral concern. It is also a prophetic one. It is about changing other people. It is about altering an environment.

. . .

Before those who are to minister healing do so, they will themselves be the recipients of the laying on of hands; they too are sinners; they too are sick.

CHRISTOPHER HAMEL COOKE

Healing Is for God

5

We find it so encouraging that you are able to recognise your anger and relate it to your lack of well-being. We all have anger but often find that hard to acknowledge.

GARETH TUCKWELL AND DAVID FLAGG
A Question of Healing

I

It's no picnic being married to a wonder worker.

I remember exactly when I realised my patience was exhausted. In the middle of November, 1988, when Mrs. Thatcher was visiting America to show them who was boss and President Reagan was slobbering at her feet, Patsy Egerton phoned to say she and Bryan were home from the States unexpectedly for a funeral and was there any chance of seeing us. I invited them to dinner on the following Friday—the eighteenth it was, a greyish sort of day, cold, revving up for that sprinkling of snow on the twentieth, the sort of November weather when I had to take the houseplants away from the chilly window-sills when I drew the curtains in the evening and do some mist-spraying in the morning if there was evidence of a dry-out. As soon as I'd spoken to Patsy I phoned Nicky at St. Benet's and asked him if he could do me a special favour and arrive home earlier than usual on Friday. He said he'd be home by seven.

He wasn't. I assumed some lame duck had claimed his attention as usual, and when the Egertons arrived I made an excuse about the heavy traffic on Friday nights, but as far as I was concerned Nicky had made his first mistake of the evening.

His second mistake was not to apologise properly when he rolled up at eight. He didn't even bother to blame the traffic. Worse still his thoughts were quite obviously elsewhere and his contributions to the conversation were embarrassingly few.

The third mistake he made was to stand up halfway through the meal and mutter: "Excuse me, but I've got to phone Lewis." He made this announcement just as Bryan was reaching the punchline of a most amusing story. I did say sharply: "Nicky, surely Lewis can wait!" but he didn't bother to reply. He just disappeared, made the call and on his return informed us that he had to go back to London straight away because there was an emergency.

I was so livid that it took me an immense effort to remain outwardly calm. But I did make the effort. Well, one always does, doesn't one? That's the rule. Patsy told me once that in America people scream at each other without hesitation when they get upset. At the time I had felt nothing but contempt for such foreign behaviour, but now it occurred to me how pleasant it would be to live in a culture where it was socially acceptable for angry people to scream with rage.

As I saw Nicky off I asked politely what the "emergency" was, and my fury was increased when he answered: "It's Lewis. He's had some bad news and he needs me."

I said: "*I* need you, Nicky. It's awkward for me if you leave now." But even uttering those understatements proved almost impossible. I'd been brought up not to complain, not to be demanding. I'd been taught that in a marriage the husband's work had the first priority and the wife always had to make allowances for him. Pre-war attitudes? Certainly. They lingered on when I was growing up in the south-west during the 1950s. But during the 1980s I'd been coming to the conclusion that the role of domestic doormat was one which I no longer had any wish to play.

Nicky was saying: "I'll sort him out as quickly as possible and be back early tomorrow morning."

That's the trouble with wonder workers. They can never resist the temptation to "fix" people. They're power-junkies hooked on deliverance, crisis-addicts mainlining on salvation. The one thing which never turns them on is dealing fairly with their nearest and dearest. I should have had priority that evening over even the most cherished of his lame ducks at the Healing Centre.

Lewis Hall, Nicky's colleague, was in my opinion a thoroughly nasty piece of work and I always thought he was a bad influence on Nicky. Dreadful old man! He drank too much, ate too much, smoked like a chimney and had a frightful temper. He'd been married once to some unfortunate woman who had immediately hit the bottle in the biggest possible way, and their one daughter—poor Rachel!—was a complete mess. Lewis had some nominal job at St. Benet's. I was never quite sure what it was but thought it had probably been devised by Nicky out of kindness to make the old horror feel useful. Lewis doted on Nicky, Nicky repaid the doting with an unstoppable stream of fraternal affection, and the whole peculiar relationship, in my opinion, was more than a little unhealthy.

Anyway there I was, abandoned at Butterfold Farm while Nicky drove back to London to rescue that nasty old brute, and as soon as Bryan and Patsy had departed, I sank down in tears at the kitchen table. My golden rule was never to cry in public—well, one never does, does one?—but by that stage of my marriage I was well accustomed to shedding a private tear or two.

That night I shed many tears, and it was when I was mopping them up that I finally thought: I can't go on.

Yet I found I could do nothing with this statement except try to forget it because in our family women always did go on. They kept a stiff upper lip and they never complained because, as Mummy had always said, that was the spirit which had built the Empire. But in 1988 the beat of a very different drum was now thundering in my ears and I suddenly found myself asking the revolutionary question: what Empire?

Then I knew my marriage had entered completely uncharted territory.

II

Later, in bed, I tried to imagine a different future, but the revolutionary drumbeat had by that time faded, blotted out by an upbringing which had taught me to believe the direst of fates awaited those who lost control of themselves and flouted the rules. To lose control in this way was the final horror; to lose control was the nightmare scenario.

Turning my back on the future in panic I fled as fast as I could into the past.

I found myself thinking of Lewis again. It was Lewis who had encouraged Nicky to enter the ministry of healing. Nicky's father had never wanted that, but Nicky had always fancied it and Lewis had led him on. Lewis had eventually taught him how to conduct exorcisms, since the ministries of healing and so-called deliverance go hand in hand. I thought the whole subject of exorcism was revolting, but what could I do? Nicky's father was dead by that time, and anyway, I wouldn't have wanted to whinge, least of all to dear old Mr. Darrow. Good wives never whinged. Everyone knew that.

I'd always tried to be supportive whenever Nicky had confided in me about the more peculiar side of his nature, but I had lived in the hope that becoming a clergyman would make him more normal. Some hope! He'd wound up on the Church's lunatic fringe. To be honest, I'd hardly expected him to wind up in an episcopal palace, since he'd never been the slightest bit interested in being a bishop, but I'd hoped he might eventually become the rector of some mellow market town. I used to picture that town sometimes. I used to picture the blissful normality of it all: the big, old-fashioned Georgian rectory by the medieval church, the beautiful walled garden, the warm kitchen with the Aga . . . It would have been the perfect environment for bringing up the boys. But the dream never came true. As a curate Nicky hated parish work and as soon as he could he escaped to become a chaplain in a large general hospital. I just couldn't understand why he wanted such a sordid, depressing job when he could have served God just as well in a beautiful market town. But of course I took care never to complain.

Before Nicky was ordained in 1968 Lewis had founded a healing centre in our nearest city, and in those days this was considered a very daring experiment. Now that the healing ministry is so fashionable one forgets what an adventurous clergyman Lewis was back in the 1960s, but he was always very much on the margins of respectability and in 1983 he went off the rails, just as I'd always suspected he would. He got mixed up with some working-class woman who had wanted her council house exorcised. She was found murdered in the end, and it was just Lewis's good luck that he had a cast-iron alibi. His car had been noticed during his regular visits to her house, and the police soon tracked him down. Naturally he was flung out of the diocese and naturally he wound up on the doorstep of St. Benet's Rectory and naturally Nicky took him in. No doubt he felt he had to "fix" Lewis because back in 1968 when they had first met, Lewis had "fixed" *him*. That was when Nicky had been going through one of his many pre-ordination phases of being very peculiar indeed.

Nicky had always had his peculiar side. He was perfectly sane and in many respects normal to the point of banality—all that Coca-Cola!—but he had his peculiar streak, and when he was peculiar he was creepy. There's no doubt in my mind that some people are psychic and have paranormal experiences; one can't live with a psychic and remain unaware of the off-beat incidents which disrupt the normal routine. I would never try to deny that Nicky was capable of foreknowledge; he had too often predicted some event which defied anticipation. Nor was there any point in denying he was capable of ESP; I had too often experienced incidents when he knew exactly what I was thinking even though we might be separated by a great distance. But I have always felt strongly that psychic powers should never be encouraged. That was why I was so outraged when Lewis decided to "train" Nicky after sorting him out in 1968. I did accept that Nicky had been going through a weird phase at the time and definitely needed some kind of help, but what he did *not* need was an eccentric exorcist adopting the role of guru. A good psychiatrist would have sorted out Nicky's problems, which basically stemmed from the fact that his mother had died when he was fourteen and his very elderly father had found it hard to cope with him. But of course I took care never to voice this opinion to Nicky.

Nicky's "training" as an exorcist took place in the 1970s when he was becoming an experienced hospital chaplain, but the "training" in the proper use of his psychic powers came in 1968 around the time of his ordination. Nicky's argument in favour of being "trained" was that as his psychic powers were running out of control and causing all manner of problems, he needed a fellow-psychic and a priest to teach him how to offer these powers to God and so ensure they were always used for the good. He said in 1968 that he'd ended up as a "wonder worker," someone who used his special powers for his own aggrandisement, and this wonder worker had to be brought under control before he destroyed not only himself but those who came into contact with him. I was careful to receive this information politely and indeed I did see that he needed the discipline of the priesthood to keep him in order, but I still thought he should have stayed away from that ministry of healing. It was the ecclesiastical equivalent of a reformed alcoholic seeking a job in a pub. But of course I never said this to Nicky.

I never said anything to Nicky which could have been interpreted as a criticism, a whinge or a complaint, although God knows, if any woman had cause to criticise, whinge or complain, I did. I thought of his decision to chuck up parish work without consulting me. I thought of his increasing involvement in the ministry of healing which had culminated in the move to London: the long hours, the frequent absences, the lame ducks, the sinister commissions—how *can* the Church still approve of exorcism?—and the neglect of his family. There were school prize-givings missed, although this didn't matter since the boys weren't academic, and sports-days overlooked, disasters which mattered very much indeed, since the boys were athletic. There were family holidays ruined because he was bored. There was my career, in which he had shown no genuine interest. There was—but why list all the grievances? Listing grievances constituted whingeing, and whingeing was for wimps. One just had to shut up and get on with it, whatever "it" was, because that was the spirit which had built the Empire.

That bloody Empire . . .

Suddenly I felt so unhappy, as I tossed and turned in bed that night after the wrecked dinner-party, that I felt more convinced than ever that I couldn't stand my marriage a moment longer, but no matter how much I might curse the Empire, I still couldn't imagine life without Nicky. We had been born in the same village and had become friends in kindergarten. The emotional connection between us now was so old and so deep that the idea of separation actually seemed not only impossible but inconceivable, and besides . . .

I knew Nicky would never agree to let me go.

III

The truth was I was really rather frightened of him. I nearly always suppressed this fear—it was wimpish to be frightened—but occasionally it surfaced and gave me nightmares. Having lived most of my life with Nicky's peculiarities I prided myself on taking them for granted, but that indifference was only achieved by willing myself not to dwell on them too deeply. Once I dwelt on them my hair would stand on end. Luckily ESP can't be switched on like a light, and Nicky's complete confidence in my loyalty and devotion made him psychically blind to my discontent, but occasionally he would read my mind with uncanny accuracy and I hated the invasion of my private self.

I hated too his hypnotic gifts, although nowadays I knew they were only used in his work and in strictly controlled surroundings. Is there anything more creepy than hypnosis? Perhaps only sleep-walking, another of Nicky's weird traits, although this seldom surfaced nowadays and was always a sign that he was overstrained in some way. I was terrified of this trait because I'd read somewhere that sleep-walkers can occasionally kill people while they're unconscious. Nicky commented once that if people killed when they were asleep they were bound to be pretty damned peculiar when they were awake, but I failed to be calmed by the thought of early warning signs. I found myself suffering a recurring dream in which a sleep-walking Nicky murdered the boys—although, of course, I never disclosed this dream to anyone, least of all Nicky. He would have thought I was getting neurotic. Sometimes *I* thought I was getting neurotic, although I knew I wasn't. We never got neurotic in my family. It wasn't the done thing so it never happened.

To be fair to Nicky I have to admit his peculiarities often troubled him as much as they troubled me. I remember in particular when we were teenagers and he told me about the poltergeist activity he had triggered. Seeing how upset he was I held his hand and listened mutely, concealing my revulsion, and my reward came afterwards when he said gratefully: "I don't know what I'd do if I didn't have you to talk to, Rosalind." I remember too, years later when we were in our mid-twenties and I'd agreed to marry him, he said urgently: "I've got to have someone normal, someone I can rely upon to stand by me, someone *predictable.*"

He put a high value on predictability, that dead opposite of paranormality. Every day at kindergarten he would arrive with his teddy-bear, the sacred totem whom no one else was allowed to touch. "Bear always moves in the same way," he said, showing me how the toy's limbs could be manipulated, "and his eyes always have the same expression. Bear's safe." Other children tried to play with the bear but Nicky fought them off. Even now, more than forty years later, I could remember him screaming: "No one plays with my bear but me!"

The other children became afraid of this consistent hostility and kept their distance. He was lonely but pretended not to be. "I like being alone," he said when my nanny first brought me to play with him, but soon it became plain that he was more than willing to tolerate my company. I was shy, quiet, non-threatening. One day I was even allowed to stroke Bear. I almost swooned at the privilege, and that afternoon his nanny said to mine: "Rosalind's very good for Nicholas." His parents thought so too. Nicky might dream of evil spirits and "see" hobgoblins; he might talk in his weird way about "The Dark"; he might sleep-walk and have premonitions which made him scream in terror; but at least he had a nice normal little friend who was willing to hold his hand and make him feel safe.

We kept in touch through adolescence but drifted apart when he went up to Cambridge and got mixed up with a fast crowd. That was when he became a wonder worker. I did go to one of the parties but was so appalled I never went to another. Nicky told fortunes and performed psychic parlour-tricks, some of which involved hypnosis. That was obscene. The worst loss of control I can imagine is being turned into a zombie and having my will vandalised. To me that's the nightmare scenario to end all nightmare scenarios.

He never again performed psychic parlour-tricks after his ordination in 1968, but I sometimes wondered how far the leopard had really changed his spots. He was a very devout Christian. There was no question about that. And he wanted only to be a good clergyman. There was no question about that either. But sometimes, although the career as a charlatan had been completely repudiated, I thought the wonder worker still lurked, like a caged beast, in the mud at the bottom of his personality. Occasionally I could sense this beast prowling around the cage and trying to escape. Then I'd feel frightened. But always the devout clergyman would step in to draw the curtain around the cage again, and the wonder worker would disappear from view.

It was only when I was furious with Nicky that I'd call him a wonder worker, but I knew that nowadays he was an honest man, and this was the Nicky I still loved. I was frightened of Nicky the weirdo and revolted by Nicky the wonder worker, but I loved Nicky my lifelong companion and Nicky the respectable cleric. I just couldn't stand him as a husband any more, that was the problem, and although I didn't see how I was going to leave him I couldn't see how I was going to go on living with him either.

As the church clock struck two in the distance, I was still asking myself what the hell I could possibly do.

But no answer sprang miraculously into my mind.

IV

Eventually I dozed in exhaustion but at six o'clock I was awakened as Nicky returned to the house and slid into bed beside me.

"Darling—"

"I'm not awake," I said. "I've had a bad night."

He said he was very sorry to hear it, what a bore insomnia was, but he did just want to apologise again for abandoning the dinner-party—he knew how embarrassing his defection had been for me but he'd make amends, he'd devote himself to me for the rest of the weekend, we could do whatever I wanted, my wish was his command—and so on and so on. Curling himself around me and snuggling close, he finally concluded with a sigh: "At least I fixed Lewis. I hated going back but it really was the right decision."

I thought: not for me, Nicky. For Lewis, perhaps, but not for me. And not for you either.

A moment later he was leaving the bed and pattering downstairs. He never needed much sleep and I assumed he had already snatched a few hours' rest in London after rescuing Lewis. Later he brought me breakfast in bed, but although I tried to eat I found I had no appetite. I knew that as soon as breakfast was over he'd want to make love. That would be all part of making amends, but unfortunately I had no desire for amends to be made in that particular way. Sipping coffee I pretended to read the Saturday papers and tried to think of a suitable excuse for postponing sex, but my brain seemed to have turned to wool.

"Are you all right?" said Nicky at last, knowing I wasn't.

"How fascinating—the gardening column's talking about that pot-plant fatshedera!" I said with genuine interest. I liked the new trend of newspapers to billow into magazines at the weekend. "And fatsia too! Fancy!"

"Look," he said, ignoring my irrelevant rapture, "I know it was difficult for you last night and I know you must feel very angry with me, but—"

"You know nothing of the kind! Nicky, I do so loathe it when you try to mind-read—and I loathe it even more when you get everything wrong. Just run off and stop agonising over me, would you? I'm still in a stupor through lack of sleep."

He sighed again and drifted away. I sagged with relief, but not for long. I was too worried about how I was going to avoid sex for the rest of the weekend. Sex was always on the agenda somewhere.

Nicky led a very predictable life when he came down to Butterfold at weekends. On Saturdays he wrote to the boys at school, wandered around the garden to see what had changed and tried to paint a water-colour. He was very bad at painting but he did it as a sort of therapy and I was careful to be kind about the distinctly peculiar results. He also spent time catching up with his reading. He read mostly books connected with Christianity, but he skimmed the occasional novel or biography as well. He prayed, of course, but always before I got up in the morning, so the habit never bothered me.

On Saturdays we often had people to lunch or dinner, but by then he would have adjusted to Butterfold life and would be capable of normal social intercourse. In the afternoon, weather permitting, he'd go for a long walk. Sometimes I'd go with him, but if I was preparing a dinner-party he'd go on his own. When I did go with him he seldom spoke. Nicky liked silence.

If our evening was free we might dine out before watching a video. He liked to browse, tongue firmly in cheek, through the early James Bond films, or, better still, to gaze dreamily at reruns he had taped of *The Avengers.* This was Nicky's favourite cult series, and during the 1960s he had been mesmerised by its star, Diana Rigg. Many were the times when I had sat hand in hand with him on the sofa and listened to him sighing as she appeared on the screen in her black leather catsuit. Diana Rigg was what he called "a steamy brunette." When young I'd been so grateful to Nicky for marrying me despite the fact that I fell so far short of this sultry sexual ideal.

In the 1960s he had tried to reassure me by saying: "I don't care what you look like. I wouldn't even care if you looked like the back end of a bus," but later I felt this was a very backhanded compliment. Surely if one loved someone one did care what they looked like? Fortunately I never looked as plain as the back end of a bus, but I did look drab when I was young; it was my sister Phyllida who had all the boyfriends. Guided by Mummy I too often wound up wearing beige, and no local hairdresser in those days could solve the problems created by my baby-fine straight hair. It was only after Mummy died that I had the courage to go bouffant, get a rinse, wear shocking pink and make sure my stiletto heels were always several inches high. Phyl had taken to ignoring my mother's chaste taste much earlier, but I never quite had the confidence to stand up to my mother. Neither did my father, hiding behind *The Times* at breakfast, hiding on the golf course at weekends, hiding at the office during the week. Poor Daddy—all that hiding! But of course he never complained. I never once heard my parents have a row. Anger was the great taboo in our family and no one was ever allowed to lose control and give in to it.

I liked being in control. I liked it when I built up my floral consultancy business to such a pinnacle that I wound up controlling not only the consultancy but three shops as well. By owning the shops I had more control over the flowers. Soon I was controlling lawyers, accountants, bank managers and the people I employed to give me the time to control everything. The irony was that I myself was not a trained florist. My only qualification was a flower-arranging diploma acquired at finishing school, but that didn't matter because my primary talent wasn't for flower-arranging but for management. I adored the power-plays, the cut and thrust of business life, the challenges met and overcome. Nothing and no one slipped through the net and escaped being managed by me. The shy little mouse had evolved into a sabre-toothed predator, and I shall never forget the orgiastic excitement I experienced when I finally sold the business after jacking up the price to the right figure.

Why did I sell? I somehow felt uneasy after the crash of '87. Of course the market rapidly recovered, but . . . well, no boom can go on for ever, can it? Better to get out while the going was good, and besides, I had a vague feeling that I wanted to go in a different direction—although what that direction was I still, even after several months of reflection, had no clear idea. Meanwhile it was nice to rest on my laurels, contemplate my bank balance with satisfaction and reflect how amazed Daddy would have been by my success.

Mummy wouldn't have been surprised in the least. She always said I was a "sticker" and not a "bolter." Phyllida was a bolter who had run away from boarding school in a fit of pique, but I was a sticker and I'd stuck it out and done well. Mummy knew then that I was as tough as she was, and when I pulled off the supreme feat of "marrying well" she was in ecstasy. Nicky's father was a clergyman with no money and no background, but Nicky's mother was a Barton-Woods, the first family in our part of the world, and she had inherited not only the family manor house but also a large estate. After she died both were eventually let, but although Nicky always said he'd return there one day, I didn't believe he ever would. He would be quite unsuited to life as a country squire, and anyway all he wanted was to swan around London practising that ghastly ministry of healing.

I don't mean to imply Nicky was entirely averse to country life. He was quite capable of enjoying his weekends in Surrey, and he particularly enjoyed sleeping with me after his solitary nights during the week. That suited me very well. I liked sex. I always saw copulation as a satisfactory method of rebelling against Mummy, who regarded "sex" as another taboo word, even worse than "anger." I didn't like orgasms much, but once I'd worked out how to be in control of them, that little difficulty was taken care of. Needless to say, I never told Nicky the truth about that tiresome mini-blot on the sexscape. He might have wanted to take control by "fixing" me, and anyway, why go looking for trouble? The idea that a married couple should have no secrets from each other, even when the secrets involve sex, has always seemed to me not only stupid but obscene.

Nicky liked sex too, and when he made the effort he could be really good at it, but nowadays he often failed to make the effort. I was unsure why. Was it because of his age? Or because his ministry was becoming increasingly exhausting? Or because he had lost a certain degree of interest in me? Or because he secretly disliked my success as a businesswoman? There was no denying that he was forty-five—forty-six on Christmas Eve—and that he worked very hard and that we had, after all, been married for twenty years, but I did wonder if the main problem was my career. It's hard for a man when his wife becomes unexpectedly successful, and although Nicky's delight and admiration were genuine enough I thought that on a primitive, unconscious level he might be nurturing various resentments. I certainly nurtured various resentments when he just banged away without finesse, but of course I never said anything to him. Well, women never can say anything in those circumstances, can they? Not if they value peace and quiet in the home. Men are so sensitive about their sexual prowess that the whole subject is fraught with danger. To complain is to risk an angry response, and once anger rears its ugly head anything can happen. The whole scene might go right out of control.

Sex, with or without finesse, would usually conclude our enjoyable Saturdays, and then we'd be all set for our more religious but almost equally enjoyable Sundays. We would start by lying in bed and reading the papers, but by ten-thirty we'd be among the congregation in the village church for the weekly parish Eucharist. I always went to church with Nicky and I always took Communion, although in fact I'd ceased to be religious long ago. I didn't exactly disbelieve in God, but by this time he seemed irrelevant. However, assuming he existed—and I felt it was always best to be on the safe side—I had no desire to make him angry by failing to go through the right motions, and besides, if one's married to a clergyman one really does have a moral duty to go to church once a week to be supportive. I had never found it easy to be married to an Anglo-Catholic but if necessary I could even tolerate Romish practices. Lewis Hall, dreadful old man, was very Romish, but luckily Nicky was what was now called a liberal Catholic and I found I could put up with that much more easily. My family were churchgoing Anglicans but Protestant, and we always felt traditional Anglo-Catholicism to be deeply unpatriotic.

After Sunday church came Sunday lunch and we were often invited out. In the afternoon we might go for another walk and after tea we would usually make love again. Nicky left Butterfold at nine and would be back in the Rectory soon after ten. The journey by car was easy at off-peak hours.

When the boys were home for the holidays our routine was different as we tended to do things together as a family. There would be outings and expeditions, since Nicky did at least try to make up for his frequent absences. Lovemaking would get cut back or indulged in at odd hours, usually in the mornings as the boys, like most teenagers, enjoyed sleeping late. Nicky never seemed to know quite what to say to the boys and I'd become tense. He and Benedict were currently going through a bad patch because Benedict wanted to rebel against Nicky's world-view just as I had longed all those years ago to rebel against my mother's taste in clothes. I understood Benedict but Nicky didn't. Benedict was gregarious and sporty and racy and adventurous—he was like Phyllida and like my father's sister Aunt Esmé. He was fun! But Nicky thought he was stupid and shallow—although of course he had taken care never to say so to me.

Nicky was no cleverer with Antony either. If only Nicky could have seen that Antony was different from Benedict, but Nicky never saw Antony properly because he was so absorbed in thinking what a problem Benedict was. Antony was neglected. Unfortunately he too bore no resemblance to Nicky, but he *was* like me. He was basically quiet and shy but copied glamorous Benedict just as I used to copy glamorous Phyllida, and this aping would get on Nicky's nerves. I worried terribly about all these tensions and often wondered where the troubles would end, but there was no one to whom I could turn for help. Once I did try talking to Phyl but she just said impatiently: "Oh, brace up, Ros, for God's sake, and don't be such a wimp!" and at once I felt I'd let the side down.

But now I knew I had to have a rest, not just from that soul-destroying spirit which built the Empire but from all manner of exhausting problems which I couldn't master. My life during the week had become a desert since the sale of my business, while my life at weekends had apparently become so fraught that I could no longer face sex. Obviously I was approaching some sort of mega-crisis. Could I be on the brink of a nervous breakdown? Absolutely not. Breakdowns were for wimps, and anyway no one in our family ever broke down. It wasn't the done thing.

But there was no denying I was currently behaving like a wimp. God, I couldn't even work out how to avoid sex for the rest of the weekend! Obviously something had to be done quickly before a nightmare scenario unfolded in which I lost control of the situation altogether and went bananas.

Staggering out of bed I reached for my Filofax and tried to convince myself I was about to make some efficient, sensible decisions.

V

I began by looking through the addresses. It had occurred to me that what I really needed to do was to get right away from Butterfold for at least three days in order to *think*. A change of scenery well away from Nicky would not only stimulate my flaking brain but would with luck produce a detachment which would enable me to visualise a viable future.

My fingers drifted to a halt in their journey through my Filofax as it then dawned on me that I had to resist the temptation to stay with friends. To get my brain ticking over briskly I had to be alone. Moreover, it was important that I didn't tell Nicky, because once he knew something was definitely wrong he'd be buzzing around trying to "fix" me. Eventually, of course, I'd have to enlighten him, but by that time I would have "fixed" myself. The whole point of beating my brains out in solitary confinement was that I had to work out how to tell Nicky without sending him into orbit and driving us both round the bend.

There was no problem about disappearing for three days between weekends. Nicky and I seldom spoke during the week, and if I left the appropriate non-committal message on my answering machine to cover all callers . . . My thoughts slithered on, twisting and turning as I worked out how to guard my privacy without arousing suspicion.

Having made the decision to flee on Monday I then had no alternative but to solve the problem of how to survive the rest of the weekend, and finally I pretended to be ill. I cancelled the lunch-party we were due to attend, and languished in bed with a Ruth Rendell mystery while Nicky brought me tea on a tray plus a little vase containing a very late flowering, boudoir-pink St. Swithun rose. The weather was about to give a death-blow to the flowers which bloomed till late autumn and the rose did look distinctly wan, but I thought it was so nice of Nicky to want to cheer me up by bringing me something beautiful from the garden. In fact he was so nice and so kind that as soon as he had left the room I plunged fathoms deep into depression. How could I conceive of leaving him? But that was the problem. I couldn't conceive of it yet it had to be done and that was exactly why I was going away to beat my brains out and come up with a viable plan. Sternly I reminded myself how utterly impossible he was as a husband.

I'd discovered soon after the wedding that Nicky wasn't very clever at being married. The problem was his compulsion to pour himself out into his ministry and be wonderful to everyone in sight. There was little space in his life, I soon realised, for a wife and virtually none for children. The problem was that he had had an off-beat upbringing; although he had been much loved his parents had been preoccupied with their own lives and he had emerged from childhood with little idea what a normal family life was like. When the children were small he was appalled by the noise and mess they generated. I suspected that his inability to cope with this disruption was the primary reason why he had escaped into a chaplaincy which, unlike a parish job, meant he didn't have to work from home. Sometimes, seeing how ill-at-ease he was with family life, I thought he should never have married at all, but of course as a clergyman he had to marry in order to have a sex-life. Perhaps, realising how difficult marriage would be for him, he had felt he could only risk a trip to the altar with a friend who could be trusted not to bolt when the going got tough.

When we were engaged I had found myself wondering more than once why he wanted to marry me. I'd always wanted to marry him, but my motives were easier to understand. I was so mousey while Mummy was alive that I had no boyfriends who were seriously interested in me and I often felt frustrated by my inability to attract the opposite sex. Nicky was the only young man who showed me affection, and even then his affection was mostly fraternal. He was rather plain in his youth. He was too thin and he had to wear spectacles, but even in his plain days he had a fluent, easy way of moving which made him stand out from the crowd, and as the years passed the plainness stealthily diminished. By the time he was forty and able to give up wearing glasses he had an excellent figure and a subtle sex-appeal which was all the more lethal for not being obvious. With his unremarkable brown hair and pale eyes and angular features he was hardly classically handsome, but these low-key looks formed the perfect backdrop to his powerful, hypnotic personality.

Before we were married he did tell me he had been "a bit wild" with various members of the fast set who had adopted him when he was younger, but he swore this period of his life was now past. He still maintained his friendships with the survivors but soon they too were settling down and becoming respectable—except for that wreck Venetia Hoffenberg. I didn't care for his friendship with that woman *at all*, but long periods would go by when they never saw each other and in the end I convinced myself she was no threat to my peace of mind. I've no time for losers who when the going gets tough just chuck in the sponge and drink themselves silly. When the going gets tough the tough should damned well get going—as I intended to do if only I could get my act together and stop being such a dithering wimp.

I got my act together speedily when Nicky moved to St. Benet's, and my God, some tough decisions needed to be made then to keep the marriage from disintegrating! I knew straight away that he'd never be able to cope with his family if we were living at the Rectory and getting under his feet, so I said the City was an impossible place to bring up children and I worked out the blueprint for the split-level marital life in which he and I were apart during the week and together at weekends. The scheme was a brilliant success, although sometimes I thought I might die of loneliness. But I solved that problem, didn't I, by starting my own business and working so hard that I had no time for wimpish self-pity. If you don't like a situation you should change it. You've got to get on top of problems, control them before they can control you.

But how could I control a divorce? That was the question. If things got out of hand . . . No, it was better not to think of that, and I had to stop myself thinking of Mummy too. I had to make up my mind not to hear her saying: "You've got to stick to your marriage. You've got to play the game and not let the side down." But it was impossible not to hear those words. I couldn't shut them out, and although in my head I screamed at her: "But I've put up and shut up for long enough, and I can't take the unhappiness any more!" Mummy just said tight-lipped: "No shouting, Rosalind, please, and no scenes. We don't behave like that in our family."

The forbidden anger turned inwards. Dragging the duvet over my head I squeezed my eyes shut to control the tears and despised myself for my lack of Empire-building spirit.

VI

Well, I got over that. Despair's for wimps. Telling myself I had to postpone all thought of the future until Monday, I bent my will towards surviving the weekend.

When I awoke the next morning I pretended I was still unwell and Nicky went to church without me. The closing of the front door seemed to give my brain a welcome jolt, and suddenly, after all the hours of brain-dead torpor, I thought of the ideal bolt-hole.

It was a holiday cottage which belonged to a couple who had once been friends of ours, although nowadays I never saw the two of them together because the husband had degenerated into a nasty piece of work and neither Nicky nor I could stand him. It was the wife who remained my friend, and unknown to Nicky I met her regularly for lunch. The secrecy was because she was my mole at St. Benet's. I was fairly sure Nicky was too immersed in his work to have the energy to be unfaithful, but the prudent wife of a one-time wonder worker should always be well informed about any groupie who tries to muscle in on her territory.

Propping myself up on the pillows I reached once more for my Filofax and phoned my old pal, Francie Parker.

6

> Anger can disrupt our emotional as well as our physical health. Anger within may well cause depression. In particular, depressive reactions to crises like divorce . . . have been linked to anger seeking expression.
>
> GARETH TUCKWELL AND DAVID FLAGG
> *A Question of Healing*

I

Francie and I had met at finishing school longer ago than either of us now cared to remember. I had wanted to stay on at boarding school and do A-levels but Mummy had thought that would be a waste of time as all I needed to know for my future as a Nice Girl, destined for marriage and motherhood, was how to cook decently and arrange flowers with flair. I took my revenge by refusing to go to finishing school in Switzerland. Daddy, who had been hiding behind *The Times* when this polite altercation had taken place, supported me when I said I hated "Abroad," but the truth was that I hated the idea of being compared to Phyllida and found wanting. Phyl had cut a terrific dash in Switzerland and had had a passionate but unconsummated affair with an Italian prince who had wanted to buy her oodles of clothes in Paris. Aping Mummy I said this was all very vulgar, but in private I was madly jealous.

"Francie darling!" I exclaimed, wrenching my mind back to the present as she answered the phone. "It's Rosalind. How are you?"

"Rosalind!" Francie sounded a trifle *bouleversée*, as Phyl would have put it after the racy year in Switzerland. "Darling, what a surprise! Why aren't you in church with Mr. Glamour-Puss?"

"Why aren't you in church yourself, you old slacker?"

"I'm too busy enjoying Harry's absence! He's gone to Hong Kong for a few days and I must say it's rather heavenly without him—no one complaining if I get the sections of the *Sunday Times* muddled or if the roast beef isn't pink in just the right places. My dear, what we girls have to put up with from these ultra-successful men . . ."

Francie rattled on. She was married to a lawyer with an acid tongue who got his kicks out of proving to her, in very elegant speeches, that she was a complete fool. Francie adored him. She worked at St. Benet's as a Befriender and said it was so good for her self-esteem to be useful to others. Nicky reported that she did the work very well, and at one stage she had considered training to be a counsellor, but Harry the Horror-Husband had put his foot down and told her he wasn't throwing money away on a course which she would inevitably fail. To my rage Francie accepted his decision meekly. Nicky said she obviously liked men to be masterful, and that Harry, by striking these revolting macho poses, actually made her feel cherished. I wasn't sure who was mad—Harry, Francie or Nicky—but someone had to be round the twist. However, that wasn't my problem. All that concerned me was that Francie was a loyal friend who could be trusted to give me accurate reports on any dangerous female shark who had swum into the St. Benet's lagoon. A recent arrival had been Venetia Hoffenberg. That news had certainly set my teeth on edge, but apparently she was being counselled by Robin, the therapist, and Nicky seldom saw her.

". . . and anyway, darling, enough of all that," Francie was saying. "How about *you?* What's new down on the Darrow ranch?"

"Well, to be honest I'm feeling very frazzled and I want to get away for a few days on my own before the boys roar home and Christmas soars out of control. Francie, would you mind terribly if—"

Francie didn't mind in the least. Harry had long since decreed that the cottage in Devon could be lent to friends at any time during the winter. "But Ros, I'm so sorry you're frazzled! Nick didn't mention—"

"Nicky doesn't know and you're not to tell him. I don't want him to start worrying about me when all I need's a short break . . . Does that neighbour still have the key of the cottage?"

"Yes, I'll ring her and tell her you're coming. When do you aim to arrive?"

"Tomorrow lunch-time. By the way I've quite forgotten the address and how to get there. It seems ages since Nicky and I borrowed the cottage for that naughty weekend."

"Number Seven, Kine Street—"

"Hang on, my pen's seizing up." I shook the Biro to get the ink flowing and pressed down twice as hard on the notepad. "Okay, go on."

Francie completed the address and gave comprehensive directions. ". . . and have a lovely time in deep seclusion," she added. "Your secret's safe with me."

I thanked her profusely before remembering to ask: "What's new at St. Benet's?"

"Well, Venetia's still seeing Robin, but Lewis is hovering on the sidelines—he's been having spiritual chats with her every week."

"How nauseating!"

"It's certainly eccentric—they meet for drinks at various grand hotels. Funny old Lewis, he's such a character!"

"Well, I suppose that's one way of describing him. Does Nicky ever substitute for Lewis at the grand hotels?"

"I thought of that and checked his diary, but he only substituted once and that was when Lewis was in hospital, so I didn't bother to mention the jaunt to Claridge's to you—it was obviously just a pastoral manoeuvre."

That made sense. Nicky would never normally go to Claridge's unless he felt it was a pastoral necessity. Did I need to be perturbed that he hadn't told me he was having a drink with Venetia? No. As a pastoral manoeuvre he could classify it as confidential and keep his mouth shut with a clear conscience. Very convenient. But as my marriage was on the rocks, did I really care what he got up to with Venetia Hoffenberg?

The awful part was I still did. How was I ever going to separate from him? I was beginning to feel like a Siamese twin; I knew I had to go it alone in order to get a life and save my sanity, but how did I ever begin to psych myself up for the sheer unadulterated horror of the necessary operation?

After the conversation with Francie I lay limply on the pillows for some time as if exhausted by my brief bout of dynamism, but eventually I tore the address of the cottage from the notepad, tucked the folded slip of paper in my Filofax and resumed the task of pretending to be ill.

But by this time I was in such a state of nervous tension that I hardly needed to pretend at all.

11

It was just my bad luck that on that particular weekend Nicky stayed Sunday night at Butterfold Farm. He was due in Chichester on Monday morning for a conference, and planned to spend the night with friends before returning directly to London on Tuesday.

"What's this conference about?" I asked him on Sunday evening as he brought me soup and toast for my supper.

"Pastoral problems caused by paranormal phenomena."

I somehow restrained myself from grinding my teeth.

"My paper deals with the importance of diagnosing poltergeist activity correctly," he said, sitting down at my bedside with his own mug of soup. "There's an increasing amount of fraud nowadays—we call it the phoneygeist syndrome. For example, people dissatisfied with their local authority housing sometimes simulate paranormal incidents in order to claim their home is uninhabitable. The council calls us in to advise."

I kept my head down and concentrated on my soup.

"Rosalind."

"Yes, darling?"

"I'm rather worried about you."

"Well, don't be. I'll be better tomorrow."

"But you're not really ill, are you? You're faking it."

"Oh, for God's sake!" I screamed at him. "Can't you ever lay off that bloody ESP?" That was when I knew how close to the edge I was. I never screamed. I also never normally used the word "bloody" in Nicky's presence. He didn't like it.

"Are you worried about Benedict? Is there some problem I should know about?"

"No, he's fine. And *I'm* fine, apart from this forty-eight-hour bug, whatever it is. Can we talk of something else?"

"Maybe you're grieving for your lost business. There's a vacuum in your life now and you may be unsure how to fill it."

"Nonsense! I promised myself a year off after all the hard slog and I'm enjoying my new leisure. Now, will you kindly stop flexing the ESP and—"

"No ESP's required to see your illness is a fake. I mean, it was plain as a pikestaff that you didn't want sex and decided to pretend to be ill so as not to hurt my feelings."

I was so rattled that I abandoned my soup, slid down the bed and pulled the duvet over my head again, but he refused either to shut up or to be shut out. "Look," I heard him say urgently, "if there's a problem with sex it's so often an indication that there's a serious problem elsewhere. If you could only tell me—"

Under the duvet I stopped my ears and prayed for him to go away, but he didn't. So much for prayer. The next moment he had stripped off his clothes and was sliding under the duvet to enfold me in his arms.

I tried to say: "Please go away," but nothing happened. That was because he was no longer the impossible partner of an impossible marriage but my oldest friend, genuinely worried for fear that I was unhappy.

"Oh, Nicky, Nicky . . ." In a wave of emotion I twisted around to press my face against his chest, but this move instantly reminded me of his nakedness and made me realise how confidently he had anticipated the crumbling of my will. He was now poised to use our intimacy as a tool to pry open my mind and pick over the contents. I froze, conscious of an enormous resentment, and as he immediately sensed my reaction he redoubled his efforts to manipulate me. Switching on the charm, he adopted a rueful, amused air and gave me an affectionate, non-threatening kiss on the forehead. "Okay," he said, "tell me all that's bothering you is that you don't fancy me this weekend. Tell me exactly how you feel and I promise you I won't be upset. I just want to know what's going on."

My great escape to Devon was in danger. I knew very well that if I started telling him exactly how I felt he would never rest until I'd been counselled, prayed for and "fixed." But I had to hammer out my own future. I had to stop him muscling in and trying to mould me into a shape which suited him but had nothing to do with the real me at all.

"Don't be silly! I always fancy you," I said, allowing my hands to wander idly around his midriff. I knew I had to get this approach dead right; if I was either too passionate or too cool he'd smell a rat. "But I admit I do feel increasingly depressed about your relationship with Benedict."

"I'll fix it!" said the wonder worker. "Just you wait and see!"

Ah, but Nicky, you're going to find out that there are some relationships which not even a wonder worker can fix . . .

"Darling!" I said, simulating relief and gratitude. "Oh God, I'm sorry I've worked myself into such a state about it all, but"—inspiration finally struck—"I read the most awful article in *The Times* a fortnight ago about this new drug Ecstasy—apparently it's spread from the London clubbers to the upwardly mobile, and—"

"I know all about E and the acid-house culture—we see the casualties at the Healing Centre."

"Well, if Benedict gets involved—"

"I'll talk to him. No need for you to worry."

"Oh, what a load off my mind! Nicky, I'm sorry I've been so stupid and beastly to you, but—"

He said I hadn't been stupid and beastly, just unlike myself, and he didn't like it when I was unlike myself, it bothered him, he wanted me to be happy and normal, just as I always was.

"Predictable," I said.

"Right. I love you," he insisted, clasping my wandering hand as tightly as he had held his teddy-bear's paw long ago. "You're the most important person in my life and I love you more than anyone else in the world."

I knew he meant that. But if he loved me—which he did—and if I loved him—which I did—why was I boiling deep down with rage and frustration and planning to spend three days plotting a divorce?

I thought: Christ, what a snake-pit of unspeakable emotions! And that thought frightened me because I was reminded how easy it would be to lose control of the situation and plunge over the emotional abyss into breakdown, possibly even into destruction. Dreadful things happened when people failed to remain in control. Daddy had been in control behind his newspaper; Mummy had been in control behind her engagement diary and her charity work; but dashing Aunt Esmé had had an affair with a married man and wound up seeking a backstreet abortion; Aunt Esmé had lost control over her life and had died.

"We won't speak of it," my mother had said, controlling the messy tragedy by sweeping it efficiently under the rug. "We won't dwell on it any more."

But Aunt Esmé still haunted me. She showed up regularly in my dreams. It was why I was so worried about Benedict. If he took to drugs, got expelled from school, lost control over his adolescence . . .

"Rosalind?"

"Sorry, darling, I *must* stop worrying about Benedict . . ."

We made love and I faked a workmanlike orgasm.

III

The next morning he left for Chichester at seven and I departed for Devon two hours later. I had spent several sleepless hours composing the farewell letter in my head but when I came to write it I still needed to do several drafts. Originally I had planned to leave no note because I had envisaged only a temporary retreat, but after that terrible bout of manipulation and counter-manipulation, after that unwanted sex and fake orgasm—after all those ghastly trappings of a marriage which was unquestionably on the rocks—I finally got my act together and realised, at about three in the morning, that either I left my husband or I suffered a breakdown.

Accordingly I wrote in my final version of the letter: "Dearest Nicky, I'm very sorry, but I can't go on with our marriage. I'm going away for a few days to plan my future and I do not, repeat NOT, want to see you during that time. I shall be in touch with you before the end of term about the boys, who, of course, will live with me, although I do accept that you must have visiting rights. I know it will be difficult for you as a clergyman to be divorced, but since the Church fortunately takes a more relaxed line nowadays I know you'll be in no danger of losing your job. There's nothing more I can usefully say at this point except that there's no one else and I'm sure I shall always be very fond of you. But I can't go on being your wife. Sorry, but there it is. Love, ROSALIND."

When I reread the letter it seemed very cold, almost brutal, but I felt sure I was right not to go into long explanations which he would immediately want to rebut. The best way of handling the mess was to be business-like—not unfriendly exactly, but just thoroughly sensible and polite. No scenes. Practical details discussed through lawyers. Civilised behaviour at all times. I thought I could cope well with a divorce conducted according to those reassuring rules, but first of all I needed to escape, recover from the trauma of the weekend and try to think coherently about the immediate future. How was I going to tell the boys? How was I going to cope with Christmas? How was I going to keep Nicky at arm's length once I emerged from seclusion? All these dreadful questions required very careful consideration indeed. I hurried on with the task of removing myself to Devon.

I telephoned my cleaner with the news that I was going away "for a few days" and asked her to come in to water my plants, just as she always did when I was on holiday. I phoned Reg, who helped me in the garden, and told him he could dig out the liriope but must on no account tug the dead leaves off the yuccas. I cancelled the newspapers and the milk delivery. Then I went upstairs to pack. This was difficult, as I now had no idea how long I might have to be away. I certainly intended to return home as soon as possible, but I had to wait until I was sure Nicky had accepted my decision. Otherwise he might crash around and . . . But at that point I rang down the curtain on my imagination. I didn't want to remind myself that I was secretly a little frightened of him and more than a little frightened of his reaction to being dumped. He would adjust, of course, since he was a mature, civilised clergyman and not some macho ape fresh from the nearest cave, but the adjustment might take some time, and meanwhile . . . Meanwhile I just didn't want to be around to take the flak.

I decided to pack for a two-week absence, but in the end I got carried away by the desire for a permanent break from Nicky, and to symbolise it I packed in addition to the necessary clothes my photograph albums of the boys, my silver-framed picture of my parents, and my jewellery. I knew it wasn't sensible to weigh myself down with all this baggage, but I told myself these precious mementos would boost my morale during the testing times which lay ahead.

Once my suitcases had been packed I went outside to bid a temporary farewell to my garden, but that was a mistake because I started to feel weepy. How stupid! I was sure Nicky would cede me Butterfold Farm in the divorce settlement, and anyway I'd soon see it again. But meanwhile . . . Meanwhile the separation was agonising. Running back into the house I suddenly remembered I had forgotten to leave a suitably neutral message on the answering machine. This proved difficult to draft but eventually I heard myself declaring: "You have reached Butterfold 843419. I'm not returning any calls at the present time, but please leave your name so that I can get back to you when I'm fully recovered from my virus." This seemed to cover all callers: my friends would do as they were told, tradesmen would hold their fire, burglars would think someone was at home and Nicky would assume I was still glum about Benedict and not in the mood for chit-chat.

All I had to do now was get myself to Devon.

Grabbing my suitcases I choked back a sob and staggered outside to my car.

I V

I arrived at the cottage early in the afternoon, picked up the key, let myself in and collapsed exhausted on the living-room sofa. When I awoke it was dark and very cold. Wandering around in a disorientated daze I drew the curtains and tried to coax the electric heating to work but after a while I remembered I had no food so I abandoned the radiators and trudged out to the car. Luckily there was no snow but I could all too easily imagine a heavy frost whitening the landscape.

Although the village shop was shut a local yokel told me that a large Tesco's had opened not far away on the A38, and when I arrived I found to my relief that despite the lateness of the hour people were still shopping. But once inside I couldn't decide what to buy. I wandered up and down the aisles like a lost soul.

After a long time I found myself back at the cottage and nibbling a grilled cheese sandwich. The heating seemed to be working better but the cottage remained icy. Interrupting my meal I hunted down the electric fires and plugged them both in. After half an hour I felt I might survive if I were to remove my overcoat. To make sure I poured myself a third whisky.

Unable to face sleeping in any of the arctic bedrooms upstairs I brought down some blankets and pillows and prepared to sleep on the sofa. The blankets were damp. In the bathroom I noticed the spiders' webs for the first time, and was reminded that the lavatory, visited on my arrival, showed signs of being in terminal decline. How different this slummish hovel was from the idyllic thatched cottage, warm and sunlit, which Nicky and I had visited for our dirty weekend five years ago! The passage of time and the owners' indifference had taken their toll. Depression began to envelop me again. What on earth was I doing in this godforsaken hole? Could I be in the midst of a nervous breakdown without realising I'd gone over the edge? With a shudder I finished the third whisky and promptly passed out.

When I awoke at eight the next morning I felt better. I switched on the fires and when I discovered that the water was at last seriously hot I had a bath. An hour later, having knocked back orange juice, muesli and three cups of coffee I felt almost normal but when I tried to survey the future my brain went dead. I wanted to run out and buy a plant somewhere but this was hardly practical behaviour. I did hope Reg wouldn't succumb to temptation and try to pick the dead leaves off the yuccas. They have to be plucked in a certain way and he'd never mastered the art.

To divert myself from the wave of homesickness which washed over me at that point I went outside to inspect the cottage's little back garden but it was bare, bleak, dead, and I felt more homesick than ever. Fleeing back indoors I made a new effort to take control of the situation by plonking myself down at the kitchen table with my Filofax and writing THINGS TO DO at the top of a blank page. I was just thinking how fortunate I was not to be a penniless woman seeking shelter in a women's refuge from a violent husband, when I heard a car draw up outside.

I told myself someone was calling at the cottage next door, but the next moment a thunderous knocking made me jump straight out of my chair. Immediately I assumed that Francie had driven all the way down to Devon to tell me that Nicky had had a terrible accident.

Gasping with fear, my imagination already visualising the tangled wreckage of his car, I rushed across the room and flung wide the front door.

Nicky shot across the threshold, shoved the door shut and shouted: "You selfish, stupid bitch, how dare you do this to me—how dare you!" And having slammed me against the wall he began to shake me till the room spun before my eyes.

V

I was plunged so deep into shock that I was even unable to scream. There was no question of struggling. My limbs refused to work. All I could do was close my eyes to blot the scene out, and Nicky, thinking I was fainting, at once took a different course. I was picked up, carried to the sofa and cradled tightly in his arms as he slumped down on the cushions. He was saying: "I love you, I can't live without you, I'm not letting you go." He said this over and over again.

I tried opening my eyes. Nothing dreadful happened. Nicky even tried to apologise but I cut him off by announcing: "I'm going to be sick."

Escaping to the kitchen I vomited into the sink.

"I'm sorry, I'm sorry, I'm sorry—" That was Nicky, resuming his broken-record act.

"Go away." When I vomit I like to do it in private. He knew that. Obediently he trailed back into the living-room.

Five minutes later I had swished away the filth, mopped myself up and filled a glass of water. I felt unspeakable. With the glass clutched tightly in my hand I staggered back to the living-room and collapsed not on the sofa, where he would have seated himself next to me, but on one of the armchairs. At last I managed to say: "You were supposed to spend last night in Chichester."

"I changed my mind because I was so worried about you. So I got back to Butterfold and it was all in darkness and then I found that disgusting note—"

"Oh God—"

"I don't know how you could have written anything so cruel, I don't know how you could have brought yourself to do any of this, I don't understand one single damned thing here—"

"I'm sorry, but I've been so desperate, so demented, so—"

"Well, how do you think *I* felt after reading that note? I went mad, I rushed back to London because I couldn't think properly, my brain felt as if someone had put a meat-cleaver through it, but Lewis calmed me down, fed me some brandy, persuaded me to get some sleep before I started searching for you—only I couldn't sleep, I tried but I couldn't, so at dawn I drove back to Butterfold and ransacked the house for a clue about where you'd gone—and at last when I looked at the notepad by the bedroom phone I saw traces of a message so I got a pencil and shaded the paper and this address came up—you must have been pressing very hard on the top sheet because the imprint was so clear below—"

"The pen was running out." I found myself remembering the old nursery rhyme about how a battle had been lost just because some horse had lost a nail from its shoe. Meanwhile Nicky was still talking at top speed.

"—and then I recognized the address and remembered that weekend we spent here, so I jumped in the car again and I drove and I drove and I drove—"

"Oh, Nicky—darling—" Wave after wave of deadening despair began to pound me. I hated myself for hurting him yet I hated him too for making me hate myself. The cauldron of unbearable emotions was boiling so hard by this time that I felt faint with the effort of keeping the lid on.

"I'm not letting you go," he said in his most obstinate voice. "Obviously there are things that aren't right but we'll sort them out. If you could just tell me, very simply, what you feel has gone wrong—"

"Everything's gone wrong." I could say no more. To my horror I was beginning to cry.

"But I'll put everything right! I'll fix it!"

"Nicky—"

"I've got to have you in my life. You keep me normal, you keep me on the rails—okay, I know you can't stand the psychic side of me, but at least you don't try to change me, you accept me as I am, and I need that support, I depend on it, I've got to have it—"

"But what about me?" I burst out, dashing away the tears. "Don't I get to have a life too? Or is my purpose solely to keep you ticking over by dishing up normality—whatever that is—whenever you deign to pay me a visit?"

He was stunned. "But you've been having such a rewarding life—you've had that wonderful career!"

"Only because you neglected me and I was so bloody lonely that I had to do something in order not to die of unhappiness!"

He stared at me in horror. "That's not true. You're exaggerating. That can't be true—"

"What's true is that I *can't go on!*" I bawled, and unable to bear his devastated expression a second longer I rushed out of the room and hurtled upstairs.

But he was too quick for me. He grabbed me before I could lock myself in the bathroom.

"But why didn't you tell me before?" he was shouting. "Why couldn't you talk to me? I'd have done anything to make you happy—you know perfectly well how much I love you!"

"No," I said, and my voice seemed to be coming from a long way away. "I was never entirely sure how much. You're so very attractive and there are so many greedy women in the world and I found I could never quite forget how you screwed around when you played the wonder worker back in the sixties."

"But that was before I was ordained—before we got married—before Lewis straightened me out and I turned over a new leaf!"

"I know. But sometimes I think the wonder worker's still around. Sometimes, when you talk of 'fixing' everything as if all you had to do was wave a magic wand, I think—"

"Wait a minute, let me just get this straight. Are you saying you seriously believed I might be unfaithful to you?"

"Yes. I was afraid that if I stopped serving up normality on weekends you'd fall in love with someone else. I've always loved you more than you loved me."

"But I adore you! I can't live without you!"

"But you do, Nicky. Five days out of seven you do live without me."

"But that wasn't my choice! It was *you* who decided not to live at the Rectory!"

"Only because I knew you'd never cope with family life if I did."

"What?"

"Oh, be honest, Nicky! Why were you hardly ever at home when you were a chaplain? I brought up those boys single-handed while you were always out somewhere being wonderful! You only turned up when you wanted sex!"

"That's a bugger-awful thing to say! You talk as if I just regard you as an upmarket tart!"

"But that's exactly how I feel! I feel I've been used and abused for years, and I can't take it any longer, Nicky, I'm sorry but I've reached the end of the line and now all I want is OUT!" And twisting away from him in a paroxysm of pain I blundered into the bathroom, bashed the door shut and banged home the bolt.

He started to break the door down.

VI

I let him in. That sounds ridiculously feeble, but I panicked at the thought of having to explain to Francie why the bathroom door had been vandalised, and the moment I drew back the bolt Nicky burst across the threshold. Grabbing me again he started bruising my mouth with his own. I choked, gulped for air, tried to scream and finally started to retch. That was when he came to his senses and released me. I retched again after staggering to the basin but there was nothing left to come up. Meanwhile Nicky was flitting around saying he was sorry, sorry, sorry, and filling a tooth-mug with water from the bath-tap. This grisly scene lasted some time but at last I drained the mug, staggered to the nearest bedroom and fell on to the bed just before I fainted. At that point I felt so ill that recovery seemed inconceivable.

When I regained consciousness Nicky was lying on the bed beside me and enfolding me in a tight, fierce clasp. As I opened my eyes he said flatly: "You've got to believe I love you and that I'll do anything to put matters right." Evidently we were back at square one.

I drank some water from the refilled tooth-mug, sank back on the pillows and managed to say: "It's not so easy for me to believe that when you crash around like a caveman with a rock-bottom IQ."

This time, when he said he was sorry, I felt the balance of power shift. He was contrite now, ashamed of the violence. Having slackened his clasp to allow me to prop myself on one elbow and drink, he made no attempt to imprison me again. Life was improving.

"I really do love you," he said humbly. "I really do, I promise."

"Okay," I said, lulled by this new, meek approach. "I believe that *you* believe that you love me—and maybe *I* even believe that you love me—I hardly know what I believe any more, I'm in such a muddle—but I feel as if your love's got nothing much to do with ordinary married love and nothing whatsoever to do with the woman I am now. In fact you don't even know the woman I am now. That's all part of the problem."

He started to feel insecure again. Grabbing back my hand he held it tightly as if he needed to keep me tethered. "Of course people should evolve as they go through life," he said, "but no matter how much you've evolved in recent years, you're still Rosalind."

"How do you define 'Rosalind'? I'm not the shy little yes-girl you married, Nicky. I'm not the retarded adolescent who adored you enough to put up with anything. That 'Rosalind' has quite gone."

"But I've been so proud of the woman you've become!"

"How can you know what kind of woman I've become when you've made no effort to share my new life with me?"

"Well, you've never made any effort to share my ministry!"

"That was because I never felt I had any place in it—you were never able to fit me in! But we're talking about my career, not your ministry, and what I'm trying to say is—"

"What we're both trying to say, obviously, is that there's been a complete breakdown of communication, but that's not uncommon, that can happen even in the best of marriages, that's something that can be put right." The thought seemed to cheer him. Releasing my hand he sat up, swung his feet off the bed and announced: "Let's go downstairs and have some coffee. Then we can work out how to restructure our relationship."

I saw then that by luring me into describing what was wrong with the marriage he had trapped me into listing symptoms which he could now pretend formed the problem itself. In other words, I'd been manipulated again. The real problem was that we had nothing in common and needed to go our separate ways. That meant no restructuring of the relationship was possible because the relationship itself was finished, but how could I convince Nicky of that when he was apparently capable of nothing except trying to manipulate me in order to avoid facing reality? I began to feel the entire situation was now slipping rapidly far beyond my control.

Following him downstairs I waited like a zombie in the living-room while he boiled water and scooped the Nescafé into mugs. At home I always served filtre-coffee, but last night I had been so dazed at the supermarket that I'd grabbed the first jar of instant I saw. I realized I was equally dazed now, thinking trivial thoughts about coffee when I should have been beating my brains out to concoct a speech which would convince Nicky our marriage was over, but the nightmare scenario of control totally lost was stealthily reducing me to pulp. Making an enormous effort I tried to think sensibly. I told myself that although the violence had been literally sick-making, I knew that Nicky would never beat me up. Or did I? Men fixated on women could be capable of any atrocity . . . although Nicky was a clergyman and so quite different.

Or was he?

My scalp prickled as I remembered the day long ago in kindergarten when he had bashed the children, male and female, who had tried to kidnap his bear. But that was a long time ago. People evolved from their childish selves . . . except that sometimes, in some way or other, they didn't. Sometimes they got stuck, went peculiar, lost control—

I shivered from head to toe.

"Here," said Nicky, returning to the living-room with the coffee. "This'll warm you up."

"Thanks." I put my hands around the mug but remained ice-cold. "Nicky," I said tentatively, "wouldn't it be better to talk about all this somewhere else?"

"You mean at home?"

"No, I mean . . . well, I mean in a controlled setting . . . with a skilled mediator present." As I spoke I realised with relief that this was the only possible solution to the current hell. I also remembered that Relate, the marriage-counselling agency, not only helped couples to achieve a reconciliation when this was possible but also assisted other less fortunate couples to part with dignity. In a burst of enthusiasm I added to Nicky: "I'm sure if we went to Relate we could find the right person to counsel us!"

"Good heavens, there's no need to bother with counselling!" said Nicky surprised. "I can sort everything out myself—I know all the right moves."

I was so appalled by the sheer arrogance of this statement that I was struck dumb. Nicky did have an arrogant streak, but it was years since I had seen it so openly displayed. Undiluted arrogance, flaunted without shame, was part of the wonder worker syndrome, and suddenly, queasily, I found myself remembering how he had performed psychic parlour-tricks at the smart parties long ago and how he had vibrated with pride afterwards when his fast set had fawned on him in admiration.

"Nicky," I said shakily, "wake up! You're dreaming."

"I could say the same thing to you—imagine inflating a run-of-the-mill breakdown in communication into a fullscale marital mess worthy of counselling from Relate! Now darling, let's just talk about this calmly and sensibly for a moment. First of all I want you to know that I accept my share of responsibility for this very painful situation and that I intend to work very hard to redeem my mistakes. It's entirely my fault that I didn't realise much earlier how unhappy you were—I'm afraid I've been using up so much energy in my work that I've been incapable of ESP when I've come home to relax! However, ESP or no ESP, I promise you I'll be a great deal more sensitive in the future."

"Thank you, but—"

"Now, the second thing I want to say is that I do understand why you're going through a crisis at the moment. With the business sold and the boys growing up fast you must be very conscious of an emptiness at the centre of your life, but I assure you that the way forward is not, as you seem to think, to smash up your life and destroy your closest relationship. The way forward is to transform your—our—present life so that our relationship is healed, renewed and transformed."

This struck me as being psycho-babble—or rather, psycho-spiritual-babble, something which I knew I ought to ignore in order to focus on the central truth that the marriage was finished. Yet at the same time I was severely tempted to argue with him. I'd suffered too much from that awful ministry of healing which had consumed my husband

and deprived me of a normal married life, and no one was now going to try to heal *me* with psycho-spiritual-babble in the expectation that I would make no attempt to talk back! As the white-hot anger, long suppressed, swept through me I managed to say crisply in the calmest of voices: "Don't play the guru with me, Nicky, and don't hand me any wonder cure which isn't firmly rooted in reality! You're just twisting the dogma to suit your purpose, but two can play at that game and now I intend to twist it back!"

"What do you mean?"

"You've often spoken in the past about self-realisation—about people growing and developing into the unique selves which God has designed them to be. You believe, don't you, that we have a duty to realise ourselves as far as possible because the more we become most truly ourselves the better we can serve God by doing what he wants us to do—by doing what he's designed us to do—and so chiming with his overall creative purpose. I've got that right, haven't I? Isn't that what you believe?"

"Yes, but—"

"Well, I want to go on realising myself. I've come a long way in the past few years, but I don't want to stop now and I don't want to go back. I want to go on becoming the person God means me to be, and the life God means me to lead has nothing to do with being married to you."

"That's not just twisting dogma, that's perverting the truth! What you've outlined is the 'me-generation' philosophy—it's individualism running wild because what you're really saying is: 'I'm the only one who counts and everyone else can go to the wall!' You don't want to serve God by taking your place in a unique network of human relationships—you just want to serve yourself by going your own way regardless of those who love you!"

"No, it's not like that—you're twisting everything again—"

"I'm twisting nothing! I'm telling you the truth, I'm speaking out for Christianity against self-centred individualism, and I'm saying that you *can't realise yourself at the expense of others!*"

"My God, that's rich!" I exploded as anger finally elbowed my fear aside. "You've been realising yourself at my expense ever since we married! And throughout most of our marriage you've certainly been realising yourself at the expense of our sons! Well, I can't take your self-realisation any more, Nicky—I can't take it, and neither you nor anyone else is going to make me!" And yet again I rushed from the room.

VII

He came after me as I stood trembling at the kitchen sink, but when I told him to keep his distance he remained by the door. I concentrated on taking deep breaths to fight off the nausea, and eventually, when I remained silent, he said in a level, reasonable voice: "Although I would deny the truth of that accusation, I do concede that in trying to care for you to the best of my ability I've nevertheless managed to get a lot wrong. Well, I'm very sorry and now I want to redeem my mistakes by putting everything right."

"Of course you're going to say that," I said, clutching the edge of the sink so hard my fingers ached. "That's the Christian game, isn't it? You confess, you repent, you're forgiven, and then everything's a glorious resurrection, but I'm sorry, I'm not playing that game any more and I don't want this marriage to be resurrected. I want—I need—"

He suddenly let his anger show. "Oh, 'I'—'I'—'I'! Rosalind, have you any idea how fantastically egotistical you sound? Unless you draw the line now your self-centredness is going to make a lot of people—including yourself—very miserable!"

"Don't you bloody preach to me!" I cried, but I was rattled. Violent anger certainly demolishes me but I'm also no good at coping with scenes when non-violent anger is on open display. I have to have the anger muzzled and veiled. That's what I've always been used to and that's what I can handle competently. Naked anger knocks me off balance.

"I'll damn well do as I choose!" shouted Nicky, careful to sound angrier than ever. Of course he knew exactly how disconcerting this was for me. "Why shouldn't I preach to you? Good preaching means telling a few home truths about reality, and a few home truths about reality are obviously just what you need to hear!"

"Don't shout at me, don't shout—"

"Shut up! Now just you listen to me! You accused me of realising myself at the expense of our sons, but what do you think you'll be doing if you smash up our marriage? In fact how can you even think of doing this to the boys?"

"But they'd be all right! They'd go on living with me at Butterfold and the disruption would be minimal—"

"Rosalind, I don't know what corner of cloud-cuckoo-land you're inhabiting, but I suggest you come back to earth right now and stop messing around with this very dangerous fantasy. You have two adolescent sons, one very disturbed, the other shaping up to go the same way, and yet you casually propose to sever them from any masculine influence in the home! Okay, I know I'm not the world's most perfect parent, but even though I haven't been around as much as I should have been, those boys know I care about them, they know I'm utterly committed to their welfare, and no matter how much they whine at some of my decisions, they know I'm *never* going to realise myself at their expense, wash my hands of them and walk out. So if you think I'm going to sit back and let you deprive Benedict and Antony of the love and security I represent—"

Guilt instantly exacerbated my burgeoning panic. "But you'd have visiting rights! I'd never, never do anything which would harm Benedict and Antony—"

"Then why are you talking of smashing up the marriage? Can't you see that if you do that you'll smash up the boys?"

"Oh, but—"

"I think it's time you took a long, hard look at yourself, Rosalind, I really do. You've been ready enough to criticise me, but I think if you turn the spotlight on your own behavior, honesty will force you to admit you're not entirely without blame yourself! For instance, you've convinced yourself that I was the one who wasn't able to cope with family life at St. Benet's, but in fact the non-coper was you, wasn't it? You couldn't face life in London without at least an acre of garden to nurture! And talking of nurturing, what about your shortcomings as a mother? If you hadn't spoilt Benedict so rotten, Antony wouldn't have felt compelled to imitate him to gain your attention! You never had a clue how to deal with them sensibly—in fact if you hadn't secretly been more interested in bringing up flowers than bringing up children, those boys wouldn't be the rowdy yobs they are at the moment and my job as a father trying to repair the damage you've caused would be one hell of a lot less tedious and painful!"

I had no strength left to fight. He'd drained it all out of me, drop by drop, with vilely skilled precision. I felt trumped, tricked, trashed and trounced.

Breaking away again I burst into tears and ran sobbing back to the living-room.

VIII

I fought for self-control and lost. I felt as if I were drowning in a rising tide of guilt and grief, and now all I wanted was to escape to some private haven where I could abandon myself to despair, but no escape was possible because Nicky was on the brink of shoring up his victory. Slumping down beside me on the sofa as I wept, he gathered me into his arms and I no longer had the strength to push him away.

That was the moment when I knew my brief, brave sprint for freedom was over. I was to be comforted, counselled, remodelled, "fixed." In the end I would be just another name on Nicky's long list of successfully treated clients, just another testament to his powers as a healer. And that would be a happy ending, wouldn't it? Obviously I'd spent years being a selfish wife, refusing to share his ministry, and a rotten mother, capable only of producing rowdy yobs. If anyone needed "fixing" I did.

The awful thing was that I knew these desolate thoughts were a gross travesty of the truth, but I found myself powerless to repudiate them. All decent mothers suffer agonies of guilt if their children become troublesome, and I'd often worried myself sick by wondering how far I was to blame for the boys' problems. By zeroing in on my guilt and magnifying it, Nicky had converted my shortcomings into a burden which I couldn't, in my present shattered state, throw off. The result was that I could only think: yes, I must abandon any idea of divorce or else the boys will be destroyed and I'll wind up being the worst mother in the world.

I thought of Mummy talking of soldiering on and keeping a stiff upper lip. I thought of Daddy playing the game and not letting the side down as he endured silently behind his newspaper. How could I even think of desecrating their memory by chucking in the towel and doing a runner? A deserting wife was beyond the pale. A deserting wife could only be condemned. A deserting wife had lost control.

My whole body seemed to throb with shame as my upbringing finally reclaimed me. I couldn't withstand it. My defences had been destroyed and my will had been broken. All I could do now was to lie like a lump in Nicky's arms and listen, wet-eyed and passive, as he talked in the gentlest and most soothing of voices.

"Now darling, don't despair," he was saying. "We're going to get over this. The thing to do is to take one step at a time, and the first step is to end this split-level way of being married—we must be together during the week as well as at weekends, and what I suggest is that we begin by living together at the Rectory until the boys come home for the holidays. We'll have to spend the holidays in accordance with the old regime because we certainly don't have time for radical reorganisation before mid-December, but if you now come back with me to London you could make a start on planning how to adapt the Rectory for family life."

He paused, waiting for a comment, but when none came he continued with increasing confidence: "During the holidays we can involve the boys in our new plans—the change should be presented to them as exciting, a move which will give them a lot of interesting opportunities. Then when they return to school in the new year you can go ahead with renovating the Rectory, making plans for the garden and so on . . . Okay, I know the garden's a wilderness at the moment and I know how inferior it must seem to the garden at Butterfold, but it's got great potential, and there are two unused rooms next to Alice's flat—they could be thrown into one to make a garden room for your plants. The boys, of course, will need their games-room but that's all right, we can divide the curate's flat; there's no need for Stacy to have so much space. Yes, I can see the house taking shape . . . and we'll be together at last, just as we should be. It's the split-level living that's undermined us but once we put a stop to that we'll be on our way to a much better relationship." Kissing my cheek lightly he gave me a reassuring squeeze.

I managed to whisper: "And Butterfold?"

"We'll keep the farmhouse as a second home," he said at once. "I know how much it means to you, and besides, we'll still want to escape to the country sometimes, particularly during the summer."

"I suppose . . . I suppose there's no question of you leaving St. Benet's in the immediate future?"

"None. It's going from strength to strength. Incidentally, I don't know if you've had any ideas yet about what you want to do next, but there's plenty of opportunities for voluntary work at the Healing Centre, and—"

"Yes."

"—and I'm sure we could use your special gifts in some creative way. On the other hand," he added rapidly as he failed to detect any sign of an enthusiastic response, "if you wanted to return to domesticity—" He broke off.

I waited before it suddenly dawned on me that he was having trouble phrasing his next suggestion. Memories of a very awkward subject surfaced, triggered by the concept of domesticity, and at once I tried to turn the conversation elsewhere. "I shall enjoy taming the garden," I said feverishly. "Would I need to get permission from the Archdeacon if I wanted to build a conservatory?"

But Nicky's thoughts were far from conservatories and he refused to be diverted. "Look," he said urgently, "I know you've always been cool in the past when we've discussed the possibility of having another child, but I see clearly now why you were against the idea. You thought, didn't you, that I wouldn't be around enough to give you the necessary support, but if we now eliminate the split-level life—if our marriage moves into a new phase—if you were to fancy a return to domesticity—"

"No, Nicky. I'm sorry, but no."

"Well, I realise we're both a bit old for that sort of thing, but women often have babies when they're over forty these days, it's not unusual—"

"It's not unusual but in my case it's impossible," I said flatly, so unnerved by this time that I could do nothing but blurt out the truth. "I had myself sterilised four years ago when I went into hospital for that D and C, and there's no way I'm going to try to reverse the operation."

IX

He stared at me in stupefaction.

"I'm sorry," I repeated, stumbling over my words, "but I just couldn't face discussing it with you."

"But why on earth did you do it?"

"I got fed up with contraception."

"But *I* would have taken on the contraception!"

"I didn't trust you not to want to skip it every now and then. I knew you always wanted a daughter because you were so disappointed in your sons."

"I was never disappointed in them!"

"Oh yes, you were, Nicky! Oh yes, you were!"

"I admit I'm sorry neither of them share my interests, but—"

"Sorry? You're devastated! In fact only someone irrationally upset on the subject of offspring would suggest that we should have another child in these particular circumstances!"

"Forgive me, but I'm not prepared to be diverted by these wild accusations—I'm still reeling from this truly appalling disclosure and I still don't understand why you decided to be sterilised. You couldn't just have done it because you were fed up with contraception!"

"Well, I did. I hated taking all those hormones and then I hated risking a perforated uterus with the coil and then I hated scrabbling around with a diaphragm—and anyway, it was *my* body! Why shouldn't I have my tubes tied if I wanted to?" Sheer fright was making me sound much more belligerent than I really was, but the effect of the belligerence was disastrous.

"I can't believe you could have been so criminally selfish!" exclaimed Nicky, turning on the anger again. "That's the kind of behaviour which gives the Women's Movement a bad name! You're talking as if you exist in isolation from everyone else and owe nothing to anyone but yourself!"

"Well, that was how I felt after being married for all those years to you!" I shouted, determined now not to collapse again in the face of his anger, and in consequence becoming uncharacteristically shrill.

"What a cheap remark! Damn it, this confession of yours makes me wonder what else you've concealed over the years! Have you ever had a lover?"

"No, of course not!"

"That's the wrong answer. You should have said: 'Don't be stupid!' and looked hurt!"

"Well, I'm saying: 'No, of course not,' and I hope I'm looking bloody furious!" I was in better control of myself now. I'd remembered that attack was the best form of defence, and that enabled me to harness my anger so that it became an asset instead of a handicap. "And what about you?" I demanded. "What have you been keeping quiet about during the last twenty years? I noticed earlier, when I said I always felt I loved you more than you loved me, that you never came right out and said you'd always been faithful!"

"I didn't think it was necessary! And anyway it's not true to say you always loved me more than I loved you!"

"Oh yeah? Would you be able to swear on the Bible that you've been faithful to me since the day we married?"

"Well, of course I would! Don't be ridiculous! I couldn't sustain my ministry—particularly this ministry—unless I live as I should. If I were to start screwing around on the side I'd be finished, just as poor Lewis was back in 1983. You can't lead a double-life and preserve your integrity—you can't exploit others without damaging not only those others but yourself and maybe innocent bystanders as well. We're all too interconnected for exploitation not to have an adverse effect somewhere along the line."

"Well, if we're talking of exploitation—"

"Okay, so you've been feeling exploited. But if I'd only known—"

"So why the hell didn't you know? The truth is, Nicky, you were never sufficiently interested to bother to imagine what I was feeling!"

"The truth is I never dreamed you were capable of deceiving me on such a cosmic scale!"

"Oh, for God's sake! Just because I had a minor operation—"

"Minor?"

"I admit it had a major consequence, but technically—"

"Forget it, all that really matters is that you deceived me. Now let's hear about the other deceptions. If we're going to start a new phase of our marriage, I'm not tolerating any no-go areas—"

"There aren't any."

"Of course I did wonder occasionally what you got up to down in Surrey while I was in London, but I always tried to have faith in you, I always willed myself to believe that for the boys' sake, if not for mine, you wouldn't go messing around with one of those bone-headed Surrey businessmen who can only talk about money—"

I suddenly had an inspiration. If I confessed, he would back off. He would see that the marriage couldn't possibly be continued. Reality would dawn. He'd come to his senses, accept a new vision of the future, release me. It was my one remaining chance of escape.

Dizzy with fear again but driven on by desperation I interrupted: "All right, I'll tell you. He was a Surrey businessman and he did talk about money, but he wasn't bone-headed. He was my accountant, and he was shy and rather sweet. If you'd ever bothered to meet him you'd have written him off as dirt-common and dead-boring, but I liked him a lot. I only broke off the affair after the take-over because I felt he was getting too involved and I didn't want things to get out of control."

I stopped. I'd been staring down at my hands, but the silence which followed my last sentence was so loud that I looked up. At once I saw Nicky was shattered. Evidently he had not after all suspected me of infidelity. The gibe about a lover had been a mere reflex, an automatic seeking of a reassurance which he had never seriously doubted would be forthcoming.

Now it was my turn to be shattered. I stammered: "I'm sorry, I never intended—never wanted—you to know, but I was so lonely, you see, and you couldn't share the business with me in any way, and Jim found my success so exciting—"

"But I thought you said your accountant was a young man who'd only recently qualified!"

"Yes, he was a lot younger than I was. I wouldn't have had the courage to approach someone older. I wouldn't have felt in control."

There was a deadly pause. Nicky's face was very pale and set, his eyes slatey and expressionless.

"I feel sorry for young men today," I said, so driven to fill the terrible silence that I hardly cared what I said. "They're so grateful to meet an older woman instead of the usual sex-mad teenage girl who expects them to know every position in the *Kama Sutra* and deliver multiple orgasms on demand."

A second, even deadlier pause began. All Nicky said when he broke it was: "How many others have there been?"

"Only two. One was a young man I met last summer when I was organising the flowers for that enormous wedding down on the Sussex border, and the second was a young American I met by chance at Fortnum's, but both affairs were very brief and I wouldn't have wanted to prolong them."

Nicky looked away. Then suddenly, wholly unexpectedly, he wiped his eyes with his cuff, levered himself to his feet and blundered from the room.

X

My heart felt as if it was bursting. Groping my way forward, unable to see properly, I followed him upstairs and found him lying face down on the double-bed in the largest room. I lay beside him, my arm around his shoulders, and wept silently for a while. It was only when he tried to push my arm away that I managed to whisper: "I didn't love any of them, but I felt so cut off from you and they made life bearable." When he failed to reply I added in misery: "I know this means you can never trust me again and that going on with the marriage is impossible, but I do care for you, I always will, and I wouldn't want us to wind up enemies."

He twisted around to face me, levered himself groggily upright on one elbow and said in a flat, dogged voice: "Okay, you've made your point. I drove you into being unfaithful because I've been a self-centred, insensitive workaholic, but I'll make amends now, I swear it—I swear that now I fully understand the situation everything will change."

"Oh, Nicky . . ." I was almost fainting with relief. He was facing reality at last. The end of the marriage was in sight. We were going to part with dignity.

"Of course I forgive you for the infidelity," he said strongly. "Of course I shall trust you again and of course we must go on with our marriage. I accept that the others meant nothing to you and that you still love me."

I was appalled.

"We're going to survive this crisis," he was saying obstinately. "All this honesty's been very painful, but at least I know now what has to be put right and I won't rest until you're happy again."

I tried to speak but I couldn't even think coherently. Indecipherable mental patterns whirled across my mind and reduced me again to a passive powerlessness. I felt as if I'd been tossed into a maelstrom so fierce that any hope of survival was futile.

"We won't mention any detail of this conversation again," said Nicky, confident now and very determined. "We'll treat all our past errors as forgiven—they won't be forgotten, but now that they've been exposed we'll be free to go beyond them and get on with building a new future." He started to kiss me.

I kissed him back because I was confused, because I was stupefied, because I was in such a mess that I had no idea what else to do. Amidst all my chaotic emotions I was aware of a longing to be nice to him, to be kind, to be generous—to be anything which would make amends for all the pain I'd given him by that dreadful confession. How could I have been so cruel to my oldest and dearest friend? I felt I was drowning in guilt again, awash with self-loathing. Here I was, married to this wonderful clergyman who was being so good and so Christian, forgiving me when I didn't deserve it, loving me no matter what I did, and what was I doing to express my gratitude? Nothing! How despicable I was, how utterly self-centred and disgusting . . . I suddenly saw that he'd been right all along in his criticism, and that

I'd been both mad and bad ever to think of leaving him. Swept on by this tide of shame I blurted out: "Oh Nicky, I'm so sorry—I didn't mean to hurt you so much, I really didn't—"

"My darling Rosalind," he said, "it's all right—everything's all right, and now we're all set to live happily ever after."

How mad can one get? But by that stage I was so demented that I believed every word he said.

7

With major conflicts, it is quite unrealistic to expect to settle them before the sun sets. What is important is not that we resolve everything immediately, but that we are open to a process both of self-examination and of constructive communication . . . with other people involved in the conflict.

GARETH TUCKWELL AND DAVID FLAGG
A Question of Healing

I

At that point in this catastrophic scene we floundered around in pursuit of sexual intercourse. No doubt we thought we were making love, but in retrospect I can see I was making amends to him while he was making a big effort to convince us both that the crisis was past. We eventually achieved a connection but Nicky came too soon and was almost beside himself with annoyance. I'd never before heard him use so much forbidden language in such a short space of time.

Knowing how upset he was I felt more guilty than ever, and my increased guilt drove me to embrace him even more lovingly—while simultaneously I wondered what the hell I was doing and where on earth our mess was going to end. But those were dangerous questions, so dangerous that they had to be instantly suppressed, and instead of trying to answer them I frantically told myself that my sole aim in life now should be to spare Nicky from further agony and ensure the boys weren't ruined for ever. I myself was of no consequence. I just had to soldier on and keep a stiff upper lip in order to avoid more chaotic scenes packed with shouting, violence and unspeakable emotion, otherwise known as hell on earth. Vaguely I started to recall pictures painted by Hieronymus Bosch.

It was too cold to linger long in the bedroom and neither of us now wanted to stay at the cottage. After the sex I gathered together my belongings while Nicky cleared up, and we departed ten minutes later. There was never any question about our destination. Nicky had said I had to be with him at the Rectory until the boys returned from school, and I now accepted that this was the first step towards restructuring the marriage and living happily ever after, just as a decent wife and mother should.

Dutifully I got into my car and followed Nicky east along the road which led to London.

II

When we stopped for a sandwich lunch at the service station on the M3 Nicky phoned Lewis and I stood by the open booth to listen to the one-sided conversation.

". . . so it depends on the traffic, but I'll cut down through Earls Court to the River, and we should be home reasonably soon . . ."

I noticed the use of the word "home" and the casual familiarity with London. I felt as if I were journeying to a foreign country while Nicky was merely returning to his native land.

". . . and could you tell Alice to make something special for dinner tonight? Rosalind and I'll eat in the flat, but Alice doesn't have to worry about that, I'll carry everything upstairs . . ."

I'd quite forgotten Alice Fletcher, the new cook-housekeeper at the Rectory. Did I really want a servant living in and getting on my nerves? No. But on the other hand I certainly had no intention of slaving away cooking communal meals and winding up a drudge chained to the Rectory sink.

The problem with the Rectory, dreadful old dump, was that it had a public, professional use in addition to being a private home. I had always treated the ground floor as a write-off, constantly subject to invasion by all kinds of peculiar people, and on my irregular visits to the house I had confined myself to our flat upstairs, but the flat was horrid, quite unmodernised, and one couldn't possibly entertain there. If the house were to be made into a decent home the ground floor would have to be reclaimed, but there was currently a major obstacle standing in the way of reclamation: Lewis. When his arthritic hip had made climbing the stairs too difficult, two of the ground floor reception rooms—formerly interconnected and divided only by double doors—had been amalgamated to provide a large bed-sitting-room for him, and the hall cloakroom had been transformed into a bathroom.

However, Lewis now had a new hip. He could be sent back upstairs to the curate's flat which he had occupied originally, long before Nicky had been permitted to take on a curate. He wouldn't want to share the curate's flat with Stacy, but Nicky had said the flat could be divided . . . to provide a games-room for the boys. If Lewis was shipped up to the top floor, where could I put the games-room? In the basement, was the obvious answer, but in that case, what happened to my proposed flower-room? My mind was just beginning to spin with the effort of trying to solve this seemingly intractable problem when I realised the phone conversation had finished and Nicky was talking directly to me again.

"When we hit London," he was saying, glancing at his watch, "don't panic if we get separated by traffic—I'll pull in as soon as possible and wait till you catch up. I'll be stopping in the King's Road to get a bottle of wine, so watch carefully for the left turn once we're through Earls Court and Kensington."

I nodded meekly, wondering why he should be treating me as if I were a learner-driver adrift in the great metropolis. London might seem like a foreign country to me, but I was not unfamiliar with it. It was true I never normally chose to drive there—who in their right mind would?—but I was still capable of finding my way from the western fringes to the City. I could only suppose he needed to boss me around a bit to boost his bruised ego.

The traffic was frightful, but the sheer volume of vehicles meant that it was easy to chug along in convoy. In the King's Road Nicky bought a bottle of champagne at an off-licence. Then we dropped down another block and began following the River all the way to the Square Mile.

The leafless trees of the Embankment were looking wan but the River was all glamour; every now and then I glimpsed the racing tide, the rippling waters and the sucking, sexy swirling of the currents around the bridges. The glamour doubled as we approached the City. Giant cranes were silhouetted against the skyline, symbols of the building boom which marked the country's prosperity, and as the skyscrapers swung into view beyond the dome of St. Paul's I seemed to feel the throbbing pulse of world-class London, revved up by the dynamism of Mrs. Thatcher to become the greatest money-market on earth. A primitive thrill of patriotism made the adrenaline surge through my veins and as I exclaimed aloud: "London's for winners!" I miraculously found myself even looking forward to the challenges my new life posed.

But by that stage I suppose it was almost inevitable that I should have been willing to retreat from a harsh reality into a euphoric fantasy-world.

Driving buoyantly around St. Paul's I followed Nicky through Cheapside towards Poultry and north up Egg Street to St. Benet's.

III

The Rectory stood next to the churchyard in a cobbled alley which ran south from London Wall. German bombs had blasted away much of the pre-war surroundings, but although the church had sustained minor damage the Rectory, unfortunately, had survived intact. There had been a house on that site for centuries, but the present Rectory had been built late in the eighteenth century and extended in the nineteenth. I could have coped with a beautiful Georgian townhouse. But the Victorian architect, intoxicated by Gothic ideas, had concocted a vast new wing full of mysterious passages and gloomy rooms and little flights of stairs, oddly placed, which made hoovering hell.

At the Georgian front of the house the basement barely peeked above ground but at the back it was on a level with the garden, a turgid little wilderness which no one, least of all me, had ever bothered to tend. On the north side of the garden was the churchyard of St. Benet's, however, and this was well kept and attractive. It was on a higher level than the garden and separated from it by a substantial wall. On the east side of the garden was the back of a modern office block, deserted at weekends, and on the south and west sides the garden was flanked by the Rectory which, thanks to the Victorian extension, now formed the shape of a reversed L.

On the ground floor, which was raised a few feet above the cobbled forecourt and therefore not, strictly speaking, on the ground at all, the Georgian rooms had been rearranged and renovated in the twentieth century when the kitchen had been resited, but the first floor flat allocated to the Rector was still a slab of rampant Victoriana; not even the Georgian rooms at the front had escaped the lust of the architect for Gothic interior decoration, and in the Victorian wing the rooms were crammed with monstrous fireplaces, dusty panelling, the occasional stained glass window in frightful taste and heavy lighting fixtures. There was no central heating, although each room had a gas fire.

The best room in the flat was the lavatory, a magnificent chamber with steps which led up to the "throne"; there was a blue-and-white flowered bowl, a mahogany seat and a long chain which reminded me vaguely of medieval tortures. Next door to this masterpiece in a room which was always freezing, even in summer, stood a long bath on legs. The rest of the accommodation consisted of four bedrooms (including one each for the boys to use on their occasional holiday visits), a dining-room and a drawing-room but not Nicky's study; he preferred to work on the ground floor in the reception room on the north side of the front door.

I had never been tempted to "take the house in hand," as Mummy would have put it, and on my infrequent visits I had simply gritted my teeth and endured the discomfort and the inconvenience. I hadn't even complained about the decor, arranged by Nicky after his arrival in 1981. He and I had quite different tastes in furnishings. I liked comfortable armchairs and sofas, ranges of chintz in warm colours, thick carpets peppered with antiques. Nicky liked austerity, a rug or two on bare floorboards, plain drugget in the passageways, stark white walls whenever there was a respite from the heavy panelling. He also saw nothing wrong with buying cheap furniture, and he had even put up DIY shelves in the drawing-room. It was not that he was devoid of taste. The furniture was pleasantly upholstered and the few pictures, all posters of modern paintings, were very striking if one liked that kind of thing—and it had to be said that they looked very odd amidst the Gothic ambience —but he had no interest in pursuing excellence in interior decoration and he was indifferent to the lack of modern comfort. Since he always ate downstairs with the others it was small wonder that the flat's kitchen was reminiscent of a 1950s slum, but he had never even bothered to buy a new refrigerator to house his Coca-Cola. The yellowish antique which wheezed and clanked in a corner could hardly manufacture solid ice-cubes.

I hated that grisly, dark, poky kitchen which made all thought of giving dinner-parties in the flat inconceivable. Even if the place had been modernised it would still have been much too small to permit any self-respecting cook to work there, but on the other hand the house's main kitchen, formerly in the basement but now covering a substantial area of the ground floor, was an excellent size because two rooms had been knocked into one in order to produce a satisfactory dining area. I liked this arrangement and thought the kitchen had considerable potential, but it did need revamping; one could have spent twenty-five thousand pounds there very rapidly with no trouble at all. However, when I reclaimed the ground floor for the Darrow family the problem would be not the shabbiness of the kitchen but the lack of a formal ground-floor dining-room. One can hardly ask one's guests to eat among the pots and pans.

In addition to Nicky's study and Lewis's bedsit, there was one other reception room on the ground floor but this was used for church business unconnected with the Healing Centre and I saw no way of annexing this space; one needed a room not only for meetings but a room in which to dump both casual callers and people who had an appointment to see Nicky in his study. Yet again I realised that the obvious solution to all the difficulties was to shoehorn Lewis out of that interconnecting double reception room and convert it into a dining-room and drawing-room, but I felt sure Lewis would tenaciously resist being shoehorned.

As I reviewed these possible changes to the Rectory, I was unpacking my suitcases in the main bedroom of the Rector's flat. This room contained my sole contribution to the house: an ultra-modern, ultra-comfortable double-bed. I can't bear discomfort when I'm trying to sleep.

Having finished unpacking I discovered that someone had switched on the immersion heater after learning of our imminent arrival and that the water was now hot enough for a bath. Nicky liked his bathrooms to be very clean so I had no cause for complaint on the grounds of hygiene, but I hated that enormous trough, so uncomfortable, and the room itself was, as usual, freezing. Back in the bedroom I crouched over the gas fire and dreamed again, like Mrs. Thatcher, of radical change.

I knew exactly what needed to be done to this floor when the Rector's flat ceased to exist and the house became one home again. I wanted a master bedroom with bathroom en suite, a guest-room with bathroom en suite, the boys' rooms with a large bathroom they could share and last but not least a sitting-room for myself, a private and luxurious space to which I could retreat when the inevitably churchy atmosphere of the Rectory got too much and I needed a breather. I knew I could have great fun designing that sitting-room . . . Idly I began to visualise carpets and fabrics.

Nicky had long since disappeared and I assumed he had gone down to the bedsit to bring his henchman up to date with the news, but I had no wish to see Lewis again that day and every wish for a large gin-and-tonic. Scanning the cupboards in the kitchen and drawing-room I found one bottle of tonic, left over from my last visit, but no gin. Nicky had probably taken it downstairs and used it to oil the churchwardens. I was just muttering a curse when I remembered the champagne and felt better. But there was no sign of it. I assumed that Nicky, wanting the bottle to chill quickly, had bypassed the clanking antique in the flat and consigned the champagne to the modern refrigerator in the main kitchen.

Having gone downstairs I found the new cook-housekeeper, a very plain girl, moving—or rather, lumbering—around her domain. She was wearing a red plastic apron over a blue skirt and a voluminous purple sweater. It's strange how often fat people wear colours which make them look fatter than ever. Alice could have benefited from some advice about how to dress properly, and as for her hair . . . I wondered if she cut it with garden-shears.

Curled up in a basket near the dresser was a cat. "Oh!" I said, very much surprised.

Alice was so startled that she dropped the spoon she was carrying. "Mrs. Darrow! I didn't hear you come in!"

"Sorry to give you a shock. Is that your cat?"

"No, Nicholas got it. Didn't he tell you?"

"Oh yes, I'd forgotten," I said airily, but that was a lie. He had never told me. I have nothing against cats but in the past I had always felt that with two children and a garden I couldn't cope with looking after animals as well. This attitude was undeniably wimpish, but I'd covered it up by taking a strong anti-animal line and declaring that I didn't want the carpets infested with fleas and the upholstery torn to shreds.

Looking at the cat which Nicky had failed to mention to me, I said to Alice: "I suppose you're the one who looks after it?"

"Yes, but I don't mind and I promise you he'll never go to your flat. Nicholas has been helping me train him."

What was all this talk of "Nicholas"? As my brain began to add up certain facts with the speed of a calculator I stopped looking at the cat and started looking at her.

"Dinner will be ready in half an hour," said the girl awkwardly. "I hope that's convenient."

I pulled myself together. "Lovely!" I said, flashing her a dazzling smile. "Thank you so much." Gliding to the fridge I extracted the champagne and caressed the bottle lightly to make sure it was chilled.

"I do hope you don't mind about James," said the girl behind me. "He's really very good."

"James? What an elegant name for a cat!" I took another look at the animal. It was a tabby. That meant Nicky had chosen it. Nicky always preferred tabbies. But why had he suddenly decided to acquire a cat? As the obvious answer occurred to me I said sharply to Alice: "Has there been a problem with mice?"

"Well, as a matter of fact—"

In disgust I thought for the umpteenth time what a dump the Rectory was. I hate mice.

"—I believe a mouse *was* spotted once before I came but since we've had James there's been no problem at all."

"Good for James!" I gave her another dazzling smile and walked out.

At Lewis's door I paused to adjust my grip on the bottle before I tapped on the panel and peeped into the room. I had seen Lewis briefly on my arrival so I didn't bother to say anything further to him. This was not, as might be supposed, because I was embarrassed that he should know all about the current state of my marriage; I had long since reconciled myself to the fact that Nicky had no secrets from his former mentor. My taciturnity simply stemmed from the fact that I was dying for a drink. Holding up the bottle of champagne I just said to Nicky: "Shall we?" and at once Nicky jumped to his feet as if he could hardly wait to take his first sip.

"Enjoy your dinner à deux!" said Lewis, putting on the excessively courteous voice he often used to disguise how much he disliked me. "Alice has devised a dazzling menu."

"Too sweet of her!" I said brightly. "Which reminds me—Nicky darling, why didn't you mention Alice's playmate, little James?"

Nicky at once looked very vague, as if he couldn't quite remember who James was, and began to drift across the room to the door. "I didn't think you'd be interested in such a trivial domestic detail," he said, as if I always had to have my mind fixed on the most exalted of subjects, "but there was a mouse problem and when Alice suggested the obvious solution I decided not to object. You don't mind, do you? He'll never trouble you. Alice looks after him."

"Yes, I can see there are all kinds of things she might like to look after."

Lewis at once heaved himself to his feet. "Don't let that champagne get warm!" he advised jovially. "If you both hang around here much longer I shall drink the whole bottle myself!"

Nicky seized the chance to escape without commenting on my barbed remark.

In silence we retired upstairs.

IV

"*Honestly*, Nicky!" I exclaimed as soon as the front door of the flat was closed. "Honestly!"

"Look, I'm sorry about the cat, but I didn't foresee you coming to live here, did I, and I knew he could be kept out of sight during your visits—"

"I'm not talking about the cat, you chump! I'm talking about Alice!"

"Alice?"

"Yes, *Alice!* God, men are so stupid sometimes—no wonder more women are staying unmarried and just raiding sperm-banks whenever they want children—"

"I'm not sure what you're trying to imply, but if you seriously think for one moment—"

"Oh, for God's sake open the champers and let's get stoned."

He peeled off the foil from the bottle while I extracted a pair of the cheap glasses he had bought at Habitat, and just as the cork yielded with a satisfying pop there was a most pleasant surprise: Alice arrived with a platter of canapés.

"I thought you might like these with the champagne," she said shyly when I responded to her knock on the door.

"Good God!" I exclaimed astonished. "How super! Thanks very much."

She smiled, peeped over my shoulder and smiled again. "Thanks, Alice," said Nicky behind me in the kitchen doorway.

Alice disappeared. The door closed. Nicky and I were left looking at each other over the luscious hors d'oeuvres.

"Well, 'Nicholas,' " I said in my pleasantest voice, "I think it's time you and I had a little talk about that girl."

V

In the living-room he poured out the champagne. "I honestly don't see what your problem is."

"That's the problem. Cheers, darling."

"Cheers."

The glasses clinked. We took a sip and subsided onto the rock-hard cheap sofa. In front of us, beyond the woolly rug which Nicky had rescued from a jumble-sale, the gas fire burned fiercely while above the chimney-piece Nicky's favourite Kandinsky poster glowed in a riot of bright colours within its plain black frame.

"Here's to our new life," said Nicky.

"Here's to our new life," said I.

We had another swill and began to gobble the canapés. Soon the memory of the sandwich lunch and the horrors of the morning began to recede at the speed of light. Not for the first time it occurred to me that there was nothing like a glass of champagne for restoring one after a short holiday in hell.

"Now listen to me, darling," I said after my third swill. "It's very naughty of you to employ that girl when you must know that she's in love with you—no, don't interrupt! Let me have my say. I'm speaking here, please note, in defence of Alice, who's obviously the most respectable of nice girls and more than worthy of being a Rectory employee. It's about time she had a woman to stand up for her in the face of all this rampant male exploitation!"

"What exploitation?"

"Oh God. Nicky, it's simply not fair to that girl to keep her under your roof when she's in love with you. I'm sure you only wanted to be charitable and Christian, but it'll screw her up emotionally if you continue to let her yearn for you with no hope of a reward."

"But—"

"It's not healthy! Can't you see you're exploiting her by taking advantage of her infatuation? She'd be much happier in the long run if she went back to Belgravia and took a job with one of Cynthia Aysgarth's pals!"

He stared down at the champagne as if he wished he was drinking Coke. All he said was: "Alice isn't infatuated with me."

"Well, if you believe that, you'll believe anything!"

He continued to stare at the champagne in his glass but now it was as if he was peering into a crystal ball which would tell him what to say. Nicky's the only person I've ever met who can make a glass of champagne last for an hour and even, if necessary, for a whole evening.

At last he said with care: "I agree the situation must be carefully monitored, but so far Alice is all right—in fact she's doing well, getting to know everyone at the Healing Centre and enjoying community life. She's not pining away from unrequited love or living in some fantasy-world. She's at last having a decent life firmly anchored in reality."

"Nicky, I do accept that you're trying to do the right thing by that girl, but you just haven't a clue how painful it must be for her to worship a very attractive man whose only response is to treat her with Christian kindness!"

"Alice doesn't worship me. She simply sees me with great clarity and values what she sees. That's different."

"Look, one of us is being very stupid and I don't think it's me. If you believe—"

"Try to see the situation within the context of the ministry of healing," he interrupted, looking me straight in the eyes at last. "A lot of people who come here are emotionally deprived. For them to experience love in any form, even in a form which you and I would consider childish, is for them a big step forward and the last thing they need is rejection. The wonder worker would exploit that love and use it to feed his own ego, but the Christian priest should accept the love—hero-worship—whatever you care to call it—and offer it back to God, the source of all love, so that the love is contained and sanctified instead of corrupted and destroyed. It's all part and parcel of treating the poor and needy with special care, as Christ did, and living out the belief that each one of us has value in God's eyes."

"Well, that's certainly very fine and idealistic, but . . ." My voice trailed away. By this time I was conscious that the conversation had become very different from the one I'd anticipated. It had become far more serious, far more profound, far more . . . But I could not quite think of the adjective I wanted. "Baffling" implied I was too thick to grasp Nicky's simple sentences, and "disturbing" implied I was being needlessly neurotic. Then I realised that the right word was "enigmatic." That implied both mystery and complexity, qualities I had never once expected to encounter in Nicky's relationship with Alice Fletcher.

I didn't care for this conclusion at all, but as soon as I had reached it, Nicky said swiftly: "Darling, you can be quite sure that if I thought Alice wasn't thriving here I'd find her a job elsewhere. So there's no need for you to worry about her, I promise. No need at all."

That sounded sensible enough. What exactly had I been worrying about anyway? The girl could hardly be considered a threat to me, and Nicky had long since learnt how to deal with infatuated females. Then it dawned on me to my astonishment that I had been identifying very deeply with Alice. Poor girl! No man, not even a man armed with ESP, can really begin to imagine the horrors plain women have to endure . . .

I drained my glass of champagne and silently thanked God that my plain adolescence now seemed like another life on a distant planet.

VI

Alice had cooked chicken forestière with duchesse potatoes and carrots followed by peaches in brandy with a sweet white wine sauce. The carrots were a trifle *al dente* but otherwise I had no complaints. During the meal neither Nicky nor I bothered much with conversation, and afterwards when I was preparing the coffee, he stretched out on the sofa and fell asleep. The drama of the past twenty-four hours, capped with the dose of champagne, had finally taken its toll.

Abandoning the coffee with relief I fell into bed and was asleep five minutes later.

At five-thirty I was aware of him having a bath and dressing in fresh clothes before going downstairs to his study. Here, I knew, he would do his spiritual exercises: reading, meditating, praying. At six-thirty he would tackle his correspondence—he conducted much of his spiritual direction by letter—and at five to eight he would go over to the church for the first service of the day. This one was too early for the office-workers; they would flock to the lunch-time Eucharist, but the principal people at the Healing Centre would all try to attend alongside the prayer-group which met regularly to support the ministry. Only the Healing Centre's personnel, however, would show up at the Rectory afterwards for the communal breakfast. The members of the prayer-group were not concerned with the administrative matters which surfaced at this daily staff meeting, and would disperse after the service to their homes.

At quarter to eight, just as I was dreaming I had won an enormous gold cup at the Chelsea Flower Show for exhibiting a wilting red rose dripping blood, Nicky woke me up and asked if I wanted to go to the eight o'clock "mass." Why Anglo-Catholics can't be decently British and talk of "Communion" I shall never know.

"Oh Nicky, I could never be ready in time and anyway I've got to revive this rose before the judges realise it's dead—"

He disappeared.

When I awoke properly half an hour later I felt guilty. I should have gone to Communion to mark the fresh start in our marriage. For a split second as I stared around the bleak bedroom I longed for Butterfold, but that anguished stab of desire was so disturbing that I repressed it. I decided to devote the morning to making a comprehensive survey of the Rectory so that I could flesh out the ideas I had already had and dream up some new ones. I still hadn't solved the problem of where to put the boys' games-room.

Having dressed in a dove-grey suit to encourage a business-like frame of mind, I borrowed some A4 paper and a clipboard from Nicky's study and retired again to the flat where I drank coffee and drew diagrams of rooms dotted with furniture. After completing the third diagram I decided I ought to make a polite appearance at the communal breakfast, but fortunately an earnest discussion was in progress about whether the proposed fax machine should be abandoned and I was able to escape in less than a minute. Apparently someone had just discovered that messages on fax-paper faded away when stored and had to be photocopied on arrival, a procedure which added to the expense involved. As I slipped out of the room Lewis was announcing with relish: "The idea that technology will save us all time and money is one of the great urban myths of the late twentieth century."

Closing the door of the kitchen I paused in the hall. I was wondering whether to inspect the garden but then I remembered it was only accessible at present through Alice's flat, known as the hell-hole in the days when it had been used to store files and other clutter from the Church and the Healing Centre. This junk was now choking the area which Nicky said I should use as a garden-room. But where was the junk to go next? The whole problem began to seem very knotty indeed, almost as knotty as the problem about where to put the games-room if a shoehorned Lewis was dispatched to share the space at the top of the house with Stacy.

I was just beginning to feel depressed when Stacy himself lolloped out of the kitchen and caught sight of me musing by the main staircase. I guessed he was probably en route to the curate's flat, formerly the servants' attics, to change from his cassock in preparation for his morning's work.

I had a soft spot for Stacy, not just because I was partial to young men but because I felt sorry for him, living alongside Nicky and Lewis, both former public-schoolboys from moneyed, privileged backgrounds. Stacy had been chosen by Nicky to broaden the social base of the ministry. I thought this was actually rather patronising, as if Nicky and Lewis were saying: "Gosh, we're so elite that we really need a yob like you to teach us how the other half live!" and I wondered how happy Stacy was not only with his clerical colleagues but with the middle-class southerners who helped to run the Healing Centre.

St. Benet's, being a Guild church, was not classified as a place where curates could be trained, but the clerical authorities in Westminster and Lambeth had liked the idea of a young priest being groomed for this flourishing, fashionable ministry, and when a legacy to the Centre had enabled Nicky to pay a clerical salary, special arrangements to authorise the engaging of a curate had been made at Church House. Stacy's interest in the ministry of healing had begun some years ago in his home town of Liverpool when his "Mam" had been in hospital for a cancer operation and the Anglican chaplain had applied the laying-on of hands. "Mam" was still very much alive, battling away in her council flat with the local authority whenever she wasn't organising a wedding for one of her daughters. There was no "Dad," who had expired in the 1970s after what was described as a "tiff" with a neighbour in a pub. Dad had been prone to tiffs, and shortly after his arrival from Ireland he had had a tiff with the local Roman Catholic priest; this had resulted in the entire McGovern family transferring their religious allegiance to the local outpost of the Church of England, an Anglo-Catholic set-up which proved to be to the right of Rome. The McGoverns had felt quite at home there.

Stacy was huge, about six foot three, and had long lean limbs which he had only a hazy idea how to control. He was always knocking over furniture or smashing things by mistake. He had beautiful red hair, glowing and wavy, and beautiful blue eyes and beautiful cheekbones. But the rest of him was very plain. Fortunately, however, he had so much energy and enthusiasm that it was easy to overlook his defects, and even the ugly Liverpool accent was alleviated by his unstoppable flow of Irish charm.

"Stacy dear," I said as he bounded out of the kitchen, "may I have your permission to go into your flat this morning? I'm making a survey of the house in order to take it in hand."

"Wow!" said this delightful overgrown child. "Help! The flat's a tip—I haven't picked up anything lately!"

"Oh, Benedict and Antony never pick up anything either, I'm used to that. Just hide the naughty pictures of page-three girls and I shan't bat an eyelid."

The child blushed. He really was rather sweet. "You're a real tease, Mrs. Darrow!" he said. "You're like my sister Aisling!"

I had told him at least three times to call me Rosalind, but he couldn't. I was so many years his senior and I came from the South and I had a cut-glass accent and I was his boss's wife. I could see him practising calling me Rosalind but could never imagine him taking the plunge and calling me Rosalind when we met.

"How's Aisling getting on?" I asked kindly. Stacy, the baby of the family, had three sisters and adored them all. The youngest had recently married, and according to Nicky Stacy had for some time been showing her wedding photographs to anyone who displayed the remotest degree of interest. He had never quite plucked up the courage to invite me to his flat for a private viewing during my occasional brief, busy visits to the Rectory, but now that I was to be staying at the house for some days I had no doubt that the courage would soon be found.

"Aisling's grand!" responded Stacy enthusiastically, delighted to have the opportunity to prattle about his favourite subject. "She's planning to go to Ibiza next year for her holiday and she said she did wish I could come with them—and I wish I could too, we could have such fun, all three of us! I've always wanted to go to Ibiza, and when I heard she was planning to go there I—"

This most peculiar speech, implying Stacy had no idea how newlywed couples felt about an intrusive third party, was terminated abruptly by Lewis, who clattered out of the kitchen on his crutches, growled at Stacy: "Get a move on!" and then, to my surprise, gave me a charming smile as Stacy fled in the direction of the backstairs.

"Ah!" he said genially. "Rosalind! Could you possibly spare me a moment, please?"

I was more surprised than ever, but told him he could have as many moments as he liked. This produced another smile and an invitation into his crowded bed-sitting-room which faced across the garden towards the church.

I realise now that I didn't describe Lewis when I mentioned him earlier; I just delivered an anti-Lewis polemic. Let me now, in the interests of accuracy, try to present a more balanced portrait of this man who had attached himself to Nicky's ministry and was now clinging to it like the most ferocious of limpets.

Lewis was one of those eccentric upper-class Englishmen who make a great show of "playing the game" according to the rules but who are actually capable of more or less any licence or lunacy. The more immaculately he behaved and the more conventionally he dressed the more one became aware of his underlying oddness. His deepset black eyes were so sinister and his tough square build was so reminiscent of a great actor portraying a Mafia hitman that I could never feel at ease in his presence, and my discomfort was exacerbated by the fact that he was sexy. Indeed in his younger days, before his hair had silvered to give him an air of bogus respectability, I had thought he was one of the sexiest men I had ever met—although it was not the kind of sexiness I liked. Even now I could feel the automatic, mindless twinge one experiences whenever one sees male sexiness on display, but every other feminine instinct told me to give him a wide berth, with the result that I had always found him wholly resistible. Nicky refused to talk in detail about his friend's private life, but I suspected that Lewis was one of those men who, although sexually normal, thoroughly disliked women. Such men are dangerous to any woman who values her sanity.

In Lewis's defence I have to admit he was a very sincere, very devout Christian and completely dedicated to the task of being a good clergyman. I couldn't help thinking this must have been an uphill struggle but he never gave up, not even in 1983 when he got in that mess in his previous diocese and was sacked by the Bishop. I admired Lewis for this persistence. But he really was a very peculiar cleric. Of course the ministry of healing and deliverance does attract these highly charismatic, potentially dangerous men, and the danger doesn't only lie in the psychic gifts they often possess; it lies in the immense power latent in the personality, and this power is all mixed up with sex. No wonder everyone says the ministry of healing is so subject to corruption! If the healers let all that charismatic glitz get out of control—if they lose sight for one moment of the integrity of that healer *par excellence* Jesus Christ—this potent cocktail of sex, power and religion explodes with the force of dynamite and destroys everything in sight.

Perhaps I ought to steer clear of that word "charismatic"; it can be so easily misunderstood because it has different shades of meaning. When I wrote just now that the ministry of healing attracts highly charismatic men, I was using "charismatic" as we used to use it in the 1960s—as a slang-word meaning dynamic and mesmerisingly attractive. But in its strict technical sense "charismatic" refers to the special gifts of God, the "charisms" listed by St. Paul which include the gift of healing. Nicky and Lewis were charismatic in both senses; they not only had the gift of healing but were also magnetic personalities. To complicate matters I should also mention that there was a third use of the word "charismatic"—this time "Charismatic" spelt with a capital C. This referred to the people, Catholic and Protestant, who belonged to the Charismatic Movement which had spread like wildfire through the Christian churches around twenty years ago and was still going strong. The Charismatics held emotional services in which they spoke in tongues, exorcised anything that moved and were allegedly empowered by the Holy Spirit. Neither Lewis nor Nicky was charismatic in this sense, and indeed they prided themselves on reflecting the respectable Anglican Catholic mainstream.

"Do please sit down," Lewis was saying, still very much on his best behaviour, and adjusting his crutches he stooped to flick an imaginary speck of dust from the visitor's armchair as if only the cleanest cushion could possibly be good enough for me.

"Now," he said when I was in my assigned place and he was seated opposite me. "I won't beat about the bush. I know we've never been the best of friends and that's exactly why I want to be straight with you here and leave no room for misunderstanding. First of all, let me make it clear that I wish you and Nicholas well in your efforts to overcome your present difficulties. Second, let me say that I regard it as my duty as a priest to do all I can to help you—and when I say 'you' I mean not just Nicholas but you as well. And third, let me spell out one or two facts which may not be obvious to Nicholas but which you might find useful as you try to visualise a future at the Rectory . . . May I proceed or should I shut up?"

I found myself reluctantly attracted to this frank approach. "I'm all ears."

"Right. Well, if you're going to make the Rectory your main home, it's important that you should feel free to make whatever changes are necessary. So here are the facts you need to know: one, I don't have to live here; there's no reason why I shouldn't take a flat in the Barbican. Two, Stacy doesn't have to live here either; nowadays curates almost always have their own home away from the vicarage or rectory. It would be too expensive to house Stacy at the Barbican, but we could afford to put him in one of the cheaper neighborhoods nearby . . . Am I being helpful or should I stop?"

"I'm riveted. Go on. What about Alice?"

There was a pause. I wondered if my eyes were as expressionless as his.

"Alice has the advantage of being immensely employable," he said at last. "In the past she's underrated her employability and not aimed high enough, but cooks of her calibre are much sought after and there'd be no need for her to return to Belgravia. She could stay in this area, where she now has friends, and set herself up as a freelance. There are four thousand people in the Barbican, many of whom are wealthy enough to hire a cook for special occasions, and as there's an active grapevine I don't think Alice would have a problem getting work. Accommodation could be difficult at first, but Daisy would fix her up—social workers always know the best deals available in local housing."

"So you're saying Alice doesn't have to live here either."

"Exactly. Indeed eventually she should move on anyway in order to develop her gifts further and broaden her horizons. For Alice St. Benet's should be seen as just a staging-post along the way."

"I see." I examined my thumbnail before saying politely: "May I ask some questions?"

"Please do."

"What happens to the new communal breakfast if Alice goes?"

"We can have a rota and take it in turns to cook. The same applies for lunch. It's been important to us to have a cook-housekeeper, I admit, but if Stacy and I are to live elsewhere, it would be hard to justify the expense of retaining live-in help."

"But surely you yourself have to live here—doesn't the Rectory need to be manned twenty-four hours a day to cope with emergencies? What happens if Nicky and I are out and someone rings up with a problem?"

"British Telecom can provide a system for rerouting calls to my flat at the Barbican."

"So technology isn't quite so black as you were trying to paint it just now!"

"Every cloud has its silver lining!"

"But supposing someone turns up late at night when Nicky's away and I'm here on my own?"

"Don't answer the door. Anyone connected with St. Benet's would always phone first, and for anyone else there's always the Samaritans or the emergency services. Nicholas and I are certainly on call in an emergency to those registered at the Healing Centre, but the Centre itself isn't manned twenty-four hours a day and there's no law saying a rectory has to be manned twenty-four hours a day either."

"I've got one final question. I don't think Nicky realises any of this. Why hasn't he worked it all out, just as you have?"

"He's extremely confused at the moment. He's had a big shock and he's in a flat spin. That's why I thought it was important that you and I should talk."

I meditated on this as I gave my thumbnail another examination. Then I said: "I've thought of another final question: why are you being so noble, ceding your bedsit so graciously? Or in other words, what's in all this for you?"

"Good point!" said Lewis benignly, not in the least disconcerted. "Well, I was quite sincere when I wished you well, but I admit my primary concern is Nicholas's stability. It's very important for his ministry that he gets his private life straight, and I am, as you know, deeply committed to that ministry of his."

That made sense. I was tempted to end our conference at that point, but it was so pleasant to have an honest conversation which was encouraging instead of deeply upsetting that I succumbed to the temptation to linger. "I've thought of yet another final question," I said. "Do you think Nicky's being dumb about Alice?"

"My dear, that's your third final question! No dictionary would support your definition of the word 'final'!"

This frothy prevarication almost certainly meant the answer to my question was "yes." "Don't get me wrong," I said. "Obviously there's no danger of him leaping into bed with her. I just think there's a level here where he's not plugged in to reality."

Lewis said politely: "I'm not sure I understand," but I suspected not only that he understood all too well but that he was surprised by my insight. Driven on by his misogyny he had probably long since written me off as a materialistic robot devoid of sensitivity.

"Yesterday," I persisted, "I told Nicky it was wrong to keep Alice here when she was clearly in love with him, but he just spouted some amazing stuff about accepting her love and offering it all back to God so that it could be sanctified—well, it sounded wonderful when he said it, so splendidly Christian, but when I woke up this morning I saw straight away it was nuts. If you're an attractive man you don't keep a lovelorn maiden in your basement, it's just asking for trouble, and anyway, as I tried to explain to Nicky yesterday, it's not fair on *her.*"

"Obviously you need to talk to him again about it."

"Obviously I do. And by the way, while we're on the subject of Nicky being uncharacteristically dumb I'm very miffed about that cat. Why didn't he tell me about it? I'm not so anti-cat that I can't see it's the best solution to the mouse problem! So why did he have to go hatching cat-schemes—as he obviously did—with that poor plain lump of a girl whom he couldn't possibly fancy?"

"Why indeed," said Lewis, black eyes inscrutable, but he set his thin-lipped mouth into the toughest of straight lines.

"Oh, face it, Lewis!" I exclaimed irritated. "After all, it was you who initiated all this straight talking! Alice *is* a lump and she *is* plain and she *is* poor, but don't make the mistake of thinking that in consequence I feel only contempt for her, because nothing could be further from the truth. As a woman I have a good deal of sisterly sympathy for her—which is exactly why I don't want her to get mangled by an ultra-magnetic healer who's taking time out from rational thinking to engage in cat-mad nuttiness . . . And talking of time out, weren't you supposed to have a convalescent holiday after your operation? I hope you're not succumbing to the urge to do too much too soon."

Lewis said he hadn't been able to tear himself away from Alice's cooking and anyway winter was all the wrong time for an English holiday, convalescent or otherwise, and talking of holidays, how had I enjoyed my brief visit to Francie's Devonshire cottage?

I shuddered. "It seems to have turned into a rural slum."

"What a pity! And when you phoned Francie to ask if you could borrow the cottage," said Lewis, "how did she seem?"

"Fine—awash with guilty relief that ghastly Harry's away in Hong Kong. Why?"

"She called in sick yesterday."

"Oh? Maybe she's subconsciously pining for Harry to come back and tell her how stupid she is."

"He's not violent, though, is he?"

"No, the cruelty's all verbal. Poor Francie! She ought to have a proper career and kick the brute in the teeth . . . but I suppose I shouldn't say that to a clergyman."

"People say the most extraordinary things to clergymen," said Lewis, finally rising to his feet to escort me to the door. "That's what makes the clerical life so interesting. Do you see much of Francie these days?"

"We meet very occasionally for lunch," I said vaguely, anxious to soft-pedal my association with my mole, and changed the subject by thanking him for his most enlightening suggestions about the reorganization of the Rectory.

I was dimly beginning to realise I'd been swindled.

8

Ruthless honesty with ourselves is required to face how much we are secretly nursing anger and resentments.

GARETH TUCKWELL AND DAVID FLAGG
A Question of Healing

I

The flat was so cold, so drab and so uninviting in that grey winter light that as soon as I entered the hall I suffered an overwhelming desire to escape. Grabbing my coat I slipped on some comfortable shoes and set off for the Barbican, that twelve-gated city-within-a-city, with its skyscrapers and mews houses, its duplexes and triplexes, its penthouses and studios, its cinema, theatres, restaurants, library, schools, offices, shops, gardens, fake-lakes and fake-waterfall. I enjoyed the Barbican. There was something sexy about all that crude concrete brutalism and that rampant, no-holds-barred architectural adventurousness which had marked—and marred—the twentieth century. I found the peculiar landscape stimulating, rather as an astronaut would be stimulated by seeing something so far beyond his earthly experience as the far side of the moon.

At Gate Six I climbed the stairs to the podium, crossed Gilbert Bridge and entered the centrally heated comfort of the Arts Centre. In the cafe I toyed with a Danish pastry and gazed out across the fake-lake to the dome of St. Paul's while I waited for my brain to thaw.

The more it thawed the more clearly I realised that I'd been swindled. It was as if Nicky had put my brain on ice in Devon but Lewis's straight talking had initiated a melting process, and I was only halfway through my Danish pastry when I said to myself: wait a minute. Just how the hell have you wound up losing your beautiful home and languishing in that horrible house which you'd be more than happy never to see again?

I tried to argue that I hadn't lost my beautiful home, since Nicky had agreed to retain it, but I knew the farmhouse wasn't suited to the part-time occupancy he had in mind. It was too big. It required too much daily attention. There needed to be someone in full-time residence—me—who could supervise the cleaner and the gardener, and besides, if a house is only sporadically occupied, it soon falls prey to vandals or burglars. I shuddered as I thought of the possible ravages. Another hazard was the central heating. Supposing it broke down in winter with the result that the pipes froze?

The truth was that unless one was rich enough to afford live-in staff, second homes needed to be small, filled with cheap furniture and designed to require the minimum of upkeep. Anyway the two-home syndrome was hell for women. It was all very well for Nicky to live in two homes—he merely had to drive down to Surrey and everything was waiting for him: food, wife, clean sheets, the lot. But if *I* had to manage two homes I'd soon be bogged down in cooking, shopping and cleaning, and in no time at all I'd be transformed into a household drudge.

The emotional cost of having two homes would also be unbearable. How would I be able to endure leaving Butterfold at the end of each brief visit and returning to exile at the Rectory? No, the scheme would never work. What was more, I was sure that Nicky had known it would never work but he had been clever enough not to suggest selling the farmhouse immediately. He had been gambling that by the time I discovered the Butterfold-as-second-home scheme was unworkable I'd be so thoroughly committed to the Rectory that I'd be willing to pull up my Surrey roots.

Nicky wouldn't miss Surrey. He had no root there to pull up, but my whole life was there, my circle of friends, my garden—everything. I loved Butterfold, and *so did the boys.* What were they really going to think of life at the Rectory? How were they going to get on with Nicky, and how was Nicky going to cope with having his family bobbing around him all the time during the school holidays? None of the old problems, the problems which had driven me to suggest a split-level marriage seven years ago, had actually been solved and none of my unhappiness had been alleviated either. In fact it had been exacerbated because I knew that this new togetherness in a place I hated would only serve to underline the fact that the marriage had broken down. I still wanted out of the marriage, I could see that now, just as I could see I had been mad to wind up playing the docile wife at the Rectory.

The full dimensions of my unhappiness finally resurfaced. The fact was that I was so lonely and so miserable with my part-time, uncomprehending husband who dropped in at weekends for sex that for some time I had been showing clear signs of coming apart at the seams. I winced as I remembered my erratic behaviour in recent months. I didn't approve of adultery. It offended my sense of fair play. It was all very well to feel smug about my dexterity in bedding beautiful young men, but the rock-bottom truth was that this kind of frolicking was very trashy and vulgar, quite unsuitable for a woman of forty-five who wanted to retain her dignity and self-respect. What was I trying to prove and to whom? Nicky the clergyman would have judged me off-centre, floundering around in a spiritual vacuum as I struggled to blot out my unhappiness, and Nicky the clergyman would have been right. The marriage was driving me not just to act out of character but to slide into lunacy, I could see that now, and unless I took action very soon there would inevitably be further shoddy, freaky behaviour culminating, no doubt, in a fullscale nervous breakdown.

I shuddered again and bought a second cup of coffee.

I then began to do what I had planned to do in Devon: to work out a better future for myself. I would stay at the farmhouse. The boys would remain there too during the school holidays, although Nicky would have visiting rights. I would finish my year's sabbatical, ride out the backchat of the village gossips, who would naturally be delighted by the spectacle of a clerical marriage on the rocks, and afterwards, strengthened by the support of my many loyal friends, I would embark on a new career. I thought I could take a diploma—or why not a degree?—in horticulture so that I had a qualification which would set me apart from the amateurs. I could study at Kew or Wisley—perhaps even qualify as a landscape architect eventually—and then . . . YES! I could start a business designing gardens. That would allow me to satisfy my business talents *and* engage my creative instincts, such as they were, on a deeper level. Flowers had served me well but now I wanted something more—a wider canvas, a bigger vision, a better challenge—AN EMPIRE! Yes, that was it. I wanted to build an empire over and over again. Each garden would be an empire. I'd be a horticultural Mrs. Thatcher, a neo-imperialist Britannia togged out in green Wellies and a Barbour jacket!

I reined myself in, smiling at this droll fantasy but recognising with excitement the alluring reality which underpinned it. I had no doubt whatsoever that such a new career would make me happy, and once I was happy I knew I'd be stable and well behaved again. There would be no more pathetic batting around with young men. I'd find someone of my own age—well, perhaps five to ten years younger, that would be quite acceptable—more or less—and it would be someone who shared my interests, some elegant widower from the National Trust perhaps, who loved beautiful houses and beautiful gardens and who believed in the great tradition of English Country Life and who voted for Mrs. Thatcher, scintillating Mrs. Thatcher, who proclaimed that every English family should have its own home—and that was such a wonderful goal, wasn't it, because deep down *every* normal person wanted their own home—and their own garden—and I was no exception to this very human desire.

I wasn't peculiar like Nicky. I was a normal English person in 1988, just one of the countless millions who had voted for Mrs. Thatcher because she alone understood what all we normal English people wanted: homes and gardens, law and order, pleasure and leisure, health and wealth—with a full orchestra playing "Land of Hope and Glory" in the background and a forest of Union Jacks stretching as far as the eye could see.

Well, was it such a crime to be normal?

No. But Nicky had behaved as if it were a crime for me to vote Conservative, just as he was now behaving as if it were a crime for me to want to lead the life that was right for me. Down in Devon he had obviously decided that I was no better than a loony criminal who needed to be radically rehabilitated, so he had brainwashed me by playing the wonder worker. The honest Christian clergyman had disappeared and I had been manipulated, browbeaten and catastrophically outmanoeuvred by this charismatic horror who had mixed power-plays with sex to such devastating effect that I had wound up conceding *everything* while he had wound up conceding *nothing*. As a Christian healer he should have tried to set aside his own wants while he explored as sympathetically as possible the reasons why I was so unhappy, yet instead he had decided, without once pausing to consult me, that my entire life-style should be destroyed. All that talk of "restructuring" our marriage! The restructuring was to be undertaken solely by me as I was compelled to slot into his London life! I was supposed to live in a horrible house with a horrible garden while he simply carried on regardless and made no changes to his own life-style whatsoever. Of course he'd still have no time for me during the week, but with luck he might come to life as usual at weekends. Big deal! In other words we'd be exactly as we were before—marriage on week-ends—but I would have lost my home, my garden and my entire cherished way of life.

I saw then that Lewis, cunning old villain, had probably deduced all this from the start but had realised it would be easier to wake me from my browbeaten, brain-dead state than to tackle Nicky with the truth when Nicky himself was too shell-shocked to think clearly. Lewis would have grasped that to talk positively and encouragingly about converting the Rectory into a family home was the best way to make me realise not only how much I hated the idea but how far Nicky had lost touch with reality. The truth was Nicky hadn't even begun to face up to this crisis. He had merely made the snap decision that if he could keep me at the Rectory like some sort of mindless lucky mascot, we would live happily ever after. What an absurdly childish dream! But he showed no sign of abandoning it. How could I get him to wake up, grow up and relinquish me? Queasily I re-membered the little boy who had declared to his class at kindergarten: "This is my bear and no one plays with my bear but me."

He still had that bear. It was wrapped in tissue paper and kept in his old school tuck-box in the farmhouse attic. Before we were mar-ried he had said he was keeping the bear for our future children, but when the boys came it had never been exhumed.

I thought: I'm not going to be shut up in a box like that bear. And amending little Nicky's declaration to the kindergarten class I added to myself: this is my life and no one controls my life but me.

I set aside my coffee-cup. No more procrastination. Procrastination was for wimps. Leaving the cafe I marched back over Gilbert Bridge and headed south out of the Barbican to St. Benet's.

II

On returning to the Rectory, however, I found I had no choice but to procrastinate as Nicky was out, slaving away as usual at the task of being wonderful to everyone in sight. In the flat I turned on the drawing-room's gas fire and crouched in front of it for five minutes to combat my incipient hypothermia. After that I realised I was yearning for a dose of sympathetic female companionship so I phoned the Healing Centre and asked for Francie. I was very put out to be told she was still off sick. Grabbing my Filofax I tracked down her home number and started to dial.

"Francie, it's Rosalind," I said after she had uttered a dreary "hullo" into the receiver. "I hear you haven't been befriending lately—what's wrong?"

"Oh, nothing serious! At least . . . well, actually that's a complete lie, I'm so depressed that I feel it could be terminal, but never mind, it's not important. How's Devon?"

"I'm not in Devon, I'm at the Rectory. I've been depressed too, but it's bloody well not going to be terminal! Let's meet. Lunch at Fortnum's?"

"God, I don't think I could make it as far as Piccadilly."

"Oh, don't be so feeble, Francie! Why the hell are you so depressed?"

"Perhaps it's the menopause."

"Oh, fuck the menopause! You're not secretly pining for Harry, are you?"

"No, I want to murder him."

"Super—I want to murder Nicky. Maybe we should do a swap, like those two men in *Strangers on a Train*, and kill each other's husbands so that we can each stage a cast-iron alibi for the appropriate murder."

"But good heavens, why on earth do you want to murder Nicky?"

"Because he's being totally impossible and I'm fed up to the back teeth," I said recklessly. "For God's sake let's meet before I start invading the Healing Centre and giving primal screams!"

"Well, maybe I could make it to Piccadilly after all," said Francie, reviving at a brisk pace. There's nothing like the prospect of a riveting gossip for dispelling the blues. "But I can't make it today. Harrods rang up this morning and said they were going to deliver Harry's new desk at one-thirty."

"Okay, let's make it tomorrow. Twelve-thirty upstairs at Fortnum's, and if you OD on tranx before we can let our hair down I'll never forgive you," I said, looking up Fortnum's number in my Filofax even before I had replaced the receiver.

Having reserved the table I realised I was feeling better. Thank

God for devoted and loyal girlfriends! To boost my morale still further I called Susie in Tetbury and Tiggy in Winchester. I was meticulous in keeping up a front for my more recent girlfriends in Surrey, but Susie and Tiggy, orbiting in different areas of the Conservative heartlands, could remember me in a gym-slip so I felt I could indulge in a modified whinge without letting the side down. ("Nicky wants to revamp our marriage—my dear, the *challenge!* I'm so stimulated that I feel ripe for a strait-jacket . . .") This veiled breast-beating let off some steam, but I was aware as I spoke that I could only be utterly frank to Francie. She was the only one of my friends who had firsthand experience of the ministry of healing; she was the only one who would understand how thin the line could sometimes be between the honest Christian healer, committed to serving God, and the shady, manipulative wonder worker, committed to serving his own interests.

Both my old pals tried to cheer me up by giving me delicious snippets of information about their current difficulties. Susie said Nigel was making so much money that he had started drinking champagne for breakfast, and Tiggy confided that Bam-Bam was so stressed at work that he spent all weekend at the golf club trying to unwind. I diagnosed alcoholism and adultery respectively and envied them their well-known marital problems. Part of the trouble with being married to a charismatic clergyman was that the marital problems were so peculiar. I had said to Susie once that I refused to sleep with Nicky directly after an exorcism because he smelt so odd, but Susie had just thought I was joking.

Having revitalised myself by tuning in to what the feminists are pleased to call "the sisterhood," I then drew up a list of food to restock the flat's empty kitchen for twenty-four hours and drove to the supermarket on Whitecross Street. I wasn't sure how long it would take to coax Nicky to face reality, but I thought it would be sensible to be well nourished as I prepared for battle. The battle itself I planned to conduct in a civilised manner which would ensure there were no further ghastly scenes, and to set the tone for the initial discussion that evening I decided to cook an elegant dinner. I would take infinite trouble over it—just as much trouble as that girl had taken yesterday—and my carrots weren't going to be underdone either. In fact I planned to omit carrots, such a boring vegetable, and serve madly fashionable mange-tout.

The supermarket contained some extraordinary people but since it was surrounded by working-class housing I could hardly expect to meet the inhabitants of middle-class Surrey. Some of the food was strange too, but I didn't mind that. Encountering exotic ingredients for recipes can be fun, but nevertheless I began to find my expedition unusually exhausting. Once I was past the check-out I was tempted to go straight back to the Rectory but I felt I couldn't face the flat without flowers. Having circled around to Aldersgate I spent some time in the florist there, and when I emerged I was only just in time to avoid getting a parking ticket for dumping the car on a single yellow line. Deciding London was impossible I retreated at last to the Rectory, placed the flowers in water, ate some soup and passed out on the bed. The entire afternoon was wasted in sleep. I hadn't realised how worn out I was by all the to-ing and fro-ing from Devon in a state of extreme nervous tension.

When I awoke groggily at four I found there was no sign of Nicky, but he seldom came back to the flat during the day. Having drunk some tea I soothed myself by arranging the flowers. The shop had been stuffed with chrysanthemums, the traditional November fodder, but I'm not necessarily snooty about chrysanthemums and can well spare the time to admire the Korean types, particularly the pink Venus and the pale Ceres. They do well in perennial borders because they're so hardy. I'm also very fond of the pink and crimson Emperor of China, always so striking and with the additional virtue of being frost-proof in a cold spell.

The chrysanthemums I had purchased weren't quite in this league, but they made a warm splash of colour, particularly when set against a daring pattern of foliage, and I felt pleased with the results. I took some time over the arrangement because it stopped me thinking about the scene destined to take place when I announced my latest conclusions to Nicky, but as soon as the last flower was in place I knew I wasn't just nervous; I was frightened.

I told myself that this was irrational. I was certain that after the scenes at the cottage Nicky would be ashamed enough to want to avoid any further violent outbursts, but there was no doubt I was still feeling very jittery. To calm myself down I opened a bottle of plonk which I'd bought at the supermarket and had a quick slurp. Then it occurred to me that a well-controlled, non-violent Nicky playing the wonder worker was a much more spine-chilling prospect than a poorly controlled, very physical Nicky playing the caveman. A caveman might just about manage some crude brainwashing whenever he wasn't bucketing around trying to break down the nearest door, but he wasn't going to be organised enough to employ the most lethal tricks of the wonder worker's stock-in-trade.

In a flash I remembered that horrible party up at Cambridge when Nicky had been an undergraduate, and naked fear rippled through me as I recalled the hypnosis.

I knew I hadn't been hypnotised down in Devon. I had certainly been manipulated but I had remained in control of my mind—by which I mean that although Nicky had persuaded me to do the opposite of what I wanted, I myself had still been the one making the decision that I should go on with the marriage. Nicky knew I'd never stand for hypnosis. Long before he had performed the parlour-tricks for his smart set, he hypnotised me into believing that he had stopped my watch just by looking at it. He said: "The second-hand's halted, hasn't it?" and I could see that it had. Then he said: "But when I snap my fingers you'll see that it's moving again." And when he snapped his fingers I could indeed see that the second-hand was moving on. Enthralled I begged him to tell me how he had done it, and he admitted the hypnosis.

So appalled was I by the knowledge that my mind had been temporarily removed from my control in this vilely sly way, that I rushed out of his house and would have run sobbing all the way home if I hadn't bumped into his father in the drive. Old Mr. Darrow had become a recluse after Nicky's mother died, but Nicky and I were only thirteen then and she was still alive. Mr. Darrow saw I was upset and as soon as I told him what had happened he said that the hypnosis was very wrong and that he would speak to Nicky immediately. I loved old Mr. Darrow. He was such a very wise, kind clergyman and always so nice to me.

Nicky arrived at my house on his bicycle half an hour later and apologised. "I'll never do that to you again, I promise," he said. "*Never.*" And I knew then his father had made him understand how wrong it was. No wonder I was so horrified when I saw him using hypnosis six years later up at Cambridge! "Your father would have hated that," I said stonily to Nicky afterwards, and at once he said in a panic: "You're not to tell him—I forbid it! You're not to make him upset!"—as if *I* would have been responsible for old Mr. Darrow's inevitable distress! That was Nicky trying to manipulate me again, and I did indeed promise him I'd keep quiet, but I made it clear that I'd found his tricks so repulsive that I never wanted to see any of them again.

Much later, during our engagement, he said to me: "You're the one girl I can trust to support me to the hilt now that I've rejected all that stuff," and I remember feeling faint with relief that he had reformed.

But although he no longer abused his gift for hypnosis, he didn't abandon it. He explained to me that he had offered the gift to God and now hoped to use it in the service of others. He took a course in the medical use of hypnosis and was very scrupulous in using it as a treatment in accordance with medical ethics. I knew he never hypnotised any of his clients unless Val the doctor was present, but needless to say I was still revolted by the fact that he continued to dabble in hypnosis and I made it clear I never wanted to discuss the subject again.

He did try to reassure me by insisting that people couldn't be hypnotised against their wills, but I was never entirely sure I believed this. I certainly hadn't wanted to be hypnotised when he had stopped my watch. How had he done it? I put this question to him but he just said vaguely that I'd been a child at the time and incapable of raising the right mental defences. What were the right mental defences? Nicky, vaguer than ever, said it was just a question of recognising the hypnotist's will and refusing to submit to it. But when I thought back to the watch-stopping episode I couldn't remember any attempt to subjugate me. I could only remember Nicky laughing and being very chummy as we drank Tizer after a game of Ping-Pong; I could only remember feeling relaxed and utterly unsuspicious. But of course, as he had pointed out, I'd just been a child at the time.

I took another slurp of plonk and pulled myself together. Nicky, regretting the caveman performance in Devon, would be on his best behaviour. Of course he'd have another go at trying to change my mind and no matter how good his intentions were he probably wouldn't be able to avoid some form of manipulative behaviour—people with powerful personalities are hardly likely to turn into soft-as-butter yes-men when they're under stress—but this time reason would triumph, ethics would prevail and he would stop well short of brainwashing, crude or sophisticated. In other words, I could stop gibbering with fright and instead steel myself for a difficult but not dangerous evening during which the painful truth could be bravely faced and honestly discussed.

Pouring myself another glass of plonk to help keep this reassuring vision nailed to the forefront of my mind, I embarked on the task of cooking a supremely civilised dinner.

III

As it turned out I only had a sip or two from that second glass of wine because I became too busy trying to remember my recipes and producing the necessary improvisation when my memory failed. For the first course I had decided to do deep-fried radicchio with goat's cheese, a very tasty starter which apart from the final frying can be prepared ahead of time. My original intention was to make a fish soup but I didn't have a sieve or a liquidiser in the sparsely equipped kitchen of the flat. For the main course I had chosen roast guinea fowl and for the pudding I was keen to produce Grand Marnier crème brûlée, always rich, sophisticated and delicious. I toiled and muttered and sweated and cursed over my hot stove for some time before I had everything under control and could retire once more with my wine to the drawing-room.

At seven o'clock there was still no sign of Nicky and I put the oven on a low setting before buzzing Alice on the intercom to enquire if she knew when the men planned to resurface at the Rectory. I was told that an important meeting was taking place at the Healing Centre and was clearly taking longer than anyone had anticipated. Returning to the kitchen I fiddled again with the oven and then roamed around the living-room with increasing irritation until finally, at twenty-eight minutes past seven, the Rector of St. Benet's-by-the-Wall deigned to appear. The first words he uttered were: "Why are you waiting up here? Alice is all set to dish up downstairs!"

I was flabbergasted. "But I took it for granted that we wouldn't be eating with the others!"

"Why on earth did you take it for granted?"

"Because I'm married to you and not to them!"

"But Alice has made fish pie for five!"

"Well, I've made honey-roasted breast of guinea fowl with glazed shallots for two!"

"But why didn't you tell Alice you were planning to do this?"

"Oh, the hell with Alice!" I cried, by that time feeling thoroughly exasperated as well as unpleasantly nervous, and swigging back the wine in my glass I poured myself some more plonk with a trembling hand.

Moving to the intercom Nicky buzzed the kitchen downstairs. "Lewis, I'll be eating with Rosalind up here," I heard him say.

"Would you apologise to Alice, please, and say we'll work out a system to ensure such a mix-up doesn't happen again? Thanks."

Abandoning the intercom abruptly he opened the door of the refrigerator, ignored the plonk and extracted a can of Coke. "Okay," he said, not looking at me. "Let's eat."

I stormed over to the stove to fry the radicchio.

When we eventually embarked on the meal he shovelled in his food with an undisguised lack of interest while I, having lost my appetite, pushed various fragments of my culinary masterpieces around a succession of plates and waited in vain for him to display at least a nominal politeness by complimenting me on my cooking.

"Right," he said at last at the end of the meal after he had retrieved another can of Coke from the kitchen. "What's your problem? Obviously you're upset."

"God, you're just not in touch, are you! You're gliding along totally disconnected with reality!"

"What do you mean?"

"You've just finished yobbishly wolfing a meal which I spent a great deal of time and trouble preparing—"

"I'm sorry, it was good. Thank you. But what I meant was, what's your *real* problem? I can feel your nerves screeching like a bunch of overstrung violins, and it can't be just because I was so hungry that I hit the food without drenching you with compliments."

"The problem's you, Nicky."

"Are you trying to say that just because I stuffed down that rather good fried rabbit-food and that very sexy bird which had smeared itself with honey—"

"I'm not talking about that. You know I'm not talking about that. I'm saying the problem is that you're not facing up to the truth here."

"What truth?"

"This reconciliation isn't going to work, Nicky. I'm very sorry, but we made a mistake down in Devon and I'm going back to Butterfold tomorrow."

He went white. For a moment I thought he was too shocked to reply but then he said very distinctly: "I'm not going to let you do this. You've got it all totally wrong."

"No, I'm the one who's got it right!"

"You? Got it right? You're proposing to smash up your marriage, your family and your entire life and you're telling me *you've got it right?*"

"Nicky, I know this is hard for you, but if you could only listen to me for a moment instead of—"

"You're obviously very sick," he said, "much sicker than I thought. But don't worry, I'm going to put things right. I'm going to heal you."

I was terrified.

IV

I said panic-stricken, stumbling over my words: "If you start trying to manipulate me again I'll never forgive you."

"Oh, don't be so ridiculous! There was no manipulation in Devon—I just showed you the truth, and the truth was you were trying to make a catastrophic mistake!"

"Nicky—"

"Okay, let's calm down while I try to understand why you want to abandon the decisions you made yesterday. Are you willing to calm down and conduct this conversation sensibly?"

"Well, of course! That's what I want, but—"

"Fine. In that case, let's take a moment to review what you decided in Devon. One: you agreed that our marriage needed to be restructured since the split-level life we've been leading since 1981 was clearly no longer working. Two: you agreed that the Rectory should be our primary home but that we should keep the farmhouse as a country retreat. And three: you agreed to stay at the Rectory until the school holidays begin in order to explore how it can best be turned into a family home. Now, would you say that was an accurate summary of what took place?"

"No. I didn't actually agree to anything. You just steamrollered me into coming here, and this morning I suddenly realised—"

"Why do you now think you can't live at the Rectory?"

"Because I want to live full-time in my own home! Is that so unreasonable?"

"But I never suggested we should sell Butterfold! I suggested—"

"The farmhouse is quite unsuited to be a second home, Nicky—it requires too much daily attention. Anyway I'm not prepared to relegate it in that way—I love that house, my whole life's bound up with it—"

"You're making an idol of bricks and mortar and worshipping it!"

"But it's my home! Surely—"

"Home is where the people you love are. Good heavens, think of all the clerical wives who regularly accompany their husbands from job to job and would never dream of whingeing like this!"

"Well, even if I was willing to leave Butterfold I wouldn't want to live here in this horrible house! It would cost thousands to make it even partially decent!"

"I'm prepared to spend the money—my money, not yours—on having the place renovated. I'll do anything you want in order to make you happy here."

"Would you get rid of Lewis, Stacy and Alice?"

"Why?"

"Because they're cluttering up the landscape and making it impossible for me to turn this house into our family home!"

"What nonsense! There's room here for everyone—and anyway their presence is absolutely essential!"

"But Lewis informed me this morning—"

"Yes, he told me exactly what he'd said to you, but I saw straight away that he was just making a quixotic, unselfish attempt to put our welfare before his own. The truth is it would be quite wrong for me to turn Lewis out; he needs to live among other people because if he's on his own he'll get in a mess. And the same applies to Stacy, who's still not adjusted properly to life away from that family of his. Stacy needs special care at the moment—and so does Alice. What you're completely failing to understand is that we're not just a bunch of independent individuals—we're a group of interdependent people living in community, and we all support each other. If you weren't so hung up on self-centred individualism—"

"Oh, shut up! If you weren't so hung up on the power you're getting out of managing this group of lame-duck losers, you'd see your family ought to come first on your list of priorities, and if you think the boys and I will ever be happy, confined to this ghastly flat because the rest of the house is being used to accommodate your lame ducks—"

"*Ghastly flat*? Have you any idea, Rosalind, any idea at all how some people in this city have to live? This flat has four bedrooms, two reception rooms, a kitchen, a bathroom and a lavatory. Convert the fourth bedroom into an extra bathroom and the place will be perfectly adequate for our needs—and don't forget you can still have a garden-room downstairs and the boys can still have a games-room in the attic. What on earth have you got to complain about? You should be excited—stimulated—brimming over with creative ideas!"

"Well, I'm not. The rock-bottom truth is—"

"The City's a great place! There'd be so many opportunities for you to build a new life here! For instance, if you could only try to take part in the life of St. Benet's—"

"I'm not churchy. You know that. It's just not my scene."

"But why shouldn't it be? We have a dynamic community on the cutting edge of reality. What's that got to do with being 'churchy'—which I always understood to be a description of people being prim and pious in some middle-class ghetto fifty years behind the times?"

"I can't help it, Nicky, this place just isn't 'me' at all, and the boys won't like it either, I know they won't—"

"But life in London will be much more fun for them than life in the Surrey backwoods!"

"No, it won't! They'll be miserable, cut off from their friends and familiar activities. They'll take to drugs, hang around the wrong places, get mixed up with the wrong people—"

"They're much more likely to do that in Surrey if they've got nothing to occupy them but sport and pop music!"

"You don't understand those boys!" I shouted in despair. "You never have and you never will!"

"I'm sorry, but I refuse to have a slanging match about Benedict and Antony. I'm going down to my study until you feel willing to stop this self-indulgent screaming and talk sensibly." He began to head for the door.

"How *typical!*" I bawled, making sure my voice was louder than ever. "You walk away and leave me shut up in this horrible box! Well, I'm not going to stay shut up here and you're not going to make me!"

He turned his back on the door. "Stop that!" he ordered in his sharpest voice. "You're hysterical. Stop that at once."

"God, that's a classic male put-down—why, I don't know how you have the nerve to trot it out! Men always call women hysterical when they want to control them!"

"Well, I call a woman hysterical when I want her to know she's hysterical."

I screamed in sheer rage. At once he tried to grab me but I shot sideways and put the table between us.

"Nicholas Darrow," I said very clearly in a shaking voice. "I am not, repeat *not,* going to let you treat me as you treated Bear!"

"Treated *who?*"

"Bear!"

"You're out of your mind! What's Bear got to do with any of this?"

"Well, since you're so busy being the wonder worker," I yelled at him, "why the hell can't you just wave your magic wand and see the answer written in the sky?" And unable to endure the scene any longer I bolted to the bedroom to escape from him.

But the key refused to turn in the lock.

V

He didn't shove his way in. He waited until I'd finished scrabbling with the key and then he tapped politely on the panel before walking in, but his restraint made no difference to the fact that he was pursuing me. By this time my stomach was churning. All the naked anger was taking its toll. Breathlessly I gasped: "I don't want to make love to you. Let me make that quite clear," but he only exclaimed exasperated: "Oh, for heaven's sake! Just because you've been screwing around lately in the worst possible way with children not much older than Benedict, you needn't think all men are panting to bed you!"

"My God, I knew you'd soon throw that in my face—I knew you would, I knew it! You hate the thought that I've been unfaithful to you, you haven't forgiven me at all and now in revenge you want to shut me up in a box like Bear and stop me living the life I was meant to lead—"

"Could you kindly stop talking such pathetic and bathetic drivel? I mean, it's actually quite funny, and if we weren't in the middle of our worst row of all time I might even split my sides with laughter—"

"Well, split away—split yourself in any way you choose, I don't give a shit so long as you go away now and *leave me alone.* Right from the start of this conversation you've been condescending, patronising, chauvinistic and just plain vile!"

"And you've been obstinate, bloody-minded, hysterical and just plain nuts—which reminds me, I still don't see the relevance of Bear! Why do you keep dragging him in?"

"You were peculiar about him. Remember that party when you brought Bear along and got into a fight with Dicky Hampton just because he tried to touch Bear's glass eyes?"

"He tried to rip the eyes out—and it wasn't Dicky, it was Peter

Woodstock. The fight took place at that party where the conjuror produced a white rabbit which made a mess on the carpet—"

"No, no, no—that was Phyllida's birthday party much later and you didn't bring Bear then, you were old enough to leave him behind. The party I'm talking about was Dicky's—it was the one where you had double portions of everything at tea because you had to eat for Bear as well as yourself, and you wound up vomiting all over Caroline Pottinger—"

"Old Potty! I never liked that girl!"

"Neither did I! She used to dribble when she screamed."

"I remember you spitting at her."

"I never spat at anyone!"

"Oh yes, you did! You pretended to be a cat because you knew I liked cats so much," he said laughing, and suddenly as I remembered the incident I found that I was laughing too. Weakly I sank down on the edge of the bed.

"Oh, Nicky, Nicky . . ." My anger had gone and I was in despair. Once more I was the Siamese twin trying to tear herself away from the much-loved sibling and once more I was failing to achieve the life-giving separation.

"Darling Rosalind," Nicky said, putting a comforting arm around my shoulders, "what on earth are we doing, beating each other up like this?"

And to my horror I felt so confused that I was no longer sure of the answer.

VI

Seeing my confusion, Nicky gave me a comforting squeeze but made no attempt to kiss me. "I love you," he said, and it was impossible to doubt his sincerity. "I love you so much. You do believe that, don't you?"

"Yes, but . . ." I struggled for the right words but they were so hard to find. "It's not real, Nicky."

"It's the most real thing in the world to me."

"Yes, but what I mean is . . . what I'm trying to say is . . . well, it's not *me* you really love. I'm like Bear. You thought it was Bear you needed, but in fact—"

"I'm starting to pine for Bear! When we go back to Butterfold for the school holidays I must get the tuck-box down from the attic and take a look at him!"

"Nicky, I don't want you coming back to Butterfold. I'm afraid you've really got to accept that I—"

"Okay, I recognise your anger—I accept that I behaved like a bastard when I raked up that confession of yours, and I'm very, very sorry I said what I did. Now, let's forget all the slanging matches, let's calm down, let's concentrate on what's really important here. You do believe, don't you, that *I* believe I love you?"

"Yes, but—"

"Right, hold on to that. Let's just pause there to think about it, let's just pause, let's not say anything for a moment, let's just think of love and how we both need it and how all human beings need it, and let's focus on love because love is good and if we focus on love we can't go far wrong."

After all the searing tension I was prepared to take time out for a breather. I went on sitting limply on the edge of the bed while he wandered around the room as if he too was welcoming the chance to unwind. I wasn't frightened now. We were friends again, the old chums who had been to the same children's parties long ago. I was very fond of Nicky when we were enfolded in this strand of our relationship. The shared memories bonded us together as if we were siblings, and this deep connectedness, I knew, would survive the disintegration of our marriage.

"All right," he said at last, sitting down beside me on the bed. "I feel calmer now. How about you?"

"Yes, I'm calmer too. Thanks for the breather."

"I got overheated. Literally." He took off his pectoral cross and his jacket and began to remove his clerical collar.

"Why are you wearing one of those old-fashioned collars?" I said vaguely. "I thought you preferred the modern clerical shirts with the plastic strip."

"I had a meeting just now with the trustees, at least two of whom are old enough to disapprove of mere plastic strips, so it seemed politic to go 'putting on the style' . . . Remember that Lonnie Donegan record?"

"Uh-huh." I watched him remove the collar and the black stock. Nicky had beautiful hands, very sexy, and all his movements were so graceful that even watching him undo a button on his jacket was an aesthetic pleasure. I noticed that his nails were spotlessly clean. His brown hair, barely flecked with silver, was immaculately cut, freshly washed, shining. Faultlessly groomed and faultlessly attired in that very conventional uniform, he seemed quite unaware of the erotic charge he generated merely by stripping to his shirt-sleeves.

"That's better," he murmured when the stock was finally set aside. "Now, where were we? Oh yes, we were thinking about love and the fact that I love you. You do remember me saying I love you, don't you?"

"Of course."

"But how well do you remember?"

"Mega-vividly. Really, Nicky, I'm not suffering from Alzheimer's!"

"So if I were to snap my fingers now, what would be the first words to enter your mind?"

"You love me. Okay, you've made your point: your feelings are important here. But all the same—"

"Wait a moment, I want to get this absolutely straight, I want to express the situation in the simplest possible language. I love you—and you love me too, don't you? I know you do, deep down."

"Yes, I was only thinking a moment ago how deeply connected we are, but—"

"Wait, wait, wait! We've established that I love you and you love me and that we're deeply connected. Now, keep that thought in front of you, hold it, hold it—okay? Right, I feel much better now I know you're thinking that. Thanks! It was very good of you to go out of your way to help me relax."

"Not at all," I said politely, and thought: anything to please an old pal.

"That wasn't so difficult, was it?"

"Easy-peasy."

"I wasn't browbeating you, was I?"

"Nope." I was thinking how sweet it was that he was so earnest and sincere. I found myself vaguely moved. Dear little Nicky, how adorable he had looked long ago with his fair hair and pink cheeks and Bear tucked under his arm . . .

"I'm still feeling a bit tense—could we do a rerun just to reassure me—for old time's sake—" He clicked his fingers absent-mindedly.

"You love me and I love you." After all, I didn't want to go on screaming at him, did I? I just wanted a respite from all the horror now, and anyway he was my oldest friend. I'll always go the extra mile for a friend.

"I love you and you love me," he was saying. "Great. Okay, I'll forget about going downstairs to work in my study. I'd much rather stay here. You wouldn't mind if I stayed here, would you?"

"Not really." I was thinking how stunning his eyes were, pale grey but brilliant and glowing like clouded white fire. It was funny how the irises seemed to change colour; sometimes they were as dark as slate and sometimes they were so light that they were almost blue. He really did have the most unusual eyes I'd ever seen . . . He was talking again. Pulling myself together, I struggled to concentrate.

"You're all right now, aren't you, Rosalind? You're totally relaxed now, aren't you, after that awful scene?"

"Yep. Finally."

"So am I. It's terrible when the future seems upsetting, but there's no need for the future to be upsetting, is there? Tell you what: let's get under the duvet and imagine a future which isn't upsetting at all. Remember how we used to play imaginary futures in the old days?"

"Of course. You used to make a tent out of that old army blanket and we'd crawl in after listening to that super Malcolm Saville serial on Children's Hour—"

"—and imagine an exciting future. That's right. We imagined—"

"We imagined we had a big house in a magic city, didn't we?"

"Exactly, I knew you'd remember. And *this* is our big house, Rosalind, and *this* is our magic city, and now we're going to resume that vision, we're going to get under the duvet and imagine—"

"—something wonderful." By that time I could hardly wait to crash out. I felt as if I were on the verge of sleep—yet at the same time I seemed to be pulsing with a curious energy, very peculiar, I couldn't understand it but wait a moment, yes, I did, it was sexual energy because Nicky was being so incredibly erotic, and I fancied him, fancied him deeply, in fact I couldn't wait to get my paws on his body and . . . Paws? No, hands. I was a human being, not an animal. Or was I?

"Nicky, I'm not Bear, am I?"

"Absolutely not. You're Rosalind, the most wonderful woman in the world," he said, snapping his fingers as if to salute a fact which was indisputable.

I said: "You love me and I love you," and all at once I felt blissfully, immeasurably and indescribably happy . . .

VII

Well, there we were under the duvet, and Nicky began to waffle away about the ideal future; it was all about a community where everyone was linked to everyone else and supported everyone else, a world where the self-centred behaviour of the individual had no place to exist, a world of relatedness powered by the dynamic of love. "The Trinity is a symbol of relatedness powered by that dynamic," he was saying. "It's a model of how reality truly is. Reality is threefold," and I was murmuring yeah-yeah, I could see that, it was all clear as crystal, and I could do with a little relatedness right now, how about it, come down out of the future, Mr. Wonder Stud, and let's go all related in the present.

And Nicky was saying fine, great, we'd pretend we'd slid sideways into a parallel world, we'd pretend we were starring in a sex movie, why not, anything could happen in a parallel world, and I said—rather woozily, as if I'd had the whole bottle of plonk instead of half of it—yeah-yeah, go for it, Miracle-Man, but no porn because Mummy wouldn't approve. Then Nicky said okay—okay, he said no porn, this would be very high-tone, like an art movie—like that famous scene in *Don't Look Now* when Donald Sutherland and Julie Christie had done a terrific number in Venice, and I said yeah-yeah, let's do it, let's do it, I said, and swore this would be better than the film because he was far sexier than Donald Sutherland—at which point Nicky said I was far sexier than Julie Christie because Julie Christie was too thin. And when I argued no one could be too thin, according to Mrs. Simpson, he just said he wouldn't have wanted to go to bed with Mrs. Simpson, it would have been like making love to a broomstick without the witch, and he'd never envied the Duke of Windsor one little bit.

Then we forgot about the Windsors because we were so busy being Donald Sutherland and Julie Christie in this fascinating parallel world—well, universe, actually—which we just happened to have dropped in on, and of course I knew it was really all a dream—Nicky said it was all a dream and of course I believed every word he said—but it was such fun, so when he said it was all a dream, this wasn't really happening, I didn't get upset, far from it. I said yeah-yeah and swam around swoonily.

After that there were no more words for a while, but it was all right because Nicky said it was all right and of course I believed every word he said. After all, ultimate reality, as Nicky had said earlier when talking of the Trinity, lay beyond the scope of words to describe and this experience of ours was ultimately real—and I remember thinking how strange it was that I'd never realised this truth before, but there it was, words were inadequate when one was engaged with the ultimately real and that was why all Trinitarian talk sounded so weird, but never mind, ultimate reality was all about relatedness powered by the dynamic of love—and wowee, was I perfectly relating to Nicky in our parallel universe, and wowee, was he being dynamic, and wowee, this was the best dream I'd had for ages, so when he said that this was the way things really were I said yeah-yeah, and when he said that this was why we had to stay together I said yeah-yeah, and when he said we were going to live happily ever after I said yeah-yeah, yeah-yeah, yeah-yeah . . .

It was the most beautiful dream but at last it came to an end, just as all dreams do, and the parallel universe exploded across the star-spangled heavens in cascades of white light. Gently we floated down to earth on a fluffy white cloud and gently we landed on a bed of white swansdown and gently, gently, gently we slipped into a shimmering seraphic sleep . . .

VIII

When I awoke later that evening, I found something had happened to my memory and I couldn't remember where I was or how I'd got there. In fright I exclaimed: "I've got amnesia!" but Nicky said at once: "No, you haven't," and snapped his fingers.

Instantly I said: "You love me and I love you," but that struck me as all wrong, weird, not chiming with what had been going on in my life—although I couldn't quite remember what had been going on. "Nicky, I really do have amnesia—"

"No, you don't. We were playing imaginary futures and I was discussing Josiah Royce's concept of the ideal community and you fell asleep. I'm not surprised either after all that plonk you knocked back."

"But did I knock back so much?"

"At least half a bottle, and that stuff's all chemicals . . . Like some tea?"

"Very much. Thanks." My memory had started working again, thank God, and I could now remember how he had wolfed down my exquisite dinner, how angry we had been with each other afterwards and how only the mention of Bear had saved us from further marital horrors. I could remember too the relief I had experienced as we reminisced about our kindergarten days and regressed into our childhood friendship. That was probably another reason why I had passed out; after the extreme tension produced by yet another row I had been half-dead with exhaustion in addition to being half-poisoned by that plonk . . . I made a mental note to spend more money next time I picked up a bottle of wine in a supermarket.

Meanwhile Nicky was sliding out of bed on his way to the kitchen to make tea, and to my astonishment I saw he was naked. My brain did a stagger. "Nicky . . ." I rubbed my eyes for fear I was hallucinating.

He was pulling on his dressing-gown. "Yes?"

"Why do you have no clothes on?"

"Because it was hot under that duvet and I didn't think you'd thank me if I sweated like a pig all over you."

"Oh, I see," I said. But I didn't. Alarm made my stomach flutter. "Wait a minute," I said slowly. "Wait a minute. I had this extraordinary dream—you said it was a dream. We were doing a remake of the sex scene in *Don't Look Now*, and—"

"Hold it, I've got to pee."

"God!" I exclaimed appalled as the memories snowballed. "That plonk must have been spiked with LSD!"

Nicky disappeared. The lavatory door closed and eventually I heard him pull the old-fashioned chain. Then the door opened and he went into the bathroom to wash his hands before heading for the kitchen. By this time I was feeling deeply confused again. I was trying to work out how on earth I had wound up with him under the duvet when I was supposed to have been talking to him about divorce. I knew—I could clearly remember—that I'd been feeling sentimental about the childhood friendship, but it was a big step from indulging in nostalgia to sliding under the duvet and playing imaginary futures with this husband I was determined to leave. Why on earth was I bothering to play imaginary futures—what a damn stupid, childish game!—when the whole point about the marriage was that it had no future whatsoever? Somewhere along the line I'd gone bananas. That *bloody* plonk! I felt like suing the supermarket. Yet I wasn't hung over. Curious. I had no headache of any kind and the only discomfort I was currently experiencing was a full bladder.

Having decided to go to the lavatory I sat up—and found to my astonishment that I too was naked. When had I removed my clothes? Nicky must have eased me out of them when I was in my stupor . . . or did I have some distorted memory of tearing them off as I slipped into the Julie Christie role? No, the sex sequence had been a dream. Nicky had said it was a dream, and of course I *knew* it had been a dream because in the present circumstances when all I wanted was a divorce—and when I had firmly said to Nicky that I didn't want to sleep with him—the very last thing I would ever have consented to was sexual intercourse.

Still feeling troubled by the peculiarly groggy state of my brain I swung my legs from the bed to the floor, but as soon as I stood up I knew something was horribly wrong.

For a second I was transfixed, unable to believe the truth which was now clamouring to be acknowledged, but then I put a trembling hand between my thighs.

There was no mistaking what I found.

For ten dreadful seconds my mind was again in chaos, but finally reason and reality snapped back into their familiar alignment, the fog of confusion was blasted apart, and my memory raced to project image after image, all pornographic, onto my mind's big, bright, blazing screen.

I only just managed to reach the lavatory before I was violently ill.

But I knew now exactly what was making me vomit.

And it wasn't the cheap supermarket wine.

9

[The anger's] expression may, on the other hand, become inhibited as in those who have suffered sexual abuse. Here inappropriate shame and guilt stir up deep anger and aggression.

GARETH TUCKWELL AND DAVID FLAGG
A Question of Healing

I

I flushed the lavatory, stumbled next door to the bathroom and locked myself in. Turning on the taps I waited for the bath to fill. My brain had seized up again by this time. I was in shock. Scrambling clumsily into the bath I began to scrub and scrub and scrub.

After a while Nicky knocked on the door. The noise startled me so much that I almost passed out. As I gripped the side of the bath and listened to my banging heart I heard him call: "Are you okay?"

"Yes, fine—I'll be out in a minute." My voice sounded casual, almost languid.

He went away.

I remained motionless for a further minute, but I was in control of myself again now after that nightmare scene when far more than my will had been twisted and violated, and at last my instinct for survival triggered some rapid rational thoughts. My first decision was that I should avoid a further conversation with Nicky about the future because as he was irrational on the subject, any attempt to discuss a divorce would be futile. My second decision was that I had to fight the urge to flee at once either to Butterfold or to anywhere else because he would only rush after me and engineer more disgusting scenes. When I left the Rectory it would be with his consent, and this meant that for a while at least I would have to pretend that the marriage was still viable. However—

However, the third decision I made was that I was never, under any circumstances, going to sleep with him again.

Struggling out of the bath I dried myself, tucked the towel around my body and went to the door to listen. All was quiet. Turning the key in the lock I opened the door and found myself eyeball to eyeball with him.

I screamed.

"It's okay, it's okay—" He backed off hurriedly.

"Christ, Nicky, you gave me a shock! What the hell do you think you're doing?" I demanded, and all the time I spoke I was willing myself to behave as I would have done if no revolting abnormality had taken place. "Did you make the tea?"

"I'll make a fresh pot," he said at once. "I didn't realise you were going to have a bath. But perhaps I should have done. Rosalind—"

"Never mind, I didn't really want tea anyway. What's the time?"

"About five to ten. Darling—"

"Oh, five to ten, good, we're in time for the ITV news. Let's goggle at the box and recuperate from all that frenzied exercise in the bedroom."

"I was just going to say—"

"No need. Naturally I've put two and two together but we won't talk about it. You were extremely silly and to be quite honest I did feel livid with you when I realised you'd pulled off one of your childish parlour-tricks, but never mind, it's all over now, forgive and forget, and we won't refer to it again. Now I want to find out who's starving, who's fighting, who's whingeing and what Mrs. Thatcher's doing to fix them, but if you don't want to watch the news with me, if you want an early night—"

"Rosalind, can you hold it right there for a moment? There's something I want to say."

When I finally summoned the nerve to look him in the eyes I realised how tense he was. "Absolutely no need to say anything," I said strongly at once. "Much better not. No need to say anything at all."

But he was apparently incapable of taking this advice. "I just wanted to tell you," he said unevenly, "that I know I've overstepped the mark, but I did so only with the very best of intentions. You see, I knew—I *knew*—that deep down you loved me and wanted us to stay together. I *knew* that because of all the self-centred crap which was cluttering up the surface of your mind you couldn't think straight. I *knew* that if I cut through all the crap and put you in touch with your true feelings everything would be all right. I *knew* that if only I could reach you on that level I could initiate a healing—and when I say '*knew*' I mean it was true psychic knowledge, I just knew I was right—"

"Uh-huh. You know, I think I've changed my mind, I feel sleepy after the bath and now I just want to go straight to bed. But don't worry, I'm sure I'll be as right as rain in the morning." Moving back into the bathroom I opened the door of the airing cupboard.

I was aware of him staring without comprehension as I pulled out fresh bed-linen. The boys' duvet covers, printed with pictures of ancient cars, were quite different from ours.

"What are you doing?"

"Oh, I'll sleep in Benedict's room," I said. "No problem. I just feel I'd like to be on my own for the rest of the night, if you don't mind, but no offence meant. I only want total peace and quiet so that I can crash out for at least twelve hours."

"But *I* can sleep in Benedict's room! You sleep in our bed which you like so much!"

"How sweet of you, darling, but no thanks. I'd rather be in Benedict's room."

"But why?"

It wasn't just because the thought of our bed was now repulsive to me. It was because I knew the lock worked on this particular door. Benedict had locked himself in during his last visit after a row with Nicky, and it had taken me over an hour to coax him out. "Just humour me, Nicky, would you, please? I'm so tired," I said, and began my journey to Benedict's room. Only a few more steps to go now until I was safe for a few hours. I'd nearly survived this terrifying and obscene ordeal. I was almost there.

"Rosalind, I really do think we should talk about this—"

"No, Nicky. I'm sorry, but no."

"Obviously you're angry, but don't forget I proved that deep down you still love me. You wanted the sex, remember—you asked for it—begged for it—"

I whirled round to face him. "Shut up!" I screamed. "Shut up, *shut up*, SHUT UP!" And bolting the last yards to Benedict's room I hurled myself inside, locked the door and began to shake from head to toe.

I'd never been so frightened in my life.

11

It was freezingly cold in the room so I lit the gas fire before I made the bed and burrowed under the duvet. At last I managed to stop shaking, but nightmarish thoughts continued to plague me. Was there a spare key to the room? Would Nicky unlock the door when I was asleep and creep in and . . . Leaping out of bed I dragged the chest of drawers across the door and switched on all the lights, even the desk-lamp. Only then did I feel safe enough to close my eyes.

But I was unable to sleep. I was trying to work out what to do. Could I seek help from Lewis? No. He adored Nicky, hated me and was enough of a misogynist to decide the whole incident was my fault. And perhaps it was. Maybe I *had* led Nicky on by finding him so sexy. After all, there he was, the devout priest. If he'd overstepped the mark, I must have driven him to do so. I'd asked for sex, Nicky had reminded me, begged for it . . . I shuddered and shivered for some time. In the end I went to the basin in the corner of the room for fear I was going to vomit again, but nothing came up. I turned on the hot tap and tried the water. The immersion heater had been working overtime after my bath and the water was warm once more. Shedding my dressing-gown I began to wash myself over and over again.

As I did so I wondered if I might seek help from Nicky's spiritual director, but I supposed that she would be as pro-Nicky as Lewis was, and anyway I'd never been keen on nuns. She'd probably say it was all my fault for wanting a divorce—and perhaps it was. I'd asked for sex, begged for it . . . Nicky himself had acted only with the very best of intentions . . . His sole aim had been to heal my debased state of mind which was making us both so unhappy . . .

I began to cry. I washed and I washed and I washed and I wept and I wept and I wept, yet still I felt filthy, guilty and degraded. My sister would no doubt have said I was being a wimp and should brace up, soldier on and stop whingeing. "So you and Nicky had a sex-orgy," I could imagine her saying robustly. "God, you're damn lucky! What the hell are you complaining about?" And I'd never be able to explain. I could never explain to Susie or Tiggy either. They wouldn't understand. My marital problems were always so bizarre, so outside the range of normal people's experience. Only Francie, as I had told myself earlier, would be capable of understanding. Not only was she so familiar with Nicky, but she was a trained listener who dealt regularly with people impaled on what Nicky called "the cutting edge of reality." I thought: Francie may not know exactly what I should do next but at least she'll empathise and sympathise. And with relief I remembered that our lunch-date at Fortnum's was less than twelve hours away.

I crawled back under the duvet as the clock of St. Benet's chimed two. I wanted to sneak out to the kitchen and finish off the plonk, but I was too afraid to unlock the door in case Nicky was there.

By four o'clock, exhausted but still sleepless, I knew that hell was nothing like the pictures painted by Hieronymus Bosch. Hell was living in fear of a wonder worker who was running amok—and hell was being crucified by the dread that this apparently endless stream of soul-destroying abuse was no one's fault but one's own.

III

I stayed in my room until eight o'clock when I knew Nicky would be at the Communion service. Then I dressed quickly and wrote him a note which read: "I've gone shopping and will grab some lunch in the West End. Back for dinner—let's eat with the others this time. I'm sorry about last night but please don't let's refer to it again. R."

I had no idea whether I would be back for dinner or not but at least I would have a few hours free of the fear that he might be pursuing me. I was now in such a state that all I wanted was to reach Fortnum's and talk to Francie.

Having left the note on the hall table of the flat I fled from the house. Up Egg Street I skimmed and along London Wall to Aldersgate where I headed for the Barbican tube station. I was walking so fast that I felt hot in my winter coat, but so relieved was I to have escaped from the Rectory that I never once slackened my pace.

Five minutes later a train was carrying me out of the City into the heart of the West End.

IV

I had thought I might spend the morning buying Christmas presents for the boys, a demanding task which would divert me from the horrors I had experienced, but I soon found that any demanding task was quite beyond me; I wound up drinking coffee in the mezzanine restaurant at Fortnum's and looking at the *Daily Telegraph* and the *Daily Mail.* I was unable to read but I spent ages examining the pictures on the front pages. After a long, long time the Fortnum's clock chimed noon and I trailed upstairs to the St. James's Restaurant to have a scotch while I waited for Francie to arrive.

I never normally drank scotch in the middle of the day and in fact I never drank scotch at all unless there was a crisis going on, but I felt I had to have something strong to calm me down so that Francie wouldn't think I'd freaked out. I didn't want to appear a complete broken reed. I could afford to appear troubled, but I had to give the impression of being in overall control of myself. Supposing Francie were to think I was having a nervous breakdown? With a shudder I hid behind the *Telegraph* but fortunately the scotch proved a most effective tranquilliser, so effective that I ordered another to ensure I stayed encased in an air of normality. By the time my glass was empty again I was no longer cowering behind the *Telegraph* but flaunting the *Mail* while silently chanting my favourite American mantra: "when the going gets tough, the tough get going."

Summoning the waitress I told her to remove the empty glass and bring me a Perrier on ice with lemon. Image was all. Straightening my back I crossed one leg over the other, adjusted the cuffs of my blouse and was just elegantly sipping my Perrier when Francie surged in.

She was wearing a scarlet jacket, a pencil-thin black skirt, and a black blouse with frills which bounced merrily over her lapels. She was just the teeniest bit fat for a size fourteen but too thin for a size sixteen, so this presented her with a tricky fashion problem to solve, but apart from one or two straining seams she looked smart and her make-up was excellent. When we kissed I held my breath to control the scotch fumes but she let a sliver of air escape and I realised to my surprise that it was ginny. So Francie, like me, had been tanking up! But of course she was depressed at present, poor thing, and had probably needed a discreet g-and-t to oil her path out of Islington.

Having solemnly decided not to have a drink before lunch, we teetered off into the main part of the restaurant to take our seats at the table.

Francie was magnificent. As soon as I started to tell her what had happened, she rose to the occasion, shed her normal air of scatty housewife and became the trained listener, oozing warmth and concern from every pore. Effortlessly she contrived to give the impression that I was the most important person in her life at that moment and that she was wholly dedicated to my welfare. Normally a chatty, bouncy soul she became faultlessly attentive, only murmuring encouraging monosyllables or helpful phrases at exactly the right moment. Once or twice the mask of the Befriender did slip and I saw she was beside herself with prurient curiosity, but I found I could forgive her because I knew she was only being human. We all like to be titillated occasionally and it was only natural for Francie to be riveted by a story about Nicky's sex-life, just as it was only natural for her to derive an almost-but-not-quite-concealed thrill from hearing about a marriage on the rocks. We all like to look down our noses at people who wallow in *schadenfreude*, but who hasn't succumbed at some time to having a similar wallow? At least Francie battled valiantly to keep her more disreputable feelings to herself and never for one moment ceased her heroic task of oozing warmth and concern from every pore.

"Ros darling," she said earnestly at last after I had completed my story and was busy draining my glass of Chablis Premier Cru, "you shouldn't blame yourself for *anything*. What Nick did was totally wrong."

I was enormously grateful to her for saying this. Yet at the same time I was terrified that she was saying it only out of a desire to be kind. "But surely," I said, "if the hypnosis uncovered my true feelings, and if I then egged him on, he's justified in saying—" I broke off as my voice started to waver. Disaster! I was on the brink of losing control. In panic I groped for the bottle in the ice-bucket, but Francie, anticipating my every need with a brilliant display of empathy, was already refilling my glass.

"My dear," she said firmly, "what the hypnosis did was suspend your will. So the 'true feelings' which were then uncovered were actually *his* feelings which he was imposing on you when you had no mind of your own." Hastily she added: "Of course Befrienders aren't supposed to offer opinions or advice, but since I'm here in a non-professional capacity—"

"Oh yes, yes, yes, never mind all that, I'm just desperate to know what you really think!"

"I think what he did was completely unethical and I'm horrified that he's brainwashed you into thinking you led him on. Ros, before he turned on the hypnosis, you didn't want to sleep with him, did you?"

"Absolutely not. I told him so."

"So what he actually did was to—"

"He took away my power to say no," I said slowly. "He had sex with me without my consent. If I'd been *compos mentis*—"

"—you'd never have agreed to it, let alone encouraged him. Right. And when a man has sex with a woman without her consent, that's—"

"No, don't say it, I don't want to hear, I can't bear to think he could ever do something so—" I broke off, overwhelmed by tears. "Don't look at me," I muttered in panic as I groped in my handbag for a tissue. "You're not seeing this, I forbid you to see it." And finally I whispered: "I think I'd rather believe it was all my fault than believe Nicky could ever treat me like that."

Francie passed me a Kleenex. The Befrienders were famous for never being without a supply. "Nevertheless," she said firmly, "it's terribly important for your sake that you don't assume a guilt that doesn't belong to you, so let me take a moment just to spell out what seems to have happened. I think Nick took advantage of all that ancient kindergarten affection which exists quite separately from the marriage and used it to lull you into a false sense of security. Then he switched on the hypnosis, and once he did that you wouldn't have been responsible for anything that happened. You'd have lost all power to control the scene."

I recognised the nightmare scenario, and although I remained physically battered, mentally shattered and emotionally annihilated I was finally able to exonerate myself from blame.

"He's very skilled at hypnosis, you know," Francie was saying. "Val told me once that he can put a willing subject under in a flash with no trouble at all. You might have taken longer, because you were fundamentally hostile, but once he'd neutralised the hostility by resurrecting those childish memories and regressing you into the past—"

"Yes. That's how it was. I can see it all now." By this time I found I was admiring Francie's skill not just in listening but in understanding the situation and handling my distress. In the past I'd always found her warm-hearted but a bit thick. Now I saw I had underestimated her. As a St. Benet's Befriender her gift of empathy was given full rein so that every ounce of her intelligence was maximised, and this made me realise how much even ordinary people could achieve when they took up work to which they were perfectly suited. I thought how clever it had been of Nicky to spot her potential and recruit her to work at the Centre.

The thought of Nicky brought fresh tears to my eyes and forced me to destroy another Kleenex. How could the Nicky who was my lifelong friend and most trusted companion have treated me like that? I felt as if I had never known him; I felt as if he had destroyed the past; I felt that all my most precious memories had been brutalised until they appeared to be no more than a string of illusions. Yet alongside my cherished memories were the memories of the parlour-tricks. I'd always known he was capable of misusing his gifts, but it was one thing to hypnotise willing girls at a party and quite another to—

"How could he have done it?" I cried in despair. "How could he have brought himself to do something so—" but I could not bring myself to say any of the words which were no longer fashionable. No one bandied around words like "wicked" and "evil" and "corrupt" any more unless they were Bible-bashing bigots or those Islamic fundamentalists who had just protested about the latest Rushdie novel. The liberalism of the sixties had destroyed our moral vocabulary, and Mrs. Thatcher had so far been too busy stoking the fires of nationalism and capitalism to reinvent it.

"Funnily enough," Francie was saying, as if trying to lower the emotional temperature of the conversation by staging a temporary retreat into casual chit-chat, "there was a case like this in the papers only the other day. Various women were hypnotised by their therapist who then used them for sex sessions. They were aware of what was going on but they couldn't resist, and it was only after they came out of the hypnosis that they realised exactly what he'd done."

Faintly I said: "What happened to him?"

"Oh, he was jailed, of course, but he was obviously just a run-of-the-mill wonder worker."

I tried to speak but nothing happened.

"Nick's quite different," said Francie rapidly, "because he's basically a devout priest. He's just gone temporarily crazy because of your decision to leave him."

"So it's all my fault after all!"

"No, no, no, I didn't mean that—" Francie, realising she'd put her foot in it, frantically tried to backtrack, but I was already rejecting another guilt-trip; I had finally seen the situation in the round. With a strength that surprised me I said: "Then isn't the truth just this:

that although we all under stress can do dreadful things, we always have the choice whether to do those dreadful things or not? And if we do make the evil choice and behave bestially, shouldn't we face up afterwards to what we've done and try to make amends to our victims? Nicky said sorry but he didn't mean it," I said, voice shaking, and suddenly anger was shoving aside my despair. "He was just going through the motions of apologising! If he'd really been sorry, he'd have taken full responsibility for what he'd done instead of telling me that I'd asked for it!"

"Oh, but that's classic behaviour," said Francie at once, bending over backwards now to support me. "Men guilty of that particular act often take that line. They're in denial."

The anger made me feel better, gave me the strength to pull myself together. I decided it was time to repair my appearance, but when I opened my compact I saw to my dismay that my state of disrepair was worse than I'd imagined. My supposedly waterproof mascara had smudged. With my shiny nose, damp cheeks, chewed lipstick and panda-like eyes I resembled a sixty-year-old clown.

"Shall I order a brandy?" said Francie resourcefully, seeing I was on the verge of collapse again.

"No, it's no good using alcohol as a crutch," I said with bravado, but then I spoilt this show of courage by dissolving into tears again. "Oh Francie," I wept in utter despair, "I'm so totally wrecked! What on earth am I going to do?"

"Well," said Francie, wonderfully cosy and sympathetic, "as a matter of fact, I *do* have one or two thoughts I'd like to share with you . . ."

V

"*First of all,*" said Francie briskly after I had begged her to continue, "you must get a divorce. No question about that. I know marriage is supposed to be for ever for clerical couples, but everything's changed so much, hasn't it, and nowadays a priest isn't automatically washed up if his wife seeks a divorce—although of course the divorce has to be handled very discreetly with nothing sordid ever seeing the light of day. So you needn't be terrified of wrecking Nick's career, and as for his personal life . . . well, who knows? Maybe he'll wind up falling madly in love with someone else."

"Oh God, if only he would! That would certainly let me off the hook, but apart from me the only woman he's peculiar about is Alice, and I can't see him ever wanting to—"

"Alice?" said Francie so sharply that I jumped. "*Alice?* Alice Fletcher?"

"Yes, they drool over the cat together, I don't understand it, but I'm sure it's got nothing to do with sex. So assuming there's no hope at present of some gorgeous bimbo enslaving Nicky with a flick of her false eyelashes, how the hell do I drill it into his head that the marriage is completely finished?"

"Have an affair," suggested Francie—very creatively, I thought. After all, she was a regular churchgoer.

"Good try," I said with respect, "but I've done that. And when I confessed to him in Devon on Tuesday—"

"*You had an affair?*" gasped Francie.

"Well, actually I had three, but two were only one-night stands so they hardly count."

"*One-night—*"

"Well, I had to do something, Francie! I was going mad with misery down there in Surrey!"

"Oh darling, I'm not blaming you—heaven forbid I should ever be judgemental!" cried Francie, fighting back her enthralled expression and oozing empathy again from every pore. "But wasn't Nick devastated when you confessed?"

"Yes, but as the infidelity was all in the past and as he realised I'd never have been unfaithful if he hadn't made me so miserable, he turned the other cheek and forgave me."

"God, that man's so Christian!" said Francie fervently, but realised a second later that this statement was hardly compatible with last night's catastrophe. At once she pulled herself together. "Sorry. Let me concentrate. You had these affairs, you said—but good heavens, how amazing, how did you do it? I mean, men do so like to take the lead, don't they, and they tend to back off if a woman comes on too strong—"

"I always chose much younger men and I took care to be either nannyish or schoolmistressy. They loved it."

"Good God!" said Francie stupefied.

I decided it was time to haul the conversation back on course before she realised she was jealous. "Well, never mind all that," I said rapidly. "Let's focus on the main problem. How do I convince Nicky—"

"Hang on," said Francie suddenly. "You've just given me an idea. Supposing you have another affair, but this time you pick a lover who'll underline to Nick that this isn't just a spot of adultery which can be blown away by a gale of Christian forgiveness; it's cast-iron proof that you can't stay married to him because if you do you'd wreck his ministry."

"You mean the best way to wake him up is to shock him to the core?"

"Yes, if you were to pick someone who from the point of view of his ministry is absolutely *verboten*—"

"Well, I'm sure I'd have no luck if I tried to seduce the Bishop, and I can't think of anyone else who—Francie! What is it? Why are you looking as if you're about to explode?"

"Because I've just had the most fantastic brainwave! Darling, the solution's simple: you must seduce Stacy McGovern."

VI

The waitress chose that moment to collect our plates but as soon as she had departed I said: "Francie, you're nuts."

"But it would show Nick, wouldn't it? It would send him slamming up against reality so hard that he'd have no choice but to face the facts. He's responsible for Stacy's welfare—the implications would be horrific—"

"Which is why I could never do it. Poor little Stacy!"

"*Little?* That huge uncoordinated red-headed hulk? Listen, if you taught Stacy a thing or two you'd be doing him a favour! He's so shy and emotionally retarded that he can only think of dating Tara Hopkirk!"

"Francie, I can't seduce the curate. I may have my failings, but there are some lines I will under no circumstances cross. Seducing Stacy wouldn't just be immoral; it would be naff."

"But it would solve everything!"

I stared at her. She was bright-eyed, pink-cheeked, vibrant with enthusiasm.

"Well, I must say, Francie," I remarked, "for someone who's been off work for depression, you've certainly made a spectacular recovery! Have you ever thought of being a marriage guidance counsellor? You'd be on a perpetual high!"

Francie immediately looked contrite. "Sorry, darling, I didn't mean to sound as if I'm deliriously happy as the result of this ghastly mess—I'm just fired up because I'm so passionately keen to help you."

"And I'm hugely grateful for the help. But as far as Stacy's concerned—"

"Ros, I don't think you can afford to pull your punches now, I really don't. Can't you see that you'd actually be doing Nick a favour by giving him the biggest possible jolt? He really does need to snap out of this dangerous fixation of his before it starts affecting his ministry."

"I agree, but I still can't see myself bedding Stacy . . . Who's Tara Thingummy-jig?"

"Oh, haven't you met her? She's one of the church cleaners and looks like the back end of a bus."

"But why should Stacy settle for anyone like that? What's his problem?"

"My dear, how should I know? I'm not the one who's the expert on young men! He can't be gay, can he?"

I paused to consider this question. "No," I said finally. "Not possible."

"Well, I have to admit he does seem to be a hundred per cent masculine."

"It's not that. It's just that Lewis would never consent to hiring a homosexual curate. He regards homosexuality as a handicap."

"Lewis is so old-fashioned," said Francie primly.

"Well, I don't know," I said, producing my compact again. "As a woman I can't help thinking it *is* a handicap not to be able to relate in depth to the opposite sex. And as a woman I personally don't like being rejected on the most fundamental level of all for reasons which make my flesh creep."

"My God, Ros, you can't go around saying that sort of thing nowadays!"

"I've just said it." Steeling myself I faced my nightmarish reflection in the mirror and finally began to make the necessary repairs. "Can you get the waitress and order coffee? If she looks at me in my present state she'll run screaming from the room."

Francie obediently ordered the coffee but was still rattled by the fact that I'd expressed my deeply unfashionable views without batting an eyelid. Apparently it was all right to advocate even the naffest form of adultery; adultery was just fine. But if one so much as breathed a word against a bunch of people prone to sodomy, one was absolutely beyond the pale.

"As a matter of fact I don't give a damn what homosexuals do," I said as I finished off my repairs by powdering my nose. "I just wish to hell they'd have the good taste to do it discreetly like the rest of us and stop whingeing about being persecuted. I hate whingers—which reminds me, I do apologise for this awful whinge all the way through lunch! I've been far worse than any homosexual activist! Now darling, tell me about *you* and *your* problems!"

"Oh, they're all trivial," said Francie quickly, "not even worth mentioning, but how sweet of you even to think of asking when you're in this terrible situation . . . Are you sure you're so dead against seducing Stacy?"

" 'Get thee behind me, Satan!' Yes, I draw the line there, I'm afraid."

"I think you're a saint," said Francie. "If I'd been through what you've been through, I'd seduce Stacy out of a lust for revenge."

"If you'd been through what I've been through, you'd be lusting only for freedom from fear, I assure you."

Francie at once invited me to stay with her but I said no, Nicky would only turn up and break the door down. She then made the more practical suggestion that I should see a top divorce lawyer at the earliest opportunity, and she promised to ask Harry to recommend someone as soon as he returned from Hong Kong. "And meanwhile," she added, "if you won't take refuge with me I think you should go to Phyllida. Isn't her husband keen on hunting? He could defend you with a horsewhip if Nick went on the rampage."

"Tommy's keen on shooting too. I don't want him reaching for a gun."

"He sounds exactly the kind of macho thug you need—fly to Phyl without delay!"

But I had no desire to appear wimpish to my sister and anyway ghastly Tommy was quite capable of siding with Nicky in the name of masculine solidarity. I began to think I might have to adopt a pseudonym and disappear for a while until the boys came home from school to chaperone me. Where would Nicky never dream of searching? Northern Ireland was a possibility, but I didn't want to risk being blown up. I could disappear into Europe but no, I had to go to a place where English was spoken because I was too upset to cope with speaking a foreign language . . .

I suddenly realised I was on the pavement outside Fortnum's and Francie was kissing me goodbye. Gratefully I kissed her back and told her how wonderful she had been. What a blessing it was, I reflected as I took a taxi back to the City, to have such a loyal and devoted friend supporting me as I struggled to survive this horrible crisis . . .

VII

When I reached the Rectory my lack of sleep and my emotional exhaustion combined to overwhelm me, and locking myself in Benedict's room again I escaped into unconsciousness beneath the duvet.

Later, when I was waiting for the kettle to boil for tea, I went into the drawing-room to pull the curtains, and as I glanced down into Egg Street I saw Stacy chatting with a stout girl who looked as if she might be Tara the cleaner. I stood watching them. They talked on, unaware that they were being observed, but at last Stacy turned away and as he did so he saw me standing at the lighted window.

He waved, smiled, bumped against my car which was parked in the Rectory's forecourt.

I waved and smiled back before drawing the curtains.

As I made the tea I realised that Francie had been right; if I were to seduce Stacy Nicky would be forced to face the truth that I was determined to end the marriage, and then once he was facing reality he would see that he had no choice but to let me go. Moreover the sooner this happened, the sooner I would be free from fear. Even if I now did a runner to Northern Ireland, I'd still be living in terror in case he somehow managed to trace me, and meanwhile what on earth was I going to do when he returned to the flat after work that evening? Supposing he wanted to have sex with me again to make sure everything really was forgiven and forgotten, as I had put it so glibly in my terrorised state last night? Supposing—and this was even more frightening to contemplate—he tried to "talk it all through" with me in an attempt to provide "healing," and somehow managed to brainwash me all over again? He didn't need to resort to hypnosis to be highly manipulative, and if he once more piled on the emotional pressure I might crack up altogether and become like one of the women in that horrifying film *The Stepford Wives*, a doll-like creature with no mind of her own, utterly subservient to her husband.

Suddenly I found I could imagine the previously unimaginable: I could see myself having a complete mental breakdown and losing all control over my life indefinitely as Nicky signed the papers which would commit me to an asylum. I could even hear him say: "Darling, I'm doing this because I love you and because I know you love me too . . ."

It was the ultimate nightmare scenario.

I thought: I can't live like this, I can't live with this constant fear, I can't live with the vile memory of last night and the crucifying dread that he might somehow manage to abuse me again.

Then I thought: why the hell should I live in such torment? And deep down in my mind the anger ignited again at last, the anger which this time was going to empower me.

I reminded myself that I'd been tricked and violated. I reminded myself that I wasn't responsible for anything I'd done after my mind had been hijacked. I reminded myself that what I had to do now was not to turn my anger inward so that I drowned in guilt and shame but to turn my anger outwards until it was focused on the correct target.

Aloud I said very clearly in the quiet room: "That bastard deserves to be punished for what he did." And the next moment I had understood that what I truly wanted was not revenge but justice. A just punishment would ensure that Nicky stopped playing the wonder worker, a just punishment would set me free to live in peace, and a just punishment was what I now had to serve up with every ounce of strength and ingenuity I still possessed.

Someone knocked on the front door of the flat.

I jumped, but in fact I wasn't entirely surprised. Luck was going to start running my way now, I was sure of it, just as I was sure that I wasn't going to sit back and wait for justice to be dumped in my lap.

Screw morality, I told myself fiercely, and who cares about being naff? Screw scruples, screw convention, screw the spirit that built the Empire, screw every damn thing that stands in the way of justice! And above all, screw being a victim! When the going gets tough, the tough get going.

I opened the door.

"Hi!" said Stacy, bright-eyed and bouncy, like a friendly puppy. "You know you said yesterday morning that you wanted to inspect my flat? Well, you can inspect it now if you like, and then I could show you the pictures of my sister Aisling's wedding!"

I never hesitated. "Lovely!" I exclaimed. "Can't wait to see them!" And leaving the flat without a backward glance I set off on my journey out of the frying-pan into the fire.

Part Four

NICHOLAS

The Escalating Disaster

Judgment, properly understood, is the logical consequences of the choices we make. So the Christian counsellor does not himself judge. He knows that he too is under judgment—having to live with the consequence of the exercise of his own free will.

CHRISTOPHER HAMEL COOKE

Healing Is for God

10

The healing movement itself becomes sick when bad pastoral practice is cloaked in spiritual phraeseology; when the "strong" insist that the "weak" believe for a cure; when "deliverance" is seen as the only resort if the helper is stuck; when carers, driven by their own needs, always need to solve everything. There is potentially a frighteningg level of abuse.

GARETH TUCKWELL AND DAVID FLAGG

A Question of Healing

I

I wrecked my marriage on Wednesday the twenty-third of November, 1988. Afterwards I slept for six hours. Wrecking things is an exhausting occupation. Nothing life-enhancing about it at all.

At half-past five the next morning I awoke and realised I was up shit creek. I knew the marriage could be fixed. That went without saying, since the alternative was inconceivable, but meanwhile it was shredded. For a time I pretended I was hooked up with God and engaged creatively in prayer. Then at six, when no further pretence of this kind was possible, I abandoned my study and knocked on Lewis's door.

Lewis always arose before six but never dressed until seven. On that morning he was looking disreputable in his thirty-year-old, custom-made, claret-coloured dressing-gown which was frayed at the cuffs and mended at the elbows with iron-on black patches. There were no buttons any more, and above the slackly fastened belt I could see the message inscribed on the T-shirt he was wearing instead of pyjamas.

The words read: MY BARK IS WORSE THAN MY BITE. The T-shirt had been a gift last Christmas from the church helpers.

I said: "I've got a problem."

Lewis raised an eyebrow but waved me without hesitation across the threshold. No astronaut lost in space could have had a calmer response from Mission Control.

There was a small table by one of the windows, and I slumped down on a chair there. The big double-room was crammed with furniture. In one half a wide bed jostled for space with a Victorian wardrobe, a tallboy and a prie-dieu, while in the other half the table with its two chairs stood cheek by jowl with a desk, a couple of armchairs, a matching pair of bookcases and modern shelving designed to hold his CDs, his LPs and even his ancient 78s; there was no television but plenty of hi-fi. In front of the prie-dieu was a miniature altar adorned with two brass candlesticks and a cross, and on the wall above this arrangement hung an icon of the Virgin and Child. Lewis liked icons. He kept several smaller ones dotted around alongside photographs of his family. In the centre of the bedroom mantelshelf was the photograph of his great-uncle, Cuthbert Darcy, shaking hands with Archbishop Davidson shortly after the First World War. Father Darcy was revealed in this picture as a silver-haired, squarely built adventurer with a vulpine look. Lewis had now reached the age when this description also fitted him.

"So?" he said, sitting down opposite me at the table and reaching for his packet of cigarettes.

"There was a scene last night with Rosalind."

Lewis could hardly have looked less surprised. I watched him as he lit the weed and inhaled some smoke.

"I think I may have taken the wrong line," I said. "In fact I know I did. In fact I realise now I made a monumental balls-up. But it seemed like a good idea at the time."

Recognising the classic epitaph on a catastrophic decision, Lewis turned a shade paler.

"Rosalind said she couldn't live at the Rectory after all, she wanted to go home, wanted a divorce. Immediately it seemed plain to me that this rabid individualism of hers had finally spun out of control and was now a destructive force which had to be neutralised straight away. In other words," I said, watching the smoke drift towards the nicotine-stained ceiling, "I decided she was someone who required radical healing."

I paused in case he wanted to make a comment. None came.

"The real Rosalind," I said, ploughing on as he took another drag of the weed, "the Rosalind who still exists beneath this false persona which has been growing like a cancer on her personality, still loves me. I know that. So I reasoned that if I were to bypass the false persona I'd be able to prove to her that the desire for divorce was madness. I figured this would be a valid path to healing and wholeness: excise the cancer, heal the damage with love, enable Rosalind to develop a new integration. It all seemed to make sound clinical sense. The therapy, in its own way, would be a form of deliverance from this spiritual sickness which was oppressing her."

"Nicholas," said Lewis, and I knew the hair was standing on end at the nape of his neck, "what exactly did you do to that woman?"

"Well, I . . . well, this isn't going to sound too good, but I administered a mild form—a very mild form—of hypnotherapy. I mean, she was barely under. I mean, I just wanted to make it crystal clear that she loved me and I loved her and—"

"Are you seriously trying to tell me—"

"All right, I know it was a risk, but I thought the risk was worth taking! I thought the hypnotherapy was a valid tool in the circumstances!"

"Nicholas, I just can't believe I'm hearing this."

"Okay, okay, okay, I made a mistake! I got things a bit wrong. Well, very wrong. I know that, because the treatment didn't work. Yet at the time—"

"Wait. I want to make sure I haven't misunderstood what happened. Are you saying you hypnotised Rosalind in order to have sex with her?"

"No, no, no! I hypnotised Rosalind in order to excise the cancer on her personality and uncover her true self! Then we had sex. Well, of course we did. Once she realised she still loved me, she—"

"But what about when the hypnosis wore off?"

I shifted restlessly in my chair. I tried to frame a sentence but no pattern of words seemed right.

"Nicholas?"

I abandoned the attempt to form a pleasing verbal pattern. "She vomited," I said. I was no longer gazing at the smoke. I was staring at a patch of worn carpet. "I found vomit later on the rim of the lavatory bowl. After the vomiting she had a bath, a long one. I waited outside the bathroom but when she came out she didn't want to talk.

She just said I'd been silly but it was all forgiven and forgotten. Then she went to Benedict's room and locked herself in. Before that she'd indicated she was very angry. That was when I realised I'd made a big mistake, but of course it's just a temporary setback. I know she loves me, and once she accepts that the hypnotherapy was a valid medical procedure adopted with her best interests in mind—"

Lewis grabbed his crutches and stood up. Moving awkwardly to the phone he picked up the receiver and held it out to me. All he said was: "Phone your spiritual director."

"Does that mean—are you trying to tell me—"

"You're an emergency case, Nicholas. You need help without delay."

II

After a profound silence I said doggedly: "I'm prepared to admit I took a risk which didn't come off. I'm prepared to admit I was too emotionally involved to attempt to heal her. I'm prepared to admit that as the result of this mistake my marriage is in a bigger mess than it was before. But what I'm not prepared to admit is that Rosalind doesn't love me and that the marriage is washed up."

"Nicholas, if I attempted any comment here I'd only be trespassing on your spiritual director's territory. Phone her."

There was another profound silence before I said: "I'm not sure I can talk to Clare about this."

Lewis slammed down the receiver and started to radiate belligerence. "So my worst fears are confirmed—you have no-go areas with your spiritual director! Well, of course I always did think it was the biggest possible mistake for a man like you to see a female about matters which are of such crucial importance—"

"Oh, sod off!"

"No, I won't sod off! You're being driven by pride! You can't bear the thought of this woman seeing you in an unattractive light! You want her to dote on you just as all the other women do—you want cosy little chats on prayer and soapy little compliments about how spiritually splendid you are, but let me tell you this: if Great-Uncle Cuthbert were here in this room with us—"

"Oh, sod off about Father Darcy!"

"—he'd say your reluctance to see your spiritual director was very unedifying, indicative of severe spiritual problems, and he'd be right.

Nicholas, if you really feel you can't talk to that woman about the decisions you made last night—decisions which call into question not only your judgement as a healer but your present fitness to work as a priest—"

"No need to exaggerate!"

"I'm not exaggerating! Moreover, let me make it crystal clear to you that if you attend mass at eight I shall refuse you the Sacrament!"

"Now you've gone completely over the top!" I said in disgust, but by this time I was disorientated, as if I'd somehow wound up driving in France without crossing the Channel.

"I may have gone over the top," Lewis was saying furiously, "but you've hit rock-bottom! Now go and see that woman, and if I find when you get back that she hasn't succeeded in banging some spiritual sense into your head, I'll—"

"Could you kindly stop referring to my spiritual director as 'that woman'? Her name's Sister Clare Veronica."

"I don't care if her name's Mother Teresa, she's no damn use here—why, she can't even hear your formal confession! If you'd only go for spiritual direction to a priest of the Church of England instead of pitter-pattering around with this Roman nun—"

"Wake up! It's 1988! We don't make nasty remarks about Roman Catholics or women any more!"

"I wouldn't have made any remarks, nasty or otherwise, about your nun if you hadn't said straight out that you couldn't talk to her about this!"

"Okay, you win, I'm going. I'll see Clare and tell her everything."

Lewis sagged with relief. The verbal bashing could now be terminated. I liked the way he gave me a verbal bashing whenever he thought it necessary. It made me feel safe. All healers need to be slammed back on course occasionally. Particularly when they're up shit creek without a paddle.

Of course the old boy had lathered himself into the most unnecessary sweat and of course he had made a number of statements which could only be classed as exaggerations, but basically he had given me the right advice. I had to take action before the acute anxiety about my private life affected my ministry, and taking action meant having the humility to tell my spiritual director I'd made a first-class balls-up. Then we'd work out what to do to put matters right. Clare would be sensible and sympathetic, I had no doubt of that. Her suggestions were certain to be helpful.

So why was I so reluctant to see her?

Mystery. Could it be anything to do with the fact that she was a woman? Of course not. What had I done which would be so tough to admit to a woman? Nothing. I'd made a mistake as a healer and this would be tough to confess to any spiritual director, regardless of gender, but otherwise I'd acted with the very best of intentions and my conscience was clear.

Wishing I could forget the road which good intentions notoriously paved, I returned to my study to phone the convent.

III

Clare lived in Fulham. The sisters had owned the house near Parsons Green since the days when the area had been deprived, and even now that the tycoons were building flats for the rich on land down by the River, there were still plenty of the less privileged around. Cuts in social services had made life harder. Drug use was rife. Beneath the glittering surface of the Big Boom, dark forces writhed as if longing for the recession and ruin which would liberate them.

I left the Rectory before eight but because of a traffic jam on the Embankment it was almost nine by the time I reached the house. The Office would have been said. Breakfast would have been eaten. The nuns would be engaged in their daily tasks. Clare was the cook. Sometimes Alice reminded me of her. Christianity, with its vision of the material world being shot through and through with the sacred, was not a religion whose founder had despised food and drink. Rosalind thought I was indifferent to both, but I'm not a teetotaller and I like to be adequately fed. I prefer plain food, that's all, and I'd rather have a dose of caffeine than a slug of some chemical which is going to make me sleepy.

The nun who opened the front door said sternly that Clare was busy peeling potatoes, so in the little room off the parlour I sat down at the table below the crucifix and prepared for a long wait. But less than a minute later Clare entered the room.

She was tall for a woman, about five foot ten, and had large hands, reddish, calloused, still scarred from the car accident long ago which had killed her husband and children. She also had a fair skin, blue eyes and a beautiful mouth, elegant, capable of a wide variety of expressions. Her smile tended to be wintry but she was neither cold nor without humour; the wintriness was an aspect of the formal, detached persona which she found helpful to adopt in certain situations. The impression she gave was of a distinguished doctor who exuded confidence without arrogance, ability without ostentation and devotion to the patient without any displays of false charm or professional flamboyance.

"This is nice," she said. "I'd rather see you than a sack of potatoes."

"Sorry to foist myself on you so suddenly and at an awkward time of the day."

"That's all right."

I'd risen to my feet on her arrival but now we both sat down. She wore a grey habit, spotlessly clean and well-ironed. It reminded me of the spotlessly clean, well-ironed jeans I liked to wear sometimes, but I wasn't wearing jeans at that moment. I was dressed in a black suit with a black stock and thick white clerical collar, just as my father would have been for an appointment with his spiritual director. I wasn't my father's clone, yet by dressing formally for the meeting I knew I was trying to present his version of the dedicated, devout priest. My father too had made mistakes during the course of his long ministry but no one had ever questioned his dedication or his devotion to his calling. Tucked safely behind the image which reminded me of him, I tried to draw strength from his memory.

By this time I was feeling nervous. Not very nervous. Just nervous. It was the sort of nervousness which makes one want to clear one's throat and fidget with one's cuffs. Not the kind of nervousness where one's sweating like a pig and trying to repress the urge to run bellowing from the room.

"I'm very upset," I said to Clare. "I want to stress how upset I am. If I hadn't been so upset I wouldn't have made such a serious mistake last night. I was upset because Rosalind had told me she wanted a divorce. She told me in a note she wrote last Monday, but since then the disaster's escalated, just as all the worst disasters do, and now there's a big mess."

Clare merely said: "Start at the beginning."

I talked for some time. I described Rosalind's flight, my pursuit to Devon, our agreement to restructure the marriage. Then I began to describe the events of the previous evening. Twice I got in a muddle, once when I was discussing my decision to use hypnotherapy and once when I described how Rosalind had screamed at me in anger before locking herself in Benedict's room. Those were the two occasions when Clare interrupted me. On the first occasion she said:

"I note you use the word 'hypnotherapy' instead of the word 'hypnosis.' Where is the therapy here?" But when I again explained how I'd been attempting to heal Rosalind, Clare asked if any attempt by me to heal my wife could be in accordance with professional ethics.

"No," I said. "I'm too emotionally involved. I can see now I acted unethically, but as the situation was an emergency—"

"And unethical therapy isn't actually therapy at all, is it?"

After a pause I said: "No."

"So we can't call this hypnotherapy, can we? What should we call it instead?"

"Hypnosis. Plain, ordinary hypnosis."

"Very well, go on."

On the second occasion when she interrupted she said: "Rosalind expressed anger? Was that all that was being expressed?" but I couldn't think what she meant.

"Never mind. Go on," she said again, but this time I was confused because half my mind was still groping for the message she was conveying and I knew I wasn't able to grasp it. Obediently I continued my story, and by the time it had finished I had put my confusion behind me. I felt I had handled the confession well. I'd been frank. I'd been more than willing to admit bad judgement and foolish risk-taking. I'd had no hesitation in saying I regretted my errors and wanted to do all I could to make amends and heal the marriage.

"It's a classic case of the road to hell being paved with good intentions," I concluded at last. "I only wanted to prove to Rosalind that she still loves me."

"And what, in fact, have you succeeded in proving?"

"I've proved that Rosalind still loves me once her self-centred individualism has been stripped away."

"You may have proved that to yourself. But what have you proved to Rosalind?"

"Well . . . This is the point, isn't it? Rosalind isn't convinced that she still loves me. That's why I know the risk I took didn't come off and that's why I know my marriage is still on the rocks and that's why I know I'm still up excrement creek without a paddle. I did pray hard for the Holy Spirit to act through me and heal my wife, but —"

"The gifts of the Spirit can be recognised by their fruits. What are the fruits here?"

"Anger and alienation on her part. Deep anxiety on mine."

"So?"

"So this wasn't the Holy Spirit in action. This was just me making a mess. I thought I was aligning myself with the Holy Spirit, but all I was aligning myself with was my own ego."

"Your ego distorted everything, didn't it? Even your great gift for hypnosis."

"Yes."

"It's a God-given gift, isn't it, and you've undergone professional training so that you can use this gift for the good, in God's service."

"Right."

"So where was God when you used your gift for hypnosis last night?"

"Well, obviously I . . . well, the trouble was . . ." I cleared my throat and started again. "Clearly my ego cut me off from God," I said. "All I could think of was what I wanted—I was self-centred instead of God-centred. But Rosalind had made me so upset that I acted out of character."

"You're saying this was all Rosalind's fault?"

"Well, no. Not exactly. No, it wouldn't be right if I implied that."

"Then what are you implying?"

"I'm simply stating that I was upset. I'm not saying I *blame* Rosalind—she's so sick at present that she's not responsible for her actions—but it's a fact that she did upset me. I mean, I know very well that if I hadn't been so upset I wouldn't have done what I did."

"And what exactly was it that you did, Nicholas?"

I fell silent at last. We sat there motionless beneath the crucifix as the silence lengthened. At last I said in an obstinate voice which sounded as if it should have belonged to someone quite other than my mature, rational self: "You've got to see this in context. My wife wrote me a cold, brutal note, she walked out, she told me she'd been unfaithful, she said she wanted a divorce, she behaved as if she wanted to go away and never come back. Then after I'd moved heaven and earth to put the central problem right, she again tells me she wants to leave. Well, I'm going to be very, very upset by this, aren't I? I mean, this is all wrong, it shouldn't be happening, this wasn't part of the deal."

"What deal?"

"Well, I married her because I knew she *wouldn't* go away and never come back. Rosalind was always there, always, she never let me down. I couldn't have stood being let down again."

"Again?"

I suddenly realised what I'd said. Too late. I sucked in some air and kept it in my lungs for a moment to calm me down. Then I expelled it slowly and said: "When my mother died, she went away and never came back. Not her fault, of course, but . . ." I broke off. Had to grab some air again.

"You never wanted another such bereavement," said Clare, "so Rosalind's constancy was exceptionally important to you."

"Right. Oh, I know how Freudian all that sounds, but Rosalind's nothing like my mother—except that they were both thoroughly normal and both good businesswomen. But I didn't know Rosalind was a good businesswoman when I married her, so—"

"Okay, let's not get hung up on Freud. Let's just focus on Rosalind. Why do you think she was so angry with you at the end?"

"Well, maybe I exaggerated a bit, maybe she wasn't so angry, maybe she was just tired, although I still don't see why she had to lock herself in Benedict's room as if I was some sort of villain. Let's face it, she wanted me to make love to her! She asked for it—begged for it—and it was all a huge success, we were so happy—"

"And on what level was that huge success taking place, Nicholas?"

"Level?"

"Of reality."

I said at once: "It was real for *me*. It was very, very real indeed."

"And for Rosalind? What level of reality operates when one's under hypnosis?"

I started to sweat. This was the moment when my nervousness changed gears. I forgot to fidget with my cuffs. I forgot to clear my throat. I stopped looking around the room for a neutral object to watch. I clasped my hands till they ached and I stared at my white knuckles and I felt the sweat prick my skin beneath my hard white clerical collar.

"The hypnotist calls the shots, surely."

I managed to nod.

"And the subject accepts the shots, whatever the shots are. But where is the reality here?"

I was dumb.

"I saw a stage-show once," said Clare. "The hypnotist made a woman believe she was a dog. She crawled over the stage and barked. Finally she even licked his shoes. She believed that he was her master and that she adored him. But was that real?"

My voice said politely, very, very politely, as if I were a diplomat at a five-star reception who had just realised he had been served cyanide instead of champagne: "I'm not sure I can accept that."

"Accept what?"

"What you're implying."

"Fair enough, we'll move on. What do you suppose Rosalind thought of the hypnosis once she'd recovered?"

"Well, obviously she was annoyed—she did tell me I'd been—quote—'very silly.' She always hated that sort of thing."

"What sort of thing?"

"Hypnosis. She always hated it, particularly in the old days when I used hypnosis as a parlour-trick to boost my ego. But of course I don't do that sort of thing any more."

"Could you please repeat that last sentence, Nicholas?"

The silence which followed screamed in my ears. I found I could no longer think of Rosalind. I could only remember my father, a man of great integrity, looking stricken as he realised how far I had been abusing the psychic gifts which I had inherited from him.

I began to feel very ill.

At last Clare asked: "Why do even skilled hypnotherapists, fully trained and working for God to serve others, need to be so careful in the use of hypnosis, Nicholas?"

I whispered: "Because it's an exercise in power."

"You dominate another person, don't you? You take away the will of that person and impose your own."

I nodded.

"So when Rosalind begged—"

"Yes."

"Whose will was she reflecting? And what relation did her actions have to the reality which she herself had been experiencing before you turned on the power?"

Sweat trickled into my eyes. I wiped it away. I said: "She does love me." My eyes blurred again but not because of the sweat. "I know she does."

"Yes. But before you hypnotised her, did she express any desire to go to bed with you?"

I moved my head painfully from side to side.

"Wasn't she asking for a divorce?"

Painfully I moved my head up and down.

"Are women who are in the middle of asking for a divorce usually willing to—"

I steered my head from side to side again.

"So Rosalind was unwilling. There was this woman, unwilling to have sex with you, and what did you do next?"

"Wait a moment," I said. "You've got to wait. Just *wait.*"

We both waited. The only trouble was I had no idea what I was waiting for. Perhaps I was waiting for the truth to go away. But it didn't. It just lay there between us. On the psychic level I saw it as a huge, black, bleeding lump. I felt sorry for Clare, having to be the midwife at such a hideous birth.

After a while I heard myself say: "I know I can't expect you to understand."

"My dear," said Clare in such a gentle voice that my defences were finally annihilated, "of course I understand. You love Rosalind very much. That's why it seems, doesn't it, that you couldn't possibly have done what in fact you did do. How could you ever have done such a thing, you're saying to yourself, to the person you love best in the world, your lifelong friend, the mother of your children, your wife for the past twenty years? It's quite literally unthinkable—so you unthink it, you deny it, you turn that powerful gift for hypnosis upon yourself and you will yourself to blot such a terrible question from your mind."

I had my elbows on the table by this time. I was shading my eyes with my hands. The mental pain was so excruciating that I wanted to slam my head against the wall until I lost consciousness. I managed to say: "Rosalind did upset me. But I'd been upsetting her for years and years—I'd upset her so much that she couldn't take it any more. So all this is my fault, not hers."

Clare said nothing.

"It's my fault the marriage is in a mess," I said. "It's my fault I went out of control last night. What happened last night had nothing to do with healing and nothing to do with being an honest priest trying to serve God. I was just a wonder worker. The only person I wanted to serve was myself."

"And where is God now in all this?"

I dug my fists into my eyes to dam the tears but said strongly: "With Rosalind. With the abused and exploited everywhere."

"God's with the people who suffer, yes. And Rosalind's not the only one who's suffering here, is she?"

I gave up trying to stop the tears. I abandoned my ruined defences. I stared at her ugly hands folded in front of me on the table as my voice said: "I don't deserve any support from God after what I did."

"Maybe not, but God's not interested in operating a brownie-point system—he's only interested in loving and forgiving those who are brave enough not to deny what they've done, no matter how terrible, brave enough to be truly sorry, brave enough to resolve to make a fresh start in serving him as well as they possibly can."

Once again it proved impossible to reply. I sat there with the tears streaming down my face, and then just as I was thinking how utterly I was cut off from Christ the Healer, that shining, mysterious figure I had tried so hard for so long to follow, Clare reached out across the table and briefly covered my clenched fists with her scarred hands.

IV

I didn't make a habit of crying. But in my work I saw people of both sexes weep as they wrestled with the cutting edge of reality, so I had no macho delusion that tears were only to be shed by women and children. Many men would have been embarrassed to cry in a woman's presence, but Clare was so much more than just her gender; that was merely one aspect of her multi-sided personality, and to me it wasn't the most interesting facet. I didn't find her sexually attractive. What intrigued me was the way her considerable intelligence was perfectly integrated with her humdrum daily activities. She told me once she was as happy cooking for eight as she was reading the New Testament in Greek. All work was for God. Manual work could provide as much satisfaction as intellectual work. Everything was all of a piece. Life was balanced, rounded, whole.

I admired this Benedictine attitude to life and could only regret how often I failed to live up to the Benedictine ideal. I was very far from being as well integrated as Clare. I had certain talents but they were mental and psychical. I hated working with my hands. It bored me. Over the years I'd tried many different kinds of manual and artistic activity—carpentry, carving, cooking, even knitting—but I was useless at all of them. In the end I found I could do no more than paint bad water-colours of Rosalind's beautiful garden; it wasn't much of a past-time but it was better than nothing. The boys thought this hobby was vaguely pansyish and that I was vaguely nuts. I'd never told them I'd once tried to buck the sexual stereotype by dabbling with knitting.

I often wished I was musical, like Lewis. He worked hard but he knew how to switch off, either by listening to his CDs or by playing the church organ. Lewis was no workaholic. But I was forever fighting the urge to work till I dropped.

I was also poor at domestic life, a failing which exacerbated my workaholic tendency. Without effort Clare—five years my junior but with the spiritual maturity of someone much older—had diagnosed these handicaps at the beginning of our relationship, and ever since had tried to help me achieve a more balanced life. Probably she had never approved of the way I had split off my family life from my work, but she had abstained from criticism. Meeting me as I was she saw me as I was. No wonder I had no conventional masculine hang-up about shedding tears in her presence! I didn't have to keep up a front to preserve her illusions. Seeing me always in the light of truth she never had any illusions to preserve.

When I had wiped away the last tear we talked further about the situation. She wanted to be sure she had fully understood the implications for my career in the event of a divorce.

"Well, there's no point in discussing that," I said, "because I'm going to get Rosalind back. It'll take a long time, I realise that, and it'll require a lot of hard work on my part, but I'm willing to do anything to save the marriage." And when she remained silent I added: "This is a call to integrate my family life and my working life, I see that so clearly now. I've got to redeem this disaster by using it as an opportunity to improve my marriage and make Rosalind much happier."

Clare made no comment on these statements but asked instead: "How would the Church authorities view the fact that your marriage is currently in difficulties?" As a Roman Catholic she was always cautious in her speculations about the rules, customs and general chaos prevailing in the Church of England. The messy open-endedness of our structures as we strive to accommodate the widest possible variety of opinions within the given parameters must so often seem weird to the Romans.

"The Archdeacon might drop in for a chat if he heard I had marital trouble," I said, "and I'm sure the Bishop would make time to see me if I asked for help, but I'm not a career priest, always on the prowl for the next big promotion, and the hierarchy tends to leave mavericks like me well alone. So long as I'm not running around with an underage girl or abusing clients at the Healing Centre, nobody's going to be asking for my head on a platter."

"Not even if you divorce?"

"Priests tend to survive divorce nowadays, particularly when there's been no scandal and the priest has done his best to keep the marriage going. The real problem is when a divorced priest wants to remarry . . . But why are we still talking of divorce when I've told you it definitely isn't on the agenda?"

"Because we know divorce is on Rosalind's agenda and that means we can't pretend the possibility of a final break-up doesn't exist. I admire, of course, your commitment to your marriage and your desire for a better integrated life, but in my admiration I mustn't turn a blind eye to reality."

The implication was that I shouldn't either. Instinctively I tried to impress her by being practical. "I'm all for facing reality," I said, "and now that we've discussed the present situation, can we talk about what I should do next?"

"First of all you must make your formal confession to a priest. I know it sounds very Roman to say 'must' when the Church of England prides itself on saying 'may,' but in these particular circumstances—"

"No need to sound apologetic. I'm an Anglican Catholic who believes in regular confession to a priest even when the confession's going to be hell, but can I confess to Lewis? Or would that be a cop-out?" I usually went to the Fordite monks to make my confession, but the idea of recounting the previous evening's events to yet another person was hard to bear.

Clare paused to consider my request. "It would be a cop-out to use Lewis if you hadn't first made a comprehensive confession to me," she said at last, "but you have. However, there's still a danger in using him. He could be sentimental about you, and you could use his sentimentality to manipulate him."

"He's too sharp to allow that."

"Is he? Lewis's weakness, so you've told me, is his attitude to women. He's also immensely fond of you. Unless you vow before God to be utterly honest you could wind up in a situation where you confess what you did to Rosalind in euphemisms and Lewis colludes with you by implying that she asked for it."

"I promise you that won't happen."

"Reassure me by pretending I'm Lewis and saying exactly what you did to Rosalind last night."

"I abused and exploited her."

"Those are euphemisms. Try again."

"I . . ." But the word refused to be spoken.

"If she suffered it," said Clare, "you can say it."

"Right. Yes. I raped her. I *raped* her," I repeated distinctly, and tried to block off the resulting agony by adding at once: "I'll say that to Lewis, I promise." Just articulating another sentence stopped me hearing that terrible word echoing in my mind, but the pain was still excruciating.

"After the confession," said Clare, as if sensing how much I needed her to keep talking, "you should think much more about what God's purpose is for Rosalind and how you can best help her fulfil it. It strikes me that you're so consumed with your fear of losing her that all you can think of is your own threatened ego. It's very natural for the wounds caused by your mother's death to be reopened by this present situation, but try to keep in mind the fact that fear is one of the strongest forces which cuts us off from God—you must fight the temptation to build a wall around yourself and hide behind it. Remember too that the best kind of love is always unselfish, not consumed with the ego's demands but with the desire to help the beloved. I would recommend that you make a short retreat—straight away if possible—so that you can think and pray about all this in the necessary depth, without distraction."

"I'll go to the Fordite monks."

"Fine, yes, that's good. In a familiar place the stress will be minimalised."

"At least it'll give Rosalind a break from me."

"To be honest, I think you each need a break from the other. Try at least a couple of weeks apart and see how the situation looks when you've both cooled off."

"You mean I should suggest to Rosalind that she returns to Butterfold?"

"I've got a hunch that in addition to making a short retreat this is the most practical thing you can do. Rosalind will regain her equilibrium more quickly once she's reunited with her garden, and that'll benefit you as well as her. The last thing you want now is for her to have a breakdown and be incapable of seeing you for months."

I flinched. "I hadn't thought of that."

"Well, think of it now—and pray for her. Pray for her constantly. Pray that she recovers from the trauma, pray that she's enabled to set aside her anger, pray that she's granted a respite from . . . Ah yes! Do you see now why she locked herself in Benedict's room? She wasn't just driven by anger, was she?"

I shook my head.

"What was the other emotion driving her?"

With great difficulty I said: "Fear."

"Yes, now that you can acknowledge what you did you can also see how frightened she must have been, so pray, please, that she's granted a respite from this fear of hers. Then you must pray for yourself. Your main task, as I see it, is to reopen the channel to God which your own fear has closed down. You need to pray for understanding, and understanding can't take place in a closed mind. Try to prise your mind open again by asking certain questions."

"Such as?"

"What exactly is the nature of this powerful feeling you have for Rosalind? Why precisely is this woman, who shares none of your interests, so vital to you? What's actually been going on in your marriage? Has it helped you to serve God, and if so, in what way? Has this marriage helped Rosalind to serve God, or does her refusal to involve herself in your ministry signal that the marriage, as it stands at present, has blocked her spiritual journey? And finally . . ." She paused thoughtfully. At once I felt sure this last question was to be the most important.

"And finally," said Clare, looking me straight in the eyes, "ask yourself this: what is the significance of Bear?"

"Bear?"

"Bear." She gave me one of her wintry smiles and added on a lighter note: "By the way, while on the subject of animals, how's the cat?"

"Doing well." I was still floundering around in my childhood memories. "Alice is very good with him."

"And Alice herself? How's she?"

"Fine. Benefiting very much from life in a community."

"Good."

"I wish Rosalind could understand me when I talk of community," I said impulsively, "but she's too much of an individualist to listen."

"Is she, Nicholas? But you know all about being an individualist, don't you? Didn't you describe yourself only a moment ago as a maverick who was happy to operate outside the Church's traditional career structures?"

I was silenced.

"Beware of projection," said Clare wryly. "Beware of projecting onto Rosalind all those qualities of your own which don't conform with your ideal image of yourself. And while we're on the subject of that community life of yours in the City, let's take a closer look at it. You actually have to hold yourself apart from those who work at the Centre, don't you? A certain detachment is essential for people in your position. And although you're sharing a house with three other people, how far is it a real community? For perfectly valid reasons you have to maintain a certain distance between Alice, the woman living under your roof, and Stacy, the pupil you're trying to train. I suspect that your only real relationship is with Lewis, but a relationship between two men who each happens to fill a need in the other—for a brother in your case and for a son in Lewis's—doesn't constitute a community."

This was tough talk. I bent my head and started to examine my fingernails one by one.

"And now let's take a look at Rosalind," said Clare. "Let's take a look at this individualist who you say is incapable of understanding what the word 'community' means. Butterfold is a large village, isn't it?"

"Yes."

"Does she lead an isolated life there, seeing no one?"

"No. She has a lot of friends there. She was a power in the W.I. before her business took off. She goes to church with me every Sunday."

"She relates well to her community, it would seem."

"Yes. Okay, you've made your point—"

"Her idea of community, perhaps, is a little different from yours. But whose idea of community is actually closer to the ideal?"

I had run out of fingernails to examine. Too bad we didn't have ten fingernails on each hand. I could have used some more fingernails at that point.

"Assuming Rosalind isn't entirely without community skills," said Clare when I was unable to reply, "perhaps I might add some further questions to those you need to ask yourself. First of all, why is she unable to relate to your world at St. Benet's? How far have you really tried to make her feel welcome? You had no hesitation in asking her to give up her own community, but what did you offer her in return?"

"I did suggest she got involved with St. Benet's but she just said she wasn't churchy. I then tried to explain that we were a dynamic organisation on the cutting edge of reality but she still wasn't interested."

"But Rosalind herself is now grappling with that cutting edge of reality—so what's your dynamic Christian enterprise doing to care for her as it's cared for Alice?"

"You can't force help on people who don't want it."

"You're saying it's Rosalind's fault that she feels your community has nothing to offer her?"

"No, I'm saying . . ." But by this time she had me in such a tangle that I had no idea what I was saying. I took a deep breath and tried again. "Rosalind's very disturbed," I said. "She's going through a mid-life crisis. One has to make allowances for her, and I don't want to blame her for anything."

"Nicholas, last night was Rosalind the only one who was very disturbed?"

Silence.

"And are we really so sure we know whom this mid-life crisis belongs to?"

Another silence.

"Of course we must be careful to make the distinction," said Clare briskly, "between the mid-life crisis and the Second Journey. The Second Journey usually begins in mid-life and is a time of profound spiritual growth; it's characterised by the desire to let go of youth and move on to explore the rewards and challenges of middle age. The mid-life crisis, on the other hand, is characterised by the desire to cling to a lost youth, the refusal to move on to the next stage of life, and an arrested spiritual development. The symptoms include not just the well-known tendency to have a love affair with someone much younger, but the clinging to a symbol of youth—a sports car, perhaps, or some other much-loved significant object which should have been set aside long ago . . . But why am I telling you all this? I'm sorry! Of course you know it all already—the subject must constantly come up with your clients."

"Yep. Sure. You bet." I was so mesmerised by this time that all I could do was sit in my chair like a robot and grunt phoney Americanisms.

Clare rose to her feet. "Come and see me again after you've made your retreat," she said. "I hope I've managed to clarify your thoughts and provide some profitable lines for meditation, but I've exhausted you now and you need to rest. Do cancel your engagements and withdraw to the Fordites as soon as you possibly can."

I nodded and levered myself clumsily to my feet. "Thanks. Sorry

I . . . Sorry I was so . . . Sorry—so stupid sometimes . . ." My voice trailed away.

Giving my hand a quick clasp she said: "You'll be very much in my prayers. Now go home and talk to Lewis."

She went away, leaving me feeling as if I'd been washed, scoured, scrubbed, spin-dried, ironed and starched. I wondered if she did the laundry as well as the cooking. It would explain why her habit always looked so exceptionally clean and well-pressed.

Staggering outside I drove raggedly back to St. Benet's for the next stage of my mid-life nightmare.

11

> The first stage of grief is a shock reaction and we cannot absorb the painful truth in one go . . . The unreality theme of "somehow I still can't believe it" recurs throughout the grief process. We hope we will wake up from the dream.
>
> GARETH TUCKWELL AND DAVID FLAGG
> *A Question of Healing*

I

"*I think* I could start to like this woman," said Lewis.

"Don't strain yourself. At your age it could be dangerous."

We were sitting in his bedsit after my return to the Rectory. Over at the church Stacy was conducting the lunch-time Eucharist with the assistance of Brother Paul, the Anglican Franciscan friar who helped part-time at the Centre, but I was bypassing the service in order to make my formal confession. Lewis had just granted me absolution. He had removed his stole and was lighting a cigarette.

"I'm glad you're mellowing towards Clare," I said, "but you don't know yet what she said to me."

"I know that you left here this morning out of touch with reality and that you've come back capable of making an honest confession! Without doubt that woman's given your soul an effective spring-cleaning—no mean task, as I well remember."

"Her name is Sister Clare Veronica."

"So you keep telling me."

"Aren't you going to ask what advice she handed out?"

"I refuse to meddle in your relationship with your spiritual director."

"Since you've just told me to make a three-day retreat as a penance, I thought you'd be interested to hear that Clare advised me to make a short retreat as soon as possible."

"So what? I don't find the coincidence in any way remarkable. Obviously you have to take a break at this point and obviously you need the kind of break that only a retreat can provide. Even an ordinand could draw such a conclusion!"

"You're cross because Clare's been a good priest to me and you can't admit any woman could be capable of such a thing!"

"Oh yes, I can! My arguments against the ordination of women are purely theological!"

"Then why in heaven's name are you being so cantankerous about her?"

Lewis sighed. "I suppose I'm jealous. I know I can't be your spiritual director any more now that we're living in each other's pockets, and I know I mustn't interfere in your relationship with this woman—"

"Sister Clare Veronica."

"—but I still mind about her role in your life. The fact that I mind is both ridiculous and pathetic. That's why I'm sunk in cantankerous gloom. Satisfied?"

"You silly old sod!" I was very fond of Lewis when he dedicated himself to presenting what he called "the unvarnished truth." It takes guts to be that honest. Reaching across the table I patted his forearm consolingly. "But you can still give me fraternal advice!"

"Not in these circumstances—oh, come on, Nicholas, wake up! I'm not getting into discussions with you about your marriage. Rosalind and I have never got on—I'd be undermined by all manner of prejudices and couldn't possibly give you the kind of clear-eyed advice you need at present. I'll stand by you whatever happens and I'll pray for you, but my role here is to be supportive, not directive."

We sat in a silence broken only by the murmur of the gas fire. Glancing at my watch I saw we had ten minutes before the Eucharist ended and the staff returned to the Rectory for lunch. Despite all Lewis had just said I remained desperate to talk to him in his old role of mentor. Tentatively I asked: "Do you think I'm unfit at present to do any work?"

"Well, you're no longer spiritually unfit; you've confessed, repented and received absolution, and I certainly believe you'll now bust a gut to behave as you should, but the trouble is you're almost certainly still in a state of emotional exhaustion and that means you could make bad mistakes—not sins necessarily, but errors of judgement which could lead you into a dead-awful mess."

"Perhaps I should make a retreat for longer than three days."

"Make the three-day retreat first and then see what your spiritual director advises."

"I admit I do hate the thought of taking time off work."

"That's what all the workaholics say. Nicholas, no problem is more pressing than your spiritual and emotional health. Take whatever time you need and I think you'll find the Healing Centre will survive your absence."

"Yes, of course," I said mechanically, but at once started worrying about Francie Parker and Stacy, two people who in their different ways presented me with a major problem to solve.

On my return to London from Devon on Tuesday Lewis had informed me that Francie had called at the Rectory on the previous evening. His conversation with her had been confidential so he had given me no hint of what she had said, but he had thought I should be informed of her visit. He had also disclosed that earlier during that same evening he had had a talk with Stacy. This conversation too had been confidential, but again Lewis had thought I should know it had taken place. In both cases I was assured that he had everything under control.

Obviously there had been trouble, but Lewis's message was that although I had to be warned so that I could be on the alert for a sudden crisis, I was on no account to go wading in and trying to fix things. This situation was not uncommon at the Centre where we dealt frequently with disturbed people and confidentiality was an important issue; I trusted Lewis's judgement just as he trusted mine, and I was prepared to stand back and let him cope, if that was what he wanted. But on this occasion it was hard not to want to know more. Stacy was my curate. Francie was the Centre's chief Befriender. We weren't talking about clients but about personnel.

My brain began to flicker over the morally acceptable ways of obtaining more information. Priests do have ways of signalling the contents of confidential conversations but Lewis and I were agreed that signalling could only be justified in a white-hot emergency. Lewis had given no signal about the contents of either conversation. Paradoxically this was itself a signal, proclaiming there was no white-hot emergency. But it could be red-hot. In fact with two members of staff it had to be. Staring into the flames of the gas fire I tried again to figure out what had taken place at the Rectory on Monday night.

Our basic concern had long since been shared. Francie we suspected of fantasising about her husband's sadism in order to win extra attention from me, and Stacy we knew was bogged down in an immaturity which manifested itself in . . . But here Lewis and I disagreed. There was no doubt that Stacy had sexual problems, but this fact distracted attention from the central question: whether or not Stacy was suited for the ministry of healing.

Cautiously I said to Lewis: "Is Francie back at work today?"

"No, I phoned her this morning and she said she wanted to take another day off. But I think she could be back at the Centre tomorrow."

"She's feeling better?"

"She must be. She told me she was having lunch with an old friend at Fortnum's today."

"What exactly was this malaise of hers?"

"Oh, she just felt a bit down. No need for you to worry. I've been phoning her every day and monitoring the situation."

"You're saying her depression doesn't justify a visit to her GP?"

Lewis thought for a moment before saying: "If she wanted to see her doctor I wouldn't stop her, but she's expressed no desire to do so."

So he did think Francie needed medical help. "Should I try to talk to her again," I suggested, "about seeing a psychiatrist who specialises in abused women?"

"No, what you've got to do is leave her well alone, Nicholas, and when I say 'well alone' I mean *well* alone. I'll deal with her."

If I had to be kept apart from Francie it could only mean that her harmless hero-worship of me had indeed spiralled, just as we'd feared, into a neurotic fixation.

Sceptically I said: "Are you sure she'll be fit to return to work tomorrow?"

"No, and neither's she. But don't worry, if she does show up I'll see she does no befriending. She can help me with the music therapy."

"What I'd like to know is why Francie's suddenly gone over the top like this! Why should—"

"Nicholas, you don't know whether or not Francie's gone over the top, and I think you should now stop your attempt to pump me for information."

I sighed. I'd been enjoying my break from lacerating myself with thoughts of Rosalind. "And Stacy?" I enquired, hoping to extend the holiday.

"Nothing I can say on that subject at the moment."

"No? How's he getting on with Tara?"

"Ask him."

No signals of any kind there. Sighing again I said: "I dislike the thought of going away when we have those two major problems on our hands. I feel I might be needed here."

"No one's indispensable."

"Yes, but—"

"Nicholas, you're behaving as if you're hooked on people needing you—as if you can't wait to grab a magic wand and go around fixing everyone in sight. But that's the attitude of the wonder worker. Now shape up, ship out and rest up before you start making some really bad decisions."

Better not to upset the old boy by arguing further. Anyway I knew I'd be fit for action again once I'd made my three-day retreat. The three days would seem like an eternity, I realised that, but once they'd been endured I wouldn't need more time off. Patting his shoulder reassuringly I headed for the door. "I must go upstairs," I said. "It's time to tell Rosalind she's welcome to return to Butterfold for a while."

It was a good exit line. Glancing back as I opened the door I saw Lewis quiver with the desire to ask me how I'd been led to this decision, but he stuck to his guns and refused to cross-question me further about my interview with Clare.

Taut with dread at the prospect of facing Rosalind, I toiled reluctantly up the stairs to the flat.

I I

At that point I received a reprieve. On entering the flat I found a note from Rosalind which informed me that she was lunching in the West End. As if to reassure me of her friendly intentions she then suggested we dined that night with the others, and as if to erase completely any lingering impression of hostility she apologised for the incident last night. She also suggested that we never referred to it again.

I sat down in the living-room and brooded on this communication until Lewis buzzed me from the kitchen to remind me I was missing lunch. I said I would be downstairs shortly. Then I resumed my examination of the letter. I noted that Rosalind had implied the incident was her fault. Confused rape victims often did assume a guilt which didn't belong to them, and I had certainly encouraged her to assume it. I also thought her desire to gloss over the incident indicated not friendliness at all but fear, while her suggestion that we dined with the others was born merely of a desire to appease me. Her flight to the West End underlined her longing to escape from the whole sordid mess.

In short the letter stank. I hated myself for driving her to write it. I hated myself for what I'd done. I knew that by repenting and confessing to a priest who had given me absolution the spiritual slate had been wiped clean, but I still felt soaked in grief, guilt and shame. The absolution had no psychological reality for me yet. And it wasn't the only thing my psyche was finding hard to grasp. As a new wave of grief swept over me I found the aftermath of the rape was providing me with a reality which was almost unendurable. I thought: this can't be happening to me. I'll wake up soon. For by this time it had occurred to me in horror that not only was I in shock but that I was behaving as if I'd lost Rosalind for ever. Although of course I hadn't. I'd get her back. Eventually. But meanwhile . . .

Meanwhile it was as if the marriage had died and I was grieving over the corpse, but that wouldn't do at all and I had to pull myself together. With determination I shredded Rosalind's letter and dumped it in the swing-bin, but afterwards I found I was unable to rest until I'd scooped out the shreds and burnt them in the sink. The letter, that terrible reminder of the true state of my marriage, had to be wholly annihilated. Only when the ashes had been washed down the drain did I go downstairs and pretend to eat lunch.

After five minutes I went to my study, shut the door and prayed hard for a while. Nothing happened except that I shed a few more tears of self-hatred. I went on grieving for Rosalind, missing her, mentally pawing over the damaged structure of our marriage. How was it going to be mended and redeemed? But perhaps my best hope of staying sane now was not to try to visualise the future but to move on doggedly, taking one day at a time, and always fighting any desire to abandon hope.

Deciding to begin this fight I dragged myself over to the Centre to attend to some paperwork. Despairing priests could never face paperwork. Therefore if I could face it, I wouldn't be in despair. My morning appointments had been taken by Lewis, who had a flexible schedule designed to cope with emergencies, and my afternoon appointments had been cancelled by him. But the committed workaholic can always find something to do, even if his colleague has decided he's unfit to work. On arriving at my office I embraced the paperwork with relief and felt almost normal again.

I dictated some letters to Joyce, my secretary, but she kept having to correct me and the letters sounded jerky when she read them back. Finally I dismissed her and started filling in a form relating to a diocesan enquiry, but I changed my mind so many times about what to put down that in the end I tore up the form and binned it. Let them send another.

By this time it was four o'clock. To kid myself I was still at work I picked up some brochures left by the computer salesman and told Joyce I was retiring to my study at the Rectory to read them. I was wondering if Rosalind was back, but there was no one in the flat. However, her coat had been dumped on Benedict's bed. So she was back but somewhere else. Still clutching my brochures I padded downstairs again to the study and began to fidget with my computer.

The Applemac was new. Benedict had taught me how to use it. It had finally given us something to talk about. Benedict was a brash, unreflective young man who was unable to bear either silence or solitude. Recently I had read an article about public school lager louts and had realised that Benedict was a prime example of this species. I found it hard to believe we were related—but perhaps we weren't. Perhaps my wife had been unfaithful to me for longer than she had chosen to admit. Maybe my happy marriage had been one long grand illusion.

Hadn't really forgiven the adultery, of course. I'd said "I forgive you" and I had indeed wanted that statement to be true, but the forgiveness proclaimed so nobly had had no psychological reality. It was a tricky thing, this business of the psychological reality being at odds with the proclamations of the intellect and the will. I'd often witnessed the phenomenon in my clients and now I was seeing it happen in myself. In this case my battered psyche hadn't caught up with the demands of my Christian conscience. The psyche was lagging behind, bruised and bloodied, still screaming silently with the pain of damage sustained and loss endured.

Drained of energy by this new insight I abandoned my computer and began to thumb through the brochures for the new Psion Organiser, the all-in-one alternative to diaries, filing systems, calculators and address-books at a price of £195.95, but in the end I had to abandon even this stimulating technological diversion. The pain was so stupefying, shredding my thoughts and stirring up profound feelings of rejection and failure. I was trying not to think of my mother and all the grief which had followed her death, but I could still feel those old scars breaking open and bleeding all over my mind. Love had been lost. Security had been wiped out. Chaos had been enthroned. And now it was all happening again—except that of course this time, with Rosalind still alive, I'd beat back the chaos, recapture the love and security and win through. But meanwhile . . .

Meanwhile I was thinking that huge personal disasters, striking at the root of one's stability, had a way of escalating until they terminated in catastrophe. My mother's death had had a variety of consequences for both my father and myself, but the most serious had been the removal from our lives of someone who personified normality. If she'd lived I wouldn't have become such a troubled, oddball loner in adolescence, and if I'd been able to rely on ordinary social skills in order to make friends I wouldn't have wound up abusing my psychic powers to impress people and becoming the paranormal pet of that fast set which had adopted me when I was barely out of my teens. My father had tried to set me straight but he'd been too old and hadn't been able to cope. In the end I'd almost wrecked my chance of being ordained. If Lewis hadn't intervened . . .

But it was better not to think of the catastrophe which had lain at the end of that escalating disaster. It was enough to recall that I was bucketing around, out of control, a wonder worker who allowed himself to be used and bruised by the powers of darkness, until the inevitable day came when I made the wrong decision and was almost wiped out. That certainly taught me a lesson. Maybe all arrogant, know-it-all, bone-headed young idiots, psychic or otherwise, should have a short, sharp brush with death to bring them to their senses. It certainly brought me to mine.

After Lewis had saved me he trained me. I owed everything to him. In 1983, when he wound up dead drunk on my doorstep, Rosalind could never understand why I'd bent over backwards to rehabilitate him, but then Rosalind had never understood how far I was in Lewis's debt. She thought I would have pulled myself together anyway after the crisis which nearly destroyed me in 1968. But she was wrong. Without Lewis I would have gone under. God had worked through Lewis to haul me back from the abyss, I saw that now, but I'd been lucky. I was well aware of how fortunate I'd been, and ever since then I'd lived in dread of the disaster which escalates, the disaster which the powers of darkness use as a surfboard to surge all the way up the golden beach into the heart of the kingdom of light.

No good talking to Rosalind in that kind of mystical language. She couldn't relate to it. I'd tried to explain to her that metaphor, symbol and analogy can convey truth which can't be expressed adequately in straightforward language, but she hadn't really understood. She preferred plain, factual statements. It interested me that although she loved flowers, what she loved best was the mechanics of selling them at a profit. Fair enough. Capitalists have their own language and their own world-view, just like any other group, but I did wish more of them could believe their language wasn't automatically superior to any other language which was on offer.

I suddenly realised I was staring at the Psion Organiser brochure, discarded earlier and now lying in my "pending" tray. I was also still shuddering with pain. Obviously I needed to move before I started banging my head against the wall. Leaving the study I headed for Lewis's bedsit to wait for him to return from work, but as I crossed the hall I saw Alice working in the kitchen. At once I knew that in her presence I would find peace and a respite from pain.

I veered away from the bedsit.

No moth could have headed more rapidly to the light.

III

Alice was rolling pastry. I was informed that we were going to have steak-and-kidney pie that night with potatoes and cabbage. Belatedly I remembered to tell her that Rosalind and I would be present for dinner but Alice said fine, no problem, she'd do extra vegetables for the second helpings. Sitting down at the kitchen table I began to watch her while she worked.

After a moment the cat sprang onto my lap and finally succeeded in making himself comfortable after much revolving and stamping and pawing. He was growing fast. Neutering loomed on the horizon. Lewis and Stacy, who knew nothing about cats, were emotionally opposed to this operation but Alice and I knew better. Tomcats have a terrible life in cities if they're left to the mercy of their sex-drive. They're perpetually exhausted, both by copulation and by fighting, and they can get badly injured, particularly if they pick up infections from dirty claws. That kind of chaotic existence shortens the life-span and makes the cat mean. What was the point of James having a full set of sex organs if he died young with one ear missing and his tail bitten off as the result of a violent and smelly career? Lewis said he recognised himself in this description and would still elect to be fully equipped. Stacy objected that Lewis was too old to die young. Alice, sensible as always, pointed out that Lewis wasn't a cat. Meanwhile James, ignorant of his approaching fate, was enthusiastically chewing our shoelaces under the table.

I stroked his fur now as I watched Alice work, and listened to his purring. Alice was very good at silences. Happiness emanated from her as the pie took shape. She was centred, focused, serene.

I sat motionless, the wounded healer, and soaked up the wordless comfort she offered.

"When you came to work here," I said at last, "you used to behave as if you could hardly believe that Lewis and I, the healers, had done you such a favour—and perhaps in our arrogance we too saw ourselves as doing all the giving, providing healing for you in various ways. But that wasn't God's purpose at all, was it? We may originally have been sent to you, but then the tables were turned and you were sent to us. It's *you* who's now the real healer at the Rectory, Alice."

She paused in her task of fluting the pie-crust. The pie was enormous, sumptuous, resplendent. Gazing at it reflectively she was too shy to look me in the eyes.

Alice was thinner now, still plump but the plumpness had an acceptable pattern. She was no longer an elongated lump with various thick appendages; she was a series of generous curves. Lewis, I knew, liked them and had remarked more than once to me recently how good it was to see Alice acquiring what he called a "non-repulsive shape." I'd agreed, although I'd never thought much about Alice's physical shape because I was so entranced by the shape of her psyche. Alice had the most beautiful psyche, supple as an athlete's body and glowing in richly patterned strands of warmth, compassion and understanding. I'd been aware of it as soon as we'd met, although at the time it had been disfigured by so much anxiety and pain. The extreme beauty of this aspect of Alice, an aspect invisible to the eye, was why I'd taken such a special interest in her. I had never admitted this to Lewis, but no doubt he had long since guessed what was going on. He himself would have been aware of Alice's psyche, although not nearly so aware as I was. Lewis always had trouble perceiving women accurately. He wasn't incapable of a clear perception but the process took him longer because he had to battle away against his hang-ups.

I suddenly realised Alice was speaking, responding to my comment that she was the real healer at the Rectory. I heard her say: "If you believe that, then I suppose it must be true, although it seems fantastic and I can't see why you should think such a thing. But thanks anyway. It's a wonderful compliment." She smiled at me briefly and for a second our eyes met. Then she returned to her work on the pie.

I noted that Alice did not ask why the residents at the Rectory needed healing. I assumed she had sensed the changes of atmosphere and the profound unhappiness which was now flowing like an underground river beneath the deceptive normality of our daily routine, but she always knew when to speak and when to be silent, when to ask questions and when to avoid comment. She was particularly clever with Lewis, who had previously terrorised all the domestic help and had at first opposed the idea of her living in at the Rectory.

Alice stroked Lewis on a psychic level and calmed him. She cooked him his favourite English dishes. She introduced him to rum raisin ice cream. She admired the photographs of his grandchildren. She visited him in hospital. But she never gushed over him or became intrusive. She just cared for him without ever striking a false note. Lewis had made a joke of identifying himself with James, but there's many a true word spoken in jest, and when I saw how deftly Alice dealt with him I was reminded of a gifted cat-lover looking after a battle-scarred old tom who had never quite recovered from being kicked as a kitten. "Dear little Alice!" Lewis would sigh, tamed and tranquillised. "I'm very fond of her."

She was equally successful with Stacy, and he had soon become confident in her presence. Non-threatening and non-possessive, she wanted only to be kind and helpful. She taught him how to use the washing machine without breaking it. When she saw the state of his underclothes after they emerged from the dryer, she offered to buy him a new set of everything at Marks and Spencer. She baked him his favourite biscuits. She introduced him to rum raisin ice cream. She praised the pictures of his sister Aisling's wedding. She showed him the best way of mending his cassock whenever the hem fell down and would certainly have mended it herself if I hadn't insisted that Stacy was to take care of his own clothes. On weekends, her official time off, she would find the time to drink cups of tea with him while he talked endlessly about Liverpool and football and his family. He never talked so freely either to Lewis or to me.

"Where's Stacy?" I said vaguely to Alice as I concluded this meditation.

"Upstairs, I suppose. He came in here a while ago and wanted to know what was for dinner."

"Was Rosalind with him?"

"No, but she's back. I heard her come in."

"That's odd. I wonder where she is. She's not in the flat."

"Oh, she's probably with Stacy—maybe he's finally had the chance to show her the pictures of Aisling's wedding."

I started to brood on Stacy's child-like naivety in relating to the opposite sex.

Lewis was sure Stacy was a homosexual, but Lewis saw the issue of homosexuality as clear-cut, like a black-and-white pattern which was incapable of ambiguity. This attitude was not, as the Gay Christians thought, because he was a bigot, incapable of sympathising with them. Nor was it, as they also thought, because he was a repressed homosexual who could only keep self-doubt at bay by condemning homosexuality in others. His main problem was that he viewed homosexuals through glasses fashioned in a previous era and he resolutely refused to acquire a modern pair of spectacles. This previous era wasn't the thirties, when he had been an adolescent, or the twenties, the decade into which he'd been born. It wasn't even Edwardian. It was Victorian, the era which had fashioned his mentor Cuthbert Darcy, who had rescued Lewis in his hour of need, dusted him down and reprogrammed him.

Great-Uncle Cuthbert had had some very Victorian views on all forms of sexual activity. Good women, he had believed, were for marriage and motherhood. The sex-drive, he had been convinced, was a considerable nuisance, interfering as it did with a man's concentration on more important matters, but if one really couldn't function adequately without coitus, then one was obliged to marry a woman of one's own class and procreate. Marriage was, of course, for ever. Fornication was not just sinful but at best time-consuming and at worst life-threatening. Those who indulged in such a fundamentally trivial activity were clearly disturbed individuals who needed to rearrange their priorities in order to lead happier, more rewarding lives. The fallen women who lured men from the path to fulfilment could only be described as the dregs of humanity, but even such dregs could be redeemed; one should never forget that because God had made each one of us in his own image, each one of us was precious in his sight; nor should one ever forget that because of the Incarnation, God was present in the world and calling us to care for our fellow men, whatever their rank or condition, as if they were Jesus Christ himself. Homosexuals—perverts, as Great-Uncle Cuthbert would have called them—were also the dregs of humanity, cursed with a handicap for which there was no cure, but again one had to remember that Christ cared for everyone: the poor, the handicapped, the outcasts—even women. So if the perverts chose to renounce their unnatural sexual activity and embrace celibacy, they were capable, by the grace of God, of leading just as good a life as their more fortunate brothers. Happy ending.

Lewis had swallowed whole at the age of fifteen this gospel according to Father Darcy, and he had never quite recovered from it. The basic theology—the idea that one should care for all people, regardless of who they were, since each individual was precious in God's sight—was as true today as it was yesterday; it was the Darcy interpretation, wedded to the sociology of his youth, which now looked like a museum-piece. To be fair to Lewis, he did accept that much more was known in the late twentieth century about sexuality than had been known in the nineteenth, and he also accepted that the Church, reflecting this new knowledge, had become more wary of uttering simplistic judgements on this most complex of subjects, but although he was capable of being both modern and imaginative in his pastoral care of people in trouble, no matter what they got up to in bed, the diverse nature of homosexuality was hidden from him behind a monolith marked SIN. In his view people were either homosexual or heterosexual. Homosexuality was a handicap. Bisexuality was either immature behavior by heterosexuals or else homosexuals pretending to be what they weren't. Either way it indicated an unintegrated personality which needed help. All forms of homosexual activity were wrong—but of course one should never fail to treat these handicapped people with as much care and compassion as if they were Christ himself in order to help them lead rewarding celibate lives.

As I always said to the Gay Christians, it wasn't that Lewis ever intended to be unkind, patronising or just plain unchristian. He was as firmly convinced as any of us that we were all of equal value in

God's sight. But on the subjects which preoccupied the gays, he was a heterosexual Victorian male and there was no changing him.

That was why I failed to take Lewis as seriously as I might otherwise have done when he diagnosed that Stacy was a homosexual. My unwillingness to support this diagnosis was also influenced by the fact that Stacy showed no interest in other men and every interest in getting a steady girlfriend. I did note that he was so nervous while trying to gain this status symbol that every date was an ordeal achieved only by a major effort of the will, but I decided this was just a symptom of immaturity. I also rejected Lewis's view that Stacy was only trying to acquire a girlfriend in order to please me, but since I saw sexuality as a complex spectrum encompassing an enormous variety of behavior, I was inevitably going to shy away from such an unsubtle opinion. What I had to remember, even as every liberal instinct urged me to discard Lewis's judgement on this subject, was that he might be right. Not all psycho-sexual puzzles are wreathed in complexity. But I was fairly sure this one was.

Stacy had ben seduced in his teens by an older man who was well educated, well respected and even, I'm sorry to say, a pillar of his local church. Despite my liberal views I don't approve of seducing minors. Nor do I approve of promiscuity, and those who persist in such behaviour have no business turning up in church and pretending they're trying to lead Christian lives. Both during and after this clandestine affair Stacy had never been to bed with anyone else so he at least could hardly be rated promiscuous, but I was prepared to bet the older man had notched up a colourful past while compensating himself for the strain of staying in the closet in order to preserve his respectable facade.

Yet life's never so simple as it seems. This man apparently came to love Stacy and was without doubt very good to him. He encouraged Stacy to read and study. He took him on cultural expeditions. He even fostered Stacy's interest in becoming a priest. So although I can only disapprove of the way this man wound up muddling and maiming Stacy's sexual development, I have to admit he must have been not only a good man in many ways but probably interesting and delightful as well. The story's a sharp illustration of how reluctant one should be to rush to judgement. Who was I anyway to act as a judge? I'd rattled around too in my time. In my own way. With girls and psychic parlour-tricks.

Stacy's ordination certainly represented some sort of redemption of the mess, but it seemed clear that the redemption was by no means complete and that Lewis and I were being called to help Stacy finish his delayed journey to maturity. Unfortunately, as neither of us could agree on the exact nature of the problem we had to solve, this was easier said than done. If Lewis was right, then our task would be to help Stacy come to terms with the homosexuality he was now busy denying. But supposing *I* was right? I thought the inevitable guilt and shame resulting from the secret love affair had turned him off sex—all sex—and that his genuine desire to live as a heterosexual was being hampered by this deep-seated revulsion. I also thought he was currently trapped in the bisexuality which is so common among teenagers with the result that he was unable to move on in the sexual spectrum to a place which would more accurately reflect his adult self. I saw the correct place as being at the heterosexual end of the bisexual middle of the spectrum; or in other words, I thought it likely that although in maturity he might experience the occasional homosexual attraction, he was not fundamentally homosexual. In which case any effort to help him to maturity by urging him to see himself as gay would do almost as much harm as the seducer who had imprisoned him in adolescence.

I did suggest the obvious: that Stacy should talk through his homosexual past with an expert counsellor so that it could be properly explored and finally transcended. But Stacy said he didn't want to talk about the past. It was done, finished, he didn't want to think about it any more. I explained that there were different ways of not thinking about the past and that some were more helpful than others. If one merely repressed painful memories they didn't go away but instead burrowed into the unconscious mind and resurfaced in some other form. On the other hand, if one faced the memories and examined them, instead of splitting them off and denying them, there was more chance of the past being successfully integrated with the present, and then all the energy wasted on repression would be set free for a more productive use.

But Stacy stood his ground and refused further help.

There are certain practitioners of the ministry of healing, notably those from the ranks of the Charismatic Evangelicals, who would no doubt at that point have tried to "deliver" Stacy by means of a traditional ritual from the malign spirit which was impairing him, but I'm a mainstream Church of England priest in the Catholic tradition and my ministry tends to be much more low-key and much more interwoven with modern medicine. I don't mean to disassociate myself from my Charismatic brethren, Protestant or Catholic, many of whom are dedicated, honourable people, and I don't mean to imply that their direct dealings with the unconscious mind are necessarily either misguided or ineffective; statistics wouldn't support such a statement. But generally speaking, I prefer to damp religious emotions down rather than rev them up, so I take care to operate within a highly conventional structure which leaves the minimum of room for histrionics. Mass hysteria is a very real danger at a healing service of any kind, and uncontrollable behaviour which has nothing to do with the Spirit of God can give religion a bad name.

I say all this to explain why I didn't play the exorcist with Stacy and, as my Charismatic brethren would have put it, attempt to "deliver him from the spirit of sexual confusion which was infesting him." I prayed for him, of course. That went without saying. I counselled him as his Rector. That too went without saying. But finally I decided that my prayers and counselling needed to be complemented by the healing skills of someone with a medical background who had specific training in this area. Rightly or wrongly I believed that this course would be more likely to produce an effective and lasting healing in Stacy's case than to deal directly, in Charismatic fashion, with the unconscious mind by using the ritual of deliverance.

One of the great maxims of the ministry of healing is expressed in the quotation: "One may lead a horse to water, Twenty cannot make him drink." When Stacy refused further help I knew I couldn't force him to take my advice and for a time I tried to convince myself that my decision to get him into therapy was wrong. But I didn't think it was. I foresaw he would go on being blocked from further spiritual and emotional development, and I couldn't work out how to break the impasse.

I consulted Lewis again, but we still couldn't agree either on the nature of the problem or on the way forward. So I decided the only thing to do was to back off and wait. I didn't like doing this. It felt too much like failure. Failure is one of the most difficult things for a healer to accept. I knew the difficulty, I recognised it, but still I found it hard to acknowledge my powerlessness and trust God to approach the problem in some other way. When I discussed the failure with Clare I admitted I felt angry with Stacy for refusing the help. It was good to admit this. But even though I tried not to be angry, I found I was steadily losing interest in him, and this made me feel so guilty that I worked harder than ever to conceal my emotional withdrawal.

I was well aware that Stacy hero-worshipped me, but I'd always felt this was just a symptom of his continuing immaturity so it had never bothered me much. Yet now, aware of my changing feelings towards him, it began to bother me very much indeed. Guilt made me desperate not to behave in any way which he could have construed as a rejection, and because by this time I was so worried about the problem he presented, my failure to help him seemed all the more difficult to bear.

Finally I decided I had to act. Merely to wait had become intolerable, and in the hope that another clerical opinion might be of use I confided in Gilbert Tucker, the vicar of St. Eadred's Fleetside. I picked Gil because he fancied himself as an expert on the sexual problems of the clergy, but I should have realised that as a gay activist he would bring his own agenda to the discussion. He said at once that Stacy was obviously as gay as a pink daffodil and that he was only pretending to be straight in order to please me. I then realised I'd come full circle. The liberal-radical (Gil) and his conservative arch-enemy (Lewis) were united in seeing homosexuality as a black-and-white issue, while I, caught between these two extremists, had wound up being even more bemused than I was before.

And now, to exacerbate my bemusement, the information had been presented to me by Lewis that last Monday night he and Stacy had been locked in a confidential discussion. What was going on? Stacy would normally come to me if he had a problem—unless, of course, I was the problem. Even so it was odd that he should confide in Lewis, whom he usually found intimidating. Could Stacy have finally sensed my ambivalent feelings towards him and confided in Lewis because he was so upset? Maybe. And if he was upset he might have exaggerated his hero-worship of me with the result that Lewis would have thought . . . Yes, I could see Lewis jumping to all the wrong conclusions, just as I could see Stacy blurting out a lot of passionate Irish nonsense about not wanting to let me down because he adored me so much. Lewis, blinkered as ever on the subject of homosexuality, would immediately think to himself: Stacy adores Nicholas; Nicholas is male; therefore Stacy is without doubt a homosexual. QED.

I sighed heavily, and suddenly realised that I was staring at the perfect uncooked steak-and-kidney pie. During my prolonged meditation on Stacy Alice had finished preparing her masterpiece and was turning aside to light the oven.

"Alice," I said, tucking James's tail closer to his back legs so that his body formed a perfect curve, "how do you think Stacy's getting on with Tara?"

"Oh, I think he quite likes her," said Alice, beginning to assemble potatoes for peeling, "but of course she could never live up to his sister Aisling."

I sensed that Alice had no doubt of Stacy's heterosexuality. But on the other hand Alice knew little about men and was hardly the world's expert on complex sexual problems.

"So you don't think the friendship will come to anything?"

"No, and that's such a shame because Tara thinks he's super! She's so nice—I'd love things to work out for her."

There was nothing bitchy about Alice. I sensed no trace of jealousy, yet I was sure no man had ever taken her out, not even a clumsy redhead who was sexually retarded. Stacy had wanted to ask her for a date and I had forbidden it on the grounds that when people live together in community it's best to avoid "particular friendships," but I'd felt guilty afterwards that I'd deprived her of some well-deserved happiness.

"I read once," I remarked vaguely, "that many women don't find redheads attractive."

"I believe Mills and Boon advise authors to make their heroes either blond or dark," agreed Alice, "although the occasional gorgeous redhead has been known to slip past the censors."

"Could Stacy be rated gorgeous?"

"No," said Alice firmly, assuaging my guilt that I'd deprived her of a boyfriend. "He's very nice-natured but he's not grown up enough to qualify as a Mills and Boon hero."

It occurred to me that despite her inexperience Alice's intuition enabled her to make some accurate observations. I made a mental note not to be so condescending in future about her lack of experience.

"Do you read Mills and Boon novels, Alice?"

"Not now, no. I did when I was younger but these days I read great big novels about amazing girls who start with nothing and end up with everything—or who start with everything and end up with nothing. Everyone spends lots of time jet-setting and shopping and having sex."

"I don't think I could take all the shopping."

"Francie's keen to take all the sex! She was very disapproving when she visited me the other day in the hell-hole and saw the book I was reading, but I noticed when I picked it up again later that it was open not at the end of the chapter but at one of the purple passages. She'd obviously been taking a peep when I was making the coffee."

I saw my chance and took it. "Have you heard from Francie this week, Alice?"

"I rang her yesterday to ask if I could do any shopping for her, but she only wanted Weight Watchers baked beans and she said they could wait. I offered to go over with some low-cal raspberry ripple ice cream, but she said no, she was too depressed to see anyone. Then she said: 'Don't worry, I'm not suicidal, I'd never give Harry the satisfaction of dying before he did!' She sounded kind of nutty."

"Hm." I paused to stroke the cat before asking idly: "What do you think her basic problem is?"

"She's waking up to the fact that her dreams can never come true," said Alice promptly. "She'd like to be twenty-nine again and have a wasp-waist and live in Monaco with a sugar-daddy husband and a blisteringly sexy Italian admirer, but instead she's forty-five and living in Islington and battling with her weight and there's not even the ghost of an admirer on the horizon."

"And not even a goldfish to play with in the bedroom," I said smiling at her.

Alice turned pink. "Don't tell me *you* read those sort of novels!"

"I read about them. So you think Francie's life's pretty drab at the moment?"

"I'm afraid I do, especially as her husband's away so much and her children are at boarding school for two-thirds of the year. Poor Francie!" said Alice sincerely, plopping a peeled potato in the saucepan.

I thought how enraged Francie would have been if she'd overheard this response. "*Poor* Alice!" she had said to me more than once in the past. "Such a nice girl, but *such* problems! It really is too sad . . ."

"You like Francie, don't you, Alice?"

"Yes, I'll never forget how kind she was to me after Aunt died. But now that I know her better . . . Well, it seems to me that Francie isn't quite the simple, friendly soul that everyone thinks she is, and to be honest I wasn't surprised yesterday when I phoned and found her in a nutty state. She was obviously heading round the bend when she called here on Monday evening."

I was transfixed. "Monday evening?"

"Oh, didn't Lewis tell you? It was late—I was watching the ITV news and they'd just got to the weather. I don't know what she said to Lewis and I didn't like to ask him about it afterwards, but at one point he buzzed me and asked me to come up to the kitchen—he said Francie wanted a woman to be present, but I could see at once she didn't and almost as soon as I walked in Lewis told me I could go. The whole scene was very peculiar—she was only wearing a nightdress under her coat and she had no shoes on, only slippers. The coat was unbuttoned so I could see the nightdress clearly—it was cut very low and her bosom was practically falling out because she was so agitated."

There was a pause while I put two and two together and made the most unpalatable four.

"Of course," said Alice, carefully examining a potato for blemishes, "Francie didn't know you were away from home that night. And I don't somehow think it was Lewis she wanted to see."

I was still staring at her, still visualising this chilling scene, when Lewis himself stormed into the kitchen and demanded to know where Stacy was.

12

> At this stage in grief, other symptoms, beside the lack of concentration that your friend has noticed, may include an inability to order [the] mind.
>
> GARETH TUCKWELL AND DAVID FLAGG
> *A Question of Healing*

I

Apparently Stacy should have arrived at the church some time ago to enable Lewis to return home and rest. Lewis hated being convalescent but knew he had to have regular rests to aid his recovery. Obliged to stay on duty for longer than he had anticipated he was both furious and exhausted.

Rosalind sometimes behaved as if she thought Lewis's job was a mere sinecure, invented by me in order to make him feel useful in his old age, but his work was vital to my ministry and how I managed before he arrived on my doorstep in 1983 I have no idea. He was the anchorman at the church, in charge of the services and the volunteers on duty there. He did do some counselling and spiritual direction at the Centre but his prime task was to keep the church ticking over briskly. In a healing ministry it's essential to have a prayer-group which meets regularly to support the work, and although I took a special interest in the members it was Lewis who organised and directed them. In short, his work, supporting and underpinning my own, enabled me to focus more steadily on the healing. Without him I would have been pulled in many directions, my energies dissipated, my concentration impaired, and so I had a strong interest in ensuring that he didn't wind up exhausted. I felt very annoyed with Stacy for not showing up on time.

"There should always be a priest on duty at the church when people start leaving their offices!" Lewis was shouting. "Ye gods, when I get my hands on that red-headed nitwit I'll scrag him! Where the deuce is he anyway? If he's bowled off to that video shop again I'll smash his television screen! That boy's terminally addicted to TV and pop music, but that's typical of the younger generation, isn't it? Forever walling themselves off from reality with filthy noises and filthy pictures—"

The phone rang, mercifully ending this tirade. Lewis reached sideways, grabbed the receiver before I could get to it and to my consternation snarled: "Rectory!" into the mouthpiece. This was hardly the way to greet a caller who might be in desperate straits, but a moment later my anxiety was relieved. Lewis's whole manner changed. He straightened his back. His eyes glowed. He beamed from ear to ear.

"Oh hullo, Venetia!" he said mellifluously. "No, no, I wasn't just about to hit someone! Wait a minute—I'll take this call in my room." Laying the receiver on the dresser he turned to us and announced unnecessarily: "It's Venetia. I'm taking the call in the bedsit." He did his best to appear nonchalant but spoilt the effect by dropping one of his crutches as he tried to leave the room at top speed.

The door finally banged. Alice and I looked at each other, but since all comment would have been superfluous Alice resumed her potato-peeling and I replaced the receiver.

Resuming my seat at the table I then spent a moment brooding on Lewis's fantasy that he was in love with Venetia. For some time I had lived in dread that he would mess up her recovery, and the more it seemed likely that she would be one of the Healing Centre's successes the more worried I became about their potentially disastrous relationship.

Venetia had made a considerable amount of progress in a relatively short time and was now preparing to start a new life in Cambridge. She would still need therapy there, but Robin was fixing that up for her with a distinguished friend of his. Meanwhile Lewis was supposed to have reconciled himself to the fact that she would soon be living sixty miles away and, for the time being, had no romantic plans of any description. It was true that I'd encouraged him to retain the hope that one day he might see her again—Lewis had needed a little hope at that stage—but I'd been working on the assumption that Venetia would disappear from his life for at least three months, an interval which would allow him to come to his senses and recognise that he had been infatuated. This unexpected phone call less than a week after their parting could therefore hardly be considered good news.

The fact was that Lewis had too many unresolved problems with women to make remarriage a viable option. After his parting from Venetia he had achieved a valuable insight into a corner of his mind which was normally hidden from him, but this didn't convince me he was in consequence destined to marry her and live happily ever after. It seemed to me clear enough that Venetia had been put across his path not to provide grand passion and/or matrimony, but to enlighten him. If he could now develop and build on that shaft of enlightenment he had received he might yet be able to beat his hang-ups, but meanwhile he was as muddled about women as ever and wallowing around in a dream which bore no relation to reality.

Lewis's dilemma was that he was attracted to sexual adventuresses but needed a very placid, conventional domestic existence in order to function properly. Volatile and eccentric, gifted but temperamental, he needed normality and predictability just as much as I did. The difference between us was that Lewis's mother had chosen to abandon him when he was in his mid-teens and my mother hadn't chosen to abandon me. In addition Lewis had been further damaged by the fact that his mother had wound up as a high-class tart, only making herself available to men who were prepared to lavish money on her. Lewis had sometimes behaved as if the only way he could guarantee himself female attention was to buy it. Secretly fearful of rejection, he found this fake-intimacy gained by the payment of money left him firmly in control and reduced the woman to a disposable facility. In this way he avoided emotional involvement, took his revenge unconsciously on the mother who had reneged on her emotional involvement with him and deluded himself that he didn't want a decent woman because he was only capable of being sexually satisfied by tarts.

Unhappy ending.

To be fair to Lewis he was fully aware that this was hardly an ideal situation, and he remained determined to keep struggling against his hang-ups, but like many people with psychological blocks he was crucially blind about the basic problem, and in his case the basic problem was very simple: he yearned for love and security yet deep down he felt so unworthy of them, thanks to his mother's rejection, that he was never able to recognise and accept them whenever they were on offer. For as long as I had known him, Lewis had never had any difficulty in attracting women, some of whom had had a great deal to offer, but always the relationships foundered because he felt inadequate. "She wouldn't love me if she knew me better," he had often said, and if a woman ever did try to know him better he made sure this prophecy was self-fulfilling by behaving badly, putting her love to the test to convince himself he was fundamentally unlovable. It was better, he obviously thought subconsciously, to take the initiative in ending a relationship than to put himself in a position where he could be rejected all over again.

Once, long ago when I was much younger, I'd made the mistake of spelling all this out to him, but he'd just said: "You're off your rocker. An inferiority complex with women? Me? That's the one problem I've never had—quite the contrary!"

As the poet wrote: "One may lead a horse to water, Twenty cannot make him drink."

I sighed deeply, and as Christina Rossetti's line echoed again in my mind, I wondered what Lewis was now saying to Venetia, who also had a poor self-image in matters of the heart. With no trouble at all I could imagine them testing each other out by jangling their hang-ups at every opportunity. The romance would be shredded in no time. So would Venetia. And Lewis would walk off, more battered and bruised than ever but still managing to say: "It was lucky she found out how impossible I am before it was too late."

"Nicholas," said Alice, mercifully interrupting this depressing vision, "while Lewis is busy with Venetia should I perhaps buzz Stacy to warn him he's in trouble?"

"Good thinking. But I'll do it." It was a relief to set aside my gloomy thoughts and move to the intercom, but there was no response when I buzzed the curate's flat. "That's odd," I said. "Maybe he's slipped out again."

"No, we'd have heard him, he always makes so much noise. Try your flat. Maybe Rosalind's taken him there for a cup of tea."

I was just about to follow her advice when Stacy at last responded to the intercom. He sounded subdued, almost groggy. I wondered if I'd woken him from a nap, but this seemed unlikely. Stacy always had a surfeit of energy.

"Are you all right?" I said sharply.

"Um."

"Good, but you appear to be suffering from amnesia. Get over to the church right away and make sure you offer Lewis a grovelling apology later." Leaving him gasping with dismay I finally tore myself away from Alice's company and returned to my study where I tried to summon the will to organise my retreat. I got as far as picking up the receiver of my private line to call the headquarters of the Fordite monks, but then apathy overcame me and I couldn't summon the energy to punch the numbers.

I was still slumped in my swivel-chair, still clutching the receiver, when Lewis, that battle-scarred old tom, sidled in on his crutches to announce that Venetia had returned to London after a reconnaissance trip to Cambridge and wanted to show him her Polaroid pictures of the flat which she was tempted to acquire. He had agreed to meet her for lunch on Saturday at the Dorchester Grill.

"But don't worry!" he added hastily. "I promise I shall behave *impeccably!*"

I assumed my most courteous expression but offered no comment.

"Booked your retreat yet?"

"I was just about to make the call."

"Then don't let me stop you. I assume you'll be leaving first thing tomorrow morning and returning on Sunday night?"

"If you're seeing Venetia on Saturday maybe I should stick around."

"No, no, no—quite unnecessary! I've got myself well in control now, and I'm just glad that I have this opportunity to part from her in a calm civilised way. It was such an upsetting mess when we parted at the Hilton."

"Uh-huh. Do you plan to rerun this final farewell often?"

"Oh, of course Venetia will eventually find out how impossible I am, but meanwhile . . . Hold it, I hear that red-headed nitwit thudding downstairs like a stray elephant—" He plunged out of the study to start venting his fury.

I allowed the diatribe to last twenty seconds. Then I followed him into the hall, sent a white-faced, silent Stacy on his way and reminded Lewis that he was supposed to be resting. On my own again I finally summoned the energy to call the Fordites, and having reserved a room in their guest-wing I realised with a sinking heart that I could no longer postpone my next meeting with Rosalind.

I trudged upstairs to the flat.

I I

Rosalind was having a bath. That was a bad sign, indicating she still felt polluted by my behaviour, but I was relieved to have the excuse to postpone the ordeal of facing her. I wandered around trying to decide what to do next and finally concluded it was time to check in again with Venetia, currently my prize client, the horse who had not only consented to approach the water but had been willing to slake her thirst.

"Hi," I said as she picked up the receiver at her house in Chelsea. "It's your Talisman." Venetia often called me that. Accepting the prediction I had made long ago that we were destined to weave in and out of each other's lives, she claimed that whenever I crossed her path something unusual happened, not necessarily pleasant. The current crossing of our paths, which had lasted since our accidental meeting that summer, had for the first time been truly beneficial, as if all the years I had spent praying for her had finally borne fruit. I'd always known that my task was to pray for her. Since I was several years her junior there'd been no question of romance when I was twenty years old and meeting her for the first time, and I'd known at once that I was merely to be a sign, a marker, a friend of the spirit, a representative of a reality which continued to exist even though she refused to acknowledge it. The call to serve her in this way had been a thankless task over the years as her life had gone from bad to worse, but I'd never given up and now it seemed the big pay-off was at hand.

My relief and joy, mingling with my terror that something might still go wrong, were so acute that I realised how much I'd come to love her. I also realised that the depth and quality of my feelings could explain why the healing was finally happening. Non-possessive, non-demanding and totally focused on her welfare, the love provided an unclogged channel for the creative and redeeming power of the Holy Spirit. All human beings have power to heal one another; it's part of the mystery of consciousness and personality. But my power to heal Venetia was being jacked up and magnified by the force which was the source of all power, all love and all creativity. In this particular case I'd finally got the alignment with God right—yet still I had to remember that I was utterly dependent on God's grace; I had to kill any desire to pat myself on the back, because if I fell into that particular trap, the alignment would be lost, the channel would be clogged and the Devil would slither in at the last moment to block the healing. God Almighty, let nothing block it now! I sweated again at the thought of me or Lewis or both of us making a balls-up, I through pride and he through lust fuelled by his hang-ups. "Keep Venetia safe," I said feverishly to God, "keep her safe, safe, safe from your all-too-human and pathetically fallible servants . . ." I suddenly realised Venetia was talking. With an effort I focused on the conversation.

"Nick, how lovely—*divine* to hear you!"

"You okay?"

"Darling, radiant!" Venetia nearly always talked like this. The fact that it was a camp, upper-class patois didn't mean she was insincere.

"Huh!" I said agreeably but infusing this useful syllable with a faint air of scepticism designed to encourage truthfulness.

"What's that grunt supposed to mean?"

"What do you think it means?"

"No, don't lob the question back at me, you beast!"

"What's so beastly about it?"

Venetia and I often had these sort of dialogues. Sometimes I thought we sounded like a certain type of married couple, the bickering kind, who masked a deep connectedness by giving vent to frequent bursts of irritability.

"I suppose you've been talking to Lewis!"

"Yep. How come he gets to see the Polaroid snaps and I don't?"

"You can see them later, sweetie-pie, but right now Lewis needs to see them more than you do."

"Huh!"

"Don't you want to ask what the hell I'm up to with him?"

"Nope. None of my business."

"What I can't bear about men," said Venetia acidly, "is their high-minded attitude to gossip. It's so inhuman—any woman would be panting to know all the details!"

"Well, since I'm not about to change sex—"

"Thank God, I can't bear mutilation. Listen, darling, it's okay about Lewis, it really is—he's being absolutely perfect and I adore him."

"Uh-huh."

"You swine, is that all you have to say?"

"I was just reflecting how vulnerable Lewis is beneath that buccaneering exterior."

"He and I are two of a kind," said Venetia, for one brief moment setting aside the patois and speaking straight from the heart. "We can be vulnerable together." Then as my heart sank at this revelation of a shared romantic illusion, the patois was resumed. "How's the Fair Rosalind?"

I quickly pulled myself together. "Having a bath."

"Dear Rosalind, always so clean. Well, my pet, much as I adore listening to your cryptic comments and sexy grunts, I'm going to have to love you and leave you now or I'll never get to the AA meeting on time. Keep praying, please."

"Take care, Venetia. Remember that you count, you matter, you're important. Remember that I'm with you every step of the way."

She told me she adored me and made various kissing noises. I barely heard the stifled sob before she hung up.

I remained motionless, praying. To Christ the Healer I said: "Give Venetia the strength to FIGHT ON!" I prayed this over and over again. Then I framed another short prayer asking for help in dealing with her relationship with Lewis. Obviously she was genuinely keen on him. That was bad news. When Lewis had been in hospital and I'd met Venetia for a pastoral chat at Claridge's, her favoured haunt, she'd been very casual, calling him "a dear old pet" as if he were some lovable pensioner whom she happened to find rather amusing. I hadn't accepted this line of hers, but I'd thought she was merely covering up the fact that she'd flirted with him out of habit and been firmly turned down. Now I realised she had been concealing deeper feelings.

I was sunk in gloom. Supposing the admirable plan to move to Cambridge came to nothing? Supposing the two of them went mad and married on an impulse? I prayed fervently for them to be delivered from such insanity, but in the silence that followed, the silence of God, I remembered Lewis talking not of Venetia but of the most important lesson that an arrogant psychic can ever learn. Twenty years fell away. I was back in 1968, a walking disaster who had finally found the mentor capable of training him, and Lewis was commanding: "Nicholas, say to yourself very calmly, very rationally: 'I CAN BE WRONG.' "

It was time to admit that I might be mistaken about the nature and potential of the relationship between Lewis and Venetia. Maybe they were destined for wedded bliss after all.

But I doubted it.

Thinking of wedded bliss reminded me of marital hell, and I was just wondering for the hundredth time what on earth I was going to say to Rosalind when I heard the bathroom door open and knew my ordeal was about to begin.

III

When Rosalind joined me in the living-room she was wearing a black skirt and jersey with a peacock-blue jacket. No jewellery. Hardly any make-up. She looked exhausted, but she still had enough energy to clasp her glass of white wine so hard that I feared the stem might snap.

I said: "Ah. There you are. Right. Oh, you're having a drink. Good. Excuse me while I just get one for myself."

Bolting to the kitchen I grabbed a Coke from the refrigerator and took a swig straight from the can. I'd broken out in a cold sweat. My heart was thumping at an unnatural speed. Somehow I got myself back into the living-room. I didn't sit beside her on the sofa in case she felt threatened. Instead I dumped myself in one of the armchairs.

"Busy day?" she enquired idly, making an enormous effort to be casual.

"Uh-huh." I did some more Coke-guzzling. "I went to see Clare. She recommended a cooling-off period for us both."

"Oh?"

"Yes, so tomorrow I'm off to the Fordites for a three-day retreat and you can go back to Butterfold. I mean, you can go back if you want, I'm not trying to dictate to you, but I expect you'd welcome the chance to get back and I just want you to know that's fine by me, I see now I was being very unreasonable, expecting you to leave Butterfold at the drop of a hat and come to live at the Rectory."

"Ah."

"Yes, so what I thought was we could stay apart, cooling off, until the boys come home for the holidays. Then we can put the problem on hold until term begins—we won't say anything to the boys, we'll just focus on giving them a good Christmas—and you needn't worry about me bothering you, I'll sleep in the dressing-room and you can lock the bedroom door every night, no problem, I accept now that the marriage has temporarily broken down."

This time Rosalind said nothing at all, not even an "oh" or an "ah." Had I gone wrong somewhere? I tried not to panic. "But it must all be entirely as you wish," I said rapidly. "Believe me, I'm not trying to impose a decision on you. We can talk about it all later, if you'd prefer, after the cooling-off period. In fact yes, I can see now that this would be best. Further discussion at a later date. When we're calmer. We can have a mediator—go to Relate—do whatever you want."

"Hm," said Rosalind.

My nerve finally failed me. I was unsure whether it failed because of her reluctance to respond positively or because the hardest part of my speech was still to come. Abandoning the Coke I marched to the kitchen, grabbed a tumbler and filled it to the brim with the white stuff. There's no doubt alcohol does have a calming effect in a time of fear. This was definitely a time of fear. Taking a deep breath I soundlessly recited Jesus' words "Be not afraid" three times, swigged half the wine and returned to the living-room.

"There's something else," I said. "Clare made me face up to exactly what I did last night. I see now that you didn't want to have sex but I forced you to have it, I raped you, I messed around with your mind and abused you and behaved like a complete and utter shit. But now I want you to know how sorry I am—well, no words can really express the horror and shame I feel, I can hardly believe I did such a thing to the person I love best in all the world, and I don't expect you to forgive me straight away but I'll do anything to make the marriage come right, anything, I love you so much—"

I broke off. The speech was degenerating into a rant which might upset her. I swilled some more wine and tried to work out what to say next. "Well, I just wanted to tell you how sorry I am," I said. "I just wanted to make everything clear." I paused again, waiting, praying, longing for a response which would give me a flicker of hope, but all Rosalind said in the end was: "I see. Thank you." However, although she spoke with such formal politeness she didn't appear to be either angry or revolted. Or was the politeness masking unprecedented depths of anger and revulsion? I nearly bolted to the kitchen for more of the white stuff, but before I could lurch into action Rosalind said abruptly: "Look, I'm sorry but I can't face dinner with the ménage tonight after all—in fact I don't think I can face any kind of dinner. I had the most enormous lunch at Fortnum's today with Francie."

I was so startled that I was jolted not only out of the fear and shame generated by my confession but also out of the confusion and panic generated by the non-event of her reply. Blankly I repeated: "You had lunch with Francie?"

"Yes, she was a bit depressed to start with but I cheered her up and by the end of the meal she was quite her old self again."

A horrific thought overwhelmed me. "You didn't tell her about last night!"

"No, of course not." Rosalind stood up, retrieved the bottle from the fridge and refilled both our glasses.

By this time I was beating my brains out trying to square this astonishing information with the bizarre scene witnessed by Alice on Monday night. Cautiously I asked: "Why did you have lunch with Francie?"

"I often have lunch with her."

"But I thought you hardly saw her any more!"

"Well . . . yes, for a time we drifted apart. But then we drifted back together again."

"You never mentioned that!"

"No, but there were a lot of things I never mentioned to you. You weren't around enough."

A silence ensued. When I could no longer stand the pain of listening to it I poured some more wine down my throat and said: "What do you think's going on with Francie at the moment?"

"Not a lot. She's pretty damn fed up with Harry, but she'll never leave him. Too much of a masochist."

"Does he beat her up?"

"That's odd—Lewis asked me that yesterday. No, the cruelty's all verbal . . . Why are you both toying with the idea that Harry's a wife-beater?"

"We've no concrete evidence. But of course we're going to wonder what's at the root of her depression, particularly when she's too low to face coming to work."

"Oh, I think it's just mid-life blues."

"Yet she perked up, you said, towards the end of the lunch?"

"Yes, by the end she was radiant, bursting with vitality! All she needed was a chat with her best friend."

"You mean it was she who suggested the lunch?"

"No, I suggested it. I felt I needed a break from all the horrors."

"And she accepted without hesitation? She wasn't antagonistic towards you in any way?"

"No, of course not! Why on earth should she have been?"

"Depressed people do behave erratically—"

"Well, she wasn't *that* erratic! I admit she was a bit slow off the mark when I issued the invitation, but that was just the depression making her apathetic."

"Yes, of course. How interesting. Lewis will be glad to hear she's so much better. In fact maybe I'll just go down and pass on the good news." Knocking back the rest of my wine I headed for the door.

"Oh Nicky, do apologise to Alice for me, please—I really am sorry to bugger up the dinner numbers yet again—"

I muttered a word of reassurance and hurtled downstairs to the bedsit.

IV

Lewis was still resting. He had changed into a heavy green sweater and a pair of grey flannels and was listening to a Bach cantata as he lay on his bed. He looked cross when I interrupted him.

"This is the best bit, Nicholas. Sit down and keep quiet for two minutes."

I did as I was told. I was by no means indifferent to music, but given the choice I preferred silence, and on this occasion I tuned out the cantata in order to worry about Lewis. I was sure he was doing too much whenever my back was turned. Worse still I suspected he wasn't obeying his physiotherapist and doing his post-operative exercises regularly. Lewis's drive to treat his recent operation as a mere minor inconvenience was all part of his fury that he was now nearer seventy than sixty.

The cantata concluded. Lewis sighed, opened his eyes and said: "Yes?"

I said: "Francie's not beaten up. She's fed up. As a result, her acceptable admiration of me has spiralled into an unacceptable erotomania and she's now showing signs of manic depression."

Lewis's eyes widened. Sharply he said: "Not *manic* depression, Nicholas. She's been a bit down because she's realised that recently she made a fool of herself, but there's been no plunge into a serious depression and certainly no corresponding manic euphoria—indeed I'd dispute that she's clinically depressed."

"And the erotomania?"

"Nicholas, this is a fishing expedition—you're just flinging out these extravagant diagnoses in an attempt to find out what's going on!"

"You dispute the erotomania?"

"Look, this is just a menopausal woman with an unhappy marriage! Obviously she needs help for her little compensating trips to fantasy-land, but I'm aiming to get her into therapy with Robin as soon as she returns to work."

"I think there's something more sinister going on."

"Nicholas—"

"Okay, try and wrap your mind round this one: Francie began her lunch-date today in a state of depression but ended up—quote—radiant and bursting with vitality. And you know who my source is? Her companion at Fortnum's, Rosalind!"

Lewis eased his legs painfully off the bed and sat bolt upright on the edge. "That's not possible."

"I thought that would grab you. So what have we got? According to Alice—"

"Alice! Triple-hell! I suppose she—"

"According to Alice, Francie arrived here on Monday night looking like a half-dressed hooker. Deduction: the erotomania's taken over—or, as our Charismatic friends would put it so robustly, the spirit of lust. You then somehow managed to defuse her—you put the spirit on ice, as it were, so that it can be dealt with properly later. In fact you handle her so skilfully that you keep the lines of communication open and pave the way for her to be coaxed into therapy. Great. Well done. But maybe, if she's rocketing around between euphoria and gloom, she's far more ill than you think."

"I doubt it. In typical cases of manic depression the move from one extreme form of behaviour to another is more gradual and each acute phase lasts longer."

"Maybe she's atypical. And even if she's not a manic depressive she's obviously unstable, so can we now, please, without breaching the confidentiality you owe her, have a discussion about this very dangerous situation?"

Lewis recovered his poise. "No."

"Why not? I'm not asking you to reveal any details of the conversation you had with her! I just want to discuss the possible diagnoses of her mental disturbance!"

"Nicholas, you're merely creating a huge diversion for yourself in order to take your mind off the problem with Rosalind. Stop playing this game at once and start focusing on your coming retreat!"

"But supposing—"

"I really can't see why you're getting in such a state just because Francie moved from depression to euphoria during what was no doubt a delicious lunch at Fortnum's! If she was starving to start with, a perfectly cooked meal alone would account for the euphoria at the end!"

"Yes, but—"

"All right, I concede it's bizarre that Francie should be lunching with your wife at the present time, but Francie obviously felt she had no choice but to show up. She's not so nuts that she wants to declare her passion to all and sundry by offering Rosalind a hemlock cocktail!"

"Even so—"

"Listen, here's the rational, sober explanation of the euphoria: Francie arrives at Fortnum's sunk in gloom; however, as soon as she hears that Rosalind has marital problems—"

"But Rosalind says she kept quiet about all that!"

"Oh, come on, Nicholas, you know what women are like when they get together! I'm not suggesting Rosalind told Francie all about the hypnosis—of course she'd never betray you by repeating such a story to anyone except a doctor or a priest—but if she didn't say a single word about how troubled your marriage is at present, I'll eat my cassock. So what's the result? Francie instantly jumps to the conclusion that the marriage is on the rocks—"

"—and starts to get euphoric," I said, beginning to accept the scenario. "In her head she hears Tammy Wynette singing 'D-I-V-O-R-C-E'—"

"Tammy who?"

"Never mind. The point you're making is that Francie's euphoric not because she's experiencing a manic-depressive mood-swing and acting irrationally but because she thinks I'll soon be completely free to respond to her grand passion."

"Exactly. And I'd just like to stress that although Francie's unbalanced at present she's only unbalanced in the area of her life which relates to you. This may look like erotomania, but true erotomaniacs are usually far more abnormal."

"So there's no psychosis here."

"There's no psychosis and there's certainly no possession. Francie's basically sane but suffering from a neurotic obsession which, God willing, Robin can treat and defuse before she has a breakdown and becomes more seriously ill."

I felt better. Lewis had more practical experience of mental illness than many doctors because he had worked in a mental hospital for ten years. He was certainly the first to admit he had received no medical training, but in this area of medicine, where diagnosis is often far from simple and understanding can be hazy, hands-on experience of working with the mentally ill counts for a great deal. I was tempted to let go of the problem, but some indefinable uneasiness made me continue to hesitate. "I'm getting a psychic twinge," I said at last. "I'm glad you're confident that you know what's going on here. But are you sure you're not overconfident?"

Lewis didn't make some flip remark to dismiss the subject. Nor did he get irritated by my irrational anxiety. He simply said in his calmest, most reasonable voice: "I'm sorry if I'm giving an impression of overconfidence. All I'm really suggesting is that you should leave the problem to me at the present time when you're not capable of dealing with it yourself. I respect the fact that you're having a psychic twinge which is driving you to stay involved in the case, but don't you think you might be experiencing anxiety because you're projecting your own crisis—your own problems which require an urgent solution—onto Francie? Nicholas, you're overstrained at the moment. You're all over the place dabbling in other people's problems because your concentration's in tatters and you lack the power to focus on yourself, so just try and let go now of the matters that don't directly concern you; try to channel all your energy into withdrawing, resting, praying and renewing your spiritual strength."

I promised I would.

Then I trailed back to the kitchen to tell Alice that Rosalind wouldn't be coming down to dinner.

V

We dined. Stacy was so pale and tense that I asked him if he felt unwell but he insisted he was fine. I wondered if he felt uncomfortable in Lewis's presence after the tongue-lashing episode earlier. Lewis had no hesitation about reprimanding subordinates fiercely when they slipped up. It was a policy Great-Uncle Cuthbert had followed vigorously in his days as Abbot-General of the Fordite monks, but Victorian authoritarianism can be of questionable value in the late twentieth century, and on this occasion it seemed that even Lewis himself was wondering if he had been too severe. He said kindly enough to Stacy: "I hope you're not still upset about forgetting to turn up at the church. We all make mistakes and that one's been forgiven now."

But Stacy could only mumble something incoherent and shovel food into his mouth. He then proceeded to eat so fast that Lewis lost his temper again and growled as Stacy failed to muffle a belch: "Disgusting! And now, I suppose, you're all set to vomit like a yob!"

Stacy fled.

As the kitchen door banged shut Alice said astonished: "What on earth's the matter with him?"

"I neither know nor care," said Lewis acidly. "My patience is exhausted." But he added very benignly to her: "My dear, could you please give me another slice of that celestial pie?"

Delighted with this compliment Alice obediently doled out a second helping and turned to me. "Nicholas? More?"

I woke up. "No thanks." I was busy worrying about Stacy. Something was obviously amiss and I ought to talk to him without delay. But since I was currently so debilitated—since *Lewis thought* I was so debilitated—and since even I had to admit that I was currently not at my best . . . Muddled thoughts about my spiritual fitness scooted around my brain and whipped my anxiety to new heights. I was just opening my mouth to speculate further about Stacy's behaviour when Lewis exclaimed: "What the deuce is he up to now?" and I heard Stacy clattering rapidly downstairs again. I guessed that having collected his coat from the curate's flat he was on his way out. A moment later, as the front door slammed, my suspicions were confirmed.

"Perhaps he's just realised he's madly in love with Tara," said Alice, trying to strike a lighter note, "and is rushing off to the Isle of Dogs to propose."

"It's more likely that he's rushing off to the vicarage of St. Eadred's Fleetside," snapped Lewis, "to have a drink with Gilbert Tucker."

Glancing up startled I was just in time to see him look annoyed with himself before he wiped the expression from his face. I knew then the remark had been an indiscretion, committed when he was too irritable to censor himself efficiently.

"Gilbert Tucker?" Alice was saying. "He's the nice, good-looking clergyman, isn't he, who helped Nicholas organise the AIDS seminar."

"That's the one," said Lewis, and in an effort to smooth over the implications of his earlier remark he declared benignly: "A very charming fellow. Not quite my kind of priest but I concede he does sound work at St. Eadred's."

"I didn't know Stacy was a friend of his," said Alice.

"Neither did I," I said, and added, looking straight at Lewis: "When did you see Stacy in the company of Gil Tucker?"

"I expect it was last Monday evening, wasn't it, Lewis?" said Alice obligingly. "I thought you were dining at the Athenaeum and Stacy was going to be out with Tara, but you both changed your minds without telling each other and went to that lecture given by the Benedictine monk." She turned to me. "When Lewis arrived home afterwards he said to me: 'No, don't bother to get me a meal—after hobnobbing with Gilbert Tucker I just need a stiff drink.' But later when I checked the fridge I found he'd polished off the mushroom quiche and a whole pot of coleslaw."

"Whisky's a great reviver," said Lewis blandly, gaze fixed on his plate, and went on devouring his second helping of steak-and-kidney pie.

"Where was the lecture?" I said, taking care to keep my voice casual.

"Sion College."

"And Gil was there?"

"With his chums, yes."

"And Stacy?"

Lewis made the pragmatic decision that any further attempt to conceal this fact would be futile. "He was sitting next to Tucker and having a whale of a time."

"Good!" I said cheerfully. "I'm always telling him he should socialise more with the London clergy! I'm delighted that he finally took me at my word."

Lewis drank deeply from his glass of claret and made no reply.

But by this time I didn't need one because I'd worked out what had happened at Sion College on Monday night. Stacy knew I was keen on Benedictine spirituality, but he'd probably decided to attend the lecture not just to impress me but to follow my advice about socialising. A fair number of priests always attended the Sion College lectures. I could picture Stacy arriving on his own, shy, a little hesitant; I could also picture Gil, who had become better acquainted with Stacy as the result of the AIDS seminar, catching sight of him and waving, just to be friendly. And finally I could all too easily picture Stacy relaxing at the sight of a familiar face and plonking himself down without a gay thought in his head among Gil and his friends.

Well, why shouldn't he sit among the gays if he felt like it?

Weren't we all followers of Jesus Christ, and shouldn't we all be concentrating on what united us rather than what divided us? Gil was kind, generous, compassionate. In my opinion he had a well-integrated personality. It was true that in his support for the gay community he sometimes displayed a fanatical streak, but most people are fanatical about something or other—football, the Green Party, the Royal Family, the ministry of healing, flowers, the entire work of J. S. Bach—and a fanatical streak isn't necessarily incompatible with being a good Christian. I was quite certain Gil would have had no sinister purpose in befriending Stacy that night. But Lewis, of course, would have seen them sitting side by side and instantly imagined them conspiring to hit every gay bar in town.

After dinner I retired with him to the bedsit and said: "Lewis, I know this is hard for you, but do try and see Gil Tucker as a real person instead of a stereotype labelled GAY ACTIVIST. I assume your confidential conversation with Stacy on Monday night stemmed directly from the fact that you caught him sitting with the gays, but all I can say is that if you seriously think Gil's now going to start preaching to Stacy about the wonders of gay sex—"

"Activists always proselytise. They can't help themselves."

"Look, is it really helpful to make these sweeping generalisations? If you could only discard those blinkers of yours and see Gil Tucker in more than one dimension—"

"It's you who's in blinkers, Nicholas! The truth is liberals like you can never bear to see anyone in the round—it destroys too many of your cosy, soft-hearted ideas about human nature!"

"I work at the cutting edge of reality. I don't deal in fey ideas about the human condition. Nor do I consider myself a liberal in the pejorative sense you've just defined—"

"I know you don't. That's the problem."

"There's no problem! Like you I'm dedicated to pursuing the truth. Like you I believe that all truth is from God and that we must therefore pursue it to the best of our ability—and that's exactly why I don't believe in making sweeping generalisations about any group of people, particularly a group as diverse as homosexuals! Sweeping generalisations distort the truth!"

"But the truth's still there beneath the distortion, isn't it? For example, the British are a very diverse race. But it's perfectly possible, as foreigners never tire of showing us, to make some generalisations about the British which are both sweeping *and* accurate. They may not be very kind but they hit the mark because they contain a core of truth. I'm sorry, I know you think I'm just a tiresome reactionary, but—"

"Okay," I said, "let's stop right there. This isn't a profitable conversation. We've wandered off course. Now if we can get back to the subject of Stacy—"

"No, Nicholas. You're creating another huge diversion for yourself because your own problems are so painful that you can't bear to concentrate on them. Let me repeat what I said earlier after our discussion of Francie: withdraw, rest, pray, recover your spiritual strength."

I gave up and wandered away.

VI

I couldn't face going upstairs to the flat. I couldn't face the possibility of finding that Rosalind had retired early to bed in Benedict's room and again locked the door to protect herself from me. I felt now that she hadn't believed I had been sincere in apologising to her, and that this was why she had made such an unsatisfactory response. Or could she have accepted my sincerity but for some reason found the apology meaningless? I replayed the scene again in my memory but found myself unable to imagine what the reason could have been.

By this time I was back in my study. Slumped in the chair at my desk I forced myself to continue focusing on my problems; perhaps I was driven by some obstinate desire to confound Lewis, who had said I was too debilitated to concentrate on them. I tried to recall the questions Clare had posed, and the next moment I heard her say: "What is the significance of Bear?"

Rosalind had talked of Bear in the scene prior to the hypnosis. "You were peculiar about him . . ." I could clearly remember her saying that, but what had she meant? I hadn't been peculiar about Bear at all. A lot of small children are seriously attached to their teddy-bears. My devotion to Bear had been normal. Besides, he'd been the most beautiful bear, golden-fleeced and supple-jointed, his glass eyes very knowing, his black-thread mouth turned down in a subtle expression of melancholy wisdom. How I'd loved him! Even when I'd outgrown my toys I'd never been able to face giving him away. He still lived in comfort in the attic at Butterfold Farm, dressed in his best pullover knitted long ago by Nanny, and kept safe in my old school tuck-box from the ravages of moths.

"You want to shut me up in a box like Bear!" Rosalind had screamed. I was even sure she had made not one but two references to being shut up in a box. What was going on? Without doubt she'd been furious at the time and probably not thinking too clearly, but why had she linked herself with Bear like that? It was true that Bear was shut up in a box. But a lot of people kept stuff from the past shut up in boxes. It wasn't unusual. Families hoarded the most extraordinary things in attics. That wasn't unusual either. So why was Rosalind implying Bear was a symbol of kinkiness and why was Clare endowing him with a weird significance?

It occurred to me that in my distraught state I might have failed to explain to Clare that the mention of Bear in those circumstances wasn't so weird as it might seem. Of course two adults in their mid-forties didn't normally waste time chatting about teddy-bears, but Rosalind and I had been discussing our shared past, and in the shared past of our kindergarten days Bear had loomed large. It was natural to talk about him in that context. Nothing weird about it at all.

I was just heaving a sigh of relief that I had reached such a satisfactory conclusion when a very disturbing thought struck me. I was almost sure that when Rosalind had first introduced Bear into the conversation we hadn't been talking about the past. But perhaps my memory was playing tricks. I tried to rerun the scene more accurately but the harder I tried the hazier my memory became. Could my subconscious mind be at work, trying to blot out this fact which destroyed my comfortable theory that the mention of Bear had been wholly natural? I decided I was being melodramatic. The most likely explanation was that my middle-aged memory wasn't as sharp as it should have been, and the subject of Bear had arisen, just as reason and logic suggested, from our nostalgic conversation about the past.

To distract myself I turned to my computer and allowed my fingers to do a short tap-dance on the keys. I typed BEAR, and then remembering how Clare had switched from talking about Bear to asking after James I typed CAT. I sat there, gazing at the screen and thinking of animals. The next moment my fingers were tapping out: "One may lead a HORSE to water, Twenty cannot make him drink."

Not quite automatic writing. But something was bubbling purposefully down there in the unconscious mind. I wiped the screen, abandoned the computer. Now there was just me and that other computer, my brain. I suddenly realised it was saying: Clare led you to the water. Now for God's sake do yourself a favour and drink.

Couldn't shut down this particular computer, that was the trouble. Very inconvenient.

Aloud I said briskly: "Right!" and allowed my memory to go into free-fall in the hope that it would trigger some crucial knowledge that I'd repressed. Had to show Lewis I wasn't quite such a basket-case as he thought. Had to show Clare I was the horse that was willing to drink. Had to show myself I wasn't some spaced-out weirdo fixated on a soft toy.

I thought of going to kindergarten for the first time and taking Bear with me for company. Nothing weird about that. I was four years old. Four-year-old kids did that kind of thing. I took Bear everywhere because he made me feel secure. On my first day at kindergarten the other children, nasty brutes, tried to grab him but I shouted: "No one plays with my bear except me!" and fought them off. I didn't like other children. I was the only surviving child of my parents' marriage and all the adults I knew treated me as if I was immensely special. My parents weren't around much but I was able to console myself for their absence by savouring the fact that I was unquestionably wonderful. Then came kindergarten which confirmed my worst fears, acquired previously at various children's parties to which I'd been dragged by Nanny: I wasn't so special after all. There were a lot of other people my size in the world. Worse still, they didn't think I was unquestionably wonderful. Innocence was over. Real life had begun.

It was easy now to look back with a smile at the bruising of my very inflated infant's ego, but at the time it had been far from funny. My whole sense of self had been undermined and I'd been convinced that some huge hostile force was trying to annihilate me by destroying my identity. As soon as I returned home from kindergarten after that first day I'd had a psychic attack, seen all the other children as hobgoblins, and screamed until I was blue in the face. Nanny thought I'd gone mad, but my father had soon sorted me out. He had made the hobgoblins vanish; he had rolled back The Dark; he had enabled me to feel safe again. But nevertheless I had refused to go back to school.

Then after a couple of days this little girl was produced for me to play with. I'd seen her around at the tea-parties and I knew she had been at kindergarten too although she'd kept in the background. She was very shy and seldom spoke. I liked that. She also understood about Bear and never touched him unless I gave her permission to do so. I liked that too. Eventually it was suggested to me that I might like to go back to school because Rosalind had no special friend there and was longing for someone to look after her. I agreed to go back, the Prince rescuing Goldilocks. I walked into the playground with Bear under my arm and as I let go of my father's hand I announced: "No one plays with my bear except me and Rosalind Maitland!" Rosalind went pink with pleasure, overwhelmed by the honour I'd done her. I took her hand and felt strong, safe, normal. I now had a friend, just as all the best children did. I was also protected from the hobgoblins because she made our classmates see me not as a hostile thug but as an ordinary kid capable of joining in the playground games. Rosalind was my passport to normality. After a while I became so normal that I even left Bear behind in the nursery when I went to school. But I didn't need Bear to make me feel safe and secure any more, did I? I had Rosalind.

I sat in my study, a man of almost forty-six, and stared for a long time down the tunnel of memory to the muddled, frightened, lonely little boy who stood facing me at the far end.

Finally I thought: so Bear made me feel safe and secure and Rosalind made me feel safe and secure. But what's the big deal about that? It's just one of the many reasons why Rosalind is the most important person in my life and I love her and come hell or high water I'm never going to let her go.

I shivered suddenly. Didn't know why. It was as if something had frightened me. Didn't know what. Maybe it was the idea of letting Rosalind go—except that I wasn't going to let her go, couldn't, we were too deeply connected. I knew we had little in common, but so long as I knew she was safe at Butterfold, tucked up in her box . . . But of course that was Bear, not Rosalind. Rosalind had a sociable life in her own form of community, the Surrey village, and she wasn't in a box at all. So why had she said . . . And why had Clare signalled . . .

Another part of my brain cut in, terminating this irrational nonsense by making me aware that I wanted to go to the lavatory. What a relief to think of a simple task like urination! Almost gasping with pleasure I tramped across the hall to Lewis's bathroom, formerly the cloakroom, and relieved myself. But afterwards I was afraid I might start thinking irrational nonsense again and trying to kid myself I was on some sort of trail to the truth, so I went to the kitchen in search of Alice.

No luck. She had cleared up and retired to the hell-hole. I wanted to go down and knock on her door, but that was impossible. Distances had to be kept. Boundaries had to be observed. Alice was very important to me. I didn't want to crash around like a wonder worker again in a new bout of destructive self-centredness.

Yet at that moment I longed for Alice. Nothing to do with bed. I just wanted to sit with her and feel enfolded by that most beautiful, most elegant psyche. Rosalind and Lewis would never have understood. Rosalind, reflecting the spirit of the age, thought all love between an unrelated man and woman was accompanied by torrid sexual urges, and Lewis, reflecting his hang-ups, thought that fornication was always just around the next corner, but Alice and I knew better. Alice quite understood she would never go to bed with me. She quite understood how devoted I was to Rosalind. She quite understood that distances had to be kept and boundaries had to be observed. *Alice understood.* That was the point. And because she entirely accepted that our relationship could only be conducted along certain lines, she wasn't living in a hell of jealousy and frustration. I would have known if she was secretly seething with misery. But she wasn't. She was radiant, glowing, serene. No wonder I sought her company! On the level where our minds met, her love, non-possessive and utterly unselfish, lit up the landscape where I had lived so long in isolation and banished the shadows I'd begun to fear.

Reluctantly withdrawing again to my study I found myself contrasting Alice's love with Francie's neurotic fixation. At the Centre we had a standard procedure for dealing with people who became obsessed with me. First Robin would begin to sit in with me on the counselling sessions. Then Val would join him and I'd drop out. But that procedure only applied if the fixated woman—or man—was a client. What made Francie horrifically different from the usual case was that she was a member of staff.

We had never before had a member of staff who had gone over the top in this particular way, and neither Lewis nor I had needed to spell out to each other just what a killer-threat this was. Unlike our pathetically fixated clients, her mental and emotional record was good. Her stability was judged to be considerable. Her credibility rating stood high. So if we now failed to defuse this illness of hers—if either Lewis or Robin or Val or I made a false move—she could blow her stack with lethal results. Supposing she announced to the world that I was rejecting her after a passionate love-affair? Then I'd really be in trouble. I'd fall victim to the no-smoke-without-a-fire syndrome where people believe any fable while kidding themselves that the worst is always true. Riding on the back of her mental illness, the demons of doubt, suspicion and fear would infiltrate St. Benet's in no time and destroy my ministry.

This was such an unpleasant thought that I stopped brooding on Francie and spent a moment praying to God for protection. Then just as I was wondering if I could finally face going upstairs to the flat I received yet another diversion.

Stacy returned from his expedition.

Without stopping to think I leapt up from my chair and hurried into the hall.

VII

As soon as he saw me Stacy looked as if he wanted to run all the way to Liverpool.

"Come in here for a moment, would you?" I said abruptly, giving him no choice, and led the way back into my study. As I spoke I wondered if Lewis would hear us, but when there was no interruption I assumed with relief that he was asleep.

Stacy dragged himself after me, and once the study door was closed he shrank back against the panels as if he longed to disappear into the woodwork.

Speaking briskly but kindly I said: "Stacy, I can't pretend I haven't noticed that you're behaving as if you've received a one-way ticket to hell. So let's tear up the ticket and take a look at this problem. What's going on?" This was certainly a direct approach but he was in such a state that a more oblique line would only have confused him. By this time I was convinced he had acquired a problem far more overwhelming than a failure to sustain a friendship with Tara Hopkirk or a dread of remaining in Lewis's bad books. Rigid with tension he stared fearfully at the carpet.

When he proved unable to reply I said gently: "I'm sorry you feel you can't confide in me. That must be my fault, since I'm responsible for keeping the lines of communication open between us."

He shook his head, apparently disputing that the fault was mine, but still he offered no information. I was baffled. He had always talked to me willingly enough before, even when the difficult matter of his sexual past had been under discussion. The obvious explanation for his tongue-tied state was that he felt he had let me down so badly that I would find it hard to forgive him, but what could he have done which was so unforgivable? Inevitably my thoughts returned to the subject of homosexuality. A homosexual incident wouldn't be unforgivable, but Stacy might think that it was. Taking a deep breath I made a new effort to reach him.

"Well, if you don't wish to talk to me," I said evenly, "I must respect your decision, but you should see your spiritual director at once to tell him what's wrong."

"I can't!" He was panicking. "But it's okay, I've just been and talked to another priest—it's okay, it's okay—"

"Which priest?"

"Gil Tucker."

I was deeply confused. On the one hand I was glad Stacy had picked a priest I respected. On the other hand I was dismayed that Stacy apparently had a non-relationship with his spiritual director and upset that my curate could no longer confide in me. What was going on? The obvious answer was that Lewis had been right all along, I'd been just a wet, woolly liberal blinding himself with trendy talk of sexual spectrums and Stacy had turned to the gays for the strength to come out of the closet. But was the obvious answer the correct one? Injured pride made me long to answer the question in the negative, but I could think of no other explanation which made sense. Then it belatedly occurred to me that if Gil had been counselling Stacy he had hardly been a success. Here Stacy was, still tormented and still behaving as if he were on the brink of breakdown.

Aware of the mystery becoming more baffling than ever I said carefully: "I'm glad you felt you could talk to Gil. Perhaps we should ask him to mediate between us."

But Stacy only shook his head violently and began to cry.

"Stacy," I said, concentrating on speaking as simply as possible in order to get the vital message across, "if you can no longer talk to me our relationship has broken down. If our relationship has broken down, this is my fault, as I should have prevented such a thing happening, and I must act to put things right. Putting things right involves—"

"None of this is your fault!" shouted Stacy in despair. "None of it!

You're the best priest in the world and I'm the bloody worst!" And before I could reply he had rushed from my study, slammed the door and bolted off again down the hall to the backstairs.

I was just asking my computer to produce Gil's phone number when Lewis, tousled and furious, stormed into my study to demand that Stacy be sacked for crashing around late at night like a drunken hippopotamus.

I shut him up with the news that Stacy had become an emergency case.

13

Grieving is hard work, and this needs recognising by others. All kinds of physical, mental and spiritual symptoms can occur . . . and we may be unable to cope with the smallest of everyday demands.

GARETH TUCKWELL AND DAVID FLAGG
A Question of Healing

I

"*I can't think* why you're so baffled," said Lewis when he heard what had happened. "The explanation's obvious: the boy's fallen in with a bad lot, gone on a cottaging spree and lived to regret it. Of course he can't bear that you, his hero, should ever know the depths to which he's sunk, so he's just made his confession to that heterosexual-bashing bigot Tucker who would—of course!—have given him absolution on demand. Stacy knew he had to confess and be absolved before he could take the Sacrament tomorrow morning with a clear conscience, so naturally he chose to confess to a priest who thinks cottaging's no more of a sin than a visit to the cinema. However, this abysmal travesty of a confession did nothing to allay Stacy's guilt. That was why, when you accosted him just now, he went straight to pieces. Where's the mystery?"

"I know that's the obvious explanation, Lewis. The only trouble is I can't believe it."

Lewis kept calm. "You mean you can't believe Stacy's capable of such activity?"

"I suppose I can just about believe he's capable of having another homosexual affair, although I think he would be very ill-at-ease in such a relationship and I'm sure it would soon fail. What I can't believe is that Stacy would ever go prowling around public lavatories in pursuit of sex."

"Why does that seem so implausible? People who are messed up about sex often indulge in seamy promiscuity. Stacy's messed up. Therefore Stacy could be capable of seamy promiscuity."

"QED."

"What?"

"Nothing. The point is—"

"Wait a minute, what's Tucker's name and phone number doing on that screen?"

"Well, I know it's late but—"

"What's the point of talking to him? He's hardly going to reveal the secrets of the confessional!"

"I realise that, but I could alert him to the fact that I know there's a crisis going on, and then—"

"Nicholas, leave that man Tucker alone. He's poison! He's just muscled in on your curate, he's behind all this battering you're getting from the Gay Christians to sack me, and in my opinion he's being used by the Devil to undermine your ministry at St. Benet's!"

"Uh-huh. Look, why don't you go back to bed now and we'll postpone this discussion until the morning."

"Oh no, we won't! Tomorrow morning you switch off and go on your retreat, and if I find you still lurking around here when I come back from mass, I'll—"

"Okay, I get the message. Relax. Tomorrow I'll switch off."

But tomorrow was another day. I waited until I heard the door of the bedsit close. Then I picked up the receiver and dialed Gil Tucker.

II

"*Gil,* it's Nick Darrow. Were you asleep?"

"No, I've just opened a bottle of claret. I always prefer Médoc to a sleeping pill."

"You're not the only one who feels sleep could be hard to get tonight. Look, Stacy's told me he visited you just now. Obviously there's a king-size problem, but when I pointed out that my relationship with him had clearly broken down and suggested you should act as a mediator, he behaved as if no mediator could be of any use. What do I do next to restore his confidence in me? Since you know what's going on, I'd really welcome your advice."

"Of course," said Gil without hesitation, yet in his voice I heard a note of . . . but I couldn't define the emotion. Embarrassment? Anxiety? Dread? From the speed of his response I picked up the message that he wanted to be helpful yet was at a loss to know how to proceed.

"Of course I don't expect you to breach his confidence," I said swiftly, "but if there's any help you can give me in finding a way out of this impasse—"

"Nick, all I can advise you to do is let the matter rest for two weeks."

I could make no sense of this at all. "Two weeks," I repeated blankly.

"Yes, then I hope the current situation will be clarified and I'll be in a position to give you the proper support."

"Support?" I had asked for advice. This could certainly be classified as asking for help, but "support" implied a degree of assistance which I hadn't sought. "If only I had some idea," I exclaimed in despair, "what I've done wrong! Okay, maybe I misread the sexuality issue—maybe Stacy really would be better off as a gay—"

"No, don't wear out your shoes walking down that particular street, Nick. Wasted journey."

I sat bolt upright on the edge of my chair. "You mean—"

"I mean you can tell that old grizzly-bear you keep at your Rectory that no, I haven't taken Stacy on a cruising expedition, and no, I don't go around trying to convert muddled young curates to the joys of gay sex, and no, I'm not some addled relic of the 1960s who believes in free love among the flowers in Nepal. I suppose Lewis has been saying—"

"Never mind Lewis," I said curtly, but I was conscious of a massive relief. I managed to add: "Thanks, Gil. But are you really sure Stacy can be left alone for two weeks? On his present showing I'm reluctant even to leave him for three days. I'm supposed to be going on retreat from tomorrow morning until Sunday evening, but—"

"Fine. Go on retreat. I'll keep checking on Stacy by phone and try to get him over here for a meal, but I think that by tomorrow he'll have recovered his equilibrium. He'll be at mass anyway, I can promise you that."

This was the signal that Stacy had made his confession, received absolution and was now in a position to make a fresh start in the knowledge that whatever errors he had made had been forgiven. But what worried me was that Stacy could have gone through the correct ritual without connecting with it in any meaningful way. His guilt-ridden, panic-stricken behaviour suggested that the forgiveness wasn't reflected in his conscience; I found myself again facing the conundrum in which the ritual of forgiveness had no psychological reality for the penitent.

Reluctantly I heard myself say: "He seemed on the verge of breakdown just now."

"Don't pay too much attention to that. There are reasons why he might not have wanted to face you, but by the time you return from the retreat I'm sure he'll have got his act together—or if he hasn't, I'll know about it and take care of him . . . Will Rosalind be at the Rectory over the weekend? I understand she's in town for a while."

"The plan's changed. She's going back to Butterfold tomorrow."

"Good, the fewer people Stacy has to face at the Rectory the better. Alice won't bother him, of course, and if you could give strict instructions to the old grizzly-bear that he's on no account to bite or scratch at the wrong moment—"

"Lay off Lewis, would you, Gil? Surely you of all people can recognise a good priest who has the guts to stand up for what he believes to be right!"

Gil laughed and apologised but added: "I just don't think he's the right person to be around Stacy at this particular time. However, leave Stacy to me and make sure you have a profitable retreat. I'll pray for you."

The conversation ended but after I'd replaced the receiver I went on staring at the phone. "I'll pray for you . . ." It was almost as if he'd known—but no, he couldn't possibly have known that I was currently worried about a great deal more than my curate. "I'll pray for you . . ." That was a natural enough promise for one priest to give to another, but Gil and I weren't in the habit of exchanging that particular assurance; our friendship, although genuine enough in its own professional way, just wasn't on that kind of spiritual footing. I did pray for him now and then. I prayed for all my colleagues who worked with me in the City, and I was sure he did the same. But I wouldn't have said to him very seriously: "I'll pray for you," unless I knew that he was in deep trouble.

Maybe Gil was psychic.

But no, the most likely explanation was that my guilt about Stacy was making me paranoid.

I decided to drag myself upstairs to bed.

III

At three o'clock in the morning I awoke and found myself sitting at the kitchen table downstairs. Horror slugged me. I hadn't walked in my sleep for years. Gripping the edge of the table as if to glue myself to a reality which had slithered beyond my control I broke out in a cold sweat of revulsion.

I was still taking deep breaths to steady myself when the kitchen door opened a crack and Alice peeped in. I'd switched on the light while unconscious. I'd also lit the gas for some reason. One ring of the stove was blazing strongly.

"Nicholas?"

"It's okay. Turn off the gas, would you, please?" I wondered whether I had wanted to burn something. Perhaps I had seen the fire as purifying, burning off the pain which was draining me of strength. Or perhaps it was just an irrational act. Who knew? I didn't. I went on sitting at the table as if this was a very normal thing to do at three in the morning, and eventually it occurred to me that I was cold. Then I realised I was only wearing pyjamas. I hadn't put on my dressing-gown. Maybe I'd lit the gas to provide some warmth.

"Would you like tea?" said Alice tentatively.

"Thanks." I went to the hall and fetched a coat from the cupboard. On my return I asked: "What are you doing up at this hour?"

"I awoke when I heard footsteps overhead, and wondered if it could be Stacy having a snack. He didn't stay to have pudding at dinner."

Naturally Alice never asked me what I was doing in the kitchen. She just got on with the task of tea-making. When the tea was poured she sat down opposite me at the table and I felt her psyche enfolding me with loving concern.

"I walked in my sleep," I said. "I do that sometimes when I'm under stress, but I wish I didn't."

The beautiful psyche enfolded me more closely and started stroking. My own psyche, beaten up and bedraggled, at once felt soothed and smoothed.

"It's no fun to sleep-walk," I said. "It's frightening to onlookers and it's upsetting to the sleep-walker when he wakes up. The whole thing's disgusting."

The beautiful psyche stroked and stroked without faltering. Alice wasn't disgusted. She wasn't frightened either. All she cared about was that I was under terrible strain and profoundly unhappy. Alice knew exactly how unhappy I was. I'd never confided in her but she knew. The beautiful psyche patted all my ragged edges and tucked them into place and poured love over the wounds to help them heal.

"I wish I didn't have to go on this retreat tomorrow," I said. "I've got no energy for it."

"Then don't go."

"No, I must. I've got to try and get a grip on this escalating disaster, and—" I broke off as I remembered she knew none of the details. Finally I said, switching subjects: "I wish I could remember what I was dreaming when I lit the gas. I think it had something to do with lighting a funeral pyre."

"Whose funeral was it?"

"That's what I'm trying to remember. I think I was back in my childhood, back in the village where I grew up . . . Yes, that was it. It was November the fifth, Guy Fawkes night. There was always a bonfire on the green and every year we went to watch the Guy go up in flames—"

"The funeral pyre of your dream?"

"Yes, but it was more complicated than that. I'm beginning to remember now . . . I was standing with my parents, and the chairman of the parish council invited me to light the torch which would ignite the bonfire. That sounds odd, doesn't it, but it wasn't so odd as you might think because my mother owned the manor house and we were the first family in the parish. I lit the torch—and then when I looked at the top of this enormous bonfire where the Guy should have been, I suddenly saw—" I stopped.

"The Guy wasn't there?"

I found I could hardly speak. "Oh my God." I was feeling very sick.

"Someone was there in the Guy's place?"

"Yes," said my voice. "Yes. Someone else. It was my bear," I said, "my old teddy-bear. I'd thought he was so happy and content in his box, but he wasn't. He'd escaped and climbed to the top of the bonfire to immolate himself. As soon as I realised what was happening I tried to run forward to save him but my father stopped me, he held me so that I couldn't move and he said: 'He'll be free now.' And then

I had to stand by and watch in the knowledge that *I myself* had destroyed that wonderful bear I'd loved so much—I'd made him want to immolate himself, and then I'd even lit the fire which was going to burn him alive—"

"And did you actually see him die?"

"No. The scene was so horrific that I woke up." I shuddered from head to toe. "I wanted him back in his box so that he'd be safe again," I said. "So that *I'd* be safe again. Yes, that was it. That was the real core of the nightmare. Deep down it wasn't Bear I was worrying about. It was me. How was I ever going to live without him? I wouldn't be normal any more. The hobgoblins would come again. I'd disintegrate." I suddenly realised I was on my feet and roaming around the room. I also realised I was talking like a maniac. What could Alice be thinking? Mustn't frighten her. Had to be normal. Otherwise she'd be repulsed and go away.

Abruptly I sat down next to her at the table. "It's okay," I said. "I was nuts in the dream but I'm not nuts now." I reached out to take her hand but managed to stop myself just in time. Had to preserve the boundaries. Had to keep Alice safe. "You don't think I'm nuts, do you, Alice?"

"No."

"I'm normal, aren't I?"

"No, but that's okay. You wouldn't be Nicholas if you were normal."

"You don't mind me being me?"

"Of course not."

I looked straight into her dark eyes, straight into her mind, straight into the bright light blazing at the heart of that beautiful psyche—and suddenly I was better, no longer split apart but stitched together, patched up, ready to face another day.

I wanted to take her hand and squeeze it tightly in gratitude, but I knew that would be a mistake. So I just said: "Thanks, Alice. Thanks for everything." Then I toiled back upstairs to my bedroom.

IV

I failed to sleep again that night. At five I shaved, dressed and went downstairs to my study, but I gave up trying to pray after five minutes. Time enough for that later. Instead I wrote Rosalind a note which read: "Darling, I'm making an early start to my retreat. Have a safe journey back to Butterfold and please give my love to the boys if they ring up. I'll phone you on Sunday evening when I return to the Rectory. I'm sorry, sorry, sorry about everything that's gone wrong, but we're going to get over this, I promise. I love you. N."

I reread the letter carefully. It seemed sensible enough, but when I tried to read it yet again the marks of my pen seemed as meaningless as a set of prehistoric hieroglyphics—or as meaningless as my nightmare, remembered in the clear bright light of day. Imagine getting in such a state about old Bear going up in flames! Of course the Freudians would say that no dream was without significance. Fair enough. Maybe I should concede that my nightmare hadn't been meaningless, but all it signified was that I hated the idea of my security being destroyed. Didn't we all. Pulling myself together I stuffed the note into an envelope and slid it under the door of Benedict's room.

In my bedroom I packed a bag and wondered what Rosalind would do once she was back at Butterfold Farm. Perhaps she would renew her affair with that young accountant. Perhaps she would approach someone new. Dimly it occurred to me that these sort of thoughts would now be continually running through my head whenever we were apart, and more dimly still it occurred to me that my life was changing irrevocably, whether I approved the changes or not. Yet this was such a terrifying thought, hinting at a situation beyond my power to fix, that I couldn't cope with it. I told myself there was nothing I couldn't fix, but I knew that was a lie. I was hearing the corrupt wonder worker talking, not the honest priest. If I hadn't tried to fix Rosalind on Wednesday night . . . If I'd asked humbly in Jesus' name for help and healing—by the grace of God and through the power of the Holy Spirit . . . If I'd tried to line myself up properly with God so that *his* will could be done instead of bucketing around in an orgy of manipulation to ensure that *my* will was done . . .

But it was no good saying "if," was it? What had happened had happened, and now that I was just a failed wonder worker who'd got his magic wand in a twist I had to take time out in order to recover my integrity.

But I didn't want to take time out, that was the problem. I just wanted to stay around, fixing things. I wanted to fix Stacy, fix Francie, fix everyone in sight.

Disgraceful. In fact, sick. I could see how spiritually sick I was and

I could see I had to go on retreat in order to get better. So why in God's name was I now shilly-shallying around like the worst kind of coward?

Because I was afraid of what the retreat might uncover. I was afraid of the thoughts I might think when I was on my own with no one to fix.

God, what a mess I was in! I tried to pray for help but nothing happened. I felt as if I were cut off in an isolated house on a stormy night while outside in the darkness my enemy, the one that wanted me dead, had just cut the telephone wires.

I looked in on Lewis, who was pulling on his dressing-gown. It was six o'clock by this time.

"Pray for me," I said.

"Of course. Are you on your way already?"

"If I don't go now I'll funk it."

"Is it really that bad?"

"Worse."

"I'm sorry. But you're doing the right thing."

"For God's sake handle Stacy with kid gloves."

"I'm already wearing them. Goodbye, Nicholas."

"And if Francie turns up for work—"

"I'll flaunt the kid gloves there too. Goodbye, Nicholas."

"And if anything should go wrong don't hesitate to—"

"Goodbye, Nicholas."

I finally tore myself away.

V

I left my car in the forecourt of the Rectory and took a cab to the cream-coloured mansion in Bayswater where I was to incarcerate myself. The monks of the Fordite Order of St. Benedict and St. Bernard were Anglicans, and the mansion had once been the town-house of their wealthy nineteenth-century founder. The Order had another house near Cambridge and yet another in the south-west where they had founded a public school. I had been a pupil there long ago. The Fordites were a familiar part of my private landscape and normally I found that a visit to any of their houses was a positive, useful experience, but unfortunately, as I was all too well aware, my current circumstances were far from normal.

I should have realised straight away that my retreat wasn't going to get off the ground, because I felt claustrophobic as soon as I crossed the threshold. Although I was occasionally leery of ramshackle lifts I didn't consider myself to be vulnerable to this particular malaise, but as the guest-master showed me into one of the small bedrooms set aside for visitors the hackles rose on the back of my neck. Once I was alone I reopened the closed door and heaved up the sash-window.

The seven o'clock service which combined Matins and Prime was followed by Holy Communion. With relief I escaped from my box—box? An evocative word!—and made my way to the chapel. I could hardly have been described as benefiting from the services, since my concentration was poor to non-existent, but it was stabilising to go through a religious routine. After the mass I attended breakfast in the guest-wing. There were several other priests there, all making a retreat, but luckily there was a tradition of silence at meal-times. I ate half a slice of toast and drank two cups of tea, but I made this meagre meal last a long time because I was so reluctant to return to my box.

When I did rise from the table, the guest-master said the Abbot-General was looking forward to seeing me, so my entombment was again postponed. The Abbot-General, who was plummy and chummy and not much older than I was, said something like what-ho, old chap, nice to see you again, what an unexpected pleasure, so sudden, nothing seriously wrong I hope, but on the other hand if there is . . . He paused to receive the necessary information.

I said: "Just general wear and tear."

The Abbot-General understood at once that I was a wreck so he murmured more platitudes to put me at ease and asked me how I wanted the retreat to be structured. Did I want to see my usual confessor or was there anyone else I wanted to reflect with, discuss prayer with, be silent with? Sometimes it was good to have a change. He himself would be more than ready to help, of course, but I was to have no hesitation in saying if that didn't suit. Perhaps I just wanted to be alone.

"I don't know what I want," I said.

The Abbot-General, who was a clever man beneath the plummy manner, was not in the least surprised or disconcerted by this remark but said in that case my first task was to find a corner of the house where I could be comfortable because if I wasn't comfortable I would be unable to think single-mindedly enough to discern what was needed. How did I feel about my room?

I said: "It seems very small."

The Abbot-General suggested that I should sit for a while in the chapel, which was large. I wouldn't be entirely alone, as someone was always there praying, but it would be peaceful, far more conducive to reflection than the visitors' common-room where I might be plagued by social chit-chat.

"Fine," I said.

I was again assured that if I wanted companionship and conversation later, this could be immediately provided. "And why don't you drop in and have another word with me after dinner?" said the Abbot-General, meaning lunch. In the Fordite tradition lunch was always dinner and dinner was always supper.

"Okay," I said. "Great. Thanks."

"Now let's take a moment for silent prayer," said the Abbot-General purposefully, so I closed my eyes and kept my mouth shut for a bit while he prayed. I did try to pray as well but I was too aware of his thoughts scratching away busily like a quill pen on parchment.

The prayer ended. Rising to his feet the Abbot-General shook my hand and said he was sorry I was under strain but very glad I had decided to make a retreat.

I hadn't the heart to tell him that all I wanted to do was run away.

VI

Fleeing to the chapel I slumped down on one of the pews in the south transept, the area which was set aside for visitors. I was breathing hard and feeling nauseated—but not by the Abbot-General, who had been kind and, in his own way, adroit. I suspected the nausea stemmed from my growing realisation that I was going to be unable to talk freely to any of the monks; it seemed that having discussed my situation with Lewis and Clare, I'd exhausted my ability to confess.

I tried to console myself with the thought that at this stage a confession wasn't compulsory. A summary of the main problem would without doubt be useful to any monk assigned to help me pray effectively, but I didn't have to say any more to him than I had said or implied to the Abbot-General. Since it was obvious that I was suffering from stress I might be asked questions about my work, but I wouldn't be asked directly about my marriage unless I signalled that I wanted to discuss it.

And I didn't want to discuss it. It was my central problem, yet it was beyond discussion. I couldn't talk about that marriage of mine at all, I saw that clearly now, just as I saw that even the thought of talking about it was making me nauseous. Hauling myself to my feet I blundered back to my box where I leaned over the basin in the corner and waited to vomit.

Nothing happened. Then just as I was straightening my back claustrophobia struck and I knew I had to get out of the room. A second later I knew I even had to get out of the house.

Grabbing my raincoat but leaving my unpacked bag, I sneaked outside and shot along between the rows of cream-coloured houses to Hyde Park beyond the Bayswater Road.

VII

As I entered the park I decided I was going to walk to Clare's house in Fulham, a journey of several miles. The decision to see Clare was made because I felt she was the only person who could defuse the extreme stress I was experiencing as I battled to keep unthinkable thoughts about my marriage from surfacing in my consciousness, and the decision to walk was made because I knew I needed to expend as much physical energy as possible in order to ward off an outbreak of energy on the psychic level. I wasn't the sort of psychic who normally experienced visions and locutions, but there are other abnormalities, all sinister, which can overtake a psychic under stress. I didn't want to foresee death or slide backwards in time or even do something so mundane as trigger poltergeist activity. Now that I was older I usually had no trouble keeping my psyche in order, but the sleep-walking episode and the uncharacteristic claustrophobia were both signs that emergency action was now essential.

I strode off rapidly into the park.

As I walked I wondered how close I was to a nervous breakdown, that nebulous condition which can cover such a wide variety of mental problems. Although I had experienced claustrophobia there had been no panic, no hyperventilation. It was also reassuring to observe, as I moved through the great open space of the park, that I felt no twinge of agoraphobia. Nor did I feel any twinge of the apathy which would signal the onset of depression. I was walking at a brisk five miles an hour. That was good. I was also walking in silence. That was even better; at this stage of the game the fact that I wasn't sobbing or shouting uncontrollably was a big plus. Best of all I wasn't heading for the nearest pub to wait for opening time or hunting for a prostitute or rushing to expose myself to the nearest middle-aged matron or racing to Soho in pursuit of pornography. All these facts meant I hadn't broken down. Yet. I was just reeling punch-drunk on the spiritual ropes and floundering all over the paranormal rubbish-heap, but neither of these two humiliating conditions was necessarily fatal.

I had a sudden longing to be sitting companionably with Lewis in his bedsit. Lewis knew all about the hell of reeling punch-drunk on the spiritual ropes and floundering over the paranormal rubbish-heap. It would have been such a comfort to sit with him. Or we could have sat in the kitchen while Alice cooked and the cat lay on my lap in a beautiful shape and purred beneath my fingertips . . .

Quashing the urge to walk east towards the Rectory, I paused to take note of my surroundings. I seemed to be in the middle of the park. The grass was frosty, the bare trees clean-limbed and stark against the clear sky. The air was crisper than usual for November, but at least there was no sign of snow or rain. I tried to work out the quickest route to Fulham, but having done so I decided it didn't appeal to me. I disliked the thought of the noise and smell which would assail me as soon as I left the park.

In the end I decided that since it was so pleasant in the park I would go on walking in green spaces for as long as I could and then take a cab to Clare when the grass ran out. I began to veer east towards Park Lane and within ten minutes I'd wound up on the brink of Hyde Park Corner. How did I cross this heaving hell without getting smashed to bits by the traffic? With relief I reflected that I had no desire to commit suicide.

Plunging into the nearest subway I padded along through the network of underground streets until I found the exit to the south side of Piccadilly. Seconds later I was stepping into my next large open space, Green Park.

I decided I liked this park very much. I sat there for a while and thought how pleasant it was to wander around London like a tourist. I was sure this was excellent therapy for me in my overstrained state. All I had to do now was avoid getting mugged. I looked around warily but found myself on my own, yards from anyone else; the nearest person was slumped on a distant bench. I drifted on downhill to Buckingham Palace.

Once I hit the top of the Mall I crossed into my third big open space, St. James's Park, which was the park I liked best. I prowled along by the lake to the bridge and spent a long time gazing across the water at the towers and minarets beyond Horse Guards. There was still no sign of a would-be mugger, but various out-of-season tourists were wandering around as if torn between Buckingham Palace on the one hand and the Palace of Westminster on the other.

Soon I was asked to take a photograph of two smiling Japanese visitors. This so exhausted me that I had to sit down to recover, but just as I was preparing for the next phase of my walk an American couple seated themselves next to me, spotted my clerical collar and began to ask questions about what kind of future God had in store for AIDS, promiscuity, teenage pregnancies, pornography and the Soviet Union. I said: "Sex will survive. A false ideology won't," and tried to escape by saying I had an appointment at Westminster Abbey, but they replied with joy that the Abbey was the next place on their schedule and that they'd be honoured to accompany me there. They were so polite and charming that I felt I could forgive them a great deal, even for interrogating me about the future plans of my boss, the founder and president of Universe Inc.

After a seemingly interminable interval we reached the Abbey and I escaped into St. Faith's Chapel. As I remembered my lie to the Americans and tried to justify it, I told myself one could always have an appointment with God.

Unfortunately the chapel struck me as having an odd atmosphere. I waited, fearful of some psychic eruption, but when none came I calmed down. At least the chapel was quiet. A verger wandered in and out, but the hardy groups of off-season tourists were being shepherded around the main part of the Abbey, and the chapel set aside for the private prayers of visitors was St. George's by the west front. Possibly only my clerical collar had won me unquestioned access to St. Faith's.

At last I decided I felt sufficiently rested to take a cab to Clare's house in Fulham. Leaving the chapel by the other entrance, a door which opened into the passage by the Chapter House, I wandered into the cloisters. I was just pausing to look at yet another green space—the grassy quadrangle—when I glanced across to the west cloister and saw a familiar figure hurrying through the colonnade.

It was Francie.

VIII

Automatically I started to run. I raced around the corner into the south cloister, and by haring all the way down it I managed to catch Francie in the passage which connected the cloisters with Dean's Yard. But when I touched her arm and she turned to face me I saw I'd made a mistake. This woman was unknown to me. With an apology I dropped back and she moved on.

It was only then that I realised how stupid I'd been. There was no reason why Francie should have been visiting Westminster Abbey that morning. Moreover at close quarters the woman had borne little resemblance to her. How had I come to make such a strange mistake? Rubbing my eyes as if this would somehow sort my brain out, I made a big effort to think straight. Obviously I had been worrying about Francie on an unconscious level, and when I had seen in the distance a woman of her build and colouring the false recognition had allowed me to bring to the forefront of my mind the problem which she represented.

I felt glad I hadn't seen her double. To see a double was a harbinger of death. But I'd acted as if I'd seen her double. I'd genuinely thought the woman was Francie. So . . .

I cut off that thought, since it led straight to the subject of paranormal phenomena and I had to steer clear of that particular web. Making a fierce resolution to pull myself together immediately I walked to the far end of Dean's Yard around yet another green space—the Choir School's playground—and sat down on the steps of Church House, the headquarters of the Church of England. Here I took more deep breaths and tried not to think of Francie. One or two people walked past but no one seemed to think I was behaving strangely. Perhaps priests often sat on the steps of Church House, like pigeons who had come home to roost. I sat staring at the Abbey's twin towers, currently shrouded in the scaffolding which was enabling their restoration, and after a while I realised I couldn't face taking a cab to Fulham. After an even longer while I thought: that's a very disturbing conclusion and I must think of something else straight away before I get upset—and unsurprisingly the "something else" turned out to be Francie, her image dragged into the forefront of my mind by the doppelgänger.

Suddenly I had a revelation. It occurred to me—and why on earth hadn't I realised this before?—that I was the only one who could fix Francie because I was the only one who could convince her that I wasn't going to wind up in the divorce court. Rosalind and I were going to stay together. The marriage was going to work out.

At once I realised I had to see Francie without delay. I had to put her back in touch with reality, no matter how unwelcome that reality was, and provided I handled her skilfully I could steer her onto the road to health and healing. Was I capable of handling her skilfully? Of course. Admittedly I wasn't quite functioning at my best, but my basic skills were still intact and I was an old hand at the tricky interview with a disturbed client. I'd pull it off. I'd fix her. One less problem to solve. A welcome success after all the failure.

I paused carefully, professionally, to review Lewis's diagnosis. Essentially this was just a case involving a normally sensible woman who had been temporarily overwhelmed by some common mid-life problems—children growing up, absent husband, menopausal symptoms—with the result that her unhappiness had taken a neurotic form in one specific area of her life: her relationship with me. There was no possession, no psychosis. She wasn't imagining that everyone at St. Benet's was conspiring against her in order to keep us apart. She didn't think her husband was trying to kill her. She hadn't sent her children away to school because she was afraid she would murder them. She wasn't hearing voices from Venusians who ordered her to kill Rosalind and liberate me. Violence wasn't on her agenda at all. Her only problem was that she was obsessed with me, obsessed enough to turn up at my house in her nightdress, and this was certainly a problem, but once she heard from my own lips that I intended to stay married to Rosalind I was sure I could delicately manipulate her into an emotionally neutral space where the fantasy could be recognised as misguided—of course there'd be no crude shattering of the delusion—and then with the appropriate help from Robin, Val and Lewis . . . Yes, with the right treatment she'd soon recover, but there was no time to lose. If the obsession worsened and the public declarations of passion started . . . if the demons rode into St. Benet's on the back of that mental disturbance . . . if the no-smoke-without-a-fire syndrome ignited . . .

But what was I doing, idling away my time by dwelling on these nightmares? I had to act. This was an emergency. I had to act *now.*

Feeling immensely better at the prospect of returning to action again as a healer I set off in search of a public phone. After enquiring at the Church House bookshop I eventually found a booth nearby in Great Peter Street, and a minute later I was asking my secretary if Francie had come to work that day.

She had, and in response to the summons from Joyce she came gasping to the phone.

"Nick!"

"Yes, it's me. Look, I need to talk to you."

"Oh, my God!" Francie sounded as if she was reeling with surprise, delight and something which came across as shock, the pleasurable kind common among bystanders viewing an exceptionally interesting disaster. Breathlessly she demanded: "Is it about Stacy?"

"Stacy!" I was so confused by this question that it took me at least five seconds to reply: "No, of course not." What was going on? In my mind Stacy and Francie represented two separate problems with no common ground. Then it occurred to me that something might have happened to Stacy that morning while I'd been loafing around the open spaces. Instantly I saw Lewis accusing him of cottaging—Stacy rushing out of the house in a panic, losing his footing on the steps and smashing his skull on the cobbles—the ambulance howling along London Wall—Mrs. McGovern sobbing up in Liverpool—

I reined in my imagination. "Has Stacy had an accident?"

"Oh no!" said Francie glibly. "No, nothing like that, but he didn't feel well this morning so he went home. I wondered if you were calling to ask me to check on him. Lewis said just now you'd gone on a retreat, but I know how difficult it must be for you to switch off from St. Benet's, and if you'd like me to go and see Stacy—"

"No, I want you to come and see me. I think we should talk as soon as possible."

"Oh, how super, yes, do let's! I'm only working till twelve-fifteen because funny old Lewis asked me to take a break from befriending today and help him out with the music therapy patients, but the session's almost over and then I'll be free as air. Why don't I pick you up at the Fordite HQ and whisk you off to Islington? I've got white wine in the fridge and one of those yummy quiches from M and S—"

"That's good of you, Francie, but I've other plans for the next few hours and I'm not with the Fordites, I'm somewhere near Parliament Square. Can you meet me at Westminster Abbey for Evensong?"

"Oh, what heaven—yes, of course! And afterwards—"

"Afterwards we'll have a short talk in the nave. Thanks, Francie. By the way, Evensong begins at five—I'll get seats for us in the stalls so look out for me as soon as you enter the quire."

"Wonderful!" breathed Francie fervently before I hung up.

I found another coin, dialed the Fordites' number from memory and left a message to say I'd gone to see my spiritual director and wouldn't be back for lunch. But as soon as I had replaced the receiver I knew I still couldn't see Clare. I needed to spend a restful afternoon so that I was in prime condition to tackle Francie. Leaving the phone booth I wandered down to the little park on the Embankment beside the Houses of Parliament and sat down on one of the elevated seats which overlooked the River. A large gull was perched on the parapet. His chest was so white that I wondered how he cleaned it. Surely there were spots his beak couldn't reach? I wondered if his partner helped to groom him. But I didn't want to think of partners. Didn't have to either, now that I was so satisfyingly occupied with Francie. As the gull flew away downstream I began to review my conversation with her.

I thought I'd been both clever and skilful. Clearly it would have been idiotic to suggest a meeting in her home or in surroundings where there would be no witnesses. To meet in a large place amidst plenty of people was the perfect solution, just as to meet for a service was the perfect prelude to our conversation; Francie would be reminded that I was a priest unavailable for fornication and adultery. It might have been awkward if we had been obliged to sit close together, but the stalls at the back of the quire would ensure that Francie had no physical contact with me, even though we were sitting side by side.

Congratulating myself on this brilliant scheme I suddenly realised I needed to eat. I left the park. Then I walked down the Embankment to the Tate Gallery, refuelled by downing a sandwich and spent the afternoon contemplating some interesting modern pictures.

Or at least, that was what I appeared to be doing. In another dimension of reality I was behaving like a lemming rushing at full speed towards the nearest cliff, but unfortunately at the time this insight never crossed my mind.

14

> In a way grief is indeed a kind of madness . . . we seem totally unable to handle anything. Our feelings may well get put onto other things or people.
>
> GARETH TUCKWELL AND DAVID FLAGG
>
> *A Question of Healing*

I

When did I first realise I had made a catastrophic error? Perhaps it was when Francie entered the quire and turned her mad, shining eyes in my direction. I made myself believe that she was merely excited by the prospect of meeting me, but my heart continued to beat rapidly, as if my psychic eye glimpsed the reality which my physical eyes were too afraid to see. Or did the awareness finally surface when she sat down in the stall beside me and in greeting put her hand briefly on my thigh? The physical contact, unsought and unwanted, was the equivalent of an ice-pack on the genitals. It was hard not to wince, harder still not to allow a vision of disaster to flood into my mind, but somehow I convinced myself that this was a mere spontaneous gesture and that my best policy was to ignore it. It was only when Francie sank to her knees to say a prayer before the service that the truth blasted my delusions aside and I sensed not her prayers but the panting breath of the demons which yearned to destroy me.

In a flash I not only recognized my error but understood why I'd made it. I hadn't wanted to convince Francie that there was no possibility of divorce. I'd wanted to convince myself. My chaotic emotions had blinded me to danger and shoved me in entirely the wrong direction. Unable to face the possibility that my marriage might be beyond saving, I had seen Francie's fervent belief in a future divorce as a threat to me which had to be eliminated so that my own fears could be kept under control. So here I was, playing the wonder worker again despite all my earlier lectures to myself on the subject, and facing the one person whom I should have avoided at all costs.

Game, set, but not quite match to the Devil.

Was I talking the religious language of metaphor and analogy? Yes. But I was describing something that was real. Evil exists. Those who forget that fact or ignore it or reject it are at best taking a big risk and at worst conniving at their own destruction.

All creation has its dark side. That's inevitable; it's built into the creative process, as I myself had discovered when I'd tried to paint water-colours. One wrong stroke of the brush and the whole picture is under threat. Then one has to sweat blood trying to make good the mess.

But I'm more familiar with the dark side of God's creation than with the dark side of painting water-colours. I'm more familiar with the darkness which can't be weighed and measured in the laboratory but which is nonetheless chillingly real. Artists and poets can represent it best with symbols because it's not easily accessible to straightforward description. The old religious code-words still bear traces of the terror they once invoked, but they've changed over time and lost their power. But the underlying reality doesn't change. The underlying reality *is.* Lives get smashed up. People, even nations, are destroyed by what appear to be huge unseen forces far beyond the control of politicians or economists or scientists. Accidents happen. Psychopaths wander around with dead eyes. And people pushed off balance by extreme stress make bad decisions and rush lemming-like to their doom.

My hand automatically clasped my pectoral cross as I expressed my intense desire to make contact with my Creator. I was so horrified that I couldn't frame an extempore prayer of any kind, but my memory regurgitated the lines from the Litany which begged for deliverance. Meanwhile Francie was sitting back again in her stall with a sigh of pleasure. My flesh crawled. I went on clutching my cross and trying to think coherently. Should I bolt or should I stay? I was aware of a strong urge to bolt, but at that moment the choir began to sing the Introit as they stood gathered around the nave altar, and seconds later they were processing into view. Bolting would still have been possible but it would have been awkward, especially as the members of the choir were now taking their places in the rows directly below us. I decided I had to stay and use the time to figure out what on earth I was going to do.

It seemed plain to me now that Lewis had seriously underestimated Francie's condition . . . Or had he? No, probably not. Probably he had played it down because he knew that if I had realised the size of the crisis I'd have wanted to postpone my retreat. He had been helped by the fact that his crucial conversation with Francie had been confidential, enabling him to censor the truth with a clear conscience. Yet Lewis had clearly said she was neither psychotic nor possessed. Would he have told an outright lie? No. So that meant . . .

I then realised that the truth could be more of a muddle than I had anticipated. Probably Lewis had both tried to play down Francie's condition *and* seriously underestimated it, although to be fair to Lewis I had to remember that Francie's illness, whatever that was, might not be in the same stage now as it was when he had made his diagnosis last Monday night. Sick people can deteriorate rapidly. The borderlines of mental illness aren't clear-cut, and in the general haziness the patterns of different illnesses can emerge, blend, fluctuate, disappear and emerge dominant. And what did we really know about Francie anyway? We only saw her at the Centre when she wore her mask of Befriender. Once that was discarded all manner of abnormality might be surfacing at her house in Islington but no one would be around to see it. I thought of Alice, who occasionally called there, saying: "Francie isn't quite the simple, friendly soul everyone thinks she is . . ." The more I thought about this the more sure I felt that Alice, who was highly intuitive, had been picking up the vibes of profound abnormality.

Francie certainly wasn't behaving normally now. She was surfing on big waves of adrenaline, living in an unreal world. By this time I was sure she wasn't unbalanced merely in the area of her life which related to me. The euphoria made me start thinking again of manic-depressive psychosis. Or if she was completely out of touch with reality maybe I was seeing some form of paranoid schizophrenia. Or maybe—

But I had to stop speculating. I was a priest, not a doctor, and anyway even if a posse of psychiatrists had been present they might well have been unable to agree on what was going on. The one undeniable fact was that Francie was sick. The second undeniable fact was that this sickness was very dangerous to me. And the third undeniable fact was that if I wanted to survive this nightmare I had to calm down so that I could correctly work out when and how to escape.

By the time I reached this conclusion the service was well under way. I had risen to my feet for the Magnificat and Nunc Dimittis, subsided into my stall for the readings and sunk to my knees for the Collects. As the choir began to sing their anthem I tried some covert observation of Francie, but found myself agreeing with Lewis that there was no sign of possession. Apart from the total absence of all the more florid symptoms, she seemed without fear and without awareness that something was very wrong. It was true that her febrile excitement was unnatural—bright eyes, dry lips, shallow breathing, hand slightly unsteady as she turned the page of her prayer-book during the psalm—but this could be explained entirely by the fact that she was sitting so close to me. Or in religious language, the demon of lust was certainly present, but there was no sign that the Devil had taken up residence. In which case why did I feel so convinced that the situation was thoroughly evil and that I stood in very great danger? I reminded myself that although I was spiritually debilitated at present there was no diminishment of my psychic powers. Quite the reverse. Stress always had the effect of rubbing my psyche raw and making it even more perceptive than usual. That was why I had been so keen earlier to fight my way clear of the paranormal rubbish tip. The trouble with going through an ultra-perceptive phase is that one picks up far too much, most of it meaningless junk. Yet I didn't think the impression I was currently receiving from Francie was meaningless junk at all, particularly now that the fog had cleared from my brain and I knew exactly why I had fallen into the trap of arranging a meeting with her. I was always wary of psychic twinges, but this wasn't a twinge, it was a thump. I knew myself in danger just as I knew Francie showed no outward sign of wishing to harm me.

The next moment I found myself toying with an unusual but not impossible explanation of what was going on. Maybe Francie's obsession with me was a way of blotting out the fear caused by the initial symptoms of possession. Maybe she was even using the obsession on an unconscious level to hold on to her identity which was being consistently undermined by an alien force. I reminded myself that at the Healing Centre she had always been completely in control of herself. If her trouble had stemmed from a chemical imbalance in the brain she would have been unable to regulate her behaviour in that way. But maybe it wasn't Francie who had been doing the regulating.

I suddenly realised I was on my knees and reciting the grace which concluded the service. Was Francie able to say the words "Jesus Christ"? Yes. I had also heard her say the Lord's Prayer and the Creed without faltering. As I had already noted, there were no signs of possession. Yet my forehead was damp with sweat and my fingers ached from gripping the cross and my psyche, picking up the disordered emotions of the woman sitting next to me, was reacting as if it were being beaten up. I felt as if I might be wiped out at any moment by an invisible assassin.

This was hardly a pleasant thought. Maybe the Devil had triggered it. With an enormous effort I remembered the saving power of the Holy Spirit and prayed in Christ's name for deliverance, but I still felt as if I were about to be liquidated by some malign side-effect of the rough, tough, brutal process of creation. I knew my Creator was there, desperate to save me, but maybe I'd jumped so far into the jaws of darkness that he would be able to do no more than toil to redeem the mess left by my destruction. All creators are omnipotent in their created world, but they can only work with the material at hand and sometimes the material proves fatally intractable.

I prayed feverishly again for deliverance.

There was no organ music in the Abbey that night so the choir and the clergy padded away in silence. After that the congregation knelt for a moment of private prayer, but a moment later, still clutching my cross, I was obliged to rise from my knees.

"Wasn't that a beautiful service!" breathed Francie starry-eyed, allowing her arm to brush mine.

"Very professional." I deliberately selected an unromantic judgement but it had no effect. She remained starry-eyed. Obviously she believed I had lured her to the Abbey for the thrill of sitting close to her and was now entirely convinced we were on the brink of an affair.

Leaving the quire we paused to exchange a few words with the canon in residence before moving to the other side of the nave. I threaded my way through the rows of chairs to the north aisle, and as Francie bobbed along behind me I realised she was still chattering about the service. On reaching the end of the row I pulled out the last chair and set it well back at right angles to its neighbour. Since I was now deprived of the protection afforded by the choirstalls I wanted to ensure that Francie and I didn't wind up sitting too close together.

"Have a seat," I said, gesturing to the chair which was now the last in the row, and sank down on the chair I had detached.

"This is so wonderful of you, Nick—such a divine idea—"

"I agree it's always a good idea to go to church and keep in touch with reality," I said dryly, "but I don't think it's particularly wonderful of me to suggest it. In fact it seems to me to be a pretty mundane suggestion for a priest to make. Now, Francie, let's try and remain in touch with that reality spelt out by the service—let's try to—"

"Now that we're away from the Centre we can really talk, can't we?"

"No, we only have a few minutes because the Abbey closes at six in winter. Francie, I just want to say—"

"I've got the car parked on a meter behind Dean's Yard. Why don't we go there straight away and I'll drive us both back to Islington?"

"Francie, you're a trained listener. Could you please listen for a moment?"

She laughed. "Sorry, darling! It's just that it's all so wonderfully exciting—the consummation of all my dreams—"

"I repeat: could you please listen for a moment?"

"Oh gosh, sorry, there I go again!" She gazed at me with glowing eyes and fell silent.

Carefully I said: "I'm afraid I've made a mistake in arranging this meeting. I now think it would be better if we met at the Centre on Monday. Then Robin can be present."

"Robin?" She looked blank. "But what on earth's Robin got to do with us?"

"I think it could be useful to include him in a discussion about the viability of your position at St. Benet's."

"About the—oh, *vulnerability!* For a moment I thought you said *viability*. Don't worry, darling, I'm tougher than you think! I can take the bitchy comments when people realise you're leaving her for me!"

I saw I had to abandon the subject. "I'm afraid you can't hear what I'm saying," I said evenly, "but never mind, we'll put the matter on hold until Monday. And now, if you'll excuse me, Francie—"

"But of course I can hear, don't be so silly! I won't let you leave until you've explained why you wanted to meet me here!" She leant forward and gave my arm a playful pat.

Hurriedly, wanting only to avoid further playful pats and terminate the conversation without delay, I said: "I'd thought I might tell you something about Rosalind, but since this is obviously entirely the wrong moment—"

"Rosalind! Oh my dear, it's not necessary for you to say a single syllable! She's told me everything—*everything*—and I must just say that although I took care to tell her exactly what she wanted to hear, my sympathies, darling, were entirely with you. No wonder you had to hypnotise her to get some decent sex! I always knew she was frigid. Promiscuous women so often are, aren't they? Always searching for the orgasm they never find!"

There was a pause. Nothing much seemed to happen. The huge shadowy interior of the Abbey was still dotted with people, and the faint drone of multiple conversations mingled with the sound of muffled footsteps. It was just the end of another day at the Abbey. No one around me knew that an entire cherished private world had suddenly come to an end.

It had ended silently, without a whimper, and smoothly, without encountering an impediment. The safe, secure world of my marriage had finally died not from confessions of adultery and not from mudslinging rows but from the knowledge that my wife had told this deeply disturbed woman details which should never have been disclosed to anyone but a priest or a doctor or some other professional qualified to help us. Moreover she had lied to me afterwards to conceal the depth of her betrayal. Could I argue that Rosalind had lied merely to spare me from pain? No. That would be giving her a moral stature she didn't possess. The truth was she had lied in order to avoid a scene. In her view anything was better than enduring a scene: lies, writing cruel notes, two-faced behaviour—anything.

I saw then how shallow she was, how unreliable, how utterly lacking in integrity, and it seemed strange to me that I should have derived such security for so long from a woman who could in truth offer me no security at all. I had trusted her love and loyalty, but I saw both had been illusions, conjured up to meet my own emotional needs. I'd been projecting qualities onto her which contained and neutralized my own flaws and problems, and beneath the projection was a woman I scarcely knew. I'd been obsessed with an image—how typical of the 1980s' preoccupation with "style"!—but reality had all the time lain elsewhere.

It was at that moment that I suffered the most horrific shock. One moment I was drowning in pain, every inch the crucified victim, and the next moment the truth had exploded before my eyes so that I saw myself in quite another light.

The trigger was the word "obsessed" which had just skimmed across my mind. I had been *obsessed*, I had told myself, by an image. I HAD BEEN OBSESSED.

My whole consciousness seemed to shift and bend almost to breaking point before snapping agonisingly into a new and unbearable position. It was like an earthquake: the grinding roar followed by the ear-splitting cracks as the earth ruptured and re-formed at lightning speed. I had been obsessed, *obsessed*, OBSESSED—as obsessed as this mad woman in front of me, and in Francie's shining eyes I finally saw my own insanity reflected.

The earthquake roared again, the ground breaking open with a volley of whiplash cracks, and at my feet I saw the abyss open up to reveal the unspeakable, indescribable darkness churning below. I shrank back, but not before I had seen the horror I had inflicted on Rosalind, the unreasonable demands, the violent pursuit, the mental and physical oppression. No wonder she had finally snapped, blurting out all her despair and terror to someone who was not only an old friend but a trained listener! I'd driven her to it. I'd broken her integrity. And to think that a moment ago I'd been wallowing in injured pride and accusing *her* of shallowness and betrayal! *I* was the shallow one, never seeing my wife in any depth, never making any effort to understand how she must be feeling. *I* was the expert in betrayal, kidding myself I'd been a loving husband yet leaving her to struggle on alone, running my home and bringing up my children. And to think I'd accused *her* of self-centredness! To think I'd sermonised to *her* about the evils of individualism and the virtues of living in community! I'd neglected my primary community, my family. I'd gone my own individual self-absorbed way under the guise of helping others. No wonder worker, it seemed to me at that terrible moment of revelation, could have gone more adrift in his arrogance and his vanity, and no wonder worker could now be better set up for the just retribution of a grisly and scandalous end.

"Nick?" Francie was saying somewhere a long way away but I barely heard her. In my head I was with Rosalind, the beloved childhood friend with whom I would always feel so deeply connected. In my head I was saying to her: "It's all right. I understand now. I understand."

"Nick, is something wrong?"

I didn't answer. I wasn't there. I'd broken free from my father and I was scrambling to the top of the bonfire to save Bear from his attempt to immolate himself. "He'll be free now," my father had said. But I didn't want my bear to achieve freedom by death. I wanted him to have freedom through the gift of a new life.

"Life." I suddenly realised I had spoken the word aloud. "Life."

"Oh *yes*, darling!" cried Francie in ecstasy, her words scoring deep gashes across my consciousness. "Life, life, life with a capital L—just you and me, together always in an utterly glorious future!"

The picture of Bear atop the bonfire was wiped out. As my mind abruptly snapped back into alignment with the present I realised that I was in Westminster Abbey with Francie Parker, who was mad. Then I remembered. I had to fix Francie. But there was a problem: I couldn't. My strength had been used up. I could only stare at her dumbly and wish she would go away.

"You'll be a new man once you get away from Rosalind!" Francie was saying with manic enthusiasm. "Poor darling, how ghastly it must have been for you to have a frigid wife!"

I said automatically: "Rosalind's not frigid."

"But of course she is! Why else would you have needed to hypnotise her to get some sex?"

"You've jumped to all the wrong conclusions. About everything."

"What on earth do you mean?"

"I mean you haven't a clue what's going on." I stood up. "Excuse me, please. I've got to go."

Francie's eyes widened. "Oh, poor Nick!" she exclaimed passionately, leaping to her feet. "Poor, poor Nick, you're the one who's jumped to all the wrong conclusions if you think that sheer Christian charity can continue to save this marriage! My dear, I know for a fact that Rosalind's planning to have another affair to drill home to you that the marriage is beyond salvation!"

I stared at her. She was breathing hard, eyes glittering, bosom heaving in an almost sexual satisfaction, lips shiny and moist with saliva, and suddenly I felt revolted. I no longer cared about "fixing" her, whatever that meant. I just wanted to shove her aside and escape. With my patience exhausted I snapped: "That's nonsense. I don't believe it."

"Oh darling!" cried Francie powerfully. "You're in denial! Listen, I know exactly what her plan is—she's going to seduce Stacy!"

At once I said: "That's not just rubbish, Francie. That's disgusting rubbish." I was moving forward as I spoke. Increasing my pace I began to hurry down the side-aisle to the west end of the nave.

"It's true, it's true, it's true!" She rushed after me. "She said she realised she could only get you to see the truth by doing something so frightful that you'd have no choice but to let her go!"

I spun round to face her. "Be quiet! Be quiet at once! You're lying, you're deluded, you're—"

"Rosalind's made up her mind to seduce Stacy, I tell you—why, she's probably already done it! That's why I said to you when you rang up: 'Is it about Stacy?' I thought you must be calling because she'd done it and you'd found out!"

I suddenly realised she was telling the truth. And as the shock swamped my mind I saw the waters of darkness roaring towards me in a filthy, annihilating tide.

Knowing I was within seconds of going under I could think only of self-preservation. I had to escape. And I had to escape immediately. No more conversation. No more delay. Even another second in her company could prove disastrous.

Sprinting from the Abbey I jumped aboard a bus which was moving forward slowly after pausing at the traffic lights on Victoria Street, and the last thing I saw as I looked back was Francie gazing after me with an adoration undiminished by my desertion.

Her mad eyes even seemed to be blazing in triumph.

II

I left the bus minutes later at Victoria, plunged across the station's forecourt and was nearly run over by a taxi. That proved the final shock. I vomited into the gutter, and immediately every passer-by shunned me as if I had the plague. No Samaritans in that particular crowd. Inside the station I lurched into a phone-booth.

Lewis answered my call on the third ring. "Rectory."

"It's me," I said. "I'm ploughed under."

"Where are you?"

"Victoria."

"I'll come and pick you up."

"No, I'm still capable of grabbing a cab but I don't want to go to the Rectory, I don't want to see Stacy. Meet me at the Barbican—that window next to the Balcony Cafe."

"I'll be there." He hung up.

Staggering outside I joined the rush-hour queue waiting for taxis.

III

The Arts Centre at the Barbican was crowded when I arrived at six-thirty. Visitors were having supper before the plays and the concert began. The multi-storeyed building, confusing as ever with its yawning chasms and acres of staircases, swallowed me the instant I was disgorged from the taxi. Unable to endure either the wait for a lift or the thought of being incarcerated in a small steel box, I fought my way up the stairs to the Balcony Cafe, which faced St. Giles Church and the artificial lake. The wall of glass nearest the cafe's entrance usually had seating in front of it but when I arrived I found no sofa and no sign of Lewis. I was just wondering if, in my distraught state, I had named one of the other restaurants, when he called my name. He was occupying one of the tables which flanked the walkway spanning level six. Beyond the table was a drop to the floor below but fortunately I was too wiped out by that time to add vertigo to my list of discomforts.

I had also been too wiped out to remember that Lewis was battling with a new hip. Immediately I saw the crutches I felt guilty that I had dragged him out of the Rectory, where he should have been spending a quiet evening. Lewis had been travelling far too much lately, attending that lecture at Sion College last Monday and bucketing around the Anglo-Catholic strongholds the day before. Even though he had done his travelling in taxis I was sure all this activity was hardly compatible with his surgeon's idea of a sensible convalescence. Supposing the new hip was a failure? By hauling him out to the Barbican that night I'd be at least partly responsible.

"You silly old sod, you should be at home! Why didn't you refuse point-blank to meet me here?"

"Cut the crap and just tell me what the hell's going on. You look like death."

I slumped down opposite him. Then I said: "I know what's happened to Stacy. I know why he's on the edge of breakdown and I understand now why he can't confide in me. He's been to bed with Rosalind."

Lewis looked me straight in the eyes, paused as if silently counting to ten and finally said in his most neutral voice: "I see. Well, that's certainly an interesting theory."

"It's no theory."

"You've got proof?"

"No, but it all makes sense—Rosalind—Francie—Stacy—everything. I'll bet Francie put Rosalind up to it and Rosalind was too desperate and damaged to resist. Oh, and Francie's psychotic. No question about that. She's not possessed, but there's a heavy demonic infestation and the Devil's using the psychosis to infiltrate—"

"Hold it. You need some sweet tea. You're in shock."

"No, I'm all right. Listen, Lewis—"

"Well, *I'm* not all right and *I* need some sweet tea, and if it wasn't for these blank-blank crutches I'd play the waiter and bring us what we both need, but—"

"Okay, I'll get it." After dragging him out of the Rectory the least I could do was humour the old boy.

"On second thoughts," said Lewis as I scrambled to my feet, "I'd rather have a brandy." Now that the battle was won and I had agreed to take the anti-shock medicine, he could afford to change his mind and indulge himself.

I hurried down the walkway to the catering outpost at the far end and bought the drinks. It was calming to go on such a mundane errand and I began to feel less severed from normality, but my heart was still banging away like a discombobulated metronome. I wondered vaguely if I was a candidate for a heart attack but thought not. Too little cholesterol, too few excess pounds, no cigarettes. On the other hand, if stress was the primary factor in inducing a coronary, I was ripe for a coffin.

Back at the table again I collapsed into my chair and drank. I hate sweet tea but one shouldn't expect to like medicine. Meanwhile the scene around me was beginning to look slightly different, resembling not a layered tower in hell after all but a futuristic railway station built by mistake in an area where there were no trains.

"I'm better," I said after tipping the last of the tea down my throat.

Lewis knocked back the rest of his brandy. "Then let's start at the beginning. How did you get this idea that Rosalind's seduced Stacy?"

"I saw Francie. She said—"

"*You saw Francie?*" Lewis shouted, instantly losing his composure.

"I know, I know—I've really screwed up—the disaster's just escalating and escalating—"

"Tell me that you didn't go to Francie's house. Nicholas, please, please tell me that you didn't meet that woman on your own with no witnesses—"

"I didn't meet her on my own with no witnesses. I didn't go to her house. I'm wrecked but I'm not certifiably insane. Not yet."

Lewis wiped the sweat from his forehead. "All right," he said, reaching at last for his cigarettes. "I'm listening. Go on."

I told him everything.

IV

"*The* most likely explanation," said Lewis at last, "is that this is Francie's fantasy, drummed up at the end of the conversation to maintain your interest when you showed signs of wanting to leave. Remember you've no proof whatsoever that what she said was true."

"But it does explain Stacy's recent behaviour."

"There's another explanation for that and it doesn't have anything to do with Rosalind."

"Yes, but once you admit he's not a homosexual, the other explanation's plainly wrong—"

"Wait a moment, Nicholas, I haven't finished outlining the most likely explanation. I want to show you how Francie could have whipped up this fantasy."

I forced myself to be patient. "Okay, go ahead."

"Because I stopped her doing any befriending she had more time to see what was going on at the Centre this morning. There was obviously something very wrong with Stacy, and she was present when I told him to go home and rest. By this time the news was also circulating on the grapevine that Rosalind had changed her plan to stay at the Rectory until the school holidays and had departed for Butterfold. Francie had access to both these unconnected facts, and during her conversation with you this evening she could have yoked them together in fantastic style to grab your attention. Obsessed people do this all the time—they fasten on a stray piece of information, infuse it with a meaning which serves their neurotic needs and then inflate the distorted truth into a dramatic lie."

I made a big effort to match his rational manner. "Okay," I said, "okay, I concede it's a plausible theory, but it doesn't quite pan out. You forget that Francie herself didn't know whether or not this disaster had happened. All she knew was that it was set to happen, but surely if she'd been fantasising she would have claimed the event had definitely taken place? I think her uncertainty gives the story the ring of truth."

"That's a valid point." Lewis paused to rearrange his thoughts. "All right, I still don't believe Francie's statement, but let's for a moment assume this event was set to happen. How do we know it's already happened?"

"Stacy's behaviour."

"Yes, but—"

"Look, this is the sequence of events. Rosalind and Francie met for lunch yesterday. Francie put her up to this scheme in order to hammer home to me that the marriage was finished. Rosalind returned to the Rectory. A little later on I was looking for Rosalind and couldn't find her. You were looking for Stacy and couldn't find him either. Alice did suggest that Rosalind and Stacy were together in his flat, but you were diverted by Venetia's phone call and I preferred to loaf around watching Alice cook. And when Stacy finally came downstairs—"

"He looked traumatised. Yes, that's true but Nicholas, there's still a huge problem with this theory. Rosalind may well have declared in a fit of bravado over an alcoholic lunch that she'd seduce Stacy, but can you seriously imagine her ever going ahead and doing it? I know that where sex is concerned anything's possible, but the sort of pathetic, self-destructive behaviour we're talking about here would be so alien to Rosalind's nature—"

"I'd driven her to act out of character. All this is my fault, all of it. I see now I've been as obsessed as Francie." I covered my face suddenly with my hands.

Lewis was silent for a moment. All he said finally was: "That's how it seems to you?"

"Yes, but I can't talk about it, not at the moment, it's too difficult." Letting my hands fall I stared down into my empty cup on the table.

"Very well," said Lewis after another pause, "let's return to your theory. I admit I'm beginning to find it plausible, but I'm still not convinced it's correct. I've queried the likelihood of Rosalind doing something so louche; let me now query the likelihood of Stacy getting into bed with his boss's wife. Even if the boy's not as queer as a coot, I can't imagine—"

"If he's the insecure, ignorant heterosexual wannabe I think he is, I can imagine it all too well."

"You mean that if he's in a state of chronic anxiety about his sexuality and desperate to prove to himself he's not gay—"

"I suspect only an experienced older woman could have dealt with all those fears which he's consistently refused to talk through with a therapist."

"Yes, but this woman was *your wife*. Surely—"

"This woman was Rosalind. She knew what she wanted and she would have set out to get it as efficiently as possible. And Stacy was Stacy—weak, muddled, little more than an overgrown child. His one previous affair was with someone much older. This present incident would have been just a repetition of the pattern."

"Maybe more of a repetition than you think. Maybe subconsciously he could have seen going to bed with Rosalind as a way of going to bed with you. The situation would have resembled those three-in-a-bed episodes where despite the presence of a woman the real action is between the two men."

"Okay, I admit that emotionally there could be a homosexual dimension to this episode, but I've never claimed that Stacy was a hundred per cent heterosexual. All I've claimed is that he's heterosexual enough to feel happiest in a heterosexual way of life." I leant forward on the table to drive my argument home. "Lewis, we can't know exactly what happened between Stacy and Rosalind, but I think we can be sure that some sort of sexual incident took place. Why else would Stacy have been unable to confide in me? Why else would he have rushed out of the house and made his confession to Gil Tucker?"

"We don't know for a fact that he saw Tucker."

"Yes, we do."

"You mean you did speak to Tucker last night? My dear Nicholas—"

"Stacy told me he'd seen Gil, and Gil signalled to me that a confession had been made."

"Well, I knew Stacy must have made his confession, since he attended mass this morning and took the Sacrament, but I assumed he'd seen his spiritual director. Surely the fact that he chose to go instead to a gay activist means—"

"All it means is that Stacy's got a non-relationship with his spiritual director and that he chose to confide instead in a priest who'd been kind to him. By the way, Gil also signalled to me that this crisis hadn't been triggered by Stacy coming out of the closet."

"Well, he would say that, wouldn't he? According to bigots like Tucker, homosexuality never triggers anything except indescribable bliss!"

"Lewis—"

"All right, don't let's get hung up on Tucker. Maybe I should concede, though with considerable reluctance, that your appalling theory is probably correct. I suppose it just proves yet again what depths human beings can sink to when the Devil muscles in and starts cracking the whip. And talking of the Devil—"

"Yes," I said. "Let's start talking about possession."

V

"*At least* we're in agreement," said Lewis as the conversation shifted gears, "that Francie's not possessed."

"In the absence of symptoms there seems no other conclusion to draw, but . . ." I hesitated, remembering my psychic thump at the Abbey.

"You're uncertain?" said Lewis surprised. "But you seemed very sure of yourself at the start of this conversation! You said she was psychotic, with a heavy demonic infestation, but there was no possession."

"Yes, I did say that. And I think I still believe it. But I could be wrong."

This statement impressed Lewis. I wasn't being a know-it-all wonder worker any more. The Christian healer had finally resurfaced. "Well, we need to get this right," he said, "or we'll bugger up the treatment and so will the psychiatrist."

This was all too true. It was no good attempting to treat by conventional medical means a person possessed by the Devil, and conversely it was worse than useless to exorcise a person who wasn't possessed. But very few people were, in the classical sense, possessed and requiring a full exorcism with priests, psychiatrists and social workers in attendance. Much more common were the cases of infestation by demons. These cases required a short rite of deliverance from the priest in combination with psychiatric care for the underlying mental illness which had made the infestation possible. The psychiatrist who supported us in this particular aspect of our work at the Healing Centre told me he thought of demons as spiritual bacilli which could invade the soul just as physical bacilli could invade the body. I myself preferred a more holistic approach to the mystery; I saw body and soul as one entity which over the years formed a unique pattern: the personality. This could be undermined by illness. Physical illness affected spiritual health. Spiritual illness affected physical health. It was all a unity, all one. Bacilli, demons—they were just technical terms for different hazards to health. We were all flawed so no one had perfect health, but we could all strive to be healthier. It was a task, a mission, a journey, a pilgrimage. The healthier we were the happier we became. The healthier we were the more ably we could serve God by giving expression to that unique pattern of personality and contributing to his overall creative purpose.

"Nicholas?"

I refocused. "Sorry. What were you saying?"

"Why have you now got your doubts that Francie's not possessed?"

I told him about my psychic thump and my off-beat speculation that Francie could be unconsciously escaping into her obsession to blot out the fear triggered by the suspicion that something was trying to take over her personality.

"That's not impossible," said Lewis at last, "but I don't think it's likely. The point about the onset of possession is that the victims can't blot it out—or at least that's always been so in the cases I've encountered. I'm sure that if Francie had been succumbing to possession she would have come to us in fear, convinced that something was very wrong."

"Well, she did, didn't she?" I said. "She presented the fantasy about Harry beating her up. That could have been a coded cry for help. Do you remember how I once speculated that the wife-beating saga might have been concocted because she couldn't bring herself to speak directly about what was wrong?"

"Yes, I do remember that." Lewis fell silent, taking time to consider this theory carefully, but in the end he said: "It would be irresponsible to diagnose possession when there are no classic symptoms present. I think we've got to act on the basis that she needs psychiatric help and the deliverance ministry but no exorcism."

"Well, an exorcism wouldn't be possible anyway—she's expressed no need for it."

"She's expressed no need for anything apart from you, has she? We still haven't solved the problem of how to get her to accept treatment."

"Maybe the illness is still evolving. Maybe she'll soon break down. Maybe—"

"Further speculation is pointless at this stage, Nicholas. The only two things that are absolutely clear are that you have to keep out of her way and I have to get her into treatment. I'll phone Robin tomorrow at his home and try to work out how we can corral her when she shows up for work on Monday morning."

"Supposing she turns up at the Rectory again over the weekend?"

"No, she won't do that. Harry arrives back tonight from Hong Kong and like all the best unreconstructed males he'll want to be waited on hand and foot."

I shifted restlessly in my chair. "Surely he'll notice something's wrong!"

"Not necessarily. She may be perfectly normal with him."

"But she's seriously nuts! My God, when I think of her egging Rosalind on—and I'm sure she did, I'm sure she came up with the whole demonic idea—"

"Obviously there's severe infestation. But we can't ring up Harry and say—"

I was barely listening. Despair had gripped me again. "Of course if Rosalind hadn't been in such a mess as the result of what I did to her she'd never have listened to Francie. All this is my fault."

"Now look here, Nicholas. Try and keep this in perspective. What you did to Rosalind was morally wrong, no question about that, but you didn't knock all her teeth out, did you, or force her to have sex with a dog? Or in other words, your behavior wasn't so degrading, was it, that she ended up a gibbering wreck who required hospitalisation? If she went along with Francie's suggestion about Stacy, that was her decision, made when she was very distressed but still sane, and you must allow her some responsibility for her actions."

"Even so—"

"I think you should set Rosalind aside for the moment. She's currently safe, back at Butterfold with her garden. And I think you should set Francie aside too. She'll have her hands full attending to Harry. But the one person you can't set aside is Stacy. You've somehow got to rescue him from the hell he must be in."

"Right." I struggled to think constructively. "But how on earth do I do the rescuing?"

"The real problem is the opening dialogue. After that you can bring in a mediator."

"Gil?"

"Yes, I'm afraid it'll have to be him, since he's the one person Stacy trusts, but maybe he'll surprise me by performing a pastoral miracle." Lewis wiped the sweat from his forehead again and groped for another cigarette. "Incidentally, did Tucker offer you any advice when he spoke to you last night?"

"Yes, he did," I said, finally diverted from my despair. "He said I should do nothing about Stacy for two weeks."

"Two weeks?"

"That's what he said."

"But what's the point of the long interval?"

"No idea."

We stared at each other. "I think he said something about giving

Stacy time to get his act together," I said at last. "He was glad I was going on retreat—and glad Rosalind wouldn't be at the Rectory, yes, I remember that now—"

"Well, that makes sense, but the two weeks on ice certainly don't. Nicholas, I know you think I'm hopelessly prejudiced against Tucker, but even if he was radiating heterosexuality from every pore, I'd question that particular pastoral judgement. He doesn't know Stacy well, does he?"

"He does now—and I'm sure the right thing to do is to ask him to act as a mediator, but I still can't think how we're going to handle our return to the Rectory tonight. What in God's name do I say to that boy?"

We stared at each other again as we tried to imagine the unimaginable.

VI

"*So this* is what we do," said Lewis after ten minutes of painful and erratic speculation. "We arrive home. I go up to the curate's flat and tell Stacy you've cancelled your retreat, you're back at the Rectory and you want to talk to him about Rosalind. If he's innocent and we've been dead wrong in all our deductions, he'll be astonished and uncomprehending. If he's guilty, as I now believe he is, he'll panic. I then calm him down by saying you've no wish to beat him up but you do want to see him. I float the idea that after this preliminary conversation a mediator should be present—"

"I'm beginning to think we should skip the preliminary conversation. Let's haul Gil over straight away."

"No, I believe that would be a psychological mistake, Nicholas. Stacy might not be able to cope straight away with an outsider being present—in fact he might baulk again at the whole idea of a mediator. You don't want to look as if you're strong-arming him into accepting this particular way forward."

"Okay, we keep the preliminary conversation. I say to Stacy—"

"No, concentrate on what you don't say. Don't mention Francie—keep her right out of it. Don't go into explanations about how you know what's happened. Just focus on the fact that you want to do all you can to redeem the disaster by easing his distress and steering him back onto a positive spiritual path—focus entirely on your position as his Rector. Your aim should be to soothe him, convince him forgiveness isn't just a Christian pipe-dream—"

"But Stacy may actually want me to be angry with him, and if I just play the spiritual pussy-cat I'm going to sound false as hell!"

"That's true, but don't forget your first task is to throw Stacy a life-line as he wallows in his self-hatred and despair, and the life-line should clearly signal that you're not going to play Pontius Pilate and wash your hands of him. You can certainly vent your anger later, but that must wait until there's a mediator present."

That made sense. I felt sure now he was right, but the trouble was I also felt sure I wanted to take a swing at Stacy, maybe even beat him up. The idea of behaving like a saint and assuring him I only wanted to guide him back to the correct spiritual path seemed to bear no relation whatsoever to reality.

"Nicholas, you've got to act! You can't afford to dither around here playing Hamlet!"

"The trouble is I feel more like playing Othello."

"Then stop thinking of yourself and start thinking about that boy! In fact the more *I* think of Stacy the more clearly I see that we have to act as soon as possible. Tucker may think this problem can be kept on ice for two weeks, but we know Stacy better than he does, we know he's now reached the stage where he can't work, can't face anyone, can't do anything except shut himself up in that flat—"

"Obviously he's in a bad way, but Gil may still be right in saying Stacy needs time to get his act together. If we were to leave him alone over the weekend—"

"Nicholas, you're adrift. You're still not plugged in."

"But—"

"Let me spell out how this hellish situation looks to Stacy right now this minute. He hero-worships you—and that's an understatement—but by a succession of bizarre events which he certainly never anticipated and still can't quite believe have taken place, he slept with your wife. He knows he's betrayed his ordination vows but what to him seems infinitely worse is that he's betrayed you. He's now living in terror because he knows that once you find out (and he's sure you will) it'll mean the end of the affair—not the consummated fling with Rosalind but the unconsummated relationship with you. He's feeling mad with grief and remorse, slaughtered by guilt, crucified by the very blackest despair—"

I finally understood. Automatically I leapt to my feet and said: "Let's go."

VII

As soon as we reached the Rectory I rushed up the backstairs. Lewis, ignoring my order that he should spare the hip and stay on the ground floor, clambered upwards more slowly. The door of the flat was locked. I started to hammer on the panels.

"Stacy!" I yelled. "Stacy, it's okay—let me in!"

There was no response. I rushed back downstairs, passing Lewis on the first floor landing, and retrieved the spare key from my study. By the time I returned to the top floor Lewis was there, waiting for me. His eyes were pitch-black in his white tense face.

I flung wide the door.

The living-room was empty. So was his bedroom. I started to open the doors of the spare rooms.

"The bathroom," said Lewis behind me. "That trap-door to the roof-space."

"Roof-space?"

"It has beams."

It also housed the rope which we kept on the top floor in case of fire.

"The door's locked." My scalp crawled. I was sweating. Rattling the handle I shouted: "Stacy! Stacy, open up—it's all right!" But it wasn't all right. It wasn't all right at all. It was all wrong, and no one replied.

"Kick the door in," said Lewis. "I'd do it myself but—"

"For God's sake stop pretending you're Action Man." I kicked and shoved. In films people break down doors by just the tap of a toe or the shove of a shoulder. The non-realism is a form of poetic license. But this was the cutting edge of reality and there was no poetry here, just nausea, sweat and fear.

"Wait," said Lewis. "There must be something in the kitchen we can use to force the lock."

He went away to look. I grabbed a wooden chair from the room next door and began to smash the panels. The wood finally caved in. Shoving my arm through the hole I turned the key and burst into the room.

He was there. The rope had been fastened to one of the beams and he was hanging below the open trap-door.

He was quite dead.

VIII

Lewis rejoined me. Eventually he led me away and made me sit down in the living-room amidst all the framed photographs of Stacy's mother and sisters. The pictures of his sister Aisling's wedding were still lying on one of the side-tables. The room was very cold.

After a while Lewis got up and began to move around the room as if he were searching for something.

"What are you looking for?" I said, but I knew.

We found the note on the bedside table. The envelope was addressed to me so I broke the seal. I didn't think the police would be too upset by that. So far we had disturbed nothing except the door of the bathroom, but I felt I was entitled to read a letter which was addressed to me.

Stacy had written: "Dear Nick, I can't go on, there's no future for me with you and the Church, you're the best priest in the world and that's why I have to stop letting you down all the time, I should never have been a priest, I'm not fit, I've no calling left, I just hate myself so much, but please never let my family know what a failure I was, it would break their hearts. This way there's a good chance they'll never know, this way I'm doing them a favour, I'm acting out of love to protect them, it's redemption, and although God will be very angry with me I think he'll understand I did it out of love and he'll forgive. I'm very, very sorry for everything—EVERYTHING—please ask Lewis to pray for me, I know I've no right to ask you. You had faith in me yet I turned out to be nothing but shit. STACY."

I read this letter aloud to Lewis because he didn't have his reading-glasses with him. I was hardly able to read to the end. Afterwards I let the paper slide through my fingers to the floor and pressed my hands against my aching eyes.

After a long time Lewis said: "Let's go downstairs. I want to get my glasses and read the letter myself. I think he's protected you but I want to be sure."

We went downstairs. While Lewis studied the note I made tea. It gave me something to do. I also needed another dose of tea and sugar. The shock was reaching me. The numbness had worn off and I kept shuddering with cold.

"We must call the police," I said, spooning sugar into both mugs.

"Yes. But not just yet."

Automatically I said: "No cover-up."

"I was hardly about to suggest we dumped the body in the river! But we need to do some hard thinking, not just for the sake of you and your ministry but for the sake of the Church. It could mean the difference between a single paragraph in the broadsheets and banner headlines in the tabloids."

I knew this was true but I remained quite unable to see the way forward. "My brain's seized up."

"Mine hasn't. Suicide's no longer a crime but the coroner could still ask some very awkward questions. Stacy's protected you in this note by never mentioning sex, but you can bet your bottom dollar that the subject of sex will come up and when it does we've got to know what we're going to say."

"You mean what we're going to omit."

"No, we know what we're going to omit: everything and anything to do with Rosalind. But if we get this right we can still respond to the inevitable questions with a succession of truthful statements."

"Can we?"

"Well, no one else is going to bring up Rosalind's name, are they? That means we won't be asked directly about her, and if there are no direct questions—"

"What about Gil? Of course he'll want to protect me, but if the police go knocking on his door—"

"Why should they? You and I are the only people who know he's connected with this fiasco, and Tucker's not going to go out of his way to break the seal of the confessional even though Stacy's dead. He'll stand by you, Nicholas."

But I was already surveying another minefield. "Supposing the press start digging and turn up details of Stacy's affair with that man in Liverpool?"

"No, that's not a problem," said Lewis at once. "The affair ended long before Stacy was ordained and so it couldn't constitute a scandal for the Church."

"But once those homophobic tabloids scent a homosexual angle—"

"I'm sure we'd survive because there's no evidence whatsoever that Stacy's had a homosexual affair since he became a priest. But what the tabloids absolutely mustn't find out about is—"

"—the episode with Rosalind."

"Exactly—and there's no way they can find out about that,

Nicholas. If Tucker, Rosalind, you and I all keep our mouths shut, there's no one else who—" He stopped.

I gasped.

In horror we had both remembered Francie.

IX

At last Lewis said: "As things stand at present Francie too is going to want to protect you. We'll worry about her later. What we've got to do now is work out our answers to the inevitable sex questions, and then call the police."

"We must tell Alice first. She's going to be so upset. We can't let her find out only when the police arrive."

"I agree. All right, you go and break the news to her while I write down a list of questions for us to consider. We've got to move fast now—if we delay too long in reporting the—"

The phone rang. We both jumped. "Don't answer it," said Lewis.

"It might be Rosalind." I picked up the receiver on the sixth ring. "Rectory."

"Nick! Why aren't you on retreat?"

It was Gil Tucker.

X

I slumped against the wall. "I cancelled," I said. For the moment I could say no more.

"Maybe that's all for the best—I was becoming increasingly worried about Stacy. Is he there?"

"No." I tried to say more but nothing happened.

"Well, I've phoned him several times at his flat but there's been no reply. So I thought I'd phone you—or rather Lewis, since I believed you to be away—to see if he had any idea where—"

"We've just found him."

"You have? You mean he's in his flat but not answering the phone?"

"Yes." I waited for him to acknowledge his worst fears before I confirmed them.

"You don't mean—you can't mean—"

"Yes. He killed himself."

There was a long silence.

"Since we last spoke," I said, "I've found out a great deal and I'm certain now I know what Stacy confessed to you yesterday." I paused before adding: "I'm sure it concerned Rosalind."

The silence returned, a stricken silence, heavy with shock and grief.

"Gil?"

"Yes, I'm still here. Nick, if I'd thought for one moment that he might—"

"Lewis and I knew him far better than you did and even we couldn't get to him in time."

"But he promised—he swore he'd be all right—he gave me his word he'd do nothing before the two weeks was up—"

"What two weeks? What was that all about? What was going on?"

Gil said rapidly: "I took him to my doctor in Harley Street at lunch-time today for an emergency appointment."

"An *emergency* appointment?"

"For the test. And you know what a long time it takes to get a result."

"You mean . . . are you saying . . ." But I knew exactly what he was saying. I knew that for the homosexual activist there was only one test which needed no qualifying description. I felt cold again, but much, much colder than I'd felt before. My lungs felt as if they were icing up.

"Rosalind told Stacy she wasn't sleeping with you, so I knew you were in no danger, but . . ."

I ceased to listen. I had ceased even to think of Stacy and his former lover in Liverpool. At that moment I could think only of Rosalind, and as I pictured her savouring her return home in blissful ignorance, I knew the escalating disaster had finally exploded into a catastrophe which stretched as far as the eye could see.

Part Five

ALICE
The Cutting Edge of Reality

We confess that there is no health in us and in doing so begin to find it. Elusive, intangible, always evading us and escaping us, it is our wholeness and our holiness.

CHRISTOPHER HAMEL COOKE

"Health and Illness, Pastoral Aspects,"

an entry in *A Dictionary of Pastoral Care*

15

We all carry pain and "disease" in some areas of our lives but because inner pain is less acceptable and costlier to share, it is more often the physical pain and disease that is readily encountered and demands attention. Yet, on listening, we may find that the root of real distress and pain is not in physical illness but rather is held within the emotional, psychological, social or spiritual experience of the individual.

GARETH TUCKWELL AND DAVID FLAGG
A Question of Healing

I

It was Nicholas who broke the news to me. I was taking in the waistband of my best skirt and listening to the television. The news presenter was droning on about the usual global disasters, but my little living-room was warm and serene. Violent death always happened elsewhere to people I had never met, and the Rectory was an oasis of peace, immune from the carnage which raged in the surrounding desert—or so I had always thought until that evening when Nicholas came to tell me what had happened to Stacy.

I knew straight away that something was wrong because no one ever disturbed me in the evenings unless there was an emergency, and besides, Nicholas was supposed to be away for the weekend. I had heard Lewis return to the house with someone half an hour before, but it had never occurred to me that the someone might be Nicholas. Normally at that hour I would have been in the kitchen cooking, but since Nicholas was supposed to be away and Stacy had retired sick to the curate's flat, Lewis had given me the evening off.

I opened the door. Nicholas was looking haggard, shattered, greyish. His normally neat brown hair was disordered. His eyes were bloodshot.

He said: "Alice, I have something very difficult and very painful to say," and at once I thought: Rosalind's been killed in a car crash. But I believe I knew, even before this pathetic sentence slithered across my mind, that the violent death didn't belong to Rosalind.

Nicholas said: "It's Stacy. Something's happened to him, something terrible. I'm so sorry, Alice, so very sorry, I know how fond of him you were."

"He's dead."

"Yes, but there's more I have to tell you."

I knew what that meant, but I found I was unable to utter the word "suicide." All I could whisper was: "How?"

"There was a rope. He used a beam in the roof."

For a split second I visualized the scene but then my imagination blacked out. I heard myself saying in an absurdly calm voice: "I'm to blame," and then as the shock curled over me like a huge tidal wave, I felt as if I were drowning, wiped out along with my cherished oasis by primitive forces far beyond all human control.

I I

Nicholas looked stupefied. "*Your* fault? But my dear Alice—"

I started to explain but after one stumbling sentence he interrupted: "You know what was going on, don't you?" and when I nodded dumbly he moved at once to the intercom in the kitchen.

"Lewis," I heard him say. "There's another angle on all this. You'd better join us." Turning back to me he gestured to the sofa and we both sat down. "I was about to call the emergency services," he said, "but that can wait. It's vital that we pool our knowledge so that we can work out exactly what happened."

I nodded, trying to wipe the tears from my eyes, and as we sat down James wriggled through the catflap; he always knew when Nicholas was around. Nicholas picked him up and arranged him carefully in my lap. I began to stroke the stripey fur.

Lewis entered the flat with difficulty, shoved the door shut with one of his crutches, laid a comforting hand briefly on my shoulder and sat down abruptly on the dining-chair which Nicholas had pulled close to the sofa. Like Nicholas he was looking haggard, but unlike Nicholas he showed no sign of being battered by grief. I was sure he was experiencing powerful emotions, but he was in control of them. I could sense his mind focusing sharply on the key problems: how to protect Nicholas, how to evict the dark forces which had invaded the Rectory, how to ensure our survival. Suddenly I felt a fraction less frightened, but the easing of fear opened the way for a fresh onslaught of grief. I began to cry.

"There, there!" said Lewis, effortlessly slipping into a paternal role. "You've had a terrible shock. Nicholas, make some tea."

"I'm all right," I said. "I'm all right." But I wasn't. I stifled the sobs but the tears kept coming. When Nicholas returned to the kitchen and James slipped off my lap to follow him, Lewis heaved himself onto the sofa so that he could sit beside me. "Dear little Alice!" he said. "I'm so sorry." And somehow when he spoke as gently as that it was hard to remember his chronic grumpiness. Very tentatively, my eyes still blurred with tears, I found his hand and held his thumb. I didn't quite dare to hold the whole hand in case he recoiled at my familiarity, but he at once curved his palm around my fingers. His customary smell of whisky, cigarettes and Pears soap was immensely comforting.

Nicholas returned with a mug of tea and sat down inches away from me in the chair Lewis had vacated. I took a sip from the mug and found the tea had been well sweetened. In relief I drank some more.

At last I said: "I knew something had gone very wrong, but the trouble didn't seem at first to be centred on Stacy. I just thought—" But I had to break off and pretend to sip tea.

Lewis said: "Take your time. Your evidence is very important. There's nothing we can do now for Stacy, but we can still fight to save Nicholas's ministry at St. Benet's."

I nodded but I was barely listening to him. I was looking back over the past week at the Rectory and trying to pinpoint the moment when everything had started to go wrong . . .

III

In my memory I saw Rosalind, arriving at the Rectory with Nicholas on Tuesday afternoon. I'm not saying life was trouble-free before her arrival—obviously we all had our problems, since we were human beings and not robots—but the problems seemed to be manageable and we jogged along comfortably enough. After all, one can live very happily with several kegs of dynamite provided that there are no matches around. But Rosalind was the box of matches, and all it takes to light a fuse is a single flame.

At the time I was blissfully content. Even *my* problems had become manageable once I had the right job and the right home. I loved my little flat which looked out over the jungly garden and I loved having a cat again and I loved being part of the St. Benet's team. Best of all I loved looking after my three men—my substitute father, substitute brother and substitute husband—and keeping them all well fed and neatly organised. Those feminists who believe women are debased by caring for men in this way just don't have a clue what real life's all about. I feel so sorry for them sometimes.

Anyway, there I was, so happy that I'd even lost interest in rum raisin ice cream, when disaster struck and Rosalind arrived. Nicholas said she was planning to live permanently at the Rectory and would be staying for a while to work out how the house could best be altered into a family home. I was horrified because she was such a malign presence; I could sense that beneath her immaculate exterior she was a mass of churning emotions, all of them unhappy. Nicholas clearly adored her, and at first I tormented myself by thinking of them having magnificent sex in their vast double-bed, but within forty-eight hours I'd begun to believe that grade-A sex wouldn't be—couldn't be—on the agenda. Rosalind was too unhappy. Sex was around somewhere, had to be, since Nicholas adored her so much, but I sensed it would be shadowed in some way, sort of maimed and off-colour—and suddenly the memory popped up in my mind of that tragic scene in the famous film *Don't Look Now* when the characters played by Donald Sutherland and Julie Christie have sex not to express their love for each other but to anaesthetise themselves from their problems.

This visit of Rosalind's was utterly different from her previous visits. Nicholas was very tense, quite unlike himself, and Rosalind, usually so silky and self-assured, was spiky and restless. I had already spent much time trying to work out why Nicholas was so besotted with this detestable woman, and now, when she was clearly infecting him with her unhappiness, I considered the puzzle afresh, but no explanation I dreamed up ever satisfied me. I accepted that love wasn't always sensible, but I still didn't see how he could even like her. She didn't share his interests. She didn't even bother to go to the eight o'clock service with him on the morning after her arrival. She obviously hated the Rectory and couldn't wait to strip it of all its quirky individuality. (Okay, the kitchen *was* a bit dog-eared, but who cared? I certainly didn't, but Rosalind the Wrecker obviously thought the entire house was fit only for the scrap-heap.) What on earth was Nicholas doing with such a creature? The whole marriage struck me as totally bizarre.

In the end I was so disturbed by the prospect of Rosalind inhabiting the Rectory on a permanent basis that I confessed my anxiety to Lewis, but he was reassuring. "Don't worry, my dear," he said. "The plan will never work—she'll lose interest and go back to her garden at Butterfold. But nevertheless," he added sharply as I sagged with relief, "we have to do all we can to try to make this experiment successful. Otherwise when it fails and they look around for someone to blame, we'll be the prime candidates."

I knew then, although Lewis was always careful never to say a word against Rosalind, that he disliked her as much as I did and was as appalled as I was by the thought of her coming to live among us. It was Stacy, not Lewis, who regarded Rosalind through rose-tinted spectacles.

"She's so elegant!" he sighed to me after her arrival that week. "So regal! I like to think of Nick being married to someone like that. Only someone really high-class could ever be worthy of him."

This sort of sentimental twaddle irritated me so much that I behaved just like Aunt. "She's not particularly high-class," I said tartly. "Her father was just a country solicitor."

"But her grandfather owned a lot of land in that village where Nick grew up!"

"Probably just an acre of garden plus a paddock for the pony."

However, Stacy was determined to cling to his vision of Queen Rosalind, the only woman in England good enough for his hero. Stacy worshipped Nicholas. It was all part of his abnormality. "Abnormality" may seem a harsh word, but it *is* abnormal for a man in his mid-twenties to dote on his boss with the passion of a thirteen-year-old idolising a rock-star. Stacy was immature, indulging in behaviour he should have outgrown years ago, and it occurred to me as I brooded on his arrested development that what he really needed was a dynamic female to blast him out of his adolescence.

Once when I was peeling potatoes—I have so many creative thoughts at the kitchen sink—I thought Francie could play the necessary *femme fatale*. She had plenty of oomph and was, as I well knew, indestructibly warm-hearted; I thought she might take Stacy on out of sheer generosity of spirit even though she was a practising Christian and (presumably) anti-adultery. However, this brilliant idea came to nothing because I soon realised that Francie was never going to look twice at any man except Nicholas. She was madly in love with him. Of course she did a wonderful job in passing off her passion as harmless hero-worship, but I was ultra-sensitive to all the feminine adoration which swirled around Nicholas and eventually it dawned on me that Francie was not only nuts about him but might just possibly be nuts about everything. I had no proof of such fullscale nuttiness. This was just my intuition working at full blast, but as soon as I sensed that Francie was far nuttier than anyone imagined I started to observe her much more closely in the hope that I would find the proof which would confirm my intuition.

I noticed, whenever we met for coffee, that her husband was usually abroad somewhere. I already knew her children were away at boarding school, but now I picked up the unspoken message that they were teenagers who didn't want their mother fussing around them whenever they were at home. In short, life on the home front was a desert. She was always saying how busy she was, but it seemed to me that her social life only woke up when her husband came home—and even then it merely consisted of attending corporate events with him or giving dinner-parties for his business acquaintances. She appeared to have no close friends apart from Rosalind, but from the tart comments Francie was now making about her I soon realised that beneath the show of friendship lay envy and dislike.

I saw then that Francie's warm, outgoing manner, cultivated for her work at St. Benet's, was no more than a mask, and beyond the mask was the real Francie: isolated, needy and simmering with convoluted emotions which were all stealthily becoming focused on Nicholas. Certainly she was much too preoccupied to vamp Stacy, who was meanwhile continuing his career as an elderly adolescent.

I was just brooding on Stacy's problems for the umpteenth time when suddenly, quite without warning, he began to act out of character.

Stacy was actually great fun. I've been unfair, emphasising the Nicholas-worship and implying he was nerdish. Sunny-natured, keen to help, keen to please, keen to be kind to everyone he met, he bounded around with a zest which only a kill-joy would have criticised. Every now and then he was downcast when reality failed to meet his joyous expectations, but he always bounced back quickly and sallied forth once more with his optimism intact. Sometimes I felt he was too innocent, too nice-natured, to cope with the harsher facts of life, and this made me wonder how suited he really was for the ministry of healing which so often involved working with the depressed, the damaged and the dying. I wondered too if he himself ever questioned his suitability or whether his child-like optimism was his way of shutting out truths which he found too difficult to face. That was why, when he began to act out of character, I was immediately very worried. I thought he might be finally cracking up, unable to come to terms with the fact that he was in the wrong job and unable to imagine a separation from his beloved Nicholas.

He began to behave oddly on Thursday, two days after Rosalind's arrival, when the atmosphere at the Rectory was so tense that I half-expected it to twang whenever I took a deep breath. Even Shirin our cleaner, who probably thought we were all odd, seemed extra-shy and extra-nervous, as if our western life-style had reached new heights of eccentricity.

At four o'clock in the afternoon, long after Shirin had trundled back into Tower Hamlets after her morning's work, Stacy came home early from the Healing Centre. I was taking a bag of rubbish out to the dustbins which stood tucked out of sight of Egg Street on the side of the Rectory which faced the office building. There had once been a basement entrance there but it had been closed off when the kitchen was moved upstairs, so when I took out the rubbish I had to use the front door.

As I stepped outside that afternoon with the garbage bag in my hand I saw Stacy chatting with his girlfriend. Tara was large, almost as large as I'd been on my arrival at the Rectory, and although she was so jolly and good-hearted she wasn't in the least pretty so I couldn't help wondering how Stacy avoided comparing her to his sisters and finding her wanting. Stacy pined for his sisters. He pined for his mother too, but he pined for those three girls more. Two were brunettes and one was a redhead. In their photographs all were slim, and his favourite—raven-haired, blue-eyed Aisling—was beautiful. Stacy had shed a tear when showing me her wedding pictures but I had pretended not to see it. I knew the Irish had no tradition of maintaining a stiff upper lip, but nevertheless I had felt embarrassed, as if I had uncovered yet another abnormal streak in Stacy's personality. Surely one didn't get so emotional about a sister's marriage? But maybe, if one was Irish, one did; maybe Stacy's habit of showing the photos of Aisling's wedding to everyone he met was the height of Irish normality.

As I began to lug the garbage around to the side of the house I waved at Stacy and Tara and they waved back, Tara calling: "Cheers, Alice!" in her usual friendly fashion. Having disposed of the bag I returned indoors, and I was just pottering around the kitchen again when Stacy bounced in and demanded to know the menu for dinner.

"Steak-and-kidney pie," I said, "potatoes and cabbage, stewed apples and custard to follow."

"Wowee!" exclaimed Stacy, typically joyous, utterly normal. I deduced that he had finally dredged up the courage to ask Tara for another date. Then he said: "Mrs. Darrow's just waved to me from her flat and I'm going up to see her."

Off he went, bounding up the main staircase in a succession of receding thuds.

I began to make the pie. Some time afterwards Nicholas wandered in, looking pale and drawn, and said he and Rosalind would be present for dinner that night after all; he was sorry for any inconvenience this would cause me. I was surprised by this decision, since Rosalind had always given the impression of being too grand for a communal meal, but I assured him there was no difficulty as the pie was large and I could cook extra vegetables. He then sat down and watched for a while in silence as I prepared the food. He liked to do that. He seemed to find it relaxing, and again I sensed the jagged edges of his profound anxiety.

I was now sure he was having terrible trouble with Rosalind, but I couldn't work out what the trouble was. Surely if he adored her he would be glad that she was planning this horrible take-over of the Rectory? But perhaps I'd got it all wrong and his troubles had nothing to do with Rosalind at all. Maybe they were spiritual troubles (whatever that meant). I knew he had been to see his nun that morning. Lewis had said so when he had been explaining to me why Nicholas would be missing both the eight o'clock service and the communal breakfast.

I had long since learnt that clergymen didn't wait until there was an emergency before they made an appointment to see their spiritual directors, but nevertheless I felt sure that on this occasion an emergency must exist. For Nicholas to pass up both the service and the communal breakfast was unprecedented. I wondered why he couldn't have seen his nun later in the day. The obvious answer was that a crisis had demanded immediate action.

I had noticed at breakfast that Lewis was barely touching his food. This too was unprecedented. As I now sculpted the pastry of the pie and recalled his lack of appetite I felt the knot of anxiety tighten in the pit of my stomach.

Suddenly I realised Nicholas was talking after a long silence. He was making a brief, moving speech about how *I* was the healer at the Rectory, and implying that the official healers were the ones who needed to be healed. I knew by this time that the "official healers" always themselves received the laying-on of hands at the healing services in acknowledgement of the fact that everyone in this imperfect world was in need of healing of some kind, but Nicholas was now giving this fact a very special slant. I hardly knew what to say—and I certainly couldn't imagine what had led him to pay me such an extraordinary compliment—but I picked up the hidden message that he was in pain and that I was somehow helping him simply by being there, so I didn't say: "What a load of old codswallop!" and look embarrassed. I just thanked him as simply as I could and got on with making the pie.

Nicholas smiled. That meant he was feeling better. He stroked James behind the ears, and as James purred I suddenly felt so happy, so absolutely at one with the world, that I didn't care about that horrible wife of his any more. At that moment I also found I could believe Lewis's prediction that the plan to remodel the Rectory would come to nothing and Rosalind would return permanently to Butterfold. I didn't expect that Nicholas would then stop adoring her and turn to me; I wasn't nuts like Francie. But at least, once Rosalind had slotted back into Butterfold, we'd all recover our equilibrium and live in harmony again.

All I wanted was for life to go on as before. I knew I couldn't expect more than that, but I felt that so long as I was living at the Rectory and looking after Nicholas as well as I possibly could for five days out of seven each week, I'd be content. More or less. Of course in my lonelier moments I'd have liked more, but that wasn't possible and one always had to recognise what was possible and what wasn't. The fact was that Nicholas was never going to desire me sexually. I was quite clear about that and was even glad my ugliness gave me no chance to deceive myself. If I'd been as attractive as Francie, I might have succumbed to all sorts of pathetic illusions and wound up just as nuts as she was.

But I wasn't nuts. I did love Nicholas but I didn't deceive myself about the situation. Of course before I'd come to the Rectory I'd been like Stacy, an elderly adolescent in the grip of hero-worship; I'd been infatuated, nurturing a big romantic dream—not a delusion, as Francie now seemed to be experiencing, but a fantasy which I knew at heart was unreal. Francie, I was sure, had lost sight of the fact that her infatuation was unreal, but then Francie was very unhappy and I wasn't, not now. I had my three men who all cared about me, and I had the respect of the people who worked at the Centre. I did a useful job well and derived immense satisfaction from it. In short, reality was so stimulating nowadays that romantic dreams took a back seat. I didn't exactly discard the dreams, but as I was able to see how unreal they were, I was able to keep them in their correct place. So although I occasionally still found myself day-dreaming of marrying Nicholas I never for one moment kidded myself that this was ever going to happen. Nicholas adored Rosalind and would stay married to her for ever. I accepted those two facts completely. But I accepted too that I loved him. I couldn't not accept it. It was the most real thing in the world for me, a gift from God (the real, living God, not Aunt's fossilised, useless old relic) and no one, not even horrible Rosalind, could ever snuff it out.

The love I felt for Nicholas enriched me. It made the world seem inexhaustibly rewarding and worthwhile. In fact sometimes I felt the gift wasn't love but life itself, but then I knew that love *was* life—or rather, love was the driving force of life, the energy which powered not only the world but the whole universe—or so it seemed to me whenever Nicholas sought my company, whenever he sat at the kitchen table in silence and watched me work.

Yes, I loved Nicholas. But by this time I loved not a perfect hero who didn't exist but a man who was as flawed as any other human being. I saw him in the light of reality. I saw all his faults: the way he worked too hard, leaving too little time for his family; the detachment which kept people at arm's length all the time he was caring for them; the solitary nature which would make true intimacy difficult; the arrogance which lurked always in the shadow of his genuine humility. I saw him as akin to Kipling's "cat which walked by himself," a splendid cat, powerful and arresting—but as dangerous as a tiger on the prowl. The staff at the Healing Centre had plenty of stories of women who had fallen for Nicholas and writhed in humiliating enslavement beneath the weight of his meticulous, professional caring which never once strayed into impropriety. He did do great good in his ministry, but the big state secret of the Healing Centre was that he also, without meaning to and while acting with the very highest motives, did much harm. It's degrading to wallow in a mire of unrequited love which can so easily slip over the edge into a pathetic infatuation. Francie wasn't the only one who had drifted onto the emotional rocks surrounding Nicholas. The shipwrecks in those chaotic waters were legion.

I kept asking myself why Nicholas didn't see what was happening to Francie. Then I realised that he probably did see but was waiting for the right opportunity to get her into treatment—and wash his hands of her. That was no doubt sensible, professional behaviour, but at the same time it implied that whenever broken people displayed too many jagged edges he disappeared behind bullet-proof glass and left others to clear up the mess. Perhaps he thought that so long as he himself behaved according to the rules, attending Communion daily and treating his clients with his morally correct but psychologically bruising detachment, his God would sort out all the boring women who fell for him and made fools of themselves. But I wondered sometimes what his God really thought of this very streetwise retreat from the damaged people who looked to him for healing.

Personally I felt that *my* God—the God that wasn't quite Nicholas's but certainly wasn't Aunt's—the God who had begun to inch stealthily into my mind and stroke all my muddled thoughts into some sort of coherent shape—*my* God, I felt, would have wanted much more co-operation from Nicholas in sorting out the human shipwrecks. Nicholas should have seen that more was required of him here; after all, he did care about people and he was so often unusually perceptive. I realised he had to be careful in order to preserve his reputation, but I still wondered if his lethal detachment sprang purely from a desire to protect his good name and play the game by the rules. Sometimes I thought that perhaps, deep down, he feared the temptation these women represented when they revealed their rampant sexual desire—but I always dismissed this theory because I knew he adored Rosalind and so therefore no temptation to commit adultery could exist.

I finished the pie and with Nicholas still watching me silently I decided to peel the potatoes.

As usual, when a spell at the kitchen sink was in the offing, I then began to meditate creatively. If I really loved Nicholas, I told myself, I was safe from madness because real love had nothing to do with wanting to control the beloved and then raging around in frustration when control proved not merely elusive but impossible. Real love wasn't possessive. Of course I was a bit jealous of Rosalind—just a bit—every now and then—but that was natural. If I'd had no twinge of jealousy I would have been inhuman. But what I wanted above all, I thought as I brainwashed myself fiercely, was the best for Nicholas, and if the best for him was Rosalind, then so be it.

I offered this conclusion cautiously to the God who was now moseying around in my mind like some clever, elegant caterpillar, inching hither and thither, laying trails, exploring the uncultivated, disorganised environment with a peculiarly unconditional acceptance of all the mess and muddle. Then I added silently to my elegant caterpillar whom I knew I would one day see as the most beautiful butterfly: "Please help me *never* to stand in the way of what's best for Nicholas, *never* to be possessive and selfish and *never* to deflect him from his job of serving you as well as he can." And in a burst of longing I tacked on an additional request which seemed to bypass my brain altogether and come straight from the heart. Soundlessly I cried to my caterpillar: "Please use me to help Nicholas somehow—use me, use me, use me!"—and then I saw this had already happened; Nicholas had been talking of how I was the real healer at the Rectory and he was behaving as if I had made him feel better.

Of course I knew the main healing power came from God—or Christ—or the Holy Spirit—or whatever one wanted to call it, so I didn't succumb to delusions of grandeur about my ability to heal. Nevertheless it did occur to me that by loving Nicholas as I did, by wanting the best for him and by shutting out all self-centred possessiveness, I was the ideal channel, not polluted, not clogged up, my own minuscule healing power aligned accurately with its source. Perhaps by loving Nicholas in this way, I thought, I might somehow help God to keep him safe not only from the dark side of his ministry but from the dark side of his personality—the arrogance, the obstinacy and that glamorous detachment which guaranteed that he stayed secretly uncommitted in a career where commitment was developed to a fine art.

I suddenly realised Nicholas was talking again. Switching off the meditation I began to tune in to what he was saying.

He was confiding in me obliquely, signalling that he was worried about Stacy and Francie. It was a relief to know for certain that he had realised Francie was a problem, but at the same time I was worried that the full extent of her nuttiness might be unknown to him. On Monday night she had arrived, overwrought and underdressed, at the Rectory in pursuit of her adored one. As Nicholas was away Lewis had dealt with her but I was unsure how much he would have been able to say about the interview afterwards, particularly if Francie had turned the interview into a confession. Casually I now mentioned to Nicholas how Francie had been wild-eyed, her breasts almost popping out of her low-cut nightdress, and at once my suspicions were confirmed. Nicholas was staggered by the information; I had the clear impression that although he knew of her visit he knew no details. Lewis, it seemed, had been superbly discreet, but I wasn't a clergyman and nothing had been confessed to me so I felt no obligation to match his discretion. Choosing my words with care and using a studiedly neutral voice I described Francie's appearance in a way which left Nicholas in no doubt she was round the twist.

I would have said more but at that point we were interrupted—which was a pity, but at least he now knew Francie was in a different league from the usual adoring groupies who haunted St. Benet's. These women—and I had met a couple of them—were still capable of dressing appropriately and keeping up appearances. Francie wasn't. After all, you don't turn up in your porn-shop nightwear at the house of your employer unless you've either received some hefty encouragement or else are totally freaked out, and I was prepared to bet my jumbo steak-and-kidney pie that Nicholas had done no encouraging.

Meanwhile, as these thoughts were zipping across my mind, Lewis was storming into the kitchen in a filthy temper and demanding to know where Stacy was. Apparently Stacy was supposed to be on duty at the church, but no doubt the chance meeting with Tara followed by the glimpse of Rosalind waving from the window had induced amnesia. This was all very typical of Stacy, well known for his scattiness, so I didn't think twice about it. Instead I concentrated on trying to calm Lewis down, but while he was still seething, that awful Venetia Hoffenberg rang up and instantly he was tamed.

Lewis was being very silly about Venetia. He ought to have been old enough to know better. I felt sad about this silliness because he had been such a splendid clergyman when he had coped with her at Lady Cynthia's lunch-party. Of course he was still a splendid clergyman, I knew that, but that was exactly why I hated to see evidence of the fact that even the best clerics can occasionally be absolute ninnies, just like the rest of us. Stacy, innocent as ever, had no idea what was going on and neither had anyone who didn't live at the Rectory, but Nicholas and I were in agony, praying that this weird bout of senile passion would rapidly burn itself out. Naturally Nicholas and I had never exchanged a single word on the subject, but we didn't have to. We each knew what the other was thinking, and that was why, when Lewis bolted to the bedsit to take the call, Nicholas and I merely exchanged looks and remained tight-lipped.

I sighed as I returned to the potatoes. It was just so obvious to me that Lewis needed a nice, kind, youngish widow devoted to Anglo-Catholicism, not this non-churchgoing old bag with a drink problem who probably couldn't even boil an egg.

Even before Venetia's call it had dawned on me that Stacy had probably taken Rosalind up to the curate's flat for her long-delayed treat: a private viewing of Aisling's wedding photographs, and when Nicholas finally buzzed the curate's flat on the intercom and found Stacy at home, I realised I had been right. Nicholas ordered him to go at once to the church. There was a nasty moment shortly afterwards when Stacy, rushing downstairs, was pounced on by Lewis, who had finished talking to Venetia, but I heard Nicholas sort them out in the hall and send Stacy on his way. I didn't actually see Stacy at that point, as I'd remained in the kitchen, but if he'd been looking upset I would have assumed he was distressed by his bout of amnesia.

An interval followed during which I was on my own, preparing the vegetables. Nicholas was in his study for a short time. When I heard him go upstairs I presumed he was going to talk to Rosalind, but soon afterwards he returned downstairs and I heard the bedsit door open and close as he slipped in to see Lewis. It was during their conversation, which lasted some time, that Stacy crept back into the house after closing the church. This was the first obvious instance of him acting out of character, because he never crept anywhere; he bounded and bounced. Unable to believe he could ever enter the house without banging the front door I looked out into the hall for fear some down-and-out had picked the lock, and as soon as I saw Stacy's face I knew that something had gone very wrong.

I V

"*Stacy*—" I tried to detain him to find out what had happened, but he rushed on without stopping. Although I heard him mutter: "Sorry—got to—" he never completed the sentence before disappearing at top speed in the direction of the backstairs.

I made no attempt to follow him, partly because the meal was now at a crucial stage but mostly because at this point Nicholas left the bedsit and drifted tensely back into the kitchen. Rosalind, he informed me, wouldn't be dining with us after all (wretched woman, messing me around again!) because she wasn't hungry; she'd had a large lunch at Fortnum's with Francie.

I was astonished. I could think of no reason why Francie, now totally bananas about Nicholas, should wish to have lunch with his wife. It was hard to believe that the fiction of bosom friendship could still be sustained.

Tentatively I enquired: "How did Francie seem to Rosalind?" At the very least she had to be tanked up on gin to avoid appearing bogged down with gloom. She had already been off sick that week with depression, and the thought of seeing her arch-rival would have made her feel more depressed than ever—or so I assumed. But I was wrong.

"She took a little time to get going," said Nicholas without expression, "but by the end of the meal she was in fine fettle. The word Rosalind used to describe her was 'radiant.' "

"Gosh!" This made no sense at all. In the silence that followed I tried to remember what I'd read in the medical column of *The Times* about that illness which drives people to be suicidal at one moment and high as a kite the next. Maybe Francie was even nuttier than I'd imagined.

Before I could dwell further on this thought, Nicholas decided to feed the cat. We kept tinned catfood for James but I cooked fish for him regularly and on that day there was cold boiled cod on the menu, disgusting for humans but James loved it. As Nicholas put the plate on the floor, James arched his back in ecstasy before thrusting his nose towards the food.

I was just about to tell Nicholas about the new vitamin-enriched cat-snack which I'd seen advertised on TV, when Lewis arrived for dinner. There was no sign of Stacy and after removing from the oven the glowing pie I went to the intercom to summon him.

Eventually I heard him whisper: "Yes?"

"Dinner," I said. "Are you okay?" But the connection had been severed before I could complete the question.

I served up the vegetables and adorned the bowl of potatoes with a sprig of parsley. By this time Lewis was making the usual greedy sighs and saying how wonderful I was. I loved his enthusiasm for my cooking, and nowadays I hardly ever cooked French recipes because both Lewis and Stacy so enjoyed the English classics. Nicholas was always polite enough to say how much he enjoyed them too, but he had no *passion* for food as Lewis and I had—although that night I wasn't feeling hungry; I was too aware of being needled by a pervasive, steadily expanding anxiety. I helped myself to only one potato, a mere spoonful of cabbage and a slimmish slice of pie.

Finally Stacy arrived, slipping into the room as silently as a ghost. Nicholas said grace. We began to eat. Stacy said nothing but bolted his food and vanished. A few minutes later the front door banged shut as he rushed out.

Knowing that Stacy's behaviour was highly abnormal but wanting to defend him from Lewis's inevitable acid comments, I pretended all was well by declaring Stacy must have been dashing off to see Tara. Lewis disagreed, saying it was more likely that Stacy had a date with Gilbert Tucker, the friendly gay clergyman who had helped Nicholas organise the AIDS seminar. I couldn't think why Lewis was implying Stacy was gay when it was so obvious he wasn't, but Lewis was very fractious that evening, overtired and fit only for a nursing home for convalescents. If ever I have to have a hip replaced (which God forbid) I'd take convalescence very seriously indeed instead of pretending it wasn't necessary. Why do men so often put the need to be macho before the need to use their common sense? I was getting cross with Lewis for being so dumb, but perhaps by that time I was as overstrained as he was.

After the meal Lewis went to bed early (common sense finally triumphed) and Nicholas withdrew to his study. I stacked the dishwasher, cleaned up, made myself an extra cup of decaf, sat around thinking of nothing in particular. After a while I realised I was waiting for Stacy to come back, but he didn't return and eventually James and I padded down the backstairs to my flat. I thought I might watch television but I found I couldn't be bothered to switch on the set. I looked in the fridge but there was nothing I wanted to eat.

At last I had a bath, put on my dressing-gown and started to read

Good Housekeeping but none of the recipes interested me. I was just yawning my way through the last pages when I heard the front door slam shut. Speeding up the backstairs I saw from the end of the passage that Stacy had returned and Nicholas had waylaid him in the hall; as I watched, the two of them disappeared into the study. Neither of them saw me. Returning to the basement I stripped off my nightdress and dressing-gown, pulled on a bra, sweater, briefs and stretchpants, and beetled all the way up the backstairs to the curate's flat.

V

Stacy arrived a minute later. He was breathing hard, having raced upstairs, and he was obviously on the verge of tears. As soon as he saw me I said: "Look, I don't want to butt in where I'm not wanted, but please, please tell me if there's anything I can do to help because I hate to see you so upset."

Stacy's defences immediately crumbled. At first I thought he'd expended so much energy on holding himself together during his conversation with Nicholas that he'd run out of the strength needed to suppress his tears, but then I realised he was merely touched by what I'd done. I'd stayed up late; I'd hauled myself all the way up to his flat to wait for him; I obviously cared. Stacy, distraught and tormented, was almost speechless with gratitude.

"Oh Alice!" he managed to say. "I do love you—you're as good as a sister to me!" Then he collapsed in a heap on the sofa and sobbed. That was the moment when suddenly, in a blinding flash of insight, I understood him through and through. His central problem was that he always wanted a sister, never a girlfriend or a wife. If only he could have grown up sufficiently to let go of those three ravishing sirens, Siobhan, Sinead and Aisling! Then he could have married jolly Tara and lived happily ever after, but that was never going to happen because Stacy had got lost somewhere along the road to adult life and now he was perpetually in thrall to the desire for loving relationships where sex was utterly forbidden.

"Dearest Stacy . . ." I put my arm around him comfortingly and held his hand in mine.

Eventually he found he wanted to blow his nose but neither of us had a handkerchief. There ought to have been some Kleenex somewhere—that staple soft furnishing at the Rectory—but he couldn't remember where the box was and the flat was such a mess that I could have searched for half an hour without success, so I went to the bathroom and grabbed the entire roll of toilet paper.

At last when he was too exhausted to cry any more he whispered: "Alice, do you know much about AIDS?"

"Well, I'm not living in a glass bubble down there in the hellhole," I said startled. "I'm not about to ask you what the word AIDS means." My first thought was that a friend of his had been diagnosed as HIV-positive.

"You know you can't get it by holding hands with an infected person or by breathing his breath?"

"Yes, I know all that," I said, trying not to sound impatient. Then I realised I was holding his hand and breathing his breath. Horror gripped me. "My God, Stacy, are you trying to tell me—"

"I think I may have HIV," he said, and started sobbing again.

I never slackened my grip on his hand and I never altered my position on the sofa beside him. I had to concentrate in order to achieve this immobility, but nevertheless I was aware of upsetting thoughts bolting around my brain, incredulous thoughts, questioning thoughts, all of which were hard to focus on. In the end I could only say: "Is that very likely?" I was trying to remember what I'd read about AIDS being contracted from a contaminated blood transfusion. I couldn't recall Stacy telling me of a time when he had been so seriously ill that a blood transfusion had been required, but perhaps the illness had been a long time ago.

"I want to believe it isn't likely," he said, "but I saw Gil Tucker tonight and he said I had to act on the assumption that it was possible—he's arranging for me to have an AIDS test tomorrow at one."

"But Stacy, why on earth did you go to Gil Tucker? Why didn't you go straight to Nicholas?"

Stacy dissolved into tears again.

"Oh Stacy . . ." I put both arms around him and gave him a hug. "I didn't mean to sound cross, I just felt so confused—and I don't want to be confused, I want to understand everything so that I can sympathise with you properly. How does Gil fit into all this? Forgive me if I'm being stupid but I can't quite see—"

"Gil knew an old friend of mine from Liverpool who used to come to London regularly to attend the Synod and who was interested in the Gay Christians. Gil told me tonight that this old friend of mine had died of AIDS. I didn't know. We'd lost touch, although I think if he'd lived longer he would have made contact again and told me—but he died quickly, he got the pneumonia, the lethal sort that AIDS patients get, and—"

"Wait a minute, when you say 'old friend'—"

"He was called Gordon. I said to Gil: 'But surely he must have been HIV-positive for years, he must have known,' but Gil said not necessarily, you pick up the virus, you have some flu-type symptoms, you get better, you don't have the test, you go into denial—until you start to get very ill—"

"But Stacy—"

"He was much older than me but he was so interesting, so kind, so—"

"You're saying—no, you can't be, I'm sorry, I know I must seem as thick as two planks but I'm not understanding any of this—" But I was. I felt vaguely revolted but above all else I was baffled. "Stacy, how could you have a homosexual affair when you're not gay?"

To my astonishment this proved to be exactly the right thing to say. Stacy sagged with relief, wiped the last tears from his eyes, clasped my hand tightly in gratitude and said: "You don't think I'm gay do you, Alice?"

"No, of course not. You're in love with Aisling."

Stacy looked appalled. "But how could I be in love with my sister?"

Instantly I realised that this subject couldn't be pursued. "Well, never mind that," I said rapidly. "Tell me why you wanted to have sex with Gordon."

"Oh, but I didn't want to! It was all his idea, but I was never keen, I only did it because it seemed to mean so much to him and he'd been so good to me that I felt in his debt. He transformed my life, Alice. I was just a boy from the backstreets, I knew nothing, and he taught me about literature and music and art and religion and—oh, it was another world he introduced me to, it was such a miracle, such a gift—a gift from God, as I saw later—but of course the sex side of it was wrong and I'm not just saying that because of the Bible, I'm saying that because it felt wrong for *me*, I never really liked it, it was just a mechanical bore like shaving or brushing one's teeth or going to the toilet, so although I was pleased to make Gordon happy after all he'd done for me, I just couldn't wait to escape into the priesthood and switch him off. I had to have a good excuse to end it, you see, because I couldn't bear the thought of hurting him, but the priesthood gave me just the excuse I needed."

"So once you went to train at Mirfield—"

"As soon as I was accepted for Mirfield I told him there had to be a clean break, told him I couldn't see him again, told him not to write to me—but oh God, how guilty I felt, poor Gordon, I was so much in his debt, but I couldn't help it, Alice, I couldn't have gone on with that kind of sex any more, I'd had it, I wanted to move on—but when I did try and move on I seemed to be sort of paralysed, I'd never done it with a girl and I was afraid by that time I'd only be able to do it with men, I was afraid—oh, I was afraid of so many things, and the pretty girls all seemed to know so much and that made me more scared than ever because I knew so little, and the plain girls—well, I can't really get interested, and sometimes I think I don't want sex at all, with anyone, ever, but of course that's not done in our society today, is it, one's got to have sex or else one's just a nerd, despised by everyone—"

"Stacy, I'm sure things will work out—"

"Not if I've got HIV they won't," he said, and slid back again into despair.

VI

"But Stacy," I said, trying to focus on the medical facts in order to distract him from his tears, "surely it's been ages since you had sex with Gordon?"

"Yes, but they now think the virus can be around for a long time before the serious illnesses begin. The big question," said Stacy, grabbing another wad of toilet paper to soak up the tears, "is whether Gordon contracted HIV before or after we parted. And that's what we don't know."

"But surely if he was so keen on you he wouldn't have messed around with someone else?"

"That's what I said to Gil, but Gil said these things do happen. You see, I didn't like doing some of the things Gordon liked, and when Gordon realised this he said okay, forget it, it doesn't matter—but maybe it did matter, maybe when I wasn't around he had one-night stands so that he could do exactly what he liked. He wouldn't have seen it as infidelity, he'd think he was being kind, going elsewhere instead of bothering me."

"But if you were living with him surely you'd have known if—"

"Oh, I never lived with him!" Stacy looked horrified. "He was a churchwarden and a pillar of the community! And anyway I had to keep it from my family, didn't I? If my Mam and my sisters had ever found out it would have destroyed them utterly—in fact I'd have killed myself rather than have them find out, and that's why, if I have HIV, I've got to do everything possible to make sure they never know."

"Honestly, Stacy, I still can't believe it's likely that you're infected! If Gordon really loved you as much as you imply he did, he'd have passed up the peculiar stuff in order to be faithful to you!"

"You can't always tell who's going to be unfaithful," said Stacy, and suddenly looked so white that I thought he might faint.

"What do you mean?" I demanded, heart beating much faster. "Why do you say that? Why are you looking as if—"

"I'm just shit-scared. Dear God, if the test is positive—"

"Stacy, I really think you ought to tell Nicholas about all this," I said, by now baffled that this wasn't as obvious to him as it was to me, but at once Stacy was plunged back into panic.

"No, I can't—I can't—"

I tried to calm him down. "Look, I know he's your hero and you don't want to upset him, but I'm sure he'd—"

"*I can't tell him.* I CAN'T. I can't face him at all."

I opened my mouth and shut it again. By this time I was so baffled by Stacy's refusal to do the obvious that I was beginning to suspect there was more to this horror-story than he wanted to admit. I wondered again why he had chosen to confide in Gil Tucker. The obvious answer was that Gil was an AIDS expert, but Stacy, I was almost sure, had implied earlier that before he had seen Gil that night he had had no idea that Gordon had died of AIDS. Dimly I realised that the chronology of the crisis wasn't making sense.

"Hang on a minute," I said slowly, "I'm getting confused again. Stacy, you were actually upset and acting out of character *before* you went to see Gil Tucker this evening and heard about Gordon. Why did you want to see Gil in the first place? What was going on?"

Stacy's pallor increased. He closed his eyes and gripped my hand harder than ever and looked like death. My heart picked up speed again. Then a second after I realised how frightened I was, memory, reason and intuition all fused in my mind to produce the key I needed to unlock the mystery.

"It's all to do with Rosalind, isn't it?" I said.

Bull's-eye.

He stared at me in terror.

V I I

"*You* were okay before you went up to see her this afternoon," I said rapidly. "You came to the kitchen and asked me what was for dinner and you behaved exactly as you usually do. Then you said Rosalind had waved to you from the window of her flat and you were going up to see her. And off you went, still completely normal, but by the time dinner's ready, Rosalind's refusing to come downstairs and you're a zombie. So what the hell happened?"

Levering himself to his feet, Stacy blundered across the room to the bookshelves and dragged out a Bible. As he returned to me he said: "You've got to swear you'll never tell Nick what I'm going to say."

"I swear I'll never tell Nicholas what you're going to say." I removed my hand from the Bible and he slumped down beside me again. By this time I was so frightened that I felt sick. I was sure that Nicholas was somehow in danger—and perhaps too I sensed we were all in danger, all of us who lived at the Rectory, everyone who worked at the Healing Centre. I could almost see the darkness swirling around us and billowing to blot out the light.

Stacy was speaking again. His eyes were swollen and bloodshot, his pale skin mottled as if bruised by grief. His voice was no more than a whisper. He said: "I took Rosalind up to my flat to show her the photos of Aisling's wedding." Then he exclaimed violently: "I never want to see those pictures again!" And he began to shudder from head to toe.

I struggled to understand. "She polluted them in some way?"

"She polluted everything. She asked me to go to bed with her."

I finally lost control over my revulsion.

V I I

I had managed to cope with the possibility that he might have HIV. I had managed to cope with the information that he had once had a homosexual relationship with someone cultured and kind who had cared for him. But what I just couldn't take was the fact that he had betrayed Nicholas. I knew Rosalind's behaviour was far more revolting than his, but that made no difference; it came as no surprise to me that Rosalind should be capable of treachery. But Stacy's behavior not only appalled me but left me feeling horribly disillusioned. I had always thought him so innocent, so nice-natured, so fundamentally good, dedicating himself to serving God among the sick. Now I felt I could only see him as a weak, pathetic creature of no integrity who should never have become a clergyman.

But perhaps I had misunderstood him. Perhaps in my revulsion I had jumped to the wrong conclusion.

"But you didn't go to bed with her," I said, making the sentence not a question but a statement. "You turned her down."

"I wanted to. But I found I couldn't."

I lost my temper. "God, how feeble can you get! Why couldn't you have just said no?"

"Well, it was like the affair with Gordon all over again—I mean, there I was, just a boy from the backstreets of Liverpool, and Rosalind was so kind, taking such a special interest—"

"But you bloody idiot, this had nothing to do with kindness! This was all about cruelty and betrayal!"

"No, she really did want to be kind! She said she could see I needed a helping hand about how to get on with girls, and—"

"But this is Nicholas's wife we're talking about—*Nicholas's wife!* How could you possibly have—"

"She said they weren't sleeping together, she said it was all over, she said they were as good as divorced, she said Nick had been very cruel to her—"

"And you believed that?" I could hardly get my words out.

"Well, it did seem to explain why she felt free to be so kind to me—"

"But you fool, don't you see she was just spinning you a line to get what she wanted? Nicholas loves Rosalind—God knows why, but he does, he loves her. And now, just because that woman's so bloody bored and so bloody decadent that she'd even seduce her husband's curate for a cheap thrill, you go crashing around, smashing and bashing everything up—"

"You don't understand! I'm sure Rosalind was telling me the truth when she said—"

"That woman wouldn't recognise the truth even if it stepped up and slugged her on the jaw! She's a lying bitch—and you're just an overgrown child with no understanding of adult relationships at all!"

"Alice—"

"I think your behaviour's been absolutely disgusting!"

"But Alice, wait—once I was in bed with her, I—"

"And how dare you try to tell me the sordid details of what you got up to! You ought to be telling me instead about what you're going to say to Nicholas when he finds out!"

Stacy panicked again. "But he's never going to find out!"

"He will if you've got HIV and infected Rosalind!"

"But Alice, if you'd only let me explain—"

"You seem to be totally adrift from reality. Even if you don't have HIV, how can you go on working alongside Nicholas as if nothing's happened? How can you live with such a deception? And do you seriously think that Rosalind's going to keep her mouth shut? She's the sort of bitch who would boast about her conquests—it'll all get back to Nicholas in the end, you'll see, and then he'll kick you out and it'll serve you bloody well right!"

Stacy burst into tears again, but this time I had no strength to help him. I was emotionally drained, physically nauseated. Struggling to my feet I began to blunder from the room.

"Alice!" cried Stacy in despair. "Alice!"

But I never replied. We were severed from each other. It was as if a foul-smelling fog had swirled between us and choked our lungs.

Stumbling all the way down the stairs to the basement flat, I threw up again and again into the lavatory.

IX

I dragged myself exhausted to bed but I slept badly, and during one of my waking moments I heard footsteps above me in the kitchen. Switching on the light I looked at my alarm clock. The time was a minute after three.

Leaving the bed I pulled on my dressing-gown and crept cautiously upstairs in the hope that I would find Stacy raiding the fridge—I was already regretting my angry words earlier—but when I entered the kitchen I found Nicholas. He was wearing pyjamas and sitting bolt upright at the table. He had lit one of the rings of the gas stove but nothing was cooking on it, and his expression was baffled, as if he was having trouble working out where he was and what he was supposed to be doing. The whole scene was shot through and through with oddness, but when he confessed he'd been sleep-walking the mystery evaporated and I realised the oddness lay primarily in the random nature of the details: the circle of flames, the smart pyjamas, the absolute silence, the clock on the wall indicating a peculiar time, the sheen of Nicholas's fingernails as he gripped the edge of the table. To restore normality I turned off the gas, plugged in the electric kettle and made tea. Meanwhile Nicholas was recovering. He fetched a coat to keep himself warm, and when he sat down again at the table he seemed to me once more so exceptionally elegant, so overwhelmingly masculine and so mesmerisingly watchable that I felt faint with my physical desire for him.

That was when the truth dawned on me. I had ranted and raved at Stacy for going to bed with someone who was married, but deep down at the bottom of my mind this was exactly the sin I myself yearned to commit. Or in other words, I was no better than poor, pathetic, pitiable Stacy whom I had so brutally condemned in an orgy of self-righteousness. A horrified remorse replaced my niggling regret but I shut it out. I would deal later, I told myself, with the mess I had made of the scene with Stacy. At the moment Nicholas required my full attention.

Repressing my desire for him by a massive act of the will, I tried to open up the channel of healing again by asking God to use whatever shreds of unselfish, non-possessive love remained in me to fill the vacuum created by Rosalind's defection.

It was only then that I recalled Rosalind's assurance to Stacy that the marriage was finished, and realised this explained Nicholas's profound tension and unhappiness. It also occurred to me that only a marriage which was on the rocks in the worst possible way could begin to explain Rosalind's bizarre behaviour. Much as I disliked her I had to admit that she normally gave the impression of being someone who was clever, well organised and in perfect control of her life. Yet Stacy's seduction indicated a woman who was stupid, reckless and possibly even as nuts as Francie. Obviously I had been too cynical in jumping to the conclusion that Rosalind had been spinning lies to Stacy in order to get what she wanted. This conclusion was now looking just plain wrong. And maybe some of my other conclusions weren't looking so right either.

All kinds of thoughts then started to crawl out of the woodwork of my mind. I was imagining a divorced Nicholas, free to marry someone much better suited to him, and the vision appalled me. I didn't see how I could stay at the Rectory if he were to marry someone I could like, someone who would live there with him and be a real wife instead of a mostly absent partner; the situation would be far too painful to bear. I still passionately wanted the best for him, but if God was going to answer my prayers and send him the best possible wife, I couldn't stay around and watch him being happy with her. I wouldn't be able to live up to my high ideal of a selfless non-possessive love. I'd be jealous as hell and wind up wanting to scratch her eyes out. And how genuine had my selfless, non-possessive love been anyway? I might honestly have wanted to attain the ideal, but reality, buried deep at the bottom of my mind, had lain quite elsewhere.

Acknowledging how much I desired Nicholas enabled me to see for the first time what had really lain behind my violent dislike of Rosalind. I hadn't been just "a bit" jealous, as I had sunnily confessed to myself many times previously. I'd been very, very jealous indeed. The jealousy had been easy to suppress so long as she hadn't been around to remind me she was the woman in possession, but as soon as she had arrived at the Rectory to stake a claim I'd promptly begun to seethe with loathing and resentment. And to think I had gone on kidding myself that my love for Nicholas was utterly pure! I felt humiliated by my pathetic romantic illusions.

But meanwhile, as all these searing revelations were roaring through my brain, I was still sitting with Nicholas at the kitchen table and Nicholas himself was still upset and I was still trying to help by enfolding him with all the love, selfish and unselfish, which I possessed. It's amazing how even in extreme distress one's capable of doing several things at once. Remorse for the scene with Stacy, shame about my own pathetic delusions and shortcomings, grief at the thought of losing the man I loved to someone else in the future—all these powerful emotions were streaming along side by side with the concern for Nicholas which made me long to be a healing presence in that room.

He was talking about the three-day retreat he was planning to make with the Fordite monks and saying that he didn't want to go after all. I knew it couldn't be because he wanted to stay with Rosalind; he had already announced at dinner that she would be leaving for Butterfold in the morning—well, of course she would be; I was sure her prime desire now would be to escape from the scene of the disgusting behaviour with Stacy. But I didn't think Nicholas knew anything about that particular incident. She wouldn't have told him. And Stacy hadn't. And I couldn't. All I could do, when he said he didn't want to go on retreat, was to beg him to stay at the Rectory, but he was still under the illusion that it would be helpful to shut himself up with a bunch of monks for seventy-two hours, and I knew I could say nothing to dissuade him. Of course he was wrong. He needed to be loved and looked after in his own home—or so it seemed to me, but then I didn't really understand all that business about retreats and spiritual exercises. I just understood how it felt to be intolerably anxious about the future and desperately unhappy in consequence, but maybe the monks had some magic mystical cure which was far superior to anything I could offer to help him endure the pain.

"Thanks, Alice," said Nicholas at the end of our conversation. "Thanks for everything." And I realised not only that he knew how hard I'd been trying to help by enfolding him with love, but that he was sorry he could only exude his notorious detachment in response.

I went back to bed and wept at the thought of losing him to the perfect wife who would inevitably appear once he was free.

How self-centred I was being! And how pathetic I was too, loving this man who was never in a million years going to find me physically attractive! Wholly immersed in the most disgusting self-pity I prayed to God for the strength to behave with dignity once the new wife arrived.

It seems so terrible to me now in retrospect that I never once prayed for Stacy.

X

Nicholas left early the next morning, well before the eight o'clock service, and Stacy never left the curate's flat until the communal breakfast had finished. I did rush out into the hall to try to catch him before he left for work but he was too quick for me. By that time I was feeling so guilty about the hash I'd made of our conversation that I could hardly wait to apologise.

But I never saw him alive again. I was at the supermarket when Lewis decided Stacy was unwell and sent him home, but it seems likely now that Stacy went not to the Rectory but to Gil Tucker's vicarage half a mile away. The appointment in Harley Street was kept but I never heard Stacy when he returned home afterwards; I think the dishwasher must have been going full blast in the kitchen as I cleared up after lunch. Normally I would always have heard Stacy shutting the front door with a crash and bounding up the stairs, but we were all such a long way now from normality, and Stacy was drifting silently through the house like a ghost.

Later I went into the hall to answer the front doorbell—the caller was just a salesman who needed to be rerouted to the Healing Centre—and when I turned back towards the kitchen I saw there was a note for me on the hall table. It said: "Alice, I'm upstairs and I've got to be alone. No meals, please. Sorry I upset you so much, but don't worry, I'm going to put everything right. STACY."

I tried buzzing him on the intercom but he didn't answer. I even went up to his flat and knocked on the door but there was no reply and the door itself, unusually, was locked. At last, realising I had to respect his wish to be alone, I reluctantly retreated downstairs.

As soon as Lewis returned from work I said I was very worried about Stacy, but Lewis, who had been overdoing it as usual, was too exhausted to pay much attention. He said: "I'll talk to him later," and then announced his intention of having a nap. He also said he was too tired to eat dinner—this was an unprecedented acknowledgement of his invalid status—and that I might as well take the evening off.

About half an hour later the phone rang, but just as I was on the point of answering it Lewis picked up the receiver of the extension in his room. I assumed he had forgotten to switch off the bell before passing out and I felt sorry his nap was being interrupted. I hoped he was still sufficiently exhausted to flop back into unconsciousness as soon as the call was finished.

But Lewis left the house ten minutes later. By that time I was downstairs in the basement and making some spaghetti bolognese for myself, so I didn't have the chance to ask him what was going on. I merely assumed it was some emergency or other and went on cooking.

When I finished I buzzed Stacy's flat again in the hope that he might now be hungry enough to share my meal with me, but still there was no answer and when I sat down with my plate of spaghetti I found myself quite unable to eat.

Just over an hour later Lewis returned to the house with Nicholas, and shortly afterwards Nicholas came downstairs to tell me Stacy had committed suicide.

The guilt I experienced was unbearable. The grief was devastating. And then, very slowly, as the full extent of the crisis dawned on me, I began to realise that I was terrified.

16

> A key area of suffering is that of loss . . . It was perhaps the major common factor in our work with those who came to stay at Burrswood: loss not only in the death of loved ones but in all experiences of life's phases. It was often true that people were helped simply by the recognition of another that their losses were real and by the shared naming of their grief.
>
> GARETH TUCKWELL AND DAVID FLAGG
> *A Question of Healing*

I

With Lewis sitting beside me I tried hard to repeat every word of my last conversation with Stacy but my memory kept blacking out. At the end all I could whisper was: "I failed him. It was wrong of me to be so angry. I should have been so very much kinder."

"Not necessarily," said Lewis in his crispest voice before Nicholas could speak. "In my opinion it would have been a big mistake if you'd repressed your revulsion and simpered over him like some half-baked social worker—it would have been a betrayal of your integrity. The plain truth is that priests have a duty to preach that adultery's wrong and a layperson has the right to expect priests to practise what they preach."

Shedding another tear I was unable to reply.

As if realising this judgement might be too brutal, Lewis added in a gentler voice: "Since priests are only human there are going to be times when they can't live up to their ideals, but if any layperson hears of a serious clerical lapse the priest concerned certainly shouldn't be surprised by an angry reaction. Stacy would have known that, and

I'm sure he wouldn't have blamed you for reacting as you did. He would have realised the fault was his for confiding in you."

"What Lewis is saying," interposed Nicholas the moment Lewis paused for breath, "is that Stacy should have confided in either his spiritual director or in some other priest. And he's saying that not because lay people need to be protected like children; he's saying it because a priest who gets in a moral mess needs expert counselling. Stacy's situation was a nightmare. You couldn't be expected to cope. In fact the scene you've described might well have floored even the most gifted spiritual director."

"Exactly!" said Lewis the moment Nicholas's sentence was finished. "Alice, the fact that you lost control of the scene doesn't mean you were either wicked or insensitive. It just means you lacked the experience to make the correct pastoral moves."

"And even if you'd made the right moves—whatever the right moves could possibly have been here—I believe Stacy would still have killed himself," resumed Nicholas, speaking equally firmly. "He had deep-seated problems which had nothing to do with you at all, and you yourself weren't in a position to solve any of them. You criticised yourself for not being kinder to him, Alice, but in fact to try to heal Stacy at that point by a display of kindness would have been as effective as trying to patch up a fatal knife-wound with a strip of sticking-plaster."

"He's right," said Lewis to me before I could draw breath to speak. Their shared speech was seamless, delivered without faltering, the manifestation of a skill developed through years of working together. Then suddenly a jarring note marred the harmony. Leaning forward Nicholas, in a wordless gesture of comfort, clasped my hand, and as I caught my breath in surprise I was acutely aware of Lewis freezing with disapproval on the sofa beside me. At once he tried to gloss over this reaction by lighting a cigarette. The flame flared. The smoke curled upwards. Through the bluish haze I saw Nicholas look away as he casually withdrew his fingers.

"We mustn't forget," said Lewis, abruptly resuming the speech, "that it was Stacy's decision to end his life, no one else's. We may all feel to some degree responsible for what's happened, but we've got to fight the urge to see this tragedy entirely through the distorting lense of our guilt." He waited for Nicholas to speak but when the silence lengthened he added incisively: "All of that means, Alice my dear, that you shouldn't assume a degree of guilt which is misplaced and unjustified. That's easy for me to say, of course, and not so easy for you to do. But for your own sake you should try."

I was grateful to him for the advice and grateful to both of them for providing me with a clearer perspective on the tragedy, but I found I could no longer talk about my emotions. It was too painful, and besides . . . I was in a state of emotional chaos because Nicholas had abandoned his cast-iron detachment when he had reached out to take my hand.

Trying to focus solely on Stacy I heard myself ask: "How likely is it that he had HIV?"

"All that matters," said Lewis, "is that it's a possibility that can't be ruled out."

In the silence that followed I was sure we were all thinking of Rosalind.

"The trouble is that scientists seem to change their mind every five minutes about AIDS," Lewis said when Nicholas remained silent. "In the beginning we were told any one-night stand could pass it on but if that's so, why aren't we seeing an explosion of cases among heterosexuals?"

"We're just about to," said Nicholas at once, finally driven to speak again. "That's why there's all this current talk about compulsory testing. It's an attempt to control the future heterosexual epidemic."

"Yes, but surely the real message there is that no one has a clue what's going on and everyone's desperate to find out? I personally think that apart from the people who are infected by needles and transfusions, this is primarily a gay disease."

"In Africa—"

"We're not in Africa. We're in England and talking obliquely—excuse me, Alice my dear—about sodomy."

Nicholas said with startling truculence: "I wish you'd stop treating Alice like a Victorian maiden!"

"I can think of worse ways of treating her."

Rapidly I said: "If we can get back to the subject of—"

"Yes," said Nicholas, suddenly taking control of the conversation. "Alice, think hard. What did Stacy actually admit to doing with Rosalind?"

Lewis did a double-take. At first I thought he was merely embarrassed again on my behalf, but then he exclaimed: "Of course! Why didn't I think of asking that question myself?"

"Sorry," I said. "I'm all at sea."

At once he turned to me. "Alice, Stacy did admit, didn't he, that he went to bed with Rosalind?"

"Yes." I couldn't look at Nicholas.

"But did he admit to a consummation?"

I finally saw the point of the questions, but as soon as I tried to recall Stacy's words my memory started blacking out again. "I'm not sure," I said in despair. "Perhaps he didn't. Perhaps I just assumed—" I stopped. I'd remembered that Stacy had twice tried to tell me something but in my rage I'd cut him off. "Maybe he did try to tell me nothing happened in the end," I said in a rush, "but I didn't want to hear any details."

"Of course you didn't," said Lewis soothingly. "Quite right too." He turned to Nicholas. "The boy was obviously impotent. I'm sure Rosalind's safe."

Nicholas at once became truculent again. "Lewis, could you please stop being so homophobic? First of all you imply that AIDS is a gay plague—a statement for which there's no evidence whatsoever—"

"How about thousands of dying homosexuals?"

"—and then you imply that anyone with homosexual inclinations is incapable of performing with women!"

"Nonsense! You're getting in such a liberal huff that you're grossly misinterpreting me—all I was implying is that this particular homosexual would be incapable because (a) he was hopelessly immature and (b) he'd be terminally inhibited by the fact that Rosalind's your wife!"

"But you said just now at the Barbican that he'd see going to bed with Rosalind as a substitute for going to bed with me!"

"Yes, and I still think I was right, but going to bed with someone and being capable of intercourse with them isn't necessarily the same thing—which is why we're having this very difficult and painful conversation!"

"But if, as I've always argued, Stacy was bisexual and not homosexual—"

"Just a minute," I said. "I don't understand any of this."

"Nicholas, if you weren't so infatuated with all this modern guff about sexual spectrums—"

"Excuse me," I said, "can I just say something?"

"Lewis, if *you* weren't so infatuated with these black-and-white views drummed into you by Cuthbert Darcy—"

"*Stop!*" I shouted.

They both jumped and started to apologise for upsetting me, but I interrupted them again.

"I'm only upset," I said, sitting bolt upright on the edge of the sofa, "because you both seem to have gone crazy! What's all this about Stacy being homosexual or bisexual?"

"My dear, naturally we wouldn't expect you to have any profound understanding of Stacy's sexual orientation, but—"

"Go on, Alice," said Nicholas. "Why are we crazy?"

"Because you've made such a bloody stupid mistake!"

They stared at me. I stared back, shocked by their absurd waffling, but at last I was able to say in a firm voice: "Stacy was heterosexual. I always knew that, and in our final conversation he confirmed it—he told me very plainly that he found gay sex a big yawn, and if you ask me, the main reason why he became a priest was to escape from that relationship with Gordon."

They went on staring at me. I waited a moment, but when there was no response I added rapidly: "He was in love with his sister Aisling. No woman ever measured up to her, that was the problem, and even if anyone had he wouldn't have wanted to go to bed with her because you don't go to bed with your sister, it's forbidden. That's why he found it safer to stay an adolescent. He didn't want to grow up because he knew that once he was grown up he'd have to snog and have sex. It was so much easier for him to indulge in a teenage crush on Nicholas and take out jolly old Tara who didn't attract him physically at all."

I stopped speaking. There was a deep, deep silence before I concluded flatly: "If nothing did happen with Rosalind, it wouldn't have been because he was homosexual. It would have been because he was so hung up on his sister that he found all sex with women taboo."

Both men appeared to be carved in stone. Then as Lewis finally exclaimed in stupefaction: "What a lesson for the arrogant priests!" Nicholas leant forward again and this time clasped both my hands in his.

II

Beside me Lewis flinched and violently crushed out his cigarette on the rim of the plate which protected the end-table from my latest pot-plant. At once I tried to detach my hands but I failed; Nicholas was holding them too tightly. I was acutely aware of his hot skin and strong bones and the flowing lines of his long fingers as I said in a rush: "You both believe me?" I knew it was immensely important to keep the conversation moving.

"Of course we believe you," said Nicholas.

Lewis added dryly: "Fortunately we're still capable of recognising the truth when we meet it eyeball to eyeball. Nicholas, I think Alice would prefer her hands to be released."

"Thank you," said Nicholas, "but I'm quite capable of reaching that conclusion myself." His fingers trailed lightly over my flesh as he withdrew them again.

"What's so extraordinary," said Lewis before any kind of pause could develop, "is that Stacy was able to confide so completely in Alice. He was never so frank with us."

"Well, of course he wasn't!" I exclaimed exasperated. "And it wasn't extraordinary at all that he always found it easier to talk to me—Stacy was so used to confiding in women! As a matter of fact I could never understand why you sent him to a male spiritual director. Why couldn't he have gone to see your nun, Nicholas?"

"Yes, Clare would have been right for him, I see that now."

"But why wasn't it obvious to you earlier?"

"A lot of things weren't obvious to us earlier."

"The fact is, my dear," said Lewis, "that it's really better if spiritual directors are priests. And of course all priests are male."

"Why is it better if spiritual directors are priests?" I said, feeling quite irrationally angry. "And why are all priests male?"

"They won't be for much longer," said Nicholas.

"If Stacy had had a woman spiritual director," I persisted fiercely, "*a woman spiritual director who was also a priest*, then I'm sure he wouldn't have ended up in a vile mess where he was so lonely and so homesick and so miserable that he—"

"No priest should have allowed Stacy to muddle on as he did," interrupted Lewis tersely, "but I hardly think our failure here is an argument for the ordination of women!"

My fury overwhelmed me. "Why, you horrid, bigoted old brute!" I shouted at him. "Have you any idea how bloody offensive you are when you act as if women were a subhuman species? I bet Jesus wouldn't have stood it! He'd have bashed your teeth in!"

And scooping the cat into my arms I burst into tears and blundered from the room.

III

I didn't blunder far. The living-room of my little flat adjoined the bedroom. Slamming the bedroom door behind me I leant back against the panels, held James more tightly than ever and let the tears flow unimpeded as I shuddered with my violent emotions. Grief for Stacy was now rapidly elbowing aside my anger with Lewis.

The door was ill-fitting, made of cheap wood. I could still hear their voices clearly. Nicholas was saying in exasperation: "You silly old sod!" and Lewis was snapping: "I was distracted. If you'd behaved properly with Alice instead of pawing her repeatedly like a wonder worker on the make—"

"Oh, for God's sake! You touched her yourself at the start of the conversation!"

"That was a justifiable professional gesture, entirely appropriate for the occasion, and I certainly wouldn't have dreamed of repeating it by grabbing both her hands and staring soulfully into her eyes!"

"I categorically deny—"

"Anyway I don't count, do I? I'm just a bigoted old brute who deserves to have his teeth smashed in!"

"You surely can't have found that judgement surprising!"

"Yes, I did! Dear little Alice, talking like a hard-boiled feminist—"

"Well, if you insist on making idiotic remarks about women at exactly the wrong pastoral moment, what the hell can you expect?"

"All right, all right, *all right*—"

"Okay, maybe it was healthier for her to vent all her anger about Stacy's death on you rather than turning it inwards on herself—maybe you performed a brilliant pastoral manoeuvre—"

"Fat chance. Dear God, why can I never get it right with women?"

"Forget it. Let's refocus. Where have we got to?"

"We've established," said Lewis, sounding unutterably relieved to be reined in, "that you'd be entirely truthful if you told the coroner that Stacy was currently only interested in dating Miss Tara Hopkirk from the Isle of Dogs. That means there's no need to get into any discussion with the police about whether or not Stacy was gay. On the other hand—"

"—on the other hand, if there's no gay angle and the police are still trying to work out why he committed suicide, they'll wonder if Tara was the only woman in his life, and—"

"—and Francie will eventually be unable to resist spilling the beans about Rosalind."

"But if we assume that Francie's so infatuated that she'd want to protect me from scandal—"

"She may want to protect you now, but will she be so supportive in future when you keep rejecting her? Remember that the dynamic behind full-blown erotomania isn't love; it's hatred. It's all about control and domination, the attempt by inadequate people to assert themselves on the objects of their desire."

"I wish," said Nicholas, "I was more confident that we knew precisely what was going on with Francie."

"Never mind the diagnosis for the moment. The only thing that matters in this context is that Francie's unreliable, and if you can't rely on Francie not to spill the beans, it might be better to head off the police by playing the gay card, admitting Stacy had a homosexual past and saying he'd just been tested for HIV. That would not only make it easier to discredit Francie's story later—it would stop the police dead in their tracks right now. It's well known that young men can commit suicide if they fear they have AIDS, and once the police know about the gay angle they'll never stop to wonder if another woman was involved."

"Yes, but Lewis, we can't push that line. We can't push it because we know it's not true. Stacy didn't commit suicide because he feared he was HIV-positive. He committed suicide because he couldn't face up to the consequences of having gone to bed with my wife."

"But the HIV possibility must have been a factor—"

"It was by no means inevitable that he was infected. He would have waited for the result of the test."

"You're assuming he was thinking calmly and rationally. But if he panicked, decided he had HIV and feared he'd infected Rosalind—"

"He couldn't have feared that if he was impotent."

"There might still have been oral sex. If there'd been a cut or a lesion—"

"This is all speculation, Lewis, and we can't speculate now, there's no time. If we could somehow work out which line we're going to take to the police so that the press pick up the right information—"

"Well, one thing at least is certain: we've got to cut out the Rosalind angle. We agreed that at the Barbican."

"Yes, but—"

"There's nothing scandalous about a young man rejecting a homosexual way of life, going into the Church and never again looking at another man. But for a curate to bed his boss's wife—"

"Wait, there's something we've entirely overlooked. Lewis, even if Francie and Gil keep quiet and even if you and I manage to avoid talking of Rosalind while making a succession of truthful statements to the police about Stacy's life prior to the seduction yesterday afternoon, the fact remains that the police will want to interview Alice. They're bound to. As a resident of the Rectory she can provide evidence about his state of mind. And how on earth can we ask Alice, of all people, to lie about his final conversation with her last night?"

I tucked James under one arm, wrenched open the door and blazed back into the living-room to sort them out.

IV

I said strongly: "You're only thinking of yourselves. But what about Stacy? And what about the family he loved so much? Is no one to speak for them?" Then as both men rose to their feet I fought back my tears, struggled to keep my voice level and declared: "I believe one should keep faith with the dead. The last thing Stacy would have wanted is for Nicholas to be dragged through the tabloid press—as he will be if the mess with Rosalind gets out. And the second to last thing Stacy would have wanted is for his family to know he ever—*ever*—had a homosexual affair. I suppose there are gays who would say that was a pathetic attitude but I don't care—I think it would be very wrong to cause extra pain to Stacy's family when they have to grapple with the horrible fact of his suicide."

I paused, waiting for them to argue with me, but when neither of them spoke I said in a calmer voice: "Tell the police the truth by all means, but tell them the *real* truth, tell them the facts which *really* lie at the bottom of this catastrophe, tell them Stacy was lonely, cut off from his family and his culture, missing his favourite sister, worried about the difficulties of finding a steady girlfriend, not doing well at his job, perhaps worried deep down that he became a priest for the wrong reasons, frightened of failing in his career and disappointing the family who were so proud of him—and frightened too of failing and disappointing his hero Nicholas. If you tell the police all that, what more do they need to know? Do you really think Stacy would have got into such a mess with Rosalind if he hadn't already been unbalanced as the result of all the problems he couldn't handle? Tell the police he was vilely depressed but then for God's sake shut up about the consequences! The only consequence the police need to know is that he wound up dead with a rope around his neck, and that's a consequence they can see for themselves."

Lewis stepped forward, propped one crutch against the wall, scooped James from my arms, dumped him on the floor and hugged me. It was a very fast one-armed manoeuvre but it was quite definitely a hug. As he turned away he said to Nicholas: "Now it's your turn to squirm at the sight of an excessive tactile gesture—and when you've finished squirming you can call the police."

But Nicholas was barely listening. He was looking straight into my eyes and saying: "If the police ask about Rosalind you must tell them the truth."

"Of course. I shall answer every question truthfully. But they don't know there are any questions to ask about Rosalind, do they?"

Lewis said suddenly: "What Alice said just now chimes with the suicide note—it's obviously what Stacy wanted us to say. So why couldn't we have seen that from the start, Nicholas? Why have we been tying ourselves in knots like this?"

"Guilt. So long as we focused on the gay issue and the Rosalind disaster we could avoid admitting how thoroughly we mishandled him for so long." Without warning he slumped down on the sofa before exclaiming with despair: "How are we ever going to come to terms with all this?"

"Shut up!" said Lewis savagely—so savagely that I knew he too was shattered. "Save all that for later. Now call the blank-blank emergency services before we're all arrested for trying to conceal a corpse."

Without another word Nicholas trudged back upstairs to make the call.

V

When we were alone I said to Lewis: "Sorry I yelled at you about teeth-bashing."

"I'm sure any woman would say I got what I deserved. Sit down, my dear, and rest for a moment. This is the kind of situation which can slice one to ribbons in less time than it takes to say 'catastrophe.' "

We sat down together again on the sofa and I stared blankly at the far wall, but eventually I dredged up the energy to remark: "I hate the thought that Francie might wind up in the witness-box at the inquest."

"You couldn't hate it more than I do." Lewis started to give me the latest report on her nuttiness. Apparently she had met Nicholas at Westminster Abbey earlier that evening and Nicholas had only been able to escape by running away.

"But why on earth did Nicholas suggest a meeting in Westminster Abbey?"

"It's a long story, but the short version is that he thought he could best defuse her there."

"I can't imagine how he came to that conclusion! Lewis, supposing she turns up at the Rectory tonight just as she did last Monday?"

"No, that won't happen because Harry's just come home from Hong Kong. The odds are we've got Francie on ice until Monday."

"And then what happens?"

"Then we've got to defuse her, but how that's going to be done I've no idea. I doubt if she'd ever consent to see a psychiatrist and so long as she can keep up an appearance of normality we'd never get her sectioned."

"Sectioned?"

"Confined to a mental hospital under a certain section of the Mental Health Act."

"But couldn't she be heading for a complete nervous breakdown?"

"Possibly but not necessarily. The trouble is that without a diagnosis by a psychiatrist who's spent time with her, we can't be sure what's going on. The whole situation's a nightmare."

"Nicholas should have left her well alone!"

"Of course he should! But Nicholas is at present as destabilised as Rosalind—which reminds me, I'd like to offer you a piece of advice. Don't make the mistake of casting Rosalind as the villainess of the piece. When a marriage founders there are almost always faults on both sides—and that leads me to yet another piece of advice I'd like to give you: don't assume that just because the marriage is in difficulties the Darrows are going to wind up divorced."

"But surely only a marriage on the rocks would explain why Rosalind—"

"Marriages can be floated off the rocks. What you may not understand is that the Darrows' marriage is very durable. If it wasn't it would have collapsed long ago."

I managed to say levelly: "I know he loves her," but Lewis just shrugged his shoulders as if this fact were hardly relevant.

"They're certainly very deeply connected," he said, "and the connection is without doubt very real, but what that's got to do with 'love' in the conventional romantic sense I'm not sure. Alice, the big question here isn't: 'Do they love each other?' It's: 'Can they live permanently apart?' And I have a suspicion that a permanent separation may prove far more difficult than Rosalind's currently willing to believe."

I heard myself say: "You're warning me off, aren't you?"

"I'm telling you the truth as I see it. What you do with that truth is up to you."

"Tell me the truth about something else: why did you make such a fuss about Nicholas holding my hands?"

"It was the way he held them. We work in a ministry where certain boundaries are essential and tactile gestures should be governed by strict rules. Nicholas should take care."

Glancing down I saw that my fists were clenched in my lap. Watching them I said: "I'm not another Francie."

"No. You're a very remarkable young woman, Alice, but you too should take care. Don't get blinded by illusions just because Nicholas is so destabilised at present that he's taken to throwing common sense to the winds."

"Fat plain women like me don't have illusions," I found myself retorting in a high, rapid voice. "They get all their romantic dreams smashed to pieces at a very early age. I've no illusions about Nicholas—I can see he's just a mixed-up mess at the moment, but so what? That means I love someone real and it's not a crime for me to love someone, particularly when I've always realised that my love's never going to be reciprocated. Fat plain women don't expect any man to love them, least of all men who are very attractive, so they don't have the same expectations as ordinary women. They don't expect ever to sit down to a square meal. They're just content if they're lucky enough to gather up a few crumbs of comfort occasionally in the form of liking and respect. They know that's far better than having no food at all and starving to death."

I was breathing very hard by the time I had finished this speech. I was also feeling nauseous, as if someone had compelled me to strip off all my clothes in public. I had never before said such things to anyone. I had never revealed such deep and private wounds for inspection by another. I thought how furious Aunt would have been by such embarrassing behaviour. Tears sprang to my eyes as I thought of her, and as I turned my head away sharply I realised I too had been destabilised by the succession of terrible events at the Rectory.

There was a pause before Lewis said in a studiedly neutral voice, as if he knew I would have interpreted any hint of kindness as pity and resented it: "My dear, you should distinguish between being obese and being plump. You're no longer obese and I assure you there are plenty of men in the world who find plump women attractive. So there's no reason why you should settle for anything less than a square meal." Without giving me the chance to reply, he levered himself to his feet. "And now, if you'll excuse me," he was saying, "I must go and find out how the mixed-up mess is getting on."

The door closed.

Screwing my eyes shut I clenched my fists again so tightly that they hurt and began to nerve myself to face the police.

17

At Burrswood we find the hours after death are a time when personal and corporate healing takes place.

GARETH TUCKWELL AND DAVID FLAGG
A Question of Healing

I

The invasion of the emergency services seemed to last for ages. The police spent ages at the top of the house; the Archdeacon, representing the Bishop, arrived in response to a phone call from Lewis and spent ages with Nicholas in the study; Lewis and I retreated to the kitchen (where he finally remembered to phone the Fordite monks to say Nicholas had abandoned his retreat) and spent ages drinking tea. Every incident resembled a nightmare in slow motion.

Eventually the mortuary van came and I wept again as Stacy's body left the house. I had barely finished mopping myself up when Nicholas and the Archdeacon entered the kitchen with two policemen and I knew my ordeal was about to begin.

The policemen were polite in their professional way and not unkind. In response to their prompting we all pieced together Stacy's movements that day and I was able to produce his note in which he had told me that he didn't want to be disturbed. The note, of course, referred to our final conversation, and soon afterwards the police asked to see me on my own.

I was surprised how calm I felt. "I believe one should keep faith with the dead," I had said earlier, and now I was keeping faith with Stacy, protecting his family and Nicholas, just as he would have wanted—and just as any one of those sisters would have done if they had been standing in my shoes. I might have failed him at the end of his life but at least now I could redeem the mistakes I had made in that last agonising conversation, and care, on his behalf, for all those people he should never have left behind.

As I wondered if Stacy's family would ever fully recover from the tragedy I felt very angry with him. The moment of anger passed almost instantly but I felt in that brief second that I had shared something of the rage which had driven him to lash out against the world as well as against himself when he had made his terrible act of rejection.

". . . and how did the deceased seem to you last night, Miss Fletcher?"

"Very down. I hate to say it but I got angry with him and we had a row—as the note implies. (The do-not-disturb note, I mean, not the suicide note.) But I shouldn't have got angry. Poor Stacy, he had so many problems."

"What would you say his basic problems were?"

I listed the homesickness, the alienation, the concern about his job, the worry that he might be letting Nicholas down, the difficulty about finding a steady girlfriend.

"And this final conversation you had with him, Miss Fletcher—can you tell us a bit more about that?"

"Well, it really focused on relationships," I said steadily. "We talked about someone he knew who had died a few months ago. We talked about Mr. and Mrs. Darrow—Stacy had always admired them both immensely. We talked about his sister Aisling, the one who recently married. Stacy did miss his sisters so much." I hesitated before adding: "That was the problem. No girl ever measured up to them." Immediately I wondered in fear if I had said too much, but the elder policeman was nodding his head as if recognising a problem he had encountered before.

"And there were problems getting a steady girlfriend, you said? What about this girl he was taking out?"

"Tara? I doubt if the relationship would have gone anywhere. He liked girls but he couldn't seem to get his act together with any of them."

The younger policeman said suddenly: "Preferred his mates, did he? Did he go off to the pub with them when he wasn't wearing his dog-collar?"

"No, Stacy wasn't keen on pubs and he only drank very moderately. That was because his father had been a heavy drinker who had died in a barroom brawl."

"But he did have his male friends?"

"He did in Liverpool," I said, "but down here he found it hard to make friends—that was yet another of his problems. Mr. Darrow wanted him to make more effort to get to know the other clergy in this part of London, but Stacy couldn't really connect with southerners."

"So what do you think the final trigger was, Miss Fletcher? The one that drove him over the edge?"

"I suppose we'll never know that for sure if he didn't explain it properly in the suicide note, but as I've already said, I do know he was chronically worried about his relationships with the opposite sex and terrified of letting Mr. Darrow down by botching his opportunities here. I'm afraid he wasn't exactly a grade-A curate."

"Is it possible that the girlfriend had broken off the relationship?"

"You'd have to ask her. I think not, though, because he didn't mention it."

"You're sure he wasn't gay?" said the younger policeman, finally ditching the euphemisms.

"Quite sure. He was just hung up and horribly depressed. I'm sorry, I wish I could provide a cut-and-dried answer to the question about what finally drove him over the edge—I wish I could round off my account of the scene neatly—but I can't because the reality wasn't neat at all, it was messy and upsetting. You must know how it is when people are vilely depressed—you reach the point where you feel fed up with them and can't take the misery any more, and that's the point I reached all too soon during that last conversation with Stacy. I cut him off, I went away, and now . . ." The tears which began to flow at that point were all too genuine, and my interrogators, deciding I had nothing further to offer them but evidence of remorse and grief, terminated the interview.

Retreating to the basement I collapsed exhausted on my bed and thanked God the police had probed no further, but of course, as I reminded myself, once they were satisfied that Stacy had committed suicide there was nothing further for them to investigate. The result of the brief enquiry into motive would supplement the pathologist's report and then it would be the coroner's responsibility to ask any questions which hadn't been asked in order to wind up the case. But

I wasn't afraid of the coroner. I knew now I could stage a rerun of my truthful statements. And I wasn't afraid of the press either. After all, nobody could compel me to talk to them. The only person who still terrified me was Francie, the time-bomb ticking less than a mile away in Islington.

Shuddering with fear at the thought of the havoc she could wreak I mopped myself up yet again and toiled back upstairs to the kitchen.

11

The police were just leaving, and Lewis, leaning heavily on his crutches as he watched the front door close, was standing in the kitchen doorway.

"Come and have a drink," he said when he saw me.

"Where are Nicholas and the Archdeacon?"

"The Archdeacon's gone to see the Bishop. Nicholas is trying to get in touch with Stacy's mother. He tried earlier but there was no reply."

Sinking down in a chair at the kitchen table I tried to imagine the horrific conversation which was waiting for Nicholas and Mrs. McGovern, but all I could do was shudder. Meanwhile the brandy decanter was already on the table and Lewis, balancing himself precariously, was reaching into the cupboard for a glass.

"I'll get it," I said hastily.

We settled ourselves at the table, and after the first sip of brandy I found I was able to say: "Were the police satisfied?"

"Thanks to you, yes . . . By the way, if any journalist phones just say 'no comment' and hang up. On no account be drawn into conversation."

Nicholas chose that moment to emerge from his study. "I still can't get hold of Mrs. McGovern," he said worried. "Either she's out very late or else she's away somewhere. I can't decide whether to wait and try yet again or whether I should get Stacy's address book and call the eldest sister."

"Why not enlist the help of the parish priest? Look up his number in Crockford's."

"That's an idea. But right now I need a short break." He turned to look at me. "Are you all right, Alice?"

"Holding up," I said, indicating the brandy, and found myself adding in a rush: "I didn't let him down. In the end I didn't let him down." My voice shook. Finishing the brandy I squeezed my eyes shut, and when I opened them again I saw that every muscle in Nicholas's face was taut with sympathy.

"You'd better have a shot of brandy yourself, Nicholas," said Lewis abruptly, interrupting us, but Nicholas took no notice.

"We need to inform the senior staff," he said, roaming around the room before pausing at the sink. "I can tell the prayer-group at mass tomorrow, but the senior staff need to be told now in case the press start asking questions."

"It's just as well tomorrow's Saturday," said Lewis. "I hardly think we're fit for work at present. In fact—" He broke off.

Nicholas froze. "What is it?"

"No, no, it's nothing—I've just remembered I'm supposed to be having lunch with Venetia, but of course I'll cancel it."

At once Nicholas said: "But it may be important for her that you should turn up."

"True." Lewis dithered for a moment. This was unusual. He wasn't normally a ditherer but in this case his desire to stay alongside Nicholas and his desire to see Venetia were locked in a fierce battle for supremacy. Finally he said: "Of course I'd like to see her, but I couldn't possibly leave you to cope with Mrs. McGovern on your own."

"It's unlikely that she'll arrive before the end of the afternoon. By the time she's got over the initial shock and made the travel arrangements—"

"Let's wait and see what happens when you finally make contact with her."

I said suddenly: "Who's going to break the news to Rosalind?" and without a second's hesitation Nicholas said: "I am. I'll leave for Butterfold after breakfast tomorrow morning."

There was a silence as Lewis and I tried and failed to think of an appropriate comment. "However," added Nicholas when he realised that the scene he had conjured up was a nightmare which had left us speechless, "there's a serious problem with that plan and that's this: I don't think Rosalind will agree to talk to me if I'm on my own."

"I'll come with you," said Lewis at once.

"No, that won't work—Rosalind knows you always support me, and if we turn up together she'll be doubly hostile."

"Take Val."

"No, that's no good either. I agree I've got to have a woman with me, but I can't ask Val because Rosalind despises homosexuals."

I suddenly realised he was looking straight at me, and a second later I saw Lewis had realised this too.

Wordless reactions ricocheted between the three of us with such speed that although I could sense the emotions generated I was unable to react to anything except my own shock.

Unsteadily I murmured: "If I could be of any use . . ." but Lewis was already saying to Nicholas: "I don't think Alice should be involved with your marital problems. Get a woman deacon to go with you."

"But then he'd have to get involved in giving her an explanation!" I found myself objecting. "At least if I went he wouldn't have to explain anything to me. And I don't mind going—I don't mind doing anything which would help."

"All you'd have to do would be to sit in the car," said Nicholas swiftly. "Rosalind and I would talk on the doorstep. She won't want to let me into the house, but she'll talk to me so long as you're there to watch what goes on."

I was astonished by this evidence of such extreme marital discord, but before I could reply Lewis said strongly to him: "I can't tell you how much I disapprove of this idea of yours. And what's more I'm sure Rosalind would disapprove of it too. She knows exactly how Alice feels about you."

Nicholas stood up so abruptly that I jumped. "Rosalind understands nothing whatsoever about my relationship with Alice!" he said in a level voice which still managed to sound furious. "I'm surprised, Lewis, that you should choose to make such an ill-judged remark about a matter which at present requires no comment at all." And he stalked out of the room. The door of his study banged a moment later.

"Triple-hell!" muttered Lewis, draining his glass of brandy.

Numbly I said: "What should I do?"

"Oh, you'd better go. There's obviously no dissuading him."

"But I want to do what's right—"

"Of course. Damn it, I might have known the Devil would launch his most lethal attack on Nicholas's ministry not through an obvious lunatic like Francie but through a woman who's integrity personified!" And having delivered himself of this vile remark he heaved himself out of the room in a rage.

Pressing the palms of my hands against my cheeks, I remained seated as if nailed to my chair.

III

After a while I started to cook. I was exhausted but I knew I would never sleep. I wasn't in the least hungry but I craved to go through a routine which was comforting, and the most comforting routine I could imagine at that moment was to make a cake. A picture floated into my mind of a light-as-a-feather sponge with jam and butter icing in the middle of the two halves and a flaky, curly white icing on the top. I would pipe the edge in pink and design a royal blue inscription. I pictured the words ST. BENET'S: 25TH NOVEMBER, 1988 grouped around a single candle.

I had just finished stirring the gooey mess in the mixing bowl when Nicholas returned.

"I got hold of the parish priest," he said. "Apparently Mrs. McGovern's been hospitalised as the result of an angina attack, but he's going now in person to see Stacy's eldest sister . . . What on earth's that?"

"Cake mixture."

"But why—"

"It's sort of therapy. I feel so awful." I bit my lip to stop it trembling and stirred the mixture harder than ever.

"I'm sorry."

But I didn't want him feeling sorry for me. I was afraid I wouldn't be able to bear it, afraid I might break down and hurl myself into his arms and tell him how much I loved him, afraid of embarrassing him, alienating him and driving him to believe he'd grossly overestimated my ability to cope with what he called "the cutting edge of reality." The last thing I wanted was to be a nuisance to Nicholas—which was why Lewis's final remark had been so vilely unfair. I wanted to be a support, not a drag, but I saw now that the cutting edge of reality had the teeth of a chain saw, and I felt as if I were tied to the bench of some carpenter from hell as the teeth advanced inexorably towards me.

"Where's the old man?" said Nicholas, sensing my chaotic emotions and striking the right casual note to help me remain in control of them.

"Gone to bed, I hope." With an enormous effort I pulled myself together. "Did you phone the senior staff?"

"I phoned Val. She said she'd ring the others. She offered to come over, but . . ." As he allowed the sentence to peter out I knew that he too was exhausted yet unable to face the ordeal of trying to sleep. Then he seemed to dredge up some fresh strength. Abruptly he said: "Don't let Lewis upset you. The truth is he's so worried about me that he's seeing disaster everywhere he looks."

"He started talking about the Devil—"

"Yes, I know exactly how paranoid Lewis gets when all his anxieties outweigh his common sense . . . Are you really willing to come to Butterfold with me tomorrow?"

"Of course, but supposing Lewis is right and Rosalind does react badly when she sees me?"

"My dear Alice, I know Rosalind very much better than Lewis does. Her first reaction when she sees you will be relief that I'm not on my own. Her second reaction will be relief that I'm not accompanied by Lewis, and her third reaction will be relief that I'm accompanied by a woman whom she'll feel free to ignore. She'd feel obliged to put up a front if she was faced with a woman deacon."

I felt better. The thought of Lewis getting things wrong was comforting. I began to spoon the mixture into the baking pans. The goo was very smooth even though I hadn't used the mixer. I had beaten and beaten it, pounded and pounded it, whisked and whisked it in an orgy of therapeutic frenzy.

Nicholas moved away, putting the table between us before saying: "You were magnificent tonight. You saved us both as we lost our footing on the high wire."

I said nothing. I just kept on smoothing the cake mixture over the surface of the shallow pans. I smoothed and smoothed the mixture. I curled it, curved it, stroked it, raked it. Finally I was able to offer the comment: "I just said what I thought."

"Anyone can say what they think. But not everyone's thoughts are as clear-sighted as yours." He paused before adding abruptly: "Would you come with me to mass tomorrow?"

I was astonished. He had never made such a request before, and indeed nowadays I never attended a service at St. Benet's. At the time of the eight o'clock service I prepared the communal breakfast, and during the midday Eucharist I was busy setting out the informal lunch. At weekends when the church wasn't officially open I never fancied tagging along with the prayer-group who attended the services held by Lewis, although I had taken to sampling Sunday services elsewhere.

I had tried St. Paul's Cathedral but it was too big and I felt lost. Eventually I had discovered St. Bride's in Fleet Street and would drift along there for Choral Evensong on Sunday night. I felt comfortable in this church because I could hide my bulk in one of the back pews and pray without feeling self-conscious. I was always sorry the time allotted for prayer was never very long. I liked tuning in to the stream of thought and adding my voice to the silent melodies produced by the group-will. I had found that once I no longer had to endure the constant white-noise of my unhappiness I could hear the cadences and rhythms which had been hidden from me before.

Sometimes I felt I wanted to join the St. Benet's prayer-group, but since I wasn't a regular communicant I was sure I couldn't possibly be good enough for them. Occasionally I'd wondered whether to mention my secret interest in prayer to Lewis or Nicholas, but they were always so busy and I didn't want to bother them. I also felt that I knew them so well off-duty that it was hard to approach them in their professional role. This was another reason why it seemed easier to stay away from St. Benet's when I dabbled in worship; besides, I didn't want to risk resembling those women who came to St. Benet's to worship Nicholas instead of God.

At first I'd wondered if my absence from the church would mean I wouldn't meet the wider community—the inner circle, of course, attended the communal breakfast—but all kinds of people were invited to the informal weekday lunches and everyone was very friendly. There were also various social events, but so far I had always been too shy to attend them. No one seemed to mind that I didn't turn up in church during the week. Neither Nicholas nor Lewis had ever put me under any pressure to do so and I suppose I had assumed the matter was of little consequence to them. Yet now Nicholas was asking me—actually asking me—to attend the Communion service with him as if I was a real Christian instead of someone who was only beginning to have one or two God-ideas and who was still far from sure exactly what she thought about Christianity! I was so amazed that I couldn't immediately think what to say.

"You needn't take the Sacrament," he said quickly as I hesitated, "but if you could just be there—at the back of the church, if you'd prefer—I'd find your presence such a support."

I was much struck by this last word. I had wanted to be a support to him and now he himself was spelling out the exact type of support he needed. Yet still I hesitated. I was so conscious of my inadequacy.

"But surely," I said, "there must be a prayer-expert who could do the job so much better than I could?"

"I don't want a mystical genius. I want someone who cares."

I stared at the baking tins. "Okay, I'll be there."

"Thanks." Absent-mindedly he ran his finger around the edge of the bowl and sampled the left-over traces of the cake-mixture. "Is it the Anglo-Catholic ideal of the daily mass which you dislike?" he asked. "Because if it is, I assure you we're really very Middle-Way in our style—in fact Lewis complains that nowadays we hardly qualify as Anglo-Catholic at all."

I said: "It's not that. I just hate the thought of everyone staring at me when I go up to the Communion rail and thinking how fat I am."

"Ah, I see." He sampled the cake-mixture again. "But the people who attend an early mass would be much too preoccupied with the service to pay you any attention, and besides . . . now that you're thinner you have less to worry about, haven't you?" And without waiting for a reply he wandered out of the room into the hall.

Abandoning the cake I retreated downstairs and tried to feel pleased that he had noticed I was thinner. But I knew I would never be as slim as Rosalind.

My profound exhaustion finally manifested itself in self-pity and to my shame I cried myself to sleep.

I V

Before the eight o'clock service the next day Nicholas received a phone call from Stacy's sister Siobhan. The local clergyman had been to see her; her mother, who was still very ill, had not yet been told of the tragedy; Siobhan hoped to be in London on the following morning. Neither Lewis nor I asked Nicholas what else had been said and Nicholas volunteered no further information. In silence we walked over to the church.

Only four of the prayer-group were present. Before the service began Nicholas told them what had happened and we kept silence for a few minutes. The service which followed was short. Lewis conducted it. I sat at the back and tried to soak up Nicholas's pain while encircling him with love. I didn't take Communion but that wasn't because I was afraid of being stared at. It was because I didn't dare break off from my task of encirclement. The members of the prayer-group were encircling him too, I knew that, but they were so experienced that they could do more than one spiritual task at a time. I envied them their gift and their skill.

As it was a Saturday there was no communal breakfast. Nicholas drank a cup of tea and broke a piece of toast into ragged crumbs and withdrew to his study after five minutes. Lewis then apologised to me for his harshness the night before, but I didn't want to think about what had been said then so I just muttered: "That's okay," and hoped he'd shut up. He did, and as soon as he had disappeared into the bedsit I was at last able to relax, but my respite was short-lived. At nine o'clock Nicholas reappeared and we left in his car for Butterfold.

V

The weather was foggy but the visibility improved as we left London, and soon I found myself surprised by how beautiful Surrey was. I had thought of it as merely the most exclusive of the Home Counties, crammed with luxurious suburbs, but in less than an hour we were driving between wooded hills through a wide valley where farms flecked the rural landscape.

"Our house used to be a farm," said Nicholas, speaking for the first time since the start of the journey. "There are a lot of fake farmhouses around this area—houses which were tarted up when Surrey got rich and spoilt."

"It doesn't seem spoilt to me."

"We're travelling at an off-peak time. Normally there's too much traffic, but it must have been a good place to live in the old days."

"If you're not keen on it, why did you choose to buy a house here?"

"Rosalind liked it. And I didn't want a long drive at weekends."

We said nothing else, but I thought how sad it was that his family home lay in a place which meant so little to him. A second later it also occurred to me how much I should hate it if the man I loved was so lukewarm about the place where we'd agreed to live. Much disturbed by this shaft of empathy with Rosalind, I shifted restlessly in my seat.

Butterfold had a village green and a pub and some cottages so quaint that they looked unreal, as if they were cardboard props on a film set. The Darrows' house was half a mile from the church, and the first thing I noticed was not the house itself but the garden. Even though it was so late in the year there were still shrubs blooming around the paved areas at the front. I pictured smooth lawns and sumptuous borders behind the house and thought how beautiful the place would be in the height of summer. In my imagination the vision of roses was so intense that I even wrinkled my nose as if I could smell their scent.

Nicholas swung the car into the gravelled drive at the side of the house and parked outside a garage which had clearly once been a barn. We were in full view of the front door. Switching off the engine he said: "With luck you won't have to do anything except stay put," and the next moment he was slipping out of the car.

I watched him move to the front door, his head bent forward, his fists shoved into the pockets of his jacket. A light wind, ruffling his hair, made him shiver as he rang the doorbell.

It was as he waited for a response that I wondered why he didn't just open the door with his key and call her name. Even if he and Rosalind were on such bad terms that they could only talk in full view of a witness, I didn't see why he had to ring the doorbell as if he were a stranger.

He waited and waited, but just as he was about to ring the bell again Rosalind opened the door.

She had the chain in place and was peering at him through the narrow gap.

With shock I finally understood. She was frightened of him. There was a window on one side of the front door so she must have been able to see who the caller was, but she had still used the chain. I realised then why Nicholas had rung the bell instead of using his key. He hadn't wanted to terrify her by entering the house without warning; he had known it would be an ordeal for her even to see him waiting outside.

Appalled by this new understanding I held my breath and watched them. She was trying to shut the door but he had wedged it open with his foot. A second later he was pointing to his car.

She saw me. There was a pause. More words were exchanged but finally he removed his foot from the threshold so that she could close the door and unhook the chain. The next moment the door opened again as she stepped outside to join him. She had slipped into a navy-blue coat with brass buttons and looked as if she was about to be photographed for the fashion pages of *Country Life*.

I was expecting a lengthy conversation but within seconds Nicholas was turning away and heading back to the car. I stared in bewilderment. Rosalind made no effort to return indoors. She was watching me just as I was watching her, but I was sure my expression was less inscrutable than hers.

Opening the driver's door Nicholas slid into the car. "She refuses to talk to me," he said, "but she'll talk to you."

I began to feel sick. "How much have you told her?"

"Nothing."

"But what on earth do I say?"

"Try and convince her that I have some very serious, very urgent news and that she's got to listen to it."

I was speechless.

"She's glad you're here," he said. "I was right about that. I'm sure she'll be friendly."

"Great."

"Look, I'm sorry—"

"Why's she so scared of you?"

"I'll explain later."

"I'd rather you explained now, if you don't mind."

"Alice—"

"No, don't behave as if it's none of my business! You made it my business by involving me like this!"

"I realise that. And I wasn't going to say it was none of your business."

"Then what the hell *were* you going to say, for God's sake?" I was horribly rattled by this time.

"I was just going to say that the subject's very difficult for me to talk about because I'm so ashamed."

"Okay, but I'm still none the wiser. What exactly is Rosalind afraid you'll do?"

"She's afraid I'll manipulate her in the worst possible way. She's afraid I'll use hypnosis to take away her will and make her do what she doesn't want to do. Of course that would be impossible now, since she's so hostile, but she still believes—"

"Wait a moment, I'm not following this. What is it she thinks you'll make her do that she doesn't want to do?"

"Have sex. She thinks I'll hypnotise her into having sex in the hope that it would heal the mess we're in."

I stared at him.

He looked away, unable to meet my eyes. He was ash-white. The knuckles of his hands shone as he gripped the steering wheel.

I heard my voice demand: "Why should she think you'd ever do such a wicked thing?" But the moment I phrased the question I knew the answer. "Because you've already done it," I said blankly, and added in my politest voice: "I see." By this time I was feeling very sick indeed. Scrabbling for the door-handle I started to struggle from the car.

"Alice, if you only knew how much I now regret—"

I slammed the door to cut him off, gathered the folds of my jacket around me and tramped across the gravel to the front door.

Having waited until we were face to face Rosalind said crisply: "He shouldn't be using you like this. It's wrong. I always said to him that he wasn't treating you fairly, but he's so damn arrogant that he always thinks he knows best." She pushed open the front door and added over her shoulder: "Come and have some coffee."

I followed her silently into her beautiful house. Pale carpets, highly polished furniture and yards of expensive curtains all formed an elegant pattern of luxury beneath the oak-beamed ceilings. The kitchen was built of oak too, a huge room it was, with all the ugly appliances concealed and every working surface wiped meticulously clean. As I stared around, absorbing every opulent detail, I could finally understand why she had detested the shabby, sprawling, awkward-to-run Rectory. This was a woman with high standards and an exacting attention to detail; she liked order and efficiency; she demanded and expected the best. A second later I saw too why she couldn't relate to Nicholas's ministry. The messy pain of sickness, the muddle of broken lives and the chaotic inefficiency of the weak would have been intolerable to her. With such a drive for material perfection she would have no patience with the losers and no interest in the pathetic and the pitiable. I could see clearly now just why her behavior with Stacy had been so out of character: normally she would have been far too busy pursuing her rigorously high standards to embark on conduct which was so shoddy and second-rate.

I saw then not only how deeply Nicholas had damaged her but how deprived she was, despite her exquisite surroundings. The quest for perfection had been misdirected. Having spent so much of her life creating and sustaining this perfect home, she had been obliged to share it with a husband who couldn't appreciate it and was mostly absent. So many of her creations would have been unappreciated by him; so much of her love would have been unnoticed and unrewarded.

My insight deepened, illuminated by this glimpse of suffering, and finally I understood why she couldn't bear the deprivation which was on display at the Healing Centre, why she couldn't stand the austerity of the Rectory. Her real life, her inner life, was in fact shot through and through with deprivation and austerity, but that was a truth far too painful to acknowledge so she'd shut it out by creating this luxurious, sumptuous world where she could pretend she was happy and fulfilled.

"I'm so sorry, Rosalind," I said. "I'm so very sorry."

She shrugged, not understanding that I was pitying her—indeed the very idea that I could be in a position to pity her would have seemed absurd. I suppose she thought I was merely apologising for my intrusion into her private life.

"Have a seat," she said tersely, moving to the percolator and producing a couple of Royal Doulton cups and saucers from the cupboard above it. "Milk and sugar?"

"Thanks." I sat down at the kitchen table, and after she had poured out the coffee she sat down opposite me.

"I've got a good idea why Nicky's here," she said, "but you can tell him I'm not talking to him except through lawyers—I'm having no more ghastly scenes . . . Did he tell you what he wants to talk to me about?"

"Yes. Rosalind—"

"Is it about Stacy?"

That was a shock. I could only nod.

"I thought so," she said wearily, as if far too exhausted to display run-of-the-mill emotions such as embarrassment or shame. "I suppose the silly child couldn't resist confessing everything to his hero—and I suppose that was what I originally wanted, I don't know—I don't know anything any more except that I've got to be shot of Nicky, but I suppose now I wish I could have told him about Stacy myself—in a letter, so that I could make it crystal clear that the marriage is utterly washed up and that it would be pointless to come down here and make a scene . . . How much do you actually know about all this? I mean, did Nicky just say to you that he wanted to discuss Stacy with me, or did he tell you—well, never mind, it doesn't matter, I don't care how much you know. A week ago I would have cared, but I don't care now, I've crossed some sort of pain threshold and I'm numb, I can't feel pain any more, all I feel is fear that Nicky might crash in here and—well, never mind all that either. Just tell him, would you, that I'm not talking to him about either Stacy or anything else, and that if he tries to bash his way in here I'll call the police—oh, and tell him I've already changed the locks. He won't have realised that, since he played the gentleman and rang the bell just now, but if he'd tried his key it wouldn't have worked."

"Rosalind," I said when she finally paused for breath, "I think you really should talk to Nicholas now about Stacy. Honestly. It's very important."

"Absolutely not!" She slammed down her coffee-cup and clenched her fists.

"But there's something—well, two things—which have got to be said. You see, Nicholas came down here because there's been a catastrophe. He—"

"Catastrophe?"

"Yes, something terrible's happened—the most frightful thing—it's not for me to tell you, but—"

"Christ, what is it?"

"If you'd only talk to—"

"WHAT IS IT?"

"Stacy's committed suicide," I said, giving up the struggle to refer her to Nicholas, and saw all the colour drain from her face as the shock exploded in her mind.

VI

"Oh my God," she said. "My God." She was motionless, no longer seeing me, her eyes dark with memories which had become unendurable.

I tried to tell her about the investigation. In particular I tried to make it clear that the police had no idea what had happened between her and Stacy, but she was too shocked to listen. I finally broke off when I saw the tears in her eyes.

"I can't believe he's dead," she whispered. "I can't believe it." But she did. A moment later she was adding fiercely: "If I'd thought for one second that he'd kill himself, I'd never have—" She broke off, too overwhelmed to continue.

I said: "If you'd speak to Nicholas, he'd—"

"Oh, shut up about 'Nicholas,' for God's sake! If it hadn't been for him I wouldn't have gone round the bend, and if I hadn't gone round the bend—"

"If you'd speak to him he'd tell you that what happened wasn't your fault."

"Of course it was my fault! Or at least, partly my fault! Thank you, but I believe in accepting responsibility for my actions—I'm not one of those feeble whingers who go howling to counsellors in the hope of being let off the hook!"

"Yes, but—"

"Shut up. I need to think about this. I need to *think.*" There was a catch in her voice but she controlled it. "Okay," she said abruptly. "Stacy killed himself. I know now. You can tell Nicky I appreciate the fact that he wanted to tell me in person, but I don't want to discuss it with him. All I want now is to be left alone."

"I understand, but—"

"Oh Christ, there's something else, isn't there? You said there were *two* things I needed to know about Stacy. If one was the suicide, what was the other?"

"Yesterday—the day he died—" I tried to go on but it was so difficult.

"Yes? Well, spit it out, for Christ's sake—I'm not going to stage a total collapse!"

"Yesterday he had a blood test," I said. "There's a chance he was HIV-positive."

Rosalind stared at me. I saw the tears well in her eyes again, and as I watched helplessly she groped her way to her feet.

I followed her as she blundered to the door. "Rosalind—"

She crossed the hall. She reached the front door and dragged it open. She stumbled outside.

I ran after her but stopped on the threshold.

In the driveway Nicholas was scrambling out of the car. She ran to meet him, and as he hurried forward she ran all the way into his outstretched arms.

For a moment I watched as she sobbed against his chest and he held her tightly.

Then I returned to the beautiful kitchen and poured myself some more coffee with a shaking hand.

18

> Crucial to all our teamwork is the interface of the medical and the spiritual. We are most unhappy that so much deliverance work, for example, is undertaken without medical support or insight, especially when there is a history of mental illness.
>
> GARETH TUCKWELL AND DAVID FLAGG
> *A Question of Healing*

I

They talked in the car for a long time. I sat on a chair in the hall and watched them through the window. Once the engine started up but I realised, when the car remained stationary, that they merely wanted the heater to run for a while. Five minutes later the engine was switched off.

I returned to the kitchen, washed my coffee-cup and saucer, dried them and put them away in the cupboard. I was just folding the tea-towel when I heard the Darrows come into the house, and seconds later Nicholas was entering the kitchen on his own.

"Alice."

He seemed calmer, as if some huge anxiety had been dispelled. "Thank you for coping so well," he said. "I'm very grateful." Then he added as he turned away: "I just want to fetch something from upstairs."

I wondered if I ought to offer to return to London by train, but before I could phrase the question he had disappeared. Obviously he was on the brink of a reconciliation with her. When the chips were down she had turned back to her oldest friend. No wonder he was calmer! He'd got what he wanted. I thought of the old-fashioned films where the hero and heroine concluded the story by walking off into the golden sunset.

He remained upstairs for some time and when he returned I saw he was carrying a little black trunk, much scuffed, with N. DARROW printed in worn white paint on the lid.

"We can go now," he said.

I made a big effort to sound as calm as he did. "If you'd rather I went home by train—"

"Home by train? What do you mean?"

"Well, if she's asked you to stay—"

"Oh, I see. How thoughtful of you, but no, we've said all there is to say for the moment, and anyway I must get back to town to hold the fort when Lewis goes off to meet Venetia."

"But surely Rosalind would prefer—"

"Rosalind's all right," he said, speaking with difficulty. "She's all right." Making an enormous effort he managed to add: "Stacy did nothing which could have infected her."

"I thought . . . when she ran to you just now . . ."

"It was the shock. I knew that in the end she'd be glad I was there."

I said nothing more. I had recognised the love which lay behind both his happiness that she'd turned back to him and his relief that she was safe. I thought of Lewis saying how durable the Darrows' marriage was.

We left the house. There was no sign of Rosalind and I was glad I didn't have to watch them bidding each other a very temporary and very affectionate farewell. When we reached the car Nicholas put the little trunk carefully on the back seat, but I was too absorbed in the bleakest of thoughts to ask him why it was travelling with us.

We drove away. The miles slipped past, and gradually I became aware of his tension returning. His hands gripped the wheel tightly again; he cleared his throat several times as if he wanted to speak but failed to find the right words; he frowned, wrinkled his nose and frowned again. At last, unable to stand the stress-symptoms any longer, I demanded: "What's the matter?" and immediately he pulled the car over to the side of the road to park.

"I want to talk to you about the hypnosis."

"I don't need to know any more."

"But *I* need to know that *you* know how deeply I now regret what I did."

"Yes, you've already admitted you were ashamed."

"I talked it all out with my spiritual director, I made my confession to Lewis, I apologised from the bottom of my heart to Rosalind—"

"In that case I can't see why you want to rake up the subject again with me."

"It's because I'm upset at the thought of you being shocked and disillusioned."

"I really wouldn't worry about it, Nicholas. There are plenty of other women at St. Benet's who are still eager to see you through rose-tinted spectacles."

"My dear Alice—"

"Oh, shut up, for God's sake, and stop worrying about the state of your image!"

"But it's you I'm worried about, not my image! I'm worried in case—"

"Forget it. Okay, maybe I *was* shocked, but so what? I'll get over it, I'll recover, I'm not some delicate little flower doomed to shrivel up at the first frost of winter—and I'm not so naive that I don't know we're all capable of doing frightful things. I discovered that when I was looking after Aunt and not getting enough sleep and feeling at the end of my tether. I used to look at her and want to . . . well, not exactly murder her, but at least hit her to vent my despair."

"But you never did. We may all be capable of doing frightful things but that doesn't mean we have to do them."

"I might have done something frightful if she'd lived longer. When you enabled her to die with dignity you also saved me from hitting rock-bottom." I paused to try to sort out my feelings. "I thought I no longer saw you through rose-tinted spectacles," I said, "but perhaps deep down I still wanted to think of you as infallible—not exactly sinless but someone who would always do the right thing and never be tempted to behave like a—like a—" I held back from the ultimate put-down.

"Like a wonder worker," said Nicholas.

"Yes. You see, after Aunt died, when I knew I was horribly fallible, I wanted you to be infallible in order to make amends for the messiness of life—"

"People often want that of clergymen."

"But it's not fair, is it? Poor clergymen! How difficult it must be for them to be burdened with so many people's unreal expectations! I can see now why you love Rosalind so much. She sees you not as an impossibly perfect hero but as the man you really are."

"She certainly has no illusions about me, but—"

"I'm glad that in the end you were finally able to talk. You'll both be all right now, won't you?"

"Maybe. By the grace of God. Yes, I hope so."

I tried to feel glad that they were reconciled. At least a new wife wouldn't be coming to live at the Rectory; at least, if Lewis was right, Rosalind would abandon her plan to live in London and the Darrows would resume their old routine of marriage on weekends. But although I realised this was the best outcome I could hope for—the outcome which would enable me to stay on at the Rectory—I still felt desolate.

Drearily I said: "Can we drive on, please, Nicholas?" and without another word he edged the car forward again into the traffic.

II

We crossed the river, which looked like undulating metal beneath the white winter sky, and headed north past St. Paul's into Cheapside. As it was a Saturday traffic was light and we skimmed with ease into Egg Street and across the cobbles to the church.

Lewis was about to depart for his lunch with Venetia; at breakfast Nicholas had again insisted that he should keep the engagement. Leaving the two men talking in the hall I went downstairs to my flat to tidy myself and when I returned to the main floor after a brief onslaught of tears I found Nicholas on his own in the kitchen.

"Has Lewis been fending off the press?" I asked, turning away quickly in the direction of the refrigerator to hide my pink-rimmed eyes. Opening the door I stared inside, looking for sandwich fillings.

"There's been no reaction. The police have obviously written the death off as a run-of-the-mill suicide. But I daresay the inquest will catch the press's attention."

I removed from the fridge some cold chicken and cheese. It was only when I reluctantly turned towards him again that I saw he had placed on the table the little black trunk from Butterfold.

"I want to show you something," he said.

I set down the food containers.

Opening the box he lifted out a bundle wrapped in tissue paper. The bundle was laid gently on the table. The tissue paper was equally gently parted. To my astonishment I found myself looking at an ancient teddy-bear, bald in places and dressed in a faded blue jumper.

A faint odor of mothballs emanated from the open trunk as Nicholas ran his finger lightly over the bear's beautiful glass eyes.

"I kept him for my sons," he said, "but I never gave him to them. I shut him up in that box and hoarded him in the attic. I thought I did that because I loved him, but I was wrong. Real love has nothing to do with the desire to hoard and control, and what I thought was love was just an obsession with what he represented to me."

He paused to stroke the patchy fur. "He represented security to me," he said at last. "I loved him because he was so predictable. He always had the same expression, his joints always moved in the same way, he was always there, unquestioningly, when I needed him. My parents . . . well, I didn't see much of them when I was young. My mother had her estate to run and my father had his ministry. I had a devoted nanny but she was frightened when the psychic side of my personality began to develop, and I was frightened too. When you know that the world can be shot through at any time by abnormality—by paranormality—you crave the normal, the predictable, the safe. When I was a child, I had my bear. When I grew up . . . Well, I thought I'd put Bear away, but I hadn't. I was still hankering after the normal, the predictable, the safe—and I suppose I found all those things, in a way. But there were a lot of things I didn't find. Things I tried not to think about. Things I tried to believe weren't as important as security."

He moved the joints of the bear's arms and turned the head a couple of inches, as if testing the perfect predictability which had enthralled him. "And now I've got a problem," he said. "I've come to realise that I've got to stop hoarding my bear but the whole weight of the past is pressing on me and I still find it so very hard to let him go. That's because I'm bound to worry about him so much. If only I knew he'd be all right . . . in a good home . . . well cared for . . . appreciated . . . cherished . . . But he's past his first youth, isn't he? Is he really capable of having a new life, or will he just wind up dumped in a dustbin after being kicked around by the wrong owner?"

I took the bear and examined him. Beneath the faded jumper his fur was thick and golden. "I think he could be made almost as good as new," I said encouragingly. "Some soap and water—perhaps a touch of dry-cleaning fluid here and there—"

"Would that be safe? I don't want his fur ruined—"

"I'm sure it would come up very nicely and he'd look years younger. It's a pity about the bald patches, but I can cover them up by making him some new clothes—a little pair of jeans, perhaps, and a T-shirt with ST. BENET'S embroidered on it—yes, that's it, I'll make him very contemporary and then he'll be a bear all set to enjoy the 1990s!"

"He'd still have to find the right home."

"Put him in Reception for a week, and someone reliable is bound to find him irresistible. I honestly don't believe this is quite such a problem as you think it is."

"No?"

"No. Have faith! And think of poor Bear, shut up in a box for so long! I do understand how difficult it must be for you to let him go, but I'm sure you're making the right decision."

Throughout this extraordinary conversation I was trying to work out why, in this time of crisis, Nicholas had chosen to focus on such an irrelevant and trivial object, but although the obvious answer was that he had finally snapped under all the strain, I saw no other sign that he had freaked out. That meant the rescue and restoration of the bear was neither irrelevant nor trivial, but the significance of the scene remained a mystery. I then wondered if his determination to "put away childish things" was symbolic of a new maturity, achieved by his reconciliation with Rosalind. It was hard to imagine Nicholas being less than mature in his personal relationships, but perhaps, as Rosalind had been his childhood friend, some childish element had lingered on into their marriage until it had finally caused the recent troubles. With the childishness now cast out, the marriage would be all set for repair and renewal.

While I was working out this explanation I altered the bear's legs into a sitting position and arranged him in a place of honour on the dresser. I was just about to ask Nicholas what he wanted to do with the little black trunk when there was an interruption.

Someone rang the doorbell.

"At best that'll be Gil Tucker," said Nicholas, "and at worst it'll be a reporter from the *News of the World.*"

"Do you want to escape to your flat?"

"No point. If it's the press they'll never go away until I've appeared in person to say 'no comment,' and if it's Gil Tucker I want to see him. I've got a hunch it's Gil."

But his hunch misled him. Psychics can't always get it right. The moment he opened the front door I heard a woman's voice exclaim richly: "Nick—darling!" and I realised with utter horror that our visitor was Francie Parker.

III

I suffered a second of total confusion. Francie was supposed to be "on ice" until Monday, entirely preoccupied with the husband who had just returned from his business trip to Hong Kong. Driven by an appalled curiosity and an acute concern for Nicholas I peeped out into the hall.

Francie had streamed over the threshold and was about to enter the study. She was wearing a smart black coat but as I watched she shed this onto the nearest chair and revealed a tight V-necked red sweater and a shiny black leather skirt. Her breasts, shoved high by some amazing push-up bra, were looking as if they couldn't wait to jump out of both the bra and the V-neck. She was clacking along in high-heeled glossy boots and looked like a bad actress playing a Hollywood hooker.

Nicholas glanced across the hall and motioned me to join them. I glided forward, pausing only when I reached the threshold of the study.

". . . and of course I just had to come the moment I heard the news," Francie was saying. "Stacy! Suicide! My dear, I was shattered!"

"How did you hear about it?"

"Rosalind phoned just now."

I saw Nicholas's left hand clench shut as he realised he had forgotten to warn Rosalind of her best friend's duplicity.

"—and Rosalind was gutted, darling, simply gutted. She rang to beg me to say nothing to anyone about—why, Alice! What are you doing, loitering in the doorway like that? Anyone would think you were trying to eavesdrop!"

"Alice doesn't need to eavesdrop," said Nicholas evenly. "She knows everything there is to know about this situation, and she came with me this morning when I went to Butterfold to tell Rosalind about Stacy."

"Really? But how odd." Francie's head turned slowly as she gave me another look. Her eyes were glittery, febrile, mad. As my scalp prickled I instinctively stepped across the threshold in order to be closer to Nicholas.

"What else did Rosalind tell you?" Nicholas was asking, and although he kept his voice calm I knew he was afraid that Rosalind, in her shock, had admitted far too much.

"Oh, we didn't talk for long because she was so upset—my dear, she even accused me of trying to egg her on when she decided to seduce Stacy! As if I'd ever do such a wicked thing! But of course I forgave her because she was crucified with guilt, poor darling, and not thinking clearly."

"What exactly did she say?"

"She said she'd bedded Stacy—well, I told you she was planning to do that, didn't I? I told you last night in the Abbey!"

"I remember, yes. Did she say anything else?"

"Oh, she said he was impotent, which I must say was hardly a huge surprise, but that explains the tragedy, doesn't it, because obviously he killed himself out of frustration and remorse and the whole disaster was Rosalind's fault. Honestly, Nick, I hate to say this, as she's my oldest and dearest friend, but the sooner you're shot of that woman the better."

"And that was all she said?" Nicholas obviously wanted to make sure that Rosalind, focusing on the seduction, had never mentioned the possibility that Stacy had been infected with HIV. It would be one less detail to worry about at the inquest.

"What else was there to say? Oh, you mean did she talk of divorce—no, she didn't, but since she'd put her wicked plan into operation, there was nothing more to add, was there? Obviously she's still gasping to be rid of you, but don't worry, darling, because I'm now poised to take over. I've just put my own utterly brilliant plan into operation!"

Five terrible seconds passed before Nicholas was able to say: "What plan?"

"*My* plan! My own utterly secret, utterly inspired, utterly stupendous plan which I've been working on for months and months! I—" She broke off as she became aware of my presence again. "Oh Alice dear, do run along, there's a good girl! I really must talk to Nick on his own now!"

"Humour me, Francie," said Nicholas lightly, signalling me to stay. Obviously the last thing he wanted was a scene with no witness. "Alice is in my confidence, as I've already explained, and I'd like her to be present. You don't really mind, do you? After all, Alice is one of your most devoted admirers—she always says she'll never forget how kind you were to her after her aunt died."

Francie preened herself. Pride streamed forth from her in a swirling black tide. "I was wonderful, wasn't I?"

"Wonderful!" I said at once, picking up the cue that she was to be flattered but glad I was still able to speak the truth. "I was so grateful, Francie."

"Poor Alice! Very well, I shall be as kind to you as Nick is—darling Nick, trying to include you in everything in order to make you feel useful! So sweet of him!"

Nicholas edged casually to the right in order to put the table between them. The study had four focal points. If one stood in the doorway, the small round table stacked with papers and books lay straight ahead in the middle of the room; to the left was the window which overlooked Egg Street; to the right was the fireplace, and on the far wall, beyond the table, was the desk with the crucifix hanging above it. At that moment the three of us were forming a distorted triangle. I was hovering between the door and the fireplace, Francie was standing with her back to the window, and Nicholas, shifting around by the table, was veering towards his desk.

Idly he said to Francie: "So what's all this about an inspired plan?"

"My dear, I've been so clever and no one's suspected a thing! I did think for one frightful moment that Lewis suspected during our conversation at the Rectory last Monday night—he asked why I had always confided in *both* of you about Harry's violence—but no, it was all right, I soon realised he hadn't a clue what was going on. Of course I shouldn't have gone to the Rectory at all that night, but I simply couldn't contain myself any longer! And with Harry away and Lewis under doctor's orders to go to bed early, I thought I'd be absolutely safe if I arrived at ten-thirty, but—"

"It was bad luck I was away that night. But Francie, tell me now what you didn't tell Lewis. Why did you, in fact, confide in both of us about Harry's behaviour?"

"Because once the police found out that you and I intended to marry, your evidence would be suspect."

There was a pause before Nicholas said colourlessly: "Evidence?"

"Yes, although you had to know how unbearable my marriage was—although you had to know I was available for you to love—I needed another witness, an impartial witness that I was being driven beyond endurance."

I saw the muscles harden in Nicholas's face as he struggled to keep his expression neutral. He said: "I'm not sure I understand you." But I knew he did. I thought I did too, but I didn't want to. I was aware of my heart thumping unnaturally fast.

"Well, you see, it was like this," said Francie cosily, leather skirt riding up over her plump black-stockinged thighs as she sat down on the window-seat. "I've known for a long time that we were made for each other, and I realised right away that the real problem was not that you were married; I was sure I would eventually get the chance to show you that your marriage was a sham—and it *was* a sham, wasn't it? You and Rosalind spent most of the time apart."

"And once I was divorced—"

"Divorce would produce a tricky situation, I realised that, but I knew you'd be all right if Rosalind was the guilty party and you went through the motions of trying to save the marriage—you'd win everyone's sympathy, even the stodgiest of the trustees. However, the *really* tricky phase would be when—"

"—remarriage was on the cards."

"Exactly! I knew the trustees and a lot of other people wouldn't approve of you marrying a divorcée. But if you were to marry a blameless widow whose husband had horribly wronged her . . ." She smiled at him roguishly as she allowed the sentence to fade away.

Nicholas's pallor now had a greyish tinge. I found I had backed away until I was leaning against the doorframe. I felt I might pass out.

"Oh, don't worry, darling!" exclaimed Francie, springing to her feet again as she at last sensed his horror. "I'd never do anything which would jeopardize your ministry here, and that's why I decided from the start that I had to be a widow instead of a divorcée! Of course it'll be a teeny bit awkward when the police arrest me, but I'll be the wronged heroine, won't I—the good Christian woman vilely brutalized by her wicked atheist husband—and everyone will want to drench me in sympathy and forgiveness and understanding, not least the judge and jury! After all, I've been so brilliantly plausible! How skilfully I've built up my chilling portrait of a marital monster! How cleverly I've played the role of the battered wife! Well, I would, wouldn't I? I've heard it all so many times before during my years as a Befriender, and so I was able to put my experience to the best possible use! I was amazing!"

Nicholas somehow managed to say: "Amazing. So when did you decide the time was finally right to—"

"Kill Harry? Well, I originally planned to do it in the new year after the children had gone back to school—I didn't want to spoil their Christmas—but as soon as I had lunch with Rosalind this week I knew I had to act without delay. After all, she was rejecting you—

you'd need me! So when Harry woke up jet-lagged this morning after that long flight home from Hong Kong . . . Well, it was all so simple. He was sitting at the kitchen table in a bleary-eyed stupor as I was in the middle of preparing lunch—which made things so much easier, because I already had a knife in my hand. I came up behind him and I stabbed him and stabbed him and stabbed him. Actually I think I cut his throat. I can't quite remember. (That bit was rather traumatic.) Anyway when he was dead I changed into clean clothes and came straight over here. I didn't bother to call the police—they can wait because it's an open-and-shut case, nothing much for them to do, and with the right counsel I know I can get off scot-free. Must have the right counsel, though—a QC—the best money can buy—but that's all right, I'll have plenty of money now Harry's dead . . . Alice dear, why are you looking at me like that? In fact why are you here at all? You should have gone back to the kitchen, you know, instead of lingering on out of curiosity. Curiosity," said Francie sadly, "killed the cat. Did no one ever teach you that when you were little?"

I felt as if I were welded to the doorframe. Something had happened to my lungs. I could barely breathe.

"Never mind Alice for the moment, Francie," said Nicholas, murdering the pause so swiftly that it was almost stillborn. "Tell me how you feel now about Harry."

Francie was immediately diverted. Having advanced several paces towards me she now turned back to him and began to move around the table to his side, but Nicholas didn't wait for her. He too was on the move, keeping the table between them. For a moment he was close to me and I felt safe, but as Francie continued to advance he moved on. When she finally stopped she had her back to the fireplace, he was standing opposite her with his back to the window and nothing separated her from me except a few feet of polished floorboards.

But Francie had temporarily forgotten me. "I feel pure joy!" she was declaring exuberantly. "I can't tell you how much I hated that man! He was always so horrible to me, but I've triumphed over him in the end, haven't I? Vengeance is mine, said the Devil, I will repay!"

I shuddered as I heard the famous quotation perverted, but Nicholas just said: "You've certainly shown great ingenuity, Francie." I saw him edge fractionally closer to his desk again even though she herself was no longer moving. Casually he added: "But I'm troubled by the haziness of your memory. Are you sure he was dead when you left?"

"There was blood all over the kitchen table! But darling, I knew you might find it hard to believe I'd been quite so resolute and brave, so I've brought the proof with me." Hurrying to the handbag which she had abandoned on the window-seat she whipped out a nine-inch-long butcher's knife, its blade dark with gore. "Here you are!" she said gaily to Nicholas. "Take it! I don't need it any more . . . or do I?" She paused, her brow furrowed in thought, the knife still clasped daintily between her thumb and forefinger. "Darling, it's just occurred to me—what are we going to do about Alice? She wasn't part of my plan at all."

"Why don't we take a moment to discuss that in private?" said Nicholas at once. "Alice, go to the bedsit, would you, and tell Lewis that lunch will be a little late today."

I knew I was being told to phone the police, but before I could escape Francie altered her clasp on the knife and ordered me to stay where I was. "There's something here I need to sort out," she said, brow still furrowed, right hand now wrapped around the knife's handle so tightly that the knife seemed to be growing out of her fist. "Alice dear—" She took a step towards me. I tried to move but my legs wouldn't work. Out of the corner of my eye I saw Nicholas reach his desk but I couldn't think why he wanted to be there. He and I were now on opposite sides of the room but Francie was almost within lunging distance of me and the knife was still thrusting obscenely from her palm.

"Of course I know you're in love with him," she was musing, "but why is he suddenly taking you everywhere with him and insisting that you're present at even the most private of conversations?"

A voice said: "I've no idea." It was my voice but I failed to recognise it. I suddenly saw that over by the desk Nicholas was unhooking his crucifix from the wall.

"Rosalind warned me about you!" said Francie sharply. "I remember now—she said there was something odd going on, but let me tell you this: if you think you can get him you're wrong." With a shock I realised that her voice too had become almost unrecognisable. I felt as if the scene had suddenly shifted into a different gear. "I'm getting him, I'm having him, he's mine!" Her eyes were now like black holes. Her face was skull-like. The familiar bone-structure was dissolving into an alien mask. She was breathing hard through her bared teeth in a steady, rhythmic hiss.

"Francie!" said Nicholas loudly, but she took no notice. She had begun to raise the knife. "Francie, look at me! Francie, *in the name of Jesus Christ*—"

I was finally forgotten. She spun to face him as if he'd cracked a whip, and as the hissing stopped I saw a change come over him. It was as if a curtain came down over his horror, his enormous tension and his fear for my safety. Holding the crucifix casually in his hands he appeared to relax, although I felt sure this was an illusion created by the sudden onset of a willed stillness. I sensed the narrowing of his concentration as he focused on Francie. His fine eyes were brilliantly clear.

Suddenly he smiled. He was very laid back now. In fact he was enchanting—in the most literal sense of the word; he was weaving an enchantment, spinning a web which would ensnare her. She was being invited to look into those remarkable eyes, which at that moment had no expression other than a peculiarly intense interest, and to read into them whatever message she chose to see there. He was luring her on to believe he would do anything she wanted if she would do anything he wanted—and once she knuckled under to his will she would be trapped. De-willed and de-skilled she would be no better than a robot which could be programmed in any way he chose.

For a second as revulsion overwhelmed my fascination I thought I was witnessing the corrupt act of the wonder worker, but then I realised I was witnessing hypnosis used not for self-aggrandisement but for healing. Nicholas was struggling to beat back deadly symptoms in a woman who was horribly sick, and as soon as I understood this I became aware of the crucifix as he unobtrusively transferred it to his right hand.

"You're going to keep looking at me, Francie, aren't you," he was saying, and he spoke so warmly, so delightfully, so sensibly that Francie became recognisable again as she gazed at him in rapture. "You're going to keep looking at me and you're going to forget Alice, aren't you, because I want you to forget Alice and you want to forget Alice and we both want to forget Alice—we want there to be just the two of us, don't we?"

Francie was starry-eyed and excited. She was herself once more. The hissing, alien presence had now vanished. "Oh yes, darling, yes, yes, yes—"

"Okay, you're going to forget Alice is here and when I click my fingers you'll have forgotten her, you won't be able to see her any more, she'll have gone away. You do believe I can do that, don't you? Of course you do. So now I'm going to click my fingers"—he clicked them—"and there you are, Alice has disappeared, your wish is my command and she's gone, no need to worry about her any more, I've taken care of her, she's no longer a threat to us, and it's just you and me now, just you and me, and that's what you want, isn't it? Okay, fine. Now Francie, there's one more thing you have to do to please me: you have to put down that knife. I'm going to count to five and when I say 'five' you're going to *put down the knife*, put it down on the table. Got that? Okay, good, I'm going to start counting. One—two—"

I was just thinking, awash with relief, that everything was going to be all right when without warning everything went very, very wrong. Francie's identity began to disintegrate again, this time far more violently. The hissing returned but at once deteriorated into groaning. She was still rooted to the spot but she was shaking violently, and the knife remained wedged in her clenched hand.

"Right," said Nicholas swiftly, breaking off the countdown, "I can see this is too difficult for you, I can see we're losing touch, but hold on to the fact that I'm on your side, Francie—hold on to the fact that I'm fighting for you against—"

Francie's identity was abruptly wiped out. It was as if a drowning swimmer had finally been pulled beneath the surface of shark-infested waters after a prolonged struggle to survive.

The next moment her vocal cords were making a noise like an animal having its throat cut.

Nicholas dumped the attempt to communicate with her, dumped the hypnosis, raised the crucifix aloft and shouted: "In the name of—"

But he was cut off. A voice which sounded male bellowed: "I hate you, hate you, hate you—I want to kill you, kill you, kill you—"

"In the name of Jesus Christ, Satan, I—"

This didn't work. The voice screamed louder than ever: "*Kill, kill, kill—*"

In a flash Nicholas had changed tack. "Spirit of murder, spirit of hatred, spirit of anger, spirit of lust—"

This didn't work either. The voice yelled loud enough to hurt my eardrums: "KILL, KILL, KILL—" but Nicholas yelled even louder: "—and all other unclean spirits, leave this woman, go back where you came from and IN THE NAME OF JESUS CHRIST NEVER RETURN!"

The thing using Francie's body raised the knife and rushed forward bent on butchering him.

I V

It was all over even before I could shriek in terror.

Nicholas moved the crucifix to parry the blow from the knife but the slash never came. Francie—the thing—or things—whatever—came to a dead halt as if slammed by a tremendous force. For one long moment she was paralysed, arm raised, knife poised, fist clenched, head thrown back. Then as her eyes rolled upwards in their sockets she gave a long howl and fell to the floor in a convulsion.

V

The convulsion probably only lasted a few seconds but at the time it seemed never-ending. When at last she lay still I thought she was dead. She had let go of the knife as she fell to the floor, and Nicholas, glancing at that long, smeared blade as he knelt beside her, said to me abruptly: "Fetch a roll of paper towel and a clean dish-cloth."

The contrast between the prosaic request and the grossly abnormal behavior I had just witnessed was so great that at first I couldn't think where to find what he wanted, and when I did reach the kitchen I couldn't remember why I was there. Closing my eyes I took several deep gulps of air as if I hoped that oxygen would kick-start my brain.

A stench greeted me on my return to the study, and I found that Francie had not only urinated but defecated. Instantly I wished my memory would go on the blink again, but I knew this was a fact I was going to remember.

"Thanks," said Nicholas, taking the paper towel and the dish-cloth from my hands. Tearing off a strip of the towel he used it to pick up the knife which he then wrapped in the clean dish-cloth. It didn't occur to me until long afterwards that he was taking such care with the knife because it was an alleged murder weapon.

"Is she dead?" I finally managed to ask.

"No, just asleep. They always sleep afterwards."

"Was it an epileptic fit?"

"More or less."

"How much more," I said shakily, "and how much less?"

"Well, the episode could certainly be described as a fit. But I don't think she's now going to start suffering from epilepsy." He stood up and put the wrapped knife in a drawer of his desk before reaching for the phone. As he dialled the numbers he said without looking at me: "I don't know how I can even begin to apologise for recruiting you as a witness to that particular scene."

"I'm okay," I said automatically without having the slightest idea whether or not this was true. "But I need to understand what happened. Then I won't feel so—so—"

"Yes. Just a moment." He turned his attention to the phone. "Val, it's me. Look, Francie's just behaved like a paranoid schizophrenic and tried to kill me—she's now out cold after a seizure. Can you—" He broke off, then merely added a second later: "Thanks," and hung up. "She'll organise an ambulance," he said, "and come straight over." He tapped some keys on his computer and when Francie's phone number flashed on the screen he started to dial again, but although he waited for a long time, no one answered. Replacing the receiver he squatted down to take another look at Francie but there was no change; she was still so deeply unconscious that she scarcely seemed to be breathing.

Straightening his back he turned to face me. "All right, let me try to offer you some kind of explanation," he said, "but it's not easy because when all's said and done this condition is a mystery—it's part of the mystery of consciousness and the mystery of personality. One day the scientists will uncover the mechanics involved but just uncovering the cerebral processes won't explain why these things happen and what triggers them. A lot of mental health is a mystery. Mental illness isn't as clear-cut as lay people think, and often diagnosis isn't easy. There's also a problem with language."

"What language?"

"The language we use to describe and categorise what's going on. People mistake symbols for reality and treat the symbol as reality itself, but the purpose of a symbol is to point the way to reality—to make reality easier to grasp when there are no precise words to describe it. Another problem is that words used to describe a phenomenon are treated as an explanation and they actually explain nothing; they just allow the phenomenon to be placed in a category."

"I don't follow." This was an understatement.

"Well, schizophrenia, for example, was originally just a description of various symptoms, yet now, if you say someone's schizophrenic, you're probably saying that to explain why someone's behaving in a certain way. In fact it doesn't actually explain anything. And take the word 'demon,' used in its modern sense. Some people think a demon really is a little creature with horns but other people think this is just a visual symbol for one of the dark forces of the unconscious mind."

"And who's right?"

"It doesn't matter because the only thing that matters is that the patient is suffering and needs help. When you're working at the cutting edge of reality, there's no time to meditate on semantics."

"But when you helped Francie just now—"

"I treated her by naming the demons and casting them out. That's the religious language. Or you can switch languages and say in the language of psychology: I dealt directly with the unconscious mind, bypassing normal thought processes and flinging out words which triggered the release of certain malign archetypes—"

"Wait, wait, wait, I'm getting all muddled and only understanding about one word in twenty—"

"Okay, let me try again. There are various medical words which can be used to describe Francie's condition but I don't think they're going to prove adequate as explanations when she makes a reasonably quick recovery."

"You think she'll *recover?*" The idea seemed inconceivable.

"She'll need a lot of treatment, but yes, I believe that in the end she'll be the same person as she was before the other personality muscled in on her."

"And when you say 'the other personality,' you mean—"

"A psychiatrist might try and float the theory that she's suffering from a multiple personality disorder, but since that particular illness usually stems from a long history of severe abuse and since Francie's abuse was a fantasy—"

"She was possessed, wasn't she?"

"That too is just a description, and in the end 'possessed' is as hazy a word as 'mad.' To be quite honest I'm still by no means certain what was going on."

"But you must be—you were certain enough to exorcise her!"

"Strictly speaking that wasn't an exorcism. The rite to exorcise the Devil takes a lot of time to set up and the patient has to consent."

"But you called on Satan!"

"I blew it and made a mistake. Well, I nearly blew the whole thing—"

"But Nicholas, if that wasn't an exorcism, what on earth was it?"

"It was an emergency rite of deliverance, but I'm not at all keen on that sort of thing—I'm not one of those glitzy Charismatics who see demons everywhere—"

"But the deliverance worked!"

"By the grace of God, yes—or did it? What exactly was the right button which switched her off? I'm not at all sure certainty's possible here."

By this time I was far more confused than I had been at the start of the conversation. "Nicholas, I don't understand why you're floundering around like this! Aren't you supposed to be an experienced exorcist?"

"Yes, and that's exactly why I'm floundering. I know enough to know how little I know for sure. Sometimes I think the Christian ministry of healing isn't so much about problem-solving as mystery-encountering." He smiled at me unexpectedly.

"You mean that even though you're so experienced—"

"This was very different from the type of experience which normally comes my way. I usually only exorcise places. That's pretty mundane; one can be well prepared and business-like. As for deliverance, I like to set up the rite well in advance after a great deal of prayer and counselling and with a doctor in attendance. My ministry's about being low-key, not about shouting at demons and waving a crucifix around like a magic wand—and it's not about using hypnosis without medical supervision either . . . Of course there are doctors who would say I overpowered Francie by the power of the will and not by the rite of deliverance at all."

"But in the end you ditched the hypnosis," I said at once. "You ditched everything except the crucifix."

He seemed surprised that I'd noticed. "That's true," he said, "I did—I had to. The hypnosis was successful in calming Francie, but I couldn't have hypnotised that other personality. It was much too strong."

"Are you sure it wasn't the Devil?"

"I'm not sure of anything. I'm shell-shocked."

On the floor Francie moaned, making us both jump, but she remained unconscious.

"I was lucky to survive," said Nicholas, looking down at her. I saw him shiver.

"But you couldn't have got killed—you called on Jesus Christ!" I was unsure how far I believed this.

"But not to save me. To save Francie—and I believe she would have been saved even if I myself had been killed in the process. But it would have been entirely my fault if I'd been killed. I'm so debilitated at present that the last thing I'm fit for is the ministry of deliverance." He finally allowed himself to sink down on the swivel-chair at his desk and close his eyes in exhaustion.

Withdrawing to the kitchen I made us both some sweet tea. I was still feeling shattered but it helped to go through the familiar routine of tea-making, and when I returned to the study I found Nicholas had also been on the move again. He had covered Francie with a blanket from the bedsit and opened a bottle of lavatory cleaner from Lewis's bathroom. A pungent chemical odour was now masking the stench from the body.

As I gave him his mug of tea I said: "Why did you call on Jesus for help? Why not just call on God?"

"Jesus is by tradition the Light that drives back the Dark, but there's more to it than that. Today we would say Christ is a symbol of integration—he was the one human being who was so totally integrated, so totally at one with his Creator, that he was divine, and Francie at that point was almost subhuman, her personality abnormally fragmented. By evoking such a potent image of integration I was calling on God to draw the fragments together by the power of the Spirit and cast out the destructive forces which were annihilating her."

I sipped my tea and restrained myself from muttering "Weird!" through chattering teeth. Then it occurred to me to wonder how the supposedly non-weird doctors would cope. "Nicholas, what will they do to her at the hospital?"

"Oh, put her on a psychiatric ward, give her a brain-scan, drug her to the eyeballs, but don't worry, she'll survive. I doubt if she'll remember much. Alice—" He broke off as if too upset to continue.

"What's the matter?"

"I'm just so sorry this has happened. I would never have wanted you to witness this side of my ministry."

"Why not?" I said astonished.

"Well, I know normal people find it a complete turn-off—"

"What normal people? What's 'normal' anyway? And why are you suddenly aping Lewis and treating me as a Victorian maiden whose purity mustn't be sullied? I don't have to be wrapped in tissue paper, you know, and preserved in a box like your bear!"

I was still smiling at him, still savouring the fact that my teeth were no longer chattering, when once more we heard the doorbell ring in the hall.

"That'll be Val," said Nicholas, hurrying forward at once, but again his ESP was malfunctioning. As I followed him into the hall he opened the door and I saw that the caller was a stranger to me. He was a tall man of about forty-five, handsome, well dressed and, quite obviously, terrified.

"Nick!" he exclaimed, swaying in relief. "Thank God you're here—you've got to help me!"

"Alice," I heard Nicholas say, "meet Francie's husband, Harry Parker."

19

There is no simple way round the bearing of griefs and sorrows. Easing the way through involves some understanding of the path of grief *and* a confidence in the Lord whose risen life proclaims that every Good Friday gives way to a new Easter Day.

GARETH TUCKWELL AND DAVID FLAGG
A Question of Healing

I

It may seem strange but I had been so absorbed in the attempt to murder Nicholas that I had quite forgotten Francie's boast that she had murdered Harry. Nicholas had remembered; he had phoned the Parkers' number after she had passed out, and I realised now, as the truth dawned, that he had had his suspicions about the throat-cutting. Francie had been too vague. I also realised that the reason why Harry hadn't answered the call was because he had been on his way to the Rectory.

"We've sent for an ambulance," said Nicholas after showing him Francie's unconscious, blanketed body, "and Val's on her way here as well."

"Who?" Having flinched at the sight of the body, Harry flinched again as the odour of lavatory-cleaner fluid and human ordure hit his nostrils.

"The doctor who works with me, Val Fredericks. Alice, sweet tea for Harry, please."

"*Sweet tea?*" yelped Harry. "Christ, don't mess around! Give me a double-brandy if you don't want a second body on your floor!"

Nicholas made no attempt to lecture him about the best medicine for shock. He merely nodded to sanction the request before saying: "You'd better sit down."

When I returned with the brandy I found Harry had collapsed in a chair in the hall out of reach of the worst of the stench and Nicholas was standing nearby on a spot which allowed him to keep an eye on Francie as he listened to Harry's monologue.

"Christ Almighty," Harry was saying in a daze. "Jesus Christ." Now that I had the chance to observe him closely I saw he had blue eyes, bloodshot with tiredness, a florid complexion, hinting at a fondness for alcohol, and a peculiarly curly mouth which conjured up vaguely repulsive images of gluttony and lust. But this impression of a sexy *bon vivant* was blurred by the shock he had received. The curly mouth no longer looked as if it longed to wrap itself around the rim of a glass of vintage claret at some upmarket restaurant. His lips trembled. He could hardly slurp down the brandy. When he finally embarked on a monologue his voice was unsteady.

"Well, I realised some time ago that she was getting peculiar," he said between gulps. "I remember coming home from Australia last spring and being greeted with the news that she was going to study for a diploma in counselling. Francie! Study for a diploma! Hell, the only academic qualification she's got is an O-level in art! Okay, I'm not saying she doesn't have a flair for dealing with the sad stuff that turns up at your Healing Centre, but she's got the kind of brain that just doesn't function in an academic setting. I tried to tell her that but then she slid even further off her trolley and threatened to get back at me by telling everyone I was cruel to her! Well, I ask you! What was I supposed to do? In the end I just laughed it off, decided it was hormones and hoped it would go away.

"But it didn't.

"You know what happens next? She says she'll tell everyone I'm a wife-beater—*me!* Christ, I can't even bring myself to give the dog a whack when he eats my slippers! Francie was always saying I was just a big softie but now all of a sudden I'm cast as a macho hard man. 'Hey, what *is* all this?' I say to Francie. 'What the hell's going on? Because whatever it is I think you ought to have medicine for it!'

"Okay, *okay*—maybe that wasn't the brightest comment to make, but damn it, I was so rattled by that time that I wasn't about to win first prize for diplomacy.

"And you know what happens next? After I drop this hint that she should see a doctor she comes at me with flailing fists and screeches that I ought to be castrated! Bloody hell! I get the real bugger of a black eye and everyone at the office wants to know what's going on. A wife-beater? Me? Don't make me laugh! All the beating was done by her.

"Well, life became diabolical then, it really did. I mean, there I was, slaving away all day sweeping up the legal crap my multinational generates and practising self-defence all night with this harpy who's for ever screeching and punching and chucking the dinner in my lap—for Christ's sake, she even threw my whisky in my face, and it was Johnnie Walker Black Label too, not some bloody supermarket's Own Brand! Christ, it's been a nightmare, it really has—and now it's become a bloody horror-movie.

"Anyway, by the end of last September I'm so desperate that I trundle along to the family doctor. 'Hey, Rupert,' I say, 'Francie's gone peculiar. Haul her in, would you, and stuff her with pills—Valium would do nicely for starters,' but all he does is mutter about her 'time of life' and give me dodgy looks. That's when I realise she must have been fantasising to him that I'm the world's number one sadist, and my God, that's when I really start to worry. How long has this been going on for, I ask myself, and who else has she been bitching to? Well, at that point I panic. 'Now look here, Rupe,' I shout, showing him the bruise on my arm where I'd parried a blow from the frying-pan, 'stop talking crap and get busy with the prescription pad! That woman's got to be calmed down!' But bugger it, he says he can't force-feed Francie pills and if she doesn't come to see him there's nothing he can do.

"Okay, I do try to persuade Francie to see him but she just says the Healing Centre gives her all the medical help she can ever need. So then I toy with the idea of coming to see you, but I never do it, do I? My mistake. The trouble is I'm not religious, as I'm sure you know—no offence meant—and I'm not really into all this healing stuff—although I'm sure you do a great job in your own way—and so I wind up telling myself that if Francie's so besotted with the Centre, you yourself could be part of the problem and maybe even compounding it.

"It was easier to reach the decision not to consult you because I knew I'd got a breather coming up—the two-week trip to Hong Kong. But I did tell myself that if she wasn't better by the time the kids came back from school for Christmas you and I would have to talk.

Normally I'm not the kind of chap who talks about his domestic problems to another chap—it was bad enough telling the family doctor, and as for telling a clergyman . . . But I could see the situation might in the end call for desperate measures.

"Well, I make my great escape—work like a dog among the Chinks—and as soon as I get back last night I see she's very much worse, not with it at all, and there were even times when she didn't seem to be there—mentally, I mean—God, it was bloody eerie, it was just as if she'd turned into someone else. Anyway I get up this morning—jet-lagged to pieces, of course—and I trail down to the kitchen and I find she's got a huge knife and a huge amount of liver—pounds and pounds of it—and she's stabbing and chopping and slicing away at all this damn offal and muttering to herself like a bag-lady. There's blood all over the table, blood all over everywhere, the kitchen's as good as a slaughter-house. I don't like to comment, since she looks exactly as if she wants to chop *me* up, so I just say airily: 'What's new?' and sit down at the table as if there's nothing out of the ordinary going on. And do you know what she says next? Now, this proves beyond all doubt that she's a certifiable lunatic. She says: 'Rosalind Darrow slept with Stacy McGovern and as a result he went and hanged himself!'

"Well, I ask you! What a fantasy! Of course we all know Rosalind would never in a million years stoop to have an affair with anyone, least of all her husband's curate! Anyway, the moment I heard this preposterous statement something in me snapped—I just felt so angry and so fed up that I threw all caution to the winds and yelled at her: 'You silly bitch, you don't seriously think anyone's going to believe that sick fairytale, do you?' and she growled: 'Arrrgh!' and plunged her knife all the way through the nearest slice of liver before rushing upstairs.

"Well, I've just finished making myself some coffee—and I'm so rattled that I spill the instant all over everywhere—when down the stairs again she comes and surges back into the kitchen. She's all cleaned up and she's dressed as if she's off to a wife-swapping party. 'What's going on?' I say but she takes no notice. She just grabs the knife and shoves it in her handbag and walks out. 'Hey, wait a minute!' I shout, but that was a bad move because the next moment she's swinging round and coming back towards me—she's making a hissing sound and in between hisses she's cursing in the vilest language you can imagine. Then comes the climax—she crowns the whole performance by vomiting all over me. Jesus! Was I shattered!

Then to my unutterable relief I hear the front door bang and I emerge from my traumatised stupor to realise she's gone.

"That settled it. It took me a while to clean myself up and put on fresh clothes, but then I came straight here to ask your advice.

"Christ Almighty, Nick, what's going on? It's got to be a brain tumour, hasn't it—she's had a complete personality change, but how am I going to explain it to the kids? I mean, I'll stand by Francie—provided she can get back to the way she was before she became someone else—but what's the prognosis? Can she be operated on, do you think? Is it certain to be cancer or is there a chance the growth's benign? And even if she survives the tumour, is a full recovery remotely possible?"

He finally stopped. His blue eyes, stricken, earnest, almost childlike in his extreme bewilderment, peered mistily, trustfully up at Nicholas. He was clutching the arms of his chair hard enough to crack them.

Nicholas said: "I think she may soon be a little better. Would you like me to come with you to the hospital to talk to the doctors?"

Harry nodded, no longer able to speak. Swallowing with difficulty he embarked on a series of rapid blinks.

The bell rang to announce Val's arrival, and as I opened the front door I heard, far away in the distance, the steady wail of the ambulance as it sped towards us along London Wall.

I I

By the time Lewis came home Nicholas and Harry were at the hospital while I was just having a very belated lunch. I had cooked myself a deep-fried banana sandwich and spooned a layer of rum raisin ice cream on top. I had a craving for at least three thousand of the worst kind of calories. I supposed it was all part of the aftermath of the trauma.

"How was Rosalind?" Lewis demanded, moving into the kitchen and heading for the percolator.

"Never mind Rosalind. She's alive and well and HIV-negative in Surrey. But just wait till I tell you about . . ." I rattled on at top speed, pausing only to nibble at the fried mess on my plate. The strange thing was that when I tried to eat this hi-cal dream I found it revolting. Perhaps I was even more traumatised than I'd imagined.

Meanwhile Lewis had extracted a spoon from the cutlery drawer and was sitting down with his coffee in front of the ice-cream tub which I had been too distracted to replace in the refrigerator.

Breaking off in the middle of my narrative I said severely: "Don't keep chiselling away at that ice cream unless you intend to finish the tub! It's not hygienic to keep having scoops with a spoon that's been in your mouth." Lewis was slobbish about that kind of thing, but the fact that I was bothering to waste time being picky about it was yet another indication of my pulped nerves.

"I'm finishing the tub," he said equably. "Your news is triggering a bout of nervous gluttony. Go on."

I resumed my narrative. Confiding in him was cathartic. By the time I reached the end I was feeling better but I still couldn't face the fried banana sandwich. I got up and shoved it in the swing-bin.

"Poor little Alice," said Lewis. "What a hellish thing to happen to you! I'm very sorry indeed to hear that Nicholas was stupid enough to put you through such an ordeal."

I was very surprised and more than a little shocked. "But what else could he have done? He had to have a witness, and it was hardly his fault that Francie went ballistic!"

"It was hardly his fault you didn't both wind up dead! My dear, it's time for you to hear the unvarnished truth: the whole scene was a disaster from beginning to end."

III

"*I've* no wish to be too severe in criticising Nicholas," said Lewis, "because it's obvious he's very debilitated at present, but in order to help you come to terms with all this, I feel you should be told where he went wrong."

I sat down abruptly again at the kitchen table.

"The first mistake he made," pursued Lewis, "was not to summon help straight away. He should have shown her into his study, made the excuse that he had to go to the lavatory and then called Val from the phone in the bedsit. He should also have sent you down to the hell-hole and told you to lock yourself in."

"But he needed a witness!"

"He needed you to survive! Francie wasn't just a sad woman with a crush on Nicholas, Alice. Not by this time."

"But there was no way of telling straight away that she was dangerous!"

"No way for you, perhaps; you lacked the experience to detect the danger, but Nicholas had already decided she was psychotic and we were both convinced she was suffering from a severe demonic infestation. It was seriously wrong that he allowed you to be present at the meeting."

"Perhaps he thought he needed my support—as he did at Communion this morning—and with Rosalind later—"

"However he justified himself he was wrong. Now let me tell you what he should have done next. After dispatching you to the hell-hole and calling Val he should have created a further diversion while he waited for help to arrive—he could have said he had to make another phone call, or if he wanted to keep Francie occupied he could even have suggested she made tea for them both. If she was coherent on arrival she might have been keen to perform such a cosy little domestic task which would have implied they were on intimate terms. But the most important thing he had to do was to avoid all serious conversation with her about why she was at the Rectory—he should have pre-empted the entire scene which actually took place."

"But that would have been so difficult! She was mad as a hatter!"

"All the more reason not to engage with her without the right medical support. However, since he did engage with her, let me tell you this: he should never have let her get to the point where she was advancing on you with a butcher's knife. He should have intervened long before with the deliverance rite, and if he'd done so he might have managed to bind the demons with the minimum of disruption."

"But you don't understand!" I persisted desperately. "Once she started talking about her brilliant scheme we had to know what she'd done to Harry!"

"Of course. The demons were luring you on. But all that could have waited until later. Nicholas should have put the welfare of his patient before his rampant curiosity."

Much disturbed by the rerun of the trauma from such a dark perspective I finally marched to the dresser and poured myself a slug of brandy. It was quite the wrong time of day for drinking but I no longer cared. I was too rattled. And I'd had enough of sweet tea.

I heard Lewis say: "I apologise for upsetting you," and making a big effort I managed to reply: "No, it's better to face the truth." Then after a swig from my glass I said: "Lewis, what *was* actually going on with Francie? Nicholas did try to explain but he was very confusing and kept talking about language and symbols and archetypes until finally he admitted he wasn't sure of anything except that he was shell-shocked."

"That was his final mistake," said Lewis tartly. "Priests should save their doubts and their theological hair-splitting for their spiritual directors. Lay people want *certainties.*"

"Do they?"

"Of course—it's human nature! When you consult a specialist in any field, you don't want to hear confused, agonised waffling! You want him to display confidence and lay the facts on the line!"

"But Nicholas seemed to be confident that in this case the facts were full of mystery and ambiguity!"

"The trouble with even the most intelligent liberals," said Lewis kindly but firmly, "is that they always have difficulty in calling a spade a spade. Now sit down with that brandy, my dear, and I'll tell you exactly what was wrong with Francie Parker . . ."

IV

"*The* one fact beyond dispute," said Lewis, "is that Francie was ill. Her illness was physical, mental and spiritual. (That's the dimension doctors tend to overlook.) We know she was physically ill because in the end she had a seizure and had to be hospitalised; her brain, which is part of her physical body, suddenly went hay-wire and various systems shut down. We know she was mentally ill because not only did she drift farther and farther from what is obviously reality but because in the end she succumbed to anti-social, violent behaviour which was deeply uncharacteristic. But we know too that in addition to the sickness which was afflicting her mind and body, she was spiritually ill. Indeed in my opinion the spiritual sickness was the primary illness, the one that generated the others.

"What was this spiritual illness all about? Let me explain. Francie had been successfully facing outwards—by which I mean she had learnt how to serve God by trying to help others in her own special way, the way to which she was uniquely suited, and this service made her feel happy and fulfilled. But gradually this outward-looking, God-centred service broke down and she became inward-looking and self-centred until the concept of 'service' was lost and her life at the Healing Centre became merely a way of fuelling the demands of her ego. There's nothing particularly unusual about this, I may add. We're all to some extent consumed by self-centredness, obsessed by our own egos. It's the human condition. In religious language it's called 'original sin.' But unfortunately it doesn't make us happy and it doesn't lead to lasting fulfilment.

"If God created us to find happiness in loving and serving others, happiness is not to be found in loving and serving the self to the exclusion of all others. There are two sorts of selves: the selfish self and the unselfish self. Self-centredness means pandering to the selfish self. God-centredness means using the unselfish self, the self that God created, to do what God created us to do—and in losing your selfish self you find your real true self. Got it? Well, never mind if you haven't. All you need to know is that the more self-centred and alienated from God you are, the more sick you become. We're all sick to some degree or other because each one of us is to some degree cut off from God. That's the human condition: no one's perfect so no one's a hundred per cent fit. There's a bit of today's Francie in all of us.

"Now, here's another fact for you to digest and one which is very relevant to Francie's illness. Human beings need some kind of God in order to feel whole, and if they lose touch with THE God, the right God, they can't rest until they've put something else in his place and elevated it into a false god. The spiritual vacuum always has to be filled. It's the way of the world. It's another part of the human condition. In religious language it's called 'the sin of idolatry.' In the language of psychology it's called—no, never mind, let's keep this simple.

"Well, anything can be a false god—money, power, politics, football, science, painting, fashion, fame, communism, pornography, food, drink, sex, atheism—you name it. The pattern is that the person alienated from God sets the false god up on a pedestal in his mind and worships it with increasing intensity and decreasing fulfilment until contact is quite lost with the real world. One thinks at once, of course, of Adolf Hitler and Nazism, but in fact this spiritual sickness is very common and not usually destructive on the global scale.

"Now, Francie's false god, specially selected by her for unstinted worship and adoration, was Nicholas. She worshipped and adored him until all she could think of was not serving God and fulfilling her true self but serving her selfish self by gaining, at no matter what cost, the object of her desire. This was unhealthy. This was dis-eased. This was self-destructive, destructive of the true self. But why did all this happen? Francie had earlier got it right—how did things then go so wrong? What was the genesis of this spiritual sickness which finally infected her mind and body and overwhelmed her?

"Well, we know that Francie's marriage had become increasingly unhappy, even though her husband wasn't a wife-beater. Harry was often away; he seems to have treated her as some sort of domestic convenience and he showed no interest in or understanding of the rewarding life she'd so enterprisingly carved out for herself at the Centre. If he did genuinely love her, he had a pretty odd way of showing it. (Do we, I wonder, hear echoes of the Darrows' unhealthy marriage at this point?) In addition Francie was beginning to feel redundant as a mother because her children were not only away for most of the year but also growing up, keen to cut loose from the maternal apron-strings. We suspect she's close to none of the other members of her family, whoever they are, because apart from her demanding, semi-invalid mother in Kent, she never mentions them. She doesn't mention her friends outside the Centre either. And why? Because she doesn't have any—apart from Rosalind, who we now know isn't her friend at all. Perhaps Francie's made the mistake of dropping her old friends to focus entirely on the Centre—and at the centre of the Centre (forgive the pun) is Nicholas, who she increasingly came to believe could give her all the love which is so patently lacking elsewhere.

"Francie was starved of love. That was the rock-bottom, unvarnished truth. That was the genesis of this illness. When Christ commanded his disciples to love one another he knew what he was talking about. Without love we get sick and wither; without love we die. Ask the doctors and psychiatrists who have dealt with unloved, abandoned people. Ask the social workers who deal with the underclass, the urban low-life. Ask the chaplains who work in prisons and mental hospitals. If people feel they're unlovable and isolated they're prey to all kinds of illness, mental and physical. Each human being is a single entity, you see; the spiritual can't be divorced from the physical and mental and vice versa. It's all one . . . You understand that, don't you, Alice?"

I said I did.

"Then let's finally consider today's most serious stage of Francie's illness. Until today Francie's physical health seems to have held up, but as we know, the spiritual sickness has been triggering mental illness for some time. She'd become neurotically fixated on Nicholas, and the more ill she became mentally the more vulnerable she was to a far more serious spiritual illness. In fact the spiritual and mental illnesses seem to have interacted on each other to permit the sickness which today spiralled out of control.

"What happened today is obvious: Francie was being driven by a force which made her both evil and violent. Now, let's switch languages for a moment and look at things from a medical angle. Most mentally ill people, contrary to misinformed popular belief, are neither evil nor violent, and the small minority who want to go around killing people are usually either suffering from a fairly rare type of schizophrenia or else they're psychopaths—sociopaths, as they're called nowadays. Sociopaths have a personality disorder. If the violent behaviour is schizophrenic and triggered by a chemical imbalance in the brain it can be treated by drugs, although drug therapy isn't always successful and there can be problems with side-effects. If the violence is sociopathic, triggered by a personality disorder, then there's a problem because sociopaths are notoriously difficult to treat. Sometimes psychotherapy helps. But not always.

"Now, Francie wasn't in either of those categories. She wasn't a sociopath, someone who can't empathise with other people and in consequence has no qualms about hurting them, and in my opinion she wasn't a schizophrenic either. There's supposed to be no such thing as a typical schizophrenic, but there are certain symptoms which can encourage a diagnosis of schizophrenia to be made, and before her breakdown today I didn't see any of them. What I did see was evidence of her neurotic fixation, but this type of disorder wouldn't normally produce a murderous outburst out of the blue. What should have happened to Francie, if one bears in mind her illness over the last few months, was a nervous breakdown. What did happen was this extremely rabid psychosis—and it's not without interest, let me add, that the murderous assault was in the end directed not at you, although she'd sensed you were her rival, but at Nicholas, the object of her desire. Obsessed people do occasionally kill the love-object, but in all the cases I've read about there was a build-up beforehand of violent threats. It seems to me, from your account of the scene, that when Francie was being Francie it was you she was gunning for, but when she turned on Nicholas at the end something else was standing in her place.

"So what's the explanation? It seems abundantly clear to me that the Devil and his cohorts used the mental and spiritual illnesses which were present in her to try to destroy Nicholas and his ministry. (You'll note that I make no namby-pamby, mealy-mouthed, liberal apology for using the robust, old-fashioned religious language to describe this all too commonplace reality: the attempts by the forces of darkness to blot out the powers of light.) But having said all that, I must also state unequivocally that Francie wasn't possessed by the Devil. If this had been the case there would have been a greater variety of bizarre symptoms, much more distress over a long period of time and an acute awareness by Francie herself that her personality was being eroded. The hallmark of this case was that Francie was convinced throughout that there was nothing wrong—the demons were invisible to her because they were embedded in the mental and spiritual illness.

"So my final diagnosis is that she was not possessed by the Devil but infested by his cohorts, the demons. The diagnosis is confirmed by the fact that when Nicholas at last got his act together and called them out, they responded—and now they've been dispatched. The result is that Francie will still have her obsession with Nicholas but she'll no longer be crashing around in a psychotic frenzy. She'll need a lot of therapy for the obsession, and a lot of love—loving care, loving prayer, loving support—to restore her spiritual health, but she'll recover. Sadly, the prognosis for a paranoid schizophrenic or a sociopath wouldn't be half so positive."

By this time I was feeling much more enlightened but the enlightenment was producing new questions.

"Nicholas said something about how exorcists deal directly with the unconscious mind when they name the demons. Would you agree with that, or—"

"Oh yes, yes, yes, I can talk the language of psychology just as well as he can, but the old-fashioned religious language is more graphic, more powerful, more evocative of the life and death struggles of spiritual illness! Of course one can dress up the phenomenon of deliverance in the latest flavour-of-the-month scientific language, but we live in the age of the sound-bite and the most effective sound-bite here is EVIL WAS PRESENT BUT WAS CAST OUT!"

"Okay, but . . ." Further questions cascaded through my mind as the brandy cranked up my brain. "Could I get infested like that if I developed an obsession?" I demanded. "Is it possible the demons only pretended to go away and are still present in Francie? Or if they've gone, could they come back and reinfest her? And what happens if she's not normal when she comes out of the coma? What happens if the doctors at the hospital think demonic infestation is a fiction and that deliverance is rubbish? And how is poor Harry ever going to understand anything that's happened?"

"Right," said Lewis efficiently, not in the least disconcerted and even appearing to relish rolling out the next bunch of certainties, "here come the answers. Number one: you could indeed get infested, if you were caught in a similar spiral of mental and spiritual illness, but rest assured that it's not likely unless you've been mixed up with the occult. If you stick to a healthy spiritual path you'll be in no danger. (And remember: no demon can withstand the power of Christ.) Francie was unlucky in that she was the ideal tool for the Devil to use in his efforts to liquidate Nicholas—but on the other hand we may yet find she's been dabbling with an Ouija board; unhappy people yearning for hope of a better future regularly get mixed up with occult practices.

"Number two: the demons quite definitely came out of Francie when she stopped trying to kill Nicholas and passed out. Number three: they won't come back so long as she receives the correct medical and spiritual care. Number four: she may not be normal when she recovers consciousness, but her prognosis, as I've explained, is good. Number five—wait a minute, I've lost track. Where have I got to?"

"The sceptical doctors."

"Ah yes. Number five: Nicholas isn't going to run around the hospital declaring that Francie's been suffering from a demonic infestation and that he cured her, by the grace of God, through performing an emergency rite of deliverance. Val, of course, will understand what happened, and she'll liaise with the doctors at the hospital when they eventually confess themselves amazed by Francie's speedy recovery; the best doctors are always humble enough to be open-minded about the mysteries of illness, particularly mental illness—they're not all reductionist robots. However in the end, to preserve the scientific proprieties, they'll write her illness off as an acute psychotic episode resulting from a nervous breakdown and everyone will be happy. 'Nervous breakdown' is such a useful phrase and makes laymen feel they understand exactly what's happened—and that answers your final question about Harry. I don't think you need worry about him being baffled by esoteric explanations."

"Poor Harry." I got up and chucked the empty ice cream tub into the swing-bin to join the fried banana sandwich.

"Quite," said Lewis dryly. "But I shouldn't feel too sorry for him. He may not be a wife-beater but I doubt that Francie would have felt so unloved if he hadn't been so lacking in sympathy and understanding. Emotionally speaking the man's obviously as dumb as an ox."

I sat down again with my brandy. "The only good thing to come out of this mess," I said, "is that no one will believe Francie now if she goes around saying Rosalind seduced Stacy, so we no longer have to worry about her spilling the beans at the inquest."

"There's a silver lining to every cloud. Which reminds me . . . My dear, I want to tell you about the cloud I've been wrestling with and the silver lining which I'm only now beginning to recognise. Harry Parker hasn't been the only man, I fear, who's made a habit of behaving like a dumb ox in his dealings with the opposite sex."

With a sinking heart I finally remembered that he had had lunch with Venetia the Vamp. Stifling a sigh I took another swig of brandy and prepared to listen to the latest gory details of his infatuation.

V

"*As usual* I had the most stimulating meeting with Venetia," said Lewis. "She's made excellent progress and I'm sure now that she'll go on to lead the rewarding life she so richly deserves. But—" He heaved a sigh and fell silent.

"But?" I prompted patiently, expecting some moan about how far Cambridge was from London.

"But I feel now," said Lewis regretfully, "that she and I really must go our separate ways."

This was certainly a surprise. Clamping down on any expression of relief I enquired cautiously: "Why do you think that?"

"She just met me today to be nice to me. I saw that at once. She was bothered because she knew I'd been upset last time and she wanted to try to put things right."

"Decent of her."

"Yes, wasn't it? So . . . No, I'm sorry, I'm not being wholly honest here. The real truth—the unvarnished truth—and I hope I'm not such a coward that I can't face up to it—" He stopped to summon the necessary courage.

I was suddenly aware of a genuine interest forming. "Go on," I said, trying to sound encouraging.

"All right, here goes. The truth is that when she saw me last time on my crutches, an old crock who looked as if he had next to no mileage left, it must have seemed to her like a vision of things to come—a blinding insight into what a relationship with an old man was likely to mean in the long run. So having seen me in the light of this chilling reality, she decided I wasn't right for her either now or later—yet at the same time she liked me enough to want to be kind, and that was why she staged this additional meeting which would enable us to part with grace and style. It was a splendid gesture and of course I was most grateful to her, but . . . there was no doubt I did feel a trifle sad afterwards."

"Lewis, did she actually spell this out to you or are you just guessing?"

"It's ESP," he said outrageously, and had the nerve to give me his broadest smile.

"ESP? It sounds more like absolute rubbish! Lewis, if Venetia really loves you she won't care how much of an old crock you may or may not be in the dim and distant future!"

"Quite so, but she obviously realises that two people past fifty should be prudent rather than romantic about their relationships. I'm certain she now feels that our friendship shouldn't be taken further, but I don't blame her because to my surprise I've come to believe she's right."

"Honestly?"

"Well, what else can I think when I'm apparently so old that the best of sirens just wants to be kind to me? Ye gods, if this is what it's like to be sixty-seven I might as well book myself into the nearest nursing home and order a headstone!"

"Oh, don't be so idiotic!" I exclaimed exasperated. Lewis was becoming increasingly prone to drivel on about the horrors of old age. "You obviously need to be reminded that a man of sixty-seven is usually described as distinguished whereas a woman of sixty-seven is inevitably written off as an old bag! Why don't you take time out to thank God you're male instead of moaning away about nursing homes and headstones?"

He laughed. "Very well," he said, "I shall abstain from self-pity and merely say: so much for my romantic dreams about Venetia; I finally woke up. I'm sure I shall always find her alluring but I accept now she's not for me. That's the cloud I've been wrestling with."

"And the silver lining?"

"This experience has made me realise that it's no good perpetually searching for the ideal mistress and then kidding myself she'd be the ideal wife. And that in turn means I've finally got to admit that my spiritual director's been right all along about my private life."

"He has?"

"No question about it. He always said I ought to marry a nice middle-class girl who could put up with all my moods and cook me excellent meals and make old age heaven instead of hell."

"Super. Lewis, talking of nice middle-class women, can we go back to Francie for a moment? I was wondering if—"

"Don't interrupt. This is important. What I'm saying is this: I don't need grand passion at my time of life. I need someone I can get on with—someone I find physically attractive, of course, but basically someone who can stand the strain when I start to go downhill—"

"Oh, do shut up about your age! Listen, I was wondering if I ought to go and see Francie in hospital later—it might be therapeutic for me. Otherwise I'll be stuck with this nightmarish memory of—"

"—so bearing all that in mind," interrupted Lewis, raising his voice to drown me out, "it seems obvious to me that there's only one woman I know who's remotely suitable for the job. How about it?"

"How about what?" I was already fed up with this new fantasy of a middle-class nurse-cum-sex-slave who could provide him with gourmet cuisine.

"How about you and I getting together? I could buy a little house in Westminster—I know that's the area where you feel most at home—"

"Hang on," I said confused, finally forgetting Francie. "I'm not following this. Are you asking me to be your housekeeper?"

"Good heavens, no! Nowadays two unrelated people can never live together without everyone assuming they share the same bed, and since I'm a priest—"

"So do you mean—are you trying to say—"

"I'm suggesting we should get married. It is, in fact, a most sensible and intelligent idea—"

"Good God."

"—and I think we'd do very well. You probably wouldn't have to put up with me for more than ten years and then you'd be a rich widow. I know I was born in 1921—and don't think I don't realise how off-putting this must be for you—but I could offer you security, a nice home, *and* (with the new hip tamed) some very decent and respectable sexual intercourse every now and then—"

"Lewis—"

"Oh, you wouldn't mind that at all, I promise you! I was always very good in bed, and besides there's nothing like a bit of practice for brushing up one's skills—"

"Lewis—please—"

"—and if you wanted children, well, that's all right, I wouldn't mind so long as it was accepted that I was a father of the old school and didn't have anything to do with the child before it had learned to use a lavatory. So you see, all in all, even though I'm sixty-seven and currently on crutches, I do still have a considerable amount to offer—to the right woman. In fact, not to put too fine a point on it, I can offer you everything you've ever wanted, so—"

"Not quite everything," I said.

We finally managed to look each other in the eyes.

VI

"*All right,*" said Lewis at last. "I see the practical approach hasn't worked, although in marriage it's the practical approach that counts in the long run. Let's try this from another angle—"

"Can I say something, please? Can I finally get a word in? Lewis, it's very, very kind of you to propose, and of course I do realise you're paying me the most wonderful compliment—"

"You sound like the heroine of a Victorian novel. Spare me the Lily Dale style of rebuff!"

"—and I know that the most sensible thing for me to do would be to say yes, but—"

"Women really are impossible!" he growled, levering himself to his feet. "*Impossible!*" He shot a furious glance at his empty coffee-mug.

"Oh God, I'm saying it all wrong, I'm sorry, but I've never been proposed to before and I've never even expected to be proposed to—if you could only understand how utterly pole-axed I am you wouldn't think I'm trying to hurt you or insult you or—"

"All right, all right, don't panic!" He sat down again with a bump. "What I'm trying to get across to you," he said, somehow managing to sound both calm and rational, "is that *this*—you and I—is a workable reality, while *that*—you and Nicholas—is a romantic dream which could destroy not only you but Nicholas as well."

Tears sprang to my eyes. "I haven't forgotten what you said last night," I said. "I haven't forgotten how you said the Devil was using me too to get at Nicholas. And now you're implying, aren't you, that I'm like Francie, infested with demons who have embedded themselves in an obsession!"

"If you've been listening to me carefully, you'll know that's nonsense. Of course you're not obsessed or infested! Obviously you genuinely love him, and no demon can embed itself in a genuine love because all genuine love is from God. But the Devil can still try to take advantage of the situation and use it for his own ends."

I tried without success to reply.

Once more Lewis hauled himself to his feet. I was aware of him moving to the dresser, opening a drawer and pulling out a box of Kleenex for me, but suddenly he became motionless. Dashing the tears from my eyes I saw he had come face to face with Nicholas's bear, seated on the dresser in front of the best Delft plate.

"Is this creature," said Lewis slowly, "what I think it is?"

"Nicholas rescued him this morning from Butterfold. He's going to give him away at last—he's going to put away childish things because . . ." I faltered but forced myself to go on. "He had a reconciliation with Rosalind. The marriage will move into a new phase. She won't just be his childhood friend any more. She'll be his wife—truly his wife—and they'll have a mature relationship and all the childish side of the marriage will fade away and they'll live happily ever after." Tears were now rushing down my cheeks. "So you see, you don't have to worry any more about me and Nicholas," I heard myself say, scrubbing my eyes with the back of my hand as Lewis remained transfixed, the box of Kleenex forgotten in his hands. "He's all right now, and even if he wasn't I know he'd never feel physically attracted to me. I'm not slim and blonde like Rosalind."

Lewis said flatly: "Nicholas has never been attracted to slim blondes. He married Rosalind not because she was a slim blonde but in spite of it. And if he's really moving on towards emotional maturity he won't be having a reconciliation with a woman who merely replaced his teddy-bear in his affections."

Then as I stared at him through my tears, he moved back to the table, handed me the box of Kleenex and sat down not opposite me but at my side.

VII

At that point he asked me to tell him exactly what had happened in Surrey that morning, but I found I had the greatest difficulty in forcing my memory to focus on the scenes at the farmhouse. I saw now that I could have misunderstood what had happened, and I saw too why I had been tempted to believe in the reconciliation.

"I'd recognised how jealous I was of Rosalind," I said to Lewis, "but I suppose deep down I knew that the best I could hope for was that she and Nicholas would return to their old arrangement of being together just at weekends. If I couldn't have him for myself—and I knew that was out of the question—then a wife who spent most of the time apart from him was for me the least painful scenario."

"Alice—"

"The one thing I couldn't stand," I said rapidly, "would be Nicholas divorcing Rosalind and marrying someone else who lived at the Rectory full-time. I'd have to leave, even though that would be the last thing I'd want to do in so many ways. I've been happier here than I've ever been in my life."

Lewis said evenly: "There are times when one's called to move on. St. Benet's has been a very important staging-post for you on your journey, but who's to say that you won't be moving on to an even greater happiness elsewhere?"

Fearful that he might propose again I abandoned the table and wandered to the dresser. The bear was looking at me with his mournful, knowing glass eyes. Picking him up I held him tightly and felt I knew something of the comfort which Nicholas had experienced long ago in his nursery. Then the moment of empathy with Nicholas coaxed my memory into action. As I recalled our conversation earlier I heard him say in describing his adult life: "There were a lot of things I didn't find. Things I tried not to think about. Things I tried to believe weren't as important as security."

"Nicholas never found a genuine companionship in that marriage, did he?" I said suddenly. "There would have been no meeting of the minds. He wouldn't have found understanding—and he wouldn't have found true peace either because he didn't care about his home and always wanted to be somewhere else. All he and Rosalind really had in common were the children and the shared memories of their childhood."

"That's all they'll ever have in common. But nevertheless—"

"They've outgrown each other," I said, not listening, wholly absorbed in reinterpreting the scene at Butterfold and the significance of Bear. "He knows that now. It'll be very, very hard to let her go but he knows it's got to be done. He wants the best for her and he realises he can never provide the new life she needs and deserves . . ." I found I was hugging the bear tightly again. "I understand now," I said, keeping my back to Lewis as I reseated Bear in front of the Delft plate. "I didn't want to understand because I didn't want to think of him getting divorced and marrying someone new who would make my life here unbearable, but it's better to face the truth, isn't it? When one's grappling with the cutting edge of reality one can't afford to start believing a lie."

I heard the chair scrape across the floor as Lewis yet again rose to his feet, but I remained staring at the bear. "Okay," I said, "I accept that there'll come a time when I have to move out of the Rectory and out of his life. But that's still a long way off, isn't it? He's a long way from being divorced and an even longer way from remarriage and meanwhile I can stay on here and everything will return to normal and we'll be just as we were before all these terrible things started to happen—"

"I think not," said Lewis in his kindest voice, and began to destroy the last of my illusions.

VIII

"*Predicting* the future's a risky business," he said, "but let me start by repeating what I've said to you before: it's by no means certain that Nicholas and Rosalind are capable of separating. They may think they are, but they could be mistaken."

"But I'm sure—"

"You can't be sure. We're predicting the future, an activity not known for dealing in certainties. However, if they do stay together, the marriage will have to be completely restructured since the old split-level arrangement has broken down beyond repair. Alternatively, if they somehow manage to separate, I foresee that it will be very difficult for Nicholas to adjust to the break-up and it may take him a long time to reconstruct his private life. During that long time he'll have to wrestle with the problem of living as a priest should when he has no wife and no gift for celibacy, and how likely, do you think, is it that he'll solve such a difficult problem satisfactorily when he's living in the same house as a woman who's in love with him?"

"But Nicholas would never—"

"Never be tempted? Oh yes, he would! He may be a very gifted priest but he's also a very ordinary man in some ways, and if he no longer has Rosalind to keep him on an even keel you'll soon become an irresistible temptation to him."

"But Nicholas would never want me in that way!"

"Why not?"

"Well, he couldn't! Marriage just isn't a possibility at all!"

"I'm not talking about marriage. God only knows whom Nicholas will marry—that's all in the remote future and may never happen anyway if he and Rosalind find long-term separation psychologically impossible."

"Are you trying to say—"

"Yes, I am. Nicholas is a good man but he's not a stainless steel saint incapable of sin. No one is. He's a human being capable of making bad mistakes and getting into a lethal mess—as the events of the past few days have made only too clear."

"Yes, but—"

"Now let me lay out the unvarnished truth for you, Alice, and this isn't a prediction which may or may not come true. This is a fact. If Nicholas were to start sleeping with you his integrity as a spiritual leader would be shot. When any religious community goes to pieces the collapse almost always begins with a loss of integrity manifested in the form of sexual licence. The leader uses and abuses the women around him—or the men—and then the whole enterprise, fueled by an atmosphere of jealousy, suspicion and anger, descends rapidly into chaos."

"But Nicholas must know all that!"

"Of course he does, and so far he's kept himself honest, but he's now facing a prolonged period of emotional stress and he's going to find it tough enough to maintain his moral equilibrium without having to deal with your feelings for him—or his for you. Do you see what I'm saying? I believe that what first attracted you to Nicholas was his great integrity. You're now in a position where you could destroy it—and once it was gone and he was just another wonder worker willing to devalue others to satisfy his needs, would you still love him? Or want to marry him?"

I said: "I can't imagine not loving him." Taking off my glasses I began to rub the clouded lenses. "But I can't believe he'd ever want to marry me and if we did sleep together I can't imagine that I'd ever satisfy him for long." I replaced my glasses but they misted up again almost immediately. "I couldn't bear him getting tired of me," I said. "I couldn't bear him becoming indifferent. I'd rather not sleep with him at all than leave myself open to that kind of pain."

I waited for him to speak but all I heard was silence. "Long ago," I said, polishing my glasses over and over again, "when I was born and for a short time afterwards, there was a man who loved me. I have a photo of him holding me in his arms and he looks happy and proud. But that didn't last long. He went away and never came back and I don't know to this day whether he's alive or dead. I'd never want to go through that sort of rejection again. Better not to love at all than risk people becoming tired of you and ceasing to care. But even so . . . despite all that . . . I can't imagine not loving Nicholas."

There was another long pause before Lewis said: "It's very hard to have a parent who rejects you."

"Both my parents rejected me. That's why in the end I was glad to be ugly. The uglier you are the less likely people are to love you, and so long as there's no love around then you can't get hurt—or so I used to think—as I ate the ice cream—and all the other stuff which helped make me so ugly—"

"My dearest Alice," said Lewis. "My dearest Alice—"

"Okay, I'll shut up now, I'm sorry if I've been embarrassing."

"I'm not embarrassed. I just want to say—"

"It's all right, I'll leave the Rectory. I see now it's the only thing to do to keep Nicholas safe and me sane. You needn't worry about him any more."

"—I just want to say this: you're not ugly. I'll never reject you. The offer of marriage still stands."

The front door closed in the distance as Nicholas returned from the hospital.

IX

He halted as soon as he crossed the threshold of the kitchen. I was scooping up the sodden tissues and heading for the swing-bin. Lewis was making a great business of washing up his coffee-mug while keeping his crutches under control. Both of us were in such a state that neither of us remembered to ask him how Francie was.

"What's going on?" demanded Nicholas. Of course it must have been obvious to him that a fraught scene had been taking place.

Lewis said airily: "Oh, just a little speculation about the future!" and I mumbled: "Oh, just a little reminiscing about the past!" We both spoke at exactly the same moment.

"How's Francie?" added Lewis, finally remembering to ask the right question.

Nicholas reluctantly allowed himself to be diverted. Francie, we were told, had recovered consciousness but she was very confused and had no memory of the violent scene at the Rectory. He himself had left the hospital when the doctors had taken Francie away for a battery of tests. Val was staying on to give Harry support and to meet the psychiatrist who had been summoned; she had wanted to gauge how likely he was to be helpful.

"I felt it was better anyway to leave Val with Harry," concluded Nicholas, slumping down at the kitchen table. "As a doctor she'll find it easier to get him the hard information which he keeps optimistically asking for."

"Good decision," said Lewis bluntly. "You look exhausted, and if you haven't yet started to suffer from delayed shock you soon will. Go upstairs and rest."

"Later. How was Venetia?"

"Extremely well."

"Thank God we occasionally get something right." He picked up the box of Kleenex tissues which I hadn't had time to hide. "Who's been using these?"

"Me," I said, "but I'm okay now."

"Well, if you're not going to rest," said Lewis to Nicholas, "I certainly am. Would you excuse me please, Alice, if I take myself off to the bedsit for a while? We'll talk again later."

"Yes, of course." I was trying to work out how "okay" I really was. I felt as if all my emotions had haemorrhaged, leaving my mind bled white. Looking around for some simple task to perform I saw the kettle and filled it. Nicholas would want tea. In relief I plugged in the kettle and reached for the tea-caddy.

As Lewis's footsteps receded across the hall Nicholas said: "Was the old boy upsetting you?"

"Yes, but it doesn't matter." I found the teapot hadn't been washed. I thought of us drinking sweet tea after the scene with Francie and how Harry had arrived before I had had the chance to clear up. Later I had simply forgotten the teapot. I had been too preoccupied with making that vile sandwich and brewing the coffee which Lewis had drunk later . . . I suddenly realised Nicholas was speaking again.

"If you're upset," he said, "that matters to me."

I rinsed the teapot and dried it carefully. I was unable to look at him.

"What happened, Alice?"

"Well, as a matter of fact," I said, "Lewis proposed to me."

There was a peculiarly blank silence. I turned, expecting to see a profound astonishment, but his expression was more difficult to read than I'd anticipated. The surprise was certainly there, but there were other emotions too, emotions which at that moment lay beyond my power to identify.

"It should have been humiliating," I said, "but it wasn't. In the end it was touching."

Nicholas finally said: "Why should it have been humiliating?"

"Oh, he was playing the self-centred male chauvinist, talking about how he needed a middle-class slave to wait on him hand and foot as he sank into his dotage, but of course that wasn't what was going on at all, I see that now. He was trying to kill two birds with one stone—trying to protect you while at the same time being generous and kind to me. He was *very* kind," I said, "and *very* generous and I know he's fond of me, but you're the one he really loves, Nicholas. He'd do anything to ensure your safety."

"I'm quite capable of ensuring my own safety."

"Lewis doesn't think so."

"That's because in the past he couldn't ensure his own safety; he's projecting his past onto my future, but my future isn't his past and never will be . . . Are you going to marry him?"

"No. I couldn't marry a man I didn't love. I suppose in the end it's all a question of integrity."

We were silent for a while. I had turned away from him again to watch the kettle coming to the boil, and even when Nicholas brought the milk-jug from the refrigerator to the counter I couldn't look at him.

At last I found myself compelled to say: "You still love Rosalind, don't you?"

"Yes, but I can see now it's not the kind of love that has anything to do with marriage. Rosalind was always more the sister I never had than the girlfriend I wanted to marry. No wonder I never understood poor Stacy's problem! I was too busy repressing the knowledge of my own failure to move on from a childhood relationship."

"But now that you understand what was wrong—"

"—I'll be able to move on? Yes, I hope so, but I can't move on with Rosalind. Brothers and sisters always in the end have to go their separate ways."

"But did you never realise—suspect—"

"I was too obsessed with what she represented to me to see the relationship for what it was. Rosalind was the one who saw the truth and faced up to it. Not me."

"How are you going to explain all that to your boys?"

"I don't know, but I hope I'll have the guts to be honest." He hesitated before adding: "I realise now that they've been reflecting all the tensions of the marriage. I'd like to think that in the end—after the divorce—in time—I'll be less of an alien figurehead to them and more of a genuine father."

The kettle boiled. I made the tea.

"I hope that'll be so," said Nicholas. "I hope it will. I've got to hope, haven't I? I've got to hope that Rosalind will find the happiness I've denied her for so long, I've got to hope we'll each go on to a better life, I've got to hope that somehow all this mess and misery will be redeemed, but hope's hard sometimes, particularly when you're in pain. It's hard when you're enduring Good Friday to imagine the dawning of Easter Day."

"But the dawn came in the end, didn't it?" While I waited for the tea to brew I took two mugs from the cupboard. "I suppose," I said, thinking of the black interval which lay between Good Friday and Easter Day, "all this will have a bad effect on your ministry."

"There'll be a downside. That's inevitable. I must expect a lot of criticism and anger as people project their disappointed expectations onto me, but perhaps in the end . . ." He hesitated again.

"In the end?"

"Perhaps in the end I might compensate them by becoming a better priest. I have this unusual ministry among the sick and the broken, and now that *I've* been sick and *I've* been broken I should have a new solidarity with those I try to help. Wonder workers are never sick and broken, of course. Wonder workers never fail. But a Christian priest acquires strength through weakness and power through vulnerability, so perhaps . . . well, as I said a moment ago, I've got to hope."

We fell silent but as I began to pour the tea he said: "The real problem will come if—when—I remarry. Francie got that all wrong, thinking there'd be no problem so long as I married someone who didn't have a husband living. There'll always be a problem so long as I'm a divorcé and not a widower."

"You'd lose your job?"

"No, I'm not in parish work where a remarried divorced priest is always an embarrassment. If the trustees at the Healing Centre back me, the Church authorities will just consider St. Benet's a useful place to stow an awkward customer and they'll turn a blind eye. If the trustees don't back me . . . but I think they will in the end. I've got to hope, haven't I? I've got to hope."

"I suppose the conservative ones will say marriage should be for ever."

"I think they'll all say marriage should be for ever as far as a priest is concerned, but I know what I'm going to say to them in reply. I shall say I only wish I'd had a relationship with Rosalind which did allow my marriage to last for ever; I shall say that although I wanted above all else to heal the relationship and keep the marriage alive I had to recognise in the end that no healing—no cure, I should say—was possible; I shall remind them that cures don't always happen, because God doesn't operate by waving a magic wand. But what he does try to do constantly is to redeem what goes wrong, and in redemption is the healing. That's why I've got to accept what's happened and learn from it. It's because the learning will in the end become part of the redemption. It'll help me find healing by building a new life with someone else."

I recognised my cue and prepared to tell him of my decision to leave St. Benet's.

X

I remember being so relieved that when the moment of truth finally came my voice was steady and my eyes were tearless. I kept thinking of Lewis saying I had the potential to destroy Nicholas's integrity. Whatever happened I had to make sure Nicholas was safe.

"There's something I want to tell you," I said, and as I spoke I fixed my mind resolutely on the fact that as he would never marry me, no future with him of any kind was possible. "I entirely understand that you'll want to remarry, and that's why I've decided—"

"It's good of you to say that," he interrupted, "but of course understanding is one thing and approval is quite another. You'd be justified in thinking, along with a lot of other people, that a priest has no business remarrying when his divorced wife's still alive."

"But don't you remember what I told you in the car on the way home from Butterfold? I said it was wrong to place the burden of unreal expectations on a clergyman!"

"Yes, but nevertheless . . . the clergy are supposed to set an example. You must still be thinking I'd compromise my integrity if I remarried."

"Nicholas—"

"Alice, I'll tell you how I see it. You don't have to agree with me, but I'll tell you anyway."

"I assure you—"

"No, hear me out. I think it would compromise my integrity if I were to pretend I'm called to celibacy. I think it would compromise my integrity if I pretended to be chaste but kept a mistress. I think it would compromise my integrity if I lived a lie by pretending that my dead marriage was still alive. Christianity's about life, not death—it's a gospel of hope and renewal, not despair and decline! I may be wiped out at the moment, I may be battered and shattered and thoroughly wrecked, but I've still got my faith and I'm going to go on in the belief that the best years of my life are still to come—I'm going to go on in the hope that in the end *everything* will be redeemed, healed and made new."

I waited till I was sure the words would come. Then I answered: "You've said what I hoped you'd say. I knew you wouldn't let me down."

"You really mean that? But I thought—"

"You misunderstood."

There was another pause before Nicholas said: "Let there be an end to all misunderstandings."

An absolute silence fell. We stood side by side in front of the counter by the mugs of steaming tea and we listened to the silence as we held our breath. Then I heard Nicholas add casually: "Of course there'll be difficult days ahead. It'll be a long haul. But contrary to Lewis's worst fears—which I can imagine all too clearly—we'll survive, won't we, Alice? We'll manage."

Yet again I removed my glasses and yet again I wiped my eyes with the back of my hand. Only then did I allow myself to look at him. For a long moment we were motionless, wordlessly communicating everything that needed to be said. Then as I waited, hardly daring to believe such happiness was possible, Nicholas slipped his arms around my waist and stooped to kiss me lovingly on the mouth.

Author's Note

Dr. Gareth Tuckwell and the Reverend David Flagg, whose book *A Question of Healing* provides the quotations at the start of each chapter, worked together from 1986 until 1994 at Burrswood, the Christian Centre for Medical and Spiritual Care (now the Christian Centre for Healthcare and Ministry), at Groombridge in Kent.

The Reverend Christopher Hamel Cooke, whose writings are quoted at the beginning of each part, was Rector of St. Marylebone with Holy Trinity in London from 1979 until 1989, and the founder of the Marylebone Healing Centre where, as at Burrswood, doctors and priests work together to help the sick.

Any resemblance between the above authors and any character in this book is coincidental. All the characters in this book are fictitious and are based on no one at either of the above locations.

The Wonder Worker

SUSAN HOWATCH

A Reader's Guide

A Conversation with Susan Howatch

Q: You've previously written about Nicholas Darrow, Lewis Hall, and Venetia Hoffenberg in the Starbridge books, yet *The Wonder Worker* isn't a sequel, exactly. What made you come back to these characters?

SH: At the end of *Mystical Paths* (book 5 of the Starbridge series) there is a flash-forward to Nicholas Darrow's ministry of healing at St. Benet's church in London in 1988. After the Starbridge books, I wanted to write a novel about the ministry of healing set in modern London. It made sense to pick up Nicholas Darrow's situation and use it, spinning off three or four Starbridge characters.

Q: You often use the viewpoints of several different characters to tell a story. What are some of the difficulties in giving each character his or her own voice, and, particularly, in speaking so convincingly through different genders?

SH: I do not find it difficult to give each character his or her own voice unless the character is very like me. Fortunately, this is a great rarity—although of course there is something of myself in each character. As for gender, it's simply an aspect of personality, of varying degrees of interest or importance. My interest in people lies way beyond the stereotypical boundaries of gender. As Jung said, a man's soul does not reside in his genitals.

Q: You've described having multiple narrators as resembling "how it is after an accident: Everyone tells a different story—and none of them is entirely right." Is there a story for you as an author that is truer than any of the individual characters' stories?

SH: There should be a story for the reader that is greater than any one of the individual narrations. This is because the reader is put by me in the position of God—i.e., he or she has the whole overview, and knows more about the characters in the end than they know about each other.

Q: Alice's narration opens and closes the book, which gives her version of the events more prominence. Why did you choose Alice for this role instead of one of the other characters?

SH: The fact that Alice narrates two sections instead of one does not make her more important than the other narrators. The story simply required her to do the beginning and end.

Q: Alice shares a name with the heroine of Lewis Carroll's *Alice in Wonderland,* something that Lewis Hall notes in his section of the book. Carroll's Alice seems to be the quintessentially sensible and down-to-earth British girl in a frequently irrational world. Do you see your Alice as sharing some of her qualities? Is she in a similar situation?

SH: Alice is certainly exploring an unknown, fascinating, and occasionally alarming world like Carroll's Alice. But the comparison with *Alice* shouldn't be pushed too far.

Q: The British title for this book was *A Question of Integrity,* while the American version is *The Wonder Worker.* Both titles seem to me to refer to *Nicholas Darrow.* Was that your intention? Did you mean for the titles to refer to any of the other characters?

SH: *The Wonder Worker* was my own choice of title, and I'm glad the Americans kept it. The name *A Question of Integrity* was purely a marketing decision made by my UK publishers. All the characters in the book wrestle with integrity versus fragmentation/corruption. *The Wonder Worker* applies not only to Nicholas Darrow but also to Lewis and indeed to anyone practicing the ministry of healing—it is the "shadow" side of every true, honest healer and can take over with disastrous results if ever they're tempted to lose their integrity. Nicholas Darrow enacts this theme in the story.

Q: Nicholas begins the book very successful in his relations with others, yet ends disastrously. Alice in turn begins

disillusioned with life, yet ends believing in Nicholas after everyone else has abandoned him. Could you speak some about the themes of fall and redemption, which these reversals suggest?

SH: Once Nicholas was destabilized (by his collapsing marriage) he became self-centered instead of God-centered—i.e., he lost his integrity, his focus on a balanced life, and allowed his pride, his arrogance, and his selfishness to gain the upper hand. The story describes how he was helped to recognize this, regret it, and try very hard to turn over a new leaf and get his act together so he could begin a new life. This illustrates the great Christian themes of sin, repentance, forgiveness, redemption, resurrection, and renewal.

Alice, on the other hand, simply develops her personality as she is finally enabled to embark on a process of self-realization. This too is a Christian theme: the more fully ourselves we become, the more we can play an individually designed part in God's creative scheme of things.

Q: One critic has written about your work, "There's a lot of demonology in these books, but done in simultaneous translation into psychodrama, so if you prefer to think of jealousy, rage and denial in Freudian terms, rather than as the devil within you, you will be comfortable." Nicholas and Lewis are both clerical figures, yet both speak in the language of secular humanistic self-help programs. Do you see a tension between religious belief and faith in modern psychology? Are you suggesting that this is a direction religion is taking in the modern world?

SH: There should be no tension between psychology and Christianity. They both deal with the soul and are both concerned with helping people to become more fully themselves and to lead the richest possible life. Unfortunately, some forms of Christianity and some forms of psychology hype up the differences and make them seem more opposed than they really are. There are indeed differences between the two disciplines, but there is no reason they should not be regarded as complementary paths to the truth. There are many Christian priests who are qualified psychotherapists/counselors/psychologists and feel comfortable speaking both languages, just as Nicholas and Lewis do in the book. I do not think it's a particularly new direction, since long before Freud, spiritual guides were demonstrating a profound understanding of the human psyche.

Q: You yourself have made a spiritual journey as a writer, from the earlier Gothic mysteries and family epics to the Starbridge series and then this book. What led you to become a writer in the beginning, and how do you feel your writing, and your relationship to it, has changed?

SH: I write because I enjoy it. I still write because I enjoy it. I think the creative high is the most powerful form of pleasure there is. Unfortunately, for every creative high there are hours and hours of hard slog, so one isn't always in a state of ecstasy!

Q: What is the function of the epigraphs before each section and chapter?

SH: I thought the quotes at the beginning of each chapter were an interesting reference to the actual traditional Christian ministry of healing as it is practiced in the U.K. today—it deals with a whole range of modern malaises and sheds fascinating lights on the healing process and God's role in it.

Q: Rosalind says that wonder workers "can never resist the temptation to 'fix' people," and even Nicholas uses this term, "fix," sometimes. Doesn't this suggest a mechanistic view of healing?

SH: Rosalind was speaking caustically about a ministry of which she totally disapproved. Nicholas uses the term "fix" when he disapproves of his own drive to power. True honest healers don't "fix" people. They heal by the grace of God through Jesus Christ in the power of the Spirit. It's the wonder workers who "fix" people to bolster their egos and satisfy their craving for power.

Q: **The crisis in the book seems to be sparked by Nicholas and Rosalind's estrangement, which is due to his devotion to his work at the church. Do you see a religious calling as fundamentally incompatible with most "normal" marriage commitments?**

SH: A religious calling need be no more incompatible with marriage than any other career. But as with other professions, marriages can suffer if the parties don't get the balance right. Some priests prefer not to marry, some priests do. It really all depends on what kind of person you are and how you want to organize your energy.

Q: **Critics frequently refer to Trollope and C.S. Lewis when they discuss your work. Who are your strongest literary influences?**

SH: Trollope. Iris Murdoch. Graham Greene. Raymond Chandler. *Not C.S. Lewis.*

Q: **What do you want readers to get out of this novel?**

SH: Pleasure. A novelist's primary duty is to entertain. If readers also get enriched or enlightened or inspired or whatever as a by-product of the entertainment, that's fine, but none of that will happen unless the book is first and foremost readable and entertaining.

Reading Group Questions and Topics for Discussion

1. This book is told from the point of view of four different characters. Do you think the author favors one character over another? If so, why and how? Which character do you feel the greatest connection with?

2. Alice is a Cordon Bleu chef with an eating disorder, which means that her greatest talent is linked to her greatest weakness. Do you see this as a theme with any of the other characters?

3. Alice's aunt doesn't seem to have given her a good sense of self-esteem, and yet Alice shows a very strong sense of duty in taking care of her. Do you see this as admirable, or as something that deprives her of her own personal growth? How would you act in a similar situation?

5. Rosalind refers to America enviously as "a culture where it was socially acceptable for angry people to scream with rage" as opposed to the stiff-upper-lip tradition of Britain. Do you think this is a fair characterization of either country? If so, how do these differences affect women's lives in particular?

6. The friendship between Nicholas and Lewis seems more durable than any of the friendships between women in this book; for instance, between Rosalind and Francie. Why do you think this is so?

7. Why do you think Francie makes untrue allegations against her husband? Do you see her as a victim or a perpetrator? Is she being manipulative, or do you think her actions are excusable because she is disturbed?

8. What is the significance of Nicholas's toy bear? What does it mean for him as a child? What relevance does it have for how he treats people as an adult?

9. Nicholas and Lewis are healers who, when they are troubled, turn to their own spiritual directors, most notably in Nicholas' session with Clare (pages 318–332). Do Nicholas's and Lewis's methods of healing differ from those of their own spiritual directors? If so, how?

10. The novel differentiates between being an "honest Christian healer" and a "shady, manipulative wonder worker," yet the title suggests that Nicholas might be more of the latter than the former. Do you think this is true? What are the differences you see between the two?

11. There is a lot of speculation about the reasons for Stacy's death. Why do you think he commits suicide?

12. Who do you think is stronger—Alice or Rosalind? Why?

13. Traditionally, religious figures are expected to be above sexual temptation, but all of the men of St. Benet's-by-the-Wall struggle with their sexuality. Lewis struggles with his celibacy; Stacy struggles with his sexual orientation; and Nicholas struggles with the attraction women have for him. What do you think the role of sexuality in a clergyman's life should be?

14. Nicholas is portrayed as the highly charismatic center of a small religious community—a role that has come to be viewed very suspiciously these days. Overall, do you think Nicholas's depiction in the book is more positive or negative?

15. What experiences have you had personally with highly charismatic figures, religious or otherwise? How did you react to them? Did you trust them as much as most people seem to trust Nicholas?

16. What do you think the reasons are for the breakup of Nicholas and Rosalind's marriage? Do you think it was inevitable? Is there anything either of them could have done to prevent it?

17. Rosalind has kept important parts of her life secret from her husband, Nicholas, because she feels he isn't really paying attention to her. Do you think she was right to do so?

18. The book shows Nicholas using his psychic abilities three times—the first with Alice and her aunt, the second when he hypnotizes his wife, and the third when he "exorcises" Francie. In each case, he oversteps what might be considered proper behavior, but with very different results. When and how are his uses of his psychic powers beneficial? When and how are they destructive? What does this say about the risks of charismatic healing? What are the ethical questions involved in this sort of work?

19. What role do religion and spirituality play in the lives of the various characters? How does their belief (or lack of it) in God affect their relationships with others?

©Barbara Pollard

About the Author

SUSAN HOWATCH was born in 1940. She obtained a law degree from London University and then immigrated to the United States, where she lived for eleven years. During that time she wrote eight novels, including her international bestsellers, *Penmarric* and *The Wheel of Fortune*. In 1980 she returned to England, where she began to study Church history. The result was the six novels that make up the Starbridge series. In 1993 she made headlines by funding a lectureship in theology and natural science at Cambridge University.

Excerpts of reviews of Susan Howatch's *The Wonder Worker*

"Susan Howatch's novel is a journey through the dark side of priestly egos, past the twists and turns of their needs and addictions to power."

—*Florida Times-Union*

"What would life be without Nicholas Darrow, [his] sidekick, Lewis Hall, perennially unsettled Venetia Flaxton? . . . Happily, all three are back in *The Wonder Worker*. . . . Howatch is unsurpassed."

—*Newsday*

"She does it again in *The Wonder Worker*. . . . By book's end, you care so much about these lives. . . . One hopes that this is the start of yet another great series."

—*The Cleveland Plain Dealer*

"Combining romantic fiction with an exploration of both Christianity and the labyrinths of the human spirit seems an almost impossible task, but time and time again Howatch has pulled it off. . . . She walks right into both the bedroom and the inner sanctum of the soul."

—*Washington Post Book World*

"The plot of *The Wonder Worker* has many twisting corridors and locked rooms. It is a testament to Howatch's skill as a storyteller that she manages to hold her diverse cast together without losing her narrative's drive."

—*Chicago Sun-Times*

"She has a special kind of courage to bring ministers and their calling to center stage, allowing them to err, to fail and to succeed. . . ."

—*Detroit News/Free Press*

"Susan Howatch is back on familiar turf . . . [a] novel of emotional, psychological and spiritual exploration."

—*The New York Times Book Review*

"[A]dmirers . . . will be in for a surprise. . . . a busy but beautifully managed story. One admires her for the courage . . . perhaps she's trying to be a wonder worker herself."

—*Booklist*

"Here she darkens her pallette and addresses the dangerous side of ecclesiastical passions . . . the self-delusions to which priests are susceptible as the deal with their own humanity."

—*Publisher's Weekly*